HE WALKED AMONG US

BOOKS BY NORMAN SPINRAD

The Solarians
Agent of Chaos
The Men in the Jungle
Bug Jack Barron
The Iron Dream
Passing Through the Flame
Riding the Torch
A World Between
Songs from the Stars
The Mind Game
The Void Captain's Tale
Child of Fortune
Little Heroes
The Children of Hamolin
Russian Spring
Deus X
Pictures at 11
Journals of the Plague Years
Greenhouse Summer
He Walked Among Us
The Druid King
Mexica

HE
WALKED
AMONG
US

NORMAN SPINRAD

TOR®

A TOM DOHERTY ASSOCIATES BOOK

NEW YORK

HE WALKED AMONG US

First published in France by Librairie Arthème Fayard

Copyright © 2009 by Librairie Arthème Fayard

A Tor Book
Published by Tom Doherty Associates, LLC
175 Fifth Avenue
New York, NY 10010

www.tor-forge.com

Tor® is a registered trademark of Tom Doherty Associates, LLC.

Library of Congress Cataloging-in-Publication Data

Spinrad, Norman.
    He walked among us / Norman Spinrad. — 1st ed.
        p. cm.
    "A Tom Doherty Associates book."
    ISBN 978-0-7653-2584-6
    1. Comedians—Fiction.   2. Prophets—Fiction.   3. Time travel—Fiction.
4. Psychological fiction.   I. Title.
    PS3569.P55H4 2010
    813'.54—dc22

                                                            2009041223

First U.S. Edition: April 2010

Printed in the United States of America

0 9 8 7 6 5 4 3 2 1

For Timothy Leary and Gene Roddenberry

"Why, you shall say at break of day,
'Sail on! sail on! sail on! and on!'"
—JOAQUIN MILLER, "COLUMBUS"

Acknowledgments

I've never done one of these acknowledgment pages before, believing, as I still do, that they somehow detract from a nicely focused dedication page, but the path of *He Walked Among Us* into this English language volume publication has been so labyrinthine, and a significant number of people have been positively involved, that in this case an exception would seem to be mandatory.

So here are my heartfelt acknowledgments:

First of all, to Dona Sadock, who was part of the inspiration for a nonfiction book proposal about the Transformation Crisis called New Worlds Coming at the beginning that I didn't even know was the beginning at the time.

To Lou Aronica, my editor and publisher at Bantam Spectra, who persuaded me that the nonfiction proposal should be a springboard for this very novel.

To Tom Dupree, who became the editor on *He Walked Among Us* and did very valuable work with me to put the novel into publishable shape after Lou became a victim of a very nasty corporate war, only to seemingly have wasted all that work when the novel became a victim of the same machinery.

(I would add a few well-deserved ripe red raspberries and juicy fingers at this point, would it not place me in danger of legal action.)

To my ex-wife, N. Lee Wood, who bore with me through a year of writing *He Walked Among Us* and the aforementioned publishing wars.

To Lilas Seewald, my editor at Editions Fayard, who more or less rescued this novel like a bolt from the blue, and was responsible for it seeing first publication in French from a major literary publisher.

Which required me to do another draft in English after a long hiatus, in which

I was greatly aided by Dona Sadock again, who in effect served as my line editor on this new English draft, and by Sylvie Denis, who provided long detailed notes in French.

To Sylvie Denis and Roland Wagner, who did such a fine job on a very, very difficult translation.

To John Schoenfelder, who so passionately wanted to publish the revised *He Walked Among Us* in English, that when his publisher decided they wouldn't, he sent it unbidden by me to Eric Raab at another house.

And to Eric Raab himself, who has godfathered *He Walked Among Us* into American publication.

And finally, however grandiose it may sound, to the people, and the literary culture, and the country of France itself. It is no small thing for a writer to be granted the rare, indeed perhaps sui generis, feeling that he has a great nation not even his own covering his back through various adversities.

HE WALKED AMONG US

1

"Have fun saving the world, Dex," Ellie said dryly. "But *do* try not to get too beered out."

"*Must* you rain on my parade?" Dexter Lampkin muttered sourly.

She pecked him on the cheek. "I just don't want you to wrap that damned thing around a tree, is that asking too much?" said Ellie. "Peace?"

"Peace," Dexter grunted and closed the door behind him. He had been going to these first Wednesday things for three years now. A dozen or so fans of his out-of-print novel, drinking beer, sneaking the occasional joint, calling themselves "Transformationalists," and convincing themselves that they were somehow going to save the world in the process.

Each first Thursday, he swore he would never go to one of these things again. Each first Wednesday, he went anyway.

Why?

Because a few of these people were real scientists?

Because *they* believed in Dexter D. Lampkin even though *he* found *them* ludicrous?

Or because, God help him, some part of him still believed in "The Transformation" too?

Out in the front yard, the Santa Ana wind rattled the sere skeletal palm fronds, set dusty swirls of dead leaves dancing, and dried the back reaches of his throat. Your average Angeleno professed a loathing for the Santa Ana, which ripped shingles from your roof, whipped brushfires up into roaring infernos, and supposedly brought out the homicidal crazies. But Dexter took a great big honk as he walked across the yard to the garage.

Dexter *loved* the Santa Ana.

He loved those negative ions sweeping in off the desert, stoking up the old endorphins, tingling his dendrites with norepinephrene, boosting the middle-aged biochemical matrix of his consciousness into hyperdrive.

He loved the way the hot desert wind blew the Los Angeles basin clear of smog, perfumed the air with bougainvillea and chaparral instead of undead hydrocarbons, the technicolor blue daytime skies and the nights like this one—crystalline, heated to the temperature of twenty-year-old pussy, redolent with the musk of the California Dream.

And if the acrid tang of far-off smoke all too often spiced the Santa Ana, well, hey, despite Ellie's endless urging, Dexter hadn't fallen into the real estate trap, now had he?

As he kept telling her, any writer who sunk his freedom money into a house and a mortgage was a prize schmuck. And anyone who thought it was a cagey investment to do so in a venue famous for earthquakes, brushfires, and mud slides, where affordable insurance usually covered everything else but, deserved what he was sooner or later going to get.

For truth be told, Dexter also loved the Santa Ana just because loving the Devil Wind was somehow a finger held high in the air to the face of LA.

Not that Dexter hated Los Angeles with the provincial chauvinism of his former Bay Area compatriots, who believed anything south of the fog bank they were so cleverly fortunate to have chosen to inhabit was nothing but Orange County roadside ticky-tacky and brain-dead yahoos.

Indeed, one of the charms of Los Angeles was the very lack of a local equivalent of that smarmy Northern California boosterism. While the Bay Area brooded endlessly over its supposed rivalry with La-La Land, people down here were only dimly aware of San Francisco's existence, crappy climate but great Italian and Chinese restaurants, right, ought to fly up for a three-day weekend sometime, we get a chance, babes.

LA didn't take itself seriously at all. In place of chauvinism, what was required of Angelenos was *attitude*. The attitude that expressed itself in hot-dog stands in the shape of hot dogs, houses built to resemble the Disney versions of Baghdad or Camelot, the Chinese and Egyptian theaters, and the Hollywood Sign itself, an enormous emblem proclaiming the obvious in towering pharonic letters a few molecules thick.

On a personal level, one knew one had achieved the proper LA attitude when, what else, one had found a soul mate of a car.

Dexter flipped up the garage door and smiled a silly boyish hello to his.

When Dexter and Ellie were living in Berkeley, they had had a fairly new Toyota and a late-middle-aged Volvo. Down here in Fairfax their two-car garage contained, in addition to cartons of Dexter's author's copies and moldy manuscripts that surely would be worth big bucks as collectors' items some day, Ellie's two-year-old Pontiac Firebird coupe and Dexter's ancient red Alfa-Romeo convertible.

By any rational automotive standard, the Alfa was an unreliable piece of shit. Its leaky gaskets caused it to slurp oil at the rate of a pint every thousand miles, the gearbox made ominous noises, the shift lever now had to be held down in second, and the electrical system had been rewired so many times by amateurs that even new heavy-duty batteries mysteriously died at the usual inopportune moments.

But Dexter loved the Alfa. Not for its all-too-obvious flaws, but because it was an authentic red Italian sports car that whipped around the curves as if on rails, snapped your head back in a satisfying manner when you came out of one and stood on it in second, and it was a hoot to drive back and forth to the mechanic, which was often.

Was it juvenile for a forty-three-year-old writer with an expanded middle and a wife and kid to support to chunk out north of three thousand bucks a year in insurance, repair bills, oil, and expensive imported Italian parts to maintain this decrepit automotive wet dream?

Ellie was certainly of that opinion.

"It's pathetic, Dex, it's your midlife crisis on wheels, when are you gonna dump the thing and get a reliable second car?"

"The upkeep on the Alfa's less than the monthlies on another new car," Dexter would point out logically.

"You piss away half of that every year in repair bills and oil."

At which point, Dexter would give her the ghost of the very leer that had lured *her* once tasty young bod to him across a crowded room more than a decade ago, the glamorous cocksman's leer of the thirty-one-year-old Dexter D. Lampkin, of a risen young star along the science fiction convention circuit.

"Cheaper than a mistress in a tight dress of the same color," he would say.

It was an old joke that had long since ceased to be funny, and an old threat that had long since ceased to have bite.

Ellie knew that he might cop one of the readily available quick ones at a science fiction convention from time to time, but she also knew that he was not likely to screw anyone at such scenes that he would care to contemplate in the morning, and he knew that she didn't really care as long as he respected her need not to know. Both of them knew what went on between writers and fans at these conventions. Both of them knew what it was to be the belle and the beau of such a masquerade ball. Which is what they had been when they met at that publisher's party at the Seattle Westercon.

Dexter D. Lampkin had won the Hugo for best science fiction novel the year before, a silvery rocketship awarded by the fans who staged these conventions. An appropriately phallic trophy for someone not entirely above using it to add to his reputation as a convention cocksman.

This was more a matter of getting stoned and/or plastered enough to lose one's sense of sexual aesthetics than honing one's jejune skills as a seducer. Any published writer who weighed less than three hundred pounds, and some who didn't, could get laid at these things. The question was, by *what*?

Why did science fiction fans of both sexes tend to be so overweight? Why did they tend to be pear-shaped and look strange about the eyes? Why did masses of them crammed into convention hotel room parties exude such clouds of antisexual pheromones?

The story that Norman Spinrad told Dexter at some con or other had the awful ring of scientific truth.

"My girlfriend, Terry Champagne, had a theory that allegiance to science fiction fandom is genotypically linked to a minimal distance between the eyes, narrow shoulders, and enormous asses. One time, we were going to a convention in some horrible fleabag on Herald Square in New York, crowds of people going into the subway, your bell-shaped general population curve on the random hoof. As a scientific experiment, we stood across the street from the con hotel trying to predict who would go inside. Terry scored better than seventy-five percent."

Ellen Douglas, however, would have gone undetected as a science fiction fan by the genetic criteria of Spinrad's former girlfriend. Dexter had known her by reputation before he ever set eyes on her, for Ellen was what was known in the science fiction world as a Big Name Fan, what in the rock biz would have been called a Super Groupie.

But in the world of science fiction fandom, one did not achieve such status by screwing stars like Dexter D. Lampkin. One got to screw the stars by achieving the status of Big Name Fan. By reputation, Dexter knew Ellen Douglas as a convention organizer, fannish panel personality, and fanzine gossip columnist.

She was also reputed to be a great beauty who knocked 'em dead at masquerades in famous minimalist costumes, but fannish standards of pulchritude being what they were, Dexter had given this a heavy discount for hyperbole until that moment when their eyes met for the first time across that sea of flabby flesh in Seattle.

All right, so this lady might not be quite movie starlet material, but oh yes, she had it, particularly in the usual convention context, and oh boy, did she flaunt it! Natural blond hair permed into an incredible afro, regular features, big green eyes the regulation distance apart, and this wonderful ripe body artfully barely contained in a tight low-cut thigh-slit black dress.

It had been a magic moment, a wild weekend, and a frantic slow-motion cross-country romance, as Dexter and Ellen fucked their way from convention to convention for about six months, before she finally gave up her place in St. Louis and moved into Dexter's little apartment in San Francisco, and soon thereafter into the house in Berkeley.

For two or three years they were the Golden Couple of the Greater Bay Area Co-Prosperity Sphere, the circle of science fiction writers, their significant others, and the surrounding cloud of fans, hangers-on, fringe scientists, and Big Name Dope Dealers to same who formed what was the largest science fiction community in the United States. Those were the days to be young, and in love, and a science fiction writer in Berkeley, and Dexter D. Lampkin!

The science fiction genre had completed the transformation from lowly pulp publishing backwater, where for a quarter of a century five cents a word for short fiction and $3000 for a novel had been considered hot stuff, into a "major publishing industry profit center." Meaning that a hot young talent like Dexter D. Lampkin could command thirty or forty thou for a novel. Dexter could take six months or even a *year* to write a novel. He could afford literary commitment and social idealism and enjoy a life of relative bourgeois ease at the same time.

He could even believe he could change the world.

A lot of science fiction writers did, and some of them had. Arthur C. Clarke had inspired the geosynchronous broadcast satellite, the Apollo astronauts credited science fiction with putting them on the path to the Moon, *Dune* and *Stranger in a Strange Land* had created the hippies and the Counterculture, and L. Ron Hubbard had turned an idea for an sf novelette into a multimillion-dollar real-world religious scam.

Dexter had even read a piece by some French intellectual who had opined that science fiction writers should get together, decide the optimal future for the species, and, by setting all their stories in that future, call it into being thereby.

Given the difficulty any three science fiction writers had agreeing on how many letters made up a word at five cents per, this kind of collaborative messianism did not seem entirely practical.

However . . .

Dexter wrestled down the top, looked under the car to see whether the size of the oil puddle demanded a look at the dipstick, decided it didn't, put the key in the ignition, and heaved the usual sigh of relief, when, after the usual catch and hesitation, the starter managed to turn the engine over.

However . . .

The science fiction community did already accept certain truths as self-evident that had yet to penetrate the obdurate brainpans of the so-called "mundanes," a.k.a. the rest of the species.

Foremost, that the Earth was the cradle of a future space-going humanity, and in a galaxy containing hundreds of millions of stars similar to our own, it would be ridiculously arrogant to assume that our evolution was unique. And therefore, advanced space-going civilizations who had achieved mastery of matter and energy and long-term stability should abound.

But no less than Enrico Fermi had asked the obvious question: If so, *where are they*? Why haven't we detected them? Why haven't they visited us or at least sent a cosmic postcard?

The answer was not that reassuring. Namely that the natural tendency of sapient species was to do themselves in before evolving to the long-term stable stage.

After all, no species was likely to develop space travel without unlocking the Faustian fires of the atom first. It was hardly guaranteed that any species would develop clean sources of power like fusion or space-born solar power before the necessary precursor technologies like fossil fuels and nuclear fission poisoned the biosphere. And these were only the most obvious means by which our own species seemed likely to expire. So it seemed logical to assume that we were only *average* dickheads, that the present crisis we had entered, say about the time of Hiroshima, was something that *all* sapient species must pass through, the historical moment, as Dexter put it, when the lunatics take over the asylum.

Sooner or later any species that developed an evolving technology was going to get its hot little pseudopods on the power of the atom, long before which its activities would have begun doing unpredictable things to the biosphere, both of which were likely to occur long before it had the technology to escape the consequences by colonizing other planets. Or, if the foibles of the human race exhibited only average shitheadedness, before it evolved the necessary wisdom to transform itself into a civilization capable of surviving even another few centuries of its own history.

The human race was going through *its* transformation crisis *right now*, and judging by the lack of good news from outer space, the chances of negotiating it successfully seemed something like slim and none.

Scary stuff.

On the other hand, Dexter's New York agent had little trouble getting him a $40,000 contract for a science fiction novel based on the thirty-page outline he batted out around this material on a hot weekend with the aid of some excellent weed.

Dexter put the Alfa in gear, pulled out of the garage, and headed toward his rendezvous with the rather pathetic latter-day fans of that very visionary novel, a novel which his agent *still* hadn't been able to get back in print.

"Transformationalists," they called themselves. Their bible was *The Transformation,* Dexter D. Lampkin's exercise in science fictional messianism, the book with which he really thought at the time he was going to change the world.

NASA picks up a funeral oration from an extraterrestrial civilization by a species not much in advance of ourselves which has destroyed the viability of its planet via atomic war and atmospheric degradation. Worse still, these aliens have received similar messages from several *other* intelligent species who have *also* done themselves in by similar assholery. This appears to be the galactic norm. If there are any intelligent species out there who have successfully passed through their transformation crises, they don't seem to have any interest in foreign aid to Third World planets.

The government tries to sit on it, but a few scientists in the know are horrified, and a secret conspiracy of "Transformationalists" gradually comes together. They know what has to be done to transform the human race into a successful long-lived spacegoing species. Big bucks have to be poured into fusion, space-born solar energy, the colonization of the solar system, artificial photosynthesis. The burning of fossil fuels and the use of dirty fission reactors must be halted, massive tracts of farmland must be reforested, and complete nuclear disarmament will probably be required too.

But *how* are they supposed to cram all this down the species' throat?

They hit upon the idea of creating an alien from outer space, a visitor from a far distant civilization that has survived its own transformation crisis, to serve as their mouthpiece.

So they recruit a sixteen-year-old hippie-dip runaway and go to work. They profile the perfect transnational wet-dream fantasy, and surgery and genetic tinkering transform her into the most stunning woman the world has ever seen, with apple-green skin and purple hair.

They raise her intelligence to super-genius level, program her with the millennial history and scientific knowledge of this imaginary advanced civilization she's supposed to be from, and erase all memories of her previous incarnation so that *she* is convinced she is Lura, ambassador from the Galactic Brotherhood of Advanced Civilizations, dispatched to save the Earth.

The Transformationalists sell Lura as the savior from space and begin to effect the great Transformation through her, presenting their visionary program as the tried-and-true path of all those civilizations who have succeeded in passing through their Transformation Crises.

Many plot twists later, the civilization of the Earth is indeed transformed, the final McGuffin being the capture of Lura by a mob of the dispossessed, and her impending martyrdom.

Some of the Transformationalists try to tell the world the truth to save her. But since Lura herself contradicts them, believing that she is a noble being from an advanced civilization, they fail, she is martyred, and the Transformationalists have no pragmatic choice but to turn her into the legend that successfully puts the seal on the great Transformation.

In the epilogue, an immense spaceship then manifests itself in the solar system to welcome humanity into a *real* Galactic Brotherhood of Advanced Civilizations. Earth has negotiated its Transformation Crisis on its own. That's the entrance test. That's why the galactic silence. The Galactic Brotherhood has no interest in communicating with species who have not yet proven themselves worthy.

Dexter poured his heart and soul into this one.

It ended up taking over his life completely, became an obsession, a mission, a cause.

Before he began, he felt he had to travel the convention circuit, pouring booze and dope into scientists of his acquaintance and scientists of *their* acquaintance; conning them into serving as his brain trust, creating something not unlike the Transformationalist cabal in his unwritten novel, at least in his own mind at the time.

By the time Dexter was ready to write page one, six months had passed in a blur since he had signed the contract, he had gone through about $5000 in travel and entertainment, and he had a dossier of speculative papers from cutting-edge scientists about two thousand pages thick.

The contract called for Dexter to turn in the manuscript in twelve months. He was eight months late. The contract called for about 100,000 words, but Dexter turned in 250,000, and after three months of cutting under editorial supervision, the final version still came in at 220,000. It took harder work over more months to write than anything Dexter had ever done, and by the time he saw the galley proofs, the $40,000 was long gone.

But Dexter knew that *The Transformation* was his masterpiece, his destiny, the work for which his name would be remembered for a thousand years, the mission he had been born to fulfill.

It came out six months later, and it bombed.

"Too intellectual for the kids who they're marketing sci-fi to these days, Dex," his agent told him. "What they want is space opera series, or likewise in wizards and dragons, *Star Trek* and *Star Wars* novelizations, role-playing tie-ins, and novels based on the laundry lists of Isaac Asimov and Arthur C. Clarke."

Broke, devastated, with Ellie now pregnant with Jamie, Dexter spent ten days listening to his wife whine and staring into the black hole his life had become.

His agent had timed it perfectly. On the eleventh day, he called and dropped the other shoe.

"Hey, it's not like your career's over, Dex. You get me a strong outline for a trilogy, preferably fantasy, and I'm sure I can get you a contract for $30,000 a book, maybe even more if there's game potential in it."

"Fuck you!" Dexter snarled and hung up on him.

"Fuck *you*, Dexter D. Lampkin!" was Ellie's take on it when he conveyed the gist of the conversation. "What are we going to live on, your Polish serial rights?"

She kept hammering at him. Bills began to pile up. His American Express card got pulled. Dying inside, Dexter was about to surrender his soul to the inevitable when he ran into Harlan Ellison at a convention in Phoenix.

Ellison, a Los Angeles scenarist and short-story writer who had flourished on a high economic level for decades, set him straight in no uncertain terms.

"Are you *nuts*, Lampkin, you got to ream out crap to stay alive, don't piss on the work that really matters to you to do it. Instead of writing three hundred pages of sci-fi bullshit and ruining your reputation for $30,000 a pop, come down to Hollywood and bang out forty-eight-page TV scripts for $15,000 minimum. Buy yourself time to do your real work and keep it separate from what you do to make the rent."

The Santa Ana ruffled Dexter's hair as he crossed Sunset and drove Laurel Canyon Boulevard up through the hills. The night was warm, the canyon was heady with vegetal perfume, he kept the tach over three thousand as he whipped through the curves, just to feel those gees, just to hear the double-overhead-cam engine growl, whoo-ee!

So it hadn't exactly worked out as smoothly as the picture Harlan had painted—prime-time TV script gigs were few and far between—but considering the alternatives, Dexter figured he was doing all right.

The cartoon shows were hot for an sf writer accustomed to writing novellas in the time it took the usual derelicts to write a thirty-page script, and while the money was pretty shitty, it was usually there when needed. There was a certain amount of magazine work, bullshit he could write in his sleep. Dexter even found that he had a knack for writing album cover blurbs, ad copy, even gags for third-rate comics.

He made enough money via the Scam of the Week to be able to spend half his time writing his novels. He was now older and wiser enough to know that most science fiction writers had a book like *The Transformation* in them, the visionary masterpiece that would express the full brilliance of their genius and enlighten the world. He was older and wiser enough to know that most of them were going to bomb.

He was middle-aged enough these days too to know that the Alfa was an extended hardware metaphor that would have Sigmund Freud chuckling in his beard—the forty-three-year-old onetime visionary with the expanded waistline zipping up over Mulholland toward his boys' night out with the ghosts of his youth in his equally superannuated red Italian dick on wheels.

But as he crossed Mulholland destiny sent him a sign.

Up from the Valley side came another old red Alfa of approximately the same vintage. The top was also down, and in the car was your prototypical California beauty, long honey-blond hair blowin' in the wind, could have been all of twenty-five.

She honked her horn.

Dexter honked back.

Her smile was radiant.

Dexter waved, and then she was gone.

But not before he remembered that it was old stogie-chomping Siggy himself who, when tweaked by some smart-ass as to the obvious symbolic nature of the cylindrical object perpetually stuck in his yawp, had proclaimed: "Sometimes a cigar is a cigar."

"*Kapplemeyer's?*" said the Bimbo. "For the tenth time, Jimmy, what the hell are we doing in the *Catskills* in November?"

"Scouting talent, kid," Texas Jimmy Balaban told her, as he turned the rented Buick off the highway at the splintery old wooden sign and up the drive that might have been last paved when George Burns was still playing straightman to Gracie.

"*Here?*" said the Bimbo, whose name was Sabrina.

"Matter of instinct, babes," Texas Jimmy muttered. "The nose knows."

What was he supposed to tell her, that since Kapplemeyer's Country Club Resort Hotel was the kind of dump that Texas Jimmy Balaban ordinarily wouldn't be caught dead in, he had reason to hope that Marsha's divorce dick wouldn't think to look for the live item here either?

You're getting too old for this shit, Jimmy, he told himself as he pulled up in front of the hotel.

Yeah, sure, that's what he had been telling himself at moments like this for about twenty-five years. You're getting too old to get married again, you're getting too old to get cleaned out again in the divorce courts, you're getting too old to chase young pussy, you're getting too old to dodge house dicks and keyhole peepers. Right. Learned my lesson. Never again.

Indeed, Texas Jimmy had had no intention at all, well hardly any, of chasing after any nookie on this trip to New York. He really *had* come to the Apple on business, but only to secure some bookings for a couple comics he already had under contract. All he had done was hang around the hotel bar for a few drinks, he hadn't been looking for any action, not really.

But let a pair of formidable young knockers like Sabrina's heave into sight, let a pair of juicy red lips start cooing seductively after he had just *happened* to mention that he was a hot-shot talent agent from Hollywood . . .

How was he supposed to know that Marsha's PI had followed him out from the Coast with his microphones and cameras? Well *sure* he had slipped the house dick fifty bucks to let him know if any wiseguy came nosing around his room! Didn't *everyone* do that? Look at the shit he'd have been in if he hadn't!

"You *get off* on this sleazing around, Balaban," wife number two used to tell him. "It's the sneaking around in crummy motels that gets your pathetic pecker up. If you weren't looking over your shoulder for detectives and divorce lawyers, you'd *never* be able to raise a hard-on!"

Well, Tanya had had the disposition of a speed freak wolverine, and Texas Jimmy would have been hard-put to remember very many situations when impotence wasn't the least of his problems, but in his more philosophical moments, he had to acknowledge that she sort of had a point.

A state of contented monogamy with a wife and kiddies and the whole nine yards was impossible for Texas Jimmy to imagine as other than the moral equivalent of condition terminal in Sun City. On the other hand, a romantic streak, or an instinctive self-knowledge he knew better than to examine, kept him from simply leading the carefree bachelor life of the disconnected playboy.

Not that he *enjoyed* being tailed by divorce dicks, not that he had enjoyed the financial consequences of his first two divorces, but he had to admit that the tummeling of it all did indeed probably do much to maintain his edge. In this, he knew, he was like the comics he managed. Comedians with sex lives that a Jewish mother could love were few and far between, and of the dozen or so in Texas

Jimmy's stable, eight of them would be going through some kind of crazy tsuris at any given time. It wasn't that doing stand-up comedy was a sure ticket to the rubber room, but that you had to maintain that *edge* to stay funny. Like a top, once you stopped whirling and twirling, you tended to fall on your ass.

Kapplemeyer's Country Club Resort Hotel was five rambling wooden stories of faded pastel green with forest green trimming. A sagging covered porch ran across the front of the building. In the summer, no doubt, the beach chairs would be filled with gorked-out old folks and the rusty green lawn tables laden with the cloyingly sweet highballs and planter's punches favored by same, but now they were deserted, making the place seem even deader that it probably was.

"Jesus Christ," observed Sabrina as an ancient bellman in a musty puke-green monkey suit emerged from the main entrance and tottered down the stairs.

Inside the lobby, a gray-haired and stooped clerk managed to remain standing behind a heavily revarnished front desk. A dining room behind closed glass doors to the left. On the right, the open entrance to the hotel nightclub, labeled "Kapple-meyer's Fabulous Sunset Room" in peeling gilt letters. Three old duffers in leisure suits and two old ladies stuffed into hideous pastel capris comprised the lobby life.

"What are we *doing* in this shithole?" Sabrina hissed in Jimmy's ear as they approached the desk.

"I told you, it's *business*," Jimmy snapped back.

"Yessir," said the desk clerk in a tired wheeze, "can I help you?"

I hope so, Texas Jimmy thought, observing the ever-more skeptical pout souring Sabrina's bee-stung lips. He had taken the precaution, didn't everyone, of schtup-ping the hotel desk in New York twenty to book this room for him. Tell 'em I'm a big-time agent from Hollywood don't want to be disturbed by no paparazzi, their discretion will be appreciated, had been his instructions. It was the truth, wasn't it?

"I've got a reservation," he said. "Name of Balaban . . ."

"*Texas Jimmy* Balaban?" said the desk clerk, emerging from his coma.

Jimmy smiled patronizingly, glancing sidewise at Sabrina, whose eyes had widened, whose pout had softened. "The one, the only," he said.

"We've reserved the Presidential Suite for you, Mr. Balaban—"

"Hey, I didn't—"

"—no extra charge, of course, compliments of the management."

Sabrina breathed a wordless Wow. That had been the point. But the freebie upgrade had been more than Jimmy had hoped for.

"Well, I do appreciate it," he said. He leaned closer, nodded in the direction of Sabrina, slid a twenty across the desk, winked at the clerk. "But if anyone asks, I'm not here, the room is registered to Joseph P. Blow, get me?"

The Presidential Suite was a living room with a bay window overlooking the deserted tennis courts, a big bedroom with a king-sized bed, a monster bathroom with double sink, tub, and separate shower stall. The air within, however, was stale as Joe Miller's Joke Book, the plush living room furniture exuded a dusty odor, the first rush of water in the toilet taps was a rusty brown, and there was a telltale rime at the waterline in the toilet bowl. Kapplemeyer's probably managed to rent it out to full-paying guests about as often as Frank Sinatra topped the bill at the Fabulous Sunset Room, which did much to explain why they had comped it as an upgrade to the big-time agent from Hollywood in the off-season.

Still . . .

"Not bad, huh?" Jimmy said as Sabrina pranced around the living room.

She came to light on the couch. Jimmy stood over her gazing down her cleavage.

"You weren't shining me on, *were* you?" she said. "You really *are* a big-time agent from Hollywood!"

Texas Jimmy smiled at her. "Would I bullshit you?" he murmured.

Sabrina took both of his hands in hers. "You know what I'd like now?" she said softly.

"What?" Jimmy purred.

"Could we . . . could we have some champagne, I mean it would be perfect, just like in the movies . . ."

"Why sure," Jimmy said. "I'll call room service. Why don't you go into the bedroom and slip into something more comfortable." He winked lugubriously. "Like nothing at all . . ."

Sabrina giggled and departed. Jimmy called room service.

"A bottle of champs."

"What brand?"

"The best in the— Uh, something classy that don't cost an arm and a leg, know what I mean?"

About five minutes later, room service arrived with a bottle in an ice bucket and two glasses on a silver-plate tray. Jimmy glanced at the label, saw that it was Moët & Chandon, a famous French brand, gave the bellboy a good tip, and took it into the bedroom.

Sabrina was stretched out across the bed on her back with her arms and legs wide open wearing only a great big smile.

Jimmy popped the bottle, did the honors. "Here's lookin' at you, kid," he said Bogart-wise, clinking glasses.

Only much later, when he took a second look at the label on the now-empty bottle, did he realize that they had fobbed him off with some knockoff version of the real French stuff that had been bottled in California.

It was an unseasonably warm autumn evening for the coast of central California, and so Amanda had moved the proceedings out of Xanadu's auditorium to the back lawn of the main building.

Here, she wouldn't be upstaged by the magnificent view of the sunset from a Pacific seacliff afforded by the front veranda, but the surf breaking on the rocks below could still be heard as a rushing rumble in the background, and the stars could be seen beginning to emerge at the crown of the purpling heavens, and the perfume of the surrounding redwood forest seemed to sound just the right note of olfactory languor for the subject at hand.

Amanda began pacing in small circles before she started talking, her simple white caftan and long unfettered black hair flowing in the wind of her passage, her dark brown eyes and aquiline nose forming the visage of a bird of prey whose gaze she kept fixed on the same central point in the audience.

"There are paths that you never see until you discover that you are already on them," she said. "There are doors you can never find until you have already passed through them."

This was the standard costume she used for "Walkabout Through the Dreamtime" and the standard opening.

"The blinding flash that transformed Saul on the road to Tarsus, Joan of Arc awakening in mid-conversation with her voices, Albert Hoffman peddling his bicycle as the LSD he has unknowingly absorbed alters the world around him . . ."

This was also pretty much the usual group she drew with this one. There were twenty-three of them sprawled comfortably on piles of assorted cushions, split roughly evenly by gender, median age in the early forties, a lot of professional creators, many of them in various states of blockage—screenwriters, painters, a sculptor, poets, a composer, the usual dilettantes and seekers, but no performers.

"Moses confronted with the Burning Bush, Muhammad finding himself frantically taking dictation from Allah . . ."

Pacing faster and faster, making them track her.

"Transcendent experiences wherein the everyday mind is transformed by powers from elsewhere before it knows what happens! The rare peak experiences of prophets, and visionaries, and God-struck saints!"

Amanda stopped dead in her tracks, arced a prophetic finger in the collective face of her audience, her visage stern and a bit feverish, as if about to summon the ineffable from the vasty deeps before their very eyes.

"*Right?*" she demanded in a voice of thunder.

Beat.

"Wrong," she said in quite another voice, sinking down into the rattan peacock chair set out for her and folding her arms across her chest with a little smile. "I'm talking about a path we all find ourselves on every night, the door we all walk through on the way to it, the path through the Dreamtime, and the door to sleep."

The opening theatrics were over, and she could open up and just be Amanda.

"We never remember the moment we fall asleep, do we?" she said, as if talking to a couple of friends in her living room. "We can never remember the moment we passed through that doorway. And when we've got insomnia, it's the agony of Tantalus trying to summon it up by act of conscious will, now isn't it?"

Amanda had a repertoire of a half dozen of what she called "experiences," not just because it was a clever marketing tool which played well on the New Age Circuit, but because *experiences* were what she truly sought both to convey and obtain.

"And then there we are in the Dreamtime, without even knowing we *are* there, more often than not. The magic land of our dreams, of beauty and of terror, of spirit messages and satori, of dire punishments and inexplicable powers, stranger than truth and wiser than fiction . . ."

Places like Xanadu had existed up and down the coastal mountains of California long before fourteen-year-old Amanda Dunston had run away from Marin County for her three-week magical mystery tour in the Haight-Ashbury's Summer of Love.

"The boys in the lab coats can tell you all about the structure and biochemistry of the brain, and how rapid eye movements are the physical signature of the dream state . . ."

Wooded mountains tumbled to the rocky coast of California starting not that far north of Los Angeles, and the farther north you went, the grander the scale of the landscape, the deeper and mightier the forests, and the emptier the wilderness of the works of modern man. This was California primeval, loamy brown and forest green, a long fog-girt jumble of seacliff mountains and misty canyons like no other coast on the planet; the secret spiritual spine of the land magically hidden in plain sight.

Small wonder that Zen monasteries and nudist communes, solitary hermits and beatnik poets, ascetics in hair shirts and blue jeans and free love libertines, and who knew what Indian shamans and secret medicine lodges before the white man came, had slip-slided away into these hidden mystic vastnesses.

"But that's like giving a detailed chemical analysis of smears of paint on the canvas and calling it a useful description of the *Mona Lisa*."

So what was now called the New Age Circuit had always been here in one incarnation or another, for the sacred orgy ranches, the seminar centers, the plush retreats for artists and writers and well-heeled pilgrims, grew naturally out of this landscape like magic mushrooms and wild marijuana.

And Amanda kidded herself not, as long as there were paying rubes to be fleeced, there would be snake-oil salesmen and sleazy sideshow gurus working the Cosmic Carney Circuit. Indeed, she had to take care to avoid becoming one herself, having better tools with which to do so than most.

For few others along this circuit also acted in TV and commercials, and no one else she knew actually coached performers. And she fretted that some of the "experiences" in her repertoire perhaps *did* have too much clever show business technique about them and too little genuine satori.

"Well, tonight, we're going to start with the unscientific notion that the visions that come to us in dreams are on the deepest reality level *the same* visions that come to us in the act of artistic inspiration, that the door to the Dreamtime is also the door to our creative imagination . . ."

Which was why "Walkabout Through the Dreamtime" was her favorite.

"So if we can learn how to open that door by act of conscious will while we're *awake*, we can summon dreams forth into our waking minds, summon inspiration forth from our own vasty deeps and gain conscious control of our own creative powers . . ."

There was a bit more of this lecture stuff—lucid dreaming, dreams as arising into the human mind from the collective species unconscious—but it was more or less by way of convincing the customers that they were getting their money's worth, timewise. The real heart of it, the techniques themselves, could be explained, if hardly mastered, in a few minutes.

"Tonight I want you to be as drowsy as possible before you go to bed. Then just lay there and watch the stream of your own consciousness. Don't try to think of anything but don't try to hold your mind empty either, just let whatever happens happen."

Amanda stood up slowly, peered at the group, narrowed her eyes slightly, as if watching for something.

"Just observe the tropical fish of thought swimming through the waters of your mind . . ." she murmured. "If you watch the right way, you'll know it when it happens. Instead of the words and images and feelings going out of your mind into the darkness, words and images and feelings will start floating up out of the darkness toward you . . ."

Amanda grinned, straightened suddenly, held up a finger. "That's it!" she exclaimed. "That's the doorway! What's coming up out of it are *dreams*. You're right on the edge of sleep, and they're coming up out of the Dreamtime for you."

Now she paced in small circles, staring at the audience like a raptor. "Pull back the teeniest eeniest bit until you feel that the words and images and feelings are coming out of *you* once more. Then do the same thing over again. And again. Several times before you let sleep take you. Do this for a few nights, and you'll learn to recognize the doorway . . ."

She stopped pacing. "What's really on the other side of the doorway? Where are the dreams coming from? Your subconscious? The Jungian Collective Unconscious? The Mind of God?"

She shrugged ingenuously. "It doesn't matter. Once you've got this technique down, you'll be able to retain consciousness of the opening of the doorway, you'll find yourself able to slip from the waking state into lucid dreams, you'll have learned how to open the doorway and step through it."

She sat down slowly. "You're creative people, but you're all different, so how you do the next step is up to you," she said. "Set up a recorder, or your computer, or your easel, whatever, by your bedside. Lay down and wait for that opening of the doorway, let the dreams start coming through . . ."

She leaned far forward and then spoke in a strong stage whisper, conveying the effect of someone imparting a secret while trying not to arouse the attention of unwanted eavesdroppers.

"And then what you've got to do is hold the door open while you sit up in bed and take up your instrument and . . . *let the Dreamtime play it through you . . .*"

Amanda laughed. "*That* won't be easy," she admitted. "But sooner or later, you'll wake up the next morning with some drawings, or some words, whatever, that will seem were put there by the elves. And then you must immediately take that work as a beginning and go on."

Amanda stood up again, and began walking slowly toward her audience. "If you persist, you'll be sitting there one morning, wide awake at your work, and the doorway will open, and the Dreamtime will come pouring through! This is not magic or supernatural mumbo-jumbo but conscious access to a transcendental reality whose existence no human can possibly doubt—the realm of your very own dreams."

Amanda detested the very concept of the supernatural, the notion that there was a level of reality discontinuous from the natural realm. That kind of superstitious drivel had perverted the metaphysical insights of the Vedas into a ludicrous pantheon of petty godlings, turned the purity of the Buddha's original vision into a series of magical formulas, and in general gave mystical experience an intellectual bad name.

The supernatural was a contradiction in terms. What is, is *real*. And what is real, is *natural*. *All* belief systems—astrology, Tarot, free-market economics, or the Roman Catholic Church—were obstacles on the path to experiential enlightenment.

Of course *science* was just another belief system conning itself into believing that it knew what was real and what was not, and scientists another priesthood holding on to the franchise of their own particular brand of Ultimate Reality. And Amanda had experienced far more than is dreamt of in their natural philosophies, moments when maya's veils parted long enough to reveal the formless clarity at the core of all being, the chaotic unity at the heart of the world.

What is, is real.

Amanda had touched that transcendent reality via acid and mescaline and some pretty nasty synthetics as a young teenage runaway during the Summer of Love, had followed the Pied Piper into the Magic Mountain for a season. But she had been unable to return to ground zero in command of the visionary powers sampled therein, and neither she nor her generation of Flower Children had returned from their journeys as Lightbringers to joyously transform the world.

But Amanda Dunston's parents had not seen it as their duty to stuff the genie back into the bottle upon her return from San Francisco, had not sternly sought to convince her that life was real and boredom was earnest, had not treated the tales of her psychedelic adventures as the demented ravings of a drug-crazed teenage hippie, to be expunged from her reality track by psychotherapy or worse if necessary.

Instead, they had listened to her babbling tales of telepathic communion at group-grope orgies, of ego-death on acid at the Fillmore, of transcendent orgasm on mescaline, of annihilation of the I-Thou interface, and discussed it all with her at endless length, sometimes with a joint being passed. They had suggested certain readings, introduced her to mandalic art and mantric music, subsidized a retreat at a Zen monastery, and rather than dismiss her experience and that of her generation as aberrant lunacy, had gently persuaded her that she had, after all, been very young, and that what she had supposed was ultimate Enlightenment had only been her first steps upon the Road that goes ever on.

"Walkabout Through the Dreamtime" ended not with some grand rhetorical flourish but with Amanda delivering the final line of the formal presentation as she walked among her audience while they rose from their pillows around her.

"There's a higher level," she said quite conversationally, "not that I've attained it, but I've talked to people who say they have, and that's when you can open the doorway any time and place you want."

And she was speaking now directly to some female poet and a blocked screenwriter, as she shrugged, and smiled a slightly wistful smile. "Some day, who knows, maybe I'll get there."

And her audience had broken up into a community of the usual seekers, and Amanda had quite naturally become just one of them, without being conscious of stepping through that doorway either.

"The first few hits are free, kid," her father once told her with a Cheshire cat smile, "or so at the time it seems, after which you finds yourself spending the rest of your life on the Pilgrim's Path to the Palace of Wisdom, to learn when you are fortunate, to teach when you are called upon to teach."

Oh what schlocky webs we weave! Texas Jimmy Balaban thought morosely as he knocked back another slug of heavily watered bourbon in Kapplemeyer's Fabulous Sunset Room.

If he hadn't picked up Sabrina in the New York hotel, he wouldn't have had to flee into the Catskills, if he hadn't told her that he had dragged her to a dump like Kapplemeyer's to scout talent and revealed his identity to the management like a putz to boot, then just maybe he could have escaped the last hour and a half of torture.

But no, when the desk called the Presidential Suite, the suite they had *comped* him fer chrissakes, to invite the big-time agent from Hollywood to catch the floor show, he was hardly in a position to refuse.

Given his admitted propensity to pick 'em for tits and ass rather than sparkling personality, Jimmy all too often found himself wishing he were elsewhere once he had gotten his rocks off, so he was not unfamiliar with postcoital depression. He even knew the fancy shrink's term for the phenomenon, having looked it up once to make sure that he wasn't turning faggot or something.

But being forced by his own cleverness to watch an endless succession of excruciating acts he wouldn't have tried to book into a prison benefit on Devil's Island die in agony attempting to rouse this audience of brain-dead zombies from its collective coma raised postcoital depression to an Academy Award–winning level.

What a toilet bowl!

The walls were painted the pastel vomit green that seemed to be Kapplemeyer's signature, only to jazz up the Sunset Room, someone had dumped cheap glitter into the bucket before they slathered it on. The stage was just about big enough to handle a quartet and an act at the same time, the lighting consisted of a single fixed spot, and the sound system seemed to have been scrounged from a bankrupt biker bar in Bumfuck, Mississippi.

The room had about thirty tables, plus a dance floor, meaning that it could squeeze a hundred thirty, a hundred forty, in the summer high season, and probably did, seeing as how the nightlife within a thirty-mile radius of Kapplemeyer's consisted of an all-night gas station and an abandoned gravel pit.

At the moment, however, there were twenty-one, count 'em, and Jimmy out of habit always did, people, besides himself and Sabrina, in the audience. Some of them might even have been alive, though it was hard to tell. The only ones who seemed to be significantly under a hundred were a traveling salesman type in his fifties with a nineteen-year-old hooker, a beefy good-old boy in his forties with the severely overweight little lady, and three Japanese guys who hunched over their drinks nervously as if slowly realizing they had gotten off the subway in Harlem by mistake instead of the Village.

It was an audience that Texas Jimmy wouldn't have wished on Adolf Hitler and the Auschwitz Boys, an audience that he wouldn't even have wished on the succession of acts actually condemned to face it.

Thus far, there had been a forty-year-old female vocalist in black leather and a pink mohawk slaughtering covers of Madonna and Annie Lennox, a black ventriloquist and his whiteface dummy, a trio of ancient hippies spastically warbling Golden Oldies from Woodstock, an actual fucking Gypsy violinist, and an Elvis impersonator gay as a tree full of chickadees.

The house band consisted of four pimply teenagers who looked like they'd cut your throat for a quarter and played like you'd be willing to pay it. The MC, a balding yutz in a too-tight tux with cuffs up to his shins and sleeves to match, had introduced himself to Jimmy before the agony began as the master of ceremonies, tennis coach, and assistant manager.

"Hey, Mr. Balaban, babes, you're in luck tonight," this schmuck had babbled, "we've booked a fabulous comic all the way from Hollywood tonight, the one and only, the incredibly talented, the world famous . . . *Ja—ack* Dunphy!"

Jack Dunphy was a name that Texas Jimmy dimly recognized, an ancient refugee from the local game-show circuit last seen doing used car slots in Bakersfield.

That had been about ninety minutes, five shots of bourbon, and a million years of stupefaction ago, and the booze had been too thoroughly watered to function as anesthesia. Sabrina, on the other hand, after sharing the bottle of champagne with him in the suite, had gone on to a series of cutely named sweet mixed drinks, most of which seemed to contain rum or gin or maybe both, and seemed to have succeeded in getting herself fairly thoroughly snockered.

At least she had stopped complaining about the acts, and sat there quietly turning green from the loathsome combinations churning in her stomach. Jimmy hoped she wasn't going to throw up, not that he could blame her, if this went on much longer he would probably puke himself.

On the stage, Elvis in drag had been replaced by a goddamn *dog act*, two horrible little yapping Yorkshire terriers in pink and blue bows being put through their pathetic paces by a fiftyish woman in a black tux and top hat who in a previous incarnation might once have been a Vegas chorus girl.

Weird, Jimmy thought, really weird. It was passingly strange to go this deep even in a dim dive like this without putting on the comic. Given the amount of time that had expired, Jimmy was beginning to have some faint hope that the ordeal was about to be over, that Dunphy hadn't shown and this was the last act on the bill.

They *couldn't* have something worse than this in the wings, could they?

The dog act ended to a smattering of applause from the salesman and polite grunts and head-bobs from the Japanese businessmen.

Beat. Empty stage. Beat.

The MC staggered onto the stage, looking backward over his shoulder with a goofy dazed expression. "Uh, ah, ladies and gentlemen, ah, I've been informed that Jack Dunphy can't be with us tonight, he, uh . . ."

"*Fell into the reactor pool and turned back into a two-hundred-pound frog!*"

A loud offstage voice, penetrating and raspy: a bit like Jimmy Durante, a bit like Popeye, a bit like a circular saw hitting sheet-metal.

The MC looked back at the audience with a sickly dumb-ass grin; given the previous level of acting ability he had displayed, Jimmy was pretty sure this was not an act of which he had expected to be part. What gives?

"But, uh, he's arranged for a replacement, the fabulous, the world-famous, the one and only, uh, ah—"

"*Ralf!*" barked the offstage voice. *Really* barked it. "Ralf! Ralf! Ar-A-El-Ef, just like it's spelled, Monkey Boy!"

"The amazing, uh, Ralf . . ."

The MC exited rather hurriedly stage right, as the man behind the voice bustled on from stage left.

He was built like a slightly overweight miniature gorilla, legs a bit too short for the body, arms a bit too long. He had thick curly black hair looked like it was combed with an eggbeater, blazed with silver here and there like he once stuck his dork in a light socket. He had dumbo ears that Jimmy would've almost bet were prehensile, and big brilliant blue eyes rolling like slot machine tumblers that just didn't seem to go with his grayish and unhealthy-looking Mediterranean complexion. Bulbous beaky nose that seemed redone by a plastic surgeon for comic effect, and a huge thick-lipped mouth in constant motion.

"Peace and Love, people to the power," he rasped, making a V-sign with his pudgy right hand.

He was wearing blue jeans, some kind of tie-dyed satin peasant blouse, Reeboks with the laces untied, and a brass peace sign on a leather thong approximately the diameter of a small Domino's pizza.

He paused, did a take, took two steps forward, shielding his eyes from the glare of the spot with his hand like an Indian scout, peered out into the audience.

"Hey, wait a minute, this don't *look* like Woodstock! Wheresa tie-dyes? Wheresa dope? Wheresa topless knockers?"

Although this failed to raise the audience from the dead, Texas Jimmy found himself moving to the edge of his chair. There was something about this guy, something about his delivery, something about that kazoo of a voice, something about the weird stance he had assumed before this audience, something about his entrance, that added up to a crazy energy that went right to Jimmy's backbrain . . .

The nose knows, Jimmy thought.

Ralf put his hands on his hips, regarded the audience indignantly. "Hey, what is this, my agent told me I was doin' the *capper* on the Age of Aquarius, not the *deathwatch* at the Sun City freezer!"

Dead silence.

"Where's Joe Cocker? Where's the Airplane? Where's Hendrix? Hey, if this is Woodstock, *you* corpsicles gotta be the ones got stuffed inna time machine!"

Beat.

Ralf stuck two fingers in his big yawp and emitted a piercing whistle. "Anybody still alive out there?"

He strutted to the lip of the stage, pointed imperiously at the salesman's teenage hooker.

"You!" he snapped. "Come on, I know *you're* still breathing, I can see your boobs moving when I stare down your cleavage, where the hell am I?"

"Kapplemeyer's Fabulous Sunset Room!" the girl managed to croak in a squeaky titter.

"*Kugglehammers's Flatulent Schlockschtick Gloom?*"

As a shriek of outrage that set the mirror ball vibrating.

Ralf's eyes rolled in horror. He recoiled a few steps back, staring around the room as if really seeing it for the first time.

"These toilet-colored walls . . . the MC in the ten-dollar funeral parlor tuxedo . . . those dumb tropical drinks with the puce plastic parasols . . ." he moaned. "Oh my God . . . oh no, tell me it ain't so, those idiots missed Woodstock and dropped me in the *Borscht Belt*!"

Texas Jimmy's antennae were twitching like a roach's on a bakery shop floor. The previous hour and a half's boredom was forgiven and forgotten.

This guy's material wasn't exactly something to write home about, and he hadn't raised a chuckle yet, but Jimmy was certain that none of this was scripted, that he was *winging it*.

Ralf balled his hands into fists. "I'm gonna *kill* my agent!" he screamed. He did a take. "Only . . . only the son of a bitch ain't even gonna be *born* for another century!"

He shrugged, stared imploringly at the audience.

"This *is* the end of the Psychedelic Sixties, right, the slagbrains at least got the *time* right, didn't they?" he said plaintively. "Didn't they? Dylan, the Beatles, Charlie Manson an' his Dune Buggy Death Commandos, all that good shit?"

"Wrong *century*, asshole," the Good Old Boy called out, "what planet you say you're from, haw, haw, haw?"

This actually drew a few snide snickers. Ralf timed it perfectly, doing a teeny take before snapping one off that turned it into a straight line.

"Planet of the Apes just like you, Monkey Boy," he mugged, scratching head and armpit chimpwise, "only back when I come from, we've actually started to *walk upright*!"

The timing drew a few laughs on its own, even though Jimmy was pretty sure even the yucks here who were laughing didn't really get it.

Ralf did a take, held his nose. "Wait a minute! *When am I?* I didn't inhale? Clarence Thomas and his Coca-Cola pubic hair? Boris Yeltsin takes a meeting with Jack Daniel's? Nixon's tricky dick? What's long and green and hangs from trees in the Mekong Delta? Not funny, Monkey People?"

"*This* is the act you dragged me to this dump to see?" Sabrina whoozed.

"Shaddap," Jimmy said out of the side of his mouth without looking at her, without conscious thought, then glanced in the direction of her bilious outrage. "I'm sorry, babe, but zip it and dig it, okay, I'm working."

"Gimme a break, willya, they told me *1969* when they conned me into the time machine, they told me *Woodstock*, not the *Borscht Belt*, my agent promised me a quarter million baby boomers on LSD would laugh at the old rubber crutch act, not twelve dead bodies an' Vlad the Impaler!"

"This guy sucks . . ." Sabrina opined before subsiding into sullen silence.

From the muttering grumbles, the rest of the audience, such as it was, would seem to agree.

"Come on, give me a hint, *what's funny now*? Billy Beer? Radovan Karadzic's Ethnic Laundromats? The Mother of All Fuckers?"

Okay, so this act was going over with this audience like a big black fart in a Williamsburg synagogue. The material was just what you might expect from a broken-down third-rate comic from the twenty-second century dropped back here with the wrong joke book. Only there *wasn't* any joke book. He was for sure ad-libbing all of it. Or rather *the character he was playing*, Ralf, the schlocky comedian from the future, was ad-libbing it.

This guy was *totally* in character.

And *that* was what had Texas Jimmy Balaban snapping his fingers for a waiter and fishing in his wallet for a business card. Because the character he was so totally into was indeed like an intrusion from another time zone, another movie.

Like an unknown comic name of Robin Williams dropped down to ad-lib his own alien into an otherwise nowhere sitcom called *Mork and Mindy*.

"Go backstage, give that guy my card as soon as he gets off, and tell him Texas Jimmy Balaban wants to buy him a drink and talk some business," he told the waiter, slipping him a card and a tenner.

Okay, so the chances were probably slim and none that Ralf was a great comic actor and stand-up ad-libbing genius in the same package like Robin Williams. But if this guy was no Williams, then there was only one thing he *could* be, and *that* was something more common, a phenomenon with which Jimmy was quite familiar.

Who in the Business wasn't?

Tiny Tim. Pee Wee Herman. Howard Stern.

Talents who were either off their nuts from the git-go or who had created one character to play all the time and gotten so far inside their singular schtick that they forgot to remember that it *was* a schtick. *Major* freak acts like that were few and far between, but the syndrome was quite common among the less stellar stable of clients who Jimmy booked onto the voracious late-night variety and afternoon chitchat circuits.

Texas Jimmy handled about a dozen real comics of varying degrees of mediocrity, and these were the clients he lived and died with. But to pay the rent, and the car payments, and the alimony, and keep up the necessary front, Jimmy, no less than the producers he dealt with, could not afford to turn up his nose at the "specialty acts." The whacked out speed-freak Madonna clones, flying saucer weirdos, yogurt enema gurus, and transvestite Marilyn Monroe channelers who filled airtime for a season or two before the boys in the white coats arrived with the nets and straitjackets.

At the very least, Ralf the Comedian from the Future would be an improvement over the usual run of such freak acts. Either the guy was a genius comic actor, or he was crazy, but either way, he had the moves and the timing. If he was sane enough to work with professionally written material and take a little coaching, who knew how far he might go?

Hopefully not quite as far as the Elvis impersonator Jimmy had done quite well with for about eight months. After which he had disappeared, and was next seen in full gear trying to crash an old pink Cadillac Eldorado convertible through the gates at Graceland. . . .

That Ralf came surging up to their table no more than five minutes after making his escape from the morosely zombified audience still wearing his stage gear and squinting at Jimmy's card seemed to betray a certain eagerness.

Up close, the outfit looked even cheesier. The tie-dye shirt seemed to be made of some kind of cheap plastic. The jeans sure weren't denim, and the phony leather label said "Levi Riders." The peace medallion reminded Jimmy of a slightly outsized Philadelphia pretzel, all it needed was the mustard. Ralf himself would need something slathered on his puss before he faced any camera. His grayish skin and big dirty pores reminded Jimmy of a moonscape, and there was something unhealthy-looking about his gums and teeth.

"*Texas Jimmy Balaban?*" Ralf said. "Funny, you don't *look* like a Texan."

He eyed Sabrina's cleavage as he plopped himself down on a chair, looked back at the card, looked at Jimmy, did a take. "But you *do* look like an agent."

"You, on the other hand, look like you could use a drink," Jimmy said, motioning for a waiter. "What'll it be, Ralf?" he said when a sixtyish character apparently still wearing his bar mitzvah tux waddled up to the table.

"Your bartender know how to make a Survival Special?" said Ralf.

"No," straight-manned the waiter, "how do you make a Survival Special?"

"A double shot of two-hundred-proof alcohol in a tall glass over ice with tap water from Chernobyl. If you survive it, you're something special."

"Hah, hah," said the waiter. "Now would you like to order a real drink?"

"That *is* a real drink when I come from, Monkey Boy," said Ralf.

"Stoly on the rocks with Evian and a slice of lime," Jimmy said quickly. "That okay, with you, Ralf?"

"You got real vodka?" said Ralf. "You got real *lime*? I hate that synthetic stuff, tastes like toilet disinfectant, and looks like snot Jell-o."

The waiter rolled his eyes and departed. Sabrina grimaced.

"Hey, you're not onstage anymore, you can relax now," Texas Jimmy suggested.

"I can't *tell you* how glad I am to hear that," Ralf snapped at him sarcastically. He plucked at the front of his atrocious plastic simulated tie-dye shirt.

"My agent tells me to learn a routine for the Sixties, they costume me in *this* and stuff me inna wayback without so much as a change of underwear, here's some period pocket money, you can buy what you need when you get there, and then they screw up and drop me back half a century or so late, the time machine's supposed to make the pickup November 15, 1969, which means it's come and gone *decades* ago, so I'm stuck here in this Monkey Boy suit, with no gig and about enough money to buy one decent change of clothes, in a century, which, as you will find out, Balaban, is not gonna be one vintage year after another, but hey, I can *relax*, no problem!"

He spit it all out like schtick, but it wasn't really funny, and his heavy brows were frowning, and those blue eyes seemed to burn with something like real anger.

Or, thought Jimmy, genuine craziness. Either that, or this guy simply didn't *know* how to turn it off.

Whichever, there was no percentage in pressing the issue. Texas Jimmy was not inexperienced in dealing with people who claimed to be straight off the boat from Atlantis or Busby Berkeley's tap-dancing cousin from Mars. The operative question was not whether such people were loco in the coco, or whether they were just determined to keep shining you on, but whether their schtick was marketable. And if so, whether they were unencumbered by previous contractual arrangements.

"Can I ask you a serious question?" Jimmy said neutrally.

"Do you expect a serious answer?"

"Do you *really* have an agent?"

"Do I have an agent?" Ralf repeated slowly. "You mean do I have an agent *now* . . . ?"

"I mean do you have a contract you can't get out of?"

"I will, in about a hundred and fifty years or so," Ralf said. He scratched his head theatrically. "But I'll be dead by then, won't I, so who cares, let the son of a bitch sue me."

The waiter arrived with Ralf's drink.

Ralf took a big gulp, smacked his lips, fished out the lime slice with his fingers, held it up to his eyes and studied it reverently for a moment like a cutter appraising a raw diamond, then popped it into his mouth, peel and all, and chewed it slowly down with what seemed like an expression of genuine bliss.

"The dim dumb past *do* have its compensations," he said with a smile.

Jimmy's brain began to feel like it was floating free in its skull socket, and given the amount of watering the bar whiskey in this joint had been forced to endure, it could hardly be the booze.

This last little piece of business had been a little *too* convincing to be a piece of business. Either Ralf was sincerely schizzy, or . . . or . . . aw, that was ridiculous . . .

"We were talking about representation," Texas Jimmy said, attempting to beam the conversation back to planet Earth. "I think your act has potential—"

"You do!"

"—needs work, needs professional material, you understand, but I think you've got it. I take thirty percent off the top, but out of that I pay the gag writers, and the acting coach, and the insurance, and if you want, I can handle your finances at no extra charge too. Interested?"

"Well, yeah," Ralf said. "I mean, under the circumstances, what choice do I have? My pickup's long gone, and it'll take another century or so for my slag-brained previous agent to even be born yesterday, so I guess you got yourself a client, Mr. Balaban."

"Hey, look, the deal's off if you've got a valid contract with another agent, the last thing in the world I need is any more legal tsuris," Jimmy admonished, "my wife is giving enough of—"

"*Your wife!*" shrieked Sabrina. "You didn't tell me you were married!"

Oh shit.

"In name only, babes," Jimmy said hastily, patting her hand in reassurance. "And not for much longer, believe me, there's only a few little legal details to—"

"You're gonna get me subpoenaed as a corespondent in some tacky—"

"Relax, will you, they can't extradite you to California for a crappy divorce action, besides which I don't think the detective—"

"*You knew you were being tailed, you son of a bitch?*" Sabrina shouted. "That's why you dragged me all the way up here to this shithole, isn't it!"

"Zip it," Jimmy hissed as the heads of a few of the less comatose patrons turned shakily in their table's direction.

Sabrina's face became hard as an IRS auditor's heart. "If you don't give me cab fare back to New York *right* now, Jimmy Balaban," she hissed back at him, "I am going to start screaming. About how you shot me up with heroin so you could jam your diseased penis up my innocent virgin bunghole."

"*Jesus*—"

"Three hundred bucks should about cover it," Sabrina said, folding her arms across her ample bosom.

"I don't have that kind of cash on me," Jimmy told her. "But tomorrow we'll find a cash machine—"

"On the count of three! One! Two! Thr—"

"We got a deal, I'll lend you the cash," Ralf said. "You can pay me back tomorrow."

From a pants pocket, he produced a roll of bills, peeled off three, handed them to Jimmy.

They were hundreds. They were so new they stuck together. The ink didn't seem quite—

"Gimme!" said Sabrina, snatching them out of his hands with a nice theatrical flourish, and flouncing out stage right.

"Could I see another one of those bills, Ralf?" Jimmy said suspiciously.

"What's the matter with them?" Ralf said nervously, forking one over. "Don't tell me those slagbrains screwed *that* up too!"

Jimmy studied the hundred-dollar bill. He was no expert judge of funny money, but if the hundred was counterfeit, he couldn't tell, and if he couldn't tell, your average cabdriver couldn't tell either. It certainly seemed like a perfectly legitimate hundred-dollar bill, if a bit hot off the presses. But then, you sometimes got bills like that if the bank happened to have gotten a brand-new supply from the Treasury. . . .

Jimmy looked again.

Did a take.

The year on the bill was 1969.

2

While the singular "Amanda" had just the right resonance in her higher incarnation along the New Age Circuit, in the world of Los Angeles maya, Amanda found it useful to spin off secondary functional avatars and name them accordingly.

Amanda von Staulenburg was the name on her driver's license, credit cards, and the bills she found in the mailbox when she arrived back home in Topanga. Amanda's right to a legitimate "von" had been the proceeds of her amiable divorce from a count of the true Staulenburg line, a love of her youth who had never been closer to the seat of his title than Solvang. It intimidated obnoxious headwaiters and showbiz princelings, and bankers when they read it on questionable checks. And in lieu of alimony, her count had caused her to retain karmic possession of the house at Big Rock. She didn't own the place, legally speaking, it didn't exactly exist.

A sailing buddy of Carl von Staulenburg, another Count of California with a limited cash flow, had acquired a huge piece of empty property in Topanga, arroyos, chaparral-covered hilltops, and a mighty mini-mountain of a boulder called Big Rock, sacred to the now-vanished Chumash.

Rich in land and nothing else, he and his wife had constructed their own rough-hewn rambling demense without regard for the building codes. A compulsive builder not content with merely carpentering endless additions onto the family manor, he had built three secondary houses on the estate, which in theory were supposed to provide income as rental properties. In practice, they mostly provided shelter from the storm for a flow-through of assorted friends, relatives, temporarily insolvent writers, artists, and film people, among whom had been Carl and Amanda von Staulenberg.

When they broke up, Carl had arranged with his friend for Amanda to stay in the house permanently. Amanda's rental agreement with this most laid-back of landlords was based on a temporal communist principle—this month according to my ability, next month according to your need.

The house itself had been built in a hollow, so it and the main house were mutually hidden from each other, preserving the illusion of wilderness solitude for all concerned. It was shaded from the Southern Californian sun by a thick grove of eucalyptus trees so that the ecological ambience was that of a mountain cabin a good deal farther north.

Built of rough planking which had weathered to a splintery gray, the house had a big back bedroom, a secondary guestroom and junk storage facility, a toilet and separate primitive bath, a semi-enclosed semi-eat-in country kitchen with a little roofed back porch, and a large rustic living room opening out onto a front porch affording a magnificent view of Big Rock. Sitting out there on the porch toward sunset with a glass of Chablis or a joint, Amanda sensed that she was *just* where she belonged.

The Santa Monica mountains were the southernmost spiritual foothills of the mighty cordillera of her dearest California, the great jumble and tumble of ranges marching up the Pacific interior, which she toured as a pilgrim seeker and sometime teacher in her latest cheap clunker. Out on her porch, watching the sun setting over Big Rock cast purple shadows across the shaggy green hillsides and inhaling the sweet perfume of the mountain evening, Amanda would feel herself humbly and contentedly seated like an acolyte at the feet of this towering mythic landscape, this great wise Buddha of rock and loam.

Twenty minutes away to the north, up Topanga Canyon Boulevard, however, was the suburban ticky-tacky of the San Fernando Valley and the smog-bound traffic of the Ventura Freeway, and twenty minutes east on the 101, if you were lucky, was Hollywood and *its* spiritual foothills in Burbank and Fairfax and Studio City.

"Amanda von Staulenburg" might have a certain cache, but it didn't letter very well, so in her showbiz avatar she was Amanda Robin, under which SAG-registered moniker she played supporting roles in TV shows, small parts in the occasional feature, did commercials when she was lucky enough, and sometimes coached talent in the rough.

Unlike most such showbiz fringies constrained to waitress or worse to support their dreams of stardom, Amanda harbored no such illusory ambitions, and as far as she was concerned, this *was* her day job, and she was not about to give it up. It was honest work, karmically cleaner than succumbing to the temptation to turn mercenary guru. It was freelance and occasional, and—since by the time expenses and what she spent on other people's seminars were deducted from what she made giving her "experiences" on the New Age Circuit she just about broke even—it paid the bills.

Of which there were the usual sufficient supply when she returned. What was more, the latest refugee from Rent-A-Wreck was showing signs of terminal fatigue. What with all the mountain driving she did and the rutted dirt road between Topanga Canyon Boulevard and her house, Amanda beat the hell out of cars.

Her solution was to buy the cheapest set of wheels still capable of getting her from point A to point B—$500 was her absolute limit—and then simply do nothing but keep it gassed and oiled until it expired. Sometimes that was three weeks, sometimes over a year. In the long run, it beat investing a couple three thousand in a used something every year or two. Her current clunker, an ancient Ford Pinto, was now guzzling almost as much oil as gas and farting out horrible black smoke. No way it was going to get past the next mandatory smog inspection.

So once she had aired out the house, put the groceries in the fridge, and tossed the bills on the coffee table, she went straight to her answering machine in hopes that it had recorded some offers of gainful employ.

Alas, there was nothing from her agent. The only call that promised anything at all was from a schlockmeister name of Texas Jimmy Balaban.

This, she knew, would not be an offer of a part. She had worked as a talent coach for Balaban from time to time, never as an actress. Texas Jimmy Balaban had nothing to do with cinematic or TV drama. He had a stable of more or less professional comedians whom he booked into clubs and lesser TV slots and supplied weirdos and so-called specialty acts to the talk-show circuit.

Amanda had worked with his down-at-the-heels comics a couple of times, but mostly a call from Texas Jimmy meant making one of his sideshow attractions presentable enough to slither past talk-show producers with slots to fill and coherent enough to more or less survive on the air. But at least Balaban was an *honorable* schlockmeister. He had never stiffed her, never even been significantly late in paying up, and after one attempt at getting inside her pants, he had accepted the entirely professional nature of their relationship, which was more than could be said for most of the masculine life-forms at his level of the business.

As Amanda Robin, she could even find Texas Jimmy Balaban *charming* after a fashion.

"Okay, Jimmy, what have you got for me now?" she asked when she got him on the line. "Another mumbling white rapper with an attitude problem? Another Marilyn look-alike with a voice like Donald Duck?"

"Would you believe a comedian from the future?"

"Coming from you," Amanda shot back good-naturedly, "I'd believe Napoleon in drag fresh off the two o'clock flying saucer from Venus."

"No, I mean, I'm serious."

"You're serious . . . You've got a comedian from the future, and you're serious. *Right* . . ."

"This is kind of hard to explain," Balaban said in an entirely uncharacteristic tone of bemusement. "You had to be there, and even then . . ."

There was a long pause at the other end of the line.

"I was in a crummy dive in the Borscht Belt," Balaban said somewhat furtively. "Don't ask me what I was doing in a dump like that, but stepping in shit is considered good luck in certain circles, and this case proves the point, there I was, a place I ordinarily wouldn't be caught dead in at the right time to catch Ralf's act fresh outa the time machine—"

"*Out of the time machine?*"

"The schtick is he's a comic from the future down on his luck bullshitted into a time machine by his sleazebag agent and dropped back here in the present where nobody's heard his stale material yet."

"This is a sitcom format?"

"No, Amanda, this guy is real."

"You mean this is his act?"

"Yeah . . . I mean no . . . I mean I'm not sure . . ."

"Another one of your refugees from the Twilight Zone you want me to help you turn into a specialty item for the talk-show circuit?"

"No, yeah, well I'm not sure, if he *is* a nutcase, he's a nutcase *comedian*, he's got the moves, he's got the timing, he's got the delivery, he can ad-lib, all he really needs is some writers and polishing."

Amanda took a deep breath. "Sounds to me like what you've got is either a comedian who's gone off the deep end or someone who's such a good comic *actor* he's got a pro like *you* going."

There was another weird pause at the other end of the line.

"Yeah, that's what I'd say if it wasn't for the thing with the money."

"Money?"

"Well, ah, I had a kind of sudden cash problem, and he whips out this roll of hundreds so new you can just about still smell the ink."

"So?"

"Dated 1969?"

"*Huh?*"

"Yeah, right, exactly. So I come right out and ask him whether these bills are counterfeit. And he says they told him that they're identical to the legal tender of the period down to the atomic level, whatever that means. Well, what it seems to me to mean is that this stuff is queer. When I pin him on it, he sez if it walks like a buck and talks like a buck and passes like a buck, it *is* a buck. Hah, hah, only he seems kind of nervous about it."

Texas Jimmy Balaban's voice came down half an octave and his delivery slowed down and softened, and if this wasn't sincere bemusement, he had a career in films.

"Well, when I get him back to LA, I pay for his ticket on my Visa 'cause I'm not gonna trust those hundreds, I take one of the bills into a bank like a dim-witted citizen, and I ask the teller would he please tell me if it's the real thing, I found it on the street, and break it into twenties for me if it is. The guy looks it over, fingers it, holds it up to the light, does a little take. He pulls a hundred out of his cash drawer, compares them. Calls over another guy, whispers something, the guy goes away, comes back with a magnifying glass and some black light thing. They shine the light on the bills, look at 'em under the glass, look at me kinda weird. . . .

"Well? I ask. Is it real? Yeah, it's real, all right, they tell me, and the teller counts out five twenties. You say you found it on the street? he says. Yeah, I tell him. And then you know what he says?"

Amanda laughed. "You sure you didn't get it out of a time machine?" she said.

"Wow, hey, what are you, psychic?"

Thursdays after first Wednesdays were seldom days when the creative juices flowed freely. Dexter Lampkin sat there in front of his computer staring at a file called "Story Ideas" filled with two hours' worth of random gibberish. Dexter was between projects. He had finished his latest novel three months ago. He had handed in the first draft of a half hour Saturday-morning script last week, and hadn't gotten the call to come in for the rewrite meeting yet. The rent was paid, the bill tray was empty, there was four months' worth of nut money in the bank, cheery late-morning sunlight was pouring in through the window of his office, a day of freedom lay before him. This time should be golden.

This, after all, was what Dexter lived for, wasn't it?

The Float.

There was a moldy oldie from the Sixties that summed it up:

A hippie and a businessman meet in a bar, and the businessman starts getting on the hippie about cleaning up his act and getting a real job.

"Look at me, I've got a house, and a wife, and two kids, and a car, and even a cabin in the woods around Big Sur where we spend two weeks of fully-paid vacation every summer, just sittin' around, gettin' pleasantly buzzed, and watchin' the flowers grow!"

"Right," sez the hippie, "you bust your balls for fifty weeks to spend two weeks doing what I get to do all year!"

Time was, Dexter identified with the hippie. In Berkeley, Dexter had *lived* like a rich hippie, writing what the spirit moved him to write when it moved him, and making a living at it. These latter LA days, with the wife, and the kid, and the two cars, and a monthly nut he really couldn't cover on a science fiction novel a year, he was of necessity enough of a *professional writer* to glumly identify with the businessman, or at least to long nostalgically for those innocent bygone days.

And now, here he was, with no bills to worry about, no assignments, no deadlines to meet, right here in the Float, and what was he doing with it?

Nada. Zip. Nothing.

Dexter sighed. The truth of it was that this was really just a standard case of the first Thursday blues. The monthly meeting of the "Transformationalist Circle" hadn't *really* been more depressing than usual.

The meeting had been at Dick and Clara Braithwaite's place out in the North Hollywood flats, bought when Dick had been pretty high up at Rockwell, and while they were no longer so flush after NASA funding went south, Clara had never lost her job at JPL, and Dick had been able to sign on with some outfit doing military stuff he couldn't talk about, so they had been able to keep up the mortgage payments.

The house had a backyard with a swimming pool, and while the night wasn't quite warm enough for swimming, it was certainly balmy enough to move the proceedings out of doors, and that's where they all were when Dexter made his entrance.

Besides Dick and Clara, there were Maggie and Doug Kappler, a pair of overweight science fiction fans; Johnnie Steinfeld, who was apparently a professional dope dealer; Drew Sanderson, a software wizard; Bobby Gomez, Jack Kahn, and Irene Farrow, wannabe science fiction writers; Hank Farmer, who still held down a middle rank position in what was left of the planetary program and his wife, Louise, who taught ecology at USC; and Bruce Torterelli, who did special effects lab stuff at Disney.

The current hard core of the Transformationalist Circle.

Dexter's loyal fans.

Sort of.

What these people had in common was in a word, Fandom.

Not Dexter D. Lampkin fandom. *Science fiction* Fandom.

Fans didn't just read the stuff. They went to science fiction conventions. Some of them dreamed of being science fiction *writers*. Some of them tried. Some of them succeeded. Some of them wrote for the amateur fanzines. On the average, their IQs were about thirty points over the norm. On the average, they were about twenty-five pounds overweight.

Science fiction Fandom was a transnational tribe. There couldn't be more than ten or fifteen thousand of them, but they formed a network that permeated the world. Anyone plugged into that network could get off a plane in Novosibirsk or Winnipeg or Brataslava and be welcomed by fellow tribespeople. Fandom's tendrils also extended into worldwide *scientific* communities, and when Dexter had been doing his research for *The Transformation,* there was hardly a scientist in the country he couldn't get to by working the fannish network, and more often than not someone embarrassingly honored to be privileged to make his acquaintance.

That was the upside.

The downside was that while there were only a few thousand dedicated science fiction fans, they could and did fill hotels with grotesque costumed mob scenes, they were vocal, they were articulate, they published hundreds of fanzines, and therefore tended to determine the literature's schlocky image to the world at large.

That was the downside of the downside. The upside of the downside was in its way worse, and it was what kept Dexter coming to these goddamn things every first Wednesday and swearing never again every first Thursday. Science fiction Fandom attracted just the sort of personality types susceptible to cultist affiliations in general and that science fiction was a literature based upon the creation of imaginary worlds only enhanced its appeal to schizoid personalities seeking to psychically inhabit realities other than what the fans themselves called the "mundane."

And where there are people looking for the Yellow Brick Road out of Kansas and into Oz, there you will have a guru-shaped hole waiting for someone to fill it, and the seductive danger for science fiction writers was to don that messianic mantle. More science fiction writers than one had become gurus of their own fannish cults, and L. Ron Hubbard had expanded *his* fannish following into the Church of Scientology.

The Transformationalists were Dexter's.

Dexter did not encourage worship of the wonderfulness of his being like so many of his colleagues who had found themselves in this position, indeed he did his best to discourage it, or so at least he told himself as he got a Bud out of the ice chest, and plopped down on a folding chair between Dick Braithwaite and Louise Farmer.

". . . the data's conclusive now, as far as anyone who's not kidding themselves is concerned . . ."

Nor had he created the Transformationalist Circle, well not exactly, certainly not *intentionally*, he had just been doing research for *The Transformation*. Okay, maybe he *had* poured a lot of beer and stronger stuff into a lot of scientists, rolled them joints, and deliberately picked their brains.

". . . a water ocean a thousand or two kilometers thick kept liquid by the pressure . . ."

And admittedly, maybe he *had* blathered on about how they could participate in the transformation of civilization by helping him make the program of his fictional Transformational Circle the real thing . . .

". . . coral die-offs nowhere near major pollution sites . . ."

But after the book was published he had walked away from it all, now hadn't he, he hadn't even *known* that a little group of fans thought they had *become* the Transformationalist Circle until the book was actually *out of print*.

"Hey, who wants a hit?"

Johnnie had a joint out and was waving it invitingly as he moved off to a corner of the yard. Bobby, Irene, and Bruce got up to join him, and Dexter decided he might as well too. Unlike the people here still holding down jobs in aerospace, science fiction writers did not have to pass piss tests. Dexter did have enough status here to get the first hit off the joint, and that much fannish deference he did not deny himself.

"So what are you working on now, Dex?" Bobby Gomez said.

"Just finished a draft of a *Captain Zero* . . ."

Irene Farrow wrinkled her nose in distaste. "Jeez, why are you wasting your time on Saturday-morning cartoon shows?"

"Because it pays four grand for twenty-two pages," Dexter shot back.

She was an aspiring writer and a sincere admirer of Dexter's ouevre, and he *had* fucked her once at a Westercon, but that didn't give her the right to come down on him for doing a little honest hackwork.

He held up his half-full beer can as if it were empty, grunted something about a refill, and used it as an exit line, moving toward the poolside ice-chest and, hopefully, less depressing conversation.

Dexter had been bemused, when Colin Moore, a JPL assistant mission controller at the time, had invited him to his first meeting of the Transformationalist Circle. Moore had been one of the people he had used as a resource when he was researching the book, and Dexter had heard that some of the scientists he had enlisted sometimes got together and had a few beers, but he had never imagined such a thing as a Dexter D. Lampkin fan club. And as it turned out, that wasn't quite what the Transformationalist Circle was.

A handful of scientists who had helped him on the project and who were dedicated science fiction fans had simply missed the bull sessions that Dexter had encouraged and started meeting on their own. They identified with the fictional Transformationalist Circle in the novel, and they took Dexter's concept of a Transformation Crisis in the evolution of all intelligent species quite seriously, or at least when it came to the current nexus in the destiny of homo sap.

Why shouldn't they? The handwriting was already on the wall for those in the know enough to read it.

Fossil fuels weren't going to last forever, fusion research was getting nowhere, the space program was spinning its wheels, the oceans were in lousy shape, an ozone hole had been discovered over the Antarctic, nuclear wastes were piling up with no place to dump them, the rain forests vital to maintaining a breathable atmosphere were going, the planet was warming up, and you didn't need to be Nobel class to know that this was the generation that would decide the future of the species for good or ill.

At first, Dexter was touched. He had poured his heart and soul into a novel that had bombed, and here, years later, were real scientists who *still took it seriously*, who believed in *his* book with a passion that he himself had done his best to forget. So Dexter had fallen into the pattern of attending these meetings, and in the early days, when the regulars had all been scientists, with a somewhat secondhand renewal of the passion that had moved him during the writing of the book. He granted any interview that the Transformationalist fanzine wanted, chaired convention panels on the Transformation Crisis, even contributed a few thousand free words to the fanzine from time to time.

Of course, all this made no noticeable progress in saving the species from its own assholery. But of course, what a fannish futurology cult whose meetings were attended by real fannish scientists *did* do was attract its own outer circle of ordinary garden variety sf fans.

". . . this ozone degradation . . ."

". . . happened at least once before, you know, the biomass changed the atmosphere and nearly wiped itself out . . ."

Dexter drained his beer, pulled another out of the ice-chest, drifted over to where the Farmers, Clara Braithwaite, and Jack Kahn seemed engaged in the sort of conversation that had been the group's main raison d'être way back when.

". . . I thought the latest is that an asteroid hit is supposed to be what did the dinosaurs. . . ."

"Not *that*," said Louise Farmer. "I'm talking about what happened when a mutant microorganism in the early oceans evolved the ability to photosynthesize and started to release free oxygen into the atmosphere—"

"Which was toxic to most of the preexisting biosphere—"

"Which almost died out as a result," Louise said. "It was a damn close thing—"

"And you think—"

Louise shrugged. "If the primitive biomass managed to come that close to making the atmosphere nonviable for its own biochemistry over a few hundred thousand years with a single accumulated *microeffect*, what makes you think that advanced critters like ourselves aren't capable of doing the same thing in a century or two with all the chemical *macroeffects* of our so-called advanced technological civilization?"

The scientists who attended the meetings were accustomed to turning over scut work to navvy lab assistants and eager grad students. First the fans become the gophers, then meetings started being held at their places so they could be stuck with the work of cleaning up afterward.

"You think we've done it already?" Dexter said. "Gone beyond the point of no return?"

Slowly, the Transformationalist Circle was itself transformed, from small gatherings of scientists accumulating a few fannish hangers-on to an excuse for fannish parties with Dexter and a few of the original crowd as window dressing. . . .

"We've certainly already changed the atmosphere enough so that our presence could be detected from a few light-years away by a civilization with instruments not much better than our own, Dex," Louise said. "What really worries me is that these processes have a lot of temporal inertia. I think what we're seeing now in terms of *effects* is only the results of the *causes* we've been pumping into the atmosphere up to maybe 1960 or so. What we've done *after that*, we won't really know for decades."

"Maybe even scarier than you think," said Drew Sanderson, who had come up beside Dex. "I mean, in light of chaos theory . . ."

"Chaos theory?" said Dexter. "Fractals? Strange attractors? Mandlebrot sets?"

Once in a while a conversation like this revealed a bit of intellectual fire still left in the embers, or so Dexter managed to persuade himself.

Drew laughed. "I'm not talking about weird patterns to stare at when you're stoned," he said. "I'm talking about the fact that huge macroeffects in certain inherently chaotic systems, like for instance a *planetary atmosphere*, can be generated by itsy-bitsy *microchanges* in the initial conditions."

"Like what might have happened when Mars dried out and froze!" exclaimed Clara. "Latest guess is it all happened within ten or twenty thousand years. And *that* was a natural process!"

"Right," said Hank Farmer. "In theory, anyway, a few last molecules of hydrogen eroded into space, the atmospheric pressure was no longer high enough to maintain water in a liquid phase, the atmospheric pressure drop accelerated, the process fed on itself, went exponential, and in a few millennia the whole planet freeze-dried itself!"

"Yeah, the math says *one* hydrogen atom more or less in the original atmosphere could've made all the difference," said Drew. He grinned evilly. "But the same math says not merely that it's impossible to *predict* what kind of macrochange a microchange in the initial conditions is going to produce in a chaotic system like an atmosphere, but that the *effect itself* is inherently nondeterministic."

"Or human civilization, right?" Dexter blurted. "That's probably a chaotic system too . . . and so are *we!*"

An elusive notion teased at the edge of Dexter's awareness. If human civilization were a chaotic system, the inherently indeterminant sum of billions upon billions of microchanges made every moment by those billions of chaotic subsystems called human beings . . .

"Then every move we make, every breath we take, can have, maybe *must* have enormous consequences. . . ."

It had long been a staple notion of science fiction that you could completely change the future by making one tiny change that rippled out into enormity up the timeline. *Give me a lever and a place to stand and I will move the world,* Archimedes had proclaimed, thus launching a thousand and one schlocky alternate world stories.

"Some of them," Drew said. "But the same math says there's no way of predicting which ones."

"Or *how!*" Dexter exclaimed.

For if he was really beginning to grasp this mind-twisting mathematical principle, you could *never* know how anything you did was going to move the world, *not even if you were omnipotent God Almighty Himself*, because . . . because . . .

"Like that Aldiss story where the guy goes back in time and steps on a butterfly and the whole future—"

"Was a Bradbury story, Doug!"

"Brian Aldiss!"

Oh shit!

The idea, whatever it might have been, was gone.

Doug and Maggie Kappler had barged into the conversation and brought it back to Earth with a leaden thump.

The pair of overweight fans rounded on Dexter. "Which one was it, Dex?" Maggie Kappler demanded.

"I dunno . . ." Dexter mumbled, even though he did, not about to settle some nitpicking moronic fannish argument that had shattered the only interesting conversation he had heard all night just when it was starting to give him an important idea he could no longer remember.

And now here he was, on another Thursday morning after, swearing to himself that last night had been the last time, that next month he wouldn't go, or at least not if he had a period of Float like this in front of him to ruin.

Although just before those asshole Kapplers had stuck their fat noses in, he *had* been starting to get some kind of idea, hadn't he?

Dexter opened a file called "Chaos."

It had been during that conversation about planetary atmospheres, and Mars, and chaos theory, hadn't it, that some kind of an idea had started to swim through the tropical fish tank of his mind, maybe he could remember it, yeah, mathematical refutation of predestination in—

The phone rang.

Shit!

He picked it up.

"Hello?" he grunted.

"Dexter Lampkin?"

"Yeah, who's this?"

"Texas Jimmy Balaban," said the voice on the other end. "I maybe got some work for you, Lampkin."

Texas Jimmy Balaban? The name rang some kind of faint bell. The guy was some kind of sleazy agent, wasn't he? Handled talk-show weirdos and third-rate comedians.

"You write sci-fi, don't you, Lampkin, I seem to remember?"

Right, he had sold some material to this character a few times before.

"From time to time . . ." Dexter said dryly.

Gag writing was not exactly his forte, but it was cost-effective work when you could get it. Not something you could sit down and agonize over for hours. You just sort of kept the assignment in the back of your mind and wrote down schtick if and when it came to you.

"Well look, Lampkin, I need some Man From the Future jokes, and I figured it would be right up your alley—"

"—you need *what*—"

"—two hundred bucks a running minute for anything gets used on the air, a hundred for club dates. Interested?"

Dexter shrugged to himself. "Why not?" he said. He wasn't doing anything but screwing around today anyway. "Course I can't promise you anything . . ."

"Tell me about it," Texas Jimmy Balaban groused. "No offense intended Lampkin, but I've been around long enough to know you guys can't turn it on like a faucet, so I've got half a dozen other writers on it too."

"No offense taken," Dexter told him. "But you mind telling me what you want jokes about a Man From the Future *for*?"

"Not jokes *about* a Man From the Future, jokes *for* a Man From the Future to tell on the talk-show circuit."

"*Huh?*"

There was a rather long pause on the other end of the line.

"I've, uh, signed a new comic," Balaban finally said. "Calls himself Ralf. His schtick's supposed to be that he's a comedian from the future—"

"A comedian from the future?"

"—shoved into a time machine by his agent to drop him back here in the past where his hundred-year-old material is still funny. Only it ain't. I mean, I gotta get him some professional material."

"Too bad they didn't send some gag writers back from the future with him," Dexter said dryly.

Balaban laughed, a shade nervously maybe, but with some real warmth. "That's the spirit, Lampkin . . . Dexter," he said. "Like just imagine that they *did*, and it's *you*, right, and you gotta come up with material, or they'll never beam you back to Buck Rogers Broadway." He laughed. "Hey, that's pretty good, like one of your sci-fi stories, right?"

Dexter laughed. "Maybe *you* should try writing science fiction, Jimmy," he said.

There was another pause at the other end of the line.

"Believe me, Dexter," Texas Jimmy Balaban said in a strangely serious tone of voice, "I'd be out there peddling the story of the last couple days to the *Twilight Zone* if the latest revival hadn't been canceled."

———

Three-fifteen found Amanda a quarter of an hour late for her rendezvous with Texas Jimmy Balaban and his man from the future due to the ordinary impossibility of finding a parking place within a reasonable distance of his office on Larrabee.

How could she have refused to at least take a meeting? Texas Jimmy certainly didn't have the imagination to invent such a schtick for one of his acts, and Jimmy had projected a rather affectingly furtive confusion, as if he halfway believed the guy's comedian from the future story but was ashamed to admit it. And that business with the back-dated hundred-dollar bills had been the clincher.

Okay, a sincere schizoid could be capable of inventing all the details without even knowing it. The subconscious was capable of amazing creative feats. Nor would it have been impossible for a good actor to have gotten hold of those old hundred-dollar bills in mint condition somewhere, or even happened upon them and created this whole story around the prop. But the probabilities would only be credible to a professional skeptic proceeding from the unshakable premise that the universe was a system of known and immutable scientific law which could not be transcended. And this was an axiom that Amanda had seen Occam's Razor slice into very thin salami on numerous occasions.

And Texas Jimmy Balaban, certainly no gullible rube at the Cosmic Carnival, seemed to be reluctantly wrestling with the unsettling possibility that a bolide from another reality had pierced the veil of showbiz maya.

All of which, if not exactly Enlightenment under the Bo tree or the moral equivalent of a thousand mikes of acid, was enough of a spirit message to cause Amanda to brave the 101 in her cranky Pinto, and, ultimately, to park way west and trudge on foot all the way to Larrabee. For the experiential transcendence of quotidian reality or the hope thereof were what the *real* Amanda lived for, those moments of lucid clarity when the mists parted to reveal not ultimate truth but ultimate mystery.

Besides which, she needed the money.

Texas Jimmy Balaban's office was on the third floor of the sort of building that accommodated small insurance agencies, travel agents of dubious repute, and not very successful dentists. There was no receptionist on duty at the empty front desk, just a dusty brown couch, and a coffee table offering out-of-date copies of *Variety*, the *Hollywood Reporter,* and *People*.

Balaban himself opened the door to the inner office when Amanda hit the buzzer, a lanky fiftyish man in a chocolate-colored suit and open-collared white shirt, with wavy brown hair thinning on top, a wide grin full of capped teeth, a Las Vegas tan, baggy green eyes, and an air of slightly overripe showbiz charm that would-be starlets no doubt found, if not exactly attractive, then hopeful.

"Come on in, Amanda," he said, "Ralf's waiting in my office."

When she stepped into the corridor, Amanda was assailed by the aroma of emergency bachelor habitation—an effluvium compounded of old pizza cartons, Styrofoam cups rimed with dead coffee, and shaving cream—which informed the feminine backbrain that some guy had been kicked out of or fled from his apartment and was sleeping on grimy sheets on a cot or fold-a-bed in a spare room.

The office, however, was show-business-like. A large teak desk. A yellowing rubber tree badly in need of watering. Walls filled with signed photos of Balaban's own clients and a few all-purpose celebrities who had deigned to grant Texas Jimmy his thirty seconds for a handshake shot.

Bouncing off the edge of a black leatherette sofa was Texas Jimmy Balaban's comedian from the future, wearing a horrible lime green leisure suit that Texas Jimmy must have bought him to look weird in.

Balaban could have saved his $49.95.

Ralf was a short burly man, with a big nose, an even bigger mop of uncombed curly black hair blazed with silver, an unhealthy Eastern winter pallor, and protruding ears, mugging at her with a rubbery grin and large rolling blue eyes as he extended a beefy hand.

"Hi there, Beauty, I'm your Beast," he rasped in a kazoo of a voice. "Jimmy tells me you're supposed to dumb down my act for the dim brains of Mr. and Mrs. Slaghead, and from what I've seen on the tube here so far, it ain't gonna be easy, current comedy seems aimed at the kind of yuks who think a fart cushion is the height of sophisticated humor and Moby Dick is some kind of disgusting venereal disease."

Particularly funny maybe it wasn't, but like Howard Stern or Dice Clay or for that matter even the unfunny attack-dog likes of Rush Limbaugh or Pat Buchanan, there was an edgy energy boiling off him like heat waves off hot asphalt—or like the aura of frenzy of an actor auditioning for a part that would mean a quantum leap for his career.

"I'm Amanda—"

"And I'm Ralf. Ar! Ay! El! Ef! Ralf! Ralf! Ralf!"

Barking it like a dog as he pumped her arm.

This guy was *on*.

Amanda almost found herself believing that he *was* an obnoxious comic from a sleazebag back-alley club in some future Las Vegas rather than just a refugee from the Borscht Belt trying to hype a nowhere career by playing the part of same.

Except that he was pushing it *too* hard. If he was acting, he was overacting to the point where the overacting itself became part of the act. He was so *on* he was *off*.

"Uh, sit down, Amanda," Balaban said, pulling up the only chair by the table so she was forced to seat herself on the sofa next to Ralf, who dropped down beside her, invisibly vibrating.

"Well, what do you think?" Balaban said.

"Well, what do you want?" said Amanda.

Balaban gave her a loose-jointed shrug. "I was hoping you'd tell me that," he said. "I mean, what we got here is talent in the raw, and a basic comic premise, and what we gotta do is build an *act* around it."

"Ralf, the comedian from the future . . ." Amanda muttered thoughtfully. "That's not nearly specific enough, it's not a full *character*, not like the neurotic nerd Woody Allen created for himself, or Phyllis Diller's original stage persona, or Pee Wee Herman, you could drop acts like those right down in the middle of an improv workshop and everyone there would be able to play off them."

"Well, yeah, that's it," Balaban said, "that's *just* the kind of thing I—"

"What am I, a can of caca-flavored People Chow?" Ralf snapped. "Whaddya mean I got no *character*?" He stretched his mouth with his fingers, stuck out his tongue, and crossed his eyes. "What do I gotta do to get a laugh in this century, fart *My Way* in two-part harmony with my armpits?"

Balaban grinned at him, cocked his head at Amanda. "Is the guy an ad-libber, or *what*?"

Amanda turned to Ralf. "Tell me about *your* century," she said.

"Huh?"

"Tell me about your century, Ralf, give us some material to work with."

"What's to tell?" Ralf rasped. "It sucks. You can't go outside the air-conditioning 'cause you can't breathe the air, the stuff you eat is recycled turds they grind up in a factory and flavor with laundry detergent and glue solvent, the population problem has been solved by terminal Third World sunburn, the national animal of every country is the mutated sewer rat, and there's about enough juice left in the wires to run the dinguses supposed to fry the giant cockroaches."

"But what's *funny*?" said Amanda.

"What's funny? *You're* funny, Monkey Girl! You Slagbrains what dealt us this mess are the Polish jokes of the future!"

Out it came, spat from the smart-ass side of his mouth by an obnoxious, frenetic gnome in a ludicrous lime green leisure suit.

But as it did, Amanda made contact with those restlessly rolling comic eyeballs, and they locked on her gaze for just a beat with a brilliant blue intensity.

But in that beat . . . a doorway opened.

That floating moment when consciousness reversed and imagery and thought began to *enter* its time stream from elsewhere rather than emerge from it. The ultimate level she had sought but never attained—the full waking dream state, called up not by craft, or discipline, or technique, or any act of her own will.

The doorway opened up before her as she sat there wide awake looking into the eyes of this wise-guy who claimed to be from the future. And something came up through it out of the Dreamtime to her.

A vision of the face she was looking at subtly transformed. The unruly mess of hair trimmed into the kind of 'do a young Albert Einstein might have gotten from a Beverly Hills stylist for a speaking brochure photo session, melding the protruding ears cunningly with the jawline. The random blazes of silver dye-matched into a spiderweb tracery. The sallow gray skin peeled or washed or conditioned into an olive glow.

Somehow it changed the whole face. The big nose lost its visual comic reference to a banana. The wide mouth with its thick mobile lips had assumed a masculine cognate of the Mona Lisa's smile. The very same eyes looked back at her out of a face that was elusively different. A face steeped in wisdom.

Wisdom . . . ?

Or the smarmy comic semblance of same?

Neither a comic low-brow from the future, nor an all-knowing retrograde Nostradamus, but *the one playing the other*, as if Mel Brooks had cast Gene Wilder in the role of a twenty-second-century Werner Erhard.

"How do you tell which Slaghead's parents went skinny-dipping in the Columbia downstream from Hanford?"

Just for a beat between one line and the next. An untrained mind probably wouldn't have even noticed it happening, or if it did, would have dismissed it as an artifact of fatigue or booze or a chance trick of lighting.

But not Amanda.

"He's the one whose ass *is* his elbow!"

What is, is real.

And what was real was that an image had come to her through the doorway that had triggered a burst of inspiration. Whether waking dream or subconscious summoning up of the creative forces or chance synchronicity of angle and lighting or something else unfathomable was a question far too deep for Amanda to even presume an answer.

What counted was that it *had* happened.

"Look," she said. "What if we play Ralf not as a *comic* from the future but as a *guru* from the future sent back from the future to enlighten the present?"

Texas Jimmy Balaban wrinkled his nose. "El Stinko, Amanda," he said. "Where do the jokes come from? What's the McGuffin?"

"The McGuffin," said Amanda, "is that he's still *Ralf*."

"Huh?" said Ralf. "Who the hell else am I *supposed* to be?"

"We take him to a stylist, get him a hairdo so fancy it *looks* like it costs three hundred dollars, frost it with silver pinstriping to make him look cosmic—"

"Hey, Monkey Girl, I'm beginning to like this—"

"—and dress him up in some kind of classy futuristic jumpsuit—so the look is like Mr. Spock done up to play Cagliostro by Christian Dior!"

"That's supposed to be funny?" Texas Jimmy Balaban said. "I don't get it."

"*He's still Ralf!*" Amanda said. "Same voice! Same delivery! The act *parodies* the Guru from the Future! I'll teach him a pompous second voice to use as his own straight man, but that's just a foil, just for setups."

"Hey, all my moldy old Slaghead jokes would still be funny back here in the dim dumb days with that kind of spin!"

Texas Jimmy Balaban bounced up off his chair, began pacing in frenetic little circles. "Keep the voice! Keep the tummeling!"

"Keep the abrasive obnoxious in-your-face-personality!" said Amanda.

"Like Obi Wan Kenobi doing Lenny Bruce!" Texas Jimmy cried excitedly.

"I'm supposed to be abrasive?" Ralf snarled in a gross exaggeration of his usual grating voice. He stuck his nose in the air, lifted his chin twenty degrees toward the ceiling. "*I* am called upon to be obnoxious?" he oozed in a fatuous goose-grease cadence that didn't quite make it but did come close.

He looked Amanda straight in the eyes. He leaned closer. She could see the coarse dirty pores on the skin of his nose, smell his cheap mass-produced aftershave, and when he opened those big rubbery lips in a huge sardonic grin, she could see the heavy mineral scale on his teeth, the unhealthy bluish tinge of his gums, catch a whiff of acetone on his breath.

"And whaddya mean, in yer face?" he rasped.

Everything was in character as he delivered the line; the cocking of the head, the voice, the twitchy energy of the body language. Everything but the eyes. Amanda was sure that those eyes were not laughing at all.

Or if they were, they were laughing at quite another joke.

3

It had been a long time since Texas Jimmy Balaban had found himself wish-ing for a cigarette. He had given up the old cancer-sticks years ago, upon cough-ing up a gross wad of brown phlegm flecked with blood, and hadn't touched one since. But now he found the thumb and first two fingers of his right hand mas-saging a phantom cigarette like some stoned-out rocker playing air guitar onstage.

Amanda Robin sat beside him on the green room couch, her dark eyes calmly regarding the badly adjusted monitor, her lips creased in a little smile. Easy enough for *her* to be cool. Jimmy had already paid her $1850 in hourly wages to tune up Ralf's voice and delivery and make his image over, and that didn't count the $210 for the goddamn hairdo and the $475 for the custom-tailored suit, not to mention what the meals and motel bills had started costing when Ralf's roll had unpeeled its last hundred-dollar bill.

When you added it all up, and Jimmy tried not to, he had thus far shelled out north of five thousand bucks on his new client, and hadn't seen jack shit back.

Now he was going to find out if he had flushed it all down the tubes. Not that the *Mark Tanner Show* was even paying scale for Ralf's TV debut, but if Ralf couldn't handle a prime putz like Tanner, there would be no point in throwing any more good money after bad. The *Mark Tanner Show* was Nowhere City—one am to two am on Wednesday night on an indie was as far out of prime time as you could get and still be on broadcast TV in the LA market.

Gino Galacci, Tanner's producer, who sat on the other side of the green room in an armchair sipping Nescafé laced with Johnny Walker Red, was under no illusion as to how far his current meal ticket was going to take him, namely no farther than this. Galacci was far too much the old pro to harbor any illusions about Tanner's ability to stand up to anything much beyond the bottom end of Texas Jimmy's client list, namely the crazy weirdos, meat for his pathetic monster, which Jimmy upon occasion was willing to toss in the cage for a couple hundred under the table in cash and a free airtape.

Which was what Jimmy had let Gino assume he was getting tonight.

"A guru from the future, Jimmy? Jesus Christ, what next? Where do you get 'em?"

"No sweat, Gino, I just hang out at the interplanetary arrivals terminal at John Wayne Airport and let the flying saucers bring 'em to me," Jimmy had told him, making with his own laugh track.

Galacci had laughed with him, but if Jimmy was right and Ralf was now ready, the joke would be on him. For while Texas Jimmy had never before gone anything like this deep into the red without a payback, long experience had taught him the nail-biting virtue of timing and patience, not to surface a talent like this until he was really ready.

Not that he had ever handled a talent like this, whatever a talent like this was.

Not that he didn't have to admit that he had so far gotten his money's worth out of Amanda Robin.

He could hardly believe what she brought back from the hairstylist and cosmetician.

Ralf's face looked like it had been gone over with a belt-sander and then tanned in a microwave. His hair had been trimmed into a Hollywood version of its previous wildness frosted with silvery pinstriping, and cut around the top of his ears to make them vaguely resemble those of Mr. Spock. And they had done something to his eyebrows to give them a kind of Fu Manchu spin. It changed his whole appearance. The nose was now just big, not comically so. The eyes had a kind of strange intensity; cosmic you might say, were you the kind of vibrating lady hung crystals over her tub.

When the suit was ready a couple days later, the effect was complete.

Jimmy had nearly shit when he saw it on the hanger. Amanda had had the thing made up mostly in white! They'd have to have two of them! They'd have to dry-clean it after every performance!

"Wash-and-wear and Scotchgarded, Jimmy, relax," she had told him, and when Ralf emerged from the toilet dressed in it, he had to grudgingly admit she had gotten his money's worth in drip-dry polyester.

A formal zoot suit from Mars.

It was in one piece like a jumpsuit, designed to be worn without shirt, belt, or tie, although integrating suggestions of same in its design. White pants ballooning a bit like riding breeches above the knees, black cuffs at the bottom, tight-fitting black cummerbund around the waist. The loose white top looked tucked into it like a shirt, the belled black sleeves with white cuffs emerged from beneath the shelf of big padded shoulders, giving it the effect of a pachuco sports jacket. A triangle of black material biased to the right on the chest to suggest a shirt, a white slash across it in the other direction to suggest a tie, a high wide collar rising to near earlobe height, white on the outside and lined with black.

In this getup, the new improved Ralf looked like Dracula playing Christopher Lee stuffed into Flash Gordon's tux.

"Peace be upon you, benighted Monkey People," he said in a phony-baloney undertaker voice, waving his hand like the pope on his balcony. "I bring you greeting from the inheritors of your stupidity in the twenty-second century . . ."

He stuck out his tongue and made with a juicy Bronx cheer.

"Real Slaghead class, right?" he barked, fingering the breast of the suit like a dead fish. "Terrific! Don't tell me! You've gotten me a gig MCing Batman's bar mitzvah, right?"

In that moment Texas Jimmy sensed that the act was there. He gritted his teeth, not to mention his bank account, and started Ralf out slow, real slow, knowing he wasn't going to see any payback for weeks or months. . . .

Amateur nights at third-rate comedy clubs, then second-rate clubs, finally the Comedy Store, integrating the gags from the writers, with Amanda polishing the delivery, working on the timing of those instant vocal transitions from put-on guru from the twenty-second century to smart-mouthed wise guy that were the basic schtick, the verbal bear-trap that Ralf sprung on the hecklers the act invited.

"And now . . . here's Mark's next guest . . . *Ralf, the Man From the Future!*"

Which, Jimmy, nervously hoped, Ralf was now about to spring for the first time on what more or less passed for an unsuspecting *professional* foil.

On the green room TV screen, Ralf walked onto the *Mark Tanner Show* set from the left, the white of his suit, like his face, like everything else on the badly adjusted monitor, tinged a sickly blue. Ralf glided across the set like a sleazy politician to an Elks Club podium, smarmy smile fixed on his kisser, glad hand outstretched.

Mark Tanner shook it dubiously. He was a big blond square-jawed onetime hunk, looked like an overaged surfer forced to take a job as an Orange County cop. With about as much gray matter in the old coconut.

"So you're from the future, huh?" he said in the deep gravelly purr of the canny local sheriff in second-rate car-chase flicks aimed at the six-pack trade.

"Here we go, Jimmy," Amanda Robin whispered beside him, giving his left hand a quick little squeeze.

"Yes, Mark, that's right, I'm what you might call a missionary to this dim dark age come to spread the light and save us from yourselves," Ralf oozed in round overripe evangelist tones.

"A *missionary*, huh? You have to *audition* for the *position*?"

"Hey, Mark," Ralf said, beaming at him approvingly, and staying with the setup voice, "why . . . why that's almost *funny*! They never told me you Slagheads had a *sense of humor* back here."

"Slagheads?" grunted Tanner unhappily, knowing he was being set up but not what to do about it. "What's a Slaghead?"

"Why *you* are, Mark," Ralf smarmed fatuously. Then he switched abruptly to the smart-ass rasp to deliver Dexter Lampkin's punch line. "Guy who thinks fishin' by-products is what they serve you in a dollar-ninety-eight tuna casserole and a toxic dump is what comes out the other end next morning."

Amanda shot Texas Jimmy a quick look and a little sidewise smile. Across the green room, the look that Gino Galacci aimed in his direction was a good deal less amused.

Jimmy attempted to give him an innocent shrug, throwing up his hands.

Only then did he realize that he had been holding his right one to his lips as if to suck a nervous drag on a phantom cigarette.

". . . yes, that's right, Mark, folks when I come from are not exactly into ancestor worship, it'd be like expecting the pope to light a candle for the dearly departed soul of Adolf Hitler."

"So they sent *you* back to punish us for our sins, like booking Whoopi Goldberg into Tehran to get even with the ayatollahs?"

"What can I tell ya, Monkey Boy?" said Ralf, switching voices. "I got busted for indecent media overexposure, and it was *this* gig or three years of telling Polish jokes in the Warsaw Ghetto."

Good, Amanda thought, he had the voices and the timing down, and the rest would improve once there were more gags in the file. Ralf was no true comic actor who could put on any number of roles and make whatever character he was playing funny. Like Pee Wee Herman, or Harpo, or for that matter Chaplin, playing *one* character in every situation was the essential nature of his running gag.

But Pee Wee Herman's career had faded fast, and Harpo and Chaplin had never been stand-up comics. So the only way to go was to split the character into straight-line and punch-line avatars and play them off each other. That inspiration was the easy part.

Another voice was no problem. She gave him one with a slower cadence and an exaggerated syrupy tone and taught him a bit of smarmy guru-speak. In a week, he had it down well enough for Balaban to let him try it onstage at an amateur night in some awful comedy club way out in Eagle Rock, where the best that could be said was that no tomatoes had been thrown.

Ralf claimed to have never worked with a straight man before, and Amanda was hard put to think of a comic who played his own. He had no trouble switching voices, but the body language was all the same, all Ralf. Just two voices coming out of the same body instead of two alternating characters up there onstage. It was too much like watching some street-corner schizo babbling to himself.

Somehow she had to teach him enough acting technique to make it work. It hadn't proven easy. Five days of trying had gotten her nowhere before she finally hit on something that worked.

Maybe something that worked better than she could have anticipated or intended . . .

These séances took place in her Topanga house. It was that or the back room of Balaban's office, for Texas Jimmy had not been about to spring for a rehearsal studio. It hadn't even taken a look back there to decide the issue, a quick whiff was more than enough, besides which, it would be far less of a hassle for Ralf to drive out to her place for his coaching than for her to push the Pinto through the traffic on the 101 to the Strip.

Only Ralf didn't have a valid license. He claimed not to even know how to drive.

"Drive a *car*? When I come from, just *hiding* one under a tarp's enough to get you three to five!"

"I'm supposed to pick him up and drive him back?"

Much rough negotiation with Balaban had ensued. Time and a half for freeway time plus gas and oil. Plus $1000 in cash if the Pinto expired in the act. Plus Amanda set the hours to avoid the rush as much as possible.

It was getting on toward sunset when the idea came to her.

They were in her living room and she was trying one more time to get Ralf to match body language to voice by conscious technique, and it still wasn't working. The door to the front porch was open, but the shadows were already deepening outside, and she had turned on the halogen lamp to banish gloom from the interior.

Amanda chanced to look in the direction of the doorway. Inside the living room, the flat white artificial sunlight of the lamp created the temporal illusion of an eternal noon. But framed by the rough gray splintery two-by-fours of the doorframe like a painting was another world in another time, where golden late-afternoon shadows played over the breeze-tossed boughs of the eucalyptus trees.

"Let's try something different," Amanda said. "Put on the costume."

"Aw, come on!"

"Humor me, Ralf. We're going to try a little sensory awareness exercise."

"*Sensory awareness exercise?* Hey, wouldn't it go better if we both just got naked?"

From someone else, it might have been a come-on or at least a tentative exploratory feeler, but from Ralf it was devoid of sexual vibe. Indeed, she had spent hours and hours alone with this guy without even a hint of a sexual vibration coming off him. It might have made Amanda feel she had gone over the hill except that Ralf projected no other sort of emotional vibe that she could detect either. Everything that came out of his mouth was schtick. What the psychologists called "flattened affect."

And when Ralf emerged from the spare bedroom dressed in the white-and-black swami suit and a bad attitude, it occurred to Amanda that maybe even his permanent stance of aggressive belligerence toward the current century and everything in it was just part of the act. If so, far from being unable to act, he was a masterful actor who had never learned how to play more than one part.

"Okay, Ralf, I just want you to stand there for a minute and be aware of what it feels like to be here inside your body right now."

Ralf cocked his head at her like a bemused parrot.

"The *sensory* reality, Ralf, the smell of the dust on the carpet and the musty earth in the potted plants . . . the visual quality of the lighting . . . the temperature of your skin . . . what it feels like to be Ralf the smart-ass, the tummeler, the guy who delivers the punch lines . . . do you have it, Ralf, do you think you've got it down?"

"I've got a certain amount of practice being me, Monkey Girl," Ralf snapped. "What next?" he said, extending his arms and rolling his eyes. "Don't tell me, I'm supposed to pretend I'm a horse's ass chestnut tree!"

"Not quite," Amanda told him.

She took his hand and led him over to the open doorway. "Think of this doorway as Alice's looking glass. On this side, you're Ralf. You feel what Ralf feels, you smell what Ralf smells, you see what Ralf sees, you walk like Ralf, you talk like Ralf, you *are* Ralf. You're a smart-mouthed stand-up comic from the future, and this is what it feels like to be you."

She pulled him through the doorway onto the front porch.

"Now you're someplace else. And here, you are *someone* else."

The late-afternoon breeze whispered up the canyons, gently rolling the crowns of the eucalyptus trees, perfuming the slowly cooling air with the sappy sweetness of resin, the sharp tang of chaparral. Long shadows darkened the dusty scrub in slices to a deeper and more verdant green. The dun-brown stone of Big Rock was barely tinged with rose and the blue sky had just begun to purple toward the zenith.

"You're a savant from the future, you're well-meaning, you're a bit of a ditz, and you're a little pompous, and *this* is what it feels like to be *you* back here with us Monkey People smelling the flowers. . . ."

Ralf stood there on the porch for a long beat with his lips twisted in the usual smirk and his eyebrows frowned down toward the inner corners of his eyes, same old Ralf.

But there was no wisecrack.

"Listen to the wind," Amanda said softly. "Hear that woodpecker hammering on a dead tree in the background . . . smell the eucalyptus . . . it's warmer out here in places but cooler in others, shadows and sunlight have different temperatures, notice that, notice how the air is alive, how it's got its own smell, how you can feel it moving on your skin . . ."

A subtle change began to creep over Ralf. The eyebrows relaxed, the crease between the lips assumed a somewhat different curve, the eyes, something about the eyes . . .

"A little softer, a little more natural, and so is he, so are you, and you naturally stand a little different out here on this side of the looking glass, a little looser, a little more erect, a little like your voice, know what I mean? No, don't try talking yet, just take a little walk around the porch feeling what it's like to be this you . . ."

Tentatively, Ralf strode to the railing.

"Loosen up the legs, step a little higher, raise the chest, feel what it's like to be him, this guy's something like a professor always walking up to his podium, just a little too in love with his own wonderfulness. . . ."

Ralf walked along the porch railing away from her, moving a little more loose-jointed, yes, head held at a slightly higher angle, it was starting to work, maybe . . .

"Turn. Walk back to me."

Ralf turned and walked slowly back across the porch. Yes, he was moving differently, yes, the body language had changed. The strides were more liquid, longer, and slower. The hands hung open as the arms swung rather than half-curled into fists, the chin a tad above the vertical. An older, somehow taller, less overtly aggressive Ralf.

He stopped in front of her. The musculature of his face had relaxed. His expression had become bland, the face smoothly unreadable. Only the eyes seemed quickened with vitality as they met hers with an unwavering intensity, as if some hidden being were studying her through the holes in a mask.

It was disorienting in a way that Amanda could not quite put her finger on. Like a photo of a human face solarized into an abstraction. Like focusing for too long on the same visage during an acid trip.

Amanda blinked. Ralf didn't. She blinked again. The effect remained.

"Talk to me," she finally said.

"What do you want me to say?" he said in that orotund and slightly fatuous voice that she had taught him.

"Tell me what it feels like for you to be here," she said. "*You,* not . . . *him.*"

Ralf took a deep breath. He raised his face to the waning sun. Somehow, without change of his expression, his face seemed to capture its radiance.

"So this is what it feels like to stand outside on a living planet," he said in the same voice. "Plants! Trees! Open air you can breathe!"

He lowered his gaze to meet hers again.

"How could I have even imagined?"

The eyes never left hers. They didn't change. They didn't blink. "But then, it's not just that I've never been *here* before, I've never been *me* before, now have I?"

The heavy fragrance of eucalyptus seemed to pour into Amanda's lungs like a viscous syrup. The golden shafts of late-afternoon light streaming through the tree crowns seemed to have tangible substance. The whisper of the wind through the leaves enfolded her in a cocoon of soft cottony sound. Time seemed like liquid amber in the process of crystallizing around her.

The eyes blinked, once, twice, very slowly, as if it were a conscious gesture.

A jay screeched!

The strange moment shattered.

Amanda grabbed Ralf by the hand and yanked him blinking back into the hard white artificial light of the living room.

"Now be *Ralf,*" she said sharply, "and tell me what being . . . *him* felt like!"

"Like Bambi meets Prince Smarming," the good old bad old Ralf shot back.

Amanda laughed. "There's your straight man!" she said. "Call up that sensory memory when you toss yourself a setup line, feel him, move like him, *be* him!"

Ralf cocked his head, gave her a narrow look.

"This is what it's like to be an actor?"

Amanda had nodded her encouragement, but of course she could hardly lay serious claim to having taught Ralf to *really* act. All she had done was create an alter ego for him and teach him a basic little trick for getting inside it. But it seemed to have been enough to make the difference. Balaban had liked it well enough to pronounce the act ready for its TV debut.

Such as it was.

Amanda found it hard to imagine any audience at all out there watching the *Mark Tanner Show* at this dead hour, but Ralf was good enough to have reduced Tanner to a permanent scowl of pretty-boy petulance.

". . . you been flapping your yap for about five minutes already, Ralfie-boy, and you haven't told us a damn thing about the future, now have you? You know what I think?"

"I haven't the slightest idea, Mark," Ralf said pompously, mugging at the camera. "It's like asking me what you get when you cross a sewer rat with your mother-in-law."

The sullen Tanner refused to feed him a setup line, but the change in voice and persona allowed Ralf to work off himself.

"The big deal ain't *what*, Monkey Boy, it's amazing enough you can do it at all!"

It was a groaner, but Amanda couldn't quite eat the smile.

Gino Galacci gave Balaban another poisonous look.

Mark Tanner's fair face was probably turning beet red to judge by the expression on it, though on the maladjusted green room monitor, the effect was blued to a sickly purple. "That's as funny as a rubber crutch in an Alzheimer's ward," he snarled. "You wanna tell me how come if you're so smart, you ain't rich? I mean, if you're from the future, you gotta know how the World Series comes out, right, and the Super Bowl, and the Derby—"

"How come I'm yakking here with you instead of calling my broker and cornering the market on dog food and chicken noses?" Ralf snapped out of the side of his mouth in his natural voice.

"Yeah, if you know the future, why *aren't* you making a killing on the market or in Vegas?"

Ralf smiled benignly, changing voice and persona again. "What makes you think that that's not exactly what I've been doing?" he oozed. "Why should I tell *you*, Monkey Boy?" Ralf rasped back. "I give out tips on my sure things on the air, and *my* payoffs go from long-shot odds to worse than even money!"

"My—"

"Besides which, what makes you think I've got any reason to do you people any favors in the first place?" Ralf cut in loudly but smoothly and insinuatingly. "You really suppose your great-grandchildren are going be grateful for the mess you left us?"

It was the straight man's voice, but he had turned it into a powerful instrument in a manner that Amanda hadn't at all anticipated.

It was the straight man's body language as Ralf looked away from Mark Tanner, and the straight man's fatuous swami-smile as he looked directly into the camera, but with the edge of the smart-ass tummler inside peeking through.

"Would I be back here doing a show like *this* if the future was going to be wine and roses?" he said. "My agent had to con me into thinking I was gonna play the *sixties* just to get me into the time machine in the first place! You're the *pits*, Monkey Boys and Girls! You screwed us! It's *your* crap that's gonna hit *our* fan!"

"So what's a nice little creep like you doing in a time like this?" Mark Tanner snarled.

"I thought you'd never ask, Mark," Ralf cooed. "You see, folks, I have seen the future, the future that *you* made for us, and it sucks."

"Wha—"

"Sucks!" Ralf barked. "The ocean's full of this green slime looks like the south end of a cesspool and the twenty-foot mutated catfish that eat it glow blue at high noon! Ozone hole? We got an *Ozone No Zone*! Ten minutes of sunshine and you're a pepperoni pizza! It's so hot outside you could fry an egg on an ice cube before it melts if there was such a thing as a live chicken! The *cockroaches* gotta wear lead jockstraps!"

Mark Tanner's mouth hung wide open. Texas Jimmy Balaban grinned. Galacci shook his head ruefully, like the old trainer in a dumb boxing movie who has just seen his punch-drunk protégé walk into a haymaker.

Ralf leered into the camera. "So you see, Monkey Boys and Girls, I'm not back here because it's so cool," he said, his voice dripping with sarcastic unction. "I'm just one of your boat people got a chance to haul ass out of a *worse* disaster area and took it. You Slagheads are not the fave raves of the future, and none of your great-grandchildren are gonna get misty-eyed playing your golden oldies!"

The camera pulled back into a two shot and caught Mark Tanner squinting at something outside the shot, the director tearing the hair out of his head by the look on his face, Amanda surmised.

"Yeah, well, I'm afraid that the future's arrived already, Ralfie-boy, 'cause that's all of this we've got time for," he babbled rapidly. "We got a lady up next who's gonna tell us all about saving big money by resoling our own shoes."

Texas Jimmy Balaban exhaled, gave Amanda a wink.

Gino Galacci levered his bulk out of his chair, waddled heavily across the green room, and stood over Balaban, weaving slightly, scowling muchly.

"You didn't tell me this guy was a pro, Jimmy," he grumbled.

"I couldn't know what I really had until I put him up against your guy, now could I?" Balaban told him. "Lay off, Gino, you got yourself a bargain. I'da known he was this good, wouldn't I have at least charged you scale?"

"Hey, Loxy, whatcha doin'?" Cory said when the shift ended at midnight. "Wanna get off with me?"

"Not for free," Foxy Loxy said, strippin' off the greasy apron, pullin' off the stupid sailor cap, and tossin' 'em inna bin.

"Thought you gave up the business, girl."

"Never was in it, you know that, Cory, but t'get it on with you, I'd haveta make an exception," Loxy said.

Actually, Cory wasn't all that bad, slick black dude only flippin' catburgers in Sailor Sal's so's he could deal his own goods across the counter, gimme a cheeseburger, a cherry Coke, anna bag a smack please, light onna ketchup, no pickle.

And actually, she *had* been in the business, well, anyway, had chipped around the edges enough to pick up the "Foxy Loxy" handle, and face it, girl, this shit-ass job goes south, you gonna turn a few now and again when you can, now ain'tcha.

But turnin' a trick here and there onna street or in an alley was one thing, and doing it serious enough to get involved with some fuckin' pimp, becoming a *pro*, that was another, she had no intention of ending up like Momma. Momma had been a *real* hooker, hot stuff in her day to hear her tell it, midtown hotels, lines a good coke, champagne, steak dinners, and all.

"Where do you think you get your looks? From your poppa?"

"How the fuck would *you* know, Mom?"

Okay, while she could see no family resemblance between herself and the bucket of blubber cached out onna couch in front of the tube with a beer can in one hand and a bag of cold McNuggets in the other, she hadda admit she could see a certain amount of herself in those old pictures of Momma in her prime, the thick brown hair, the cool green eyes, the neat straight nose, the way the lips curled . . .

But how many johns had Momma screwed in the five years between the time she arrived in New York from Columbus and the time she got herself knocked up, even at only one trick a day, say three hundred workdays a year . . . well, Foxy wasn't never no good at arithmetic, but it hadda add up to plenty.

So poppa could be *anyone*, right, 'specially if Momma wasn't completely bullshittin', she had worked midtown hotels, all kindsa fancy johns hung out there, didn't they, movie stars, judges, senators, who knows, you believe half of what you read inna *Star* and the *Enquirer*, she coulda banged a *Kennedy* or, who knows, even *Elvis*.

Girl was entitled to have a few fantasies, wasn't she? Of course, likewise might very well apply to a fat old load unlikely to make it blowin' garbagemen coming off-shift at the docks at a dollar a pop. Fact was, they was already on Welfare and living inna crappy projects on Avenue D in her earliest memories, in which Momma had always been far too gross to make a credible midtown hooker.

But bullshit or stone truth, growing up with Momma had been more than enough to convince Foxy Loxy that fucking for a living was a sucker's game. Sure, it was easier than flippin' burgers in grease pits like Sailor Sal's, and what with the lines you might cadge, anna drinks, and maybe a meal inna real restaurant, a lot more fun too, not to mention that it paid a fuck of a lot better than the minimum wage even if a pimp *did* have his fangs in your pocketbook. But how long could you last? The Pig Apple was up to its twat in teenage pussy, and more fresh meat came pourin' in through the Port Authority every day, so before you was thirty, you had better get yourself knocked up so's you could collect ADC, 'cause even if the bod didn't go like Momma's, the market value of your ass wasn't gonna pay no rent.

Okay, a freelance fuck or a quick blow job was good for better than a whole day's wages after deductions in a shit-ass job like this, so why not, but better don't get hooked on the good times.

It was like smack or crystal, you were okay chippin' at the stuff, snortin' a line when you could get it, poppin' it with a spike now and again, why not, but only assholes let themselves turn into fuckin' *junkies*.

Foxy Loxy had seen too many of 'em holding long conversations with lamp-posts with snot pouring out of their noses laying onna sidewalk in their own vomit to let herself slide into *that* toilet bowl, and far too much of Momma to fall for any pimp's sweet-talkin' high-life bullshit.

"Hey, come on, Foxy Loxy, why you giving me such an attitude?" Cory said, running a comb through his eraserhead hairdo. "I don't want to *fuck you*, girl, well, if you was real nice to me, maybe I could be persuaded, I just want to show you a good time."

"Uh-huh."

"You really a hardcase, girl, you know that? I say wanna *get off* with me, I'm talkin' gettin' *high*, stoned, like *fucked up*, okay, I got to draw you a picture? I'm talkin' *for free*."

Loxy's attention sharpened at this, hey, whose wouldn't, but on the other hand, she didn't exactly find it easy to believe. "I never heard of you givin' out no freebies, Cory. . . ." she said suspiciously.

Cory laughed. "Hey, be real, I'm not talking about *my* shit," he said. "I'm going to a kind of a party, trade show, you might say, some of my customers, some of my suppliers, I ain't even bringing a *bag* of my own, *they're* gonna be laying out, and I'm just inviting you to come along as my date."

"Date?"

"Hey, come on, no one's ever asked you out on a date before, you know, just like on the TV, hearts and flowers, and teenage romance, and a great big shitload of skag."

"An' just what do you expect to be in it for you?" Loxy said. But she had already decided, hey, why not, Cory was a good-looking dude, fucking him wouldn't be hard to take in return for getting seriously stoned, especially if she was still ripped at the time.

Cory, though, shuffled his weight back and forth a bit, and his smile became a little sly, a little little boy. "Well, Loxy, you *are* kinda Foxy," he said, "and I *do* got an image to maintain, and it won't hurt for me to show up with you on my arm . . ."

"And me bein' white, that ain't gonna do you no serious harm either, now ain't that right, Cory?" Loxy said evilly, letting him squirm for a second before she laughed to take the sting out of it.

And so they left Sailor Sal's arm in arm, and walked south on First Avenue to Third Street. With all of Cory's talk about dates and parties and dealers higher up than he was, Loxy had gotten her hopes up that they were gonna turn west, away from Alphabet fuckin' City and toward the Village maybe, or at least Second Avenue, someplace witha little class. . . .

No such luck, when was there ever, east they went instead, into side streets fulla semi-burnt-out buildings, dead car bodies, cracked streetlights, and never-collected garbage; where the people you saw onna street did not exactly give you a sense of security; and first you were glad to be holding on to the arm of a black guy of a certain size with a rep as a dealer and then you got t'worryin' that maybe that wasn't gonna be good enough.

"Here we are," Cory said outside a five-story tenement that looked like the landlord was gonna torch it in the next five minutes if the junkies and crackheads inside didn't do the job for him first.

"We are?" Loxy grunted unhappily. "Far fuckin' out."

The panes on about halfa the windows was smashed and maybe half of 'em replaced with cardboard and plywood covered with speedfreak graffiti. A few dim lights behind the ones still there looked like they were bein' run off old car batteries or bad meter-jumps. On top of the stoop, the outer entrance door was hanging open on one hinge, the inner door didn't seem to be there anymore, and Loxy would as soon have stepped into Dracula's meatlocker as enter that pitch dark hallway with anything short of a machine gun.

"Fuck that, man," she said, "you ain't gettin' me up in there."

Cory laughed. "No sweat," he said, "it's in the *cellar*." And before Loxy could react to *that* with the scream of horror it deserved, he had pulled her into the well under the stoop and was bangin' hard on the sheet metal–covered door.

He stopped when he heard footfalls inside and stuck his face close to the peephole to ID himself. Deadbolts clunked, a police-lock bar scraped through its slide, and the door was opened by a large Puerto Rican dangling a machine pistol from his paw. He nodded at Cory, gave Loxy a fish-eyed stare. Cory shooed her inside, and the guard closed two locks behind them.

Half a dozen naked sixty-watters hangin' from extension cords nailed to the low ceiling lit a basement room about as big as a whole floor of the building with cones of ugly light. The center of the room was taken up by a very dead-looking furnace and boiler thing, the pipes leading from it to the upper floors draped with cobwebs and half-rusted out. The light cords that ran along the ceiling met at the main meter console, which had been jumped with car-battery leads. Another extension cord connected the power to an old TV jammed up against the furnace where some stupid toothpaste commercial onna broadcast channel tried to pretend it was MTV.

The only furniture was about twenty gray cot mattresses stinkin' of mold and rat piss scattered around the cement floor, two Con Ed cable spools someone had copped to serve as tables, and maybe half a dozen assorted fruit crates and canned goods cartons.

There were maybe two dozen people, you wanna call 'em that, sittin', squattin' an' layin' around on the mattresses in various states of consciousness and otherwise, mostly guys, mostly black or Latino, a few of 'em decked out inna chains an' leathers and dude-threads of dealers and pimps, the rest wearing shit from the Salvation Army or 14th Street.

The place was a shithole. The people were scurve.

That was the bad news.

The good news was there were spikes lying on the spool tables, tubing, spoons, razor blades, mirrors, plastic baggies of white power that could have been coke, or smack, or crystal, maybe all three. People were shootin' up. People were honkin' lines of whatever through dollar bills. People were smoking some shit in little glass pipes.

High-fives, blah, blah, blah, yo, my man, lookin' good, an' so on an' so forth, about which Loxy couldn't care less, including the names of the dealers Cory displayed her for like she was a phony Rolex from Taiwan or a gold chain too heavy to be anything but two-carat bullshit plating.

Nor was she really pissed off when he parked her onna roach-infested mattress in front of one of the spool tables and slithered over into a far corner with three a these turkeys to hunch over, bobbing and muttering the usual dealer bullshit to each other.

"Help yourself, girl," a dude wearing some kinda fancy red and yellow dashiki thing over black jeans and cowboy boots said, "it's on the house."

The white powders inna baggies might have been anything or any weird combination and probably were, an' stepped on by a herd a elephants besides. But since some pimply girl on the other side of the table just shot up was noddin' inna normal manner instead of droppin' dead, and while a certain number of bodies were layin' around the basement, none of them had turned green or purple and all of 'em seemed to be still more or less breathin', whatever all the shit was, and whatever crap they might be using for cut, seemed like none of it was fatal.

The works onna table was something else again. The junkies here musta never hearda AIDS or be too far gone t'do one of these clean needle dealies. The spikes were the old-fashioned reusable kind, of which, from the look of the crud inside 'em, they had seen plenty, there was even a fuckin' jobbie home-made out of a medicine dropper looked like it belonged inna museum or somethin'. Even the yellow rubber tubing seemed to have mold on it. Looked like you could get something disgustin' just from being in the same time zone with this shit.

Loxy had nothing in particular against chippin' a bit a smack or crystal or coke with a nice fresh needle, far from it, no other way you could get that surge. But shootin' up with any of *these* setta works was like playin' Russian roulette with a dum-dum in every cylinder. So Loxy layed out a couple lines from the nearest open baggie, fished out a five-dollar bill, rolled it, and snorted.

Coke, from the flash of it, not exactly primo, an' probably stepped on with crystal to make it seem stronger, judgin' by the bitter back-bite.

Not too terrific.

Loxy tried a couple lines from another baggie. Made her mouth taste like a cat box, made the lights burn her eyeballs like permanent flashbulbs, sent electric confetti zippin' around her brain, set muscles here and there t'twitchin' and jerkin', and the screen of the TV set up against the furnace strobed in time to the blabble of some fuckin' newshead.

Crystal meth, pretty ordinary.

Practice maybe don't make perfect, not when the shit you're practicin' with, whatever it all is, is only maybe half a cut up from what you can score inna school-yard, but if you try all of it, an' you work fast enough, it *do* finally get you pretty nicely fucked up.

None of this stuff was good enough to turn the grungy basement into like a real fancy disco or make it smell like anything but rat shit an' cockroach dust, or convince Loxy that the scurve infesting it were uptown princes, but after a while, however the fuck long that was, she was able to forget however the fuck long she had been wherever the fuck she was and who the fuck had dragged her there and get seriously involved with the light show inside her own head.

At some point, it seemed like she musta been bounced up onto her feet, 'cause, yeah, she was walkin' around, boppin' on tiptoes in jerky circles, dancin' you might say t'stretch a point to the music coming from the TV, some kinda elevator music comin' from this spastic sorta jazz quartet looked like it was bein' beamed down from Mars in about 1953. . . .

"Hey, yo, girl, blurg appa do gah . . ." said this deep wet voice suddenly in her face, or at least that was what it sounded like, kinda hard to tell, with the TV, anna blah-blah, an' this sound the lightbulbs was makin' like bees in a blender.

This face emerged from the wall of neon graffiti and eyeball static right in front of her nose so she could smell the speed-freak breath and hair grease, kinda Latino, eyes looked washed in Lysol, mouth hangin' open like some kinda ma-roon, actually *drooling*, an' it was sorta bobbin' up and down jerkily like a balloon onna string over a steam vent.

It came through that she was dancing with this guy, or anyway they were both more or less movin' up an' down to the music under the same fuckin' lightbulb, for how long this had been goin' on, Loxy had no idea.

It took her a couple of minutes or a million years, or whatever, to kinda come to the understanding that the thing he was trying to stick in her mouth wasn't some kinda weird glass dick.

Glass, all right, but not even big enough to be a poodle's pecker, some kinda *pipe*, yeah, that's what it was, it had a little bowl like one a those hash pipe dealies, and he was holdin' a Bic or somethin' over it, not a cock at all, but the idea was in-deed to stick it inya mouth and suck—

Some dim awareness, some kinda fire alarm bell going off in her brain a half beat or a thousand years after the fact, told Loxy that oh shit this was a bad idea girl, fuckin' *crack* was what it was and from what she had seen—

But by then it was too late. She had already done it. She had taken a great big greedy drag, hey who wouldn't, and this sledgehammer banged her on top of the head, and this atomic bomb went off behind her eyes, and a rocket flew up her spine, and—

—and—

She exploded.

She was suddenly as big as th' Empire State Building! As powerful as Godzilla! A zillion fuckin' volts of electricity lit up her skeleton like Times Square at New Year's! Her joints crackled and popped! Lightning bolts shot out of her fingertips and her nose and her nipples! Her cunt could crack coconuts!

The world was too small for her, too frail, not really there inna same way she was, her head shot through the ceiling, an' th' concrete floor was so much fuckin' Kleenex, if she came down too hard, she'd stomp all the way to China. Her teeth gnashed. Her fingers popped. Weird gabbling sounds were coming out of a mouth somewhere far away.

What she was seeing, whatever the fuck *that* was, smashed apart into crystal fragments like someone threw a brick through a stained-glass window and the pieces of brightly colored glass swarmed and swirled like clouds of butterflies dissolving into whirlwinds of light and—

Power! Light! Strength! Electricity! Energy! Zip! Zam! Pow! Wham! Whoo-fuckin'-ee!

Never in her life had Foxy Loxy felt this strong! She *knew* she could walk through the fuckin' walls, so why bother? Never in her life had Foxy Loxy felt this good! The whole fuckin' universe was suckin' on her clit, who needed anything more?

Power! Light! Energy!

Nothin' else was really real here inna perfect white light center of everything. Perfect! And so was she! She was the light! She was the Power!

She was the Power! The Power!

Was! She! It! The Power!

After a second, or a million years, impossible to tell since no one was there at the time to do the telling, there was an awareness of pure white light, some kinda noise, and the white light began to break up into a million glittering colors, and the colors began to whirl and flicker and sparkle—

—and this sorta face floating right in front of her.

A face-shaped space, made of a zillion little points of pale flickerin' glitter, black hair flashin' with electric fire, strobing like a cheap light show, standin' there in a circle of light shovin' some big disgustin' gray thing coulda been a fuckin' *elephant's dick* in her face, and those eyes, was *holes* inna face, somethin' glowin' blue behind 'em, trail a blue lights goin' down, down, down inta someplace where they stickin' fuckin' *coat hangers* in your brains, hee, hee, hee—

Jesus!

Loxy blinked.

Came back down, more or less, into her body.

Which was kneeling on dirty bare concrete inna scummy cellar with her face about six inches from a TV goin' nose-to-nose with some weirdo onna screen.

Head vibrating like a fuckin' Jamaican steel drum. Mouth tasted like a used tampon. Legs hurt like a million red-hot needles. Eyeballs like rotten eggs been boiled a couple weeks in Tabasco.

Foxy Loxy shuddered, slithered backward away from the TV like some kinda reptile, managed to sorta scramble upright, all kinda twinkling things still floatin' in the air in front of her.

So this was fuckin' *crack*!

She remembered the flash—well, sorta. Remembered not exactly bein' there to remember anything.

Heavy stuff!

But she remembered Power! She remembered Light! She remembered Strong! She remembered somethin' like this orgasm better'n any sex felt like it went on *forever*!

Supposed to be instant jonesy.

'Course, the dickheads said *that* said the same thing about coke and heroin, now didn't they . . . ?

She'd been chippin' a little coke, a little crystal, a little smack, a long time now, right, and hey, no problem, she hadn't turned into no crystal freak or no junkie, now had she?

Yeah, this stuff was *strong*! Made you feel like Wonder Woman screwin' Godzilla! Walk through walls! Jump over the fuckin' Empire State building! Whoo-eee!

So yeah, you hadda be careful. But, hey, she could handle this stuff too.

She just *had*, now hadn't she? She wasn't snarkin' and droolin' around the floor after the next fix, now was she? Was she?

Hey, you could handle *anything* was you careful. All you hadda remember was three little letters and it wasn't as if what the dealers charged was gonna let you forget it: O.P.D.

Other People's Dope.

You stuck to that, you never bought your own, you couldn't get hooked on *nothin'*!

Loxy looked around the cellar, where the fuck—?

Yeah, *there* he was, over there near Cory, the guy with the little glass pipe. . . .

4

"Hey Dex, look at this," Ellie said, shoving some clone of the *National Enquirer* across the breakfast table.

"Uh," Dexter Lampkin grunted around a slurp of coffee by way of reply, but he refused to reach for it.

He considered reading at the table barbaric, besides which he detested the moronic supermarket tabloids Ellie found so humorous, and the last thing he needed now was to be distracted from his psychic gearing up for the coming day's work by the birth of sextuplets to a six-year-old virgin lesbian in Bangladesh.

A joint and a snifter of cognac had jolted his memory into recalling at least the vague gist of something Drew Sanderson had said at one of those Transformationalist Circle meetings, and three more jays had allowed him to elaborate it into an outline for a new novel called *Chaos Time*, and his agent had gotten him a $40,000 contract for it.

You never knew, did you?

Nor *could* you.

Which was the McGuffin.

The notion that tiny changes in the past could produce enormous changes in the future was a moldy sci-fi oldie, but the sexy new chaos physics said that in a chaotic system, the effects produced were not only unpredictable but *inherently nondeterministic*. So, assuming time travel, you could indeed produce major alterations in the future with minor changes in the past. But if human history was a chaotic system, those macroeffects would not be merely unpredictable, but would have no inevitable causal relationship to the microcauses introduced.

But *was* human history a chaotic system?

It *would be* if meddling time-travelers kept trying to change it. The more various time-police agencies or whatever from assorted potential futures tried to bend history in the direction of their competing visions of the true path by altering the past, the more riddled with indeterminacy and chaos the battlefield of the present would become until you had a *literally* chaotic mess.

Like for instance . . . *now*!

World wars. Mass genocides. Deadly plagues like AIDS appearing from nowhere. Gurus and messiahs crawling out of the woodwork. Economic systems imploding from their own internal contradictions. The biosphere falling apart, and even the atmosphere itself in the process of uncontrolled mutation.

You sure could make a good paranoid science fictional case for it! How *else* could you explain how the most technologically and scientifically advanced civilization the Earth had ever seen had managed to succeed in fucking up so royally?

For fictional purposes, *why not* because various time-traveling factions from the future were converging on the very era when everything went so wrong, trying to fix it by tinkering with this and that without realizing that they were *creating* the chaotic breakdown that generated their own screwed-up futures in the first place?

It had seemed like a hot idea at the time, and he had come up with a bunch of characters and the bones of some kind of story in white heat and shipped his killer outline of it off to his agent without really rereading it in the cold clear dawn of the morning after.

But then he had to *write* the thing.

Getting into this one was like shitting bricks. Dexter had never tried to write a time-travel novel before, and as he was remembering the hard way, he had never found the whole apparatus of the time-travel novel, with its unresolvable paradoxes, its exfoliation of logical loops, its fracturing of causality, scientifically credible or literarily coherent. Okay, as a vehicle for getting into an alternate world novel where Hitler was a science fiction writer or the South won the Civil War, time travel was a useful instrument, but trying to write a whole novel about the breakdown of causality itself—

"Come on, Dex," Ellie insisted, "you say you're having trouble with the time-travel novel, maybe this'll help."

"Maybe *what'll* help?" Dexter muttered distractedly.

"Earth to Dexter Lampkin!" Ellie cried in a phony robot voice, shaking her tabloid in his face.

"Mars to Daddy! Mars to Daddy!" Jamie chimed in.

Dexter shot his daughter a look of bleary fatherly annoyance. "Eat your

Cap'n Crunch," he ordered. But he sighed in resignation and took the paper from his wife.

It was some rag called *Whole Truth*, the gag no doubt being that it was filled with everything but. It was folded over to page six. Next to a doctored photo of a two-headed woman holding a two-headed baby was a head-and-shoulders shot of a somewhat strange-looking man who looked perfectly normal by comparison.

He had a large bulbous nose, a smirky mouth, intense eyes, and a carefully trimmed bush of curly black hair frosted with jagged pinstriping. He was wearing some kind of light-colored jacket or shirt with a high Drac collar. He looked like Leonard Nimoy trying to play Mr. Spock on methedrine and not quite making it.

COMIC FROM THE FUTURE PREDICTS OWN SUPERSTARDOM

Ralf says he's from the 22nd Century—No kidding!

Ralf—just plain Ralf—the comedian who seems to have arrived from nowhere to burn up the late-nite chat-show circuit, wasn't born yesterday. According to him, he won't be born at all for another hundred years or so!

"What can I tell ya, Monkey Girl, I was having a few career problems back when I come from, so I let my agent stuff me in a time machine and drop me back here where I *know* I'm gonna be a star," said the so-called comedian from the future in an interview with *Whole Truth*.

When asked how he could be so confident of success after only a dozen or so TV appearances, Ralf replied: "Because I read all about myself in moldy old back issues of *Variety* before I left! You think I'd let my agent talk me into a dumb gig like this if I hadn't?"

When pressed to prove that he really was from the future by predicting something that would come true for readers of *Whole Truth*, Ralf declared: "Hey, no problem, I predict that I'm gonna be a big superstar back here, I'm gonna have my own TV show, I read it in an old *TV Guide* a hundred and fifty years from now, so it's gotta happen."

In the meantime, Ralf can next be seen on a forthcoming *Larry King Show* and is being considered for a guest-host slot on *Friday Night Live*.

Dexter shook his head. "Weird," he said.

"Uh-huh," said Ellie, "he sounds a lot like the novel you're trying to—"

"What's weird is that I think I write gags for this guy and this is the first time I've ever seen him."

"You *think* you write gags for him?" Ellie said, giving Dexter a fish-eyed look. "Do you *think* you've been paid too, Dex?"

"Oh, I've been paid all right, nine gags at $200 a pop for a total of $1800 so far," said Dexter, who had a photographic memory for his accounts receivable. "Some talent agent name of Balaban wants man from the future jokes for some comic, and he hasn't bounced a check on me yet."

He shrugged. "I *think* he said the guy's name was Ralf," he said, but his memory for names was at best indifferent.

"You *think* you've been writing jokes for a comedian who's supposed to be from the future and goes by a single name?" Ellie said incredulously. "I mean, come on Dex, how many of them can there be?"

If this was *Chaos Time*, maybe an infinite number, Dexter found himself thinking.

It had been a rare clear cloudless day in Big Sur, and Amanda had broken into a sweat in the Rabbit before turning off the coast road. But here, deep in the forest shadows, the resinous air was already cool, and Los Angeles seemed very far away as they sat in nests of paisley pillows on a deck planking behind a small cabin deep in the redwoods.

Hadashi handed her the cup. He had heated the water for the tea on an old black cast-iron hibachi. Amanda grimaced as she gulped it down. A taste-treat magic mushroom tea it wasn't, a bit like drinking a hot solution of loam.

Hadashi was an extremely mysterious character. Amanda had never known him by other than the single name. And she had known him all of her life. He had been her parents' guru and something like her own favorite adopted uncle, and something like a spiritual master. His dark eyes had enough of an epicanthic fold to pass for Japanese but he could just as well be of Chinese or Korean or American Indian ancestry. He had no regional or ethnic accent that Amanda could detect.

He would have to be at least in his seventies, but while his hair was steel gray and his skin had leathered to a finely lined patina as if the woods had absorbed him into themselves, his trim body seemed not much older than a healthy fifty, and sometimes there was something positively pubescent in his smile, though at other times he seemed a thousand years old.

He always seemed to have dressed right off the rack at the Gap; now he wore pressed stone-washed Levis, a red-and-black-checked lumberjack shirt, and an off-brand pair of garish chartreuse and black running shoes. Nor could anyone seem to ferret a private life beyond his existence within the event-horizon of their own, though he was amused to furnish any number of possible alter egos upon request.

"I'm a traveling salesman for an extraterrestrial health food company. I'm the reincarnation of a Tibetan lama who much prefers sunny California to the Himalayan snows. I'm a time traveler looking for the Lost Chord. I'm a schizophrenic Japanese gardener from Gardena. You pay no money, and I make no choice."

Which was proof positive, as far as Amanda was concerned, that Hadashi was the real thing.

The territory between the Mexican and Canadian borders abounded in spiritual snake-oil salesmen, none of whom had ever paid for her meal and half the time not even their own. But eat in a restaurant with Hadashi, and he'd reach gracefully and swiftly for the tab.

Hadashi appeared out of nowhere into Amanda's life from time to time, as he had in her parents', and there were other people on his circuit, whatever it was, with whom she was acquainted. He seemed to show up when you most needed him to, though you didn't necessarily know it before the fact. With whatever you seemed to need at the time, whether you knew what that was or not.

And yet there was nothing mysterioso about it. He'd call and say he was in town and invite you to dinner or allow you to invite him over, and he'd show up driving some rented compact. If you wanted to get in touch with him, there was an unlisted number in San Francisco with an answering machine on it. Leave a message, and he'd call you back.

Amanda had given up trying to figure it all out in her teens. She had grown up with Hadashi in her life and it was, well, normal. So it had seemed perfectly natural to call Hadashi when she knew it was time to cleanse her soul of the smog and bullshit and just as natural that he had invited her up here for a recentering ceremony that was just what the witch-doctor ordered.

Four months locked in LA, locked in her Amanda Robin avatar, locked in the Business, was just about her limit.

Not that she was complaining about her the greenness of her recent showbiz karma. Amanda Robin had been a busy girl. Six weeks of part-time work coaching Jimmy Balaban's comedian from the future had netted her close to $3000. There had been a walk-on with a speaking line in a detergent commercial. And eleven whole days in a soap at SAG scale. And a supporting role in a limited local run of some incomprehensible experimental play which actually paid *money*. Amanda Robin had done well by Amanda von Staulenberg's bank account, which now had over three thousand dollars in it, even after paying off the credit card balances and buying the Rabbit when the Pinto died.

But now it was time for the two of them to take a well-earned rest and for the other Amanda to come out and play. She had enough bookings to keep her on the New Age Circuit for two months without depleting her bank account, she was headed north, and this was the perfect first station along the Way. . . .

Magic mushroom tea might not taste too terrific going down, but the ride up was sweet and smooth. No queasiness or unpleasant body-image distortions. The somatic change was a gentle melding into the feel of the pillow beneath her buttocks, the cool breeze on her skin, the golden sunlight filtering through the gaps in the canopy, the perfume of evergreen and damp earth, the song of bird and wind, the shimmering dance of primeval life.

Amanda sighed. Hadashi smiled. The welcome stillness between them went on for a time out of time. Amanda inhaled the essence of the forest deep into her lungs, into her bloodstream, her brain, her consciousness, her spirit. Held it a few beats. Breathed Los Angeles slowly out. Established a rhythm. Felt her musculature relax into a different and sweetly familiar configuration. Felt her chakras open up and her spine tingle with chi. Grinned.

"Hello, Amanda," Hadashi said.

"Hi, Hadashi."

"So," Hadashi said after a suitable interval, "what brings you back to this neck of the woods?"

Amanda had attained a familiar oneness with the trees, with the birds flickering and chittering from branch to branch, with the patterns of green shadow and golden light, with the natural realm from whence she came, a harmonic awareness of her unity with creation, of the immortal universe of which she, as a conscious being, was the self-aware crown.

"Whatever keeps me away?" she said.

"A wise-ass has said, even if you live in an ivory tower, you've got to pay the rent," Hadashi said.

He laughed, he opened his arms to embrace it all.

"The perfect place to visit," he said, "but who can live here all the time?"

"You," said Amanda.

"Who *me*?" Hadashi said with a disingenuous twinkle. "Only the avatar you're talking to now, Amanda. We meet here every once in a while, take off the masks, but don't we put them back on again? Don't you go back to Hollywood? Don't I go back to picking lettuce for minimum wage when I'm not cornering the market on cattle futures?"

"So tell me, great swami, why do we do it?"

"Because the price of liberty is taking care of business, as Confucius said to Lao Tse. Because there's no business but show business, as the Bodhisattva said to the Buddha."

Amanda laughed. "And we are all in it," she said.

"And it's the only game in town."

Amanda laughed.

And so doing, passed beyond the world of maya but not beyond the Dance, for she had been reminded of what she already knew—that there *was* no other business but this Busby Berkeley production number of mask and pattern, form and essence, that there was *no* other game and *no* other town.

By this time, she was peaking on the mushroom tea, aware that this was what was happening—that the glowing shafts of light, the shimmering auras, the symphony of birdsong and wind, the kinesthetic sensation of flesh melting into air, of time becoming the changing angle of sunlight through the branches, were, like all of creation, the dance of energy and pattern, of molecule and mind.

What is, is real.

What is real is natural.

And Amanda knew full well in the state thereof that she was really and naturally quite gloriously stoned.

And, of course, Hadashi was right. She had just spent four months paying the rent on this ivory tower, and yes the price of such liberty was taking care of business, and indeed, being *the* perfect place, this *was* the perfect place to visit. But you couldn't live here forever, for to cling greedily to this timeless transcendence was to lose it, was the worm that lurked inside the cosmic apple of the tree of knowledge, was the dark junkie alchemy that turned true sacrament into mere dope.

For this was the Cosmic Green Room, where you came to strip away the costume and greasepaint of the previous role and cool out for a bit before making up for the next. The center of the Great Wheel was Void, and so a true ceremony of recentering could only be a transition. The transition from her Hollywood role of Amanda Robin to the avatar of Amanda the Pilgrim who followed the path hidden in plain sight that ran along this very coast, that wound through these very forests, that ascended these very magic mountains to California's mystic heart.

And voila, that which she had sought had been attained.

She was now *that* avatar, *that* Amanda.

Who now knew that she had passed through the transition. She was content to sit there under the greenery in the waning light of the cooling afternoon and contemplate the ever-changing mask of Hadashi's face.

She was sophisticated enough in such matters to realize that the recessional montage that appeared on the face before her was the product of a complex synergy between chance lighting and the altered chemical matrix of her consciousness, projection and perception, spiritual insight and visual artifact.

But what is, is real.

And when the doorway opens, you see what comes through it.

The movement of the sun across the sky had chanced to change the angle of a golden beam passing through a gap in the forest canopy so that it shone full on Hadashi's face like a celestial spotlight, literally solarizing his visage, and the wind through the trees, the passage of random birds and insects, cast moving shadows that broke it up into an ever-changing mask of abstract features.

That recombined to display a flickering sequence of avatars both strange and hauntingly familiar. . . .

Hadashi's sunlight-gilded vaguely Japanese face transmuted into the golden head of a statue of Amida. Into a vine-covered Buddha of ancient crumbling stone. Into the living flesh of Gautama himself.

Amanda unfocused her eyes and let herself fall into the cosmic light show, into the kaleidoscope of images, into the kinestatic mandala of Hadashi's face, flick, flick, flick . . .

Buddha. Krishna. Northwest Indian totem.

The masks kept changing along some vector whose elusive meaning kept her transfixed.

Shiva. Quetzalcoatl. Loki.

But the eyes *never* changed, unwavering blue eyes that she had seen somewhere before. . . .

Coyote. Hanuman the Monkey God.

Time seemed to crystallize like liquid amber around her, around the uncanny feeling of déjà vu . . .

King Kong. Bonzo the Chimp.

Eyes gazing back at her brilliantly and unblinkingly from behind the avatars' masks. . . .

Bozo the Clown.

The spirit behind the veils, the essence behind the dance of forms . . .

Ralf.

Ralf's eyes.

The same eyes she had seen peering back at her in a dopplegänger of this moment out there on her porch from behind the mask of the comedian from the future's face.

A bubble of laughter rose through Amanda's throat and burst through her lips, and she laughed, and laughed, and laughed.

"Mind letting me in on the joke?" Hadashi said.

And he was just Hadashi again.

"You had to be there," Amanda said. "You had to be really stoned." And so saying, realized she no longer really was. She shrugged. "It's kind of hard to explain," she finally said.

"Most jokes are."

Amanda did her best, though by now the nature of the cosmic punch line eluded her, and she was reduced to reciting the mere visual phenomenology, the parade of avatars from godhead to farce.

"I guess I should be flattered," Hadashi said dryly. "That's a pretty classy set of avatars to incarnate."

Now he did laugh. "Although I'm not so sure about Bonzo, Bozo, or Ralf!" he said. "That's the joke?"

Was it?

"The eyes . . ." Amanda muttered. "The eyes that never changed . . ."

"The eyes of Vishnu himself behind the dance?" Hadashi said. And he gazed into Amanda's with that very same unwavering intensity. "The immutable soul behind Maya's veil?"

Hadashi laughed. But those eyes didn't. The eyes behind all the masks. Or what in that moment what seemed to be looking back at her through them again.

"Or perhaps only visual fixation on the eyes as the center of a narrow focal plane caused by the physiological effects of the mushrooms?" whoever was doing the talking said. "Such as what I'm causing you to experience right now?"

He laughed. He winked. The spell was broken.

"An effect not exactly unheard of in the literature, Amanda," he said dryly, becoming her old familiar Hadashi again.

"But Ralf ran the very same number on me, if a number is what it is," Amanda told him. "And I hadn't had so much as a glass of wine. And *I* taught it to *him*!"

"Did you, Amanda?" Hadashi said, grinning slightly as he playfully attempted to catch her with the vacuum of his eyes again.

"I *thought* I did. . . . I was trying to give him a secondary persona to serve as a kind of in-house straight man. And I was teaching him a sense-memory exercise to call it up with, and there was a moment there when . . . when there seemed to be *someone else* looking back at me from behind the mask of his face—"

"*The very same someone?*" said Hadashi.

"The very same someone as *who?*"

Hadashi's voice laughed, but his eyes didn't. "As who's lookin' at you now, kid," he said, doing Bogart.

And there, in the waning afterglow of the mushroom tea, looking into the eyes of her old friend and spiritual master, a doorway opened.

A doorway into a mirrored recessional of doorways looping möbiuslike back on each other in time. Hadashi's eyes became the eyes that had become doorways into the Dreamtime out there on her porch. Became the eyes that had looked back at her for an unsettling moment before that in Texas Jimmy Balaban's office. The eyes behind the avatars' masks outside of linear time.

The eyes she was looking into now.

Could déjà vu run in reverse? Could she have been the instrument whereby some spirit of the Dreamtime future had opened itself a doorway into the past of the now?

"Who are you?" she said. "Who are you really?"

"Who else?" Hadashi said in his own natural voice. "The very same someone behind all the masks, including your own. From a certain perspective, who else is there? The Buddha. Krishna. Shiva. Roll your own avatar. Don't we all?"

"Loki? Coyote?"

"Oh *especially* the Tricksters!" said Hadashi.

"Even Ralf?"

He laughed a quite human laugh, and the doorway closed.

Or did it?

"The zeitgeist works in wondrous ways its marvels to perform," said Hadashi. "At certain karmic nexuses, it throws up an avatar for the times, a Buddha, a Jesus, a Gandhi."

"A *Ralf*?" Amanda exclaimed dubiously.

Hadashi shrugged. "The times *do* tend to get the avatar they deserve," he said. "God may or may not play dice with the universe, but if history teaches us anything, it's that He, She, or It is not above throwing the occasional Cosmic Custard Pie."

"New! Improved! Tastier than ever—"

"That stuff is gonna rot your brain," Momma said, gargling another halfa can of warm beer, flipping to another channel again at the same time. "It's really screwin' you up, girl!"

"—overnight lows in the fifties, but by tomorrow morning—"

Foxy Loxy just couldn't *believe* she was hearing this shit again!

All fuckin' day and so far inta the night half the time she passes out onna couch, she lays there pourin' the cheapest beer she can find so's she can afford more of it down her throat, fuckin' living room stinks like the Polish navy uses it for its regular pisser, and *I* chip a little crack makes *me* some kinda junkie dope fiend!

"—chops, minces, dices, slices, even grates Parmesan cheese!"

"How the fuck would *you* know, Momma?" Loxy snarled. "You see it onna fuckin' *tube?*"

Look at this shithole, Loxy thought, make a garbageman puke!

The Welfare was payin' for a two-room apartment, or what they called two anna half, like the toilet anna stand-in kitchen was supposedta add up to half a room. When Loxy was a kid, Momma had the bedroom and she hadta crash onna convertible inna living room, so simple a little kid could pull the sucker down like they showed onna TV if their momma was too fucked t'figure it out as usual.

These days Momma hardly ever left the fuckin' livin' room except to go to the john or get somethin' to scarf or more beer outa the fridge or once inna week maybe to actually waddle on down ta McDonald's or the bodega when she couldn't make Loxy do it.

She laid there on the couch all fuckin' day gorked out in fronta the tube witha beer can in one hand and the zapper in the other, and just maybe, if she wasn't too fried, she might get it together to pull the bed thing down outa the couch an' crawl inta the dirty sheets before she passed out, but don't fuckin' count on it!

Besides the convertible and the fuckin' TV, about all there was inna way of furniture in the shitty little livin' room was this fuckin' coffee table with the legs kept comin' off, a red beanbag chair leakin' those little pieces of foam Loxy found inna Dumpster, and a coupla foldin' chairs. Course that *did* make room for alla old beer cans an' pizza cartons an' *TV Guide*s an' McDonald's boxes an' puke-awful old underwear piled up in between visits from the Welfare investigator when Loxy dumped the mess inna garbage an' made ten million fuckin' cockroaches happy.

"That's right, I seen it on the news, smokin' that crap turns your brain to a loada mush, like snortin' Ajax, or mainlinin' Drano—"

"—rock star Ricky Speed, and special guest, Ralf, the comedian from the—"

"Since when you watch the *news*, Momma?"

"I watch it sometimes," Momma whined. "Gotta keep up with current events." She zapped channels again and got some dude doin' the sports. "See?"

"—knocked off the Knicks, 131 to 117—"

"Oh wow, Momma, I didn't know you was such a heavy thinker, ball scores an' all, next thing you know, you'll be readin' the *Enquirer*!"

Momma actually managed to look away from the tube and more or less in her direction.

"You listen to me," she said, "I seen it on *Oprah*, that stuff you smokin' isa devil's dope, turn you inta what you see out there in Tompkins Square sleepin' in a garbage can and mugging little old ladies and barkin' at the moon!"

"Yeah, anna few linesa coke or a snorta smack t'cool out's gonna turn ya into a werewolf with hair on your teeth," Loxy told her. "An' turnin' a few tricks gonna send you burnin' to hell. I ain't noticed that *you've* gone and lived your life like you believe such tightassed bullshit, Momma!"

"I lived the high life, and I'm not tellin' you I wouldn't honk up all the free coke and smack some high-rolling john'd lay out was one to walk inna door right now," Momma told her. "I ain't never fed you no Sunday school bullshit about that, now ain't that the truth?"

"—one moment of pain, and then eternal—"

Her eyes were bloodshot and kinda tobacco-stain yellow and her fuckin' breath woulda melted glass and there was beer dribblin' down one corner of her mouth, and she was still zapping through the channels like the spastic TV junkie she was, but she was looking right at Loxy insteada starin' at the fuckin' tube, and for a minute there, it seemed to Loxy that she was really trying to get it together to be human sorta, trying to remember what it was supposed to be like to be a real mom.

"—*heal* this boy, Lord—"

"So?" Loxy said.

"So if an old drunken whore and garbage-head like your momma tells you the stuff you been doin' is changin' you into a low-life piecea shit no one wantsa see around, it ain't the Salvation Army talkin' to ya, girl!"

"What the hell you talkin' 'bout, Momma?" Loxy snarled, reaching into her jeans pocket and rubbing the cool smooth glass of her pipe.

"You really so far gone on that shit you don't know?"

"Know what?"

"Know you goin' through changes. And they ain't been good."

"I don't know what the fuck you're talkin' about, Momma!"

"Bullshit you don't, girl!"

Well, okay, so you hadda be careful with the stuff, be kinda stingy with it, not get carried away, a little puff'll do ya, and okay, okay, maybe once or twice, she *had* gone a little over the top, like when she threw the fuckin' toaster against the wall, or the shit with that asshole down at Sailor Sal's; okay, maybe throwin' the fuckin' fries wasn't too fuckin' cool, but she hadn't taken a hit at work after that, now had she, well only a couple three times, and nothing bad had happened, big fuckin' deal, whaddya supposed t'do, take shit from every dickhead came upta the window with two ninety-five, shithead who said the customer's always right never worked flippin' no burgers on First Avenue, better believe it, not like she'd done anything could get her *busted* or something, and Mario hadn't *canned her* yet now had he . . .

"Right," Loxy drawled, pulling her hand out of her pocket and her pipe with it, "the stuff *I'm* doin' is turnin' me inta Dracula's daughter, but pourin' a zillion gallons a beer a day down your fuckin' yawp, hey, that's okay, that what you tellin' me, huh, Momma?"

"—Ricky Speed, singing the current number one—"

Duh, duh, duh, the old slob's lips was movin', but nothin' was comin' out, an' flick, flick, flick, her fat thumb zapped through the channels, like some fuckin' zombie goin' through the motions. An' *she's* tellin' me that the stuff *I'm* doin' is rottin' *my* brain?

"—in the brimstone and fire of Armageddon—"

"So maybe you'd like to explain to me how come it's *you* layin' there all fuckin' day doin' nothin' at all but gettin' your useless fat ass fatter and fatter, and it's this crackhead zombie slaverin' junkie what's holdin' down a job?" Loxy demanded, extracting the vial from her pocket and thumbing it open.

Momma tossed the latest empty onna floor, yanked a new can off the current six-pack, popped it, and took a swig. Loxy tumbled the remains of the rock into her palm, flaked off a chip with her thumbnail, put it in the pipe bowl, tamped it down onto the dirty screen.

"Big deal," Momma said. "Flippin' greaseburgers for the minimum wage, I useta make that in about thirty seconds!"

"Yeah, right, *useta*, Momma!" Loxy shot back, fishing in another pocket for her lighter. "You so disgusting now, you couldn't make four bucks inna *week* suckin' dick inna AIDS ward!"

"Don't you go givin' *me* that bad mouth in my own house, girl! Save it for your junkie friends on the street!"

"*Your* house! You mean the *Welfare's* house, don't ya, Momma? Whensa last time *you* made a dollar, huh? Maybe it pays shit, but at least *I* gotta job!"

"An' you're burnin' every dollar you make up in that little glass pipe!"

"I gotta right to spend my own money how I want! You want me t'give it ta you so's you can glug *more* fuckin' beer down your big fat throat?" Loxy snarled back, defiantly sticking the pipe in her mouth and giving her Bic an angry flick.

"Don't you talk like that to me! I'm your *mother*! And don't you go smokin' that shit in here or I'll throw your ass out! You of age, girl, you ain't worth no more ADC, and I ain't gonna live with no crackhead, least not one gets herself fucked up in here!"

Loxy took the pipe out of her mouth long enough to shout "Fuck you!"

"I mean it! You start doin' that stuff here, I'll throw your ass out! I'll have the Welfare do it! If I gotta, I'll call the fuckin' cops, I ain't havin' it, that shit turns you inta something scares me bad!"

"Boo! Grrr! I'm a big bad crazed crackhead monster gonna bite your head off!" Loxy snarled, rolling her eyes, giving Momma the finger, makin' a crazed animal face, an' laughin' her head off before she took herself a nice little hit.

Pow! Zap! Boom! Wow! Oh *yeah*!

The charge seared down her throat, burned into her lungs, flashed through her bones, an' lit up her brain likea zillion flashbulbs, smooth as good coke it wasn't, but it was fuckin' *strong*, an' it was fuckin' *fast*!

And it made you feel so *good*!

Not beer-guzzlin', pot-smokin', smack-snortin', reds-poppin', laid-back, fuzzed-out, floaty goooood, none of that junkie shit made you happy ta stare inta a lightbulb or the fuckin' TV for a whole fuckin' high like the disgustin' glob a blubber onna couch, oh no!

Made you feel kick-ass good! Bopadop good! Finger poppin' foot-stompin' top a th' world get your fuckin' dumb ass outa my way boogaloo good! Baaad good! Whoo-ee!

Bullfuckin' shit, this stuff was too hot to handle! Whole secret was you wasn't *supposedta* handle it, you let it handle *you*, make you strong and bright onna top a the world, yeah! Those what could *ruled*!

Loxy bounced up offa the couch, and danced around the room, zippity-zip, zappity-zap, onna tip of her toes, bop-bop-ba-do-bop, to the music of some asshole rock group onna TV, drummin' with her fists on the wall, onna foldin' chair, bam-bam-bama, onna coffee table—

Ker-rack! Fuckin' leg fell off again, anna stupid thing went fallin' apart onna fuckin' floor, hah, hah, hah, beer cans, anna telephone, an' old *TV Guide*s an' McMaggots, an' all, flyin' all over the place, hee, hee, hee, kick the motherfuckers, boom, bam, wham!

"Goddamn it!"

"Rule! *Rule! RULE!* Ker-rack! Crack! Crack! Quack! Quack *rules*!"

Momma raised herself off the couch inna cloud of beer cans an' chicken bones like some dead fuckin' whale all gross an' bloaty poppin' up t'the surface of the Hudson fuckin' River never can tell what's gonna bubble up outa the sewers in this town, now canya!

"Sit the fuck down, damn it, you're tearin' the place apart!" Momma screamed, lumbering after her like a crazed elephant.

"Hey, come on, Momma, don't sweat it, it's a fuckin' shithole anyway, hah, hah," Loxy said, dancin' in circles around her, kickin' aside a foldin' chair.

"I'm gonna call the cops!" Momma yelled and made a move inna general direction of the phone layin' onna floor.

"Fuck that!" Loxy told her, and beat her to it, pickin' it up and yankin' it away.

Maybe a little too hard, fuckin' cord pulled outa the wall. "Whoops!" Loxy giggled, and flung the fuckin' phone across the room.

"Shit . . ." Momma muttered, backin' away all wide-eyed and blubbery fluttery like Loxy was gonna bite her nose off or somethin'.

"Come on, Momma, let's have some fun!" Loxy said, chasin' her down and grabbin' her by the free hand, the one that wasn't still holdin' the fuckin' zapper that is. "Let's dance!"

And tried to whirl her around real nice like, tried t'get her inta the beat, but the fat slob musta weighed three or four hundred pounds, an' even Mighty Loxy What Got the Power couldn't do all that much with sucha load, was like tryin' ta dance with the world's biggest sacka shit!

Around, and around again about halfway, just about break your fuckin' ass ta do it, uh, uh, uh, an' then gaplowie, the old lardbucket shakes loose, and goes reelin' and staggerin' back across the room, splat up against the wall, kinda oozes down it real slow like a booger down a windowpane, ends up puffin' an' groanin' onna floor on her ass.

"—those hard-to-clean stains under the rim—"

Whimperin' and blubberin', fuckin' disgustin' t'see, tryin' to crawl backwards on her ass like through the fuckin' wall if she could, and all the time, one hand's grabbin' for a fuckin' beer can ain't there, and the other's still zappin' the fuckin' TV through the channels, drive you fuckin' NUTS!

"—send in whatever you can spare, even if it's only a dollar—"

"Stop that fuckin' shit, willya!" Loxy screamed, and she grabbed for the fuckin' remote.

Momma yanked it away, tucked it up against her tit, tried to slither away across the floor.

"You leave me alone! You leave me alone!"

"—whose future, Jay, yours or mine?"

Loxy kicked her inna fat gut, grabbed the fuckin' remote outa her paw, threw the motherfucker down on the floor as hard as she could, and stomped on it again, and again, and again, with the heel of her shoe.

"Fuck-in' T-*V*! Fuck-in' T-*V*! Fuck-in' T-*V*!" she sang, poppin' her fingers to the beat as she stomped the son of a bitch into teeny-tiny little pieces, whoo-eee, felt so fuckin' *good*!"

"—remember reading *Variety*, you could tell me when I'm gonna be canceled around longer than Letterman is, right?"

"Hey, maybe this is gonna be *my* show next year Monkey Boy, but I won't forget who gave me my break—"

"My remote!" Momma screamed at the top of her lungs like someone shoved a red-hot donkey-dick up her ass. "You busted my *remote*!"

Her fuckin' face turned red, veins throbbin', snot leakin' outa her nose. "You busted my remote, you crazy crackhead bitch!" she howled even louder. "Get the fuck out of here!"

An H-bomb went off in Loxy's brain. "You care more about that fuckin' piece of shit you ever cared about me you fuckin' fat useless old cunt!" she howled, shaking a fist.

"Stay away from me! Stay away from me!" Momma blubbered. "You come any closer I'm gonna scream!"

"You goddamn fuckin' TV junkie!"

"HELP! POLICE! RAPE! RAPE! POLICE! NIGGERS! SPICS! RAPE! RAPE! RAPE!"

And then she started screamin' like a fuckin' siren! Like the fuckin' cops was showin' up already! Some asshole next door starts poundin' on the wall! Some dick upstairs bangin' onna steam pipe with a fuckin' hammer!

Loxy freaked, whirled, turned, saw—

—some stupid wise-ass fucker witha nose like a cucumber, eyes like holes inta someplace you don't wanna go, flat-face, not a human face, a fuckin' *TV face*, yammerin' at one a those talkin' deadheads—

"Rot your brain, girl!"

"—seen the future, and it sucks!"

Tryin' to suck her on through into the TV junkie place!

"Muggin' little old ladies and barkin' at the moon—"

"—like snortin' Ajax or mainlinin' Drano!"

Bang! Smash! Scream! Siren! POLICE! RAPE! POLICE!

"—out there sleeping in a garbage can—"

"Fuck you, you fuckin' TV zombie junkie cunt!" Loxy screamed. "Fuck you, you TV face asshole!"

And kicked him inna chops with all her might.

KA-BOOM! KER-ASH! KA-POW!

Whoo-ee! The whole fuckin' shitpile exploded with a tremendous bam! crash! flash! flyin' crud! broken glass! Far fuckin' out! Hah! Hah! Hah! An' up yours!

An' Foxy Loxy roared out of the apartment into the red-hot night, slamming the door behind her hard enough to knock the stupid fuckin' pictures off the living room wall, she fuckin' hoped!

Texas Jimmy Balaban was not impressed by a Century City address. The shopping-mall-cum-hotel-cum-cinema-complex-cum-office-building-park-cum-clipjoint only existed in the first place because Fox had been forced to sell off half its studio real estate in order to bail itself out of the *Cleopatra* disaster. Built without a city street within walking distance, it was gotcha, starting with the outrageous rates in the nightmare maze of underground parking garages. The Century Plaza Hotel was overpriced enough to impress midwestern politicians, but drop it in Vegas or Miami Beach and no one would look at it twice.

The office towers ran to anodized aluminum, smoked glass, and elevators like this one, crooning at you in orchestral versions of Sinatra's golden oldies fit to throw you into insulin shock.

Just the sort of place where an outfit like the Gold Network would choose to occupy a top-floor tower suite.

Gold was a cut and a half down from the majors. Strong on the West Coast, where it filled its own full-time channel on most cable systems, not quite as good penetration in the South and Midwest, where it functioned more like a syndicated packager for independent broadcast channels, and growing on the East Coast thanks to a sweetheart deal with a major New York independent, Gold had good cash flow but not the capital to afford more than a dozen or so original dramatic series a year. So they filled the rest of their airtime with game shows; cut-rate soaps; talk shows; strange things imported from Mexico, Brazil, and Poland over-dubbed on the cheap; and taped coverage of such stellar sports events as Demolition Derby and Bobtail truck races.

Hungry, in other words, for low-budget programming.

So when Archie Madden, Gold's resident boy genius programmer, invited Texas Jimmy to take a meeting, Jimmy had been, if not exactly blinded by the light, willing to hear what the guy had to say.

For something like this was what he had been positioning Ralf for all along. Ralf was now the hottest item he had ever had on his client list, but that didn't give Texas Jimmy delusions of headlining at Caesar's Palace or Circus Circus or going head-to-head with Letterman or Leno.

The Man From the Future schtick was good enough to make Ralf a fave rave in the tabloids, sufficiently famous to command fees above scale for the kind of chat-shows he had originally done for a few bucks in cash under the table, and to get him work here and there as an opening act in Vegas, and the *Tonight Show* and *Saturday Night Live* had even more or less come after *him*.

All the money Jimmy had invested in Ralf had come back to him two or three times over, but as Jimmy knew all too well, what goes up comes down, and when it's something that relies more on novelty than talent, chances are a lot sooner than later. With an act like Ralf, you'd get one chance to grab the brass ring, and Jimmy had a feeling that this meeting was going to be it.

He found his right thumb and forefinger stroking a phantom cigarette as the elevator finally reached the top floor, and he heard his voice squeaking up an octave as he babbled final instructions to Ralf.

"Now let me do the talking at least at first, at least until I cue you, okay, you don't want do to anything to piss this guy off, make him think you're some kind of wiseass except when you're on, right?"

"Hey, come on, relax, Monkey Boy, whaddya think I'm gonna do, whip it out and piss on the floor?"

"Just can the Monkey Boy schtick, all right?" Jimmy told him as they exited the elevator right in front of a huge set of teak veneer doors. "This guy's *black*, or Afro-American, or whatever they're calling themselves these days, so he might be a little sensitive . . ."

"Hey, Jimmy, how many Afro-Americans does it take to—"

"*One* to say no in this case, so shut up!" Jimmy snapped anxiously as he pushed open the double doors.

That Madden had insisted that he bring the talent in question along for his perusal was understandable, but not exactly a dose of Valium to Jimmy's nerves.

He still had no idea of what was really going on inside the guy's head. Okay, he had had plenty of clients with whom his relationship was pretty coldly professional, and there were those who would say that Texas Jimmy Balaban specialized in weirdos. But Ralf was something else again.

The question was, *what?*

He had a real apartment now, a one-bedroom off the Strip that came furnished down to the cheap silverware and the plastic garbage cans. Jimmy picked him up there fairly regularly 'cause he *still* wouldn't learn to drive, and the only personal items he had ever seen there were a TV, a VCR, stacks of books and magazines, a microwave oven, and the wardrobe of clothes that Jimmy himself had helped him buy.

For this meeting, Jimmy had dressed him in a presentable-looking tan short-sleeved safari suit, white shirt, and cordovan loafers. But left to his own devices, Ralf would dress like a traveling encyclopedia salesman clown from Ringling Brothers—running shorts with white shirt and tie, business suit with tank top and Reeboks, blue blazer and green velour shirt with jeans and sandals, whatever he happened to grab off the rack.

If he ever got laid, or had any friends, or even hung out in a favorite saloon, not even the tabloids had been able to come up with anything juicy. Texas Jimmy had *never* seen the guy step out of the character of "Ralf the Comedian From the Future." Despite himself, Jimmy had almost come to believe that Ralf, however preposterous it seemed, *was* really what he claimed to be.

Because the only alternative, though more likely, was a lot scarier—that he was not only a skilled enough actor to keep up this schtick twenty-four hours a day seven days a week down to the teeniest little detail but that he was crazy enough to *want* to.

The thought that he was maybe walking into the most important meeting of his life with a talent who was stark staring nuts did not exactly soothe Texas Jimmy's nerves as a receptionist guided them from the standard reception area filled with stiff modern black leather furniture, show posters, and the token rubber tree, down a corridor lined with the usual standard-issue office doors.

Nor was he exactly set at ease when, instead of showing them to the oversized portal at the end of the corridor leading to Madden's corner office, they were ushered into the conference room next door. And to make matters more unsettling, Archie Madden wasn't alone.

Flanking him on one side of the usual standard-issue oval teak veneer conference table were a man and a woman. The man was gray-haired, somewhat overweight, about sixty-five, and wore a fancy pearl-gray suit, clear gold-rimmed glasses, a big nugget ring, and a gold Rolex. The woman was maybe in her early forties, shoulder-length black hair without a strand out of place, good-looking and well-preserved in the manner of a statue of a Fifties actress in the Hollywood Wax Museum, and wearing a kind of softened and skirted feminine version of the standard black business suit.

Madden himself looked maybe all of twenty-seven. Clear coffee-colored skin looked like he shaved it twice a day with a laser, except for this little Fu Manchu mustache which seemed to be drawn precisely a quarter inch past the corners of his mouth. One of those pencil-eraser haircuts, bald, and maybe even waxed on the sides. Wearing ironed blue jeans, a white dress shirt with a button-down collar, a black tie, and a satin jacket featuring a blazing orange sun setting behind a tropical isle.

"Have a seat, people," he said in a tone of instant familiarity. "This is Max Baker, our money guy, and Liz Papadopolis, executive vice president in charge of keeping me from doing anything *really* stupid. I'll come right to the point 'cause I've got a lunch date in a half hour. We're interested. What about you?"

Texas Jimmy sank down into a chair wishing there was something stronger on the table than the ice bucket of Perrier and orange juice.

He knew Archie Madden by reputation. Who didn't?

Trouble was, there were two of them.

According to one school of thought, the Gold Network had hired themselves a black front man who looked good in the trades and served as a mirror of the median IQ of the audience. According to the other, Madden was an authentic boy genius with the instincts and showbiz reflexes of a tiger shark on speed.

"Interested in what?" Jimmy said cautiously.

Madden flashed him a smile that did much to support the tiger shark theory. "I think we can safely assume that we're gathered here today to talk TV, not real estate or the music biz."

"You want give me my own TV show, that's the deal, right, Monkey Boy?" said Ralf.

Shit! Jimmy fetched him a kick in the shins.

But Archie Madden just widened that smile into something magnanimous and lordly and all the more unsettling, coming from this young kid.

"I've been thinking about it, Ralf," he said.

"You're going to do it, and it's going to be a big hit," Ralf said, flashing his own exaggerated version of Madden's smile back at him. But he did it in that other voice that Amanda Robin had given him, smooth and vaguely snooty in a comic sort of way that just managed to take the edge off.

Madden's expression changed not at all.

"Beat," he said, holding up his right hand and cuing the next line with his forefinger.

" 'Cause I looked it up in old *Variety*s before I let 'em drop me back here in the sticks," said Ralf, coming back with the familiar smart-ass voice.

Archie Madden moved his head up and down about an inch and a half. "Nice timing," he said.

"What are we *really* talking about here . . . Archie?" Texas Jimmy said quickly before the meeting slipped even further out of his control. "I mean, no insult intended, but I can read the numbers, and I somehow doubt that you're going to come up with enough money to make it worthwhile to see my guy chewed up as gunfodder in a losing ratings battle with eight-hundred-pound late-night gorillas . . ."

Max Baker, the money guy, nodded, eyes only.

Madden nodded. "We can't go head to head with the majors in postprime. Our strategy is to keep costs down low enough so we can do a ten share and show a profit. I find a way to up it to fifteen, they give me another gold star, isn't that right, Liz?"

Liz Papadopolis sat there stone-faced.

"So?" said Jimmy.

"So I've come up with one of the brilliant ideas that have made me a legend in my own time," Archie Madden said.

"Which is?"

Another of those smiles, Sylvester after finally getting to devour Tweety.

"Redefine the time slot," Madden said. "Begin our late-night entertainment programming half an hour earlier, while the competition is doing the late news. While they're going head to head with each other for the newsnerds, we scoop up the lion's share of everyone else by entertaining them for a half hour instead of depressing them with the latest disaster stories and unemployment statistics."

If a grin could have gotten even more pleased with itself, Archie Madden's would've.

"Like shooting fish in a barrel with an Uzi, don't you think, Jimmy? A half hour to hook everyone whose idea of serious news is what they see on the covers of the *Enquirer* and the *Star* on the checkout line."

"Like Ralf. . . ." said Texas Jimmy.

Madden nodded again. "Not only do they escape the news, but they get to convince themselves that they *are* keeping up with the headlines in the process," he said. "If that's not worth at least a fifteen share, then I'll be the first person in history to lose money underestimating the intelligence of the American people."

He shrugged. "Course, when the big guns come on, our market share is gonna drop, but if we hold half the audience for the second half of the slot, we average over ten for the hour, which will be comfortably in the black if we keep our production costs down."

He folded his arms across his chest.

"Well Jimmy, what do you say?"

"What do I say to *what?*" Texas Jimmy asked in something of a daze. Am I missing something here? he wondered.

"Five days a week, eleven to twelve, but we'll stunt it around in markets where they run the news at ten-thirty," said Archie Madden.

"But—"

"Production budget of forty thousand a show, you keep what you don't spend," said Max Baker.

"But—"

"Guaranteed for thirteen weeks, renewable for another thirteen, same deal, at our option," said Liz Papadopolis.

"But—"

"But what, Jimmy?" said Archie Madden.

"But what format are you *talking about*?" Jimmy finally managed to say. "What are we supposed to fill the time with?"

Archie Madden shrugged. He threw up his hands. His smile lit up the room in ultraviolet.

"Surprise me, Jimmy," he said. "Come up with something brilliant. I like surprises. And I do respect brilliance."

"And do it under budget," said Baker.

"But—"

Madden shot his left cuff, consulted one of those black plastic Casio computer watches, which, in addition to dialing your telephone and serving as a TV remote, also managed, somehow, to tell you the time.

"Lunchies, people!" he said, rising.

He gave Texas Jimmy a stage wink.

"Oh yeah," he said, "and *do* have it for us by next Friday."

5

The bourbon that Texas Jimmy Balaban hadn't gotten to drink during his prelunch meeting with Archie Madden he made up for at the office. Not that he got pissed or anything, but a couple three quick jolts did seem to be called for to lubricate the old machinery.

The numbers were sweet and sour.

A budget of forty thousand a show. Keep all you don't spend.

That was the sweet.

The sour was that it meant he had to come up with an hour format that could be produced for as much less than forty thousand as possible, but by the time he had paid for a crew, a director, studio time, and whatever, there'd hardly be anything left to dip his wick in. Meaning he'd be screwed if he had to pay anything at all for guest talent. Meaning Jimmy had to come up with a format that would enable him to fill an hour a night with just Ralf.

Archie-fucking-Madden!

After two slugs of Jim Crow, Texas Jimmy could not come up with one single comic in the entire history of show business who would be able to fill five hours of airtime a week doing nothing but straight stand-up. After his third drink, Texas Jimmy was forced to face the fact that he hadn't a clue. He needed . . . he needed . . .

He needed a writer.

This was what those guys were for, wasn't it?

The town was full of screenwriters, maybe ten percent working in film or TV at any given time, and the rest of them happy to get any work at all. Hadn't he been able to buy gags from writers with prime-time credits as long as your arm at a couple hundred bucks a pop?

Texas Jimmy began thumbing through his Rolodex. He had the names of dozens of writers in here with scribbled notes on their credits; broken-down gag writers, sitcom hacks with credits back to *My Mother the Car*—

Jimmy paused at "Dexter D. Lampkin."

Wasn't he some kind of sci-fi writer?

Jimmy perused his notes. Yeah, the guy wrote sci-fi novels, cartoon shows, no feature credits, hardly any prime-time either. A few pages by next Friday figured to be no big deal for a guy like that, and he figured to probably need the dough, how much could it cost . . . ?

It seemed like a good hungry sign when the phone was pounced on before the end of the second ring.

"Yeah?" grunted a distracted voice on the other end. Not so good.

"This is Texas Jimmy Balaban, Dexter. I've got a job for you."

"Not interested. I'm working on a novel."

"No more than ten pages, Lampkin," Jimmy said off the top of his head. "Gotta have it by next Friday. Two thousand dollars. Want me to call the next guy on my list?"

Beat.

"I might be able to squeeze it in," Lampkin said in a somewhat more polite tone of voice. "Tell me what you're looking for . . ."

Jimmy did.

"*A series format for a lousy two grand?*" Lampkin snapped when he had finished explaining. "Are you out of your mind?"

"It's not like we're talking even a treatment," Jimmy told him. "Just a concept, a springboard, talent like you could bang it out in a couple hours, who's kidding who?"

"If it's so easy, why don't you write it yourself and save the two grand, Mr. Balaban?"

"I'll . . . I'll give you a piece if it goes," Texas Jimmy said impulsively. Shit! Was that the bourbon talking?

"How much?" said Dexter D. Lampkin much more gently.

Well, what the hell, fair's fair, right?

"Five hundred bucks a show for the duration," Jimmy told him magnanimously.

"Fifteen hundred," said Lampkin.

"Be real!" Jimmy exclaimed. "For ten pages? For a couple hours' work? Seven-fifty."

"A grand is a nice round number, don't you think?" said Lampkin. "The zeros make the accounting so much easier you'll almost save the difference right there."

Texas Jimmy laughed. "Deal," he said.

He could get to liking this guy.

If he delivered the goods.

It took Dexter Lampkin about five minutes to drive the Alfa from his house to the vicinity of Texas Jimmy Balaban's office off the Strip, but fifteen minutes to find a place to park. A pain in the ass, and on one level, so was this job of work. But on another level that attitude was a con job that Dexter was running on himself, and on the third level, he knew it.

Sure, he was working on *Chaos Time* and it always annoyed him to break work on a novel to do something else, but at $2000 for a hour or so's meeting and a day or two's work, he could afford to be annoyed. Besides, there was the possibility, however small, that he'd come up with a format that actually *sold*, in which case he'd be raking in five thousand a week for the duration, no less than thirteen weeks, according to Balaban.

Dexter sighed as he entered the lobby of the tacky little office building. Such fantasies were a cardinal danger of being a writer of any sort in Hollywood. Retire for life on the proceeds from a single series format! The hell of it was that it was all *possible,* it actually *did* happen. A writer could luck into more money for a month's work or even less than a full-time novelist could make in a lifetime.

What a temptation it was to waste all your time and energy chasing after the Big Hit instead of actually doing real work for real money!

What a mistake it was to succumb!

It was all too easy to forget that one spec feature script out of a hundred got bought, that one series format out of five thousand ever went into production, that money would get you through times of no luck a lot more surely than luck would get you through times of no money.

On the other hand, breathed there a writer within a thousand-mile radius of downtown Tinseltown who dreamed not of rolling the bones and beating the odds? Who wouldn't be willing to roll the bones for the Big Hit no matter the odds when some schmuck was *paying him* $2000 to do it?

Dexter laughed to himself, for the inevitable line had run through his head as he opened the door to Texas Jimmy Balaban's office.

What the hell, at least I'm still in show business!

There was no one at the front desk in the outer office, and when Dexter hit the buzzer, the man himself emerged from somewhere in back, glad-hand first behind a slightly world-weary smile full of perfect white teeth, maybe forty-five or fifty, brown hair only thinning on top, tired but lively eyes, artificial swimming pool tan to match the teeth, and wearing a blue-and-white-striped seersucker suit.

"Dexter? Hi. I'm Texas Jimmy Balaban. Call me Jimmy."

"Call me Dex . . ."

Jimmy Balaban's handshake was firm and manly.

"Ralf's back in my office, Dex," Balaban said, "and I've got to warn you, you just might find him a little strange."

If Dexter had tried to cast the part of a sleazy talent agent by putting out a cattle call in a downtown Vegas casino, he couldn't have done much better. But there was a certain indefinable charm to Texas Jimmy Balaban that Dexter found himself liking.

His office was about what Dexter expected. Half-dead potted plant. Black Naughahide sofa. Walls decorated with signed photos of the tacky and famous, plus those of the tacky and merely anonymous who must've been clients, with the place of honor given to a poster-sized blowup of Ralf on the cover of the *Enquirer*.

"So this is the guy that's gonna make me a star," said the real live item sitting on the couch.

The face was the same as on the tabloid cover, but no still shot could capture the twitchy energy of those eyes. Ralf was a physically smaller man than Dexter had somehow expected, but his presence seemed larger, as if it had been shoe-horned into a body a size too small. Nor did the short-sleeve silk chartreuse shirt and rose-colored linen pants seem exactly calculated to make him disappear in a crowd.

"Dexter Lampkin," Dexter said, holding out his hand. Ralf's handshake was nothing out of the ordinary, though the vibe the guy gave off had him half-expecting a joy buzzer.

Balaban produced a half-empty bottle of not very good bourbon with no ice, but under the circumstances, Dexter thought he'd better, and the three of them settled in around the coffee table, Ralf and Balaban on the couch, Dexter presiding on a hard-backed folding chair

"So," said Balaban, "you come up with any brilliant ideas yet, Lampkin?"

Dexter, of course, hadn't a thought in his head. But of course he couldn't admit that. Bullshit time! Think of it as just one more dumb story conference pitch.

"Well, just off the top of my head, Jimmy, I think we have to go with this Man From the Future concept—"

"Terrific, Monkey Boy," Ralf cracked, "and here I was thinking maybe I should dress up in a top hat and a tutu and do Fred Astaire in drag!"

"What I mean is," Dexter shot back, disconnecting his mouth from his brain and letting it do the talking, "that before we can flesh out the format, we've got to, uh, sharpen the character—"

"*Sharpen my character*, you gonna square off my chin with a laser-beam and turn me into Dick Tracy?"

"Will you shut up and let the guy talk!"

"Look," said Dexter, "what we have now is a character who claims to be a comedian from the future, and insults the twentieth-century Slagheads with a stream of one-liners that are mostly rewritten Polish jokes . . ."

"So?" said Balaban.

So? thought Dexter. So what? Duh. What the hell was I thinking, if anything?

"So, er, for a whole Ralf show, we need more than a *generic* comic from a *generic* future . . ."

"I don't get it," said Balaban.

"If we're gonna do a situation comedy, then we need a real *situation*—"

"Forget it!" cried Texas Jimmy Balaban. "I told you, we got no budget for sets, or actors, or hardly anything at all but Ralf—"

"Then *Ralf's* got to be the situation!" Dexter exclaimed.

"Huh?" said Balaban.

The two of them sat there in silence for a long beat waiting for two thousand bucks worth of pearls of wisdom to drop from Dexter's lips.

So did Dexter. Without at all knowing what they would be. But knowing in this strangely familiar moment that they were going to come.

Dexter had done his share of story conference pitches, most of them for Saturday-morning cartoon shows where the story editors you were bullshitting were just about intelligent enough to serve as backboards for outrageous conceptual three-pointers and the formats were so idiotic that walking in with actual story ideas in your head would've been pointless.

So you winged it. You turned off your brain and let your mouth do the thinking for you. When you were off, you babbled gibberish and shot nothing but air balls. But when you were on, when you had that feeling of crazed certainty that Dexter had now, swish, you could do no wrong, you had found the groove.

Dexter looked squarely at Ralf. "Let's just pretend you really *are* a comedian from the future," he said. "Tell me about the future that you're from."

"What's to tell, Monkey Boy?" Ralf snapped back. "It sucks!"

"Sucks, schmucks," Dexter said. "We need *specifics,* Ralf! We need the *situation*! *What* sucks?"

"What *doesn't*?" Ralf snarled with startling bitterness. "You Slagheads killed the whole fucking planet! You can't breathe the air, stepping outside's like sticking your head in a microwave oven, it's hot enough to melt the devil's hard-on, and the only things you can grow are kudsu and crotch-rot! The food's made out of some gray goo they make in vats out of toe-jam and tastes as good as it looks! Whaddya expect, Monkey Boy, downtown Disneyland?"

Wow, the guy could *act*!

There had been convincing vehemence in his voice and an angry energy in his eyes as he sat there glowing black and boiling out fire and brimstone.

Hmmm. . . .

"And *we're* responsible?" Dexter said slowly. "*We're* the sinners, *this* is when it all went wrong?"

"Better believe it, Monkey Boy!"

"Chaos Time, you might say, huh, Ralf?" Dexter blurted.

Click.

Having arrived, Dexter now knew where his mouth had been taking him.

In *Chaos Time,* his novel, many factions in a baleful future are *also* sending time travelers back to the present when humanity took a series of wrong turn leading to the mess in which they find themselves. But they fight over which ones they were and what the right path to a better present should've been—governments, religious groups, nut cults, all send their agents back to change history according to their own pet theories.

Truman is persuaded to drop an atomic bomb on Hiroshima to shorten World War II and prevent an atomic war in the 1950s. A little tinkering with the Cook County voting machines elects John Kennedy instead of Richard Nixon. Khrushchev becomes Soviet Party Chairman instead of Beria.

And so forth.

But the meddling never stops. Factions keep sending back agents to rejigger the rejiggering. JFK is assassinated and Lyndon Johnson becomes president. The United States stumbles into Vietnam anyway. Nixon beats Bobby Kennedy and wins the war with tactical nuclear weapons. Bobby is assassinated and Ronald Reagan becomes president and nukes the Russians. A neat idea for a tailored virus to cure cancer mutates into a deadly plague.

The more the future tinkers, the worse things get, the more desperate the ever-mutating factions of the future become to set things right, the more they tinker, and it all goes chaotic as causality breaks down utterly . . .

Producing everyone's worse-case scenario—a greenhouse effect that will melt the ice caps, a deadly sexually transmitted plague, crime waves, gurus, would-be messiahs, mass unemployment, economic collpase, mass genocides . . .

In other words, the present in which the readers of the novel find themselves living.

Not exactly material for a TV format?

Unless you dumbed it way down, and turned it into a comedy!

A one-character comedy set in the present!

"So the double-domes back when you came from sent *you* back to show us the light and change history!" Dexter exclaimed.

"Huh?" said Ralf.

"They only had the budget to send *one* guy back to preach to the Monkey People, *one* chance to convince the Slagheads to stop being such assholes before it's too late—"

"*Whaa—at?*" Ralf grunted, his eyes widening in confusion.

"—one shot at changing the past to save the future! So who do they send back here to play messiah? Their best scientist? Their top politician? Naw, how would they get anybody to believe them—"

"What the fuck are you *talking about?* Hey look, I'm a comic, is all, I'm not doing so good, they tell me my material is getting moldy, so my former and future agent stuffs me in a time machine to—"

"Yeah, right, we can keep that, Ralf," Dexter said airily.

Ralf's eyes flicked from Dexter to Balaban and back again. "Jimmy, what the hell—"

"Shaddap and let the guy talk!" said Texas Jimmy Balaban. "He's on to something! Go ahead, Dex, go!"

"They send back a scientist or a politician claiming he's from the future, we're not gonna believe him, we're gonna throw a net over him and stuff him in the funny farm," Dexter babbled, feeling it all bubbling up through him. "But if they send back a *comedian* . . ."

"Yeah, yeah!" Balaban chanted like a worshipper at a tent revival suddenly beginning to see the light.

"If they send back a comedian, no one's gonna believe him either, but no one *has* to! As long as he's *funny*, he can get the word out, because instead of throwing him in the nuthouse, the Monkey People will give him a *TV show!*"

Dexter folded his arms across his chest in a gesture of self-satisfied triumph.

"That's it?" said Balaban. "But *what* show?"

"Don't you get it?" said Dexter. "*Our* show! *Ralf's* show! Which is called . . . which is called . . . which is called *The Word According to Ralf*!"

"Which is *what*, goddamn it?"

It took a mighty effort for Dexter to calm himself down, play it cagey, and not tell him right then and there. But his own experience and the collective scriptwriter folklore told him *never* to make it look too easy no matter how easy it really was. *Never* let them know you could really knock out a twenty-two page cartoon half-hour in four days. Let it age for a week before you hand it in.

So if Texas Jimmy Balaban was to feel he was getting his two thousand bucks worth, much wiser to turn in his ten-page format a whole day under deadline four days from now than to let Balaban know that he had the whole thing already and would bang it out in a couple three hours as soon as he got his ass out of here.

Three hours?

Actually, he could write the whole thing down in a page or so in fifteen minutes.

Concept:

The powers that be in a terminal future bullshit a failing comic named Ralf into letting them stuff him into a time machine and send him back to the present to change history by acquainting the Slagheads with the future consequences of their present assholery. This he will do by preaching to them via this very show.

Voila, Ralf, the *Comic* Messiah from the Future, a piss-take on TV evangelists and the foibles of the present all rolled up in the same package! And not only could Ralf keep his current act, this concept would key right in to everything in the tabloid PR campaign that had made him semi-famous!

Format:

El cheapo. A single standing set, a live studio audience. Ralf begins each show with a stand-up routine in character as the Comic Jeremiah from the Future designed to exacerbate the audience and then lets the Monkey People exacerbate him back. All that has to be scripted is the opening monologue, the rest is all ad-lib.

The Word According to Ralf.

Th-th-th-that's all, folks!

Of course, he could hardly hand *that* in and expect to be paid $2000 for it! When the deal called for ten pages, you had to hand at least ten pages in.

So . . .

"I think I've got the right vector here, Jimmy," Dexter said, "but it needs some fleshing out, you understand, but this meeting's been a big help . . ."

He paused, took a sip of raw warm bourbon, gave Texas Jimmy Balaban a little frown of worry. "You say you need it by Friday? Is that really a hard deadline, I mean—"

"Absolutely!" Balaban said, the angst in his expression conveying total sincerity. "I gotta have it on time, or I got no deal, meaning you don't get paid, we understand each other, Lampkin? You're not telling me you can't do it, are you?"

Dexter sighed. He shrugged. "Well, it's a lot to ask, it's gonna be a ballbuster," he said in his best world-weary tone, "but a deal's a deal, Jimmy. Ten pages by Friday, no play, no pay . . ."

"You got it," said Texas Jimmy Balaban.

Dexter choked back a sudden impulse to laugh, for Balaban's three words were far truer than it would have been wise to let him know.

He did indeed have it. He had the outline on which he had sold *Chaos Time*. He had already worked out in fine detail not merely one but a whole mutating series of futures like the one Ralf supposedly came from. He would hardly have to write a damn thing to make a fast $2000. Just bat out a page and cut and paste the other nine from stuff already in the computer that he wouldn't even have to retype!

The problem would be to keep it *down* to ten pages! So why bother, why not give Balaban twenty, overproduce the quota like a champ little Hollywood Stakhanovite and make him happy?

Two thousand dollars for maybe a couple hours' work, hey, not a bad wage, huh?

And although Dexter had been around long enough to know that one could not afford to pay such showbiz succubi serious heed, a seductive little voice in his ear seemed to whisper, hey Lampkin, who knows, this sucker might even *sell* . . .

Texas Jimmy Balaban had been angling for this moment ever since he had discovered Ralf in Kapplemeyer's Fabulous Sunset Room. There he stood on the set as the audience filed into the studio, the producer of his own client's national TV show. For the first time in his life, he was going to be rich—well, okay, maybe not rich by Hollywood standards, but thickly insulated from the possibility of financial pain.

He had reached for the brass ring, and he had caught it. It was a golden dream come true!

Well, gold-filled, anyway.

The backdrop was a blowup of some sci-fi magazine cover from about 1935 that Lampkin had gotten the rights to for next to zip. It depicted a city that looked like something out of *Flash Gordon* under a shimmery transparent dome. The surrounding countryside looked like the ruins of the South Bronx and the gray sky above it all boiled with angry clouds the color of shit.

The set was a waist-high space-ship control console flat acquired on the cheap from a failed TV pilot and a prop space-captain's command throne. The theory was that Ralf would preside from the captain's chair, but in practice, Jimmy knew, Ralf would end up working on his feet most of the time, pacing behind the control console, or coming out in front of it to work the audience closer.

The Word According to Ralf arched across the top of the backdrop in tinfoil letters, giving the whole thing the effect of a title card from something like *Plan Nine From Outer Space*.

Since there was no budget for anything that wasn't tacky, Jimmy and Lampkin had come up with the reverse of the tired old one-liner—if you *don't* got it, flaunt it! If it's gonna end up tacky anyway, make tacky work. Texas Jimmy had come to respect Lampkin's instincts for creative schlock, and therefore Archie Madden's insistence on making his participation a condition of picking up the show.

Not only had Lampkin come up with this set design and found the cut-rate backdrop and props, the guy had turned out to work surprisingly well with Ralf, the two of them already had the first two weeks of monologue material on paper.

Jimmy was a lot more pleased at what he was getting for his fifteen hundred bucks a show now than he had been with the twenty-one pages Lampkin had handed him for his $2000 on the Thursday morning before the decisive Friday meeting with Madden. It had seemed like a one-page springboard padded out with twenty pages of crap Lampkin had probably cannibalized from his old sci-fi novels.

"For *this* I'm paying you two grand?" Jimmy had groaned.

"For ten pages on Friday, you're paying me two grand," Lampkin had said. "And I'm giving you twenty-one on Thursday. You don't like it, don't pay me. Maybe you think you can find someone to do better by tomorrow morning?"

Jimmy did not at all feature being dicked around like this, but as Lampkin knew all too well, he had no choice, it was pay up and go into the meeting with Madden with his twenty-one pages, or don't, and arrive naked.

This time around he was told to come alone and was shown into Archie Madden's office.

Two picture windows looked out from on high over magnificent smoggy views of nothing in particular. Madden's desk looked like a stainless-steel flying saucer. The carpet was pure white. There were four soft chairs in the form of giant up-turned human hands. A huge flat-screen TV ran a tape-loop of the action in a fancy fish tank. Eerie electronic music seemed to mutter in the background, though it was so faint you couldn't quite be sure.

Madden was alone, perched behind the desk on a double-height double-width director's chair made of padded ostrich hide and ebony. He wore a white, ruffled tux shirt with a black velvet bow tie under a ragged blue denim jacket.

Jimmy shitted pickles while Madden flipped through the format. The guy turned the pages at the rate of about two a minute. Then he gave Jimmy a fish-eyed stare for about a full minute, as if waiting for a cue line.

"So?" said Jimmy.

"So go," said Archie Madden.

"You mean . . . you mean you're *picking it up?*" Jimmy stammered.

Madden shrugged. "It's cheap, it's flash, it's worth a thirteen-week shot," he said casually, as if the whole thing was about as important to him as whether to go to Vegas or Mazatlán for the weekend.

Which, Jimmy realized, after catching his breath, it probably was.

And if it made him feel like a cockroach snagging crumbs of cheese off the table of this high-rolling kid, hey, he had just made the deal of his life with no hassle and no bullshit precisely *because* it was nothing much to Archie Madden.

"So, uh, now what, uh, Archie?" he said.

"I'll have legal draw up the contracts," Madden said, glancing at his watch. "Look 'em over, sign 'em, get 'em back as soon as you can, I want this on the air in, say, six weeks."

"That's . . . *that's it*, Archie?"

"I pick 'em, I don't develop 'em," Madden said.

He stood up, extended a hand, a polite dismissal.

Jimmy shook it, turned to go.

"Oh, yes, one thing, Jimmy," Madden said behind him. "I want the guy that wrote this format on staff."

"*What?*" Jimmy exclaimed, whirling.

"Dexter Lampkin," Madden said blandly. "Head Writer, story editor, assistant producer, whatever. The deal's contingent on you getting him."

"But why?" Jimmy asked, knowing that every extra dime he had to pay Lampkin would have to come out of his end. "What do I need *Lampkin* for?"

"Just a hunch," Madden said airily. "Call it instinct."

"Call it instinct!" Jimmy exclaimed. "On this you want me to saddle myself with this guy?"

And pay for it out of my own end!

"That's right," Archie Madden had said. "After all, Jimmy, just between you and me, what *else* do you think they're paying me for?"

An exit line if ever Texas Jimmy Balaban had heard one, and he took it, repairing to a Century City saloon for a hideously overpriced shot of Wild Turkey to celebrate his good fortune and get his wits together to deal with Dexter Lampkin.

And once outside the disorienting presence of Archie Madden and under the influence of the good bourbon, Jimmy had realized that while the bad news was that Lampkin now had him by the short hairs, the good news was the vice versa.

True, the deal rode on getting Lampkin to sign on, but true too that *Lampkin* had $65,000 riding on Madden's pickup of the show, namely the thousand bucks a show for the guaranteed thirteen weeks that he had extracted in return for writing the format for a lousy $2000.

A schlockmeister demon whispered in Jimmy's ear that it wouldn't be too cagey to let Lampkin know that Madden had made the deal contingent on his participation, but something, maybe a Madden-like hunch, maybe even, he liked to think, a certain code of ethics, told him to be a mensch about it.

So before he could have second thoughts, he called Lampkin, told him to meet him in the bar to hear some good news, and nursed a single additional Wild Turkey for half an hour until he arrived.

And when Lampkin arrived, he bought him a double, and laid out the truth.

"Let me get this straight," Lampkin said when he had finished. "You're telling me you expect me to work for nothing?"

"For thirteen weeks, you gross sixty-five thousand!" Jimmy reminded him "That's by you *nothing*?"

"You're telling me that's all *you're* gonna make off this?"

"What am I, a Jerry Lewis telethon?" Jimmy blurted. "My client. I gotta produce this thing. I fronted you two grand. I made the deal with Madden. For this my end doesn't deserve to be bigger than yours?"

"Point taken," said Lampkin. "But I don't work for nothing."

"Work, schmurk, Dex. Don't you get it? All you gotta do is sign a contract putting you on staff. You do as little or as much as you want to, hey, it's not like I can fire you for goofing off, now can I?"

Lampkin took a long sip of bourbon while he thought that one over. "Look, Jimmy," he finally said, "I could be a prick about this, couldn't I? Because from what you've told me, there's no deal without me . . ."

A surge of anger boiled through Texas Jimmy Balaban's arteries. But some instinct told him not to show it. Instead, he took a sip of bourbon, looked right into Lampkin's eyes, and said, quite softly: "Have *I* been a prick with you?"

Lampkin exhaled. He smiled. "No, Jimmy, I've got to say you haven't," he admitted. "So I'm not going to be a prick either. But don't you think I should get *something* extra, man-to-man?"

Jimmy slugged down the rest of his drink. "Yeah, yeah, okay," he grumped. He shrugged. "Look, as long as we're being mensches with each other, why don't we cut the rest of the crap too, okay Dex?" he said. "I mean, you're gonna ask me for an extra grand a show, I'm gonna have an embolism and offer two-fifty, you call me a cheap schlockmeister and demand seven-fifty, I say five hundred and that's the deal, so what do you say, Dex, let's not and say we did?" And he extended his hand.

Dexter D. Lampkin had laughed a real laugh and shook it.

As far as Jimmy was concerned, Lampkin had earned his money when he put his John Hancock on the papers that let the deal go through. But Dex hadn't put up much of an argument when Jimmy wheedled him into maybe just seeing if he could help Ralf put together the opening monologues for a while, just till things get rolling, Dex, you understand . . .

And then he had somehow gotten involved in coming up with the idea for this set, and then had dealt with that weirdo for rights to the sci-fi cover for the backdrop, and known someone who knew someone who had heard about these sci-fi props and flats that maybe could be picked up for next to nothing . . .

Texas Jimmy Balaban turned to check the studio clock. Five minutes to airtime. The studio was as full as it was going to get, maybe two hundred and fifty people in an auditorium that seated four hundred. The cameras were manned. A gaffer laid Ralf's shotgun mike across the seat of the space ship's chair like a scepter across a throne.

Texas Jimmy could feel the tension mounting. Tsuris, agro, ulcers, hassle! Show business!

Weren't for the money, who would put themselves through this shit?

Texas Jimmy grinned to himself as he cleared the set.

Who *wouldn't*, given half a chance?

"And now, from *Hollywood*," warbled Jimmy Balaban's cheap-jack prerecorded intro, "the show that gives you what for—from the man who's gonna let you know why—*The Word According to Ralf*!"

"Okay, Ralf, uh, break a leg," Dexter Lampkin said.

"Break a leg?" Ralf parroted sarcastically. "Next thing ya know, Lampkin, you're gonna be telling me to go out there and lose one for the Gipper," he said, pirouetting on the exit line, and strutting onstage to an ovation from the studio audience heavily augmented by canned applause.

Dexter laughed, whether nervously, to cover up the rubeness of his remark, or because he had actually come to develop a certain strange affection for his creation. And he *had* come to think of the character who had just gone onstage as his creation.

Balaban had *told* him that Ralf was strange, but in that first meeting, he and Jimmy had done most of the talking, and Ralf hadn't done much more than throw schtick, so Dexter hadn't really begun to understand *how* strange until Balaban wheedled him into helping Ralf get a few set opening monologues together just to get the ball rolling, and he started spending some time with the guy.

The guy?

Or the character?

Was there a difference?

Dexter had gone to enough science fiction conventions to be all too familiar with people who took role-playing way over the top. At any given major convention there might be more than a hundred people who spent the whole weekend in costume, and a goodly portion of those strove to spend it all in character.

But *they* had other identities to go home to after the party was over. Ralf seemed stuck in his role full-time, like the occasional schizoid fan who put on a mercenary costume, dropped his first hit of acid at the masquerade, and ended up dodging bullets for the French Foreign Legion in Africa.

"Hello there, folks, yes, here I am, though I wish I weren't, Ralf, the voice of your pissed-off great grandchildren twice-removed, though not far enough as far as I'm concerned," Ralf said on the fly as he bounced like a bantam cock to the center of the stage.

"I mean, what a zoo just *getting here* tonight! A cloud of muck over the Ventura Freeway so brown it's *green*, and a couple of Slagheads duking it out with Uzis over whether a blow-up bimbo doll really counts as a passenger in the diamond lane, and then there was this Monkey Boy driving right along with a great big grin and this thing coming out of his fly plugged into one of those autosuck gizmos gives your dumb love affair with the smog-wagon a whole new meaning, and *this* Slaghead was a *cop*. . . ."

Not even Dexter could pry a Clark Kent out of the Superman suit. Could *anyone* be a good enough actor to maintain a role like that all the time, or was Ralf stark staring nuts?

Having been endlessly subjected to all sorts of schmucks who went to conventions dressed as barbarians and belligerently insisted that you play along and relate to their "convention character," Dexter had little patience for such assholery.

". . . first thing I think is it's his *tail*, I mean, what a relief when I realize it's just his *dork* . . ."

And since Ralf's chosen convention character viewed the present as one big Polish joke, it was more obnoxious than most.

". . . you don't *really* have tails do ya, why some of you Monkey People even look kinda *human,* know what I mean, clothes and all . . ."

As a human, Ralf was a prize dick, but as a *character,* Dexter could not help finding him technically intriguing, having never met a first draft of a *person* before.

Had Ralf been a character one of his novels, he flattered himself that he would realize that it needed a rewrite job. Which was just about what Texas Jimmy Balaban had conned him into doing. And for free.

". . . you wanna breathe the future, go down to Torrance when it's been a hundred degrees of temperature inversion for a week, no, that ain't what's *outdoors* in the twenty-second century, Slagheads, that's what comes *in* through our *air conditioners.* . . ."

Ralf strutted and tummeled near the front lip of the stage, in the audience's face with his monologue and wearing the new costume, a white ice cream suit that Mark Twain might have rented from the Salvation Army to attend Wonder Woman's wedding to Elvis.

". . . could shove one of your V-eight brontosauruses into the time machine, you could just pull the gas-cap and run the engine on the *fumes.* . . ."

For better or for worse, this was the Frankenschtick monster Dexter had created, and it *still* needed more work. . . .

"Aw come on, Dex," Balaban had wheedled, "*you know* we need more than the twenty-one pages of bullshit you handed me!"

"Archie Madden didn't."

"The Boy Genius don't have to produce this thing, Dex, and he don't have to come up with five ten-minute monologues a week either, I mean what do we really have, a thin premise, and a talented ad-libber without even a real bible let alone a joke file to work off."

"So hire some writers."

"Come on, Lampkin, you know the budget!"

"I'm working on a novel, Jimmy."

"Come on, all I'm asking is for you to come over to the office after you finish your day's work, have a couple drinks on me, bullshit with Ralf for an hour or so, and we'll just record it and have it typed up, that's not work, now is it . . . ?"

"I dunno . . ." Dexter had muttered, but that was the moment when he was hooked. Where, he wondered, had a character like Texas Jimmy Balaban learned the writer's precise technical definition of honest labor?

"You know, you got money riding on this show making it too, Dex. It's another sixty-five thousand gees if they pick up the second thirteen weeks."

"Well . . ."

So he would spend about two hours between knocking off on the novel and dinner at Texas Jimmy Balaban's office working with Ralf.

If that was what they were doing.

Balaban would set up the recorder on the coffee table alongside the booze, and disappear behind his desk and shut up almost entirely.

This was not the first time Dexter had engaged in this sort of baloney. There wasn't a writer within a two-hundred-mile radius of Hollywood who hadn't, for this sort of so-called story conference was precisely as far as any writer would go without getting paid.

"You want to explain what we're supposed to be doing aside from getting swacked on my agent's booze?" was Ralf's opening line in this creative collaboration.

"We're supposed to work on improving your character," Dexter had told him. "We're supposed to bullshit up a more detailed bible for you to work off."

"A new Bible? What's wrong with the old one? Hey, the reruns are still doing fine up the line in the twenty-second!"

And so it had gone. What Jimmy Balaban had in mind was never too clear, and what Ralf conceived these bull sessions to be besides a pain in the ass never quite emerged from the sour mash mist either.

But as Dexter saw it, the only possible point was to rewrite the role of Comic Jeremiah From the Future into something with enough depth and detail for Ralf to create his own monologues off of it. Because he was *not* gonna be roped into banging out thirteen weeks' worth of them for nothing.

Having achieved this pragmatic focus, Dexter decided to have Ralf do as much of the work as possible; play the role of interlocutor in this Socratic story conference, and by clever questioning induce Ralf to create his own material. But Ralf, like far more directors than could be tortured into admitting it, had no real creative imagination. The ability to pull imaginary detail out of general concept was beyond him.

"Look, Ralf, we need more than a dingo act, your twenty-second century's got to have detail, the audience has got to feel you know the place the way Fred Flintstone knows Bedrock."

"Look, Lampkin, they dropped my ass back here to take the piss out of you Slagheads, not your victims, namely *us*!"

It was exasperating. Ralf refused to drop out of character for a minute, but he refused to even attempt to contribute anything useful to the creation of that very character's background.

"Come on, Lampkin, I'm just an ignorant schmuck from the twenty-second century Borscht Belt," the little bastard said slyly. "So why should I know more about when I come from than what your average Polo Lounge wise-guy knows about the sex lives of the Gnomes of Zurich or the price of crack in downtown Detroit?"

"Then tell me about *show business* in the twenty-second century. Don't you know any Twenty-second Century Fox jokes?"

"Har, har, har," Ralf cackled mechanically. "Look, Lampkin, *you're* the science fiction writer, why don't *you* do it, you can make this shit up a whole lot easier than I can remember it!"

But then he smiled, and while it was not unlike the usual cynical smirk, something about the eyes gave it a deeper nuance, and his voice, when he spoke again, had become a more subtle instrument, capable of skating the edge between sarcasm and sincerity.

"Look, either I'm what I say I am, or I'm a nutcase, or maybe an actor playing a part for keeps, or all three, but I can't be anything *else*, now can I?" he said. "None of which qualifies me as a sci-fi writer."

A smile? Or a leer?

"*You* can write me a lot better than I can write myself, Lampkin. *You* can make me real."

Dexter couldn't tell which, any more than Faust had when Mephistopheles held out a lollipop of only a slightly different flavor. But Dexter could hardly resist it.

What novelist could?

After all, to create without actually having to write anything was every novelist's most slothful wish-fulfillment fantasy. Add the hubric lust of mortal writers to extend their secret godlike powers beyond the printed page. Dissolve in a beaker of showbiz glamour, and you have a cocktail capable of turning mild-mannered literary Jekylls into ego-tripping hairy-assed Hydes.

It was usually manifested as nothing much worse than the allure of the Hollywood honeypot for literary lions from Faulkner and Fitzgerald to William Goldman and Stephen King, with results more bathetic than sinister.

But in the pocket universe of science fiction, it tended to get out of hand. Where writers created realities entire, where the process was even *called* "world building" and the creator of a successful novel series might "franchise out his universe," where it was all too easy to meet readers playing characters from your own stuff, the development of a literary Jehovah complex was not exactly discouraged.

There was a line you had better not cross, though it was not always easy to know when you had along a continuum that could progress from creating a literary universe, to marketing it to people who might take it a tad too seriously, to selling T-shirts and tribbles as cult objects, to administering secret oaths to your followers at conventions, to finally disdaining to survey anything of which you were not god like L. Ron Hubbard.

But hey, come on, creating a fictional twenty-second century for Ralf to come from was hardly founding the Church of Ralfology!

So Dexter set about creating Ralf's twenty-second century. No sweat. He already had most of it worked out in *Chaos Time* and *The Transformation*, so all he had to do was distill a consensus future out of this existing material and get Ralf to absorb it. With Balaban recording everything, it could all be transcribed into a bible for the show.

But Ralf just couldn't absorb material directly from the printed page. The guy was a tummler, not a reader.

So they sipped bourbon and jackpoted about the fictitious twenty-second century as if both of them had been there, the science fiction writer expostulating woozy expository lumps, and the Comic From the Future, never breaking character, turning it into schtick.

"Forget those dumb domed cities. When the atmosphere becomes lethal, they just retrofit NASA life-support technology to the air-conditioning systems of existing major shopping malls, and subdivide the parking garages into condos."

"Dirty fish tanks for humans."

"Hey, Ralf, it's the American suburban dream. We *already* work, shop, eat, go to the movies, score dope, and pick up girls in the air-conditioned comfort of mall-world. *Living* in 'em too will eliminate the need for cars, solve the parking and traffic problems, and make it all *perfect*!"

"Yeah, sure, stinking like the Beverly Center with all of West Hollywood camped out in it permanently!"

With the biosphere reduced to vanishing remnants and the surface unfit for farming, artificial photosynthesis would produce the bottom of the food chain in factories and feed it directly into the gullet of the top and only predator.

"Right, gray goo comes out of the vats loaded with vitamins and minerals, and they color it and flavor it and stamp it into turkey legs and pizzas and chicken chow mein and sell it to you as TV dinners which taste like thirty-one flavors of rubber cement."

They really *could* do it. They probably *would*.

As long as the nuclear fuel held out or they could cover the wastelands with enough solar collectors to power the machinery to run the life-support systems and the food factories, a certain number of humans in countries advanced enough to have created shopping malls *would* survive.

"And there we sit, Monkey Boy, stuffed into stinking aquariums under grow-lights like hamsters, breathing our own recycled farts, and eating People Chow made out of our own shit! Welcome to Deathship Earth!"

Deathship Earth began to assume a reality, a reality that Dexter found all too unpleasantly credible, and Ralf's contribution of bitter specifics only made it worse. For this *was* the high probability future, given the current vector of the Monkey People, the future of a simian species which had failed its Transformation Crisis, and survived only as a hermetically sealed self-made exhibition to its own terminal folly.

Sure, the denizens of Deathship Earth would send someone back to change things if they could! Or at the least read the riot act to the Slagheads responsible for the mess they found themselves in. . . .

"All right, Slagheads, now it's *your* turn to talk back to your victims," Ralf said, extroing the monologue and retreating to the captain's chair. "Sorta like giving the Nazis a chance to explain to the Jews that genocide has its upside, after all, it's a sure cure for the common cold."

Oooh, Dexter groaned inwardly, that one was really over the top!

An ugly sound muttered through the studio audience. Insult humor might not be a subtle art form, but the line between what got you a laugh and what got you a punch in the nose could be razor-thin when you worked the edge.

At least Ralf seemed to realize that the bomb he had just laid might be toxic.

He attracted the audience's attention elsewhere by picking up the shotgun mike, doing a take at the long rubber-padded barrel, eyeballing it lugubriously, running his hand up and down the shaft.

"Hey, what's this thing, Monkey People," he said brightly, "Queen Kong's dildo?"

Not what you would call sophisticated humor, maybe, but at least it got a ration of barnyard laughter.

Under cover of which Ralf seated himself, now miming a pilot's joystick with the shotgun mike.

"Well, okay, passengers, this is your captain speaking, welcome to Deathship Earth," he said, the arrogant edge taken off by the fruity voice and the fatuous mugging.

"We'll be flying kind of low tonight, Monkey People, right above the tarpits we'll be sinking into a few time zones from now, so fasten your seat belts, extinguish your fossil fuels, and try to return your species to an upright position . . ."

For better or for worse, this seemed to blow by the audience.

"Okay, so who's ready to make television history? Hey, this show is gonna be a big hit, you think I let my agent talk me into this gig without looking at the old reviews I was gonna get back here? You're gonna tell your grandchildren you was there!"

An indistinct male voice yelled something from the dark depths of the audience. "Yeah, back there, we got a live one!" Ralf called out, pointing his shotgun mike uncertainly.

A wobbly white spot tried to follow it, expanding and contracting as it played across random faces, finally zeroing in on the only standing figure, a big beefy guy in a lime-green leisure suit that made him look like an exiled Central American generalissimo trying to blend in with the tourists in Miami Beach.

"If you're from the future, sucker," he bellowed, "then what am I thinking?"

"I don't do no mind reading act, Monkey Boy, and even if I did, your print would be much too fine for me."

A few dry laughs from a few dry people.

"Come on, bright boy, tell me what I'm thinking!"

Ralf stood up, still pointing the shotgun mike. "Why don't *you* tell *us* what you're thinking, pal?" he said.

"I'm thinking you sound like some kind of *liberal communist weenie*, bright boy! I'm thinking some real American oughta go up there and punch you in the nose!"

"That'll get you on page one of the tabloids, Slaghead, but it'll also get you three to five!" Ralf shot back, whipping the mike away, and the spotlight with it.

Terrific, Dexter thought glumly, just terrific.

"Any higher life-forms out there?" Ralf stage-muttered, pointing around the room with the shotgun mike like someone jabbing a stick into the monkey cage, while the spotlight operator went nuts trying to follow it.

Onto a little old lady who may or may not have been from Pasadena or come equipped with tennis shoes, but had a primo example of the bluish gray teased frightwig and the eyes like a lemur on methedrine.

"Yes, you lady, Harpo Marx's grandmother!"

"Tell us about the Rapture!" she said in a breathy voice. "If you're really from beyond the Millennium you must've seen the Coming of the Beast, and the Second Coming, and passed through the glory of the Rapture itself!"

"*What* rapture?" Ralf said, peering down into his crotch. "Last time I went to the toilet, everything *seemed* to be in the right place."

The pun fell into silence with a leaden thump. A silence, however, not entirely unpunctuated by a few righteous Christian growls.

Ralf stood up and cocked his ear as if trying to make them out. "Oh, the *Rapture!*" he said, making a nice barroom recovery before any born-again bottles could start to fly. "Sorry lady, the book's still selling, but the movie hasn't come out yet, hey, when I left, Elvis hadn't even gotten back on the flying saucer from Mars!"

He moved the shotgun mike again, onto a girl in her twenties in a snow white sweater an alluring two sizes two small for her boobs, which thrust out before her like a pair of 1959 Cadillac front bumper guards.

"Yes, you over there, with the rocketship knockers!"

"Wow, yeah," she said in a nasal Valley Girl accent, "like I can *see* how you guys are like *pissed off* at your ancestors, I mean like our *parents*, you know, they had a great big *beach party*, and after they had pigged out in the grossest possible manner and barfed all over *everything*, they like retired to Palm Desert and handed us the bill."

"And what are *you* gonna do with it, Sweetheart?" Ralf graveled back in a Bogie voice.

A long silent gum-popping duh.

"You're gonna keep racking up charges on Momma's overdrawn credit card, and as long as you keep paying the interest, nobody's gonna stop you, 'cause no one wants to be caught holding your rubber . . ."

Ralf paused, lowered the shotgun mike.

"And one day, the interest is gonna be more than you make, and they take your credit card away, and they kick you out of your apartment, and there you are, out on the street, up the creek, no place left to take a leak. . . ."

He shrugged at the audience.

"Hey, *we're* the ones who'll get stuck with the tab for *your* beach party, Monkey Girl," he said. "And thanks to *you*, we don't get to have one of our own either! Where you used to lay around in your cool mirror shades and tan your tender buns, we get the broil cycle in the microwave oven!"

Dexter groaned. You could get laughs insulting the audience, you could even get laughs insulting their intelligence, but you couldn't do much insulting a level of intelligence they didn't have.

"I don't think this is going too terrific, Jimmy," he muttered at Balaban backstage. "*How* did you say you got these people in here?"

"The usual way," Balaban told him. "Ran up some flyers and stacked 'em at a couple dozen supermarkets and Seven-elevens."

Meaning, Dexter realized, that what was out there was a random cross-section of whatever was attracted to freebie tickets for less than famous TV shows. Which figured to be a collection of everything from retired schoolteachers to obstreperous wrestling fans, from waitresses aspiring to be actresses to Valley Girls and Boys out on a cheap date, from the Moral Moron Majority to muscle-bound Surfer Nazis.

"Yeah, you, that's right, the guy with the turban . . ."

Life had turned inta one fuckin' hassle after another for Foxy Loxy since Momma had eighty-sixed her ass from the apartment. Okay, so she had gotten a little outa line, y'might say, but hey, she was really doin' Momma a *favor* smashin' the TV. Now maybe she'd move her fuckin' ass an' pretend to be human! She should be thankin' me for savin' her life!

But Momma had been too fucked up to see it that way when Loxy had come down and came home. She hadn't even let her in the door, had the couch or some-thin' jammed up against it and just screamed at Loxy through it.

"*Let you in?* You out of your fuckin' mind, girl! You ever show your worthless crackhead ass around here again I'm gonna pop you to the cops!"

She spent that night inna cheapest wino flop she could find, what she got paid at Sailor Sal's wasn't gonna get her nothin' better and let her score at the same time.

Course, on second thought if you could turn yourself a john a day who was in for an all-nighter, you could crash inna better class a fleabag an' come out with more than you came in with.

Okay, Loxy had chipped around the edges from time to time, hey, why not, but she had never really taken hookin' seriously before, for just the reasons she now found herself remembering.

A dick was a dick, right, an' fuckin' it or suckin' it was no big deal when you came down to it, it was over in fifteen minutes max. But the hassle that surrounded that fifteen minutes was a severe ass pain, especially when you was anglin' for a full eight inna sack insteada just tryin' to turn a quick one behind the nearest Dumpster.

She wasn't exactly the only piecea ass onna street, alla good spots near the hotels an' all were already taken by the competition who were more than ready t'fight for their turf if some fuckin' pimp didn't hit on you at knifepoint first.

So it was get what you can onna fly, by a cabstand, inna subway, atta stoplight, whatever. Loxy was a lot foxier than mosta the junkies an' drunkies that passed for the Pig Apple's gypsy hookers, so she got t'turn as many quick tricks as she could handle in her daily search for Mr. Hotel Room.

But since you could hardly find a hotel desk clerk inna whole fuckin' city not hot t' provide his own room service to the guests, she spent as many nights payin' for her own cheap flop as she did sharin' a freebie room witha john.

And when she *did* score an all-nighter, it was usually because the guy was some kinda disgustin' ol' pervert wanted her to piss in his face, or let him tie her up an' bugger her all night, or some such shit.

And the only way to get through *that* without freakin' out was to duck inta the crapper from time to time, take another hit, and let the White Tornado take over. As long as she was high, she felt no pain, nothin' could make her puke, she could bugaloo through anything, ba-ba-ba-doo-ba-ba-ba-wham!

But that tended to keep her from gettin' more than a taste a the eight hours' sleep onna reasonably roach-free mattress, which, though she tended to forget it at the time, was what she was puttin' herself through all this shit for inna first place.

So she was kinda wanderin' around inna daze onna mornings after, rushin' around to score her rocks before she hadta get her ass over to *Sailor Sal's* before Mario really *did* can her.

Loxy didn't need no computer to figure out that she could make a hell of a lot more money usin' the hours she put in at Sailor Sal's to turn a few more quick streetside tricks. But that woulda made her a fuckin' *professional*, just one more bottom-of-the-line whore who couldn't afford t' turn down even the most disgustin' special, instead of a girl witha job just tryin' t'make a hard life a little easier.

Sailor Sal's was a fuckin' greasepit, the customers themselves were the sorta scurve had trouble getting it together t'slither into a classier joint like McDonald's, Mario sat behind the cash register with a baseball bat in plain sight to keep 'em from thinkin' about pissin' him off and a .44 Magnum under the counter in case it didn't, and the job sucked, but given the alternative, Loxy wanted to keep it, even t'the point of puttin' up with Mario's bullshit war on drugs.

His mean old face would squeeze as tight as Nancy Reagan's asshole, an' he'd maybe cough a wad a smoke from the dried dog-turd he was suckin' on just to let ya know who was the boss.

"You scumbags can shoot yourself up with Drano on your own time," he'd wheeze, "but I own the time I'm paying for, and if I ever catch any of you pieces of shit polluting my premises with crap that could get the place busted, I'll call the cops myself."

Right. Sure. *Mario* would call the cops.

Like he didn't know what Cory was doin'. Like he didn't know that all of Cory's customers had to go through the motions of buying one of his greaseburgers an' maybe a Coke every time they scored. Fact was, Mario made fuckin' *sure* he always had one dealer a shift onna payroll, 'cause the only real reason anyone had to be caught dead in a shithole like Sailor's Sal's was to score.

But of course Mario hadta make like he had no idea such awful things was goin' on in his family restaurant. So to keep on bullshitting himself inta believin' he was a solid fuckin' citizen he hadta give *her* a hard time about just doin' what it takes t'keep doin' the fuckin' job.

Now Loxy wasn't *hooked* or nothin', you unnerstand, hey, under ordinary circumstances, she wouldn't start droolin' inta the fry oil an' chewin' up the soda cups if she couldn't take a hit onna job. But what with all the tricks she was turnin', an' all the hassle scorin', and all the sleep she wasn't gettin', it was kinda hard t'keep upright without a boost every now and again, was all.

She wasn't flippin' burgers with her pipe in her mouth, now was she, so what fuckin' business was it of his if she took a hit in the crapper when she took a piss?

"I know *someone's* smoking crack around here, either that or the toilet's filled with some pretty strange-smelling farts," Mario went around muttering to himself out loud so's you'd be sure to hear him. "Whoever it is better stop before I catch 'em, and have 'em busted for possession."

Well, fuck you, Mario! Loxy thought, as she slid the bolt onna toilet door inta the worn wooden hole.

Another one of those days, ain't they all?

She'd failed to find herself an all-nighter, kinda lost tracka time tryin', and by the time she scored herself a rock an' checked inta a flopjoint she ordinarily wouldn't been seen turnin' a ten-minute trick in, it was somethin' like five am. This left her seven hours to crash, get her shit together, an' get over to Sailor Sal's for her noon-to-eight shift.

Her sleep kept getting interrupted by slobberings, grunts, screams, an' wet squealin' sounds coming from the rent-a-cells around her, an' she woke up late an' feelin' even shittier than usual, and by the time she got to work, ten minutes late, the hit she had taken to get her there had just about worn off.

She hadn't hadda chance to do anything about it for two fuckin' hours 'cause right away Mario was on her case, readin' her out and just about shovin' her behind the counter before she could dare to open her mouth about havin' t' take a piss.

Could be she was gettin' a little obvious, the bags under her eyes *had* looked a little blacker than usual in the mirror this morning, and for sure the situation couldn't have been improvin' her looks any more than her condition, 'cause every time she went to the crapper fuckin' Mario had stood outside smoking one of his Italian stinkers just so she'd smell the fucker was there.

On the other hand . . .

Loxy dropped her pants, sat down, and sniffed.

. . . if you smell the cigar smoke when he was there, if you didn't, then he wasn't, right?

Nothing but piss, farts, an' Lysol as far as she could tell.

So she fished her pipe out of her pocket, and fixed herself a hit while she took a piss. She pulled her pants up, sniffed the air again, sat down, lit it, sucked hard—

Smooth this shit wasn't, annit tasted like toilet bowl cleaner, made your fuckin' lungs ache too, but y'didn't have t'hold it too long before your bones lit up like neon, an' your snatch got filled with this electric donkey dong wasn't exactly there, and a lightning bolt went up your spine an' exploded into your fuckin' brain inna big white light sorta filled everything, an' you wasn't exactly there either for a while, an' when you come back there's a band in your head playin' white-hot metal, whoo-ee, boo-ba-pa-dah, an' Loxy was bouncin' off the toilet seat, karate-choppin' the crapper door open, an' out front ready t'flip fuckin' burgers an' bite the head off the world!

Mario was too fuckin' cheap t'hire more'n one counterman, that was Cory, an' one flipper, bein' her, a shift. So when one of them wenta the can, the other one hadda keep the stuff onna stove from burning and deal with the customers at the same time.

Which was what Cory was tryin' to do right now, hee, hee, hee, flippin' burgers, takin' an order from some wino looked like Schwarzenegger on reds and muscatel, tryin' to put one onna bun he had missed with the ketchup, while some fuckin' Hell's Angels sweathog glared at him with eyes like a speedfreak Nazi an' rapped her hand on the counter for her bag.

"What you *doin'* in there, girl?" Cory snake-hissed at her. "Leavin' me here with this load of monkey burgers burnin' on the griddle when I got business to do!"

"Monkey burgers, monkey business, Monkey People, like whatshisface onna tube says," Loxy babbled at him as she slid in front of the stove. "If ya wanna know, I was takin' a great big disgusting shit, Cory, kind ya make from eatin' here, hee, hee, hee, an' I didn't flush it down when I was through, I left it there for you to smell 'cause *you're* so fuckin' *cool*!"

Cory squinted at her knowingly like the dealer he was. "Fucked *up*," he said in a flat voice.

"Fucked up, fucked up, fucked up," Loxy parrot-voiced back at him.

"If you two assholes are through quackin' yourselves off, I'd like my fuckin' goddamn order right fuckin' *now*, Cory, know what I mean?" the Hell's Angels momma snarled, lookin' like she was ready t'twist his head off. Cory looked like he woulda turned white if he could've.

"Comin' right up, mister!" Loxy told her.

She flipped one was kinda black on one side red on the other onna bun bottom, squirted a double dose of ketchup, sorta leaked all over the paper plate, whoops, slapped the top bun on, an' plunked the whole thing down on the counter in front of Cory, ta-dah, just as he was palming a bag inta the customer's hand!

"One Sailor Sal's special witha side a smack!" she called out, plenty loud enough for fuckin' Mario to hear at the register.

Mario gave her a look woulda turned piss to vinegar, fuck him, nobody gives shit to th' White Tornado, what's he gonna do, calla cops, hee, hee, hee!

The Hell's Angels sweathog seemed to be pissed off too for some stupid fuckin' reason. "Shut your stupid fuckin' face you crackhead deadbrain you wanna get us all busted?" she shouted.

"Keep it down yourself, you dumb cunt!" Mario shouted back across the sit-down tables, where three more a Cory's scurvy junkies anna couple a meth monsters were waitin' to score.

"Who you calling a dumb cunt, you dickhead wop bastid?"

"You, that's who!" Mario told her.

Hey, this was gettin' kinda funny, like onea those shows y'see onna TV, where this great fight starts up an' they trash the whole fuckin' saloon!

The Hell's Angels momma took a step and a half toward Mario, an' the creeps at the sit-downs tried to scramble inta the corners like the roaches onna stove when ya turn the lights on.

Mario grabbed up his baseball bat, lifted it about level with his chest, and she froze.

"Hey, lighten up, Mario, doncha know that bashin' the brains outa diesel dykes all over the furniture's bad for business!" Loxy called out, hee, hee, hee.

"Who you callin' a dyke, sister?" the Hell's Angels sweathog screamed, north of a hundred and fifty pounds of raw biker meat whirling around gnashin' and droolin' to take it all out on her.

Whoops!

But on the other hand . . .

Loxy whipped up the all-purpose knife y'hadda use for bread an' onions an' cheese, a great big fuckin' ugly old thing was cleaned only last month you really wouldn't want shoved in your gut, and things started gettin' to be fun again.

"Don't you go sisterin' me, Momma, I'm a drug-crazed fuckin' maniac, an' I'm liable t'carve an improvement an' send you the bill for it, hee, hee, hee!" Loxy said inna slasher flick voice, waving the dirty knife under her chin.

The Hell's Angels momma froze again. Purple veins stood out so far on her flaming red temples it looked like her head was gonna explode.

Far fuckin' out!

"Hey, whatsa matter, don't you believe me?" Loxy gabbled, rollin' her eyes, stickin' her tongue out, waggin' it around, and doin' her best to drool.

Ha! Ha! Ha! The dumb bitch looked like she was gonna shit! Great big fuckin' biker chick looked like she cracked coconuts with her twat and Loxy had her *scared*!

Too fuckin' much!

Loxy sidled out from behind the counter, waving the knife. "Slice your tits off like salami," she cackled as she brought the tip up to face height, still making like Freddy Krueger. "Shove it up your nose!"

The biker chick started backing toward the door.

What a trip!

"Put it down, Loxy!" Mario wheezed at her from across the room.

Loxy felt the power.

"You gonna make me, Mario?" she shouted back at him. "You still got the balls left to try, you dried up old fart?"

Mario hefted his bat and took a step forward.

Loxy burned. White-hot waves blasted off her skin. Crappy flickerin' fluorescents turned her inta a rock star. Knife made her strong. Just gettin' off so fine on lettin' herself play stark starin' nuts made the world shit in its pants.

Whoo-eee!

Mario gave her a real careful look, ducked back behind the cash register booth. "Get the fuck out of here," he whined in this stupid angry old voice.

"Get the fuck out of here, get the fuck out of here, get the fuck out of here," Loxy mimicked back at him.

Mario pulled the pistol from underneath the register stand and pointed it across the room at her. Three of Cory's customers actually *crawled under the tables*!

It was so fuckin' funny, Loxy started laughin', rockin' sockin' great big ones fit ta bust a gut—

—an' all ofa sudden, the fuckin' stupid biker dyke is reachin' for *her* knife—

"Hey, get your fuckin' paw off *my* knife!" Loxy screamed, pulling her wrist out of the biker's grab and the knife with it, slashin' a neat line of blood across the bitch's cheek inna process, hee, hee, hee—

—stupid cunt screams like a cat with its tail caught inna hamburger grinder an' throws a fuckin' punch right at her head—

—Loxy ducks, catches just a little edge of it cross her cheek, fallin' forward, strikin' back, and the knife goes three or four inches inta the biker momma's big fat thigh—

"*BA-DOOM!*"

Like someone put a garbage can over her head and dropped a fuckin' safe on it! Snowflakes fallin' on her face!

Slow-mo instant replay time.

Mario had fired the .44 Magnum with a blast Loxy felt likea fist as the slug slammed inta the wall about three feet from her head an' plaster exploded all over her.

And the Hell's Angels sweathog is screaming and falling with Loxy's knife still in her thigh, an' Loxy still attached to the knife, an' ain't that a siren already out there somewhere—

—Loxy yanked the knife out an' stood there lookin' at the ripe red blood, the biker momma rollin' on the floor clutchin' at her bleedin' leg with both hands and blubberin', no fuckin' class at all—

And Mario had scuttled out from behind the register, come halfway across the room, and was pointin' the gun at the tip of her nose from maybe eight feet away, lookin' like maybe he was kinda pissed off at the way things was workin' out, like his eyes was poppin' out of his head, an' she could hear his fuckin' teeth gnashin' and he was sorta breathin' funny like he might have a heart attack or somethin', hee, hee, hee—

"You got about three seconds to get your ass out of here, you crackhead piece of shit before I blow your goddamn head off!"

"Hey, c'mon, Mario, ain't you got—"

"One!"

"—no sense a humor?"

"Two!"

Siren up the avenue! Biker momma pissin' and moanin' and rollin' around inna puddle a blood onna dirty floor! Lights flickerin'! Roaches pourin' outa all the corners like Cory's scumbag customers running out the door! Not such a cool scene, fuckin' .44 Magnum shakin' in Mario's hand as he makes t'pull back the hammer with his greasy ol' thumb—

"Three!"

"Hey, if ya gonna be *that* way about it, y'can take this job and shove it!" Loxy shouted at him, givin' him the finger with the bloody knife, and bugalooin' out into the street.

"Hey, Ralf, what's your sign?"

"Moby the Dick, Monkey Girl, what's *yours*? Sure don't look like Virgo the Virgin to me, I'd bet on the sign of the Crabs."

Time oozed on in agony as Texas Jimmy Balaban stood in the wings watching his boy bomb.

Ralf had come to the very front of the stage, as close to the brink as he could get.

In more ways than one.

After forty minutes of bouncing lame lines off this dead meat, Ralf's anger at the audience was developing a dangerous razor edge. Insult humor that showed a comic's contempt for the audience before which he was bombing had never been a way to win laughs and influence rednecks.

"Hey, Monkey People, you better show some signs of life soon, or they're gonna declare you dead and freeze your heads, and when you wake up a hundred years from now, you're gonna find your brains installed as the voices of talking elevators or the automatic transmissions in garbage trucks!"

Jimmy had seen it all too many times before. The comic began to forget that the purpose of the zingers was to make the audience laugh and slid into a zone where the reason for insulting the audience became because they *weren't*.

Maybe you could get away with it for a while with an audience of showbiz wannabes in a comedy club in New York, but *this* audience seemed to be a cross-section of Valley mall rats, the six-pack polyester crowd from Orange County, the barrio boom-box set. Not the sort of folks with a healthy sense of humor for insults aimed at them, especially when too many shots started coming in below the belt.

Once it dawned on the likes of *them* that you really weren't *trying* to be funny anymore, you'd better get offstage fast before the bottles started to fly.

Not that Jimmy could entirely blame Ralf for what was happening. Jimmy had to own up to the fact that he himself had seriously screwed up. The guy had the timing and the moves to work off an audience and make *something* like Lampkin's Lenny Bruce from the Future number work.

But not with *this* audience.

"Yeah, lady, the good news is that they *will* find a cure for cancer, but the bad news is that it's gonna turn you into a four-hundred-pound lesbian communist hamster. . . ."

Texas Jimmy's previous experience with rounding up studio audiences had been limited to the occasional low-grade live variety hour, where all you needed was to run a laugh track and be able to do audience reaction shots without showing empty seats. If you piled enough handbills on checkout counters, no problem.

It would seem, though, that the biz held new mysteries even for an old dog like Texas Jimmy Balaban, who thought he knew all the tricks. He could see that he had missed one this time, but he couldn't quite figure out what it was.

"This isn't working at all," Dexter Lampkin whined sourly somewhere left rear.

Jimmy didn't bother to turn. "I'm not planning on sending out for caviar and champagne, Lampkin, if that's what you mean," he said over his shoulder.

". . . *knew* I might have some trouble with the natives, seeing as how they cast a chimpanzee's straight man as the Prez . . ."

"Is that all you have to say about it?" Lampkin muttered indignantly. "It sucks!"

Jimmy shrugged, still not bothering to turn around.

"If I slit my wrists every time I watched one of my clients die, I'da gone broke on the Band-Aid bill a long time ago," he said.

Which, upon sour reflection, was a better one-liner than most of the crap Ralf was burping up out there now.

Lampkin, though, didn't even grant him a snicker.

"How can you be so *calm* about it?" he demanded.

Perversely enough, Lampkin's amateur opening-night panic had a calming effect on Texas Jimmy's jangled professional nerves.

"Lighten up, will you, Dex?" he said.

"*Lighten up!*" Lampkin exclaimed. "Can't you see what's happening out there?"

"Sure I can, Dex," Jimmy told him avuncularly. "Ralf is as flat as last week's tortillas, the folks out there don't appreciate it, and—"

"Well—"

"Look, will you relax, we've got a thirteen-week guarantee written in stone, and this is only show one of week one. Okay, so Ralf isn't breaking out of the starting gate like a Triple Crown winner, and the format needs serious rethinking, but—"

"The format! Is that what you—"

"Hey, come on, Lampkin, relax, I'm not pissed off at you 'cause your format turned out not to be perfect," Jimmy said, favoring him with a magnanimous smile and a brotherly pat on the shoulder. "Madden bought it, didn't he, so who am I to contradict the Boy Genius?"

Lampkin gave him a peculiar look, halfway between a dumb stare and a scowl. "Meaning what?" he said suspiciously.

"Meaning we got time to fix it," Jimmy told him in the reassuring manner of a sophisticated lady explaining that one wilted hard-on was not the end of the world.

Dexter had to admire the way Balaban was taking things. One moment he had been pissed off at Jimmy for stupidly scooping up this dim audience out of random shopping malls and blaming the resultant fiasco on *his* format, and the next Balaban had disarmed his ire by reassuring him that there were no hard feelings about it.

And after all, Jimmy was at least partially right. We *do* have time to fix it.

We?

Could it be, Lampkin, that the thought of the money to be made on a second thirteen-week pickup is beginning to draw your serious attention?

"Yeah, that guy over there, the one with all the buttons on his T-shirt that weighs about three hundred pounds!"

Oh shit!

There, captured in the magic circle of the spotlight was *Oscar Karel.*

Oscar Karel was a familiar figure at science fiction conventions. With his massive paunch flowing seamlessly into his enormous ass without benefit of a waistline and his narrow shoulders and chicken-chest, Oscar Karel was shaped like a giant overweight penguin. At a science fiction convention, his physical appearance would have hardly been noticed, since this was a dominant fannish genotype, and many of these pear-shaped fans also had vaguely unfocused eyes made even weirder by the magnification of thick glasses, and favored tentlike T-shirts festooned with name badges from their last dozen conventions and elaborately illumined buttons bearing such bon mots as "Fans Are Slans," "I Grok Mr. Spock," and "Frodo Lives."

But here, cruelly pinned like a bug on a microscope slide by the spotlight, the spectacle he presented had the visual impact of a terminal wino beamed down into happy hour at the Polo Lounge.

Dexter's visceral reaction was instant mortification. *He* certainly didn't identify with the embarrassing likes of Oscar, nor did he believe that these fan-boys were his typical readers, and he was more than prepared to deliver an angry half-hour lecture to any asshole who claimed they were. But it was all too horribly true that anyone who wrote science fiction found groupies like Oscar identified in the mind of the Great Unwashed with *them.*

"Hello, Ralf, *my* name is Oscar *Karel,*" he honked in that strange flat voice and mechanically syncopated cadence. "And *I* was *working* on life-support systems for *NASA* before the *funding* got canceled . . . ?"

"Life-support systems, huh? The folks they dragged in here sure could've used some of that tonight! Where were you when we needed you?"

Oscar beamed at Ralf like a happy robot. "We were designing *long-term* closed-loop systems for L-five *space colonies. . . .*"

"Sounds like a better gig than trying to squeeze blood out of stones for a living or getting laughs outa these Slagheads," Ralf shot back.

But a bit of rough edge seemed to have been sanded off his voice, as he stood there like a fisherman examining some weird deep-sea denizen his net had chanced to dredge up from an alien ocean.

"Actually, Ralf, synthesizing *plasma replacement fluids* out of basic lunar *material* presents no major theoretical *problem*," Oscar proclaimed, apparently waiting for a laugh as if he thought he had delivered a punch line.

It wasn't that fans like Oscar were stupid, nor exactly that they lacked a sense of humor. In fact, on a Martian intellectual level, they tended to be just this sort of Mensa heavyweight. And Dexter was pretty sure that Oscar himself found that line funny. Which it might have been on Pluto.

"And I suppose you guys were also working on turning dog doody into dollar bills?" Ralf said, artfully converting it into a straight-line and actually raising a few faint snickers.

Something resembling a laugh issued forth from Oscar Karel, three sharp braying squeals that might be reproduced by goosing a donkey with an electric cattle prod.

"Actually, Ralf, *we* were working with *human* waste," he said.

"No shit," Ralf lip-synced silently, mugging at the audience, wrinkling his nose, backing away from the front of the stage, and pointing the shotgun mike in Oscar's direction like a dowager aunt pointing her umbrella in the direction of Fido's no-no.

Real laughter.

Something weird was happening. Ralf was now using his gross-out reaction to stagger back toward the captain's chair.

"It's *impossible* to design a *space* colony which doesn't accumulate great big *piles* of it," Oscar said. He giggled. "Have you ever *thought* how much the average *human* produces in a *year*?"

Ralf and Oscar didn't even seem to be in the same solar system, but at least Oscar seemed to have finally given him someone he could work off.

"Two hundred and sixty-three pounds!" Oscar said, as proud of his calculation as if he had delivered up his own contribution on a sterling silver platter.

Big laughs, guttering away into an undercurrent of nervous snickers.

True, the propensity to laugh at the merest allusion to shit seemed to be hard-wired into the species' genetic coding, but true too that Ralf was using Oscar Karel to alter his poisonous relationship with the audience.

"*Working* with a theoretical *population* of ten *thousand*, we calculated that our space colony model would produce *thirteen hundred tons* a year . . ."

"Piled high and deep," said Ralf, seating himself with a grin at the audience, and somehow, in that moment visibly regaining control of his show in the closing minutes.

"*Fortunately*, it's a *very rich* raw *material*. . . ."

Ralf sat there mugging at the audience and waving his shotgun mike up and down to Oscar's singsong cadence, conducting him like a comic maestro.

Somehow the chemistry had turned right with the advent of Oscar Karel. Somehow the format was now working.

"It's a *very rich* raw *material*, is it, you hear that, folks?" Ralf said.

"You can *use* it for fertilizer, you can *convert* it into a *hydrocarbon base* for plastics, you can polymerize it into a lightweight high-tensile *building* material, you can even use it as a *fish tank nutrient* . . ."

Ralf rolled his eyes, gagged, and the audience roared.

"You don't know the half of it, Monkey Boy," he said, and the edge had come back into his voice. But now he was using it *for* the audience rather than *on* it.

Oscar Karel tried to say something, but Ralf had laid his shotgun mike across his knees, and Dexter couldn't catch it without the amplification. The star of the show, though, was always miked, and Ralf drowned out whatever it was through the studio speakers.

"Back when I come from, Oscar, we *eat* it," he said.

Dexter's mouth fell open. The audience gasped, laughed, muttered, tittered nervously.

Ralf laughed, fracturing the tension.

"They pipe it right from the source through the middle of a nuclear reactor to kill the stink and into vats where they mix it with chemicals that turn it kinda rubbery and turn it into People Chow. . . ."

Confused uncomfortable laughter. Dexter glanced at Texas Jimmy. Jimmy shrugged. He nodded at the studio clock. The show had entered its closing moments. Maybe Ralf was watching the clock too, he seemed to be leading up to an extro.

"And then they pour it into molds and stamp out hamburgers and pizzas and chicken McSludgeIts that have so few calories you can cram 'em down your throat nonstop with both hands all day long and *still* stay thin as a starving alley cat!"

Ralf stood up, smeared a moron grin across his face, and did Oscar Karel wickedly enough to leave 'em laughing just as time ran out.

"That's *right*, Monkey People, the future you're gonna leave your *grandchildren* won't be *all* bad after all. Thanks to the wonders of science and *dreknology*, they're gonna have the *perfect* junk food!"

6

Foxy Loxy figured that while bein' a serious professional maybe wasn't
gonna be no bed a guns an' roses, at least hookin' full-time wasn't gonna be like
pullin' no stupid nine-to-fiver. Even with the cost a crack bein' what it was and
food and flop an' all, a girl should be able to keep it together on six or seven tricks
a day, like three or four hours actual work max.

What she hadn't figured on was the fuckin' pimps.

The greasy motherfucker bastards had carved the whole fuckin' town up into
turfs, or anyway anyplace a girl could figure to score a john without standing
around for hours or gettin' rousted by the cops, an' they had a real bad attitude
they saw you workin' their girls' streets. Girl couldn't even suck an honest cock
behinda garbage can without one of these pieces a shit kickin' her ass outa *his*
fuckin' alley, maybe whackin' her around, an' tellin' her she was gonna hafta let
him take care of her.

Well, y'didn't need to be Albert fuckin' Einstein t'figure out that if you let one
of these scumbags sink his meat hooks into your ass to the tune of half the proceeds or worse, that was twice as much work for you for half the bread.

No fuckin' way, Gold Chain Jose!

So Loxy had kept onna move, kept the fuck out of the obvious hooker scenes
where the pimps ran their stables, lookin' for tricks in weird places where there no
pimps figured to go, like th' Garment Center, Chinatown at Mott and Canal,
even outside St. Patrick's, hey, y'never know.

Course, where there weren't no pimps or their stringers, there was usually a
reason, like the tricks were too few an' far between, or the fuckin' cops had it inta

their heads to be bad for business, so it was an hour or more of runnin' around an' hassle t'score each trick, a workin' girl really wasn't doin' much better than a *workin'* girl, what the fuck is this country comin' to. . . .

What it had come to on *this* shitty Tuesday long about eight was what she had heard call the Diamond Center, hey, that figured to be fulla high-rollers right, she hadn't scored a single fuckin' trick all day, she didn't feature crashin' inna alley again, maybe there weren't too many pimps up there, a girl could hope, an' she didn't have any better idea.

So she boogied on up to Fifth and 47th to see what she could see, and what she saw was *this* shit. Jeez! No fuckin' pimps, but the fuckin' street was all these jewelry stores with steel shutters comin' down an' kosher delis an' Greek luncheonettes insteada the bars she had expected, an' insteada high-rollers, it was Jewish guys with beards in long black coats and these weird curls fallin' outa their black cowboy hats.

Not what you'd call promising, but what the fuck else was there to do, so Loxy paraded west, shakin' the goods, winkin', grabbin' at her crotch, "Hey, wanna fuck, wanna suck, makeya a deal," like things were gettin' desperate.

The older Jews gave her looks like she wasn't speakin' English, or they didn't understand it, an' the younger ones either looked at her like she was a walkin' talkin' piecea shit, or stared right fuckin' through her.

Fuck this!

Time for a nice big hit.

Wasn't like she was addicted to the shit, y'unnerstand, okay, maybe she was usin' a bit more these days, but hey, it was a legitimate business expense right, without it how could a girl get through a day's work, suckin' off these fuckin' creeps, doin' it against the wall inna alley stinkin' a piss an' rat turds, dealin' with *this* kinda shit, y'couldn't change your workin' conditions, so you like hadda do somethin' for your attitude.

So Loxy ducked into a phone booth.

Might seem like takin' a bit of a chance doin' it inna phone booth right there onna corner in plain sight with all these people boogeyin' by, but Loxy had it down. Duck into a phone booth, make like you're talkin' inta the receiver holding it down by the mouthpiece, palm the pipe with the same hand so no one sees it who ain't lookin' real hard, make like you're pickin' your nose with the other, no one's gonna be too innerested in clockin' *that*, take a couple a quick hits.

Inta the ol' phone booth like Clark fuckin' Kent, out the other side in about thirty seconds like the White Tornado inna Superman suit, whoo-eee, hah, hah, hah!

Oh, yeah, did wonders for your attitude, set your brain *movin'*! No bread in her purse to pay for a night's flop, but what she *did* have inna survival bag wasa fuckin' great big ol' *knife,* so fuck your goddamn attitude, assholes, the White Tornado ain't gonna take no shit from none a you pimps tonight, you just better let me peddle my ass, or I'm gonna shove *my* fuckin' attitude right up *yours!*

So she boogaloed toward Broadway, bah-bah, bah-do-bah, figurin' that the chances of scorin' somethin' to turn before she reached Eighth Avenue, where the pimps were thick as cockroaches inna flophouse crapper an' too much for maybe even the White Tornado to handle, were pretty fuckin' good. . . .

An' hey, when you're not you're not when you're hot you're hot, this creep reels outa this crummy wino bar, takes one look at the goods, an' gives her a real subtle come-on, like he puckers up his disgusting purple lips, makes a sound like the air leakin' out of a tire someone jabbed witha ice pick, and grabs at the crotch of his dirty navy blue pants with a hand looks like he just had it up an elephant's asshole.

Okay, he ain't exactly what they call *suave,* like he's wearing these dirty work-boots, and some kinda red-and-black-plaid shirt looks like it mighta been puked on a few times, an' his skin is this kinda scaly-purplish-gray-brown color you can't tell if he's black or white or Puerto Rican or maybe some kinda *reptile,* but hey, th' White Tornado is an equal-opportunity hooker, an' business is business, 'specially since this is the only action she's seen all day.

"Okay, sweet thing, you talked me into it," she told him, "now you unnerstand I don't do this shit for a livin', it's just 'cause you're so fuckin' *handsome,* turn me on an' all, ten bucks a suck, twenty-five a fuck, an' for fifty plus a room with a toilet, I'll do ya an all-nighter, hey whaddya say, you ain't gonna get a better deal than that."

The creep gave her this woozy, clearly fried to the fuckin' bloodshot eyeballs look, hmm, Loxy thought, first time it occurred to her, wonder how much he's got, just might be able t'roll him . . .

"Whatsa matter, gorgeous, pussy got your tongue, hee, hee, hee, hey come on, I ain't gonna bite, or I *could* if ya want, but it'll cost ya ten bucks extra, bein' like a *specialty,* y'know . . ."

"You . . . you . . . you fuck?" he finally managed to say in some kinda goddamn communist accent or somethin'.

"Yeah, yeah, I gota hand it to ya, you got it all figured out, you Tarzan, me Jane, fuckee-fuckee, dig it? You got twenty-five bucks?"

Guy reached into his pocket, pulled out a wad a greasy bills. Loxy's brain kicked inta high gear at the sighta it, hey, why not, if she could get him inna alley might not even hafta fuck the pile a shit. . . .

She hooked a finger into a belt loop and pulled him toward her. "Well, come on, then, man," she said, "let's go find ourselves someplace private, right?"

The creep just about dragged his fuckin' knuckles onna ground as she led him west to where the down and dirty action faded inta an empty street y'might find kinda scary was you not the White Tornado packin' a great big knife and plannin' t'be kinda scary yourself. There were little service alleys, shadowy garbage can caves under the stoops, Dumpster looked like it hadn't been emptied in years, and . . .

"Hey, whaddya say, big boy, don't that look cool?"

An old car body, the wheels long gone with the glass, so rusted out you couldn't tell what the fuck color it had ever been, but the backseat still there, all you hadda do was shove all these old newspapers an' beer cans onta the floor . . .

Loxy pushed and shivvied the john inta the back, crawled in after him. This close up the smell was more than she could take, he musta used a dead rat for toilet paper an' spent five years gargling with cat piss, unless of course . . .

"Hold on a second, willya?" she told him as he started unzipping his fishin' out her pipe and loading it with a double hit, or maybe a triple, who knows, hey why not.

While she was suckin' down two great big tokes, the creep whipped out something looked like it belonged on a dead donkey, and he grabbed it an' shaked it at her like a fuckin' firehose, jeez.

Anna great big flashbulb went off inside her head just like inna cartoon, anna White Tornado was whirlin' and twirlin', rockin' and rollin', and her mouth was so fuckin' *brilliant* was faster'n her brain, so she just sat back an' let her talkin' do the walkin', oh yeah, whoo-ee!

"Oh hey, that's fuckin' charmin', I gotta tellya, y'got me creamin' in my jeans, here let me," she babbled at him, an' started giving him a hand job. "Hey, you got me so turned on, tellya what, I don't do this for everyone, but I'm gonna give you somethin' *for free . . .*"

Still jerkin' his disgustin' dong, she stuck her pipe into his slobbery yawp. "Hey, willya hold it, huh?" she told him. "I ain't got three hands, y'know."

The john hooked the pipe in his grimy paw, an' Loxy lit it. He took a big greedy hit, then coughed the pipe back inta her palm all slimed with spit, sorta like *she* woulda done with his cock afta ten bucks' worth, an' then he just laid back there with this fuckin' moron grin an' eyes like boiled tomatoes. Jeez, no way she's gonna fuck *this* piecea shit, girl's gotta have *some* standards right, so she kept him droolin' happy with one hand while she dropped the pipe inta her bag with the other, fumblin' around for the handle of the knife—

"Hey, bitch, what you think you doin' on the Space Ace's fuckin' street?"

An' some fuckin' goddamn ape's got his paw on her shoulder, diggin' inta it real hard, and yankin' her backwards up an' outa the car body. Loxy whirled around outa his meat-hook burnin' and screamin' with fearless white-hot White Tornado fury.

"Mother-*fucka!*"

Big black son of a bitch with coppery mirror-shades and shoulders a yard wide an' this stupid fuckin' pencil-eraser haircut, and he's wearin' this cream-yellow baggy-pants suit, anna red silk shirt open to the fuckin' navel so's he can show off fifteen fuckin' poundsa gold chains, an twenny-seven rings on each finger, an' a fuckin' gold Rolex, what else, an' cowboy boots made outa some kinda green fuckin' dinosaur.

Fuckin' goddamn pimp! Fuckin' *perfect* goddamn mother of all fuckin' bull-shit pimps!

E-*nuff*! E-fuckin' nuff!

"YOU KEEP YOUR FUCKIN' HANDS OFF ME, YOU FUCKIN' PIECE A NIGGER PIMP SHIT!" Loxy shouted right into his face.

"Shut the fuck up, you honkie junkie bitch!" Wham! He backhanded her across the chops so hard she felt a coupla teeth come loose as she got knocked backwards against the car body.

Loxy could feel something that was probably pain somewhere far far away, and she was tastin' somethin' she figured was blood, an' yeah, this guy was about the size of King Kong, an' for sure she had spent the last two fuckin' weeks gettin' chased, and slapped, and hit on by every fuckin' sleazebag pimp inna city, an' maybe if she thought about it, this one woulda scared her shitless too.

But the White Tornado had had it with these scumbags. The White Tornado knew no fear. The White Tornado was pissed off. The White Tornado wasn't gonna eat no more of this shit!

"You better leave me the fuck alone, asshole," she told him. "You just better leave me alone t'do my fuckin' business. You bastids don't own me. You don't own no fuckin' street. You don't even own your own fuckin' dick, you pimp faggot piecea shit."

Space Case, or Space Ace, or whatever the fuck he called himself, sorta just froze there steamin' like *she* had just whacked *him* inna chops back, hee, hee, hee.

"When I get through with you, bitch, you ain't gonna have enough face left to suck dog dicks for a quarter," he said, whippin' an' snickin' a six-inch switchblade outa somewhere, an' slicin' her across the cheek faster'n she could feel it or think.

But not fuckin' fast enough, whoo-ee!

'Cause *her* big dirty ol' knife was already in her fist, an' she was jammin' it up into his fuckin' armpit with all her weight behind it.

He screamed this awful slasher-flick scream, hee, hee, hee, far-fuckin' out, an' Loxy yanked the knife out of his armpit with both hands, feelin' things gratin' and suckin' onna way out, an' then she stabbed down real hard inta the wrist holdin' the switchblade, musta got her knife in two or three inches, twisting and yankin' and tearin', an' all this blood kinda pumpin' out, an' after he drops the switchblade, she rips out the bloody knife, and it's like she's not there anymore, he's grabbing at the wrist with the other hand like he could hold in the blood with it, and just blubberin' and screamin' and howlin', mistah big tough pimp, whoo-ee!

And the john has oozed out of the car body, an' he's standin' there, well, sorta, with his eyes rollin', an' his mouth hangin' open and his cock hangin' out, just like inna movies, funniest fuckin' thing you ever saw, hah, hah, hah!

"Grrr! Yowl! Brraaa!" Loxy bugged her eyes out like a fuckin' nutcase, stuck out her tongue, and took a couple a steps toward him wavin' the bloody knife just for the hell of it, hey why not, hee, hee, hee!

"Police! *Police!* POLICE!" he shouts at the top of his lungs and lurches and staggers down the street as fast as he can, which ain't much, hah, hah, hah!

By this time, the pimp is rollin' around inna gutter inna buncha blood, tryin' to grab at his wrist and shoulder with his one good hand at the same time, which ain't exactly easy.

Loxy gave him a boot in the back an' another inna nuts for bad luck, an' took off the other way toward the river.

"You want me to take a meeting with you next Tuesday, Jimmy?" Amanda said, allowing a certain sitcom naïveté to leak into her voice. "What about?"

"About the show, Amanda, what else, you been watching it?"

"I catch it from time to time," Amanda told Balaban with a faint air of no-blesse oblige. Actually, how could she not? On a survival level, the gig as Ralf's acting coach had become her major source of income, so she could hardly not keep tabs on his act, and on a karmic level, she could hardly deny she had had a hand in foisting it upon the world, so she had been expecting this call to come for some time now.

"Well?" said Texas Jimmy Balaban with an edge of anxiety in his voice.

"Well, *what?*" Amanda couldn't refrain from setting him up, perhaps itself a product of watching too much Ralf.

"Well, what do you think of the show!"

"How can I put this to you delicately, Jimmy?" Amanda drawled.

She had seen what was wrong from show one.

When you put a comic up there on a stage all by himself in front of an audience, it was *theater*, and whoever had decided that an angry gnome from a grim Deathship Earth future could get laughs from Mr. and Mrs. Joe Sixpack by blaming them for the disaster didn't know the first thing about it, which was that you had to play *to* the audience, not *against* it. And Ralf was acting as if he was still up there in the twenty-second century telling Monkey People jokes to an audience of their angry disinherited grandchildren.

It was all too exactly like trying to get laughs by telling Polish jokes in Warsaw.

"To be frank about it, as they say in Washington," Amanda said, "it's dreadful."

"Hey, come on, for a show that ain't been on even two months, the ratings aren't *that* bad," Balaban said. "I don't see why Madden's panicking this early—"

"*Madden?*" Amanda exclaimed. "We're talking here about *Archie* Madden?"

"Who *else* do you think we're talking about, that's who the meeting's with on Tuesday."

"You want me to take a meeting with you and *Archie Madden*? May I ask why?"

"How the hell should I know?"

"Huh?"

"*Madden* called the meeting, you think *I* go around causing tsuris like this for myself?" Balaban said. "The Boy Genius wants you there."

"To talk about *what?*"

"Whatever boy geniuses like to talk about, what the hell do you think?"

"You're saying that I am being asked to *take* a meeting with Archie Madden *by* Archie Madden?"

"Yeah, so can we cut the crap, Amanda? Or are you gonna try to tell me that you're the only person in town who'd refuse to take a meeting with Archie Madden?"

That would indeed be a line that would not exactly drop trippingly from the lips of anyone whose destiny was at all linked to the Business. If you were invited to take a meeting by Archie Madden, you thanked your astrologer for your lucky stars and took a meeting with Archie Madden.

"Well, when you put it that way . . ."

Only after she had hung up the phone did Amanda begin to realize what she had just unthinkingly done. She had committed to involving herself into maybe saving a show she found painful to watch without being at all convinced that it was worthy of salvation. Without the least idea of how. And no one, herself included, had even raised the subject of money!

Why?

Because it was the price of the showbiz magic of taking a meeting with Archie Madden.

Say what you like about Black Magic or White Magic, the Green Magic of Showbiz was real, and it worked. It worked because the business was set up so that nothing else would.

There was always an Archie Madden or two or three around. The Business couldn't work without such sorcerers so it created them by granting some ordinary mortal a singular magic power.

As the gods of Greece endowed Hercules with superhuman strength and a crippled newsboy was transformed into mighty Captain Marvel by pronouncing the word "Shazaam," so did the Business grant the Archie Madden of the hour the magical power to say "Yes."

In a business where a single "Yes" could commit some transhuman entity to an investment of scores of millions of dollars, the power to say No was granted to every two-bit predator along the corporate food chain from script readers and appointments secretaries on up to where the Bankers did battle with the Suits.

But if the buck did not sooner or later reach *someone* whose word was a certified check, nothing would ever get made or picked up. Hollywood could not function without *someone* who could say the Magic Word.

Yes, you've got a deal that will make you independently wealthy for the rest of your life! Yes, the show is picked up for another season! Yes, it's a go, have your agent draw up the contracts!

In Washington, Yes Men might be a legion of toadies, but in Hollywood, they were singular, and theirs was the Power.

Which was why both she and Texas Jimmy Balaban knew full well that no one turned down a meeting with the current incarnation of Archie Madden.

He Who Could Say Yes was He Whose Meeting Could Not Be Refused.

Even if you had nothing you wanted him to say Yes to. Just being admitted to the Presence was sufficient motivation, as she had just found out.

If *that* wasn't magic, what was?

After all, why on Earth *was* she taking this meeting with Madden?

Upon reflection, Amanda realized that there were more spells being spun here than were readily apparent, as witness the fact that she had just been snake-charmed by one herself.

But for what?

Unless Archie Madden had snorted a major portion of Colombia's production, it wouldn't be to give Jimmy an early pickup for another thirteen weeks. She had been asking the wrong question.

Ask not what Archie Madden can do for you, ask what Archie Madden thinks *you* can do for *him.*

To which there was only one answer. To help fix a show he was stuck with for another two months, a show he had said Yes to, a show he would therefore rather be able to pick up than cancel and admit that he could be wrong.

But why should she?

No one had mentioned money, and if she gave Madden her honest opinion, it would be to seal up the body bag and give the turkey a decent burial.

Yet she *was* taking this meeting.

Amanda did not believe that the stars ruled her destiny, or that there were times when actual tutelary spirits seized control of it for their own higher purposes. But she had spent her lifetime seeking to delve beneath the surface of phenomenological consciousness, to summon the spirits of creation from her own vasty deeps, to will herself into the Dreamtime with her eyes open wide. And she had experienced those depths, that higher realm, where the Dreamtime and creative inspiration, the collective and the personal, the zeitgeist and the collective unconscious arise as steps in the same dance.

And some spirit message therefrom had not merely told her to take this meeting, it had moved her to do it without even asking her considered opinion, had made her an offer she couldn't refuse and still couldn't understand.

Or could she?

What had Hadashi said about Ralf? That there were karmic inflection points when the zeitgeist throws up an avatar for the times? That the times tended to get the avatar they *deserved*? That sometimes it's a Buddha, and sometimes it's a Jesus, and sometimes it's a Cosmic Custard Pie?

Considering the current state of the species' karma, that *did* make a certain case for Ralf.

Acting on this would admittedly be about on a par with reading the leaves in the bottom of your teacup or consulting a tarot reader in a shopping mall, were it not for one hard phenomenological fact.

She had already done it.

Generally speaking, Amanda found her Amanda Robin persona ideal for interfacing with the biz, but this time Amanda Robin had dropped her into waters that seemed to be far over her Hollywood head.

A transformation was clearly called for, and she had only five days before the meeting in which to achieve it.

Fly to San Francisco, rent a car, a day's drive in, a day's drive out, another day's drive back to LA. . . .

Amanda caught herself in midthought.

Just like that, Amanda realized that she had already embarked upon the Long Path.

"You only make the pilgrimage to the Long Path monastery once," Hadashi had told her, "and you'll know it when your time comes."

And now that it had, she did.

The Long Path was one of those legends of awareness of which were self-limited to those in tune to the music of such spheres in the first place.

Amanda had heard the legend years before Hadashi had entrusted her with the knowledge of the stages of its way as a thirty-fifth birthday present.

The Long Path monastery was supposed to be a one-shot satori, a trip that wouldn't work twice. Those who returned from the Long Path were enjoined not to speak of their experiences upon it lest prior knowledge pollute the karma of subsequent pilgrims, which made it rather difficult to verify the existence of the actual artifact.

"Oh, it's there all right," Hadashi had told her, "and these directions are the true path to it."

"Whose monastery is it?"

In the legend, there were many versions. Refugee Tibetans. Aliens from space making the most cautious of high-level first contact. Zen monks from Japan, or possibly Aspen. Northern Californian dope barons under advice from their guru to perform a karmic mitzvah.

Hadashi shrugged.

"Whoever needs it at the time," he said.

The flight to San Francisco was uneventful, and stage one of the Long Path was a boring high-speed run up an arrow-straight freeway through flat, dull agribusiness country. Farther north into wine country around Russian River the land began to roll itself up into hills, and the farms and ranches became, well, more picturesque, with their mustard and green checkerboards of crops and woodland and Norman Rockwell farmhouses.

But the six-lane freeway rolled ever on, and by now Amanda had traveled far enough from her Southern California avatar to resent this imperial intrusion from the south, for to Amanda the pilgrim it seemed that the engineers who had built it had conceded little more to the mighty Sierras as their roadway rose up into them than the Romans punching their tunnels by brute force through the Alps. Ascending from hills into mountains and from mountains into mountain vastnesses rising toward great snowcapped Shasta on mighty I-5, Amanda felt as if she was taking the Ventura Freeway between Katmandu and Shangri-La.

Maybe not quite the Himalayas, but Shasta too had a reputation for strange tribal rites and mountain-dwelling man-apes, and the Sierras *were* awesome, the crown of no mean mystic continent themselves.

Though gliding up into them with the obligatory gas station and Denny's at regular intervals *did* mar the purity of the experience, turned it into a bit of a Disneyland ride.

It was hardly dinnertime when she reached Redding, but according to what Hadashi had told her, there would be no place to spend the night farther in, so she took a cheap motel room.

After eating a hamburger, there was nothing to do but gaze up at the snowcapped peak of the vague vast shape of shadowy Mount Shasta shimmering through a fog layer in the moonlight.

Or, of course, watch television.

She could stare out the window and contemplate the Magic Mountain.

Or she could tube out.

It was a beautiful mountain, and a gorgeous night, but the vantage from which she beheld it was across the motel in plain sight of the freeway.

Had she been a painter, she might have worked all night to capture this fleeting and powerful ironic image, but having no such talent and inclination, once its sardonic satori had been imprinted on her memory track, there was nothing left to kill time with but the tube.

Should she do it?

Should she sit in a crummy hotel room sucked into the electronic black hole just like two hundred million other Monkey People while outside the window, obscured by the neon, dimmed by the distance, trivialized by the freeway, beaconing in the moonlight, was a manifested icon of cosmic vastness?

She checked her watch. It was just about time for *The Word According to Ralf*.

Should she watch?

How could she not?

So Amanda put herself through yet another hour of *The Word According to Ralf*, the tacky set, the insulting opening monologue, the vicious repartee with the dim audience, hoping that at least it would be boring enough to gork her off. After forty-five minutes or so, it seemed to be working. She lay there in bed with the remote by her side beginning to doze . . .

But then, on the edge of sleep, she was granted a vision.

Not a vision arising out of the Dreamtime into which she had been peacefully drifting, but a vision coming up at her out of the schlocktime from which she had been escaping.

The eye of the spotlight and Ralf's shotgun mike scepter pinned a woman of that indeterminant age between fifty-five and sixty-five, with the requisite bluish-gray hair and dress straight off the rack at Kmart to match, the sort of audience member you saw a dozen times a day in what was sometimes still referred to as the real world.

People who had been supermarket clerks, bank tellers, waitresses, for twenty years and whose future was twenty years more. People whose whole life story would never be even the smallest sidebar to the teensiest subplot in the schlockiest soap.

"Yes, lady, you, hey sure, why not, what's on your mind except that poodle-cut hairdo?"

"Can I ask you something *serious*, Ralf?" she replied with a certain threadbare dignity that Amanda found strangely touching. "Uh . . . uh . . ."

Ralf let her hang there for several agonizing beats before giving her a cynical world-weary look that lacked only the politically incorrect cigarette, and delivering the line as Bogie.

"Let's hear it, Sweetheart, we're all ears."

She blinked, once, twice, thrice.

Ralf narrowed his eyes, gave her the thousand-yard stare, and switched to Eastwood. "Go ahead, make my day."

"What?" the woman grunted.

It might as well have been "duh" as she stood there frozen stupidly in the cruel limelight.

"Come on, Monkey Girl, don't blow it, you're *on television*," Ralf finally said in his own voice.

"I . . . I'm on television . . . ?" the woman stammered, her blink-rate increasing to the panic level. "I'm on television . . . ?"

"That's *right*, lady, this is *your* star turn, *this* is the moment you've waited for all your life, you've won the *grand prize*," Ralf gabbled at her with the oleagenous smarm of the perfect game-show host. "*You* . . . are . . . on *TELEVISION!*"

The woman turned slightly, as if achieving awareness of the camera. She smiled at it horribly, barbled by the presence of it, by the magic red light, her lips moving but nothing coming out.

And then to mercifully hide the awfulness of it, the director cut to a medium close-up on Ralf.

"Say the magic words, *any* words, and achieve immortality," said Ralf doing Groucho.

And then . . .

And then he seemed to look right at Amanda, leering at her knowingly, convincing her beyond reason that he was speaking directly to *her*, that he knew she was there.

"Monkey People will do *anything* to be on television, won't they?" he said in an insinuating voice. "Stick a camera and a mike in their face, and they'll give you a sound bite while they're treading water in a cesspool."

Amanda knew it was an artifact of the camera angle, she knew there was nothing behind the eyes gazing so deeply into hers but phosphor dots over a vacuum, but . . . but . . .

But through the magic of Showbiz, a being from a higher reality was indeed manifesting itself in the realm of maya.

"They would *die* to be on television," that being said.

And a doorway opened.

Amanda was staring at a plate of glass impregnated with chemical phosphors excited by patterns of electrons. The Presence behind it was an illusion. It could not be real.

But from another perspective, Amanda realized with sudden satoric clarity, nothing could possibly be realer.

For she was sharing this intimate personal communion with the nonexistent entity on the screen with millions of other people, who, via the magic of Showbiz, were quite convinced *It* was realer than *they* were.

And who was to say they were wrong?

"You grin up off stretchers into the camera, and do the color on your own sucking chest wounds!" It told them. "You'd do it for your own funeral if they'd give you the airtime."

For this artifact of the electronic circuitry was indeed realer than they were in that enchanted realm where average Americans spent a third of their waking lives, namely the world of Show Business, where they were mere demographics, and It was a Star.

Here was the collective unconscious evolving archetype before Amanda's very eyes in a manner and with a speed entirely undreamed of by Jung or Joseph Campbell. For the process whereby the collective unconscious had evolved in the species via the slow accumulation of myth and archetype encoding wisdom hard-won in the Dreamtime had long since been superseded by the Showbiz collective unconscious of the Schlocktime.

Here archetypes came and went, here more collective myth was crammed down the throat of the zeitgeist in a year of Prime Time than in all of pre-TV human history.

Here, the *Star,* not the Hero, was the archetype imposed upon the Dreamtime as the Secret Second Self, the higher level of being that ordinary mortals might aspire to attain.

And if the Hero had a Thousand Faces, the Star had a million of 'em, baby, and if you don't like this one, we'll put a new writer on it, and recast the lead, and get back to you on Tuesday.

Like the rest of the audience, Amanda knew there was a flesh-and-blood Ralf in a studio somewhere behind the entity on the screen. But it didn't matter as far as the collective unconscious of the television audience was concerned.

For in their Dreamtime what was real was not a comedian who might be suffering from schizoid fugue, or a character created for him by someone's format, or her coaching, but the entity they had in every sense of the word produced . . . the Star of *The Word According to Ralf.*

"Hey, who should know better?" that entity said. "Don't *I* die on television every night and still come back for more?"

It was a groaner, but Amanda found herself laughing a zen sort of laugh anyway.

"Indeed you do," she found herself telling the apparition on the screen as she killed it with the remote. "Or anyway for a guaranteed thirteen weeks."

Amanda did not sleep well that night, dreaming in dead sitcoms and extinct series formats, but things looked better when she woke into the gilded blue of a mountain morning. Back on the I-5 at first it was still six lanes of freeway with road signs, gas stations, and fast-food joints; mighty mountains and verdant virgin forest reduced thereby to video images on the windshield.

But the Long Path called for her to leave the I-5 north of Shasta, and once Amanda did, the mountains not only began showing her their true spirit, they gave her a dose of their sense of humor as well.

Rude country style it was, too.

The off-ramp put her on a nice modern four-lane road as the foothills ascended toward mightier ranges. It was a glorious day, there was soon hardly a farmhouse to be seen, and the reality of Showbiz seemed to belong to the another geological age up in here, as she journeyed inward and upward into the mystic mountain uplands of the primal continental heart.

By the time the road approached the canyon pass that led up into actual fir-forested mountains, it had narrowed to two lanes, and then the road narrowed a bit more, and the car rumbled over some crumbly pavement they hadn't repaired since last winter's snows. . . .

At about the time the road left the sunny upland plain and entered the shady green defile of the forest, it broke up again. But the map assured her that this road went two hundred miles straight across the Sierras to Eureka, so it couldn't all be like this, *could* it?

Just as she was conceptualizing this eensy shadow of doubt, she was jolted out of all such maya by a mighty vision.

Around the bend, a bridleless palomino mare, eyes rolling, mane tossing, nostrils flaring, came down the road out of the mountains right at her at full frothing gallop.

Here was a Manifestation in flesh and blood, not phosphor dots, neighing madly as it pranced past her near enough to smell, a living metaphor of the untouchable continental heartland, the pure pristine wild spirit of the planet itself come to greet the pilgrim!

Amanda was so transfixed by the glory of this apparition that it was quite a while before awareness descended from pure perception into the conceptual realm where such signs might be interpreted.

Longer still before it dawned on her that where wild horses roam and you haven't seen another human in an hour, maybe this isn't unfinished repair work you're on. . . .

At which point she had to concentrate on her driving, because there weren't any guardrails and the road was winding higher, and there she was, creeping along on a dirt road full of ruts and boulders, crossed by a veining of tree roots, halfway up the wooded flank of a huge massif looking straight down a geologically impressive drop into an undergrowth-choked ravine.

That the VW camper car body at the bottom of it, which was the only sign of humanity, had rusted out into a vine-choked shell that seemed to have attained perfect oneness with Gaia was less than reassuring.

She might have considered terminating her pilgrimage, but the prospect of attempting to execute a broken-U on a pitted and rock-strewn dirt road no wider than her car carved into a mountain face overlooking an abyss told her that this far along the Long Path, the only way out was the way through.

The road crawled ever on, winding higher, and higher, a crude shelf bulldozed into the wooded hide of enormous feral beasts of mountains. Not a road sign to be seen. Not a farmhouse. Not a paper cup by the roadside. Aside from the ancient VW car body, she had seen no human artifact for hours.

Amanda had never before experienced this total disconnect from civilization, from the human realm itself. No backpackers could penetrate here, where whole wagon trains had disappeared, where, in the Donner Pass not so far away, survivors thereof had reverted to cannibalism.

This land had been untouched by human hands since before the Indians had crossed the Bering Strait from Siberia. She could now understand why Shasta and environs had their reputation for Big Foot and flying saucer landings and Druid cults.

This was the California Primeval.

That one might only presume to ascend to its mystic Himalayan heart by car seemed karmically appropriate.

Finally, with the sun slinking through the zenith beyond the fir trees, and the light just beginning to take on a slightly golden tinge as it filtered through the branches, Amanda reached what Hadashi had called the "parking lot."

The cliff face had been bulldozed a little wider so that a car could be pulled off the road. Two rough-hewn planks had been nailed to the nearest tree trunk to form an "X" that marked the spot. A length of raw branch sharpened into a minimalist arrow and spiked to another tree trunk marked the beginning of the footpath.

Amanda felt no twinge of trepidation as she entered the forest. Why would anyone be afraid of a walk through these fragrant woods, with the afternoon sunlight through the branches dappling the loamy forest floor and lighting her way? The trail was clearly marked every few yards, and there was no rough underbrush to impede her, nothing more than clumps of mushrooms, glades of ferns, a few low bushes easily avoided.

But as the path got steeper and steeper, as her legs began to feel somewhat leaden and her breathing became noticeably labored, and the afternoon light began to wane, she began to wonder with something sharper than bucolic awe exactly how much farther the monastery was.

A little while later, she began to notice sounds in the underbrush, they had probably always been there, there were animals in this forest of course, rabbits, and deer, and birds, and, uh, coyotes, wolves, were there still *bears* . . . ?

At which point, it occurred to her that it might be major stupidity to still be out here when the sun went down.

And then she had a not-too-pleasant little satori.

She was scared.

And there was nothing irrational about it.

This was not Disneyland. Any large predators she encountered, and they *were* out there somewhere, would not be cuddly creatures. There was no one close enough to hear any cry for help. She had no gun. She had no flashlight. Nine-one-one would not answer. Scotty would not beam her up.

This must be what it had been like to be a human animal before Adam and

Eve ate of the Silicon Apple, a naked primate somewhere in the middle of the food chain.

This was Nature.

But no succoring Earth Mother was in evidence.

This was not a simulation.

But it had always been a test.

It was with as much awe as relief that she finally emerged from the forest into the waning afternoon light of a small flat meadow atop what must have been the tallest peak in the area that could be reached without climbing equipment.

One moment she had been a frail creature fleeing through the forest before the fall of predatory night, and the next she bestrode the very continent itself like a Titan! She stood atop a crowning peak of the very spine of the Sierras themselves, or so it seemed as she gazed eastward, down across a landscape that fell away in great green folds and tumbles, a royal carpet unrolled at the feet of the queen of the world.

To the west, however, rose an even mightier cordillera, as if to whisper in her ear, "thou art mortal still."

And as such, not exactly protected from *anything* up here by the view.

This certainly seemed to be the end of the Long Path.

But where was the monastery?

And then she realized that the hillock in the center of the meadow must be it.

Oh no!

It was a ruined hippie dome so overgrown with vines she hadn't even noticed it at first.

Amanda approached the remains with a sinking sensation in her gut. During the hippie era, half-assed wood-framed Fuller Domes had sprouted all up and down the mountains of Northern California. They leaked in the rain, and came complete with their own internal greenhouse effect thanks to the minimally adjustable windows.

There weren't many of them left, even as ruins, and this one had subsided so far back into the landscape as to be virtually invisible at first glance.

When she reached it, she saw that it had been erected on a circular stone platform constructed of massive rounded blocks fitted together without mortar. No lichen grew upon it. Wasn't that rather odd?

She ascended the platform via one of the four sets of stairs that seemed to have been set at the cardinal points of the compass. Thick vines overgrew a framework of weathered gray pine faceted with hexagonal panes of glass that had weathered to a matte Coke-bottle finish. The nails were a rich old bronze green.

But—

Why did the vines follow the wooden framework and leave the panes clear of obstruction?

Amanda bent closer, touched the dome frame, examined it more closely as the masterpiece of cabinetwork that it was.

The wood had been impregnated with something that made it as hard and apparently impermeable as glass, as if it had been lovingly weathered for looks and then petrified with some kind of Space Age polymer.

And the struts appeared to have been joined not by stoned-out hippies from Mendocino but by master temple carpenters. Upon careful inspection, she found no broken panes. Some of the windows were open, some were closed, some were angled somewhere in between. The frames were gasketed with neoprene tubing, and pivoted on pins set into them.

Was it her imagination that some of them were *moving* ever so slowly?

Due north, where the craftsmen's bonze might have told them to site the entrance, there it was, a round-topped wooden door set in a rustic frame.

When Amanda gave it a push, it opened smoothly. When she stepped inside, a counterweight sucked it into the weather-sealed jamb behind her with a discreet limousine-door thunk.

Equally discreet track lighting across the top of the dome came gently up to a candlelight glow, dispelling the afternoon shadows and revealing the nature of the interior.

There wasn't any.

Not exactly.

She *felt* as if she stood in an open-air arbor in a forest glade.

The panes of the dome, which had appeared to be weathered green glass from the outside looking in, became color-neutral from the inside looking out, fading away into conceptual invisibility. Banks of them were open to admit the fragrant breezes of the pine forest, mightily enhancing the effect by telling the backbrain via the nose and the skin that this was *not* the interior of a man-made building, not the *indoors*, but the *outdoors*, the natural chemical and kinesthetic realm in which it had evolved.

Furnished, nevertheless, like something out of *Architectural Digest*.

A soft spotlight highlighted a kitchen and dining island sitting on a disk of matte green tile. Black and chrome microwave and fridge, breakfast bar to match.

What had first appeared to be a beaten earth floor was wall-to-wall deep-pile chocolate-colored carpeting. Rounded chairs and chaises upholstered in earth-tone velvets. Low tables that looked as if they had been laser-turned by Swedes out of tropical hardwoods in Kyoto.

Another soft spot drew the eye's attention to the center of the dome, where a round bed made up like something in a four-star hotel sat atop a low circular stone dais, every so slowly rotating.

"Welcome to the Long Path monastery," said a resonant sexless voice, just as the magic of the initial effect began to wear away. "I am the voice of your user-friendly voice-activated control system. Please enter the name by which you wish to be addressed now."

"Uh . . . Amanda . . . uh . . . What do I call you?"

"You have the option of personalizing this interface now."

Amanda did a take.

That was just a coincidence, right? It didn't really understand what she was saying. There was no "It" there to do it.

"Hadashi," she said, with a certain sense of devilment.

"Hadashi" conducted her along a programmed introduction, tiny spotlights coming on over each station as the voice told her the functions and commands.

She could control the lighting. She could control the bed's rotation. She could change the thermostat setting, but the computer controlled the opening and closing of the panes to maintain it. The refrigerator was stocked with the kind of micro-waveable gourmet meals sneaked in through the back door of mediocre French restaurants. The wines, however, would have been no disgrace to a serious sommelier.

No television, no radio, no telephone, no contact whatever with the outside world. No music player, no game machine, no computer screen. Not a single book or magazine. Not a single work of art. Not even a meditative mandala. No images at all. And the only spoken words other than her own the synthesized stock phrases of what amounted to little more than a talking elevator.

Never before had Amanda experienced such a pure symbolic vacuum. Never before had she been so far from the nearest human. Never had she imagined such sophisticated cybernetic pampering in the depths of the wilderness. Never could she have conceived of such perfect harmonious annihilation of the interface be-tween inside and outside, between the civilized and the natural realms.

Amanda was certain that whoever had manifested this artifact had meant it as a kind of koan.

Not one, however, which she was prepared to contemplate on an empty stom-ach, having driven all day and climbed a mountain on foot without so much as a Twinky since breakfast. She perused the contents of the freezer and selected egg-plant lasagna provolone, which sounded like it might microwave into something digestible.

By the time she had popped the sealed package in the microwave and set the timer, the sun had already slid behind the western ridgeline and the sky was purpling into twilight through the lattice-work of vines overhead, and a cooling breeze had begun to waft the resinous perfume of oncoming night through the windows.

She could *see* banks of the dome windows moving now in sequence, adjusting to the hour, the weather conditions, breathing the forest air, even as it tamed it to the heart's desire.

Amanda set an ebony lap-table inset with fitting nooks for plates and silver, selected a bottle of twelve-year-old Premier Cru St. Emilion, and when the microwave chimed, she killed all the lights except a pair of soft spots over a mustard-colored chaise, and ate her dinner off it al fresco.

Her eggplant lasagna provolone turned out to be far and away the best TV dinner she had ever tasted, layers of eggplant, pasta, and ricotta baked in a spicy sausage-and-mushroom sauce, with smoked provolone melted over it. The St. Emilion was a massive Bordeaux of a pedigree she never would have dared order in a restaurant.

It sure beat trail-mix and warm Gatorade at the end of a long day's journey into the wild heart of the continent! It sure was strange to recline on velvet cushions, centered in her own private candlelight circle, sipping fine French wine, and then to look up from her crystal and china and be reminded that that was exactly where she really was.

By now, all that was visible beyond the circle of civilized light was shadows and greenish shades of darkness. Just outside the range of her cybernetic campfire, she could hear the rustlings, and calls, and cries in the surrounding forest, while she sat there elegantly sipping a fine vintage out of crystal.

She laughed, as she extracted the koan's first level of satori.

"So this is what it's like to be human!" she said aloud.

There she was alone atop a mountain peak, a naked and essentially defenseless primate in the vast primeval forest. That breeze on her skin, that pine forest perfume, were the caress of the planet itself, no synthesized substitutes.

Never before had she felt more oneness with Gaia.

But being human meant that, even here, *you* decided how much oneness with nature you wished to take with dinner, which certainly did not extend to reverting to your natural precarious position in the food chain.

Amanda lifted her glass in toast to her unknown benefactors.

Whoever had manifested the Long Path monastery had been master of more than technology and craftsmanship. The technology was no more arcane than that at the disposal of Disney, and the craftsmanship, while impressive on an artistic level, was hardly unsurpassed anywhere else in the world.

But the Zen of what they had done with it was something else!

Sated, pleasantly exhausted with honest physical labor, pleasantly buzzed on a fine vintage, Amanda now felt ready to ride the Long Path to the end.

"Dim all lights to zero, Hadashi," she commanded.

The two overhead spots extinguished themselves gently into darkness.

A darkness that lasted only as long as it took her eyes to adjust to the starlight. It was a clear moonless night maybe ten thousand feet up a mountain two hundred miles and two hundred centuries from the nearest human exhaust fumes. The sky dazzled with stellar diamonds.

Amanda had never seen such a sky before. She was drawn out of the dome into the naked night, where the sky was a blaze of energy, the Milky Way a glowing gauze so sharp that its edges had contour, and it seemed as if she were seeing stars in subtle hints of color. Her backbrain floated on a resinous tide. The great shadowy body of the landscape fell away in starshine-glorified immensities. It seemed as if Earth itself was about to inhale her spirit.

Owls hooted mournfully. Unseen wings flapped through the branches. Far away a coyote howled, or was it a wolf, and another canine voice answered. Crickets chirped. Nightbirds called. Something catlike snarled.

Something else shrieked out its last moments in terrified horror.

And one of Maya's veils abruptly lifted.

Amanda had never really questioned the benevolence of nature or the synergy of the biomass or her place as a node in the interconnected web of all being.

But that one satoric scream had stripped a deep level of deception away.

Eat and be eaten, the law of the jungle, these were no literary metaphors out here. This was nature without Bambi and Thumper.

It was, she suddenly noticed, maybe twenty degrees colder out here than the human optimum temperature conjured up by the dome's machineries, and there was another sort of chill to the silvery sheen on the tree-shagged mountain slopes, a cool cosmic indifference that made her shudder.

In all that stellar vastness up there, she could detect no benevolent eye looking down. In all that forested vastness shimmering below her in the cold starlight from horizon to horizon, there was no glow of sentient encampment.

This was nature without illusions. This was the remorseless and mindless process of natural evolution.

For better and for worse, this was what humanity had transcended.

For here she was, at the end of an arduous journey as deep into that realm as it was possible to go, backwards in time to the days when we too were wee cowering timorous beasties. But she had only to turn, and there *it* was, banks of windows slowly closing for the night like the petals of an enormous flower, growing out of the landscape but not subsumed in it, right here at the end of that Long Path backwards from its future.

Craft, art, technology, food, wine, a cosmic sense of humor.

In a word, civilization.

"All lights slow fade up to level one," she commanded.

There in the darkness, soft buttery lights emerged, paler but warmer than the cool blued white of the indifferent stars, and the dome itself seemed to come alive, a cradle of vines cupping the wondrous man-made magic of Promethean dawn.

And the light of a high-flying jet or perhaps a satellite soared northward across the eternal firmament.

Amanda laughed in delight.

Even here, even now, even at the end of the Long Path from Hollywood to the Magic Mountain.

Wherever you go, there we are.

It had been a long day and there was much to sleep on.

Amanda was already half asleep by the time she crawled under the covers, turned out the lights, and sat there snugly ensconced, sipping the last of the wine in a heated bed rotating almost imperceptibly in majesty beneath a canopy of stars, serenaded by the Darwinian lullaby of the forest.

She finished her wine, sliding deeper under the covers just as she felt herself sliding into sleep.

But something within her resisted, made her conscious mind fight for more than its fair share of awareness, kept random bubbles of verbal thought intruding, kept her skittering about like a waterbug on the surface of the ocean of sleep.

Who had manifested the Long Path?

Why had she embarked upon it?

Had she gotten what she came for?

And if she had, what was it?

A flotsam of images swirled slowly up out of that sea within. The road through the windshield . . . Hadashi's face grinning at her over mushroom tea . . . a rude arrow nailed to a tree in the forest . . . Ralf's face popping through a TV screen as if it were a pane of taffy as he turned to look at her . . . Big Rock at sunset . . .

Elusive messages seemed to hover just beyond her comprehension in the sea of stars above, twisting, writhing, slithering out of her grasp . . . and . . .

And . . .

And she was riding right in the curl of the wave, surfing the interface, wakening into the Dreamtime in full sentient awareness.

There were techniques designed to induce such lucid dreaming, to awaken in a dream and know you are dreaming without shattering the reality in which you find yourself and so become the god of your own Dreamtime creation. To the extent that they *could* be mastered, Amanda had, and she even taught them, so she was no stranger to this Dreamtime lucidity.

So too was she familiar with this queasy slippery feeling of summoning up the doorway in the waking world and allowing imagery to emerge from the other side.

But what was happening now was both and neither.

She was lying in a bed in a magical glade deep in the woods atop mighty mystical mountains under preternaturally brilliant stars. She was as aware that this was true in the phenomenological realm as she was aware that she was presently experiencing the very same reality here in the Dreamtime.

There was an ecstasy in this strangest and most natural sense of unity, akin not to orgasm but to permanently sustained clitoral stimulation on the edge thereof. The feeling of enormous power moving through her in perfect balance was awesome. The very heavens above quite literally revolved about her. She was the very navel of the Earth.

She was the doorway.

Images were passing through her, the babbling brook of the collective unconscious bootstrapping itself out of the nothingness within, but if she stepped into that stream, *became* the void through which it was flowing, why then . . .

Why then, she *was* the Tao, the flow of symbol and image was merely her manifestation, and all she had to do was reach out from within as she was doing now and shape it to her sentient heart's desire . . .

And stand there naked beneath the stars like a goddess, why not? And spread her arms, and summon up tutelary spirits from the vasty deeps.

"Speak to me now, oh Genie of the Long Path," she commanded.

"My speech recognition circuits have been activated," said the androgynous voice she conjured. "What do you want me to say, Amanda?"

"Tell me who built the Long Path monastery, Hadashi," she said, here in the lucid Dreamtime where her word was natural law.

"Your wish is my command, little master," said Hadashi with a dry martini wryness unsettlingly inappropriate to an entity of her own imagining, subject to her creative control.

"It was built by Monkey People infesting the third planet of a crummy yellow sun in a tank town universe not particularly famous for its southern hospitality," Hadashi told her in Ralf's raspy voice as he emerged from the forest.

He was wearing a white ice cream suit over a saffron T-shirt. He had his old familiar friendly face, but his hair had turned into a curly black hedge shot with silver streaks of lightning.

"Hey, whose lucid dream is this?" Amanda demanded, clothing herself in the white dress she favored for performances on the Circuit just to be sure she could do it.

He shrugged as he walked out of the porch's bright sunlight and into the gentler illumination of her Topanga living room. "If we could answer that one," he said, "wouldn't we become the Buddha?"

"Why not?" said Amanda, and they did.

She sat there under the Bo Tree with Gautama himself, all heavy-lidded wisdom and golden smile, not as a disciple but as his doppelgänger, the two Living Buddhas in robes and full lotus regarding each other while another Amanda watched from an outside viewpoint.

"Whose dream is it now, wise guy?" that Amanda said.

"Why does a pilgrim cross the road?" rasped Ralf's voice out of Gautama's broad smiling lips.

"Does it have to be a road? Do we really need a pilgrim?" said Amanda's Buddha self in what she somehow knew was Archie Madden's voice.

"Jeez, do we gotta take a *meeting* on that?" groused Texas Jimmy Balaban.

"I'll have to check my appointment book," said Jehovah, perusing a set of stone tablets.

"Ri-ght . . . *now!*" sang He Whose Meeting May Not Be Refused in the leering voice of Johnny Rotten.

It was a crowded meeting. The boardroom table was six lanes wide and it kept climbing into higher and higher mountains. The whole gang was there. Balaban. Hadashi. Ralf. Buddha. Jesus. Muhammad. A pudgy nerdish man wearing a propeller beanie. W. C. Fields. Albert Einstein. Anyone who was anyone who was everyone.

He Whose Meeting May Not Be Refused chose to manifest himself as a young black yuppie dressed in whites for tennis, picture perfect down to the precise angle at which his powder-blue sweater was casually slung over his shoulder.

"Now I've gotta tell you Monkey People that the way the ratings look now, your show is not gonna get picked up at the end of the millennium, in fact there's not even a guarantee for another thirteen weeks," he said, his arms folded silkily across his chest, smiling a Buddha smile as he delivered the bad news in Ralf's imitable style.

"What can I tell ya, Slagheads, you're bombing out, we could do better numbers in your slot with cockroaches or slime molds, which is about all we're gonna have the budget left for after you assholes have finished stinking up the joint."

He looked straight at Amanda with brilliant slow whirlpools of stars in his eyes, and the bland capped smile of an Industry Lawyer telling you to trust him.

"I do believe you're right, Amanda," he said. "Let's seal up the body bag and give the turkey a decent burial."

"You told him *that*?" Jimmy Balaban groaned, and took a long gurgling pull from a bottle of Jack Daniel's.

"You asked who built the sets, Amanda?" Hadashi said.

"You asked who is the dreamer?" said the Buddha.

"Does there have to be a dream?" said Archie Madden. "Do we really need a dreamer?"

It was, she suddenly noticed, maybe twenty degrees colder out here on the mountaintop than in the comfy industry boardroom, the tree-shagged slopes far below her were rimed with ice as pitilessly cold as the burning black spaces in the cruel dead sky above them. In all that cosmic vastness, no benevolent eye would ever again look down on any hearthfire glow of sentient encampment.

"Will you lighten up already, fer chrissakes, Amanda, this is *your* production, remember!" Texas Jimmy Balaban reminded her.

"And we're all in it, Monkey Girl," said Ralf.

"Hey, it's *your* lucid dream, Amanda," said Bert Parks, "so *you* get to play Queen for a Day!"

"So since we're all just a format of your collective unconscious," said Archie Madden, "I guess we're going to have to leave it up to you."

He shrugged. The legion upon legion of faceless Industry Suits tiered up behind him nodded in the usual eerie unison.

"We've tried every format our best writers could come up with," Texas Jimmy Balaban whined. "The Vedas, the Bible, the Tao Te Ching, what do you guys call that, cut-rate schlock?"

"We've recast the part any number of times," said the Buddha in tennis clothes, as his face morphed into Amida, Krishna, Jesus, Muhammad, Hanuman, transmuting endlessly around the same changeless eyes full of void and whirling stardust.

Ralf shrugged. "You think we woulda stuffed an act like mine in the wayback if we weren't getting desperate?" he said.

"In Prime Time as tragedy," said Groucho Marx, "in the reruns as farce."

"God may not play dice with the universe," said Albert Einstein, "but if history teaches us anything, it's that when the show's sliding down the tubes and nothing else is working, He, She, or It, even as mortal men, is reduced to throwing a desperation Cosmic Custard Pie."

Ralf gave her a sickly smile. "And if *I* get the hook, kiddo," he told her, "there's nothing left backstage to go on but a chimp act and a gypsy violin."

"So here's the bottom line, Amanda," said the natty black youth in tennis togs with eyes of vacuum. "We need an avatar that can do at least a twelve share or the show gets canceled. We need a manifestation out of this Dreamtime of yours and into the collective zeitgeist that will persuade the bankers that we can turn the numbers around."

He favored her with the sweet reasonable smile of your favorite tyrannosaur. "It's *your* dream, Amanda, this is *your* format, but hey, no sweat, even *I'm* just a figment, right? But I *do* want it by Tuesday," said He Whose Meeting Could Not Be Refused.

He gave her a hearty wink fit to warm the cryogenic cockles of her heart.

"And I *know* you won't want to let me down."

7

"Whaddya mean, get my junkie ass outa here, whaddya think this fuckin' shithole is, the Waldorf-Astoria?" Foxy Loxy shouted, through the plastic window over the cash slot of the desk clerk's armored booth. "I been givin' this dump plenty a my business!"

The window was all scratched an' yellowy, so all you could sorta see was a mouth fulla brown teeth anna big nose witha pimple. The steel box itself was decorated with speed-freak graffiti an' a million years' wortha old snot an' squashed roach bodies.

There wasn't nothin' else inna so-called lobby 'cept the elevator door, the bottom of the emergency stairwell, a dirty blue couch give ya crabs justa look at it, anna framed picture of some kinda firehouse dog. Jeez, about the lousiest hooker flop inna Pig Apple still hasa crapper inna room, roaches are bigger'n most tricks' dongs, and this sleazeball is tellin' me I'm too fuckin' uncool for the joint?

"Heya, lady, whena is the lasta time, you look inna the mirror?" the guy behind the window said in some kinda weird Polack accent or somethin'.

"What the fuck you mean by that?" Loxy demanded.

"Whena isa lasta time you come inna here witha customer insteada for to sleep by yourself for the night?"

Somethin' hot an' white flashed down Loxy's arm from her brain, made her hand reach inta her bag and stroke the handle of her knife, how'd you like this up your asshole, you fuckin' creep! But she'd bust the fuckin' knife if she tried to ram it through the window, an' besides, it was a pale kinda flash, real tired like, she had saved up all week to make the price of a flop, and all she really wanted now was a fuckin' shower anna crash.

"I been takin' my johns elsewhere, whaddya think?" she said. "T'classier joints than this."

"Thatsa nice, so why donta you takea your crap to the Plaza ora the Hyatt, you doin' so good?"

"Because *I'm* payin' tonight, you fuckin' shitbrain, not my usual high classa john!"

Right, usual high classa john, these days a five-minute blow job or a stand-up between a couplea parked cars with one eye watchin' for the cops an' the other for the local pimp action!

Whether the fuckin' Space Ace had croaked or not, Loxy didn't know and didn't care, but a conversation witha cops was not her idea of a good time under any circumstances, an' she couldn't be sure they weren't after her ass. An' for sure a lotta pimps *were*.

Jesus fuckin' Christ, she hadn't actually *cut* another one of the motherfuckers, now had she, didn't really have to, whoo-ee, allya hadda do was scream an' wave a great big fuckin' knife crusted with dried blood in their faces, an' somehow they figured it really wasn't worth it t'give you no more shit, hee, hee, hee!

But was that any reason t'give her such a hard time?

This whole fuckin' month or however the fuck long it had been, was a harder an' harder time, what they call it, a vicious circle-jerk, the pimps keep chasin' your ass, so you gotta work streets where the action sucks so bad they don't care, so it's harder an' harder t'score tricks, so you gotta stay on your feet longer an' longer t'make the same bread, so you gotta do more rock t'keep goin', so you need more bread for the pipe, so you ain't got much left over at the end of a hard day's work for a flop, so you gotta crash inna subway or an alley or some such shit, so you don't get a chance to freshen up an' look your best, and okay, maybe you don't smell too good, so it gets harder t'score tricks and you're too scungy to even think about gettin' an overnighter, so you gotta drop the price, so you gotta work longer for the same bread, so you gotta feed more of it inta the pipe, so . . . so . . . so . . .

So I need a fuckin' hit!

Loxy let go of her knife handle, fished around in her bag, came up with her pipe and vial.

"Heya, whaddya think youra doing?" yelled the pimple-nose and brown teeth behind the window when she thumbed open the vial, spilled out the rock, flaked off a nice chip witha fingernail.

"Fixin' t'take a hit, whaddya think, asshole?"

"You can'ta do that ina here!"

"Oh yeah, I'm doin' it, now ain't I?"

"I'ma gonna calla the cops!"

"Hey, come on, don't get your balls inna uproar, hee, hee, hee," Loxy told him as she lit up an' took a nice big hit.

Whoo-ee! Zap-kapow!

Just what the witch doctor ordered, hah, hah, hah!

She exhaled, took another hit, an' took a great big bath inna Bright White Light, ah, *that's* more like it, an' hey, she was even feelin' kinda mellow toward the poor dumb shitbrain locked up in his little booth, so hey, what the fuck, why not. . . .

So she got down on her knees, natural position right, hee, hee, hee, stuck her mouth inna cash slot, an' blew a nice freebie up in his face.

Cough! Gargle! Some fuckin' growl in Haitian Chinese or Puerto Rican Russian or some such shit!

"You getta your crazy junkie ass outa here right now and you don'ta come back!"

"Hey, come on, grandpa," Loxy told him, getting to her feet, "y'supposed t'say *thank you!*"

"You get outa here or—"

"Or what, shitbrain? Y'know, I'm beginnin' not ta like your fuckin' *attitude*," Loxy told him. The fucker won't even rent me onea his roach motels, an' I give him a free hit anyway just 'cause I'm so cool, an' he's gotta give me *this* shit?

So she whipped out her knife and waved it in front of the window, rolling her eyes, an' shrieked at him inna spray of spit—hey, it works real well onna motherfuckin' pimps, now don't it!

"I WANNA ROOM RIGHT NOW OR I'M GONNA SLICE YOUR FUCKIN' DICK OFF!"

"That's it, I'ma callin' a the cops."

And the nose and mouth disappeared.

"Hey! Hey!" Loxy shouted, adding a few more scratches to the plastic window with her knife. "You fuckin' better not!"

"Yeah, youa notta gonna believe this, but I gotta a crazy crackhead smokin'a the stuff righta here inna the lobby—"

"HANG UP THAT PHONE YOU MOTHERFUCKIN' SONOFABITCH!"

"—anna she's trying to a stab ata me with a greata biga knife—"

Loxy almost lost it, as she scratched and scraped at the window with her knife, almost snapped the fuckin' tip off, she was so pissed off—

"—no, she can't a do anything, but you betta get a cop here—"

"I CAN'T DO ANYTHING, HUH, OH YEAH, DICKBRAIN!" screamed the White Tornado. And she whirled around, boogalooing inna rage around the fuckin' lobby lookin' for somethin' ta kill. Wasn't much. Just the stupid fuckin' dog picture onna wall behind the disgusting blue couch.

So she bashed out the glass with the handle of her knife, and ripped out the paper pooch's throat, an' gouged out its eyes, an—

"Hey! Hey! Stopa that shit!"

"*Stopa that shit*?" Loxy mimicked back. "Sure, why not, anything you say, Grandpa, maybe you like *this* better?"

And she plunged the knife all the way to the hilt inta the seat of the couch, whoo-ee! Again, again, and again! Stabbing, and tearing and ripping, felt so good, hee, hee, hee, moldy foam rubber, an' dead cockroaches, an' pieces of plastic shit flyin' all over the place as she ripped out the motherfucker's guts, hah, hah, hah!

"They gonna putta you in jail anna throw away a the key!"

"Y'know, you gotta point, Grandpa," Loxy shouted back. "Hey, it's been fun, but I guess I gotta split."

But the Power was with her. She grabbed the corpse of the couch by the two left-hand legs, lifted the whole fuckin' thing almost off the floor, an' kinda flipped it inna general direction of the desk clerk's booth before she danced out into the street laughin'.

Dexter Lampkin had committed himself to being Guest of Honor at LostCon months before Texas Jimmy Balaban called to tell him he had been summoned into the presence of Archie Madden on Tuesday.

"You're going to a science fiction convention? Well, for chrissakes, Dex, we gotta spend the weekend getting some kind of act together. Cancel."

"I can't. I'm the Guest of Honor."

"The which?"

The whole concept was difficult to explain to Balaban, as it always was to any normal human being who was not a member of Fandom.

"The people who read your books?"

"Well, not exactly."

It was easy enough to explain that the fans of science fiction threw enormous weekend bashes where they took over whole hotels to listen to their favorite writers bullshit, and have a masquerade, and watch movies, and buy books and comics and merchandising tie-in items, and party.

Texas Jimmy understood that since they picked up the whole tab for the Guest of Honor and his wife, that he couldn't cancel out at the last minute, it would be real lousy for his professional reputation. But Jimmy could not understand why any man in his right mind would take his wife with him to a long weekend in a hotel with several hundred female groupies.

"*Hundreds of groupies?* And you're taking your *wife*?"

Dexter found himself unable to explain *that* in a manner Jimmy found credible.

"Hey, come on, Dex," Texas Jimmy said in a voice drooling with pheremonic fantasies, "you can't tell me you wouldn't be screwing your ass off otherwise!"

"The odds are not what you think."

"A couple hundred to one, that's not good enough for you?"

Jimmy refused to believe in the concept of a fannish genotype. "Come on, Dex, you're putting me on, reading sci-fi makes them put on a hundred pounds and get funny eyeballs? It's a little early in the day for me to be *that* bombed."

They had both given up soon thereafter, after Balaban had begged him to at least *think* about the meeting with Madden over the weekend, pick some brains maybe, come up with what Madden probably wanted, whatever that was.

But Dexter remembered the phone conversation as he pulled the Alfa into the hotel parking lot, for the voice of sanity told him the moment he arrived at a convention hotel that for the duration it would *never* be too early to get bombed.

With hundreds of con-goers checking into the hotel at the same time, with book dealers hauling in cartons of their stock, with paintings and sculpture and fixtures arriving for the art show, even if you were Guest of Honor, it would be pure fantasy to pull your car up to the chaos of the entrance and expect a bellman to magically materialize. Instead, you found a space in the parking lot, and schlepped your own luggage into the lobby, around which the restaurant, cafeteria, bar and check-in desk were sited.

The fannish hordes had already occupied most of it.

Lines of grubbily dressed and overweight people with piles of strange untidy luggage stretched from the door to the check-in desks, creating the effect of a crowded bus depot in a Third World metropole. Scores of them lounged about the available free seating and reluctantly oozed into the bar where there was an overpriced one-drink minimum.

This early in the convention, few of them were in hall costume yet—a few Spocks, a brace of wall-eyed barbarians, a three-hundred-pound harem girl from Pluto, a squad of teenage mercenary spaceship storm troopers, nothing out of the ordinary to a jaded con-goer like Dexter—but even without them, Fandom presented an alien spectacle to the naive viewer.

Such as the waiters and waitresses, the desk personnel, the groaning bellmen, who were already getting that thousand-yard stare as it sunk in that they were going to be locked up for the next three days with several hundred of these people.

Most of the hotel personnel would never have seen so many grossly overweight people together at the same time, and even if they had, certainly not wearing T-shirts and capris and jeans and harem costumes in such perfectly blithe disregard of the exceedingly unfortunate fashion statement.

Globuloids, Bob Silverberg called them.

Even fans whose physiognomy would pass unnoticed did not exactly accouter themselves in a manner designed to reassure a nervously pretentious maître d'. T-shirts with incomprehensible slogans and amateurish illustrations with rows of buttons up and down them in similar mode. Toting shopping bags and backpacks and briefcases overflowing with books and magazines. Loudly gabbing and shouting with each other as if the whole place had become their own private living room, which, for the duration, it had.

Fortunately, one of the committee's volunteer navvies recognized him and ushered Dexter and Ellie through the slow-motion melee to the desk, and priority-summoned an actual bellman to show them to their suite.

What had been laid on was a parlor suite on the VIP floor. The con committee had placed a bouquet in the bedroom and a bowl of fruit on a parlor table, and when Dexter checked it out, he found bottles of Jack Daniel's and Remy under the bar counter and two six-packs of Bud and a bottle of Concannon champagne in the fridge.

"Not so bad ta be the King," Dexter said, doing a bad Mel Brooks imitation, and giving Ellie a little hug.

Even if it is king of the Monkey People, a Ralf-voiced demon insinuated in his ear.

For Dexter could not help viewing science fiction fandom from an inverse Marxist perspective. Groucho had voiced his skepticism about joining any club that would accept him as a member, and Dexter had his doubts about the hypocrisy of sucking up egoboo from an unwholesome tribe of nerdish wonks.

But "egoboo" was itself a fannish concept, and a cunningly clever insight into human reality.

And boo for the ego was what it was all about.

You could be a maladjusted three-hundred-pound postal clerk or computer jockey in the mundane world, but here, if you published an amateur fanzine, or created a hall costume that people remembered, or worked on enough con committees, or collected more of something than anyone else, or just knew how and where to hang out, you could become a Big Name Fan. BNF had been famous for being famous long before Andy Warhol got *his* fifteen minutes' worth.

Pure uncut egoboo—ego-gratification with as much relationship to achievement, or talent, or any form of intrinsic worth, as that felt by a newborn avidly sucking its mother's tit.

The lust for egoboo was maybe *the* basic human drive, and a saving grace of Fandom was that this was not only openly acknowledged in these circles but with a sense of humor.

With the writers however, aka the "Dirty Old Pros," it got a little more twisted. A science fiction writer at a science fiction convention could indeed fuck his brains out if he could achieve a sufficient state of suspension of disbelief in the reality of his own actions, and at a con the means of dissolving critical judgment were impossible to avoid.

There were few science fiction writers who had not committed indelicacies at these things that they would wish to have expunged from collective memory, emphatically including their own, and Dexter was not one of them.

In the mundane world, science fiction writers were not exactly figures of glamour fawned upon by hordes of beauties ripping their clothes off as they hung on your every word. Nor were they a tribe of suave and handsome sophisticates able to charm the same out of trees.

Tending toward the endomorphic spread as a genotype themselves, science fiction writers were ordinary guys or worse when it came to scoring with women. So how much fastidiousness would such an ordinary guy maintain when dropped down for three or four days in a sealed starship where the very pleasure of his company could become a means of counting feminine coup, if by a good deal less than his wet-dream fantasies?

Better I don't remember! Dexter thought, stealing a sidelong glance at his wife. He was not above getting himself a little at a con from time to time, not that he would have been eager to whip out wallet-photos of most of his easy conquests. But as far as he was concerned, those of his colleagues who denied their wives their fair share of the egoboo of a Guest of Honor turn were, well, cads.

Dexter still loved his wife after all these years, if not with passion, then certainly with a sense of lifelines inextricably entwined, and their marriage being the old-fashioned single-career affair that it was, with a feeling of responsibility for, well, *husbanding*, her sense of self-worth, of pride in her own identity.

And science fiction writers' careers being what *they* were, such a Guest of

Honor weekend was about the only time when she got to bask in his reflected glory, and more to the point, these conventions were the only place where she still enjoyed a measure of her own fannish fame.

For though in a certain sense it galled him to think of it to the point where he might slug someone who said it to his face, his wife, Ellen Douglas, was still a Big Name Fan.

These days, her fan activity might be confined to letters and pieces in fanzines, but though it had been years and years since Ellie wowed 'em in next to nothing at all at a masquerade or served on a convention committee, Fandom's institutional memory was long, and still remembered her glory days as Queen of the Convention Hop.

That had been the Ellen Douglas he had wooed and won and/or vice versa in plain sight of a publisher's con party! They were both riding pretty high already, Fandom relished public spectacle and juicy gossip, Ellie had it and was dressed to flaunt it, so why not give them a turn as Scott and Zelda?

So after a round or two of public gropings and smoochings, "smoffing" as the fanzines had it, Dexter had snatched up a bottle of tequila from behind the bar in a flamboyantly open gesture, and off they went to her room, having declared their open intention of banging each other's brains out.

Dexter found his cock stiffening with the memory, fuzzy as it was. The fabulous Ellen Douglas was at the time the best-looking woman Dexter had ever bedded. Brian Aldiss had declared fame the ultimate aphrodisiac, but the drools of envy on the part of his male colleagues as he exited with his prize had been no mean added turn-on either.

It had been the fuck of Dexter's life never to be topped or repeated, a space-time nexus into which no one could slide his dick twice, a youthful blaze of glory ignited by psychosexual synergies which might not bear the weight of excessive mature introspection.

So it was not without a cotton-mouthed trepidation that he gingerly pulled back the sheet to reveal the waking reality of last night's dream girl.

And what to his wondering eyes, snoring lightly on the bed next to him was not the dreaded three-hundred-pound globuloid but what could fairly be said to be the most beautiful naked woman he had encountered in fleshly reality.

He just lay there watching her for a long time while willing her eyes to open.

When they finally did, *she* looked *him* up and down appraisingly before smiling and delivering the line that was to win his heart.

"Nice to see," she said, "that you're not just another pretty mind."

Dexter smiled at his wife, at the fabulous Ellen Douglas of yore, and found, to his uneasy delight, that the sight of her here in the Guest of Honor suite at a science fiction convention was giving him a hard-on of an insistency seldom achieved out there in the mundane marital world.

Here within this charmed circle, this housewife and mother was still *Ellen Douglas*. Still a Big Name Fan rather than just another faceless writer's wife. Still a glamorous legend in the collective memory of Fandom. And she had matured into an older version of her younger self, which, while it might not draw her much attention in a Beverly Hills supermarket, was still good enough to let her shine within a con hotel's walls.

And while *he* might not have maintained the Adonis-like perfection that he never had in his youth either, he was still a reasonably normal specimen of middle-aged primate maturity.

Which was to say as Guest of Honor and Big Name Fan at a science fiction convention, they were both still far enough up the local pear-shaped curve to pass for hot shit.

Dexter Lampkin kissed his wife lightly on the lips and then he went to fetch the free champagne. He popped the cork and brought two foaming glasses back.

"Not so bad ta be the King and Queen," he said again as they clinked them, turning the line into something softer and sweeter than what was dreamt of in Mel Brooks's philosophies.

Even if it's the King and Queen of the Monkey People?

"Noblesse oblige," said Ellie, and guzzled her champs down.

"I'll drink to that, Zelda," said Dexter, doing likewise.

A half hour's lovemaking with the latter-day incarnation of the fabulous Ellen Douglas, like most incarnations of convention fantasies, might not have been quite up to the memory of glory days, but it had been sweet enough to send him out into the maelstrom of the convention wearing virtual rose-tinted granny-glasses.

Which stood him in good stead when the elevator door opened on the tenth floor and he was immediately confronted by a battle-ax-wielding barbarian in plastic chain mail, a Hagar the Horrible helmet, and a pair of urinous jockey shorts.

"Uh, uh, uh, me berserker!" he squeaked in a high-pitched semblance of a Viking battle-grunt as he whirled the ax about his head.

Dexter's present state of magnanimous glow allowed him to ignore this hall-costume asshole with a sense of amusement rather than pique, as well as the other costumed "convention characters" he encountered on his way to the bar.

The main bar tumbled out into the lobby, where the crush around the check-in desk had more or less evaporated and the fans had taken over, an invasion from Irwin Allen's Mars from the stupefied viewpoints of the airline hostesses and pilots constrained to pass the gauntlet of mutant ninja globuloids and punk tribbles in furs on the way to their company-booked overnighters.

But the back of the bar room, where you could sit around a semicircular bar in dim neon-tinted gloom or huddle at the surrounding tables, was well out of the fray, and, at this stage at least, this was where the writers would hang out.

There were less than two dozen people here in the deep end, two tables of whom consisted of an overweight fantasy writer in a flowing rose gauze gown holding court with her recently pubescent fans, and a gaggle of animation writers trying to corner the producer of a show that had already ripped him off.

So Dexter defaulted to the bar, where Ollie Peterson sat sipping bourbon with George Clayton Johnson. An odder couple could scarcely have been dreamt up by a cartoonist's imagination. Ollie looked like Sargent Slaughter stuffed into an author's elbow-patched jacket, and George, with the visage of an Indian brujo replete with long flowing gray warrior locks and an incongruous desert-rat beard, looked like the Old Man of the Mountain and had probably done twice as much hash.

Ollie wrote "hard science fiction," tales of the exploration and colonization of the solar system with currently envisionable technology, science fiction's own brand of Socialist Realism, the sort of stuff that had placed the youthful feet of so many real-life astronauts on the path to the Moon.

George seemed to live on ectoplasm. For years at a time it would seem he wrote nothing at all. But his credits, while few and far between, tended to the major. Half of a successful science fiction novel which became a film and a TV series. A handful of prime-time television shows. A major motion picture staring Frank Sinatra and his Rat Pack at the height of their sleazoid glamour. In the long in between, he tossed balls in the air like any other out-of-work Hollywood writer, and he talked. Oh, how he talked!

"Hello there, Dexter, Ollie and I have just come up with a brilliant plan to rescue the space program. Within five years we can have a huge station in space and be on our way to the stars!"

Dexter ordered a bourbon and gave Ollie an inquisitive look.

"George wants to sell it to Disney," Ollie said with an air of fatuous amusement.

"Space Station Mickey!" exclaimed George. "A zero-gravity Disney World in space!"

Dexter drummed his fingers impatiently on the bar. This was not something to listen to sober. "Disneyland in orbit?" he muttered weakly.

"And a feature film about its heroic construction *actually shot* in space!"

"George doesn't seem to have any idea of what it would cost," Ollie said blearily.

"Sure I do, Ollie, I figure on a production budget of four billion dollars."

"Three times as much," Ollie muttered.

"Not if we use those empty fuel tanks you told me about, Ollie," George told him. "That's what inspired my stroke of genius."

"Fuel tanks?" said Dexter.

Ollie got his own brand of faraway look as he sipped at his bourbon. "Every time NASA launches a Shuttle they have to *burn extra fuel* to dump a great big empty fuel tank into the ocean," he said.

"They are great big empty mothers the size of barns, aren't they, Ollie? Easy enough to pressurize and install life-support equipment. You could put them together like a space erector-set. You could do it all with a modified Shuttle for half the price of NASA's silly little toy space station . . ."

"*Jesus Christ* . . ." Ollie whispered, and Dexter could see that he had been drawn into George's web.

Mercifully, Dexter's drink arrived. "Aren't you forgetting something, George?" he said, taking a hefty slug.

"I don't think so, Dexter."

"Why would Disney spend four billion dollars on this thing?"

George grinned. "Be real, Dexter," he said. "We are talking the biggest grossing film of all time plus a completed orbital Disneyland, plus a spin-off TV series, no, wait, why not, a whole *series* of them plus three times the merchandising tie-ins of *Star Trek*!"

"*Four billion dollars' worth,* George?" Dexter reminded him.

"Don't be silly, Dexter, they'd only have to come up with a fraction of the money, the rest would come as long-term loans from banks against both the movie and twenty years of profits from Space Station Mickey, besides which they can lay off the entire construction cost as a legitimate production expense, so the whole thing *never* shows a taxable profit . . ."

Dexter downed another slug of bourbon. "I don't get it, George," he said, "what's in it for you?"

"You mean besides the spiritual satisfaction of rescuing our civilization from its terminal decline and putting our species on the path to transcending the petty planetary bounds of Earth and striding like gods to the stars?"

"Yeah," Dexter said dryly, "besides all that."

"Why the screenplay for the feature, of course, Dexter!" George Clayton Johnson told him. "And if our agents structure the deal carefully enough, the series pilot, a piece of every show, and our fair share of the merchandising rights too."

"What do you mean *our* agents, Red Man?" Dexter drawled.

"Well, since Ollie gave me the inspiration, and you are my friend, and I am such a generous fellow, I'm willing to bring you guys into the project," George said magnanimously. "I've got the entire concept in my head, Ollie will get the science right, and then all you have to do, Dexter, is turn it into a screenplay, and I'll pitch the project to Disney."

For a mad moment Dexter was almost tempted. "You, ah, have an in to Disney, George?" he said.

George Clayton Johnson beamed at him brilliantly as only George could beam. "Why, I was counting on you for that, Dexter," he said ingenuously. "You sold *The Word According to Ralf* to Archie Madden, didn't you, Dexter?"

"Uh, well, not exactly, it was my format, but—"

"Well then, surely your friend Mr. Madden—"

"I've never even *met* Archie Madden, George—"

And then a lightning bolt hit as he said it—

"—but I'm taking a meeting with him on Tuesday."

Pick some brains Texas Jimmy had told him?

Where would he find a more fertile brain so promiscuously avid to be picked than that of George Clayton Johnson?

Dexter leaned forward. "Let me buy you something a little better than that bar whiskey you're drinking, George," he cooed. "You too, Ollie."

He ordered three double Wild Turkeys straight up and laid it out for them.

"So Balaban thinks that if we don't come up with something to make Madden believe that the ratings will pick up significantly, there'll be no second thirteen weeks."

"And you wish to have the benefit of my instinctual brilliance?" George said. "You want to pick my brains? You want me to give you the magic word that will charm Mr. Madden?"

"Something like that," Dexter admitted.

George Clayton Johnson grinned at him. "Why, I'd be delighted, Dexter," he said. "And I can give it to you right now."

George might have an ego the size of the Ritz, but his generosity with the products of his imagination, as long as it did not involve putting them down on paper, was legend.

Pause. Beat. Nod of the head.

George grinned even wider.

"Fandom!" he said.

"Oy," said Dexter, a sound that emerged from his lips like that of a tire deflating.

Down through the years, George had come up with any number of crackpot schemes to seize the reins of Fandom, including a plan to move them all to lightly populated Nevada and vote him in as the philosopher king of a science fiction utopia.

Not that he was the only one.

Ever since L. Ron Hubbard had proven that it *could* be done by turning a fannish cult into the Fortune 500 Church of Scientology, science fiction writers of a messianic and/or pecuniary bent had been trying to roll their own with somewhat more modest success.

Ever since Gene Roddenberry had tapped into the fannish network to save the original *Star Trek* and then watched it exfoliate into a whole clade of spin-offs, producers of anything remotely science fictional had dreamed and schemed to do likewise.

Ever since his own pass in this direction, *The Transformation*, listening to this brand of bullshit had given Dexter an upset stomach.

"How different is your problem from what Roddenberry faced in the very first season, Dexter?" George said, leaning forward and locking eyes with Dexter. "They were going to pull the plug on *Star Trek* too."

"We all know the story, George," Ollie said tiredly.

George ignored him. "Gene got a few thousand fans to dump *zillions* of letters on NBC and Paramount, saved the show, created a great tribe of Trekkies, and changed the course of television history and popular culture."

"I don't think Archie Madden is gonna respond real well to a letter-writing campaign, George," Dexter told him.

George Clayton Johnson's eyes sparkled with the purity of their intensity. "Of course he won't, Dexter," he said, "but do you not think he might be suitably impressed if he could come to believe in the prospect of a *Ralf* fandom?"

A bubble of bourbon soured Dexter's stomach. "Urk," he said.

"Against their will, the Suits of the shark pond were taught a happy lesson as they watched science fiction fandom turn a canceled TV show into a major media marketing industry," George went on, his voice suffused with a superlubricated loquacity. "By now every executive in Hollywood with the intelligence of an earthworm knows how Gene did it, but they'd all be quite pleased to be had in the same manner, now wouldn't they, Dexter?"

"Shit," said Dexter.

Dexter had been present at a party where the host was accosted angrily for having slipped LSD in the punch by the outraged date of a lady who was sure she was on acid. But there was no acid in the punch. She had simply been having an intense conversation with George.

Now Dexter was beginning to understand how she must have felt.

George could just about suspend anyone's disbelief in anything.

"Whisper *Star Trek* in his ear?" Dexter said, unable to deny that the notion had a certain nauseous credibility.

"Great minds run in the same circles," said George.

"But . . . but how would you go about creating a Ralf fandom, George?" Dexter found himself asking.

George Clayton Johnson shrugged. "*I* wouldn't," he said.

"Why not?"

George laughed, broke eye contact, took a sip of Wild Turkey, smacked his lips appreciatively, and the spell was broken.

"Because it's not *my* project, now is it, Dexter?" he said.

Dexter wasn't what he would've called properly sloshed when he and Ellie arrived at the Meet the Pros Party, but at least he had a decent anesthetic buzz on.

And of course, he needed it.

The Meet the Pros Party was being held in the main hotel ballroom. Most of the folding chairs that would convert it into an auditorium had been stacked on the stage, and a bar had been set up to the right of the entrance. A wall of noise smacked Dexter in the face as he made his grand entrance; three hundred or so people not noted for the civilized modulation of their conversational tone all trying to make themselves heard over the collective din they were creating.

An unruly mob scene surrounded the bar, where three bartenders were doing their inadequate best to pour watered drinks at high prices as fast as the fannish hordes could consume them. A miasmic odor of sweat, booze, ripened sweatsocks, Cheetos crumbs, crushed peanuts, and stale secret farts was already beginning to build.

To be fair about it, Dexter had to admit, stuff any three hundred people in a room this size, and the resulting noise and odor might not be that dissimilar. But the visual impact of fandom en mass was something else again.

It wasn't just the preponderance of overweight people, but that whatever of how much fans had, they dressed here to flaunt it, they let everything hang out, most of which you wished they didn't.

172 • NORMAN SPINRAD

Gross paunches peeked out under triple-X promo shirts and over belt lines. Immense asses strained neon pink and chartreuse capris to the awful bursting point. Size 49-triple-D-cup boobs filled out sweaters or bulged out of elephantine décolletages. Hairy thighs the size of tree trunks depended from cutoff jeans and Bermuda shorts.

And these were the fans who *weren't* in "hall costumes."

Maybe two or three dozen people *were,* and how often did you walk into a crowded room and behold barbarians, Mr. Spocks, a giant pink rabbit wearing a space helmet, an overweight harem girl painted blue and sporting antennae, and assorted other characters from stories no one cared to have admitted writing, holding converse with the citizenry as if it were the most natural thing in the world?

Norman Spinrad once told Dexter a story that he had arranged to meet Timothy Leary at con hotel to go out for dinner. Only they never made contact.

"How come you didn't show up, Timothy?" Spinrad asks Leary a few days later.

"I did, I was there for about half an hour but I couldn't find you, and that was about all I could take," says the veteran guru of a thousand acid trips. "Those people were just too weird for me."

But for this weekend they could not be too weird for Dexter D. Lampkin, Guest of Honor, who was constrained to smile, and nod, and make idle conversation, and press the flesh, and pretend to know people he could not remember.

It often appalled him how few names his memory could put to their faces, though all of them seemed to know him personally, to remember conversations they had had years ago, to remember things about him that he had forgotten himself, or wished to; a phenomenon that sometimes made him worry that maybe his brain was going.

He had to remind himself that within this little pocket universe, he was famous as no writer could ever be out there in the mundane world, famous like an actor or a rock star—the fans not only knew his name, *they recognized his face. Hundreds* of them had actually spoken with him. Over the years, he had autographed books for *thousands* of them.

Easy enough for thousands of fans to remember their encounters with a few score writers, impossible for those writers to remember meeting each of those thousands of fans.

"*Nice ta be the king, huh?*" Ralf's voice seemed to rasp in his buzzing head.

"Noblesse oblige," Ellie reminded him sotto voce, giving his hand a little squeeze. "And do try not to get too blotted."

———

As far as Dexter was concerned, the problem was getting blotted enough.

Blotted enough to sign endless program booklets. Blotted enough to make earnest idle conversation with nerdish kids who shouted right in his face, spraying him with spittle. Blotted enough to do his duty as Guest of Honor and mingle with the fannish proletariat rather than join most of the other writers huddling in little closed circles against the wall or escaping to private-room parties or the bar.

Why do I do this? Dexter found himself wondering woozily.

He had *never* gotten blotted enough to believe that he did it to sell books. Since there were less than ten thousand fans in the whole country, if all of them bought a copy of your paperback and no one else did, the sales figure would still be catastrophic.

By now, Dexter was at least blotted enough to face the fact that in his younger, hornier, and less discriminating days, he had done it mainly to get laid. Where else, face it, Lampkin, could you find yourself awash in so much avidly willing pussy of *any* kind?

But the tide of testosterone no longer ran hot enough to suspend his disbelief in the fuckablity of ninety-five percent of what was available at a con party like this. Dexter D. Lampkin might get himself a little at a con from time to time when he chanced to encounter a willing fan who came up to his minimum standard of pulchritude, but it had been a long time since he had come to a convention with the simple glandular imperative to get his ashes hauled, period.

Dexter gulped the last of his so-called screwdriver and made his way to the press of fans around the ballroom bar to secure another.

The sad truth of it was that he did it for the same reason just about every science fiction writer of his acquaintance did it: egoboo. SF writers could no more resist the free lines of the straight uncut stuff laid out here than junkies could resist smack. Dexter would be hard pressed to think of a single one who eschewed conventions entirely—not Spinrad, who blamed them for most of the genre's literary ills, not Ellison, who flagellated the fans mercilessly with his razor-sharp tongue, not even Maltzberg, who had written several vicious heartfelt satires on the subject.

"Can I get you a drink, Mr. Lampkin?"

A female voice had called out to him from the front of the crowd around the bar. "A screwdriver!" Dexter shouted without conscious consideration.

A couple of minutes later, he found himself wishing he hadn't, as she emerged from the wall of fans bearing two plastic cups of yellowish liquid.

Somewhere between twenty-five and thirty. About five-foot-two. She might have weighed anywhere between a hundred and ten and a hundred fifty pounds, for she was wearing a red muumuu that hid most of what it hinted at; heavy bra-less breasts, meaty thighs, sloppy ass, bulging belly. Long bleached-blond hair cascaded over her shoulders. Her chubby face was creamy white, save for the blotches of angry acne rouging her cheeks. A tiny rose was painted, or maybe tattooed, on the right nostril of her well-formed nose. Her thick lips glistened moistly with a purplish lipstick.

Her eyes were large and green and dramatically framed by heavily made-up brows, lids, and lashes and they were locked on him like sniperscope laser beams.

"Here you are, Dexter," she said in a voice obviously made sultry by theatrical act of will as she handed him his drink. "My name's Cynthia. I *can* call you Dexter, can't I?"

"Uh . . . thanks, uh Cynthia . . ." Dexter grunted suavely.

"It's the very *least* I can do for a man who's given me so many hours of *plea-sure*," she said breathily.

Dexter took a big gulp of the drink, not knowing what else to do. "I, uh, have?" he muttered inanely. Where the hell was Ellie?

"You're my absolutely *favorite* writer," Cynthia said, oozing forward well into his body space until he could smell the heavy jasmine perfume mingled with her sweat, all but feel the heat of her flesh as she stared up into his eyes with absolutely unabashed adoration.

"I am?"

By fannish standards, she really wasn't all that bad—well, at least what he could presently see of her—and Dexter knew all too well that there had been a time when, in another half hour or so, with a couple more drinks under his belt . . .

"*Of course* you are, Dexter," she said. "I've read everything you've ever written, it's one of the dozen most significant bodies of work in the entire history of the literature, and I've read *The Transformation at least* a dozen times."

"You have?"

"The world would be *such* a better place if it had gotten the recognition it de-served."

Dexter found himself gazing straight down into her eyes as she leaned even closer, her breasts about an inch and a half from pressing against him, if only to gauge the sincerity or lack of same therein.

How could he not? Was she not expressing what he believed himself in the privacy of his own heart? What was he *really* doubting if he doubted this fat fan girl's intelligent sincerity?

"Am I embarrassing you, Dexter?" she said somewhat more softly, her gaze never wavering, the sincere worshipfulness, the naked lust, or Christ, was it *love*, in her eyes held up to him like an offering on a silver platter.

"I'm not exactly used to hearing it said quite like that," Dexter admitted, favoring her with a little smile, for what a cad he would be not to.

"Of course you're not," she said. "I've read every word you've ever written, Dexter Lampkin, so I think I'm as informed an expert on your spirit as any woman could be who has not had the honor of fucking you."

Jesus.

Cynthia leaned even closer, allowing her breasts to touch his rib cage. Dexter could see her trembling.

Surely by now he had had enough booze for it to have finally really affected him, for Dexter found his knees turning rubbery, his head whirling around, his entire being sucked down into those eyes regarding him worshipfully as if he were a god.

Or was that just a bullshit story he was telling himself to avoid admitting just how deeply touched he really was? Face it, Lampkin, was this a maiden fair instead of an overweight homely fan girl, you'd be sweeping her up into your arms.

As it was, that intelligent gleam, that utterly frank and open admiration for precisely what he wished to believe of himself, in the eyes of this poor unlovely human creature, was now bringing him to the verge of tears.

Cynthia smiled a brave little smile up at him, full of sad wisdom. "Any time, Dexter, anywhere," she said softly, running a fat pink tongue around those thick moist lips, and just lightly touching his hand. "It would be the finest moment of my life."

"There you are, Dex," Ellie said waspishly behind him.

Dexter yanked his hand away from Cynthia's, whirling around blush-eared to confront his wife just like the poor little hubby caught with his pants down in some dumb film, and probably with the same stupid sickly grin.

Ellie looked into his eyes appraisingly, gave him a tired knowing grimace. "You look like you've just about had enough."

"Thank you *so* much for *talking* to me, Mr. *Lampkin*," Cynthia quacked in a moronic voice, painting an expression of ducklike fannish stupidity across her face.

"Come on," Ellie said, grabbing his hand, and dragging him not unwillingly away.

Nevertheless, something made him glance back over his shoulder.

Cynthia stood there meeting his gaze with total intensity. She smiled. She slowly slid her right forefinger deep between her thick wet lips, withdrew it ever so slowly, and blew him a big puckery kiss.

Dexter managed to drag himself to his eleven o'clock panel on "Science Fiction and the Noosphere," held in a secondary room, with only a mild hangover that kept him from saying very much but at least allowed him to look alert. There couldn't have been more than a hundred people in the audience at this bleary hour. Ellie was there in a show of solidarity and, disconcertingly though hardly unexpectedly, so was Cynthia, seated front row center with one hand resting on the inner thigh of her voluminous jeans, her eyes meeting his with unwavering ardor every time his gaze was drawn in her direction, which Dexter tried rather unsuccessfully to make as seldom as possible.

His three o'clock panel, "Sci-fi Trash and Critical Mass," promised to be a crashing bore, but after a lunch with Ellie and the Farmers featuring cocktails and two bottles of chablis, and after cadging a couple of quick tokes in a stairwell courtesy of an obliging fan, Dexter was ready to face it.

Or so he thought as he took his seat on the stage of the largest function room after the ballroom, with seats for about five hundred, about half of which were filled, and yes, there was Cynthia, front and center, a sight he was beginning to resign himself to seeing.

Take a couple of Big Name Fans with reps as fanzine reviewers of low-brow space opera and elves-and-dragons schlock, inveigle an innocent academic critic into taking part in the animal act, add a science fiction writer with pretensions to literary ambitions, namely Dexter, toss the question "Can science fiction be literature or would it be better off back in the gutter where it belongs?" into the piranha pond and watch the denizens thereof sink their fangs into each other for the delectation of the fannish masses.

Dexter, cast with the academic as a defender of literary elitism against the voices of fannish populism, might have had a serious go at the Philistines if his academic ally hadn't been a prime dickhead whose incomprehensible deconstruction of the ineffable made Professor Irwin Corey seem like a model of clarity.

Occasionally Dexter would attempt to get a few words in edgewise just to keep up appearances, but his heart really wasn't in it. Toward the end of it, he chanced to glance in the direction of Cynthia, something he had been assiduously avoiding. As their eyes met, she pulled a ballpoint pen out of her purse, and, smiling knowingly back at him, held it in her crotch with one hand, while masturbating it with the other.

God help him, Dexter was unable to prevent himself from grinning and nodding his agreement.

The seats had been laid out in the ballroom for Dexter's five o'clock panel, "SF in
the Media," and there must have been four hundred people in attendance, including virtually all of the writers at the con, pros and wannabes, hoping to hear
something that might aid them in cadging a scripting assignment.

This was not an entirely unreasonable expectation, since the panel was a cattle
call of everyone who had a sci-fi film or TV show to promo—the dimwit producer of a low-budget horror flick, a flack from the Star Trek federation of spin-
offs, a representative of the official Star Wars fan club, someone from the Sci-fi
Channel, three Saturday-morning cartoon story editors, and Dexter himself, "Head
Writer" of *The Word According to Ralf*.

With an hour for the so-called panel, it was obvious that this wasn't going to
be a discussion at all, that each of them was going to have about five minutes to
rap out their breathless spiels in sequence.

They had seated Dexter down toward the left end of the table, between the horror
movie producer and the story editor for a Saturday-morning sword-and-sorcery
cartoon called *Avenging Angels*, and then started from the right.

This meant that Dexter was constrained to maintain a mask of rapt attention
for the better part of the hour while enduring a series of promo spiels, schlockmeister flim-flammeries, and studio flackeries that had all the appeal of being
marinated in a vat of tepid cat-piss. Ordinarily, he wouldn't even have been in the
audience, preferring to spend the time in more intellectually gainful pursuits, such
as getting plastered.

But there he was with the rest of them, and your assignment, Lampkin, should
you choose to accept it, which you already have, asshole, is to go thou and do likewise for *The Word According to Ralf*.

So for the first time in many a convention moon, Dexter was actually giving
serious thought to what he was going to say on a panel. After all, he had a large
amount of money riding on it: his share of the second thirteen-week pickup.

True, the fate of the show hardly rode on the support of a few hundred
convention-going fans, but the bug that George Clayton Johnson had planted in
his ear wouldn't stop buzzing in his brain, still less so as he contemplated his fellow panelists. These people, after all, had been sent here by studios and production companies to win friends and influence Fandom. What was it that they and
George knew that he wasn't quite getting?

It seemed to him that he was about to capture some elusive meaning hovering just below the surface of the wall of noise, something he already knew and had only to remember, something to do with chaos theory, with the way a tiny change in initial conditions could—

"Well, now it's time for our Guest of Honor himself, Dexter Lampkin, to tell us something about *his* show—*The Word According to Ralf*!"

Shit!

The brilliant perception, whatever it might have been, flitted through his mental fingers, and there he suddenly sat—staring stupidly at about four hundred people without a thought in his head.

There was nothing for it but to turn off his brain and run his mouth.

"Well, uh, we're not hiring writers because we don't need them and couldn't afford them if we did, if you haven't seen it, the format's real simple, just an audience off the street, and an exiled comedian from a pretty damn rotten future talking to them, so, er . . . ah . . . so . . ."

So?

Dexter's tongue seemed to freeze on the word like the needle of an old phonograph caught short in a bad groove.

So?

So what, Lampkin?

And then, as he stared out over that sea of upturned faces, that flowerbed of glazing eyes, it came to him.

"So why don't I just *demonstrate* the format?" he said with what he hoped was an eagerly inviting grin. "I'm no Ralf, but go ahead, ask me anything you want to about the show!"

An endless beat of stupefied silence.

The moment seemed to expand into a horrendous eternity, giving Dexter far more than all the time he needed to contemplate what Ralf must experience up there on the stage trying to work off a collection of yuks scooped up at random off the street. No wonder Ralf's spiel tended to turn so hostile! If *he* could've thought of a cleverly vile one-liner, he too would've said just about anything to break the deadly silence!

"Yes, I've got a question for you," a familiar female voice called out from somewhere near the middle of the audience, and Cynthia stood up. "Uh . . ."

She paused, she locked eyes with him, her lower lip seemed to tremble, and it came to Dexter that she had broken the silence and stood up to rescue him without the foggiest notion of what *she* was going to say either.

In that moment of public exposure, of embarrassed hesitation, of less than ept bravery in his service, she won a little piece of his heart.

"Uh, *where* did you get that *tacky* set from?" she said. "It looks like something you stole from the Ackermansion's garage!"

And she grinned winningly as she sank back into anonymity to a decent spattering of laughter at the inside joke, at the reference to Forrest J. Ackerman's houseful of books, moldy old magazines, bits and pieces of old monster-movie props, and vastly assorted ancient futuristic dustcatchers, the genre's tawdry collective unconscious made attic artifact.

"Hey, closer than you think!" Dexter said. "The backdrop really is a blowup of a *Planet Stories* cover we borrowed from Forry Ackerman's collection, and the space ship set comes from a stinker called *Starship Cowboys* that lasted about a week and a half!"

A few jagged titters, but thanks to Cynthia, the awful silence had at least been broken.

"Yeah!" someone shouted out without standing. "How do we get tickets for the show?"

"Uh, ah, there aren't any tickets, you just show up at the studio," Dexter answered.

"How do you decide who gets in if there's too many people on line?"

Dexter shrugged, grinned foolishly. "Unfortunately, we haven't had to deal with that problem yet," he admitted to a few more dry laughs.

"Is Ralf an *actor* playing a *part* you wrote for him, or is he *real*?"

There over toward the back of the audience stood all three hundred pounds of Oscar Karel—the Truefan and former space program scientist who had engaged the star of *The Word According to Ralf* in a learned discussion of the recycling of human shit into junk food.

" Real?" Dexter stammered.

"An *actor* or a real *comedian* from a real *future*? Science *fact* or science *fiction*?"

"Are you *serious*, Oscar?"

Oscar Karel's headed bobbed up and down like that of a jack-in-the-box on the end of its spring, with the same sort of fixed grin painted on his face and a similar goofy stare. But on him what was conveyed was a weird species of earnest intensity.

"Uh-huh, uh-huh, uh-huh," he chanted.

Time seemed to stop for Dexter again, and in that long moment he believed that he understood chaos theory all too well. For he himself would seem poised to become one of those microcauses about to generate mighty but inherently unknowable macroeffects.

As he sat there contemplating an audience of four hundred science fiction fans awaiting his answer to this exceedingly dumb question, he understood what George Clayton Johnson had been trying to tell him—what these producers and flacks were doing up here with him, what Gene Roddenberry had discovered, what L. Ron Hubbard had perhaps lucked into himself.

This was one of those rare moments when you could give the universe a teeny-tiny push, and it would move.

How much, and where, however, was inherently unpredictable.

He could generate a Ralf fandom right here right now.

Maybe it would encompass half the people in this room. Maybe it would be enough to save the show. Maybe it wouldn't.

The very mathematics which told him that he could generate such a macroeffect by telling an itsy-bitsy lie also told him that all he could do was toss his little pebble into this fannish tidepool and watch the ripples spread in the quantum sea.

But he *could* do it. They *wanted* him to do it.

Fans were addicted to what they called the sense of wonder. They were not only willing to have their normal human disbelief in the marvelous suspended, they *yearned* for it. It was what drew them to science fiction in the first place.

In *Cat's Cradle*, Vonnegut had invented the concept of the "foma," the noble lie which makes you feel strong and brave and happy. Had not Vonnegut also stated the obvious when he declared that all fiction was lies?

Could it not be said, therefore, that all *lies* were *fiction*? That what he was about to do, and oh yes, he *was* going to do it, was no worse than the foma he regularly committed within the pages of his books?

"Well, Oscar," Dexter said, "I don't really know. What I *can* tell you is that if Ralf isn't the greatest actor the world has ever seen, then he surely believes he's a time-traveler from the future. He's *never* out of character, not for a minute. I can truthfully tell you that whatever he is or isn't, the Ralf you see on the tube is the Ralf *everyone* gets."

He paused, having brought himself up short. For having made the decision to tell a little white lie, he now found, upon listening to the words as they emerged from his mouth, that, much to his surprise, he was telling the truth.

All he had to do was get off without destroying the suspension of disbelief he had already created, without really having to lie at all.

"Me, I find it hard to believe he's a phony," Dexter found himself saying. "Leaving two possibilities: he's nuts, or he's telling the truth."

He shrugged. "Seems like the mundanes and the tabloids say phony or nuts, because the ratings are worse . . ." He paused for half a beat, and ghosted them a wink. ". . . are worse than *Star Trek*'s first season on NBC."

Dexter smiled ingenuously. "But *we're* not mundanes, are we? We deal in the possible, not the probable. And it's just barely *possible*, isn't it, that our poor descendants up the line on Deathship Earth, in their utter desperation, will indeed stretch their dwindling resources to the limit, and the best they'll be able to manage will be to send back a broken-down comic as their last hope."

He shrugged again, he scrunched up his face, roughened his voice, essayed a crude Ralf.

"But hey, the last joke's on them, 'cause what do *you* do with your own future's last chance, Monkey People?"

He paused, then he delivered the line, he did the deed, he threw the pebble.

"The ratings suck, so you cancel it after thirteen weeks," he said.

Beat. Wink.

"Or who knows, maybe not."

Convention masquerades had once been masquerade parties, but they had long since devolved into masquerade contests, where fans spent many months and beaucoup bucks creating elaborate costumes paraded across a stage in front of an audience in a deadly serious competition for prizes and trophies.

No thanks, was Dexter's iron-clad rule. Fortunately, Ellie liked judging the damn things, so it was easy enough to placate disappointed con committees by fobbing off such Guest of Honor duties on her, and repairing to whatever pro party was available for the duration.

At a World Science Fiction Convention or a really large regional, the pros would huddle at the Science Fiction Writers of America suite, no fans allowed, or better yet at a publisher's party suite where *they* paid for the booze. Here though, there was neither an SFWA suite nor an editor with an expense account. Dexter's Guest of Honor suite was the largest private venue available, he was otherwise on the Con Committee's tab, so what the hell, he sprang for some basic cheap stuff smuggled in to avoid the hotel corkage fees, and threw the Saturday-night pro party himself.

But alas, Dexter found that after a long day of booze and blather, his party energy had evaporated, nor had he reached the state of sotted stupidity where it was possible to believe that he could prop himself up with more. So he found himself wandering listlessly about his own party like, well, like a novelist, observing the proceedings from the detached third-person viewpoint of the proverbial Man from Mars.

Here I am in a room full of my esteemed colleagues, he thought sourly. Intelligent all of us or we wouldn't have gotten this far. Visionary dreamers at some point in our lives even if it was just the age of twelve or we would never have chosen to write the stuff.

And where are we?

Drinking crummy booze while hordes of our socially retarded and strangely shaped fans parade around in costumes that were originally based on our characters but which, like Fandom itself, have long since become expressions of the collective schlockgeist of sf rather than anything of our willing literary creation.

And what are we doing with our lives?

Most of the people here had probably just handed in the fifth volume in their latest trilogy and had already started peddling the game rights, and most of the people still naively dedicated to writing decent novels were either hanging by their economic thumbs or making it on the Hollywood hackwork they did to survive.

Like . . . what's his name, the guy who's Guest of Honor at this thing, with a groupie after his bod and stars in her eyes. Who, while standing here in his free hotel suite, bemoaning the unwholesome schizoid tendencies of the weirdos picking up the tab, has just nevertheless not been above his own attempt at using them to keep his money machine on the air?

Lampkin, Lumpkin, something like that, wasn't it, the guy who tried to do it to save the world with a book many long years ago?

The first time as naive messianic tragedy, the second time as self-serving schlock-meister farce.

It was time to see what the boys in the backroom might have.

The dope smokers at a convention suite party usually repaired to the bedroom thereof. Half a dozen people were sprawled on and around the king-sized bed, and a couple of rather parsimoniously thin joints were indeed going around.

Louise Farmer reposed against the headboard, holding court with Jack Kahn and Irene Farrow. Squatting at the side of the bed, bogarting both of the joints, were those three famous convention motormouths, George Clayton Johnson, Emory Pollock, and the great Cameron Carswell himself.

Pollock had once been high up at S.R.I., a laboratory complex so arcane that there were no words behind the initials, where anything they could con intelligence agencies into funding mated in the shrubbery to produce sci-fi toys for the spook-shop boys.

George was, well, George Clayton Johnson.

And Cam Carswell was the great Dr. Carswell himself—triple threat particle physicist, astrophysicist, and cosmologist, author of *Quantum Cosmology*; perennial also-ran in Nobel categories yet to be invented, and lifelong science fiction fan.

"—*mass* can't but *information* can, geodesics exist in four-space, don't they, Cam, all sorts of phenomena arise in temporal loops outside of sequential causality—"

"Such as, Emory?"

"Such as time and the universe itself, bootstrapping themselves into existence out of the random quantum flux! Before the Big Bang, no statistically significant events, hence no time. Before time, no four-dimensional matrix for statistically significant events to occur in, hence no causality—"

"Hello Dexter, have some dope," George said, offering him a joint, "we are engaged in a serious discussion of life, the universe, and everything."

Dexter took a hit, sinking slowly onto the floor as he exhaled.

"Actually, Dex, we were talking about time travel," Cam Carswell said. He was a large, loosely fleshed man in his sixties with shoulder-length gray hair and the brilliant dark eyes and infectious smile of a genius-level pixie. "Emory has been trying to convince me it's possible, but I haven't smoked nearly enough of this stuff yet."

"Not time *travel*, Cam, even I'm not stoned enough to believe you can flip *mass* up and down the timelines like a bead on an abacus! But why can't *information* exist as a standing wave pattern in a massless atemporal matrix?" Emory Pollock babbled.

"Transtemporal standing waves in a massless matrix?" Cam Carswell mused.

Pollock nodded enthusiastically. "Causes produced by their own effects!" he exclaimed. "Effects calling into being their own causes!"

Cam Carswell took a big hit off his joint, blew out a long plume of smoke. "An Ouroboros of temporal quantum determinism wherein shit exists in an endless feedback loop with Shinola!" he exclaimed grandly.

"Like public opinion polls or the Nielsens!" George said.

Cam looked at George narrowly. "Would you mind explaining that, George?" he said.

George grinned brilliantly. He snatched the joint from Dexter's fingers and took a puff for emphasis.

"Expectations of lousy future ratings based on past Nielsens create the very budget squeezes and stupid rewrites in the present that create them!" George proclaimed.

"If the president decides to nuke the whales because the polls show his ratings will go up by seven point three percent as a result, and he *does*, and they *do,* what then, I ask you, is the cause and what the effect?"

Cameron Carswell laughed. Dexter snatched the joint back from George, realizing that he was already feeling better.

For this was what really kept him coming back to these things.

Dexter had gone to Hollywood parties. He had attended learned scientific symposiums. He had listened to some of America's foremost literary intellectuals declaim their papers at the MLA. He had attended meetings of PEN and the Author's Guild and had even been lured once to Mensa on the broken promise of getting laid.

The intellectual level in the smoke-filled bedroom of a pro party at your average medium-sized convention like this was superior. The number of brilliant and entertaining lunatics was higher. The mix was far more sophisticated in some ultimate sense than anything in the groves of academe or the tanks of think.

The highest pleasure of con-going was the talk.

"By that Klein-bottle logic, George," said the sooner-or-later Nobel Prize winner, "Dexter's comedian from the future is like Schrödinger's cat."

"*How* is Ralf like Schrödinger's cat, Cameron?" Dexter straight-lined.

"The cat in the box lives or dies depending on the random quantum state of a particle, so not only can't you know whether it's alive or dead till you open the box, according to the Copenhagen Interpretation, it isn't *either* until you do and collapse the probabilities," Carswell said. "So Niels Bohr and George would agree that a man in the present claiming to be from any given future exists in an inherently indeterminate quantum state until the ratings collapse the show and the future in question does or does not emerge from the probability wave."

"Yeah, right," Emory Pollock gabbled, "I mean, if you've got an actor playing the part of a man from a made-up future, he could be making that future real by the effect he has in the present, or if a future sends someone back, he could cancel the very timeline that would have existed to send him back if they hadn't sent him back to . . . uh . . ."

Pollock grinned feebly at Dexter. "You can use that if you like, Dex," he said, "but I would appreciate being credited if the story gets published."

"Gee thanks, Emory, just what I needed, a dumb idea for a time paradox story," Dexter drawled. "Haven't you forgotten something?"

"Forgotten what?"

"The future's always made up!" Dexter told him. "From the viewpoint of the present it doesn't yet exist. And so, until it becomes its own present, it never can."

"Maybe," said Cam, and in a tone of voice that reminded Dexter than while this was Cam the longtime convention fan speaking, it was also Dr. Cameron Carswell, his good buddy the Nobel candidate.

"Maybe?" Dexter said.

"And then again, maybe not," said Cameron Carswell. He smiled a rather serious smile at Dexter. "This one you *can't* use unless perhaps we collaborate on a story. I've been trying to get one published for eighteen bloody years, so I can't afford to give any ideas away. Want to hear?"

"Sure, Cam," Dexter told him, feeling a delicious thrill, the thrill of private intellectual congress with a scientific savant up there with the immortals.

And, he realized with a sudden burst of empathetic insight, a thrill that must not be all that different from what the teenaged fan inside that great scientist must feel getting to pitch his story ideas to real-live published science fiction writers!

"The future is indeed nonexistent to any observer in the present, and so all we can do is make up stories about it, but it isn't made up to *itself* when its probability wave front collapses and it happens, now is it?" Cameron Carswell said, snatching the joint from George.

"Then it will become as real as we are," he said, and paused to fortify his train of thought. "Or so those caught in the causality of a clockwork universe might be led to think." He grinned at Dexter. "But of course cosmological sophisticates such as ourselves know better, don't we, Dex? We know that the nature of our comprehension of time is an illusion of our genetic programming."

"We do?" said Dexter.

"In the relativistic universe events do not occur as beads strung neatly along the string of time, they exist as points in a four-dimensional space-time matrix," Carswell said. "We only perceive time as our one-way linear passage through the other three dimensions from birth to death because that's the way our consciousness works, one might easily enough imagine a species which perceives it otherwise, and I've read at least a dozen stories which do—"

"Which leads to the conclusion that we're really living in a *deterministic* universe where cause, effect, and free will are illusions too!" Dexter blurted.

Cameron Carswell waved his joint over his head in the manner of a center sinking a hook shot.

"Two points, Dex!" he said. "The relativistic universe *is* a deterministic universe, an Einsteinian God not only doesn't play dice with events in it, He's not about to give *us* a chance to roll the bones either."

He paused, took a hit, and blew out a ragged cloud of smoke in a failed attempt to do a ring.

"*However . . .*" he said.

Cameron Carswell paused dramatically to survey the room, and yes, Louise, Jack, and Irene had ceased their conversation and all eyes were on him.

"However, Albert was wrong about quantum mechanics," he said. "Events in space-time *cannot* be neatly defined as nice clear points. One must picture the whole four-dimensional matrix that we call the universe as a volume bounded in space in the conventional manner, and bounded in time by the Big Bang and the Big Collapse and all events within not as fixed points, not as deterministic particles, but as *probability waves* oscillating within it, so that nothing actually happens until its probability wave is collapsed into actuality by an observer. . . ."

Cam paused. "Are you with me this far?" he said.

Maybe it was the dope, maybe it was the writing that had gone into *Chaos Time,* maybe it was working with a guy who claimed to be from the twenty-second century, maybe it was Cameron Carswell's formidable powers of explication, probably it was the conjunction of all four collapsing the probabilities into this moment of clarity, but Dexter actually thought he *was.*

"There's only one thing wrong with that picture," Cam said. "Do you see it?"

Dexter actually thought he did.

"The probability wave can *never* really collapse!" he exclaimed. "Because each event is observed by a multitude of observers up and down the timeline and *each observation* changes the probabilities!"

"Two ears and the tail!" exclaimed Cameron Carswell, beaming delightedly at the prize pupil. "From the point of view of observers caught in the illusion of linear time such as ourselves, probability waves collapse definitively into events, as our present moves up the time-axis through them toward the future. But from the point of view of some Ultimate Observer sitting outside our universe, all events exist as probability waves oscillating about their attractors, and therefore *nothing ever definitively happens!*"

"I've been at story conferences like that," said George.

Cam Carswell laughed, leaned back, took a little puff.

His demeanor changed entirely. Now he was just another fanboy wannabe writer anxiously seeking the approbation of the pros. "All of the . . . *time.* And *that* is my story idea!

"Well, Dex," Dr. Cameron Carswell said nervously, "am I on to something?"

Dexter shrugged. "The Nobel maybe," he said, "but where's the story?"

"You don't get it?" Cam said unhappily.

" 'Fraid not."

Cam sighed. "What it implies is that since all events in four-space exist as probability waves, since nothing ever happens definitively, the so-called future *can* affect the probability oscillations of the so-called past just as easily as the past affects the probability oscillations of the future!"

"But . . . but that's a tautology, Cam!" Dexter pointed out.

"The *universe* is a tautology!" Cam proclaimed. "Time *travel* isn't possible because linear time is an illusion, so there's nothing to travel *through*, but the so-called future *could* make changes in the so-called *past* that change the so-called future precisely *because* there's no causality involved, just a feedback loop perturbing the probability waves in four-space."

He paused. He puffed nervously on his joint.

"Well?" he said anxiously.

"Well *what?*"

Dr. Cameron Carswell, future Nobel Laureate if the probabilities collapsed properly onto their just attractor, peered owlishly at Dexter with the sweet bashful hopefulness of every teenage wannabe sf writer who had ever babbled his creative heart out to him at a con suite party.

"Well, what do you think, Dex?" he said in a shy little voice that Dexter found infinitely endearing. "Do you think I'm finally on to something we could turn into a story that might get published?"

Dexter's schedule for Sunday was mercifully light, just an autograph session in the huckster room at three o'clock and his Guest of Honor speech at five. Having made dozens of speeches at cons entirely off the top of his head, he felt no need for serious preparation, but it *did* seem like a good idea to stay sober and straight until after the big event.

So he ate a long leisurely nonalcoholic room service brunch before descending to the "huckster room." Time was, they had been known as "dealers' rooms," when they were filled with tables of scruffy semiprofessional book and magazine dealers lovingly purveying rare collector's items, moldy old paperbacks and magazine back issues, and amateur fanzines. But that was once upon a time in a galaxy far, far away, and a convention huckster room these days was a roomful of hucksters indeed.

Aisles of folding tables had been set up in a big windowless space in the lower depths of the hotel. Many of them had been turned into kiosks by cardboard flats advertising the tie-in items of the Star Trek, Star Wars, Marvel, and assorted other sci-fi commercial empires. A whole section was devoted to chain mail, armor, and assorted medieval and sword and sorcery weaponry, most of it plastic. You could buy video game cartridges, sci-fi T-shirts, comics, costume items, DVDs both pirate and commercial, slick commercial fan magazines, trolls, hobbits, tribbles, smurfs, vampire munchkins.

And here and there a few anachronistic old-timers still quixotically sold books.

They had set up a place for Dexter and they actually had a supply of three of his most recent books, not something that was guaranteed in these days of the instantly vanishing backlist.

And so Dexter sat down and signed.

He didn't draw a nonstop one-a-minute line halfway down the aisle, but at least there were relatively few embarrassing moments when he was left staring into space with no one at his table.

One of these days, he vowed, as he always did at these things after three or four fans had showed up with shopping bags full of old used books of his to sign without buying any current item, I'm gonna refuse to sign anything they don't buy new on the spot.

But he never did. It took much less time and effort to sign everything placed before him than to argue about it. And how could he not feel a fondness for those whose burgeoning shopping bags demonstrated that the only reason they weren't buying was that they already owned every book he had written?

The endless procession of LostCon program books thrust in his face by people who probably had never read a damn thing he had written got a signature and a reasonably polite response to any direct question.

That most of these were about *The Word According to Ralf* rankled on the ego-boo level as much as it seemed like a good sign on the level of pragmatic ratings survival.

But Dexter had only to glance at what surrounded him to be reminded that to half the people here, Norman Spinrad and Harlan Ellison were known only as the authors of famous episodes of *Star Trek*, and Dexter D. Lampkin, your genial Guest of Honor, was the creator of *The Word According to Ralf*.

It might have depressed him even more had he not become obsessed with quite another matter as the digits on his watch counted ever so slowly toward his four o'clock release, namely Cynthia.

All through the autograph session he had been dreading what he had supposed would be her inevitable appearance with what would no doubt be a shopping bag full of his books, and yet perversely enough, as the session approached its end without her advent, he found himself feeling somehow disappointed, let down, almost pissed off.

And then, at about four minutes of four, after he had signed two final program books, and the space in front of his table had become quite empty, and he was thinking of making his exit a wee bit early, there she was.

She was wearing a loose-fitting red-and-white-patterned African dashiki against the front of which her heavy breasts bulged suggestively. Her hair had been carefully brushed out into waves that broke over her shoulders. Her face was made up with something which gave her the shiny plastic tan of a surfer mannequin. Her brows and lashes were done in a black so deep it was almost purple, but the eyeshadow was gone, and on her lips she wore only something which made the natural shade glisten. She still had the little rose on her nostril, apparently the tattoo was genuine.

"Hello, Dexter," she said, "I hope you were expecting me," she said.

"Uh, hi, Cynthia, well, uh to tell you the truth, I was a little surprised when you didn't show up earlier."

Her eyes locked on his. She smiled at him, an openmouthed smile, the tip of her tongue protruding slightly. "I know how to be patient," she said throatily.

Dexter found himself constrained to smile back. A queasy feeling was building behind and below his breastbone, a slightly nauseous twinge of dreadful precognition.

And then he realized that she carried no bag full of his books, nothing at all to sign, not even the convention program.

"You, ah, didn't bring anything for me to sign?" he said in some confusion.

"Oh no, I brought my entire collection of your books to the convention with me," she said.

"But then—"

"I'm such a completist, and they're so *heavy*!" She looked straight at him. "I've got them all in my room," she said evenly. "I thought it would be much . . . nicer for both of us if we just went up there and had our own little private . . . session."

She didn't leer, she didn't lick her lips, she didn't wink, but then again she didn't have to. Dexter knew all too well what he would be getting himself into.

And with that very thought, with that bubble of visceral self-loathing still churning in his breast, he felt a treacherous stirring farther south, and he knew, that oh yes, he would.

Why was another matter. Dressed like this, made up like this, she didn't look all that bad, but he certainly wasn't turned on by her, and worse still, he knew full well that the naked reality would be something for which he would be hard-pressed to keep his pecker up.

He sighed. He shrugged. He made a show of checking his watch.

"Well, what the hell, I've got an hour till my speech, so why not?" he said casually. "Wouldn't want to let my most sincere fan down."

Jeez, Lampkin, he thought even as he said it, could that line of fatuous self-serving bullshit be *the truth*?

Dexter had expected Cynthia's room to be strewn with dirty laundry, assorted fanzines, sticky paper cups, and half-empty packets of munchies, which in his experience was the state of your average fan's room by the last day of a convention.

But instead the room was neat and virtually spotless. Sandalwood incense smoldered in the lap of a little brass buddha, and the only other items not of standard hotel issue were the books layed out neatly on the bed.

His books.

First editions of every book he had ever published laid out in chronological sequence. All in excellent condition and protected by clear plastic jackets, even the paperbacks.

Dexter was rendered quite speechless.

"Have a seat," Cynthia said. She smiled. The only chair was a spartan thing jammed under the dressing table. Dexter sat down gingerly on the bottom end of the bed.

"I'll be right back," Cynthia said and disappeared into the bathroom.

Dexter half-expected her to emerge stark naked with a rose in her teeth, but instead, she emerged mercifully dressed as before bearing a water glass and an open bottle of Courvoisier. Dexter hoped he avoided showing his relief as she filled the glass and handed it to him.

He took a grateful gulp, retrieved a book at random from behind him, reached for the ballpoint in his breast pocket.

"Oh no," Cynthia said, staying his hand with her own, "I've got something special."

She flitted over to the night table and withdrew an unusually thick pen from the drawer. She returned to the foot of the bed, knelt there between his dangling legs, and handed it to him in the manner of a squire presenting the mystic sword to his knight in some high fantasy novel.

It was a Mont Blanc fountain pen with a black cap and barrel. "Dexter D. Lampkin" was chased on the barrel in golden Gothic script.

"Oh, I couldn't—"

"Of course you could!" Cynthia interrupted forcefully. She folded her legs under her. She gazed up at him with admiration so total and sincere that he found it impossible to believe that he merited it. "A gift from a sincere admirer who will smile every once in a while remembering that you have it."

What could he say to that?

Not a goddamn thing. All he could manage to do was take another drink of cognac, and autograph the first book to her.

If you counted the short story collections, which she had, Dexter had published twenty-six books, and it certainly seemed to him that under these circumstances each one required a personalized dedication.

Sincerely trying to say something meaningful but at least slightly different to the same person twenty-six times in a row was an arduous literary exercise, made more poignant, but hardly easier, by the way Cynthia squatted there between his legs gazing up adoringly at him while he did it.

He found himself taking another drink of cognac every time he laid one book down and reached for another, and every time the level in his glass sank much below the median level, Cynthia topped it off from the bottle.

By the time he had finished signing the last book, he was drunk enough to feel nicely buzzed, genuinely touched, and warmly happy.

He laid the final book back on the bed, capped the Mont Blanc, smiled down at Cynthia, and clipped the pen snugly into his breast pocket, using the motion to check his watch surreptitiously.

Four thirty-seven. Twenty-three minutes till his Guest of Honor Speech.

An excellent excuse to make a genteel departure.

He finished the last cognac in his magically bottomless glass, made to rise. "Well, I've got to—"

"Wait!" Cynthia said, laying a palm atop his right thigh.

It froze him.

"Please wait, Dexter," she said in quite another voice. He could see her body shaking, he could feel her hand trembling.

"You've been everything I could've asked for," she said softly. "You've been a prince, Dexter Lampkin. This must happen to you all the time, and—"

"I—"

"Please let me finish," she said, stilling him with a tremulous hand to his lips. "You're the writer I most admire in all the world, and I know I'm just a fat little fan who's been mooning around the whole convention after you—"

Jesus.

"Look, Cynthia—"

"—and you've treated me like a real human being."

Tears glistened in her eyes as she looked up at him. "I'll never be able to tell you how much that is going to mean to me for the rest of my life," she said. "I admired you before I met you, and now I know I could love you."

Oh my God!

She nibbled at her lower lip, and there was a look on her face of such forlorn bravery that Dexter found his heart going out to her, his own eyes burning.

"But I know that's not to be," she said. "You're a married man, you've got a daughter, and . . ." She actually managed a smile. "And the last thing you need is an overweight fan following you around from con to con."

Dexter couldn't help it. He found himself placing his hand on hers, it was all he could do not to gather her up in his arms and hug her. He felt exalted. He felt a perfect fraud. He felt terrible.

"You don't have to worry, Dexter," Cynthia told him. "I'll never bother you again, you've given me all that I could reasonably expect, and I'll not repay your kindness by doing anything to endanger your marriage or make you uncomfortable at conventions."

She paused, she averted her gaze. "But . . ." she said.

"But?"

"I . . . I know I have no right to ask this, but . . . but it would make everything complete, it would make me so happy, it would . . . it would . . ."

"Go ahead, say it," Dexter told her, and he couldn't help it, he reached out, cupped her chin, and raised her eyes to meet his. In that moment, he knew that if she asked, he would be an absolute shit not to fuck her, and if his dick wouldn't—

"Let me suck your cock," she blurted.

"*What!*"

"Just this once, I'll never ask to do it again, I won't tell anyone, please let me do it, I want to feel you come and keep a piece of you inside me forever," she babbled, as if summoning up the courage to say it in four-letter words had unblocked a torrent.

Dexter couldn't move. He couldn't say a word. He couldn't even think.

"Okay?" Cynthia said softly, reaching tentatively for the zipper of his fly.

"Okay," Dexter finally managed to mutter hoarsely.

There were tears running down her cheeks as she unzipped him. It might not have been the most expert blow job he had ever experienced, but it was certainly the most sincere, and when at considerable length, he came, he knew that in the years to come, when the world seemed dark and his life seemed shitty, this would be a moment whose light he would remember. An adulterous act he could be proud of.

By then, it was four fifty-eight, and no time for lingering farewells. She tucked his dripping prick back into his pants and zipped him up so he at least wouldn't face the audience in the ballroom with his fly open.

"Good-bye, Dexter D. Lampkin," she said, as she opened the door, "I know you'll give a wonderful Guest of Honor Speech."

And, for the first, and last, and only time, she kissed him.

"Ah, and here he is now, our Guest of Honor . . . *Dexter D. Lampkin!*"

Dexter staggered up the stairs to the stage, the audience applauded, and there he was behind the podium on the ballroom stage in front of maybe six hundred people, out of breath from the mad dash from Cynthia's room, reeling from cognac and confusion, with his dick still leaking the after-effects of a blow job he could never explain to anyone into his jockey shorts, and not a coherent thought in his head.

He let the applause go on far too long as he stood there catching his breath, which probably would have felled a horse, and desperately trying to get his shit together.

"Sorry I'm late, folks," he finally managed to say, "but I was stuck between floors with a Klingon, a gorilla in a human suit, and a three-hundred-pound transvestite hobbit, you know how the elevators are at conventions."

The thud of silence which greeted this attempt at levity was all but audible.

"But seriously, folks . . ." Dexter yammered lamely, trying to find a friendly face to focus on. But the lights had been dimmed, and a spot thrown on him, and all he could make out was the reflected gleam of hundreds of impenetrable eyeballs.

Fuck it! Dexter thought.

Indeed, in the state he was in, he wasn't quite sure he hadn't just *said* it.

"Seriously folks," he repeated, "I've given a couple dozen of these Guest of Honor speeches, and you've probably heard a couple hundred, so what should I do, stand up here and lay on the bullshit about the wonderfulness of my latest novel, or tap dance down memory lane like Fred Astaire in a propeller beanie . . . ?"

This was greeted with a low subliminal rumble like the awakening ire of an enormous lion.

But this wasn't *really* the Roman Coliseum, no matter what he said, he wouldn't *really* get torn to pieces. This was just a Guest of Honor speech, fuckin' fans is all, they weren't even paying him a penny a word to do this, he didn't even quite know why he was doing it, so how could they expect him to know what he was doing?

"So I'm just gonna speak from the heart this time around," he said, "and I hope it won't embarrass you."

Which was a lie, of course; if he was lucky, a foma. For if there was anything that made science fiction fandom squirm and sweat, it was the open expression of emotion.

But Dexter, empowered with loquacious moral courage by cognac, his dick connecting him to the poignant memory of an arcane moment of twisted tenderness, *wanted* to make them squirm and sweat, *wanted* to pierce that nerdish facade, *wanted* to speak to the deeper humanity of these socially maladroit, maddeningly unselfconscious, highly intelligent, cult-prone, subspecies of Monkey People.

And who knows, in the process maybe figure out why a nice boy like himself was standing up here drunk out of his mind in front of them in the first place.

"Fans are Slans, right, mutant super boys and girls in hiding," he proclaimed grandly, "perceiving the future destiny of humanity as a transcendent space-going species evolving upwards and onwards, while the poor benighted mundanes presently in charge of this world have trouble seeing far enough ahead of themselves to keep from tripping over their dicks as they rush like lemmings toward the terminal abyss of planetary catastrophe."

Whoo-ee!

Not a sound was to be heard, nor could Dexter read a single expression, but something had changed in the pheremonal soup out there, his backbrain could *smell* that he had them. Why not? Wasn't this sort of masturbatory crap just what they most loved to hear?

"Science fiction and its gallant band of secret heroes and heroines cleverly disguised as meek mild-mannered Fandom are the hope of the world, the best and the brightest, aren't we?" he declared, switching off some inhibitory circuit in his brain that ordinarily would have prevented him from babbling on like Benito Mussolini.

And why not, it was probably just an inside joke between him and himself anyway, he folded his arms across his chest and mugged at them just like Il Duce.

"You *do* believe, don't you?" he said. "Science fiction can save the world! You know it's true because science fiction has already *changed* the world. It's inspired generations of boy geniuses and would-be space cadets to actually become scientists and astronauts! It's given the world the space program, and cyberspace, and the Church of Scientology!"

He slammed both palms down on the podium and gazed upwards like a comic-opera tent-show preacher. "We got the power!" he raved. "Give us three or four visionary science fiction novels on top of the best-seller lists, and *we* will *move* the *world*!"

The room had begun a stately rotation like a space station spinning on its axis to create artificial gravity, a subtle hint that he was quite shit-faced, that perhaps he was even making something of a fool of himself.

But how could that be possible before such a Spaceship of Fools? And even if it was, was it not in a good cause, whatever it might be? And if he went on, would he not learn what it was?

So he lowered his head, straightened his arms, using them to lean against the podium for support, stared unflinchingly ahead into the muttering vacuum, and, morally fortified by the memory of Cynthia's touching courage, dared sincerity.

"You think I'm insulting you, don't you?" he said in a much more intimate tone. "You think I'm taking the piss out of you, right? Well, maybe I am. And maybe you need it."

He shrugged, he did his best to plaster a sheepish grin on his face. "But if I'm taking the piss out of you, I'm taking the piss out of myself, now ain't I?" he said. "Because I believed it too."

The muttering died down into silence.

"Sure I did," Dexter said softly, thinking of last night's stoned-out bull session, thinking back over decades' worth of cons, thinking about what it had been like to be surfing the wave of the future, to be naive enough to believe that what you did could and should move the world.

"I believed that there was more to what I was doing than writing wish-fulfillment power-fantasies for adolescent nerds. I saw the Monkey People of planet Earth destroying their world, and I knew where the true transcendent destiny of our species lay, don't we all. . . ."

And despite all the booze, despite the pathetic ludicrousness of what he was doing, or perhaps because of it, Dexter found himself teleported back into the sensory memory of what it had felt like to believe in himself with such egomaniacal intensity, the electricity in his bones, the warmth in his breast, the brainless courage in his heart.

"So I tried to save the world through science fiction myself, any of you out there still remember?" he said. "I wrote a book called *The Transformation*, which I was sure would do the trick, hey it worked for Hubbard and Roddenberry didn't it, so why not in a higher cause, and I made a public schmuck of myself running around the convention circuit like a chicken with its head cut off preaching transformational salvation to the only ten thousand people who knew what the fuck I was talking about, to *you*, oh visionary superheroes in globuloid clothing, in hall costumes, in Trekkie drag. And what happened?"

Dexter laughed, he even laughed sincerely, for it was a pretty good joke, wasn't it, even if it was on him. He shrugged. He threw up his hands.

"It sold about five thousand hardcovers and fifty thousand paperbacks, and then it went out of print, what else?" he said.

A few titters of nervous laughter.

Dexter found himself stepping out from behind the hierarchical security of the podium, and moving shakily forward to the more egalitarian front of the stage.

"So you see, folks, I've got *experience* making a public schmuck of myself like this," he said. "It's easy once you know how. All you've gotta do is go to a science fiction convention, look around at what you see with open eyes, and think about what's really trapped inside all that costumed blubber with an open heart, about what we all really are and what we could be, and just say what you feel, and you can do it too."

Gasps and moans punctuated the silence. Dexter sat down, letting his legs dangle over the lip of the stage, why not, floor-sitting with the fans was an old con tradition, hadn't he done it last night with a fan-boy future Nobel Laureate?

"And y'know, what makes us schmucks is that we never learn," he said conversationally. " 'Cause here I am doing it again."

He leaned forward conspiratorially, did an exaggerated stage wink, put a finger to his lips. "I'm gonna tell you a little secret just between me and six hundred of you," he said. "I want to *use* you, folks, I want to use you the way Gene Roddenberry used you, to save a TV show and make myself a buncha bucks."

He laughed. "I *must* be a schmuck because I'm being up front with you about it," he said. "I would dearly love to have you drop ten zillion letters on the Gold Network telling them what an immense cultural tragedy it would be at this fateful nexus in the evolution of our species to cancel *The Word According to Ralf*. This will enable me to buy a nice house in the Hollywood Hills for my wife and an Italian racing red Porsche Targa cabriolet for myself, so you can see it's in a good cause."

Dexter sat there poleaxed by what was coming out of his own mouth. What the fuck am I doing? he wondered. Why the fuck am I doing it?

He hadn't the foggiest.

Some impulse made him decide to finish on his feet, no mean task under the circumstances, which was somehow reason enough for him to prise himself shakily upright, and stand there like a man.

"Now a lot of you people have been asking me whether Ralf is just an act, or whether just maybe he really is a messenger from the Deathship Earth future, and because I'm a schmuck I've been telling you all the truth, which is that I can't say because I really don't know. . . ."

He paused, not for dramatic emphasis, but simply because he had no idea where this was going or what he was going to say that would get him off this stage before he passed out or puked, whichever happened first.

And when it came to him, it rocked him in his socks, but instead of finally knocking him on his sodden ass, it was like a bolt of electricity up his spine, a fountain of energy holding him upright with its passage.

"*But it doesn't matter, after all, does it?*" he exclaimed. "Of course not! Because one thing we don't have to suspend any disbelief in at all to know is that unless something happens to change it, the future ol' Ralf claims to come from is what we're gonna get, Monkey Boys and Girls, and it ain't gonna be no joke!"

Dexter's physical equilibrium was still shaky and he had the woozy precognition that after this was over he would spend some time kneeling before the porcelain throne, but a wavefront of clarity had collapsed the probability fog in his brain onto a strangely obvious attractor.

"So what the hell, a comedian from the future, a cynical act, an escapee from the funny farm, what does it matter, the little bastard is holding up a mirror to the future, and what we see in it we know is gonna be true," he said.

He walked forward a few steps, somewhat surprised that he could do it. He peered out there into the darkness against the glare of the spotlight, where he could just about make out all those gleaming eyeballs looking back at him.

"Or can I bullshit you into suspending your disbelief one more time?" he said. "You'd like me to do that, now wouldn't you? Sure you would. Hey, isn't that what we're all here for? Don't we all want to believe that science fiction can save the world?"

He shrugged. "Hey, I'm not gonna insult your immensely evolved mutant intelligence by asking you to suspend your disbelief in the possibility of time travel, I'm not gonna ask you to believe that the future has sent back a comic emissary to save itself from our assholery," he said.

He shrugged again. "All I'm asking you to suspend your disbelief in is the notion that teeny tiny causes can have great big macroeffects that are inherently unknowable, and hey, that's chaos theory, that's hard science."

He smiled wolfishly. "Like for instance, if *The Word According to Ralf* doesn't get canceled, if some bullshit comic just trying to make a sleazy buck keeps ragging the Monkey People for thirteen weeks longer, or hey, who knows, even another twenty-six, then maybe it makes some kind of difference."

Dexter felt the energy leaking out of him, felt the moment passing, knew that he was not going to be able to remain upright for too many minutes more.

"Who knows?" he said. "Who can? You suspend your disbelief and toss your little pebble in the fannish tide pool and watch the ripples spread in the quantum sea."

He felt his knees going rubbery, he knew that he had nothing left to say, and it was time to get off.

"So send in those cards and letters, save *The Word According to Ralf* and save the world," he said, flipping a valedictory salute.

"Or not," he said, as he backed toward the wings. "But hey, I kid you not, I really *do* want that Porsche."

8

"Archie will be with y'all in a few minutes, just give a holler if you need any-thin'," said the receptionist with the corn pone and hominy grits accent.

"How about a whip and a chair?" Texas Jimmy Balaban muttered under his breath.

And there Jimmy was, with his animal act in the lion cage of Archie Madden's office without the tools of the trade. Or even a cigarette.

Jimmy had costumed Ralf in his signature ice cream suit and an open-collared lime green shirt, and had chosen a powder blue Italian job and a red silk shirt for himself, the idea being to show some flash.

Dexter Lampkin had shown up in a black and white business uniform that looked like he had worn it to his high school graduation and was planning on being buried in it, all wrong for a meeting with the likes of Madden maybe, but at least a sign of seriousness.

The pallor of his skin and the dark bags under his bloodshot eyes, however, were somewhat less reassuring.

"Jeez, Dex, that must've been *some* convention for you to still be hung over on *Tuesday*."

Lampkin had given him a sickly green look.

"You gonna be able to handle this meeting?" Jimmy asked nervously.

Lampkin nodded. "Yeah, I'm okay, Jimmy, more or less, and in fact I've got some ideas that—"

At which point, Amanda had blown into the reception area like a Rodeo Drive commando, wearing a pale lavender jumpsuit with an outsize collar suggesting a cloak, her long dark hair jouncing free behind her.

"Who's *this*, Jimmy?" were the first words out of her mouth as she looked Dexter up and down.

"This is Dexter Lampkin, our head and only writer," Jimmy told her. "Dex, this is Amanda Robin, I guess you could say she's—"

"My personal charm trainer," cracked Ralf. "You notice what a terrific job she's done, right?"

If Lampkin's crappy old suit had been less baggily tailored, you could've seen his dick come to attention. Amanda, though, gave him a fish-eyed stare.

"Do I know you?" she said in a strangely distracted tone of voice. "I get the feeling we've met before somewhere."

"I think I would've remembered," Lampkin came back lamely.

And there they were, waiting for the Boy Genius to make his grand entrance.

Amanda seemed to float about an inch above the floor with a disconcerting faraway look in her eyes. Dexter stood there like an East Coast Suit who had just stepped off the red-eye from New York expecting the executive suite at the Black Tower and found himself instead in downtown Oz.

Not that Jimmy blamed them. Madden's office was weird enough with the Boy Genius behind the desk, but in his obviously calculated absence, the weirdness too seemed to be calculated.

The white carpet to make you feel like you weren't good enough to walk on it. The desk shaped like a flying saucer to make you *expect* any meeting here to be presided over by something from outer space. The jangly progressive jazz in the background at the edge of audibility to make you wonder whether you were hearing things. That the only place to plant your ass was in one of those crazy chairs done up like giant human hands did not seem contrived to put you at ease either.

What the tape-loop of the silently squawking parrots on the big hanging TV screen was supposed to do was anyone's guess. Which was maybe the point.

Ralf paced around the room like a horny rooster in a henhouse, cocking his head and mugging at the video parrots. "Hey, how about a great big hand for the star of the show?" he rasped. "No? Well then I guess I'm gonna have to take one for myself." And he plopped himself down in the palm of one of Madden's hand chairs.

Jimmy caught himself rolling a phantom cigarette between his thumb and forefinger again. "Okay, now listen," he said nervously, "we don't know what this is about, but with the ratings the show's pulling—"

Archie Madden breezed into the office, and breezed was the word. He was dressed in tennis whites far too perfectly pressed to have actually come from the courts, and the peach-colored cashmere sweater rakishly slung over his shoulder seemed to have been blown into picture-perfect place by a studio wind machine.

"Sorry I'm a little late for this meeting, people, but hey, if we didn't all play our little games, we wouldn't still be in show business."

He sailed across the room, perched himself on the chair behind the desk like King Shit upon the throne, motioned for them to be seated. Dexter sat down gingerly on the edge of one of the hand chairs. Jimmy planted himself deeper in another, not wanting to seem as nervous as he felt.

Amanda stood there for a long beat staring at Archie Madden as if she were seeing something she could not quite believe.

Madden looked right back at her with a toothpaste ad smile. "Do I remind you of someone?" he said. "You look like you're seeing . . ."

He laughed.

"A spook."

Amanda had considerable experience surfing the interface between the waking world and the Dreamtime, but this . . . *this* . . .

Archie Madden was a smooth-skinned black kid in his twenties. He wore tennis whites and a sweater slung jauntily over his shoulder. The sweater was peach instead of powder blue. . . .

But otherwise this was the Archie Madden of her Dreamtime vision of this moment before the fact.

This was He Whose Meeting May Not Be Refused.

"Would you believe me if I told you that I dreamt about you?" Amanda said. "That I dreamt about this meeting?"

"Would I believe you if you said you *hadn't*?" he said. His smile didn't change. Or did it? "This year, everyone in town dreams of taking a meeting with Archie Madden."

He didn't laugh. He just stared silently at her with eyes that seemed to be made of vacuum.

"So let's get started," said He Whose Meeting Had Not Been Refused.

Oh great, thought Dexter, just what we need, a vibrating lady!

That any good-looking woman looked all the more stunning after a weekend at a science fiction convention, some pheromonic attraction, the way she happened to fit his parameters of feminine pulchritude, had all combined to give Dexter a hard-on as soon as Amanda Robin walked into the room.

And it had seemed that she might have felt something similar, giving him a long speculative look, maybe even a little tentative come-on.

But he wondered whether the lovely Amanda wasn't just a ditzy Laurel Canyon space case prone to giving everyone that Scientology stare. And while his erection didn't wilt entirely, he found himself pissed off at her lack of professionalism under these economically critical circumstances.

After all, *he* had made an effort to prepare himself for this meeting that might be fairly called heroic under the circumstances.

Said preparation had consisted of many cups of coffee, megadoses of vitamin B, carefully rationed puffs on a joint he made last all day, and hours spent contemplating the computer screen, diddling with the keys but writing nothing. For, as he realized once the fog had sufficiently cleared for him to play back the memory track of the last three days, he had already set himself up for the meeting with Madden.

He was reasonably certain that he had already caused a dozen or so fans to begin writing letters, that the chain had already reached the sf Web sites and would reach the fanzines before the thirteen-week pickup date, that the faxes and e-mail and letters would soon be pouring in on the Gold Network, if not by the thousands, then at least by the hundreds.

So if he told Archie Madden that a fannish cult had already arisen around *The Word According to Ralf*, sufficient evidence thereof would soon enough be forthcoming to convince Madden that thirteen more weeks was a gamble well worth taking.

After all, Madden could hardly be ignorant of the golden bottom line of Paramount's Star Trek empire, and in the unlikely event that he wasn't up on the means by which it had been originally created, Dexter needed no further preparation to regale him with the tale of how Gene Roddenberry and science fiction fandom had shoved vast riches down the throat of a boobishly reluctant network and studio.

But maybe he *should* have talked it over with Jimmy, gotten their signals together, he realized as Amanda Robin finally sat down without taking her eyes off Madden. He hadn't even known that this woman was going to be here.

What the hell did she think she was doing? Was she coming on to Madden? It hardly seemed like a productive strategy; okay, she was a looker, but she was at least ten years older than he was, and a guy in Archie Madden's position could pick and choose just about any would-be TV star in town.

———

Archie Madden folded his arms across his chest. "Now we all know it's not time for me to make my go no/go decision yet," he said, "but I've got to tell you, people, that the way the ratings look now, your show is not going to get picked up for the second thirteen weeks."

Amanda blinked, took a long, slow deep yogic breath and held it, trying to clear her mind of everything but the moment.

But what moment *was* this?

She might not be in a corporate boardroom filled with mythic personages, Archie Madden's lines might not be quite the same as they had been in her dream, but his body language was eerily identical, and she suddenly knew why Dexter Lampkin had looked familiar.

She *had* met him somewhere before.

The somewhere had been the Dreamtime.

Archie Madden had appeared in her dream of this meeting, and Texas Jimmy, and Ralf, and Hadashi—all people that she knew, if in Madden's case only by name and reputation, and all the other personages had been archetypes of the contemporary collective mediated unconscious. Everyone who had put in a cameo appearance was someone.

Except for a slightly overweight figure in a propeller beanie. Amanda had no idea what that beanie meant, and he wasn't wearing one now.

But in her dream the man in the propeller beanie had definitely been Dexter Lampkin.

What is, is real.

Amanda exhaled slowly, contemplating those words as a mantra.

What is, is real, what is, is real.

And the supernatural is a contradiction in terms.

What is, is real, and what is real, is *natural.*

And this *is* happening.

And if she needed phenomenological proof, there it was sitting right beside her in the form of Dexter Lampkin.

"It's bombing out," said Archie Madden. "We could do better in your slot with the Godzilla rip-offs and giant cockroach movies we already have the rights to."

Amanda shuddered at the line's strange semifamiliarity. It was common enough for memories of the waking world to dissolve into the personal unconscious to emerge later in the Dreamtime. But here the Dreamtime vision had come *first,* and the waking world template was intruding itself into the time-stream of her consciousness afterward.

He Whose Meeting Could Not Be Refused shrugged, made eye contact with Texas Jimmy, Dexter Lampkin, and then Amanda.

"Now we *could* just seal up the body bag right now and give the turkey a decent burial," said Archie Madden.

Was it coincidence that he was looking at *her* when he said it?

"Unlike everyone else in this room, you've got no financial interest in the pickup, now do you, Amanda? It's always a good idea to ask a disinterested member of the audience."

Was she imagining the reptilian coldness in those eyes?

"So what if *you* get to play Queen for a Day, Amanda?" said Archie Madden. "What would you say if it was all up to you? Do we have to have this show? Do I really need the hassle?"

Was that smile really so saurian?

She was merely being asked a question by a schlockmeister network programmer. Surely that sudden chill she felt was merely autosuggestion. Surely there was really nothing more at stake here than the fate of a failing TV show whose meanness of spirit she detested.

Surely . . .

Then why had her pilgrimage to the end of the Long Path deposited her in a lucid Dreamtime vision, the memory of which was now allowing her to anticipate the rough shape of what Archie Madden would say before he said it? And from whence had come her precognitive vision of Dexter Lampkin?

If you could answer that one, Hadashi's voice said inside her, *wouldn't you become the Buddha?*

"Why not?" Amanda said aloud, just as she had in the Dreamtime.

What is, is real.

The Dreamtime vision. This meeting. The presence of Dexter Lampkin uniting them. This very moment.

You might indeed need to be the Buddha to understand it.

But not to know that it *was* happening.

Perhaps this *was* merely about another thirteen-week pickup for *The Word According to Ralf*. But up there in her cold mountaintop vision of this moment, standing beneath a pitiless black sky from whose cosmic vastness no benevolent eye would ever again look down on the hearthfire glow of sentient encampment, it had been about infinitely more.

All her life, Amanda had always waited for this moment to arrive.

When Maya's veil would not merely be teasingly breached by fleeting visions out of the beyond within which might be dismissed by the worm of doubt as subjective manifestations.

When that higher reality which she sought would reveal itself in a manner whose connectedness to the phenomenological world of matter and energy could not be denied.

But now that that moment had arrived, it was not at all what she had sought or imagined. No ultimate Enlightenment. Not even understanding. Not a solipsistic epiphany but a karmic test.

She did not comprehend what was happening.

She could not become the Buddha.

But she was being called upon to act as if she had.

She was being called upon by she knew not whom or what to act as the Buddha would under these circumstances.

The Buddha would enter the moment.

The Buddha would proceed under the assumption that every step you make, every breath you take, would have consequences to the web of all being.

Why not?

"Why *not* give us a chance to save the show before you decide to close it all down?" Amanda told Madden, looking right back into the vacuum of those eyes full of void and stardust. "What've *you* got to lose?"

She gave him her best Buddha smile. "If that wasn't what you had decided to do already, why would you have called this meeting?"

Archie Madden shrugged. "Don't you ever play a hunch?" he said. "Don't you ever . . . listen to what your dreams tell you?"

The voice remained that of the schlockmeister Boy Genius, but those were the eyes of his Dreamtime avatar.

"Would you believe that you're here just because this is the way I dreamt it?" said He Whose Meeting Could Not Be Refused.

He laughed. He winked.

"Sure you would, Amanda."

"*Whose* dream was it . . . ?" Amanda found herself muttering softly.

Archie Madden shrugged. "Do we really need a dream?"

"Does there have to be a dreamer . . . ?" Amanda whispered.

The words seemed to move her lips as they emerged unbidden, a beat ahead of thought.

"Will you lighten up already, fer chrissakes, Amanda!" Texas Jimmy Balaban said, as she somehow knew he would.

"Yeah, Monkey Girl, can we cut the crap and get to the bottom line?"

"I thought you'd never ask," said Archie Madden, glancing at Ralf. "You want the bottom line?"

The kid in the immaculate tennis whites seemed to be addressing the entire room with his voice, but his eyes returned to Amanda's.

"The bottom line is that I can't wait till week thirteen to tell the bankers I screwed up," he said. "I've got to go to them *now* with a format change that will convince them that the numbers will turn around."

He favored her with the sweet reasonable smile of her favorite tyrannosaur.

"Which means you guys need to come up with a concept that I believe is gonna be doing at least a twelve share before the thirteenth week before this meeting is over, or I cut my loses, pay out what the contract says I have to, and pull the plug."

He gave her a wink fit to warm the cryogenic cockles of her heart.

"Your move, Monkey People," he said, as the phenomenological time-stream merged with the unresolved conclusion of Amanda's Dreamtime vision. "I *know* you don't want to let me down."

And then passed beyond, leaving her flying blind through the uncharted skies of the eternal now.

Texas Jimmy Balaban had not gone into the meeting expecting good news, but *this* curveball had certainly caught him off stride.

"Am I hearing this right, Archie?" he said. "We're supposed to convince you we can fix the show before we walk out of here, or you're gonna cancel it *now*?"

"He can *do* that, Jimmy?" Ralf asked unhappily.

Can he? Texas Jimmy wondered. The contract had been the usual thirty pages of bullshit boilerplate, and he had paid most of his attention to nailing down the payment schedules and the subsidiary rights, so that when it came to a buy-out clause, he really couldn't remember.

"Sure I can, Ralf," Madden said. He gave Jimmy the needle-capped smile of a legal weasel. "Section eight, clause twelve, paragraph E, you could look it up if you don't trust me."

"Hey, why shouldn't we trust you, Archie?" Jimmy groused. "I'm sure the check's in your mouth, and you won't come in the mail."

Madden chuckled about as convincingly as a game-show laugh track. "Hey, what's the problem?" he glanced at his watch. "I've got nothing on my schedule till four-fifteen, so I'm all yours for the next thirty-seven minutes."

Decades of contending with the schlockmeisters and sleazebags and outright crooks infesting the lower end of the Business, and Texas Jimmy Balaban had never slugged anyone. But on the wide screen of his mind he was squeezing Archie Madden's throat till the bastard's eyes popped out of his head onto his desk.

And while he was at it, his imagination decided to do a Schwarzenegger on Lampkin too for disappearing over the weekend. He would've done something similar with Amanda for waltzing in here like Miss Ditz and playing guru-farm mind games with the Boy Genius, but apparently his subconscious was too much of a gentleman to come up with a convincing scenario.

And while you're at it, Balaban, why don't you give yourself a nice big kick in the ass too for completely losing control of this situation?

"No sweat, Jimmy, he's not going to cancel the show," Lampkin said with idiot confidence.

"I'm not?" said Archie Madden.

"No you're not, Mr. Madden," Dex said, "and I'm gonna tell you why."

Lampkin pried himself up out of the ridiculous hand-shaped chair, and started pacing in little circles while he spoke, transforming himself, to Jimmy's amazement, into a tummler, a bullshit artist, a Hollywood writer making his pitch at a story conference.

"You ever hear of *Star Trek*, Mr. Madden?" he said. "The biggest grossing TV syndicate package in history, the features, the spin-off series, the comic books, the video games, the merchandising, the novelizations?"

"No," drawled Archie Madden, "I've been in a coma for the last twenty-five years."

Lampkin held up the thumb and forefinger of his right hand about an inch apart. "Do you know the schmucks came *this* close to canceling it after the first thirteen weeks?" he said.

Madden just sat there without reacting, but Jimmy didn't see how suggesting that he was a schmuck was going to be terribly productive.

"The bright boys were set to do to the golden goose *just* what you'd do to *The Word According to Ralf*, and flush all of that down the tubes before it had a chance to happen," Lampkin said.

He stopped in his tracks, paused for a dramatic beat.

"And do you know what saved them from their own assholery?"

"Let me guess," Archie Madden said coldly. "The same thing that's gonna save me from mine?"

Oy.

Lampkin beamed at him. "They don't call you the Boy Genius for nothing, do they?" he said.

"Oy," said Jimmy, this time unable to keep from groaning aloud.

"What saved *Star Trek* and made all that money for the very corporate powers that were going to kill it was . . . *science fiction fandom!*"

Lampkin said this as if it were some kind of great revelation, but Madden just gave him the fish-eyed stare.

"You mean, what do they call them, the Trekkies?" he said.

"Much more than that, Archie," Lampkin said, switching to a first-name basis, and sitting back down again. "There's a big fan subculture grown up around the kind of stuff I usually write, which is science fiction. They put on a big convention somewhere practically every weekend of the year."

"Yeah, right, the sci-fi fans," Madden said, "strange nerds in space cadet costumes and propeller beanies."

"Ten, twenty, maybe thirty thousand of them, nationwide, Archie," Lampkin said.

Madden shrugged. "Big numbers for the hotel business, I guess," he drawled.

"But with enormous leverage, Archie."

"*Leverage?*"

"The Church of Scientology was started by a penny-a-word sci-fi hack as a little science fiction fandom nut-cult," Lampkin said. He flashed Madden a royal flush grin in dollar signs. "Net worth now over a billion dollars. Star Trek, Incorporated, likewise. "*Leverage.*"

And bingo, Dex had him!

Jimmy could see it in Archie Madden's body language, as he hunched his shoulders just a little bit forward, as his nostrils seemed to flare at the sniff of mucho dinero.

"Gene Roddenberry launched a letter-writing campaign to save the show, got a few of the sci-fi writers who had written for it to put the word around, figuring a couple thousand letters from the fans delivered in a hurry was something NBC and Paramount would a least have to factor in at pickup time. . . ."

Dex spread his arms, did it as a take on Carl Sagan. "Instead, they got *thousands* and *thousands*, tens of thousands, week after week, and *pickets* outside the studio and the network offices, they *never knew* what hit them!"

"More letters than people writing them?" said Madden. He flashed Lampkin a wise-guy grin. "Does not compute."

"Fans! *Fan-a-tics!* Literally, Archie. Highly intelligent obsessive people who believe in science fiction with a burning passion, who build their whole *lives* around it, who believe that it makes them *special*, who believe they have a mission to convert *the world*! Tens of thousands of letters written by maybe a thousand volunteer public relations troops armed with computers and faxes and telephones ready to man the media barricades for anything to do with science fiction, or space, or the future! *Star Trek! Star Wars!*"

Dex paused, folded his arms across his chest, glanced in the direction of Ralf. "Or a comedian from the future."

Madden gave Lampkin a long, squinty, speculative stare that Jimmy did not find reassuring.

"Am I supposed to take that as a threat?" he said.

"No, no, no!" Lampkin blurted hastily. "It's a *promise*. Roddenberry was just trying to get himself another thirteen weeks, but his letter-writing campaign snowballed gloriously out of control into a goldmine of reruns and spin-offs and tie-ins. All thanks to a few thousand fanatic science fiction fans."

Curiosity seemed to soften Madden's eyes a notch or two. "But how?" he said. "The original *Star Trek* never got as high as twentieth place in the ratings."

Lampkin shrugged. "If history teaches us anything, it's that a few thousand dedicated culties can produce a great big humongous effect," he said. "Leverage! What else explains how a little nut-cult called Christianity ends up taking over the whole Roman Empire, how a few hundred Nazi skinheads in a Munich beerhall end up starting World War II, how a few thousand Trekkies end up creating a mass cultural phenomenon that made a lot of reluctant people real, real rich. . . ."

"Leverage . . ." Madden muttered thoughtfully.

"We're sitting on another potential *Star Trek* here, Archie!" Dex declared. "Think about it! Imagine a few thousand science fiction fans fanatically dedicated to spreading . . . *The* Word *According to* Ralf!"

Madden did seem to be thinking about it, and Texas Jimmy found himself doing likewise, trying not to grin or drool.

The show being what it was, the Gold Network lawyers hadn't bothered to play hardball on any subsidiary rights beyond syndicated reruns of the show itself. If he remembered the contract right, he had retained the lion's share of *everything else*.

"You're saying we can create a cult like the Trekkies for this show?" Madden finally said.

Dex gave him the grin of Wile E. Coyote holding a dead Roadrunner upside down by its feet, of a comic having been fed the perfect straight line for his capper.

"I'm saying *it's already happening*," he said. "I was out at a big science fiction convention over the weekend, and *there they were*—Ralf fandom, small but growing, you're gonna be seeing it in your In-basket—"

"I've got a *fan club*?" Ralf exclaimed. "Hordes of hot little Monkey Girls wanna hump my bod?"

Madden eyeballed Lampkin suspiciously, not that Texas Jimmy could blame him.

"Right . . ." he said. "Just arose spontaneously. You just *happened* to be there, you had *nothing* to do with it. . . ."

It was a dicey moment. Jimmy did some quick and dirty calculations as Lampkin and Madden stared at each other for a nervous beat.

"Look at how sweet the numbers are, Archie!" Jimmy said before either of them could break the uneasy silence.

"Sweet?" said Madden. "With these ratings? Why do you think I called this meeting in the first place?"

"Check out the bottom line, Archie," Texas Jimmy told him. "Even with *these* ratings, you can't be losing more than fifty, sixty thou a week on it, right?"

"So?"

"So fer chrissakes, Archie, you give us the five weeks before pickup to turn the ratings around, what's it really cost you, a quarter mil minus what exercising the buyout clause will run you anyway, maybe a hundred thou net!"

"So?"

"So? So maybe the odds on winning aren't even money, but all you're betting is a hundred thousand to win *hundreds of millions*! You couldn't get a payout like that betting Francis the Talking Mule to win the Kentucky Derby!"

Amanda watched Archie Madden glance at his watch conspicuously, a broad theatrical gesture.

"Thirty minutes left till the ax falls, people," he said, leaning back and folding his arms across his chest like an old-time studio mogul lacking only about twenty more years and a big fat cigar.

"You've got a point, Balaban. Sure, I'd gamble a hundred thousand against hundreds of millions at just about any odds," he said. "Except zero. Which are the chances of this turkey turning out to be another *Star Trek* instead of another *My Mother the Car* unless you come up with a format change that convinces me otherwise within the next . . ."

Another bit with the watch.

". . . twenty-eight minutes."

While Dexter Lampkin had blathered on about *Star Trek* and Texas Jimmy did his showbiz rap about the numbers, Amanda had sat there trying to return herself by every meditative technique she could think of to the state of multiplexed consciousness into which her first waking sight of Archie Madden had transported her. But she had fallen out of it when the waking reality of the meeting had moved beyond her Dreamtime vision of it, and no conscious act of will would bring it back.

It had all descended to a mercenary writer trying to convince a schlockmeister that the chance of hyping a failing show by manipulating a pathetic bunch of neurotic science fiction fans into worshipping it was worth another five weeks of low-budget production.

"We were just getting to that, Archie, now weren't we, Dex?" Texas Jimmy gabbled nervously.

"Were we?"

"Yeah, sure, remember, that terrific idea for a format change you told me on the phone yesterday? Jeez, Dex, we were jackpotting for over an hour."

From the befuddled look on poor Lampkin's face, Balaban had resorted to an outright lie to put him on the spot.

"Do tell," Archie Madden said slyly, the little grin of wicked amusement making it clear, at least to Amanda, that he was on to Texas Jimmy's game.

It was getting hard and harder for Amanda to credit her dual memory track of only minutes ago, when this low sitcom farce had seemed to be taking place in another realm, where the whole thing was being played for illusory ultimate stakes.

Now it was about nothing more than showbiz as usual: numbers, money, Balaban's comically desperate manipulation of Lampkin, and Lampkin's sleazoid cynical manipulation of . . . what had Madden called them? Strange nerds in space cadet costumes and propeller beanies?

Strange nerds in space cadet costumes and *propeller beanies*!

And that which no amount of conscious will or meditative technique had been able to summon up returned in a satoric flash, as she regarded Dexter Lampkin with suddenly doubled psychic vision.

Amanda didn't actually see that phantom propeller beanie on his head, but the memory of its presence atop the head of the Dexter Lampkin of her precognitive dream illuminated what had then been a silly and meaningless accouterment with the present's symbolic comprehension.

Forcefully reminding her that she *had* dreamt of this man before meeting him, that he *had* been wearing the emblematic headgear in the Dreamtime, before it could have meant anything to her.

That therefore her Dreamtime vision *had* to have been a time-warped message from she knew not who or where, that it *had* indeed happened.

And once more, the doorway was open.

Dexter could have killed Texas Jimmy for flipping him the hot potato, but he could hardly deny that Balaban's lie *should* have been the truth.

He *should've* worked out *some* concept for this contingency instead of waltzing in here under the blithe assumption that running George Clayton Johnson's Fandom rap on the likes of Archie Madden would be enough to do the trick.

One look at Madden told him that this guy knew damn well that he had walked in here without anything else in his head.

On the other hand . . .

On the other hand, how many times had he walked into a story conference, had the springboards he had prepared shot down in the first five minutes, and ended up blowing smoke? And how many times had he walked out with a script assignment anyway? Maybe four times out of ten, which was a better lifetime batting average than Ty Cobb's.

Do not attempt to think under such circumstances was the prime directive, just turn off your brain and talk.

So . . .

"Jimmy and I worked out four really solid premises for sitcom formats, but they all mean budget for sets and actors and scripts, which I don't think you're gonna spring for, am I right, Archie, so we gotta stick with our boy Ralf and an audience, and since we can't change Ralf, we've got to . . . we've got to . . ."

Dexter paused for a beat, not knowing what he was going to say next. But in the next beat he realized where his mouth had inexorably taken him.

"We've got to change the *audience!*" he declared.

Madden leaned forward slightly. "Change the audience?" he said speculatively.

"Uh . . . uh . . . throw a better class of meat to our monster," Dexter said, observing with bemusement as the relentless skein of logic seemed to emerge from his mouth slightly before unfurling in his brain.

"*Now* you're talking!" said Ralf. "What's been dragging itself in off the street is about as funny to work off as a barrelfull of *dead* monkeys!"

"Right, so what we need is to fill the seats with real live *Monkey People!*" Dexter exclaimed.

Hadn't he just spent three days in a hotelful of people who would make the ideal studio audience for *The Word According to Ralf*? Hadn't he just finished telling Madden that there was already a Ralf fandom out there? Why not turn it into a self-fulfilling prophecy?

If you were as adept at lucid dreaming as Amanda was, you could sometimes reenter a dream out of which you had awoken, and she seemed to be experiencing something akin to that now, to have reentered that dual perception of reality she had experienced while events had been following her precognitive vision of the meeting.

But now real-time words were ghosted by Dreamtime enhancement, so that simple lines summoned up deeper and more multiplexed meaning than the words themselves should have implied, expressed as mutating imagery on the screen of her mind's eye.

As if she were dreaming while wide awake.

"Monkey People?" said Archie Madden.

Behind the face of the Gold Network's programmer, Amanda saw the bottomless and ageless eyes of He Whose Meeting May Not Be Refused.

"*Science fiction fans!*" Dexter Lampkin exclaimed. "Colorful, strange-looking, weirdly dressed motormouths who *want* to believe in Ralf," Lampkin said, the words summoning up images from Amanda knew not where.

Amanda could see Lampkin's sci-fi fans; overweight, oddly shaped, strange about the eyes, wearing propeller beanies and Spock ears and T-shirts and buttons proclaiming their obsessions with outer space and alien beings and imaginary futures.

"The perfect cageful of Monkey People for Ralf to work off, what more could you ask for without busting the budget?"

Looking into their eyes, peering through those windows into their souls, she could feel them; intelligent but spiritually stunted primates who believed passionately in the transcendent evolutionary destiny of their species while remaining sadly ignorant in their frustrated hearts of what either transcendence or destiny was.

Ralf's caricature of the human race made flesh.

The Monkey People incarnate.

Meat for the monster, just as Lampkin had said.

"Well, Archie . . . ?" Dexter said, crossing mental fingers behind his back.

"Well . . . I don't know," said Madden, "chimp acts don't have much of a track record, and the hard-core sci-fi audience would be good for about a four share . . ."

"I *love* it!" said Ralf.

". . . but it might be worth at least another five weeks."

"We don't play *to* them, we play *off* them. Ralf uses them as foils to play *to* the folks out there in Peoria," Dexter said, jumping on Madden's hesitation with breathless speed. "And we make it look spontaneous, just plant a dozen or so fans in the audiences . . ."

Now that his mouth had shown him the way, his brain was back in the circuit, and it was zipping along in warp drive.

Dexter knew all too well what he was on the verge of selling to Archie Madden—science fiction fandom as a freak show, a monkey cage whose bars Ralf could rattle for the barnyard delectation of the gawping mundanes. Yet wasn't he giving them just what they always pretended to want? If science fiction really *could* save the world, then here's your chance, space cadets, your bluff is being called.

"You can guarantee a dozen of these sci-fi fans a night five nights a week?" Madden said dubiously. "Looking nice and weird and able to talk funny?"

"No sweat," Dexter assured him. "We'll have a waiting list a mile long, we can pick and choose."

Of course, Dexter could hardly avoid knowing that he was running a mind game on himself, no less than on the fans. For he knew that there was still a part of him that was part of them, the part that still believed that science fiction could save the world. Or at least that it was incumbent upon sci-fi guys like himself to do what they could.

And couldn't he pursue his own deeper agenda? It didn't have to be all Spock ears and three-hundred-pound Darth Vaders, now did it?

"Well . . ." Archie Madden said again, and Dexter recognized in the tone of the drawn-out vocable the production executive's mildly sadistic prelude to a reluctant yes.

Archie Madden made a show of reluctance, but in the eyes of He Whose Meeting May Not Be Refused, Amanda saw the predatory trance of a hungry cobra contemplating a juicy mouse.

"You'd be willing to, uh, procure the audience?" he said.

"Yeah, sure," said Dexter Lampkin.

Amanda knew that the inevitable hung on the yes that Archie Madden would allow the next cue-line to extract from his lips as surely as she knew that in showbiz reality bullshit flowed uphill.

But by the logic of that reality, Amanda realized with sudden satoric clarity, there was no reason for her to have been here at all.

No reason for Archie Madden to have summoned her to this meeting.

No reason for her to have taken it.

Yet here she was, brought here by forces intruding from a level of reality beyond showbiz.

By He Whose Meeting May Not Be Refused.

She must be here to do *something*.

It suddenly seemed twenty degrees colder than on that visionary mountaintop, and her psychic vision doubled as the Dreamtime poured into the frozen moment.

Here in Madden's office, Ralf sat there studying Archie Madden anxiously just like the star of a failing show waiting to hear the word of reprieve.

In the Dreamtime, Ralf's eyes were on her, and something beyond them was commanding her, perhaps begging her, to act.

We need an avatar that will turn the numbers around, she had been told up there. "You think we would've stuffed an act like mine in the wayback if we weren't getting desperate? This is *your* dream, remember, Amanda, this is *your* format, and I know you don't want to let me down."

The times tend to get the avatar they deserve, Hadashi had told her.

And *that* was the angry god of the Monkey People that Dexter Lampkin's animal act would summon forth—Shiva the Destroyer wearing Hanuman's mask.

But that was no avatar to turn the numbers around.

Times like these could not afford the avatar they *deserved*.

If the show was not to be replaced by cockroaches and slime molds, it must have the avatar it *needed*.

"We can't afford that dream!" Amanda found herself proclaiming aloud.

"What?"

"Jeez!"

And there she was, squarely in the schlocktime, with a network programmer, the star of a failing show, his agent, and a cynical science fiction writer looking at her as if she had suddenly spoken in tongues.

And from this perspective, perhaps she had.

But the vision remained sane and clear.

"It won't work," said Amanda Robin.

What is this woman doing here? Dexter found himself wondering behind his red rage.

"Why the fuck not?" he snarled.

What had Ralf called her, his personal charm trainer? Yeah, sure, his personal piece of dingbat ass was probably more like it!

"Because it's not what the times need."

"*Amanda!*" groaned Jimmy Balaban. "Why did you have to say a thing like that?"

"Because it's true. Because it will fail."

"Bullshit!" Dexter shouted, bolting out of his chair and rounding on her. It was a new experience to feel such contemptuous rage at a woman whom his pheromonic receptors told him he should want to fuck. "What business is it of yours anyway? Who asked you your opinion?"

"*I* did," said the voice of Archie Madden behind him. "So let the lady talk."

"It's a mean-spirited concept far too narrow for mass audience appeal," Amanda told Madden, thoroughly back inside her professional avatar now, and bringing it all back home to the showbiz level.

"Hey, come on Amanda," said Ralf, "it's a mean-spirited narrow *century*, or hadn't you noticed, and I ain't exactly doin' a Bambi act myself."

Amanda turned, locked eyes with him. The musculature of his face was set in just the mask one would have expected from a comic whose show she was maybe pulling out from under him, but the eyes were cool and calm and seemed to be telling her to go on.

"No, you're not, Ralf," she told him. "But you don't want to be a geek act either, now do you?"

She looked back at Archie Madden. "You could probably hype the ratings for five weeks by having him eat slugs and bite the heads off live chickens," she said. "People would watch it for a while just because it was so disgusting, but they'd tune it out in a few weeks for the same reason."

"She's got a point," Archie Madden said.

The one on top of her head! Dexter managed to avoid saying, winning the fight to keep his anger under control.

"We're not talking about a circus side show," he said tightly. "We're talking about a television talk show. We're talking about *comedy*. We're talking about an audience that Ralf can work off and be consistently *funny*."

"The *perfect* collection of Monkey People for Ralf to work off?" Amanda Robin said.

"*So?*" Dexter snapped, glaring at her, the fact that she was mimicking his own delivery not contributing to the cooling of his ire.

"Colorful, strange-looking, weirdly dressed motormouths who want to believe in Ralf . . ."

"Why are you doing this?" Dexter cried, his anger becoming overlaid with a mental anguish he didn't really want to understand.

Amanda Robin met his angry gaze unflinchingly, her face infuriatingly calm. Her eyes seemed to see right through him, or at least uncomfortably far beneath his surface.

". . . who believe in science fiction with a burning passion," she said, softening her voice, making her words somehow all the more insinuating, all the more wounding.

"Who build their whole lives around it, who believe that it makes them special . . ."

"Hey, come on, Amanda, get off it!" Jimmy Balaban said. "What the hell's the point?"

". . . who believe they have a mission to convert the world."

But Dexter knew.

"It's wrong to take the highest spiritual aspect of pathetic vulnerable people and hold it up to public ridicule," Amanda Robin told him quite gently. "You *do* know that, now don't you?"

He didn't want to, but he did.

"Hey, Amanda," Texas Jimmy Balaban said, "this is a business meeting in Century City, not a crystal-gazing act in Topanga, so if you *have* to mix in, could you at least try to stay on Planet Hollywood?"

This wasn't the Amanda Robin Jimmy had worked with. He would never have imagined her freaking out like this in a meeting with *Archie Madden*. Had she really flipped? Or was she trying to kill the show?

But why?

"On Planet Hollywood, Jimmy," she said, "shooting comic fish in a barrel is not going to keep getting laughs for very long either."

"And I suppose *you* have a better idea?" Lampkin snapped.

"As a matter of fact, I do."

Oy.

Was that it? Was all this her way of angling for a piece of the action? The Amanda Robin he knew had never seemed capable of that brand of dirty hardball, but then, she hadn't seemed capable of this kind of unprofessional crap either, you never knew.

———

Amanda found herself in a here and now where higher vision and show business, the Dreamtime and the schlocktime, merged onto a single focal plane whose Hollywood pragmatics were crystal clear.

"Ralf and the sci-fi fans would be a one-joke act with appeal to only a small niche audience," she said. "Today's *mass* audience is an audience of spiritual seekers."

"Hey, why not the Age of Aquarius while you're at it!"groaned Dexter Lampkin.

Amanda ignored him and spoke directly to the man behind the desk. Was it Archie Madden studying her so intently now or was it He Whose Meeting May Not Be Refused? Did it matter?

"You can read all about it in the supermarket tabloids. A religious revival, an astrology boom, a flowering of interest in alternate healing, Elvis cults, Wicca, Gaia worship, all going on at the same—"

"What next? Gypsy tea-leaf readings? Khalil Gibran?" snapped Lampkin.

"What next indeed?" said Amanda. "There's a great spiritual longing being expressed in popular culture, it's all a manifestation of the same transformation struggling to be born."

"Right," sneered Lampkin, "it's vibrating ladies and wishing can make it so that's gonna clear our karma and save the world!"

"Shut up will you, Lampkin, *I* wanna hear this, and it's *my* show on the line, now ain't it?" Ralf rasped.

One glance at his eyes, knowing and bottomless, and the barely perceptible nod and thinnest of smiles with which he acknowledged it, told Amanda that yes, this was what she was here to do.

That behind the mask was indeed a Presence calling upon her to midwife its incarnation for the age; not the avatar that the times so richly deserved but the one that they needed, not the Breaker of Worlds but the Opener of the Way, not a Curser of the Darkness but a Bringer of the Light.

"I *knew* I brought you here for a reason," said He Whose Meeting May Not Be Refused.

Archie Madden's smile was twenty degrees colder. "So let the lady talk," he told Lampkin. "Because I would like to know what it was."

Dexter did not expect logical sanity from the Hollywood powers that be. That a kid like Madden was in a position of power like this was proof positive that the town was no longer in Kansas, beside which a comic who insisted he really *was* from the future was merely from a minor suburb of Oz.

That his dingbat girlfriend should be on the verge of torpedoing the salvation of *his own show* with New Age psychobabble, however, was major lunacy even by the standards of La-La Land.

"So instead of saddling Ralf with a studio audience of sci-fi fans with whom only a three or four share of the viewing audience can identify, we give him a studio audience demographically representative of the national mass audience. . . ."

As Amanda Robin gabbled on, her droning voice became the forlorn dopplering hum of Dexter's Italian racing red Porsche Targa receding back into his dreams.

". . . an audience that *really* keys into the zeitgeist—"

E-nough!

"You wouldn't know the zeitgeist if it bit you on the ass!" Dexter shouted.

He wasn't a TV hack, he didn't have to eat this shit for a living! If he was going to lose the quick easy money, he could at least do it with some intellectual pride, without having to listen to any more of this macrobiotic vegetarian baloney!

"And you would?" Amanda Robin shot back.

"Yeah, I would! I do! It's how I make a living."

"Writing power-fantasies for socially retarded computer nerds?"

"*Science fiction*, lady, not *sci-fi*!"

"There's a difference?"

"You ever *read* anything I've written? Naw, why bother, when you can just channel the comic book version!"

"And I suppose you make a deep study of the place of being in the universe every time you write one of your space fantasies?"

"Deeper than what's in the bottom of your herbal teacup!"

"Hey, come on, cool it!" shouted Texas Jimmy Balaban.

What a disaster this was turning into! What next?

What next, to Jimmy's not entirely unwelcome surprise, was Ralf.

"I *love* it," he said, bouncing up out of out of his chair. "*This* is the format we're looking for! The sci-fi nuts versus the New Age loonies! Hey, Archie, ain't this more fun than a bowl of tropical fruit granola or a barrel full of space monkeys?"

Texas Jimmy had told Ralf to keep it zipped, fearing the worst if he started throwing insult schtick at Madden, but now he had suddenly reminded everyone in the room, Jimmy included, who the performer here was.

"Clock this," Ralf said, shooting a broad stage-wink at Madden, and dancing over to his desk. He turned and pointed a pantomime shotgun mike at Dexter and Amanda, who sat there grinding their molars at each other.

"Okay, folks, here we have Mr. Gizmo J. Slaghead, a real sci-fi guy, whaddya say, Giz, why don't you tell the Monkey People out there how you're gonna solve all the world's problems with high-tech chewing gum and nuclear baling wire?"

Poor Lampkin, unaccustomed to being cued for a straight line by an improvising comic, sat there and puffing like a grouper instead of feeding him one like a trouper.

But the way Ralf was cooking, he didn't need one.

"All we gotta do is build steam-powered robots outa paperclips and toothpicks an' have 'em mine outer space for beer money, right?"

Ralf turned, mugged at Madden, played to him as if he were the camera.

"You say you don't really trust the whiz kids what gave the world thalidomide and Chernobyl and talking birthday cards? Hey, no sweat on *The Word According to Ralf*, you don't like vanilla sludge, we got rocky load, stuffed with fruits an' chock fulla nuts . . ."

Ralf turned, shoved his phantom shotgun mike at Amanda.

"So let's have a sweet simian welcome for Miz *Diz* Slaghead, who ain't no material girl livin' in the material world, come on Miz Diz, read us our fortune in the stars, or at least feed me a decent straight line."

Archie Madden's face was still as deadpan as a Vegas poker hustler's. But the nose knows, and somehow Texas Jimmy's was beginning to like what it was smelling now. Smelled like victory.

Amanda smiled. It had all come down to the simplest of improv exercises. Dexter Lampkin was no actor, but Amanda Robin could do this bit in her sleep.

So she widened her eyes, goofed a kooky grin, and gave him Miz Diz Slaghead.

"Well, like dig it, Ralf," she said in a spacey Valley Girl voice, "I mean, you know, it's the *flying saucers* from Lemuria pumping all the *bad vibes* into the air that's making us all *crazy*, and the dolphins are dying in the tuna nets for our meat-eating sins, and what with rays from outer space giving surfers skin cancers and all, we've got to *get our spiritual shit together*, and clean up our *karma*."

"Ri-ght! So what we gotta do is give the planet a nice organic mudpack and a good stiff high colonic?"

Jimmy Balaban laughed. Archie Madden made a dry coughing sound. Even Lampkin seemed to stifle something.

"Now, if we would *all* only meditate on the secret meaning of the Pyramids, build our shopping malls on ley lines, and stop eating inorganic *pizzas*—"

"Then the crystal vibrations of Jane Fonda's exercise tapes will bring back the flying loxboxes from Atlantis to rain down pennies from heaven!"

Ralf delivered this capper whirling around to face Archie Madden with one hand on his hips and the other palm up for applause, like a matador finishing a neat piece of capework with a flourish.

Beat.

"Well?" said Ralf.

Madden gave him steady eye contact, but nothing more.

"Fer chrissakes, what do we have to do to keep the show on the boards, get down on our hands and knees and pray?"

Archie Madden didn't move. He didn't crack a smile.

And when he spoke it seemed to Amanda to be the voice of He Whose Meeting May Not Be Refused speaking. Nor could she detect any humor in it.

"You could try it," he said.

Ralf fell to his knees, eyes rolling toward the cciling, hands steepled in supplication.

"Oh great spirit of the Holy Nielsens, oh Monkey Boy Genius of the Network of Gold, grant us a lousy five weeks to save our show from the wrath of the ratings," he chanted. "Or. . . ."

The pause served to extract a straight line from Archie Madden.

"Or what?" he said.

Ralf raised himself slowly off the floor, and when he came fully erect, it seemed to Amanda that he towered over Archie Madden, reduced this god of the Nielsens Whose Meeting May Not Be Refused to just another kid in tennis clothes, filled the room with his presence.

"Or *you* will be responsible for the consequences," he thundered, pointing an evangelist's wrathful finger right in Madden's face.

"And lo, I have read them in the twenty-second-century trades!" he declaimed in the same vein.

"My agent here goes back to booking flying saucer nuts and two-headed chickens and drinks himself to death. Lampkin dies of an embolism after another twenty years of writing schlocko sci-fi novels and Saturday-morning cartoon shows. Your own ass gets canned and you end up as an independent producer of low-budget slasher flicks. The ice caps melt. The ocean rises. The atmosphere turns to shit. The whole fucking biosphere croaks, what's left of the human race chokes slowly to death in stinking sardine cans cursing your name, after which there's nothing left but a dead rock circling the sun forever!"

Ralf backed off a step, shrugged, threw up his hands, mugged a sickly grin.

"And all because *you* pulled the plug, wise-guy, all because *you* wouldn't give us one last chance to turn the numbers around," he said. "What do you have to say to *that*, Mr. Bones?"

Archie Madden clapped his hands very slowly, once, twice.

"I say not bad, Monkey People," he said. "Good enough to get your act five more weeks."

"*That's it?*" Jimmy Balaban stammered in breathless relief. "It's a go?"

Archie Madden flicked his gaze at Amanda, then back at Jimmy.

"As long as she's on the team," he said. "As long as Miz and Diz Slaghead book the peanut gallery."

"Oh shit," Dexter Lampkin groaned.

Now Madden did smile, at Lampkin, with all the warmth of Amanda's favorite tyrannosaur.

"That's the deal or no deal," he said.

"Fuck," said Dexter Lampkin.

In the laugh that followed, no benevolent eye looked down on the hearthfire glow of sentient encampment.

"No one said you had to like it," said Archie Madden. "The chemistry's probably better if you don't."

He stood up, swung a phantom racket.

"Gotta go now, people, or I'll be late for my match with Arnie," he said breezily. "Relax, people, hey, come on, it's just show business, just the numbers talking, nothing of . . . cosmic significance."

The exit was all Archie Madden.

Almost.

Except for the vacuum in the eyes that turned on Amanda in the half-beat catch before those last two words. Which seemed to her to have been deliberately delivered in quite another voice.

9

Dexter Lampkin sopped up the final bit of egg yolk with the last of his toasted bagel, anxious to be in his office and get to work.

Ellie had become all-too-practiced at reading that furtive look in his eyes. "Back to playing Hollywood producer, huh?" she said, grimacing. "Still not even thinking about a new novel?"

"Give me a break, Ellie, I just finished *Chaos Time*."

"So why don't you try some short stories?" Ellie said, automatically refilling his half-empty cup like a coffee shop waitress, a habit he had always found irritating.

"Damn it, Ellie, with what's at stake here, you expect me to waste my time futzing around with *stories*?"

"If you ask me, Dex, you're taking the damned show far too seriously."

"*I'm* taking it too seriously? *I'm* the one dragging *you* around the hills looking at houses?"

"You never used to let this Hollywood stuff get to you like this."

"We never had this kind of money riding on any of it, now did we?" Dexter snapped at her peevishly.

Ellie's show of concern for the state of his creative consciousness transmuted itself into a hard and not entirely sympathetic glare.

"It's that *woman*, isn't it?" she said, accenting the word with a wifely snarl of feline scorn.

Dexter shrugged, for he could hardly deny that the tone of voice in which she referred to Amanda Robin was what she had picked up from him.

A good thing that Ellie had not yet laid eyes on Amanda, at least she wasn't yet misinterpreting the crackling energy between them as lust in Dexter's heart. And nothing could be further from the truth.

Well, okay, admittedly in his *dick*. Amanda was the sort of looker most men knew damn well they would get to fuck only in their dreams. Amanda had it. And, being an actress, it was her profession to flaunt it. She dressed like something out of a movie, and she moved as if a phantom spot were following her; she had that Hollywood aura that was designed to establish a mainline from a guy's eyes directly to his cock with his cerebral functions entirely removed from the circuit.

Working with her, or against her, or both at the same time, was a novel form of torment.

Have dabbled in TV, and worse, cartoon shows, Dexter was accustomed to being forced into creative collaboration with people whose intellect he estimated to be about that of the average turnip, but none of them had ever had him walking around with a hard-on in their presence before.

Worse still, while intellectually vapid, Amanda Robin was not someone who could be dismissed as stupid, as witness the way she had taken that meeting away from him, warped his format, and razzmatazzed her way onto the staff of the show. She had first-class cerebral hardware.

But the software running on it was a load of New Age gubbish, and Dexter hated that stuff. Not only was it pig-thick scientific ignorance of such basic fundamentals as the difference between astronomy and astrology or the fact that not even bullshit could travel faster than light, it was just the sort of mystical claptrap that people who saw no difference between fusion-powered starships and flying saucers confused with science fiction.

Meaning that it was precisely the shit he had been unsuccessfully trying to scrape off his literary boot heels all of his working life.

And now here he was, forced to collaborate with Amanda Robin in turning *The Word According to Ralf* into a shotgun marriage between fortune-telling and futurology, between New Age mysticism and science fiction.

It had been war from the start.

He and Amanda Robin had to salt the studio audience with ten ringers each per show. Dexter had found, to his dismay, that booking the first week's shows had turned into almost a full-time job. He had to find fifty people for five shows, space out his reliable heavy hitters sparingly, and fill the rest of the seats with randomly chosen fans.

His part of the audience had certainly supplied the freakshow visuals he had promised Archie Madden from the very first show, replete with T-shirts festooned with a four-star general's chest worth of buttons and medallions, freebie satin

crew jackets from obscure science fiction movies, and even, god help him, a globuloid in starship trooper black with a plastic raygun.

Dexter's intellectual heavyweights were Roger Crayne, a cyberpunk writer;
Dabney Braithwaite, a middle-level tech with the Planetary Society's SETI program; and Hank Farmer out of JPL and the Transformationalist Circle.

Amanda Robin's New Age loonies were less obviously costumed, or so it seemed
to Dexter as he stood backstage with her and Jimmy Balaban, trying to pick them
out while Ralf did his opening monologue.

The blond surfer girl in the white robe? The swami-looking old duck with the
long carefully trimmed snow-white beard and the long wavy locks to match? The
bald guy in the saffron running suit?

Quien sabe? This was, after all, *Southern California.*

The sci-fi fans versus the New Age loonies.

". . . and now it's time to shake the old family tree, Monkey Boys and Girls, and
see if something halfway human comes falling out," Ralf said, extroing from the
monologue, picking up the shotgun mike, and bopping to the front of the stage.

"Yeah, you over there, the *gorilla* in the *human* suit with the ray-gun, what're
you gonna do, King Kong, hijack a banana boat back to the planet of the apes?"

The spotlight pinned the globuloid fan playing with his fancy plastic pistol in a
vaguely obscene manner.

He blinked myopically, stood there like a yuk for a beat.

Then he grinned in triumphant anticipation and pointed the thing at Ralf.

"Zap!" he cackled. "You're sterile!"

"You kill it, you eat it!" Ralf shot back, holding the shotgun mike in front of
his fly lubriciously, and drawing a nice big laugh from the audience.

Texas Jimmy laughed with them. Amanda gave Dexter a fish-eyed stare.

Ralf waved the shotgun mike around, the spotlight following it over the audience, onto a teenage girl with curly black hair and dental braces waving her hand
excitedly.

"*Me? Me?*"

"Yeah, kiddo, *you!*"

"Ooooh, I'm so *excited*!" she squealed, covering her mouth with her hand as
she bounced up and down. "I could just *shit*!"

The rubes guffawed. Ralf rolled his eyes toward the ceiling, and quickly motioned with the shotgun mike for the spotlight to move on.

"One of yours?" Dexter asked Amanda dryly. "I've got to admit, she's organic."

She gave him a look that would melt heat shield ceramic.

"You there in the captain's uniform from the Yellow Submarine!"

The spotlight picked out Dabney Braithwaite, a dark black man in his thirties wearing wire-rim glasses, resplendent in a cadmium yellow suit with television-blue shirt and matching yellow tie.

Dexter held his breath.

"Yes, Ralf," Dabney said in his characteristically pedantic voice, which played strangely against the clotheshorse image. "My name is Dabney Braithwaite, and I work in the Planetary Society SETI program—"

"Set Tea? What's that, the Blue Plate Special at an English greasy spoon?"

Dabney flashed a brilliant though humorless smile. "Search for Extraterrestrial Intelligence," he said.

"Hey, good idea, there sure ain't any *extra* down here on Earth. Whaddya do, keep an eye on the sky for flying saucers?"

"We listen for broadcasts from advanced galactic civilizations."

"Must be hot stuff! I hear tell that the porn channels on Venus feature chicks with six boobs."

"Seriously, Ralf," Dabney said with total techie implacability, "if you're from the twenty-second century, then I'm sure we'd all like to know whether we've finally picked up any broadcasts by then or whether we're still all alone."

"One of *yours*?" Amanda said.

"A real scientist," Dexter told her. "Not one of your crystal-channeling saucer-nuts."

"Do *we* get TV from *outer space* on *Deathship Earth*!" Ralf groaned with a Borscht Belt intonation.

"*Really?*" said Dabney, feeding him the straight line with perfect naive enthusiasm. "What are you picking up?"

"What do you *expect*, Monkey Boy?" said Ralf. "The same kind of crap they been getting from us—a hundred channels of schlockola television!"

He folded his arms across his chest, taking the mike off Dabney, took a little step forward, shook his head.

"You think *our* TV sucks?" he said. "Hey, Monkey People, you ain't been bored out of your socks till you've suffered through *Wheel of Fortune* played by twelve-armed Squid People! Moldy old sitcoms featuring Chicken People an' giant weasels in kilts with laugh tracks sound like happy hour at the hyena ranch! Cockroach People monster movies with giant *humans* doing the Godzilla act on hundred-story Roach Motels!"

Ralf went right up to the lip of the stage. The comic snarl suddenly seemed to acquire a bitter edge that was almost frightening. His eyes seemed to burn with a dark vision having little to do with humorous schtick, and he delivered the next lines with an emotional intensity that Dexter found quite startling.

"Yeah, sure, *saviors from outer space* telling us how to save our dumb monkey butts from the Deathship we made of our planet!"

Ralf rolled his eyes, jabbed an angry finger at the audience.

"Where did you get the birdbrained idea that so-called intelligent races what evolved from squids or cockroaches or banana slugs were gonna be any smarter than *we* are? Why should *their* TV be any better than ours?"

He shook his head, grimaced in disgust. "And those schlocky shows ain't the worst TV from outer space, oh no, Slagheads!"

He laughed mirthlessly. He shrugged. He heaved a great sigh. For the life of him, Dexter couldn't tell how much of this was stagecraft and how much . . . something else.

"Imagine how we feel," he said in a suddenly much softer voice. "There we sit sealed up in our sardine-can malls, eating our own recycled turds, on a Deathship planet *we've* deep-sixed, and on comes some slimy green thing with tentacles coming out of its nose and hair on all sixteen eyeballs with the Words of Wisdom we been waiting for. . . ."

Beat.

"And what does this enlightened mound of hairy Vaseline do?"

His voice hardened as he snarled out the capper.

"It pisses and moans about what a mess *they've* made of *their* planet, and it gets down on all twenty-five hands and knees and whines for *our* Words of Wisdom to tell *them* how to save *their* stupid asses!"

The audience sat there in stunned silence for several long beats, obviously not knowing how to take this. But Dexter did, and he couldn't help flashing Amanda Robin a look of smug self-satisfaction.

For the studio audience, for this representative slice of the national demographics, for a moment at least, the suspension of disbelief in the possibility that this really *was* an angry comic from the future hovered on the edge of emotional reality.

"But there *are* elder and wiser beings for us to learn from!" a feminine voice called out. "I work with them."

Crack!

The spell was shattered.

Ralf mugged as he waved the shotgun mike around, and the spotlight went seeking over the audience, and then there she was: the pretty and tanned young blonde in the plain white robe, standing there like something out of a granola commercial.

"You work with alien gurus from outer space, huh?" Ralf said. "What's a nut-case like you doing in a good-looking girl like that?"

Terrific, thought Dexter sourly. Back to low schtick.

"They don't come from *outer* space, but from *inner* space," the girl said in a voice bursting with sweet virginal sincerity, "and they were singing their songs and telling their tales in our seas for a million years while our ancestors were still swinging by their tails through the trees."

"Yeah? Then how come we never see them on TV?"

Her grin was fetchingly brilliant. "But we do, Ralf," she said triumphantly. "All the time! They're stars! We *love* them!"

She paused as if waiting for *Ralf* to cue *her* with a straight line. Ralf let her hang for a few seconds, then opened his arms, held up his palms, invited her with a little bow.

"They're the people of the deep, the whales and the dolphins!"

A groan went up from the audience.

"*People?*" sneered Ralf. "Flipper, Moby Dick, and Save Willy?"

The dolphin girl fairly vibrated with a clear-eyed Scientological purity.

"Beings who have been conscious for millions of years, with bigger brains than we have, with language, and music, and poetry, higher spiritual beings living in perfect harmony with the environment, and Gaia, and each other, with so much to teach us if only we will learn how to listen."

One of yours? said the curled-lip look that Dexter gave Amanda Robin.

She favored him with a smug sphinx-smile back.

"Oh yeah?" said Ralf. "If they're so smart, how come they're still jumping through hoops in Marineland for unpickled herring? How come they're starring in Disney movies and don't even get *scale?*"

"They're not covetous creatures like us, Ralf," the dolphin girl said with daunt-ingly humorless intensity, ignoring the modest spattering of sniggering chuckles. "They swim their whole lives in a boundless, bottomless ocean, so they have no sense of territoriality, no nationalism, no war, no concept of ownership or prop-erty."

Ralf peered out at her silently for a beat, cocking his head.

"Jeez, lady," he said, "you make them sound like some kind of saltwater *Com-munists!*"

"Nuke the Commie whales!" some yokel bellowed out to raucous laughter, and it was pretty much downhill from there.

That first show seemed to have set the pattern. A reasonably intelligent fan would feed Ralf a rap about virtual reality that Ralf turned into a neat little routine about the crazed machine successors of vanished humanity trying to re-create life out of freeze-dried rat brains and fossilized bubble gum, followed by a yogi demonstrating the efficacy of pranic healing by turning himself into a pretzel.

Science fiction fans and holistic psychopharmacologists. Science fiction writers and buddhist monks. Particle physics and high colonics. Space scientists and space cases.

Dexter came to see the battle between himself and Amanda Robin for the soul, such as it was, of *The Word According to Ralf* as a mirror of the contretemps between fantasy writers with their dragons and sorcerers and science fiction writers who attempted to confine their worldview to the realm of the merely improbable possible.

Which reflected the schism between people who could not con themselves into a disbelief in the cold equations, in the existence of certain immutable constraints upon the universe of matter and energy in which they unfortunately found themselves, and those whose desperate passion to believe in the infinite power of wishing to make it so was boobishly boundless.

And given the current state of the planet, you didn't need either a Gallup Poll or a crystal ball to know which side was winning.

Dexter sighed. He took a final sip of coffee.

Maybe Ellie was right, maybe it was *that* woman.

Maybe he should relax, and take the money and run after the pickup or not as the case might be.

Maybe this was the famous midlife crisis.

Maybe all this angst over a stupid Hollywood talk show was merely an intellectual sublimation of his dick's primitive simian tropism to throw Amanda Robin the mother of all grudge fucks.

But maybe not.

Maybe it really did matter.

Dexter would've needed several grams of cocaine to truly convince himself that the survival of the species or the fate of the planet depended on what happened on some seedy low-budget TV show.

But on the other hand, maybe *one more molecule* of hydrogen in the atmosphere, and Mars would have become a living world.

Maybe one more molecule of carbon dioxide, and Earth becomes a dead one.

Maybe one man couldn't move mountains or the destiny of the biosphere, but . . . *one little molecule of gas?*

Shouldn't we all toss our little pebble into that quantum sea and hope for the best while we're making an easy buck in the process?

Amanda had decided to throw a party, a meeting of true shamans of the New Age tribes, no more than twenty or thirty people, to spend a Saturday afternoon and evening eating, drinking, organizing a network to funnel top-quality guests of the right kind into the audience of *The Word According to Ralf,* and meet the man himself.

For she was forced to admit, at least to herself, that her slapdash contribution to the audience of *The Word According to Ralf* had too often come off as the collection of dingbats, ditzes, and vibrating cranks Dexter Lampkin proclaimed it to be.

She still didn't know very much about the hermetic little world of science fiction, but she knew more about the leading edges of a certain spectrum of sciences than Lampkin supposed, enough to realize that he was larding *his* collection of weirdos and dingbats with some serious people.

Amanda had even toyed with the idea of inviting Lampkin himself. She had found it prudent to read several of his novels, and they did have their moments. Particularly *The Transformation,* from which much of the background of Ralf's future seemed to have been lifted, and which revealed a consciousness which just might find more in common with the serious people on *this* Circuit than its constipated insistence on its own logical positivism might pretend to suppose.

But in the end, she decided against it. After all, the point of the party was to organize a network to balance the one *he* had already set up, so Lampkin's presence would be counterproductive.

Ralf himself had played hard to get, bitching and moaning at the cost of the cab fare when she told him that as hostess she could hardly be expected to pick him up and chauffeur him to the event.

"*Topanga?*" he had whined. "It'll cost me *forty bucks*! And forty bucks back!"

He still refused to even try to learn how to drive.

"Come on, Ralf, that's less than what people in this town who aren't making half of what you are shove up their noses in ten seconds! And these are really interesting people."

"Yeah? What kind of people?"

"Sufis and psychopharmacologists, poets, and shamans, and psychic researchers—"

"New Age fruits and nuts? Hey, come on, Amanda, don't you inflict enough of these loonies on me during the week?"

"*These* folks are different, Ralf, they're highly evolved beings, and they want to help you."

"Help me? Help me what?"

"Improve the quality of the audience. Stay on the air. Get the show picked up."

"Yeah?"

"*Yeah,* Ralf, and they've got the connections to do it!"

"Well, when you put it that way. . . ."

And so, as the sun slid through its zenith, there they were, awaiting the inevitable fashionably late advent of the star.

Not that it was time wasted, for by the time Amanda heard the protesting engine-revving of a taxi inching its unfamiliar way to the unpaved parking lot up the dirt road, the pragmatics had pretty much been dealt with in characteristic multinodal New Age style.

From what Amanda had gathered, the science fiction community had an old and well-established network of fan clubs, professional organizations, mailing lists, phone trees, publications, and Web sites which Lampkin had been able to plug into, with all access to his allotted audience slots going through him.

This hierarchical control-freak model must require him to make at least a hundred phone calls a week to fill his fifty seats, a stiff pain in the ass that Amanda certainly did not need.

So she divided responsibility for filling her slots among ten people she trusted. Meaning that each of them had merely to fill a single seat a night. Meaning that she herself need do nothing more than transmit the combined list to Jimmy Balaban.

For this, Amanda Robin, Associate Producer of *The Word According to Ralf,* would pull down $2000 a week.

It was a matter of trusting that the collective wisdom and creativity of one's true community was greater and more interestingly multiplexed than one's own.

Sri Dranda working the yogic ashrams and zen monasteries. Sara Warburton on the mental sciences. Ivan Davidoff on altered mental states. Donna Deluria seeking out the secret beat remnants. Sunshine Sue booking alternate communal lifestyles. Rob Cole and his Third World shamanism troupe. Maya Gonzalez, humanity's self-appointed ambassador plenipotentiary to the dolphins and whales. Steven Kingston on parapsychology. Bobby Falkenburg, the soft tech magician. And of course, the ever-popular Hadashi playing the Joker.

While Lampkin ran himself ragged trying to keep his one-man band act going, Amanda could simply conduct the New Age Symphony Orchestra.

Or so she hoped.

Of course, it was all largely dependent on how her circle of mages interacted with Ralf, on what manner of Ralf they collectively called forth.

The Ralf that came puffing and grunting along the rough path through the underbrush around the side of the house and up onto the deck wore a snappily tailored clay-colored bush jacket, pants to match, and brown jungle boots, looking as if he had been dressed for a safari at Abercrombie & Fitch.

He brushed phantom burrs out of his hair, squinted around at the unfinished weathered planking of the house and the solar panels on the roof, at the unruly vines dripping from the overhead trellis, at the rustic home-built hot tub, like an inveterate apartment-bound New Yorker.

"Who built this place?" he said loudly. "Tarzan of Tarzana?"

Everyone within earshot stopped what they were doing and looked at him. The star had made his entrance.

"Please, no pictures!" Ralf cried, shielding his face with the back of his forearm. "Hey, come on, Amanda told me you were highly evolved mutants and big-time Hollywood gurus, don't tell me you guys never got to meet a real live TV star before!"

"Sure never got to meet a man from the future in a Great White Hunter suit from 1938!" someone called out from the food-and-drink-laden picnic table.

Ralf laughed. "You mean this *ain't* the staff cafeteria at Lion Country Safari? The cab took a wrong turn and dropped me in *Appalachia* instead?"

He squinted, peered around, scratched his head. "But where do you keep the rusted-out car bodies?"

That much obligatory schtick having been thrown, Ralf stepped up to the table, poured himself a glass of wine, filled a paper plate with food, and allowed Amanda to introduce him around. By the time she had introduced him to everyone, Ralf had acquired a joint from someone, which he had stuck in the corner of his mouth Bogiewise, had his feet up on a packing crate, his elbow on the table, and was more or less holding court.

For at this stage of the game, the collective consensus was to play gurus at the Industry garden party and let Ralf play your humble just-plain-star. And so it went through the afternoon, people drifting in and out of the star's orbit, a Topanga party superficially like so many others Amanda had attended.

Yet the game within the game was already in motion. Casually, all the people whom she had already handed her audience slots off to managed to engage him in showbiz patter about the sort of human foils they could provide for the show, without really ever being so crass as to tell him overtly that *could* was going to become *would.*

By the time the shadows began to deepen in the ravines and the light began to golden toward sundown, the party was beginning to thin out, and it was easy enough for Amanda to assemble an inner circle by suggesting that Ralf be shown the full glory of sunset from the top of Big Rock.

"Up *there?*" Ralf groaned. "Where'd you park the helicopter?"

Big Rock was a boulder the approximate size of a ten-story apartment house, rosy tan in the waning afternoon light, fissured, speckled with hardy colonies of chaparral, but, from the point of view of the deck, relatively sheer, and apparently unclimbable by neophytes without equipment.

"The Chumash used the Rock for vision quests," Rob Cole told him. "They carved a path up the other side, or maybe it was always there."

"Hey look, guys," said Ralf, "I'm a city boy from a century when you can't even take a walk in the woods, 'cause there *ain't* no woods, and you couldn't breathe out there anyway, so my experience with scampering up old Indian trails is zilch, and I got a major ambition to keep it that way."

"The path's been improved a little more recently," Amanda reassured him. "The nasty bits have stairs and handholds and railings."

"I've been up there many times," said Sara Warburton, with her wrinkles and white hair, obviously past the midpoint of her sixties.

"I'm coming too, and I'm well over seventy," said Sri Dranda. Though truth be told, the shape *he* was in after half a century or so of yogic practice, he could've passed for a youthful fifty.

"Well. . . ."

Ralf took a long stagey look up the towering facade of Big Rock, and the set of his lips, the tilt of his head, as he mimicked the terrified city boy contemplating a fearful outdoorsy adventure seemed to Amanda to be pushed just a tad over the top into parody.

But when he turned to look back at them with a palms-up shrug of reluctant surrender, there was no fear in his bottomless eyes, and the amusement there seemed to have little to do with satiric humor.

Amanda, Ralf, Sara, Sri Dranda, Rob, and Hadashi made the climb. Amanda led the way around the back to the more fractured and fissured side of the Rock, where even the novice could make out the path to the top, a trail strung together out of natural crevices and shelves, short rude stone stairways linking them, wooden poles driven into cracks here and there for handholds, a few of them supporting rope railings for psychological security at the scarier places.

Ralf ran his eyes up along the trail. No show of stage terror now. Instead, his posture became more erect, more graceful, and somehow without gaining an inch in physical stature, he seemed like a much taller person.

And when he turned. . . .

It was as if a mask had fallen away.

Or been revealed.

The physical features hadn't changed, this was still the face of the comedian from the future. But now, somehow, that face had become a stylization of itself, an image, a totem mask. Only the eyes were alive, and they were the event horizons of holes whose bottoms did not seem to exist in this continuum.

"Time to climb your magic mountain and see what's up there under the stars," he said. The voice was Ralf's, but the cadence seemed to belong to some other being. "What's the matter, this game of Monkeys and Ladders was *your* idea, remember?"

Amanda blinked.

Nothing changed.

No one moved for a beat.

"Monkey see, monkey do," Ralf said. "After you?" He shrugged. "Follow me."

And he turned, loped over to the beginning of the trail, and began to climb.

The ascent of Big Rock was not really difficult, each step of the path upwards was more or less self-evident from the vantage of the previous one, and Amanda had made the climb many times.

So she knew that there was nothing really preternatural about the way Ralf ascended so easily, climbing smoothly and steadily with no mistakes, and at a pace that only Rob Cole, a strong middle-aged man well-familiar with the climb, could quite keep up with.

Not preternatural, Amanda thought as Ralf pulled himself up onto the broad flat shelf that was the top of Big Rock, but certainly out of character.

Whatever *that* really was.

Rob hauled himself up over the lip a minute or so later. It took Amanda and Hadashi several more minutes to reach the top, and a few minutes after that, they were giving final helping hands up to Sara and Sri Dranda.

And there they sat on the cooling sun-warmed stone, catching their breath on the very crown of this little corner of creation.

There were big mountains in the distance to the northwest, and even the ridgeline of the Santa Monica mountains to the south was high enough to hide the Pacific from sight, so Big Rock was not really the highest point in the vast panorama of the horizon's circle.

But Big Rock rose from a hilltop in a big bowl, and the mountains were distant, so from the perspective up here atop this pedestal of stone, the rest of the visible world was *down*.

It was a vertiginous effect if you stood peering over the edge, but if you sat, or if you walked a few paces away from the lip of the degree cliff, it was soul-stirring.

From this vantage, nothing of the suburban sprawl of Los Angeles was to be seen, the only visible works of man were the scattered houses on the fringes of the Angeles National Forest, and few roadways. The surrounding nearby and distant mountains rose fractally into greater and greater foldings of primeval landscape, sere and majestic.

With the sun just beginning to slide down behind the sharp-edged western ridgeline in a mighty rosy and violet blaze of smoggy glory, the mountain slopes were tinting lavender and umber, and the ravines were filling with a darker shade of green, and the sunset perfumes of the chaparral went straight to the backbrain, and the air was tinged with a golden glow.

Amanda could well understand how the Chumash had held this place sacred. For even now, it retained the power to hold Los Angeles and all that it implied at bay.

As Amanda rose to her feet, she saw that Rob Cole was standing a few feet away looking west into the incipient sunset, while Ralf had walked to the center of the mesa, and stood there, with his hands on his hips, a silhouette in purplish black fringed in fire by the sunset.

For a moment, it was impossible to tell which way the shadow-man was facing, backward to the future, or forward from the past.

Then the cinematic illusion fractured as the frame unfroze, and Ralf came walking across the mesa toward them.

"I suppose you guess I'm wondering why you've gathered me here today," he said with the familiar raspy delivery. But there was a reverse English to it, a softening of the edge that rendered it eerily unconvincing as a wisecrack.

And he seemed to wear the face of the comedian from the future like a mask. The smirk lines were gone from around the mouth, the tension was gone from around the eyes, and via a trick of the light the eyes themselves had become opaquely glistening violet marbles, all surface, upon which only nothingness could be read.

No one spoke for a long moment.

"What next?" said Ralf. "A good old-fashioned powwow?"

Once again, the unreadable eyes, the uncharacteristically placid face, a certain toneless muting of the voice, nuanced a silly line with a strangely out-of-place seriousness.

Out of place?

This *was* a place held sacred by the Chumash, and in Native American terms, a powwow *was* indeed more or less what Amanda had intended.

"Why not?" Amanda said. "It's an old tradition up here."

"Time out of mind," said Sara.

"Mind out of time," said Ralf.

Amanda cocked her head at him quizzically.

Ralf laughed, voice only, not so much as cracking a smile. He shrugged. "You're running out of one," he said, "and I'm the other."

Another long moment of silence.

"The Chumash had a special place for their ceremonies up here," Rob Cole finally said, and he led them back toward the middle of the mesa. "The center is the power point."

"Or vice versa," said Ralf, "or so they tell you in Zen 101."

And he sat down, folding his legs into a classic lotus position, eyes focused inward, thinnest of Buddha smiles, palms upward atop his knees. With, however, the second fingers of both hands pointed skyward.

"And both are Void," said Sri Dranda, seating himself in the same posture, minus the finger, before him.

"Speak for yourself, Monkey Boy," said Ralf.

"And who do you speak for, Ralf?" said Amanda.

"Who do you want me to speak for, Amanda?"

"*Seriously!*"

By this time, they were all seated in a semicircle facing Ralf and the setting sun, acolytes before their backlit master from a certain perspective, the Spanish Inquisition from another.

"*Me*, you're asking seriously?" Ralf said tonelessly, working against the line's expected Borscht Belt cadence.

"Come on, Ralf, who are we *really* talking to, what's the bottom line?"

Ralf laughed, and this time, the Buddha mask *did* crack a smile, and Amanda thought she could see something sparkle beneath the surface of those eyes.

"Do you really need to know?" he said. "Does there have to be a bottom line?"

Amanda sat there staring into those eyes without blinking, mesmerized by this punch line that had meaning only in her Dreamtime delivered by a . . . being she could have met nowhere else.

"Yes" was all she could manage to say.

"You may not like this," said Ralf, "for yea, I do speak for that highest of ultimate realities, for the bottom line which indeed is sacred!"

"Which is?" said Sara.

"The Nielsens, what else?" Ralf said in perfect deadpan. "The numbers by which the whole show lives or dies." And he delivered the next line doing W. C. Fields. "Ah yes, the means by which emptiness bootstraps itself into show business as the perfect voice of the perfect void!"

Only Hadashi laughed.

"You were expecting the Word from on High from the Throne of King Shit?" Ralf said. "Well, don't hold your breath, 'cause the lunatics have taken over the asylum, or haven't you noticed yet?"

"I refuse to accept an amoral universe without karmic justice!" Sri Dranda declared.

"The karma you get is the justice you make, so go do something about it," Ralf told him.

He laughed, a sound now somehow mirthlessly chilling up here in the waning light. "But don't complain to the management, 'cause there ain't any, Monkey Boy, and I ain't it."

"That's all there is?" said Rob Cole. "We're out here all alone?"

"Naw, I was only kidding," Ralf said. "Actually, at the end of act three, Big Daddy in a long white beard and a bathrobe shows up chompin' a two-foot stogie with a bottomless Swiss bank account to bail your bankrupt production out."

The sky immediately overhead was darkening toward a dusky violet, and a smattering of faint stars was barely visible just at the zenith, but a burnt orange sliver of the sun's disk still hovered on the western horizon, illumining the sky behind Ralf's head with gorgeous rays of purple and fire, courtesy of the neon amplification of the omnipresent smog.

"So now that I've enlightened you about life, the universe, and everything," he said, "maybe you'd like to tell me what this little séance is really all about?"

Amanda blinked. No one said anything. Nothing seemed to move.

"The idea is to turn me into a guru act, right?" Ralf said. "Stuff my audiences with warbling mystics, measure me for one of Obi Wan Kenobi's secondhand togas and Merlin's dunce hat, and have me proclaim that the Farce is with me."

"Would it be worse than tearing the wings off Dexter Lampkin's sci-fi nerds for laughs?" said Amanda.

Ralf shrugged. "I'm an equal opportunity tummler," he said.

His head was haloed in fading glory, but his face lay deep in shadow; the strangely distant smile that seemed to creep across his lips might have been an artifact of the lighting. Or not.

"But you knew that going up the mountain, now didn't you?" he said. "You want more than that."

"More than what?" said Sara Warburton.

"More than is dreamt of in your cockamamie philosophies."

A long beat of silence. A breeze blew upward from the cooling vastness of the primal landscape below them, redolent of chaparral, and sandy earth, of sunset, and musk, and off in the far distance a coyote called.

"The format says I haven't been born yet, so I couldn't exactly have been born yesterday either, now could I?" Ralf said, delivering the line in that incongruously flat tone.

Somewhat closer, a high-performance engine howled, and rapped, and howled again, as someone put a sports car through its paces along the bends of Old Topanga Canyon Road.

"What's the matter, Monkey People, cat got your tongue? It's not like you've got all the time in the world. . . . Hey, *I* don't even have a guarantee that *my* show is gonna be picked up for another thirteen weeks."

He paused, then delivered the unfunny punch line in a much harder voice.

"But then . . . who does?"

The sun had slid down past the horizon while Amanda wasn't noticing, Ralf's head lay completely in shadow now, outlined only by a deep violet glow so pale as to verge on invisibility, the temperature had dropped suddenly, and overhead in the crystalline blackness of the eternal sky, hundreds of stars shone somewhat faintly, dulled even here by the equally eternal invisible photochemical fog.

"You wouldn't be getting a little afraid of the dark, now would you?" Ralf suggested slyly. "What's the matter, Monkey People, we getting a little too close to the bone?"

The silent laughter of long-vanished cold-blooded species seemed to echo up at Amanda from their boneyards in the dark and distant mountains formed aeons ago from the tortured uplifting of the beds of ancient dried-up seas.

"*Come on*, this is *your* format, and the meter is running. . . ."

The red running lights of a light plane, its motor buzzing like no dragonfly, passed by them to the north, seemed to glimmer in Ralf's eyes for a moment, turning them into something reptilian.

". . . and if you want to imagine the future if it goes down the tubes, picture reruns of *Godzilla Versus the Cockroach People* forever."

For a moment Amanda indeed found herself imagining the land below this obelisk of stone once more as it had been when indifferent reflex-machines with teeth and claws fought pitilessly for survival in the once and future jungle, as devoid of sentient benevolence as the black void above her.

"Are we having fun yet?" said Ralf.

You had to have a *really* strange sense of humor to find it funny.

"No?" said Ralf.

He unwrapped himself from his lotus posture. "Well, if nobody's got any more cosmic comic stories to tell, maybe us White Folks shouldn't let the sun set on us here," he said, rising to his feet.

No one else moved. The five of them sat there silently for a long beat.

"I've got a koan for you," Hadashi said. "You know the difference between a comic from the future bombing out onstage and the avatar of the zeitgeist we need for the age?"

"According to you, who should know better, right?" said Ralf.

Beat.

"If the first one gets the hook, well, those were the jokes," Ralf said as Groucho. "But if the second one croaks," he said as Porky Pig, "th-th-th-that's all, folks!"

No one laughed but Ralf, with three sharp barking yocks.

Nor did Amanda find it particularly funny when a pack of coyotes, like a feral laugh track out there in the darkness, answered him back.

Ba-ba-ba-ba-*doo-bah*, ba-ba-ba-ba-*bum-bum*, the beat of some fuckin' dumb old rock song kept bangin' away in Foxy Loxy's brain, and she tapped it out with her fist on lampposts, trash cans, tree trunks, bench backs as she boogied her way through Tompkins Square Park toward her nest, singing along with the karaoke machine in her head the only line of the fuckin' thing she could remember.

"Bend y'back to the basics, bend you back to the jungle, where the natives are restless an' the stone walls crumble, hee, hee, hee. . . ."

Hadda fuckin' point, right, back t'the basics, rock for the pipe, a bite a this anna drinka that, place ta crash, an' hey, what the fuck else didya really need when it came right down to it?

As for a fuckin' jungle, well shit, whoever wrote that song musta done time here afta midnight!

She passed the occasional solid citizen walkin' his pet pit bull, lookin' paranoid an' tryin' to pretend she didn't exist, and there was half a dozen of 'em comin' back acrossa park inna task force from some party in Alphabet City, too many t'hit up for spare change, but once the dark really came down, even mosta the street people livin' in the packin' crate camps kinda hunkered down around their sterno, an' left the paths to the dealers and their customers, hey, wouldn't you.

The cops was always tryin' to clean up the park, right, upgrade the property values around it, uh-huh, send inna TAC squad, roust the fuckin' dealers an' all those fuckin' scumbag creeps livin' under the bushes an' whatever, an' then it'll be cool for Mr. and Mrs. Claude and Maude t'take their midnight jog.

Right. So they surround the park, an' a zillion bad-ass cops go in an' rip up the squat camps, bust the obvious dealers, break a buncha heads, throw the fuckin' riffraff inna tank, occupy it for a while so's the citizens can walk their French poodles at night.

An' after awhile, they pull out again, anna floodlight bulbs start t'get busted, an' the natives start oozin' back in through the cracks like the roaches behind the fridge you *never* gonna get rid of, an' before you know it, the Yups are figurin', hey, maybe it'd be safer t'take a swim inna shark pond, whaddya think, honey, jeez, that guy's got his *cock* out. . . .

Loxy looked around for trouble when she came t'the pigeon-shit-smeared bench under the lamppost witha busted light, saw nothin' worse'n Manny the Mouse sellin' some shit to a couple a punkie-lookin' kiddies, gave him the usual crazy-eyed Knife Lady look, coupla new junkies onna block she didn't like the look of started comin' in her direction, changed what mighta been left a their minds when she made t'reach inta her nose, yank out a big booger an' pop it inta her lip-smackin' yawp, and the coast bein' cleared, she slipped behind the bench, through the bushes to home sweet home.

Loxy had copped two pretty fuckin' good refrigerator cartons outa a Dumpster, opened 'em up, put 'em together to make this like cardboard pup tent at the roots of a big old tree, covered it with blue garbage bag plastic, an' then piled it with mud and dirt and leaves, all kindsa disgustin' shit from the garbage bags over that, so's you tended not t'notice it from the path, an' had the idea t'stay upwind an' far away from whatever lived in it if you did, like even the creeps from the packin' crate camps an' tent cities thought twice about givin' the *Knife Lady* no serious shit. . . .

For sure, the natives been known t'get restless, an' y'might say a girl woulda haveta be brain-damaged to crash inna park like this without havin' the right kinda friend.

But Loxy had it right in her all-purpose shopping bag witha pipe anna vials anna candy bars anna roll a toilet paper an' the rest of the *basics*, next best thing to a rich boyfriend namea Tough Tony—the Big Ripper, her great big lovely dirty old knife.

You'd be surprised how even the fuckin' creeps an' low dealers an' muggers an' all which crawled out from under the rocks in here lost their appetite for a free fuck or a rip-off when the sweet little victim chickie started howlin' and droolin' so hard snot started comin' out of her nose wavin' a great big knife so fulla crud it looked like she'd been usin' it t'chop the heads off leather faggots with AIDS an' wipin' it off onna wino's bunghole.

Loxy crawled into her nest, pulled out her pipe, a vial, the knife an' this kitchen knife sharpener she had managed to boost. She clawed a teensy little flake offa the rock, just a little taste before beddy-bye or you could be up all night, took a nice little drag, whooee, well, what the fuck, one more ain't gonna hurt, an' havin' taken care of herself, she took the sharpener to Rip, running his big sharp length carefully back and forth, squealing through those little metal rings, uh, uh, uh, rubbin' back any of the greasy black mung mighta been disturbed inna process.

Loxy had learned how to care of the Big Ripper an' ol' Rip had learned how to take care of her.

Rip, he didn't care jack shit about keepin' clean an' tidy, the skankier the better out here inna jungle, you looked like you was dirty as a subway toilet bowl drippin' with all kindsa disgustin' diseases an' fuckin' crazy enough to sink your filthy fangs inta the nearest throat for kicks, surprise, surprise, the natives tended ta wanna leave the Knife Lady alone, an' when you asked one a the tourists for a little spare change so's you could score somethin' t'get off with, they weren't inta no Bible-thumping arguments.

Clean was just *askin'* for trouble. *Dirty* meant maybe you *was* trouble and no point findin' out. Thing was to look baad and keep sharp.

An' t'keep *herself* sharp, sharp enough to scare what needed to be scared, she hadda keep that edge, hadda *know* she'd fuckin' well let Rip do his thing if she hadda, might enjoy it too, asshole, don't give me no shit, or I'll slice your fuckin' dick off!

When she started feelin' a little less than razor, her edge came from what she stuffed inna pipe every day an' wasn't too easy t'boost from those what had it, seein' as how they tended to have guns an' what y'might call a shitty attitude.

Kind of a rat race, Momma might say, tricks bein' few an' far between an' about five bucks a pop in her condition, matter of scorin' enough spare change offa tourists anna spare change artists what didn't have no friend like Rip to score enough rock to keep enough edge t'score enough bread t'score enough rock to keep her razor sharp.

Bend y'back to the basics. . . .

But hey, y'could say she had it made, right, no nine-to-fiver, no hassles witha Welfare, no suckin' fifty-seven dicks a day t'make a flop, what else did she need, she had it *all*, place t'crash, enough shit t'stay high. . . .

Bend y'back to the jungle. . . .

Foxy Loxy grinned happily as she slowly and oh so tenderly ran her thumb up the full hard sharp length of the greasy blade.

. . . an' a girl's best friend, the Big Ripper, a nice great big razor-sharp dirty ol' knife!

Ba-ba-ba-ba-*doo-bah*, ba-ba-ba-ba-*bum-bum*!

"The *Second* Coming?" said Ralf. "Hey, I ain't even startin' to *breathe hard* the *first time* yet!"

The audience watching the show in Alec and Mary Duncan's living room groaned, but the studio audience tittered nervously. It seemed to Dexter Lampkin that those who got the joke were afraid to laugh aloud at the blasphemy, and those offended by the blasphemy were leery about admitting to themselves that they had really heard the joke lest Christian honor demand that they do something un-Christian about it.

The Duncans were wealthy science fiction fans who had been holding these invitation-only salons for something like a decade before the advent of *The Word According to Ralf*, each one devoted to a theme, sometimes with a speaker. Tonight the focus was on the tube, and the theme was the show toward which the science fiction community had developed a proprietary interest, and giving Dexter grief at the way it was slipping from their grasp into the nether reaches of the crapola mysticism which the general public so often confused with science fiction and which they therefore so heartily despised.

"This is your idea of Transformationalism through television?" said Alec, giving Dexter a fish-eyed stare.

Not that Dexter could really blame them.

That Deathship Earth and its irate emissary to the Monkey People had become a minor staple of popular culture might in the long term end up contributing something to planetary survival. But that it was in the form of crummy Man From the Future and Monkey People gags trading on obtuse ignorance of the difference between the Space Age and the New Age, between his space *visionaries* and Amanda Robin's space *cases*, did not exactly sit well with Dexter either.

Worse still, Ralf had started playing to this pinheaded popular perception of himself as the envoy of a future that was equal parts Deathship catastrophe and supermarket tabloid mysticism.

Dexter shrugged unhappily. "Don't blame this crap on me," he said. "I just write the opening monologues."

Truth be told, Ralf was taking more and more to tossing away Dexter's material and ad-libbing his way through that too these days. *His* character—and not just the comic playing it—seemed to have mutated not only beyond Dexter's control but into something not to his liking.

Now the spotlight had pinned a black man in a blue blazer, rose shirt, and white ascot whose heavy-browed eyes burned with zealous intensity.

"Surely twenty-second-century humanity will have achieved a superior level of moral consciousness due to their very knowledge of the tragic results of our own despiritualized age," he intoned in a powerful theatrical voice.

Another of Amanda's vibrating loonies!

"Okay, I admit it, I've been conning you all along, the twenty-second century is gonna be a Golden Age and I am its prophet, oh yeah!" Ralf declaimed, mugging regally at the audience and waving the shotgun mike like a comic scepter, tackily resplendent in the Suit From the Future, as called for in the contract with the rag-merchant to whom Texas Jimmy Balaban had sold the rights.

The Suit From the Future was made of cheesy white polyester, cut like a cartoon zoot suit, with a built-in elastic cummerbund and a trademarked black silhouette of Ralf's head on the breast pocket to verify authenticity. It was designed to look futuristic, be dirt cheap to manufacture, and go straight to the discount racks.

"We're gonna learn the Secret Knowledge of Vegetarian Dianetic Diuretics from the Thousand-Year-Old Man when we rediscover the Lost City of Atlantis under the North Pole and find the missing pages of the Darth Vedas!"

Modest laughter from the people in the Duncans' living room, who welcomed any deflation of the vibrating bubbleheadedness that had come to infect the show. But not much from the studio audience, the majority of whom, these days, were the sort of people who wanted to take Ralf all too seriously and whose collective sense of humor about themselves was severely limited.

Dexter's science fiction writers, scientists, and futurologists attracted nothing worse than the goonier fringe of science fiction fandom, but Amanda Robin's New Age snake-oil salespersons seemed chosen to *encourage* the trend to religious culties seeking signs and portents, flying saucer nuts, and devotees of high colonics and Pyramid Power, whole tribes of humorous but humorless weirdos.

And all too often these days, Ralf was stumbling over the fine line between playing *off* them and playing *to* them.

P. T. Barnum had asserted that no one had ever gone broke underestimating the intelligence of the American people, Dexter reflected, but how many comics had bombed out underestimating their gullibility?

———

"Whoo-eee, oh yeah, what the fuck, who gives a shit?" Foxy Loxy shouted in relief as the smoke filled her lungs anna White Light exploded in her brain.

"Hey, I really *needed* that one *right now!*" she told no one in particular. "An' fuck ya mother, I'll have another!"

Okay, so maybe y'could say there was somethin' uncool about trippin' through the park even late at night suckin' onna pipe like Popeye for alla slimeballs and dickheads t'see, but hey, this had *not* been a cool day!

Fact y'wouldn't be pushin' it t'say it fuckin' sucked, was real off-pissin', like almost gettin' busted three or four times, fuckin' goddamn tourists *screamin'* just because she pulls a knife, cops comin' after her just fer stickin' her paw inna gypsy's Dixie cup, I mean, what kinda shit is that, not a fuckin' trick t'be turned, even for a dollar, all fuckin' goddamn day an' half the night t'come up with enough bread for one stinkin' little rock, an' jeez, first three dealers don't even wanna *talk* t'her, whatsa matter, her money got AIDS, okay, so maybe she was inna kinda *state,* like hurtin', like ready t'bite the heads offa sackfulla live kittens an' spit 'em inna cocksuckers' face, hey, was that any reason t'tell her to fuck off, the customer is always right, ain't that what they say, ya stupid piecea shit.

After all that crap, she finally she managed to make a connection with some dealer looked in not much better shape that she was, an' so fuck it, she was not about to wait till she got back to th' nest, hey, come on, you chuggalug five gallons a beer, you gonna wait till you get home ta take a piss, an' besides, any a you assholes thinks you can screw around witha Knife Lady after a day like *this* just like ta see ya try!

Oh shit! Oh fuck! Oh great!

Loxy could see the bench under the broken light that marked the path to her nest, and wouldn't ya know it onna day like this, there were these two *guys* sittin' on it!

Well sorta. If you pushed it a little an' took another big hit, which seemed like a pretty good idea at the moment, y'could almost convince yourself they passed for human.

One a the fuckers was a big black guy wearin' this Mets jacket looked like the whole team used it for a snotrag for a full season an' cruddy old Levis. Other creep looked t'be some kind a PR inna bomber jacket so oldie moldy some kind a green mung was growin' on the brown leather. They was layin' back lookin' yellow around the edges, eyes like sunnyside up with ketchup, passin' a quart plastic Coke bottle filled with somethin' kinda pink looked like bubble gum dissolved in horse piss.

Loxy paused under a tree t'take a big one, and figure out what next, sensible thing was maybe t'wait 'em out, but on the other hand, this had been a real fucker of a day, an' her patience was kinda thin, and it could maybe take *hours* if ever for these assholes t'pass out, who the fuck did they think they was t'give the *Knife Lady* this shit!

So she reached into her bag an' grabbed the handle of the Big Ripper, an' boogied on up the path, thingta do was maybe just kinda slide past them inta the bushes like she was gonna take a piss, an' if they made ta follow her, just like ta see ya try, motherfuckas!

When she got near enough to the bench t'see that the black guy's fly was half open, no jockey shorts neither, that was his pubic hair hangin' out, the wind musta changed 'cause the smell a shit stuffed inta Frankenstein's old sweat socks socked her inna gut.

She just couldn't help it. It was scream or puke.

"Pee-fuckin'—yoo!" she shouted, holding her nose. "Hey, don't look now, but I think one a you fuckin' zombies just dumped a double load inya pants!"

"Yu gotta problem, cunt?" said the black guy.

The PR pushed out his cracked purple lips like a big dead fish, jerked the air in fronta his crotch like an invisible dork, and made this disgusting wet slobbering sucking sound.

"Yeah, you, ya goddamn fuckin' pieces a stupid shit stinkin' up the neighborhood!" Loxy screamed at the top of her lungs.

"Suck my dick, bitch," the black guy suggested, lurching up off the bench in her general direction an' fishin' out somethin' limp and squishy looked like six inches a rotten old garden hose.

An' the PR was up an' tryin' to get his own crummy fly open, makin' to circle behind her.

"Aaaaaaaah!" Loxy shouted like somethin' in onea those karate movies, as she whipped out the Big Ripper, raised it high above her head, stepped to one side, and brought it down with all her strength into the black guy's back as he stumbled past her.

He shrieked as the knife went in a couple a three inches, then Loxy grunted in pain as it hit bone and the shock went up her arm.

"Goddamn motherfucker, ow, that *hurt!*"

Really pissed off now, she yanked Rip outa his meat just in time t' see the fuckin' spic come grabbin' for her with both filthy claws an' his cock hangin' out. He got one hand on her shoulder before she turned an' rammed the knife inna sweet uppercut inta his fuckin' gut, no goddamn fuckin' bone this time, hee, hee, hee, felt sorta like punchin' it inna a sticky old pillow, a horrible gurgling scream, and then—

Wouldya believe it, the sonofabitch hasa *nerve* to throw up all over her *head*! Gross! Disgustin' thick smelly puke all over her *hair*! Jesus!

Loxy yanked her knife outa his gut an' made a pass at kickin' him inna nuts as he fell, clutchin' his stomach an' whinin' and blubberin', face forward onta the pavement.

Black guy is screaming bloody murder, tryin' to claw at his back like when you try t'get at an itch back there an' can't make it, woulda been kinda funny the ass-hole wasn't still comin' for her, anna buncha creeps from onea the packin' crate cities come humpin' up the path like fuckin' chimps howlin' an' gibberin', anna bloody puke dribblin' down outa her hair inta her eyes, fuckin' burned like hell, she cleared it away witha back of her knife hand, stomach heavin' like she gonna toss it herself, hey who could blame her, she slashed at the black guy's face, sliced his cheek real good, an' *he* starts t'scream, fer chrissakes, and—

"Fuckin' Knife Lady go apeshit!"

"Get her ass!"

Whistles!

Creeps scattering every which way!

"Here come da fuckin' cops!"

What a day!

Loxy ducked behind the bench, slid through the bushes to her nest, but shit, there was all that noise and screamin' an' commotion behind her, and oh shit, was that a siren, can't stay here!

She paused just long enough to catch her breath, well sorta, wipe mosta the puke outa her hair, she hoped, with a wad a toilet paper, smoke up the last of her rock t'keep herself from barfin' from the smell, an' then she was off through the park, besta stay off the paths, head east, where like they say the fuckin' *squad cars* gotta go in pairs, an' like lay low, go underground, gotta find some way to *disappear*!

That Ralf had achieved the face-recognition value of a soap opera lead was some-thing that Amanda was prepared to handle in public, but when he emerged from the dressing room still wearing the Suit, she decided that it would be necessary to have this tête-à-tête in the sort of place where *no one* got hassled.

So she opted for an oriental joint with a rather strange cross-cultural menu, and a clientele of working-class family ethnics and down-at-the-heels wise-guys. Even here the damned Suit From the Future proclaimed Ralf's trademarked iden-tity as surely as if the pope had waltzed in wearing his full clerical drag. But at least the attention was confined to nods, and pokes, and whispery stares, these not being the sort of folks to float up to the Guru From the Future with a zodiac of stars in their eyes.

"So?" said Ralf, after they had ordered Singapore noodles, shrimp in hot black bean sauce, Thai sausage salad, and beef teriyaki.

"So what's with the tent-show Maharishi act?" said Amanda. "And why must you wear that awful thing offstage?"

Ralf fingered the ludicrously wide lapel of the schlocky white suit as if the crummy polyester was the finest linen, smiled at her like Shiva doing a Kmart salesman.

"What's the matter?" he said. "Don't you like the material?"

"It reminds me of a comic opera swami out hunting ashram-rats in a Banana Republic safari suit."

"Come on, Amanda, isn't this just what you and your witch doctors ordered?" he said, picking up a shrimp neatly with his chopsticks and popping it into his mouth.

Was it? Amanda wondered. What did we think we were *really* conjuring up there on Big Rock?

If there was a fine line between donning a satirical mask and becoming the very character out of which you were supposedly taking the piss, the criterion for telling which side of it you were on was hardly subtle. The audience laughed or it didn't. A simple enough distinction for the millennia between the moment when one caveman first slapped another across the keister with an inflated pig's bladder for the tribal delectation and the invention of television.

But now it no longer mattered if the live audience didn't get the joke as long as the Nielsens showed numbers sufficient to persuade the powers that be to keep the show on the air. And the ratings for *The Word According to Ralf* were holding up even while a hefty proportion of the studio audience seemed not to be doing much laughing at the basic McGuffin, or even to realize that there *was* one.

Because from the point of view of the *television* audience, the joke was on *them*.

For there was also a line between following the difficult spiritual pathways to the Palace of Wisdom and standing around on the cosmicomical checkout line waiting for the Saucer People from Lemuria to arrive to take you on the Magical Mystery Tour of Graceland.

And *that* line was so fuzzy that most people didn't really know it existed.

To most people, there was no difference between Zen satori and crystal channeling, between Bodhisattvas and Operating Thetans, between transcendent states of consciousness and being royally fucked up.

To the mass television audience, Ralf and his tribe of sci-fi nerds and vibrating New Age weirdos were just another sitcom format. And a clown in a tent-show preacher suit making fools of them for the amusement of the audience *outside* the tent could easily enough be taken for the Second Coming of the Seventh Son by the rubes *inside*. And there were all-too-many hucksters of medicine show enlightenment working the desperately willing gullible to the general disrepute of anything that got called mystic or New Age.

Amanda had always know this galling truth, but tonight Ralf had rubbed her nose in it in a manner she could not ignore.

Ever since that party at Big Rock, she had turned up backstage to catch the show once or twice a week. From that perspective, the studio audience was an even tackier spectacle than what you saw on television in selected bits and pieces.

Dexter Lampkin's scientific savants were generally intellectually respectable, but the people they attracted were a geeky collection of sci-fi fans prone to standing up at random and babbling techie arcana and cultish gibberish. And while her A-team was equally credible, the sort of people their presence attracted hardly resembled serious seekers at a cutting-edge symposium on the Circuit. Nor did the merchandising tie-ins improve the TV image, especially since Jimmy Balaban had installed tables hawking schlocky T-shirts in the lobby.

Tonight, as usual, Ralf had given roughly equal time to the sci-fi nerds and the New Age fruitcakes, though when they were wearing a tie-in T-shirt or the Suit and going on about burrowing wormholes in the Swiss cheese of reality or curing cancer via quantum-level manipulation of prana by act of will, the distinction began to get blurry.

"Are our destinies written in the stars?"

"For sure, if we're a major motion picture studio."

"Ralf!"

"Hey Ralf!"

"Yeah, you, the guy in the yellow warm-up suit, what're you supposed to be, the captain of the Hairy Krishna track team?"

"Who were you in your last incarnation?" said the spaced-looking middle-aged man in the saffron sweats.

"Who was I in my last incarnation?" said Ralf, mugging at him for the benefit of the audience. "Hey, who knows, maybe *you!*"

He strutted closer to the lip of the stage, jabbed the shotgun mike here, there, everywhere. "Or you! Or you! Or *you*! Or *YOU!*" he cried.

He let the shotgun mike droop, and a strangely ironic little smile steal onto his face, and spoke in a much lower and slyly insinuating voice.

"Think about it, folks," he said. "*I won't be born for another hundred years.* So I could be the reincarnation of *anyone* alive today, now couldn't I?"

Ralf gave a cartoon grin, but when Amanda glanced at an air-feed monitor, his eyes seemed utterly humorless in close-up.

Dead stony silence.

"Hey, what's the matter, folks, these are *your* jokes," Ralf crooned. "I've *already* stolen schtick from comic greats of today that those guys haven't even *made up* yet. And when they *do*, you're gonna hold your noses, and throw dead cats, and say, pee-yoo, they stole those moldie oldies from *Ralf*!"

A scattering of nervous laughter did little to ease the strangeness of the moment. Nor did Ralf's oddly pensive expression as he slowly retreated toward the captain's chair, playing straight to the camera as it moved into the standard show-closing close-up.

"*Re*-incarnation?" he said. "What about *pre*-incarnation?"

There was not a hint of comic irony in that expression of shaky bemusement. "I'm copping material from comics who haven't thought it up yet, and when they do, they'll be stealing it from *me*! How's *that* for one of your time-travel paradoxes, sci-fi fans? *I'm stealing my own stolen jokes!*"

He shook his head.

And then. . . .

And then Amanda checked the air-feed monitor. And what she saw there, what those millions out there in Nielsenland must be seeing now, was the visage she had seen atop Big Rock; the fleshly mask, the eyes that seemed to be gazing through it from beyond the song and dance.

"So . . . *who's writing the jokes, folks?*" he said quite somberly.

The gaze never wavered.

"In the beginning was the Word, or so the Good Book says. . . ."

The Laughing Buddha smiled a beat before the credits rolled.

"So *the jokes* must be writing *me*."

It was the strangest exit Amanda had ever witnessed, a line that seemed funny only from the point of view of the entity who had delivered it.

The entity presently stuffing Singapore noodles into his mouth with chopsticks.

"Tonight was way over the top, Ralf," Amanda told him. "You're starting to take this guru act a little too seriously."

"What, me take myself seriously?" Ralf said ingenuously, flashing her a perfect plastic grin. "I'm just a stand-up comic, Amanda, remember?"

The eyes belied the line as they locked expressionlessly on Amanda's, as if challenging her to join him outside the parameters of some game she did not quite understand.

"You're not just playing it for laughs anymore, you're leading these spiritually gullible people on. You're deliberately encouraging a . . . a personality cult."

"So? I'm a *personality* . . . ain't I?"

Are you? wondered Amanda.

For the voice seemed to be coming from a great distance now, the eyes burnished ball bearings mirroring nothing but the void.

"Just like Elvis."

"Jesus . . ." Amanda muttered.

"Hey, *his* show's been on in Prime Time for *two thousand years*, and just *look* at the tie-in merchandise it's *still* moving," said Ralf, dropping effortlessly back into the realm of schtick-throwing Maya.

"And look what happened to *him!*" Amanda found herself wisecracking back in kind.

Ralf's lips smiled. But not those eyes.

They looked right at her, giving away everything and nothing as he reached out with his chopsticks and picked up a morsel of beef teriyaki and a slippery piece of tofu dripping with sauce with the skill of a zen master.

"If the show business of history teaches us anything," he said, "it's that when you keep bombing out with tragedy, you've got to take your last best shot with farce."

He winked, mugged a take, and dropped his chopstick load quite deliberately into his lap.

Ridin' the Broadway train down t' Penn Station shakin' an' hurtin', but at least sittin' down, after comin' up dry at 125th, *Harlem*, fer chrissakes, an' no luck, Foxy Loxy didn't have nothin' better t'do than think about the good news anna bad news about her new life down here inna subway.

The good news was that once you got in, you could stay down here forever, y'didn't hafta get cold or rained on, y'could always finda a place ta crash, an' you could fuckin' *make yourself invisible.*

All you hadda do was be somethin' people didn't wanna see.

People didn't wanna see that wino snorin' two seats down with alla scabs anna piss stain in his lap. For sure no one wanted to see those nigger kids across the aisle about ready to blow ya away for a quarter. Or the twitchin' junkies, anna nutcase pickin' his nose an' eating it an' maybe ready t'offer them a bite.

People didn't wanna see a lotta things inna subway, 'cause there was a lotta things down here they hoped wouldn't see *them*, an' if you just sat there starin' inta space or readin' your paper, then was maybe a good chance that the punks witha boom-box, droolin' maniacs, pieces a human shit, might decide t'notice some *other* asshole insteada *you*.

So all you hadda do was be one of 'em, an' you could fuckin' *disappear*! You pissed an' shit where you could long as there was no cops around, no place t'wash anyway, so y'didn't, no change a clothes, so y'got nice and raggy, an' anybody dumb enough t'give ya the fish-eye, shit, y'just gave to 'em back, held out your paw for spare change, started gibberin' "fuckshitcuntcockmotherfucker," and you'd be surprised how innerested they got inna ads onna wall or cracks inna platform floor or the insides of their own eyeballs.

You got one of 'em alone near the edge of the platform maybe thinkin' you just might give 'em a shove whenna train comes in, might even getta few coins in it.

And hey, Loxy had even gotten herself this seat just by hangin' over this old lady what had it, clutchin' at her gut, an' gaggin' for a couple a stops like she was gonna puke. Jeez, if you could manage a bad enough fart, you could probably clear yourself a whole subway car!

Lotta people lived down here an' *never* came up for what passed for air, hey, what the fuck for, you'd hafta pay again t'get back in, an' there was *everything* you needed right inna subway, pretzels an' cuchifritos an' hot dogs and candy bars an' all from the stands inna big stations an' all the piss coffee an' Diet Coke y'could drink. There was plenty a dark corners t'crash in, or you could sleep inna subway car all night.

The bad news was how fuckin' hard it was t'stay high.

You could panhandle or scrounge or steal a few coins atta time, so gettin' it together t'score a rock that wouldn't really holdya all day was an all-day thing, so you was *always* hurtin', kinda hard t'keep your thinkin' onna main line with a headache alla time an' that pain in your gut, an' nerves felt like you was plugged inta somethin' leakin' from the third rail, ya hadda eat an' drink once inna while too, and that could really set ya back hours. . . .

An' once y'finally got the bread together, then you hadda hassle witha scurve passed for dealers down here, an' that was when the job really got disgustin'!

Where there was people, there was dealers, better believe it, an' it was not exactly an occupation what attracted class acts, but when the customers was what you found down here, the dealers tended ta be a lot fewer an' far between an' the kinda slimeballs had just about enough left upstairs t'hold out their mitts for the bread, hand ya the shit, and maybe blow ya away you gave them any crap, was they packin' an' still sorta seein' straight.

T'make matters worse, the cops was always roustin' 'em, they was always gettin' ripped off, usually by each other, was inta the goods too much for their own good too most of the time, so the cast kept changin', nobody seemed to have no regular spot, an' every time you hadda score, like every fuckin' *day*, fer chrissakes, it was like some dork hittin' the scene for the first time.

Like Union Square station was usually good fer scorin', but t'day it had been crawlin' with cops, so it goes, over to 34th Street, but th' only dealers there were these two assholes punchin' at each other in slow motion, well shit, it's gonna hafta be 125th Street, long fuckin' ride uptown, an' not exactly a station made a white girl feel at home, but what the fuckya gonna do, and then there's nothing up *there* wouldya believe it, so by the time she finally slithered offa the train at Penn Station, Loxy was really hurtin', twitchin' inna gut, head felt likea sewer rat inside was tryin' t'bash its way out witha sledgehammer, an' not exactly inna mood t'put up with much more shit.

But she was gonna have to. 'Cause there was no dealers onna downtown platform. An' no dealers inna crossover space where they usually hung out. An' no dealers onna uptown platform station. No dealers inna subway station at all!

Loxy just about lost it, hey wouldn't you?

The subway station here connected up with a commuter train terminal, and she remembered once seein' a place in between where there just *had* t'be a dealer, but it meant she was gonna hafta pay again just t'get back inta the subway after!

"Cocksuckermotherfuckersonofabitch!" she screamed in outrage.

But things bein' what they were, which was gettin' t'be pain city, an' not another fuckin' idea in her head anyway, there was nothin' else t'do but score first, an' think about later later, law of the concrete jungle, right.

"Whathefuck you starin' at, ain'tcha got nothin' better ta do?" she shouted as she stormed through the crush by the subway exit, rollin' her eyes, practically droolin' blood an' in no fuckin' mood t'put up witha looks the assholes were givin' her as she elbowed 'em aside.

Make matters worse, this whole fuckin' place was a maze a subway station platforms, big railroad waiting rooms, all kinds a disgustin' fast-food joints, souvenir shops, newsstands, all connected by stairways, ramps, corridors—you could get lost in here forever, an' in her condition, Loxy almost did, sorta staggerin' around at top speed, hurtin' more an' more, gettin' more and more desperate, more an' more pissed off, better believe it ya stupid assholes, get the fuck outa my way or I'm gonna slice your nuts off, seemed like it took fuckin' hours to find the place she was lookin' for, an' then y'couldn't really say she found it, more like she just kinda finally managed to slide down into it like a turd down the bowl.

There was this kind of big long wide corridor thing between the railroad waiting rooms anna subway lines, some kinda awful bat cave made outa concrete, fuckin' low ceiling made it seem even bigger an' more cramped at the same time somehow, anna light was this dim yellow gray like right before a snowstorm, anna walls an' ceiling were subway fungus filthy green under alla graffiti, anna fast-food joints in here seemed t'have grown outa the general mung like poison mushrooms, anna smell a old grease an' rotten gorilla armpits comin' from 'em was enough t'take a wino's breath away.

And there was maybe people *livin'* in here.

If ya could call it that.

Around a corner an' down the middle of the cave went these streamsa more or less solid citizens with their briefcases an' umbrellas and goodies from Macy's an' all, inta the office, backta Long Island, whatever, starin' straight ahead like fuckin' robots an' keepin' well away from the sides of the passage between the LIRR an' the subway like they was gonna catch AIDS for sure if they touched what was there or even *looked at it*.

An' hey, who knows, maybe they hadda point. 'Cause the people camped out onna floor in torn up cardboard boxes an' million-year-old sleeping bags an' nests a plastic whatever an' all looked like they'd slit y'throat for a nickel an' ate cockroaches for breakfast when they could get 'em, which wasn't too often, maybe *could* give ya some disgusting disease just by lookin' atcha.

Fuckin' hundreds of 'em. Looked like one of them movies a some fuckin' Kraut city after the blitz or whatever ya call it the Warsaw Ghetto, all these raggy starvin' refugees livin' inna ruins an' pickin' through th' garbage heap for a chicken bone some nearsighted old lady mighta overlooked, hey you never knew, you got anything better t'do.

Street people. Bag ladies. Winos. Junkies. Blacks and PRs looked like they hung out here waitin' for someone with a wallet or a purse t'take a wrong turn. Half-dead old bums, maybe dead ones too, who knew until they moved or started to *really* stink. An' whole goddamn families livin' with momma an' poppa in huts made a packin' crates an' tents made a used garbage bags, wearin' th' kinda rags finally got thrown away by gypsy beggar tribes, eatin' better you don't ask.

An' there was cops. Maybe a dozen or so standin' around here an' there kinda twirlin' their billie clubs an' lookin' at the ceiling with that zookeeper stare they got which said don't make me *notice* nothin' on this beat an' I ain't gonna notice *you* less you do major stupid, trade gonna help both ballclubs, asshole, less you want one laid upside your head.

It was, even by Loxy's standards, whatcha hadda call a heavy scene, an' that was the downside, there was somethin' about it all she couldn't put her finger on that didn't just make her wanna puke but royally pissed her off.

The upside, though, was that it was pretty fuckin' obvious that the pope himself in Mother Teresa drag could score himself a rock in about five minutes down here.

"Look, Dexter, I know what you think of me," had been Amanda Robin's opening line on the phone. "I'm a crystal-channeling New Age ditz who's screwing up your neat sci-fi scenario with mystical mumbo-jumbo, but it's high time the two of us had a little private talk anyway."

It had been an irresistible hook, so Dexter had agreed to meet her for lunch, but insisted on El Gaucho, an Argentine grill where they served margaritas in half-liter pitchers and the closest thing to politically correct New Age fare was the french fries that came with the barbecue.

To his surprise when he arrived a barely trendy ten minutes late, Amanda Robin was already there, had secured a table and ordered a pitcher of margaritas. She was wearing a mannishly tailored gray skirted suit, a plain white man's dress shirt, and she had her hair up in a severe bun, as if to declare that she was here to talk business.

She poured them drinks as he sat down, and they sat there awkwardly for a beat sipping at them silently.

"Look, Dexter, I know that you don't like me—"

"Nothing personal—"

"But I'm the enemy."

Dexter had no idea what to say to that.

Fortunately, at that moment the waiter arrived with the menu, so Dexter had a legitimate excuse to bury his nose in it to cover his utter lack of savoir faire in these strange circumstances.

Said circumstances being having lunch with an attractive woman who even now was causing his brain to argue with his pecker, protesting that this was indeed the enemy and a person for whom he had considerable contempt.

Dexter ordered himself a skirt steak and black sausage, and was surprised when Amanda went for the full mixed grill, replete with liver, sweetbreads, and kidney. It seemed entirely out of character. Or was that the point? Or would he be trying to read the hidden meaning in the patterns of the sawdust on the floor next?

"This is probably a lot more difficult for you than it is for me," Amanda said when the waiter had departed.

"Is it?"

Amanda nodded over the lip of her margarita glass as she took a sip. "I know you a lot better than you know me."

"You had your astrologer read my horoscope?" Dexter snapped.

"I've read four of your novels," Amanda said.

"*You have?*" Dexter exclaimed.

Great Ghu, was the woman a closet *fan*? Funny, you don't *look* fannish, he was sorely tempted to say.

"Including *The Transformation*, which I found . . . very interesting under the circumstances."

"What circumstances?" said Dexter, eyeing her narrowly.

"The current circumstances," said Amanda Robin.

"Look, lady, *you* called *me*, remember, so would you mind telling me what the hell this is about?"

"Ralf, what else?"

"Ralf?"

At which point, the food arrived, which seemed to provoke some kind of transformation in Amanda Robin's attitude. Even as she forked liver and skirt steak onto her platter and went at it heartily, she became more tentative, uncertain, almost furtive.

"It's hardly the kind of thing I can talk to Jimmy about, but you, those books, that one book in particular, you think I'm some kind of weirdo anyway, and a lot of people probably think you're coming from outer space yourself . . ."

"En ingles, por favor," said Dexter, washing down a bite of steak with a significant belt of margarita.

"Have you noticed anything strange about Ralf?" said Amanda Robin.

"Have I noticed anything strange about Ralf? Have you noticed that Adolf Hitler had these latent anti-Semitic tendencies?"

"I mean lately."

"You mean since you conned your way onto the staff and started stuffing the audience with your jive-ass New Age mystics?"

Dexter was rewarded by a visible flash of anger in those big green eyes. But he watched with no little admiration as she controlled it completely and came back at him in a calm, disciplined voice.

"You may be gratified to hear that I don't like it any better than you do. That's why this conversation, Dexter."

Somewhat shamed by her measured response to his overt hostility, Dexter paid his enemy, if that was what she was, the honor of cooling himself down, looking her straight in the eye, and taking at least her sincerity seriously.

"We *are* talking about the same thing?" he said. "The guru act? It's stopped being funny? That's what you're worried about?"

Amanda Robin took a sip of margarita, resumed eating. "Oh, it's still funny to most of the people watching it on television. But it's attracting an audience that's taking it *seriously. Ordinary* people too. True Believers, Dexter. In *The Word According To.*"

"That isn't what you wanted?" Dexter asked in genuine surprise.

"Is it what *you* wanted, Dexter? Look deep. Think carefully."

For some reason, Dexter did.

He had certainly thrown that pebble into the sea of fandom *knowing* it would ripple outward into some kind of tacky fannish cult. In order to save the show.

But why should he care if Ralf was seduced by the allure of sleazy guruhood? Why should he give a damn if Amanda Robin and her cronies were warping the fannish cult into something beyond his heart's desire?

But he did.

It really pissed him off.

And when you came right down to it, what other real reason did he have for the hostility he felt toward this attractive and intelligent woman?

"Yes and no," he was forced to admit.

"Me too," said Amanda Robin.

She put down her knife and fork, took a drink, leaned forward slightly. "Can we be honest with each other?" she said.

"We could try," said Dexter, and found that he meant it sincerely.

"I've read *The Transformation*, and I do believe I understand what you were trying to do then, and what you've been trying to use Ralf to do now. . . ."

"Do you?" Dexter said.

Dexter found himself also leaning forward, if not into her body space, then closer to it. How could he not? She was attractive, her eyes were locked on his, and she was holding forth on his favorite subject.

"You believe that our species is passing through a karmic nexus inherent in the existential position of consciousness arising in a material matrix, of spirit in the realm of Maya, which will destroy us unless we can transform ourselves into beings worthy of attaining a higher evolutionary level."

"Not exactly how I'd put it," Dexter stammered, "but. . . ."

But this was a better one-paragraph thematic summary than anything in the reviews the book had received, including the raves.

She grinned at him, perhaps manipulatively, but not without a certain saving irony.

"We vibrating New Age ditzes aren't *all* airheads, Dexter," she said. "And we both know that there are more legitimate viewpoints through which to ponder ultimate matters of human destiny than are dreamt of in your logical positivist philosophies, now don't we?"

Dexter found himself reminding himself that the woman was an actress, that this sudden revelation of intellectual depths could be craft, and that his response to it could not be said to be unaffected by the flattery.

"What does all this have to do with Ralf?" he demanded with not terribly convincing gruffness.

"You wrote that book *about* a conspiracy to bring about the great transformation in order to *create* that transformation yourself."

"Uh. . . ."

Dexter burned with the embarrassment of an adolescent dream of having one's pants fall down in a roomful of beautiful and sophisticated women to reveal a throbbing and jejune egoistic hard-on.

But Amanda Robin's smile was warmly knowing rather than cruelly sophisticated. "We were young, burning with noble ideals and passions, the vision was in the air, we were surfing the wave of the future. . . ."

She laughed. She raised her glass and toasted him. "Anyone who was worth anything at the time had to take their best shot at midwifing the Great Transformation."

She shrugged. "And of course, none of us succeeded."

Admit it, Lampkin, Dexter thought, you're not falling in love with this woman, you don't even really like her, but you *are* becoming fascinated. And you wouldn't kick her ass out of bed either.

"Ralf?" he muttered rather weakly. "We were supposed to be talking about *Ralf*?"

"But we are, aren't we?" Amanda said. "Ralf was your second chance, the answer to your midlife crisis—"

"Not funny!" Dexter snapped belligerently.

Amanda Robin reached out and touched his arm. Contrary to conventional expectations, there was no flash of electrical energy.

"Not meant to be, Dexter," she said. "What's a midlife crisis but the mature adult confronting the unfulfilled dreams of youth? And if a chance to fulfill them comes along, however crazy . . . ?"

She shrugged rather fetchingly. "Who wouldn't?" she said. "Not me. Not you. Right?"

"Right," sighed Dexter. "But I never meant this Guru From the Future crap to be taken seriously!"

"Didn't you, Dexter?" said Amanda Robin.

"No, I didn't!" Dexter insisted. "I wanted to use the show to transform public consciousness through humor. I never wanted to create a cult of vibrating loonies and space cadets that took Ralf *seriously*! And I *certainly* didn't want *Ralf* to start *playing* to it seriously! Believe me, in my little world of science fiction, I've seen far too much of that shit already!"

He paused, taken aback by his own sudden vehemence, calmed himself by taking a slow drink of his margarita while he pondered the woman who was pondering him.

"Haven't you, Amanda?" he finally said. "Surely in your little world of astrologers to the stars, and ninja zen gurus to the rich and fatuous, you have had some occasion to observe what happens when the dealers get hooked on their own charismatic snake oil?"

Amanda Robin just cocked her head to one side and nodded almost imperceptibly.

"That's it, isn't it?" Dexter said slowly in dawning comprehension. "*That's* why this conversation."

Amanda picked up her knife and fork, took a piece of sweetbreads off her grill, put it on her plate, and regarded the act of cutting it carefully. "Yes," she muttered. "Sort of." She put a morsel into her mouth and chewed it reflectively.

"Sort of?" said Dexter.

Amanda looked up at him, seemed to be studying him nervously as if trying to reach some sort of decision. Then she shrugged, refilled her half-empty glass, and slugged half of it down like one of the boys chugalugging a boilermaker.

"What if *we're* not using Ralf for *our* ends at all?" she said. "What if some entity is using *us* to . . . to manifest itself in the realm of maya?"

"*Entity?*"

Amanda seemed to be regarding him furtively out of the corner of her eyes even while looking straight at him. "I don't suppose I could persuade you to take a conceptual system involving material avatars of a transmaterial godhead seriously?" she said.

Now it was Dexter's turn to seek a stiff belt of liquid fortification. "Somehow I doubt it," he said dryly.

"Could I sell you the Zeitgeist at least, maybe?" Amanda suggested.

"*Maybe* . . . in a metaphorical manner of speaking."

"How about an untimebound collective species unconscious that manifests itself at times in our individual consciousness through dreams and creative inspiration—"

"What's this got—"

"—attempting in desperation to incarnate itself on the cusp of our species' Transformation Crisis, in order to save us from our own otherwise soon to be terminal shitheadedness and see us through into the transformational stage of our—"

"Hey, wait a minute, *I* wrote that!" Dexter exclaimed. "Well, uh, sort of . . ." he added uneasily, realizing what he was saying.

"Where do you get your crazy ideas, Dexter?"

Dexter groaned.

Amanda laughed. "Right," she said, "the question writers hear most often and most dread. But where *do* those inspirational flashes and images come from? Similar to what emerges from somewhere into our individual consciousness when we're dreaming, isn't it?"

Dexter found himself eyeing her narrowly. "Well, yeah . . ." he muttered.

"Something moving *through* you, something emerging from the beyond within, but while you're awake, you've felt that happening, now haven't you?"

Dexter found himself regarding Amanda Robin now in no little amazement, and there was a slippery slidy feeling in his head that seemed to have nothing to do with tequila. "How did you—"

"I've been working with dream states and creativity for a long time," Amanda said. "I've worked with a lot of writers and artists. I've developed techniques for summoning up what I call the doorway to the Dreamtime in a *consciousness* state."

She sighed. "I can summon the doorway sometimes, if not reliably, and images *will* come forth from the vasty deep beyond," she said. She shrugged. "But the true nature of the realm beyond the doorway remains a mystery to us both, doesn't it, Dexter?"

Dexter took another drink. His physical surroundings seemed outside his sphere of focus, almost as if they had entered that very elusive and allusive space, the existence of which no one who wrote fiction, let alone science fiction, could rationally deny.

"But . . . but what does all this have to do with Ralf?" he said.

"*That* is the question," said Amanda Robin. "Is the Ralf we see on the tube really *our* creation? You and me and a one-schtick pony Jimmy Balaban found in the Borscht Belt? Some comic came up with the basic gimmick, I polished the act, and you gave him a detailed future to come from?"

"Of course!"

"Then where did *all that* come from?"

"We made it all up."

"Sure, we made it all up. Just our own crazy ideas. And where do we get our crazy ideas from?"

"From . . . from. . . ."

"From what lies beyond the doorway," said Amanda Robin. "And what is that? A question whose answer I've sought all my adult life. And I don't know. Do you?"

"You're losing me, lady," Dexter protested.

But it wasn't really true. Somehow she had led him by a relentless train of rational logic into a place where, rationally, logic no longer applied.

No, she hadn't lost him. But he found himself wishing she had as she looked deeply into his eyes and he found himself unable to look away.

"A scientist locks a chimpanzee in a room with some bananas in a sealed box and various tools with which the chimp may be able to open it," she said. "After a while, he comes back and peers through the keyhole to see how the chimp is doing."

She paused for a perfect theatrical beat.

"But what he sees on the other side of the doorway is an intelligent eye studying *him*."

"What are you trying to tell me?"

"That lately I know how he feels," Amanda said. "Don't you?"

"I haven't the slightest idea what you're talking about," Dexter told her.

"I thought we had agreed to be honest with each other."

"I *am* being honest with you," Dexter insisted.

"You can honestly tell me that you've never had the feeling that there's someone or something on the other side of the doorway, in the place where your crazy ideas come from, looking back at you, using you, and me, and a broken-down Borscht Belt comic who calls himself Ralf to . . . to. . . ."

"To do *what*?" Dexter demanded.

For of course, he *did* know what she was talking about, he *had* had that feeling. . . .

Amanda Robin shrugged. "I was hoping you could tell me," she said.

"Tell you *what*?"

"Come on, Dexter, we've both been using a Ralf we've created, or so we think. You've been trying create a public awareness of what you call the Transformation Crisis, and I've been trying to manifest the avatar of the Zeitgeist that these times *need*—Prometheus the Light-Bringer—rather than what we've been conjuring at least since Alamagordo and would seem to deserve, namely Shiva the Destroyer, Breaker of Worlds."

Her eyes burned with passionate sincerity. "Okay, so maybe you can't buy my intellectual framework," she said, "but you're not going to sit there and tell me it doesn't amount to the same thing!"

Dexter found himself confronted by an intellect he could hardly deny was the equal of his own, yet working off a conceptual framework that he could not at all accept. An intellect who was going him one better by acknowledging that dichotomy of worldviews, accepting it for what it was, and moving on.

An intellect who would have proven herself his superior if he could not rise to the occasion and do the same.

"No," he said, "I'm not."

"And you're not going to tell me that Ralf hasn't evolved beyond whatever we thought we were creating into something that neither of us controls?"

"No," said Dexter, "I'm not."

"So what are we dealing with?"

"There's a story told about L. Ron Hubbard, who started Scientology as a science fiction hack and became a god to millions of paying customers," Dexter told her. "If you asked him if he was really the messiah, Hubbard would tell you it was all a con. If you asked him if it was really all a con, Hubbard would rise up on his high white horse and declare himself the Great I Am."

Amanda Robin eyed him narrowly.

"I knew a junkie who claimed that his drug of choice really *wasn't* addictive. 'Every year I stop for three days to make sure I'm not hooked,' he told me, 'and then, when I see I can do it, I go back to shooting heroin.'"

Dexter paused, shrugged.

"And *that*," he said, "was only smack."

"Point taken," Amanda said, "but there's a lot more to it than that."

"He's a third-rate comic no one ever heard of until he lucked into this messianic dope, which is the strongest and most seductive and most addictive stuff there is."

"Unless it's the real thing. . . ."

"There *is* no real thing!"

"There is a certain school of thought that contends that there is *nothing but* the real thing," said Amanda Robin. "That we are all dreams, and all that is real is the Dreamer who awakes at the end of each Great Age to bring an end to the dance of Maya's veils."

And for a moment, her eyes became windows, doorways you might almost say, behind which Dexter could see . . . could see. . . .

"Your conceptual framework or mine, you can hardly contend that we are not living at the ending of such a Great Age," she said. "And there have been times when I've looked behind Ralf's eyes and seen the Dreamer stirring from his sleep."

Amanda Robin sighed, leaned backwards, and some spell seemed to have been broken. The sounds of the room, the smells of the cooling meat, came whooshing back into Dexter's sphere of awareness.

He blinked.

"But of course, I'm just a vibrating lady," she said.

And when he looked at her now, there was nothing out of the ordinary at all, except a knowing little smile that seemed to say that some connection had been made, that like it or not, they had become reluctant partners in the same elusive dance.

A tremendous string a stinkin' loud farts from the wino crashin' nexta her woke Foxy Loxy outa some awful dream about these fuckin' robot things made outa junkyard scraps, razor blades, an' shrunken rat heads comin' after her with giant dentist's drills inta somethin' not much better.

There she was, twitchin' and jerkin' onna filthy asphalt floor of th' Penn Station bat cave, the wino fartin' on one sidea her, fat old bag lady babblin' t'herself on the other, a zillion other creeps snorin' scratchin' their nuts eatin' crap whackin' the fuckin' whinin' kiddies stealin' each other's shit, anna gorilla a jackhammer inta her brain t'tell her it was fuckin' time to get her ass in gear an' *score*, bitch, 'fore y'start pukin' up blood!

Y'could get usedta *anything*, Foxy Loxy had discovered since she became one a the cave bats—'cept of course not gettin' high!

Y'could get usedta crashin' right onna floor without screwin' around scroungin' up cartons or plastic or shit, hey who needed it right, somebody gonna steal it anyway, whaddya need, *privacy*, right, go ahead, try an' rape me, asshole, it's a buck a pop or a knife inna gut, besides which wasn't much down here could still get it up, y'couldn't even sell a blow job for a nickel.

Y'could get used t'eatin' candy bars an' hot dogs looked like boiled poodle pricks only they didn't taste as good an' gave ya the trots, y'hadda wipe yer ass witha *New York Times* or *El Diario*, an' y'could get used t'the smell anna noise of a few hunnered people fartin' an' belchin' around you, an' the light was always the color a piss through a dirty window, an' there was a stream of fuckin' commuters prancin' through your bedroom day and night like you wasn't there, anna cops standin' around, anna dead body here an' there for a few days until somebody bothered t'pick it up never really hurt nobody, y'came down to it, not like they waited for th' maggots t'start crawlin' around first, after all. . . .

Y'could get used t'all that real easy 'cause livin' here had its compensations. Their stuff was low-grade shit, but there was always half a dozen dealers slimin' around almost like havin' *room service,* fuckin' cops didn't care *what* the fuck you did as long as y'didn't hassle the taxpayers on *their* beat, which they were none too happy to have gotten stuck with lemme tellya, all y'hadda do was crawl over t'onea the hot-dog stands once inna while, finda dark corner of which there were plenty down here t'piss an' shit when y'hadda, an' the rest a the time y'could just light up an' watch the show. . . .

That is, when you wasn't clutchin' your gut t'keep your insides from fallin' out witha hammer in your head like now, an' facin' the awful hassle a figurin' out how th'fuck t'get enough coin together t'score the next hit, which was fuckin' mosta the time, couldn't get used to *this* shit inna million years. . . .

First week or so down in here, Loxy had left every day t'work the subway platforms an' stations, commutin' t'work just like the citizens, right, panhandlin', snatchin' coins from the gypsy kids, blind beggars, usual shit, comin' back to score an' crash.

But it cost to move out an' in every day, so she started out behind, an' it became harder an' harder t'hold herself together for alla time it took to scrounge up the money an' then drag her twitchin' ass back here t'score, felt like she was crawlin' around on her hands and knees half the time, her condition it was hard to tell was she imaginin' it or not, started takin' too many chances, purse snatches, pocket pickin', always almost gettin' busted, taking kicks t'the ribs, whacked inna chops, kinda foggin' out alotta the time things was gettin' kind dicey.

So somewhere along the line, who could tell when, was no days or nights down here, y'lost track a time, Loxy had just stopped leavin', what the fuck for, y'could just as well work the cave alla good it didya, right. . . .

Lotta th' locals was crashed out halfa the time, maybe dead, who knew, was coins inna pockets sometimes, cops didn't give a shit about nothin' didn't make the fuckin' taxpayers give 'em any shit, wasn't like she was the only one doin' it, after all, those what was awake always crawlin' around inta this an' that like cockroaches, all she hadda do was flash ol' Rip often enough whenna cops wasn't lookin', which was mosta the time, t'keep the worst of 'em afraid a her, not try t'roll anyone in any condition t'give the ol' Knife Lady shit he happened t'wake up atta wrong time, an' it usually didn't take much longer than workin' the subways t'put it t'gether like all fuckin' damn day.

Loxy rolled over, went through the fuckin' wino's pockets, comin' up dry, managed t'pry herself upright more or less, bumble down th' corridor along the wall an' away from the commuter traffic so's the two fuckin' cops clockin' her would keep lookin' right through her 'steada givin' her no shit an' inta th' main drag.

This had maybe been a passage to a street exit once from the look a the shop fronts linin' both walls, but these days most of 'em was shuttered, an' if the exit was still open, the citizens didn't wanna know about it, 'cause here it was just about wall-to-wall cardboard huts garbage bag tents sleepin' bags crashed out street people lurkin' muggers an' dealers an' general scurve an' all crammed inta here witha cops kinda just sealin' it an' lettin' what passed for nature take its fuckin' course. . . .

Y'hadda be careful here, was these pissed off young guys some of 'em witha wife an' kiddies just down on their luck y'piece a fuckin' street shit, would beat the livin' crap outa you they thought you was even *thinkin'* a goin' through their kit, anna gypsy mommas with enougha their fuckin' little monsters t'give ya a problem an' all kinds a fuckin' junkies an' your all-purpose ravin' maniacs plus y'tried t'roll a *dealer* sleepin' whatever th' fuck off even if he didn't blow you away or cut y'head off, you'll never score nothin' down here again you stupid fuckin' cunt!

So Loxy kept one hand onna handle of the Big Ripper inside her bag as she sank t'the floor an' melted inta the wrigglin' action, movin' around real slow, stickin' her hand here, pokin' around there, them that saw what she was doin' wasn't inta givin' her no shit about it, 'cause most anyone who had it together that far was also doin' likewise t'them what was more or less out cold.

Seemed t'go on for the usual three or four fuckin' years, nickel here, fuckin' dime there, goddamn quarter once or twice, shakin', an' jerkin', these fuckin' pains in her gut, brains felt like they was about to explode out her nose, seemed to have pissed in her panties somewhere along the line least didn't take a shit big fuckin' deal, an' about as close to comin' up witha bread as she was t'bein' elected Queen a fuckin' England was beginning t'seem. . . .

Hmmm, maybe this dude got somethin' more than a fuckin' dime, Loxy thought, anyway hoped, as she slithered over t'this fat old black guy flat on his back an' snorin' with his belly inna air, that was a half-empty fifth a Old Crow in his paw, not your usual white port muscatel piss musta set him back a couple bags' worth 'less he'd boosted it. . . .

She flopped over on her side nexta him like she was passin' out, twitchin' an' jerkin' like some kinda fuckin' junkie goin' through withdrawal, not that it took too much effort under th' circumstances, muttering, an' gruntin', and blowin' little bubbles a drool, not the sorta scene anyone was gonna be innerested in noticin', an' when that didn't seem t'wake him up none, she figured it was safe t'assume he was out cold enough.

So she walked a hand across the dirty asphalt like a big ol' spider and inta a pea-coat pocket, feelin' around, somethin' squishy maybe ya didn't really wanna know, was all, snaked it out, under the coat, inta a front pants pocket, jeez is that a wad a fuckin' *bills*—

"WHUT DUH FUCK YOO DOOIN'!"

Bam! Crash! Yow! Ow! Fuck!

Hard t'tell what happened first, somehow th' motherfucker's got her by the wrist with one hand, awful fuckin' pain makin' it hard t'see or think stink a bourbon, really dizzy, 'bout t'pass out, bastard's cracked her onna top of her head with th' bottle, an' he's holdin' th' jagged end of it in the other hand, lookin' like he's gonna shove th' broken glass right in her fuckin' *eyes*!

Anna Ripper is already outa her bag, an' she's screamin' an' jabbin' the knife hard as she can inta the arm a' the hand that's holdin' her wrist.

"Aaaaaah!" He howls as he lets go, she manages t' roll away from th' broken bottle, just a sharp pain across her cheek, yankin' out the knife, staggerin' t' her feet—

"Fuck!"

"Get her!"

"Cops!"

"Shit!"

Everybody what ain't too dead t'the world is up on their feet, screamin', and cursin', an' carryin' on, 'steada mindin' their own fuckin' business, whole place boilin' around like someone just turned onna light inna crapper fulla cockroaches, some of 'em comin' at her, some of 'em tryin' to get away, the black guy is gettin' t'his feet, he's a BIG motherfucker, one arm's got all this neat red blood like pumpin' out, but he's still got the broken bottle in the other hand, an' from the way his fuckin' bloodshot eyes seems like t'pop outa his head, anna screamin', and lurchin' toward her an' all, seems like for some reason y'could say he's like kinda *pissed off*, and she ain't feelin' too good herself, head like a garbage pail fulla smashed Coke bottles an' rusty razor blades, not too steady around the knees, smella booze all over her face, all this warm sticky stuff must be *blood*, an' she's standin' there hunched over holdin' a big bloody old knife, which could get kinda embarrassing, since *here come the fuckin' cops!*

Two of them, runnin' down from the main corridor, wavin' their billy clubs, trippin' an' slippin' over cardboard boxes, gypsy kids, winos, dead bodies, whatever, shovin' their way through the confusion, an' comin' for her!

"Police! Drop that fuckin' knife!"

"Stay right where you are! Police!"

Well, somehow, even in her present condition, Loxy managed to figure it didn't seem like whatever they wanted t'talk about was gonna be somethin' she wanted t'hear, an' lettin' go a the Big Ripper didn't seem like too bright an idea either unner the circumstances.

So Loxy started to run.

She headed for the right-hand wall, tryin' t'put as many people between her anna cops as she could, kickin' over boxes, sendin' sleepin' bags and whatever flyin', shovin' a couplea kids in front of her, wavin' the bloody knife an' screamin' to keep it all stirred up, an' before the cops can get across the mob scene to her, she gets t'the wall, an' she turns, an' she's runnin' back up along it to the main corridor, the cops have turned too, an' they're comin' up behind her now, or tryin' to, shovin', an' kickin' people outa their way. . . .

An' oh shit, one of 'em pulled out his fuckin' *gun*!

But by that time, she's reached the corridor fulla commuters, an' she jumps out right inta the middle a the stream, screamin', and droolin', an' wavin' her big bloody knife, causin' somethin' of a commotion, everyone tryin' t'get outa her way an' nobody about t'stop her, makes it kinda hard for the cops t'start shootin', keeps 'em from catchin' up. . . .

Up the fuckin' corridor t'the subway entrance, mob a people as usual, line a pay gates blockin' off the entrance to the platforms, she sticks bloody ol' Rip inna face a some bitch t'persuade her to let her squeeze through behind, likewise persuades the citizens t'get the fuck outa her way as she races across the access area toward the steps down t'the downtown platform, an' pauses t'look behind.

Shit they were still comin' after her, looked to be three or four of 'em now, she ran down the stairs, or tried to, trippin' over some stupid asshole comin' up, watch-whereyagoin' ya stupid prick, stumblin' down the last few stairs, knockin' over some old lady starts cursin' in Italian or whatever, fell onta the platform fulla dickheads waitin' for the next train on her goddamn hands and knees.

Shamblin', crawlin', gettin' more or less to her feet at the same time somehow, like some kinda ape thing shovin' through the crowd onna platform, cuttin' her way through the human jungle with her machete, pantin', groanin', about outa breath, hard t'see through the blood, feel like pukin', over her shoulder she saw, oh shit, cops still comin', five, six, a million of 'em now, wavin' their fuckin' guns, citizens screamin', scatterin, gotta—

Oh shit.

End of the platform about three feet in front of her, an' half the fuckin' cops inna Pig Apple comin' up behind!

No time t'think, not much left t'think *with* atta moment neither, nothin' else t'do but—

Loxy got down on her hands an' knees, slithered to the lip of the platform, turned her ass to the three-foot drop, an' shoved herself over, landin' onna tarry wooden ties between the rails with a painful whack of her shins, an' then she's scrambling forward, half-runnin', half-fallin', inta the fuckin' tunnel, dark enough, but not so dark as y'might think, what with all these little blue lights. . . .

Crack! Whang! Pa-*chung*!

Jesus fuckin' Christ!

Behind her, outlined inna bright light from the platform, was four or five fuckin' cops, motherfuckers *still* comin' after her—

Crack! Crack! Scree!

—an' now they were *shootin'* at her!

Snot was dribblin' outa her nose, a million razor blades was skinnin' her ribs from her flesh from th' inside, she couldn't hardly breathe no more, all kindsa colored lights sparklin' and flashin' in her eyes, hard t'remember what she was doin' somehow, oh yeah, runnin' deeper inta the dark, round the bend, Whing! Plang! things zippin' past her bouncin' off the walls, gotta stop an' puke—

What's that sound like a giant gut rumblin' whole fuckin' place is shakin'?

Oh look, here comesa big bright light!

A big square a yellow light comin' up the tunnel at her, two little lights to the side like headlights, an' this strip a letterin' lit up above it she couldn't quite read, what th' fuck—

Subway train comin' right atcha, asshole, that's what!

Loxy had about ten seconds t'think, anyway t'move, she squished herself backwards against the tunnel wall, pipes, cables, some such shit, screamin', an' droolin', an' yellin, pissin' in her pants, she kinda oozed along the wall, an' then, just as th' fuckin' train was about to smash her flat, she sorta popped backwards inta this little empty space or something, anna train came roarin' an' rumblin' an' screechin' by about six inches from her nose for what seemed like forever while she did plenty a screamin' an' yellin' herself, better believe it, anna great big loada burnin' hot shit exploded outa her asshole an' slid down her thighs. . . .

And then . . .

And then the train was past her, an' everything was suddenly different. Like she had died an' gone someplace else not exactly nobody's idea of fuckin' heaven, maybe, but a big improvement over where she had been before, better believe it.

Whether the train had squashed the fuckin' cops chasin' her was none a her business, who gave a fuckin' shit, but even if they *had* gotten outa its way, there was now maybe half a dozen subway cars between her and them.

Loxy leaned forward an' let it all go, nice big disgustin' acid puke hurt the back a her throat comin' out but, ah gettin' rid of it sure felt good, an' she could breathe now, an' suddenly it was real quiet, as she peeled herself outa the little empty space inna wall had saved her ass, an' stood there all by herself onna subway track ties lookin' down the tunnel into the endless and bottomless night.

Not as scary as y'might think.

Considering where she just come from.

One after the other, these little blue bulbs kinda lit the way farther in, seemed t'go on down forever inta the secret world beneath the city where no cops was about t'go, where no one was gonna find her, where y'could *really* disappear, who knows how far y'could go, who knows where y'might come out the other side if you ever did, who knew what was down in there in front of her in the dim blue darkness, who cared, 'cause for sure Loxy knew what was waitin' back there for her at the other side of the subway train.

Her thighs smeared with her own shit, her head ringing like a great big church bell, her only friend, the Big Ripper, clutched tightly in her hand, big hollow feelin' in her gut, dizzy kinda, twitchin' and jerkin', all kinda little colored thingies sparkin' an' flashin' in front of her like some screwed up TV set, but somehow feelin' kinda weirdly floaty an' peaceful just the same, Foxy Loxy started walkin' down down down into the cool damp quiet of the welcoming dark. . . .

Life had really turned sweet, Texas Jimmy Balaban reflected when the furniture delivery guys left. The judge had awarded his latest ex half of his salary as producer of *The Word According to Ralf,* but thanks to the accountant he had hired after the judgment but before Archie Madden picked up the show for the second thirteen weeks, Jimmy had had the last laugh.

The accountant set up a production corporation with himself and Ralf as shareholders to receive all monies due them. So the alimony she ended up with was whatever salary he chose to have the corporation pay him as line producer of the show.

Which—since the corporation owned this fancy new apartment above the Strip, everything in it, plus the Cadillac, was no more than what he needed to eat, drink, and live the high life—amounted to bupkis. Which smelled like victory on a bright sunny morning like this.

Jimmy chose a Montecristo Churchill from the selection of cigars in the big walnut humidor, what the hell, it wasn't as if he *inhaled* the things. He poured himself a Wild Turkey on the rocks, and went out on his second-floor balcony to clock the action around the pool.

This bachelor pad only a block north of the Sunset Strip was maybe a little downscale from what he could've afforded, but he was free, a big-shot TV producer with dough, and under those circumstances, he preferred *this* view.

Namely a balcony overlooking the pool of a fancy Hollywood apartment complex where the friendly neighbors ran heavily toward aspiring actresses and airline stewardesses living two and three to a nest.

Yeah, you couldn't say that things were exactly perfect, when were they ever, Jimmy thought as he puffed contentedly on contraband Havana, but in the real world, this was as good as you could reasonably expect it to get.

Too bad Dex and Amanda couldn't learn to lighten up. What was the point of good fortune if you made yourself too uptight with worrying how long it could last to enjoy it while you had it?

That lunch meeting with Amanda full of Actors Studio malarkey!

Oy! Archetypes! Personas! Actors being taken over by the characters they were playing and going schizo! Ralf being taken over by the little man who wasn't there or the schlockgeist or something, the way Shatner got to forgetting he wasn't really Captain Kirk.

After all, as he had gently pointed out, while the Method had produced quite a few successful actors and actresses, who had ever heard of a Method *comedian*?

And then Lampkin comes on with *his* crap about how the character *he* had created had escaped from his laboratory like Dr. Frankenstein's monster and was turning into the Thing That Was Gonna Eat Its Fan Club!

As if he was talking to a guy who had never handled a comic before. When it was Dex who had had no previous experience with the mental health or lack thereof of comedians.

"Relax, Dex," Jimmy had assured him, "take it from me, there's no such thing as a comic playing with a matched set of marbles, if they're not refugees from the bin, they're on their way there, why do you think they call it the funny farm in the first place?"

Jimmy had patiently explained that since most jokes worked off the grotesque exaggeration of the real world, it should not be so surprising that the guys who made a living telling them developed a warped outlook, or to put it the other way around, if you didn't see things through schtick-colored glasses, it was gonna be kind of hard to make it as a stand-up comic.

On the other hand, Dex and Amanda singing in harmony on anything being about as common as a pit bull making goo-goo eyes at a pussycat, and his golden meal ticket having admittedly been a little less funny since the pickup, Jimmy *had* decided that maybe it was time to sit him down for a Dutch Uncle talk.

This he had done in the dressing room after a show in which Ralf had drifted way too far into the nether reaches of caca with another endless dumb routine on toxic dumps, tummeling the creeps in the audience like Don Rickles standing in for Charlton Heston in one of those biblical epics, and not exactly gotten wall-to-wall laughs with any of it.

Ralf bombed into the dressing room reeking of sweat and adrenaline, tapping his fingers frenetically on the dressing table with one hand while wiping the makeup off his face with the other, normal postperformance behavior on the part of your average nutso comic in Texas Jimmy's professional opinion.

"Well, Jimmy, how was I?" he said, missing the wastebasket as he tossed away the tissues.

"Well, let me put it this way, Ralf, you didn't exactly die out there tonight, but I wouldn't want to have recorded the audience response to use as a laugh track."

Ralf popped himself a Perrier and took a long hit direct from the bottle. "That your subtle way of telling me I stank?" he said.

He looked at Jimmy, and his eyes, previously spinning like the chrome hubcaps on a Corvette doing ninety down the freeway, had turned cool and calm, weirdly sane, you might almost say.

"There's El Stinko and there's mediocre, Ralf," Texas Jimmy told him carefully. "Let's just say that lately the act's been getting a little moldy around the edges. . . ."

In his experience, comics were like one of those cross-country balloons—huge egos full of hot air, deflatable with a pinprick, that required delicate treatment to be kept aloft.

But to Jimmy's surprise, Ralf took it like a mensch.

"Five nights a week in front of these sci-fi nerds and Little Old Ladies from Atlantis, and you expect the Second Coming of Groucho?" he said not unreasonably. "It's like playing the psycho ward in the Twilight Zone."

Jimmy laughed, not unsympathetically, and used the mood to ease into it. "A place which Dex and Amanda have been trying to convince me you're maybe heading if you're not careful," he said in what he hoped was an offhand scoffing manner.

"Are they?"

Ralf's eyes gave away no more than a traffic cop's mirror-shades. But it was too late to back off now.

"They seem to think you're pushing this Guru From the Future number a little too far, Ralf, maybe taking it a little too seriously, kind of maybe forgetting it's a joke."

"And what does my agent have to say, Jimmy?"

Jimmy couldn't tell whether that curl to the line between his lips was a smile or a frown. So he opted for the truth.

"Well, let me put it this way, Ralf, I've been around, you've got to admit it's a temptation . . ."

"Temptation?"

"Come on, Ralf, when I found you, you were bombing out at Kapplemeyer's fer chrissakes! And now, here you are, the star of your own show, with a fan club, and audiences full of rubes who *want* to convince themselves you're—"

Ralf made with a raucous horselaugh.

"*That's* your idea of temptation?" he said. "Playing Messiah of the Monkey People? Give me a break, Jimmy! Have you looked out there? Would you?"

Jimmy laughed, beginning to feel relieved. "Then why are you pushing the guru act so hard?" he asked. "And don't tell me you're not."

Ralf reached into a dressing table drawer, extracted a bottle of Hennessy, poured a couple of belts of cognac into plastic cups, handed one to Jimmy, took a sip, and hey presto, with that piece of business, who was Dutch Uncling who did a flip-flop.

"Hey, come on, Jimmy, isn't that the format I got handed this time around?" he said in a soft, soothing, almost insinuating tone of voice. "What am I supposed to do but do the best I can with it?"

"Well, yeah, but—"

"It at least got the show picked up for the rest of the season, didn't it, Jimmy? It's sure moving the tie-in merchandise, now ain't it?"

Jimmy took a sip of cognac, caught by the guy's eyes, by something he didn't remember having seen there before; a reasonable facsimile of brotherly sincerity, not the real thing maybe, but a pretty good Hollywood version.

"What do Dexter Lampkin and Amanda Robin know about doing stand-up comedy that you and me don't?" Ralf said. "You gonna let these amateurs rain on our parade?"

And then Ralf had given him the look of a tiger-shark producer leering at his victim, everything but the big fat cigar, bugged his eyes, clinked plastic cups with him, and delivered the line like Bela Lugosi.

"*I* yam from de *fu*ture of *Holly*vood," he said. "*Trust me.*"

That had indeed been reassuring, and they had laughed, and drunk to it, and Texas Jimmy raised his Wild Turkey on the rocks and silently toasted the memory.

"Hi there, Mr. Balaban, whatcha drinkin'?"

Down at poolside, one of the kids with a few walk-on credits and a real friendly attitude had rolled over on her beach chair, and was waving up at him, her red string bikini leaving just enough to the imagination, and not an inch more.

"Nothin' but the best, babe!" Jimmy called down. "Like me to bring you one?"

"Y'all don't mind if ah just come up an' get it?" she shouted back in a thick mock Southern accent not likely to win her fame and fortune.

"Not at all, honey," Texas Jimmy called back contentedly. "Don't mind if y'do."

10

The scene backstage reminded Texas Jimmy Balaban of one of those old boxing movies, the fighters in the locker room with their trainers; Dexter, muttering last-minute tips into the ear of *his* boy, the world famous best-selling Dr. Fritz Kaine, champ of the futurology division, and Amanda Robin with *her* contender, some talk-show-pug Jimmy had seen right up there with the likes of Letterman and Leno; he had a head of white hair made him look like Albert Einstein's hippie brother and fought under the handle of Sammy D.

But the third man in the ring was not the ref, but *Jimmy's* boy Ralf, bouncing nervously on the balls of his feet, looking a little too punchy for the comfort of the bookies.

Texas Jimmy flipped a Maalox tablet into his mouth, crunched it up loudly, and wolfed it down dry. Jimmy wasn't the kind of guy to find a cloud in every silver lining, but the state of his digestion was telling him that Archie Madden, like the producer in the moldy old joke, was going to prove what a creative genius he was by turning gelt into drek.

However much of this was really the Boy Genius's bright idea in the first place . . .

True, it *had* been Madden who had summoned Jimmy and Ralf to lunch, and true too that the idea of a summer season had been Madden's, but . . .

Archie Madden had chosen a posh joint in Beverly Hills with no sign outside, where movers and shapers did their power-lunching, this one called Natural Roots. The room turned out to be more or less what Texas Jimmy had expected:

burgundy-flocked walls, full formal setting on the tables, waiters in tuxedos, and patrons in conservative business suits and dresses.

Except that about three-quarters of the diners were black, and all the waiters were not only white but bleached blond and blue-eyed.

And who could have even imagined a vegetarian soul-food restaurant?

Black-eyed peas, spiced and veggie-stuffed cornbread, fried greens, organically grown corn on the cob, candied yams, six different kinds of baked beans, sweet potato pie, pecan pie, apple pie, pineapple pie, kiwi pie fer chrissakes, every conceivable side but no main courses, not a rib or chitterling or ham hock in the house, and a wine list running to whites whose prices would've given Jimmy an embolism if he thought he was going to get stuck with the tab.

Madden was already there when Jimmy arrived wearing a subdued charcoal suit, the Boy Genius himself resplendent in black and white reverse pinstripes that looked like a New York Yankee home uniform tailored for a Wall Street banker.

Ralf made his entrance just as they were shaking hands, costumed in, what else, The Suit From the Future. Even in the high-class joints on Rodeo Drive where autograph hounds would've been eighty-sixed for even thinking about it, this costumed entrance by the star of *The Word According To* would've gotten him bug-eyed stares, a sudden increase in sound-level from the customers, and a certain amount of bowing and scraping from the staff.

But here, all he got were curled lips from the waiters, and, far from impressing the clientele, they acted as if they earnestly wished he would speedily become invisible.

After the usual bullshit with the menu and the wine and mutual congratulations on having a show with ratings sufficient to be picked up in the fall, Madden had come to the surprising point.

"We're going to make a move, people," he said. "We're going to do a summer season."

"Gimme a break, Monkey Boy!" Ralf groaned. "I need one!"

"Yeah," said Jimmy, "I thought we'd take it easy, just do a few live dates in Vegas, Tahoe, maybe Hawaii . . ."

Archie Madden shook his head. "That's *no* move, and no move is a *bad* move," he said. "Okay, the show's good enough to pick it up for another thirteen weeks in the fall. But we're going to take a shot at prime time!"

"*Prime Time!*" exclaimed Texas Jimmy. "You gotta be nuts!"

The Boy Genius slurped up about five bucks' worth of French Chablis and grinned at him like William F. Buckley doing his lounge lizard act.

"Sort of *Prime Time*," Madden said. "We start half an hour early when the first half of the show's only up against local programming leading from the news into

Prime, and we do it in the summer when the second half of our new live shows are up against mostly reruns. I think we can average third nationally in that slot."

"And in the fall?" demanded Jimmy. The whole thing still seemed completely nuts. The show might survive a summer season in such a slot, but it'd be eaten alive when the nets came back with new Prime Time episodes in September.

Jimmy studied the kid more narrowly. "What is this," he said, "a deliberate shaft? You got some reason you want to kill the show and you're gonna drop it in a death slot to do it?"

Madden did a take and looked at him as if he were crazy. "Why would I grind up a Golden Goose for greaseburgers?" he said innocently. "The idea is to make it last—"

"Make it last! How do you expect—"

"One hour a week should use up only—"

"One hour a week?"

"Didn't I—"

"No, you didn't, Archie!"

"I *didn't*?" said Archie Madden. He grinned. He shrugged. "Sometimes I'm so brilliant I'm thinking ahead of *myself*. Look, what we've got now is a cult show mostly watched by the same demographic five nights a week based on one basic piece of business. How long can you keep throwing the same pies at the same Monkey People before it burns out? About another thirteen weeks max is my estimate before the ratings start to go Tube City."

Madden took another sip of wine, a much smaller one this time, put down the glass, steepled his fingers. "So we cut back to one show a week to stretch out our welcome," he said.

"Yeah, well, maybe that makes sense," Jimmy admitted. "But why the hell in Prime Time?"

"You ever hear of a successful one-day-a-week late-night talk show?" said Archie Madden.

"No," Jimmy was forced to admit. *But I never heard of a successful Prime Time talk show period*, he could just as well have added, but pointing it out impressed him as something less than a brilliant tactic.

"But why do I have to do it in the summer?" Ralf whined.

"Think of it as an out-of-town tryout for a Broadway production," Madden told him. "I want all the kinks worked out of the new format before we hit the boards big time in the fall."

"*What* new format?" said Jimmy

Archie Madden threw up his hands, smiled, shrugged. "Something with longer legs than what we've got," he said. "Something hot that will make my day. Something better than the present one-man band."

Oy.

And that was when it had happened.

Ralf sprang erect, as if someone had stuck a tire pump nozzle up his ass and was inflating his stage presence with it. His eyes sparkled like a squirrel's. Had he been equipped with a bushy tail, it would've been waving frantically.

"*Something better than the present one-man band!*" he exclaimed. "It's brilliant, Archie! I can see why they call you a genius!"

This, of course, sufficed to focus Madden's attention entirely on him.

"Of course it is, of course I am," Madden said. "And now you're going tell me how—"

"You *know* how, don't you, Archie?" Ralf said. "An animal act, a raving Nazi and an Israeli general, a Black Muslim and the Grand High Wizard of the Ku Klux Klan, the head of Greenpeace and Senator Nuke the Whales, and there I am with a whip and a chair rattling the bars of the cage!"

"I don't know—"

"It sucks," Jimmy said, "that's all we—"

Ralf flashed him a shut-up look which burned with a wired energy that was just short of terrifying.

"Not *political* crap, Jimmy!" he said. "*The kind of crap we already got!* The New Age Gurus and Crystal Channeling Fruitcakes versus the Stink Tank Futurologists and Sci-Fi Nerds!"

All at once he was projecting his voice at just the right level to rivet the attention of the room, just like an actor playing a ninety-nine-seat theater.

"But like you say, that's what we've already got," Madden pointed out. "So what's the difference?"

"We bring it up onstage!"

"Bring the audience up onstage?" Jimmy groaned. "Jeez—"

"I said the audience?" Ralf shouted.

"The audience is the problem," he said, still projecting to the back of the room. "All this cheapjack format gives me to work off is amateur geeks and weirdos— okay as stand-up in a club, but in Prime Time I gotta be fed *professional* geeks and weirdos!"

By now, the whole room was listening in while pretending not to, people were staring at their plates, at the walls, into space, anywhere but at Ralf, the waiters were standing around like zombies, and the maître d' was rattling a menu nervously wondering how to shut up a TV star.

Ralf suddenly pivoted the chair around on one leg, so that all at once he was looking right back at a restaurant full of people caught in the act of staring at *him*.

"Whaddya say, folks?" he said, converting that roomful of embarrassment into an instant audience. He shot a sidewise stage-glance at Madden without really breaking eye contact with the audience. "Whaddya say, Mr. Madden, let's run it up the old flagpole, and let the Vox of the Monkey Populi speak."

Madden shrugged, smiled, sat back, crossed his arms over his chest. The maître d' started to make a tentative move toward Ralf as he rose to his feet, but Madden stopped him with a look that would've frozen a charging bull in its tracks.

"What do *you* want to see, Monkey Boys and Girls?" Ralf declaimed, pacing back and forth in front of his chair like a very stir-crazy panther in a very small invisible cage, waving a pantomime shotgun mike, for all the world transported to the set of the show.

"You want to see the Great I Am take on the heavyweight gurus and double-dome wise-guys, the pointy-headed intellectuals and stars of the tabloids that pass for the best and the brightest of this forty-watt age?"

His eyes clocked the mesmerized faces out there like a mongoose on methedrine tracking an audience of cobras, the mad charisma all but visibly coming off him like heat waves off a hot car hood.

And that wired intensity really *did* scare Jimmy now.

Because he didn't have to be Dr. Freud to see that his major meal ticket had gone over the top into grand mal Comic's Cafard, a condition with which Texas Jimmy Balaban was all too familiar. Every comic he had ever handled had at least skirted the edges from time to time.

How could they not?

In order to stand up there by yourself and believe you could hold an audience with nothing but your own wit and wonderfulness, you either had to be an egomaniac in the first place or have some trick that let you con yourself into believing that you were for the duration.

And how could you be funny without being at least a little nuts, without seeing things from a bent angle, without forgetting you had a sense of personal embarrassment, without at least halfway believing your own schtick?

A certifiably noncertifiable comic would be like a surgeon who puked at the sight of blood.

It was the lurking possibility of Comic's Cafard which gave a comedian the Edge, without which he was chopped liver. But what lurked always remained in danger of emerging. And while Texas Jimmy's experience handling comics who had achieved stardom was limited to Ralf, long observation of other people's talents had led him to believe that the ego-inflation thereof was what usually triggered lunacy like this.

For them that could ride it, it could be what Billy Shakespeare had called a *divine* madness long before Lenny Bruce or Robin Williams burst onstage seemingly a half-step ahead of the guys in the white coats with the net.

At least for the onstage moment.

And in *this* moment, Ralf could've held them reading the phone book, not that the stuff he was babbling made a whole lot more sense, and while Jimmy hadn't quite had to throw a net over him to get him off before the management came far enough out from under his spell to call the cops, it had been reasonably close . . .

Or so it had seemed at the time.

But that look on Ralf's face as he allowed Jimmy to calm him down and drag him back to his seat in the nick of time . . .

"Showtime in two minutes!" called out the production assistant, and Ralf quit his bouncing around and moved to the edge of the wings, ready to follow his intro out onto the new set.

The backdrop was a high-resolution blowup of a NASA photo shot of the Earth glowing in the starry darkness. There was a standard talk-show desk-and-chairs setup. Except for the thing painted on the front of the desk—some kind of Hindu idol with more arms than a convention of congressional lobbyists wearing The Suit From the Future, with a face more than vaguely resembling Ralf's.

Jimmy had to admit that the new set had class, but there was something about it that he just didn't like the look of . . .

"And now," said the announcer's voice, "with a whole new look, but the same old star who won't even be born till the day after tomorrow, here's the Man From the Future himself . . . and . . . The Word According to Ralf!"

Nor did he like the look that Ralf flashed him a half-beat before he pranced onstage.

For it was the same look that Ralf had given him in Natural Roots just as Jimmy had managed to snare him by the elbow and sit him down. The look of a comedian who had gone over the top, the eyes shining with too much adrenaline, the sweat ready to break out at any moment as if the thermostat had been turned up too far.

But behind those eyes, something that knew what it wanted and knew how to get it.

Whatever the hell *that* was going to turn out to be.

Something crazy?

Like a fox?

". . . but by the year 3000, most of the human race may not be living in bodies made of flesh at all . . ."

Amanda had to admire Fritz Kaine's style as he flashed a plastic smile into the camera and delivered the outrageous sound bite like the experienced talk-show rat that he was.

"What're we gonna do, turn ourselves into robots and move to Deathship Disney?"

In fact, Kaine being the best-selling author of *The Year 3000* without a current book to promote, Amanda had been impressed that Dexter had been able to get him for the show at all.

"Closer than you think, Ralf. By the year 3000, the death of the biosphere won't be a problem—"

"Right, hey, no people, no problem!"

"—because we won't need it anymore. We'll download our personalities into computers and install them in titanium bodies and become whatever we choose—flying machines, submarines, interstellar spaceships!"

Sharply dressed, his collar-length salt-and-pepper hair elegantly coiffed, author of half a dozen volumes of popular futurology, onetime NASA space scientist, Dr. Fritz Kaine was perfectly cast as Mr. Think Tank Wizard.

"Yeah, sure, hey why not turn ourselves into X-ray machines in the girl's gym or Madonna's electric toothbrush?"

"Most of the universe is hard vacuum existing at cryogenic temperatures, deadly to flesh, but ideal for the metallic life-forms we can become . . ."

"Come on, Doc, what the hell for?"

"How about . . . *to live forever?*" said Kaine, favoring Ralf with a perfect mad scientist grin of Faustian triumph. "We can escape the Deathship you say we will have made of Earth and go as a race of immortal beings to the stars!"

Is this man serious? Amanda wondered.

On a show business level, Kaine was slick as goose grease and this kind of popularized scientific transcendentalism was his stock in trade. Yet Amanda sensed the desperate passion of a man who held the possibility of the existence of anything beyond the universe of mass and energy in intellectual contempt, and yet who could not go gentle into that good night.

"Can I ask you a dumb question?" said Sammy D, rolling his eyes in a pantomime of clownish perplexity. He had just been sitting there smiling beatifically, your basic million-year-old stoned out hippie. Now he seemed to have snapped himself into sharp focus out of the virtual cannabis smog.

"Do you believe in the soul?"

"That depends on what you mean by the soul," Kaine said cautiously.

"How about a pattern of meaning that transcends matter and energy?" suggested Sammy D.

"Mystical mumbo-jumbo to me. *Nothing* exists but matter and energy."

"You really believe that?"

"Of course I do!"

"Oh yeah?" said Sammy D, mugging at the camera. "Then what about a movie?"

"A *movie?*"

"Sure, like, oh, *Gone With the Wind,* I'd say that one's got *soul,* wouldn't you, folks?" Sammy D said with a wink. "But it's not matter, and it's not energy. It's not the film stock, or the release prints, or the copy you made with your video recorder. It's what you get when you play any of 'em back, that's the . . . *soul* of *Gone With the Wind,* and frankly, Scarlet, as long as there's a copy somewhere, Gable won't give a damn."

The studio audience may not have laughed, but Amanda did. Good old Sammy D!

"Oh, you mean *information?*" said Fritz Kaine. "Not some immortal essence that exists on a so-called higher plane?"

"Maybe," said Sammy D. "Maybe not. So you want to live forever by downloading yourself into a robot. But would you really be there? Does the robot have your *soul?* Is it really *you?*"

"Or is it Memorex?" said Ralf.

Sammy D was the modern version of Nasrudin and Lao Tze and Bodhidharma—the wandering zen sufi monk incarnated for the television age as a professional talk-show guest.

"Of course it's really me," Kaine insisted with something that seemed a good deal less than certitude. "Who *else* could it be?"

"That's my dumb question," Sammy D said. "If the *real* you, the only soul you have, is a just a pattern of information stored in your brain, then if you download it into the computer memory of a robot, it's just like copying *Gone With the Wind* onto a videotape, and the robot *is* you, right?"

"Right . . ." Kaine muttered grudgingly, and it seemed to Amanda that the

Good Doctor now saw the logical black hole that Sammy D was sucking him into, but not at all how to avoid it.

"But if you can make *one* copy of a movie, you can make *two*, or a hundred, or a million. And if you can make *one* copy of Fritz Kaine, you can run off a whole bunch of 'em, stamp 'em out like CDs!"

Kaine just sat there blinking.

It was Ralf who suddenly came alive, as if remembering that this was, after all, his show.

"Or make 'em all *different*!" he said. "Fritz Kaine the robot spaceship! Fritz Kaine the robot vacuum cleaner! Fritz Kaine the robot food processor!"

"Fritz Kaine the automatic cappuccino machine!"

All at once, Ralf and Sammy D had become avatars of the same Cosmic Joker, or at the very least an instant temporary incarnation of Fric and Frac.

"Fritz Kaine the automatic electronic self-cleaning toilet bowl!"

"So?" said Kaine belligerently, the burn almost visible on his ears.

A strange thrill of time-warped knowledge crawled up Amanda's spine like a sneak-attack satori as the line emerged into her brain before they said it, and she mouthed it silently with them as Ralf and Sammy D delivered it together in eerie comic unison.

"So . . . *which one is you?*"

"After all," said Ralf on the afterbeat, "either you're a whole department store full of major appliances, or you're not there at all!"

It was the strangest moment of television that Amanda had ever seen, as Fritz Kaine, the audience, the viewers, were confronted with both a logical proof of the transcendence of the body by the soul and the transcendence of the boundaries of the format by a talk show which had just boldly gone where no such schlock had gone before.

Ralf sat there staring at the camera for an uncomfortably long beat, his eyes blank and fathomless, as if *his* soul had gotten lost in the transmission.

In ordinary time, it couldn't have lasted more than thirty seconds, but in air-time it was an eternity.

Amanda glanced at Dexter Lampkin, and though Dexter tried to shrug it off with body language, when their eyes made contact, the reluctant acknowledgment *was* there, the memory *was* shared.

The aspect of Ralf now revealing a glimpse of itself on the air might be new to the television audience but not to the two of them.

For this—whatever it really was—was the same aspect which had been revealed to them in such unsettling depth last Tuesday in Ralf's apartment.

As far as Amanda had known, Ralf had never invited anyone there, so when he had asked Dexter and her to his place to discuss the new format before the show went on the air, her curiosity had certainly been piqued.

The address was out in the flats of the Valley and all that it implied, hardly the usual haunts of nouveau riche TV stars, but Ralf still didn't drive, and here he was within walking distance of two maxi and several mini malls. The building seemed to have been built last month of limousine glass and aluminum. No doorman, and the interior lobby, black pseudo-marble trimmed with stainless steel without a place to plant one's ass or even the usual piece of institutional art, was so bleakly forbidding that despite the heat and the smog, Amanda found herself preferring to wait for Dexter outside.

Fortunately for the state of her lungs and ocular mucosa, Dexter Lampkin arrived a few minutes later in a red Porsche Targa with the roof-panel removed and chromework that seemed to have been polished with a toothbrush within the past hour.

She buzzed Ralf's apartment, he buzzed open the door, they took an elevator to the top floor, went down a pristine white corridor to a black-lacquered door, and hit the bell button.

A minute later, Ralf opened the door wearing pressed white jeans, black running shoes, and a Deathship Earth T-shirt, and led them through an entrance area devoid of pictures and furniture and into the living room.

It was large and white, and it had a view.

The ceiling was white with a simple chrome-and-frosted-glass lighting fixture. The white walls had nothing at all on them. Sliding glass doors led out onto a balcony with a magnificent view north across the awfulness of the San Fernando Valley, a zillion miles of ticky-tacky shimmering grayly in the smog. The wall-to-wall carpeting was pale gray.

There were two large black leather couches arranged at right angles, a Scandinavian teak end table and a matching coffee table, plus a large TV set along one wall, and a built-in bar with two teak and black leather stools accessing a kitchen that looked like the control room of a nuclear power plant. Amanda imagined the bedroom as equipped with a king-sized waterbed from a Las Vegas casino hotel, or maybe just a hook from which the inhabitant could sleep hanging upside down from the ceiling.

Amanda made eye contact with Dexter as they entered this generic living room, and was gratified when he gave her a little shrug back.

They had hardly become friends, but they had cleared some of the bad air between them, at least to the point where each could acknowledge to the other that they both had goals in this common enterprise which transcended ratings and money, and she found his human presence beside her in this eerily neutered domicile vaguely reassuring.

And maybe the feeling was mutual, for when she sat down on one of the couches, he sat down beside her.

When Ralf offered drinks, Dexter took bourbon on the rocks and Amanda found herself asking for a gin and tonic instead of the usual ladylike and politically correct white wine, and wishing for a joint instead.

"Well," said Dexter, when Ralf had taken a seat on the couch across from them with his own bourbon neat, "to what do we owe this honor?"

"We need to come to a . . . meeting of minds," Ralf said, his mouth smiling while his eyes regarded the two of them with all the human warmth of the apartment itself. "To the extent possible."

"Why no Jimmy?" Amanda asked uneasily.

"Oh, Jimmy and me have already talked about where things are going," Ralf told her. He took a very small sip of bourbon, a piece of stage business. "To the extent possible."

Amanda took a quick sideways glance at Dexter, trying to read whether he was getting the same strange vibrations as she was. He didn't send her any answering signal, but the tone of his voice when he spoke was enough to give his state of unease away.

"I don't really know if we should be doing this behind Jimmy's back."

"Relax, Lampkin, this ain't about money, this is about the . . . creative end."

"Jimmy knows more about comedy than either of us," Dexter insisted.

"And *I'm* the comic, so I know more than he does," Ralf said. "And comedy's not exactly the point anyway."

"Then what is, Ralf?" Amanda demanded.

"What you guys have been throwing at me," Ralf told her. "If this new format is gonna do what it needs to do, you gotta can the Tom and Jerry act."

"Tom and Jerry act?" Dexter said ingenuously.

"The punching match between the New Age and the Space Age is getting old, Monkey People. If you can't bring yourselves to crawl into bed with each other the way the Bible says good little lions and lambs are supposed to at times like these, then at least work together to book me guests for each show that work *off* each other instead of *against* each other."

"You're not exactly getting through to me, Ralf," Dexter said unconvincingly.

"Right," Ralf said dryly. "You just *creamed in your jeans* when Madden made Jimmy hire Amanda. And of course, getting rid of her and her New Age fruit-cakes would be your idea of a fate worse than death."

Amanda could all but see Dexter Lampkin's ears burn red. And strangely enough, she found herself stifling an impulse to reach out her hand to comfort him.

"Just where is all this going, Ralf?" she said instead.

"To the next level," said Ralf, and the eyes he turned on Amanda seemed to be looking at her from somewhere far beyond the mask of his face, which in that moment held all the human expression of the decor in the room. "And on the next level, the old Tom and Jerry act's not gonna get the job done."

"Get what job done?" Amanda said softly, making herself look right back at whatever she was seeing.

"The job that has to get done," said Ralf. "The job we all want to get done."

"Which is?" said Dexter.

Ralf shifted his gaze, pulled back the focal plane, so that both of them were within the sphere of its influence.

"The job I'm here to do," he said. "Just like your format says, Lampkin. Me, I let them send me back here because this was the best booking I could get, but the folks on Deathship Earth expect me to do more than pull ratings—"

"We're not talking show business anymore, are we, Ralf?" said Amanda.

"Sure we are. Last time I looked it was still the only game in town."

"Then could we can the crap and cut to the chase already?" Dexter demanded.

"We already have, Lampkin," said Ralf, rising slowly from the sofa. "We're finally talking about our hidden agenda."

"*What* hidden agenda?"

Ralf crossed behind the sofa, placed his hands on the back of it, leaned forward, eyeing the two of them a bit like a predator, a bit like a coconspirator. "The one that's hidden in plain sight."

"I don't know what you're talking about!" Dexter Lampkin insisted lamely.

But of course it was quite obvious that he did.

"Come on, Lampkin, *you're* the guy who wrote it, remember?" Ralf said, his voice sly, his smile insinuating, his eyes windows into precisely that hidden agenda, that next level, whose reality Dexter Lampkin sought so unconvincingly to deny.

It might be impossible for Dexter to believe that he confronted a creation out of his own Dreamtime that he had made manifest in the universe of mass and energy, that some avatar of the collective unconsciousness, some desperate dybbuk of the Zeitgeist, had used him to incarnate itself in Maya's realm.

But what is, is real, and Amanda had the utter conviction that one or the other, and somehow both, was what was gazing back at them now.

"Who are you?" Amanda said. "Who are you *really?*"

"I yam what I yam and that's all that I yam," said Ralf doing a perfect Popeye. But no spinach-chomping Sailor Man had ever gazed back from the screen with that empty-eyed bodhisattva smile.

"*Seriously!*"

"Would I give a serious answer to anyone crazy enough to believe me?" Ralf Grouchoed.

"Try me," Dexter said, and to Amanda it seemed like a small act of spiritual heroism, which he would never deign to recognize as such.

"Do I know?" said Ralf. He shrugged, deliberately or not, a humanizing piece of business. "We are what we remember, right?" he said.

"And what *do* you remember, Ralf?" said Amanda. She stood to face him. She looked right back into those eyes. And the doorway to the Dreamtime was open.

But whose Dreamtime was it?

"I remember staggering onstage in Kapplemeyer's," Ralf said. "I remember them stuffing me in the wayback. I remember my agent telling me what a great career move it was gonna be . . . ."

There was a strange dreamy sense of sincerity in his voice. A sense of . . . conviction.

"You remember the future, huh?" Dexter said dubiously. But the softening around the hard edge of it told Amanda that he could not help but feel it too. "You remember Deathship Earth?"

"In great gory detail, Monkey Boy."

"Even though you and me made it all up over all that bourbon in Texas Jimmy's office?"

"Or you could've dreamt all that, now couldn't you Lampkin?" said Ralf. "How would you know?" His lips creased in the faintest of Buddha smiles. "We remember . . . what we remember. We *are* what we remember."

Last Tuesday in his apartment.

Now, on the air, facing the camera . . .

That same long frozen beat of silence.

That same half-smile on Ralf's face.

The same blank and fathomless eyes, as if something behind them had been tuned to an empty channel, was trying to find . . . to find . . .

Then, Ralf had broken the silence with a laugh.

"The trick part," he had said, "is remembering what we are."

Now, Ralf broke the dead air by snapping his fingers in front of Fritz Kaine's face and returning the proceedings to Planet Hollywood.

"Wake up, Dr. Monkey Boy," he said. "Hey, your . . . *soul's* still gotta be there, 'cause if it ain't gone off to Hardware Heaven, then *where is it—*"

"—and where the hell are *you?*"

A goddamn good question, Dexter Lampkin thought, watching Fritz Kaine gasping like a grouper after having been passed back and forth like a basketball by the backcourt Bobbsey Twins, Ralf and Sammy D.

"Right in the middle of one of those singularities like Zeno's paradox," Kaine finally managed to say.

"Ze new pair a docs? Ze new pair a *ducks?* What's that, a proctologist and a urologist fresh out of med school sharing the same office, or the latest reincarnation of Donald and Daffy?"

A sprinkling of laughter from the studio audience, but Dexter groaned inwardly anyway.

Why am I starting to sympathize with *Fritz-fucking-Kaine?*

Kaine was not one of Dexter's favorite humans. Dexter's conviction that *The Year 3000,* the cornerstone upon which Kaine's career as a semi-best-selling author and TV personality was based, drew heavily on a ten-foot shelf of science fiction novels, *The Transformation* most prominent among them, did not endear him to the non-best-selling author thereof.

"*Zeno's paradox,*" Kaine said, making a standing creature with the first two fingers of his right hand, placing it on Ralf's shoulder, and walking it slowly across it, up his neck and across his cheek as he spoke.

"Which mathematically proves that a chicken can't cross the road, that this little guy can't walk from your shoulder to your nose, because first he must go half the distance, and then half the distance remaining, and then half of what's still left, and so on, and the formal logic is irrefutable. However . . ."

He reached Ralf's schnozz and gave it a comic yank in the manner of Moe Howard giving what for to one of his Stooges, extracting a decent laugh from the studio audience.

He was a pro at *this* sort of stuff, you had to give him that, which was why Dexter had let the unholy combination of Louise Farmer, Emory Pollock, and George Clayton Johnson convince him to lead off the first show of this new format with ol' Fritz.

If that was what had really happened.

If it hadn't been Ralf's doing.

Dexter had to admit that his grasp of causality had not exactly been improved by that séance last Tuesday in Ralf's apartment.

And *séance* did seem to be the word for it, even though it had occurred in that clean room of a living room rather than some gypsy fortune-teller's patchouli-scented tent.

Dexter had believed himself immune to the old Scientology Stare, but what was looking back at him through Ralf's eyes seemed to be trying to prove otherwise before breaking its own spell with a laugh a beat before the punch line—

"The trick part is remembering what we are."

At which point Dexter had come blinking out of it.

Whatever *it* had been.

"And what do *you* think we are . . . Monkey Boy?" he had managed to crack back.

"I think it's still up to us," said Ralf. "And that's why we're here today. To remember the future."

"Remember the future?" Dexter scoffed.

"Sure, Lampkin, why should that surprise a smart sci-fi guy like you?" said Ralf. "It's easy . . ."

He walked toward the glass doors to the balcony, and Dexter found himself following, Amanda beside him.

"Hey, presto—the future!" said Ralf. "You remember *this* one, don't you, Lampkin? You wrote it yourself."

He suddenly slid the doors open and a horrible front of hundred-degree San Fernando Valley smog blasted into the air-conditioned living room as if an astronaut had mistakenly and fatally opened his spaceship cabin to the naked atmosphere of Venus.

"Welcome to where we're headed," said Ralf, grabbing Dexter with one hand and Amanda with the other and dragging them right into the face of it toward the balcony. "Welcome to Deathship Earth!"

He just about shoved them outside, into the heat, into the membrane-searing, eyeball-burning, vision-graying photochemical pea-souper; more or less bearable in short doses if you prepared yourself for it before you ventured out of the shopping mall air-conditioning.

But to be instantly and unexpectedly plunged into it like this was like being kicked into a vat of simmering sulfuric acid, not that far, after all, from the literal truth.

Dexter reeled backwards out of it, and Ralf resealed the doors behind them.

Now there was something sinister about the cool filtered air of the sterile white apartment, something ultimately artificial, something claustrophobically, frighteningly, irrevocably . . . *dead.*

Dexter knew that Deathship Earth was his literary creation. But in that moment it attained a physical presence and a sensory reality for him that it had never had before and that he had the feeling it would never lose again. For he could hardly now deny that this awful vision was the future toward which the planet *was* inevitably heading unless someone or something somehow managed to intervene.

Ralf crossed the living room to the sofas, picked up his drink, and took a big slug of bourbon before he reseated himself. Dexter did likewise, and even Amanda sought refuge in liquid fortification.

"Why is a comedian from the future like a character in one of your sci-fi novels, Lampkin?" Ralf said.

Beat.

"So he's *not* like a character inna sci-fi novel." Ralf shrugged. "Or maybe he is. Does it matter? And is arguing about it gonna get us any closer to where we're supposed to be going?"

"Which is?" said Dexter, knowing the answer.

"Someplace better than *that*!" Ralf said. "Can we agree on that much, Monkey Boys and Girls?"

He took another sip of bourbon, leaned back and became the performer.

"Let me tell you a story, Mr. Sci-Fi Guy, hey, let me give you four for the price of one, you pays yer money, and you takes yer choice," he said.

"In the first story, desperate scientists on a dying planet drop a poor schmuck of a comic in a time machine to try and save it by changing the past, not because it's such a terrific idea, but because they just can't think of anything better to do. In the second story, a comic pretends he's the guy in the first story because he's otherwise out of marketable material. In the third story, the guy in the second story hooks up with a sci-fi writer and becomes such a big hit that he goes on a nutso ego-trip, and thinks he's the real thing. In the fourth story, he is all of the above and something . . . *more.*"

Ralf shrugged. He grinned like Burt Parks on methedrine.

"Which story do you prefer, Lampkin?" he said.

Dexter found himself just sitting there blankly.

"Doesn't matter all that much, does it, Mr. Sci-Fi Guy? Because it doesn't change the job whoever I am is supposed to be here to do."

"Which is?" said Amanda Robin quite rhetorically.

"To save the world, what else?" Ralf declared.

He laughed maniacally. "There, I've come out and said it! I'm the Comic Messiah! I'm the Zeitgeist Incarnate! I'm the Roadrunner of the Eightfold Path! I'm the Last Best Schtick of Man!"

The fit passed as suddenly as it had come, and then Ralf was leaning forward, elbows on thighs, giving Amanda one of those Scientology Stares.

"Which avatar do *you* prefer, Amanda?" he said softly.

"It doesn't really matter, does it?" said Amanda Robin.

"See?" said Ralf. "I *knew* we could come to a meeting of the minds."

And perhaps they had.

Science fiction's whole raison d'être, after all, was the notion that there was no such thing as *the* future; that multiplex futures radiated from every moment of the now, that collectively the future we got was the future we made. And the nutso comic messiah from the future, the mystical lady, and the science fiction writer agreed that Deathship Earth was the future toward which the Monkey People were headed unless something was done in the now to alter the probabilities.

And there was indeed a popular TV character named Ralf whose basic McGuffin was that he had been sent back here to do just that through comedy.

Lunatic? Character of Dexter's creation? Cynical comic actor? The Zeitgeist Incarnate?

In the most absolute terms, it really didn't matter.

Because you had only to open those balcony doors and take a deep choking breath to believe that whatever the star of *The Word According to Ralf* really was, the Word *was* what mattered, for the way things were going it could indeed be the Last Best Schtick of Man.

Sitting there in that dead white air-conditioned room, Dexter had not found it so difficult to fantasize that Deathship Earth itself *had* somehow reached out to them in its time-warped desperation to remain unborn.

Nor had that vision implanted in his brain turned out to be a transitory will-o'-the-wisp. For he knew that Deathship Earth *was* the high probability future, that these thoughts in his brain were real, and so in that sense at least, a future in which humanity had murdered the biosphere *had* succeeded in flashing its dire warning down the timeline—

—into the right here of this studio, into the right now of Prime Time, into this attempt by a nutso comic, a mystical lady, and a science fiction writer to turn it into a self-unfulfilling prophecy.

Fade and float, float and fade . . .

You could get usedta just about anything so long as you followed the little blue lights, Foxy Loxy had discovered, you didn't hardly need nothin' down here inna tunnels, was all taken care of like the Welfare, just float and fade, fade and float, for days, weeks, months, who knew, who cared, follow the little blue lights t'who knows where, tunnels went alla way out ta *Queens* fer chrissakes, didn't they, was those Port Authority tubes unner the Hudson, could be Newark up there, fuckin' Jersey City, who knows how far the blue lights could take you, Boston, Philadelphia, China, Africa, not that it mattered 'long as you stayed safe down under an' never stuck your head up.

Float and fade . . .

Hadn't always been like that, Loxy seemed to remember, hadn't she been layin' there twitchin' an' jerkin', shittin' an' pissin', fuckin' ice picks jammed inta her eyeballs, razor blades, broken bottles, pieces a bricks smashin' around inside her head, like in onea those stupid fuckin' movies where th' fuckin' cops put ya through the fuckin' cold turkey number, hey no sweat, ya can kick the stuff, hah, hah, hah, take ya only a few days, weeks, years, a pukin' up snot, an' blood, an' this yellow green stuff, don't worry, hurts you a lot more than it hurts us, hee, hee, hee . . .

Fade and float . . .

Or it coulda been a fuckin' nightmare, who the fuck knew, 'cause there wasn't no cops down here, now was there, an' when she woke up out of it, there she was, walkin' down the tunnel, feelin' all light and floaty, not exactly like afta a nice big hit a th' pipe, but sorta, everything all sparky . . .

Really *was* like bein' high, like those little blue lights had done something real neat to her brain, wired it up real good so she didn't *needta* score no more, go through all that fuckin' shit justa feel like this, all y'hadda do when y'knew the secret was t'keep followin' the blue lights right outa all those fuckin' horrible dreams.

Float and fade . . .

This was bein' awake, all that other shit musta been a nightmare right, such a fuckin' bummer, once inna pond of time up there inna Pig Apple witha dealers whack you fer a quarter believe it, cops whackya with their billies 'cause they didn't like your face, streets fulla fancy restaurants y'can't eat in, cars an' taxis, pimps with rusty razor blades cut ya throat for suckin' an honest dick on their turf, fuckin' housing projects, an' Sailor Sal's, anna animal life in Tompkins Square Park, an' it was hotter'n a fuck inna summer, froze your tits off inna winter, anna dogshit an' all, a fuckin' jungle, hurt y'head justa think about it. . . .

So why fuckin' bother, right?

Down here was no weather, no time, no dealers, no johns, no cops, no hassle, nothin' ever changed, all you hadda do was follow the little blue lights, and you could float and fade . . .

Never rained, never boiled ya brains, was always kinda cool an' a little wet an' musty like a cellar fulla rags an' old newspapers turnin' t'moldy old gray cheese like the stuff between your toes, an' the concrete an' stone had this smooth soft feel to it, almost slimy, 'cept where some pipe had busted, or this icky green fuzz grew.

No sun t'go up, no dark t'come down, was always somethin' like five inna am, the dirty gray light a' empty streets waitin' for the dawn's never gonna come, dim blue lights along the walls, red and green signals goin' on an' off, an' when there wasn't some train tear-assin' by so's y'hadda duck inta one a the slots all along the walls, no sweat t'let 'em blast by right in fronta y'face when y'got the hang of it, was so calm an' still an' quiet y'could hear the rats chitterin' and scrabblin', th' water drippin' somewhere, bulb about t'go sizzlin', trains rumblin' through your gut a million miles away, your feet slappin' the ties, breath movin' in an' out . . .

Fade and float . . .

Didn't hafta worry 'bout findin' no crapper, y'just dropped 'em an' did it, no one here t'give a shit about your shit, hee, hee, hee. Slept where y'dropped, what the fuck. Was puddles an' little ponds all over the tunnels t'drink from.

Float and fade . . .

Food wasn't as big a problem as y'might think when you didn't have nothin' else you hadda do but scrounge up enough a this an' that t'keep y'self goin' t'keep on scroungin' and otherwise didn't really give a rat's ass about what you crammed into your yawp.

Fact was, rat's ass once inna while when you couldn't find nothin' better wasn't all that bad when y'got used t' eatin' it raw, hey, half the shitholes like Sailor Sal's was gettin' good money sellin' it squished inta burgers an' fried in axle-grease any- way, an' here it was fresh an' free, the fuckers dropped dead all the time, an' once inna while, good ol' Rip even managed t'nail her a live one. . . .

An' there was people down here luggin' goodies, few an' far between, and a good thing too far as Loxy was concerned.

Mostly day-trippers hidin' out from the cops, or their pimps, or some fuckin' busted dope deal, or the Maf, better you don't ask, just disappearin' till the coast was clear, if ever, you could hear 'em clutterin' and clatterin' an' cursin' to them- selves from three fuckin' stations away, you could stalk 'em, an' follow 'em, an' check 'em out, an' the assholes would never know you was there.

Lot of 'em had this an' that with 'em, shopping bags a food even, they thought they was gonna be stuck down here awhile. Mostly they were the kind of bad-ass fuckers you really didn't want to know you existed Big Ripper or no, probably packin' pieces an' for sure a bad attitude, but hey, even Arnold fuckin' Schwarzenegger witha Uzi hadda sleep *sometime*, now didn't he, hee, hee, hee. . . .

Fade and float . . .

There was another kinda people down here too, mostly you didn't see 'em, mostly you didn't wanna, once inna while you sorta heard footsteps inna branch tunnel, decided to go elsewhere when you heard someone gruntin' out a dump, saw something raggy goin' by through the dividers between the uptown and downtown tracks.

Float and fade . . .

Why she didn't wanna meet the other real tunnel rats or why they didn't have no curiosity about her neither she didn't wanna think about, sorta like tigers passing each other inna jungle, hey who wantsa know, and the one time it happened, didn't make her wanna have it happen again.

She rounds a bend an'—

—she's just about smacked inna face by this yellow-green skeleton head covered with mungy gray hair an' beard like a rotten potato sproutin' this fungus stuff, crumbly black teeth, eyeballs like pigeon-eggs boiled in bloody cat piss, hunched over like a fuckin' ape!

Freezes.

Stinks like a dead elephant's armpit!

Takes one look at her—

"Aaaieeeeh!"

Screams like she's kicked him inna nuts, a wind right in her face like somethin' howlin' outa the bottom of a Port Authority toilet bowl.

And he's tear-assin' back up the tunnel one way just about draggin' his knuckles. And she finds herself doin' likewise the other before she even knows why.

But after that, Loxy made even more of a point of stayin' outa sight of the tunnel homeboys an' girls if there was any, an' seemed like they was ready an' willin' to do the same.

Yeah, once you got the hang of it, once you just sort of let yourself melt into the cool gray twilight an' follow the little blue lights up and down, in and out, down and around, to no place in particular, you could just drift along, sorta like comin' home y'might say, only Loxy couldn't, not really, she had never known a timeless place and a placeless time as private and peaceful as these endless secret wormholes deep underneath the skin of the Big Apple, where you could just forget all the hassle, and just fade and float . . .

Float and fade . . .

Mother Tucker's was a cut above a biker bar, murky air-conditioned gloom, your standard bar and stools tended at this dead afternoon hour by a fifty-year-old broad in a blond beehive looked like she might've once been a chorus girl in downtown Vegas, café tables in front of the little stage where a bored topless dancer was dutifully going at it to some kind of reggae jazz fusion, booths along the wall, where Texas Jimmy Balaban and Ralf sat drinking like extras playing barflies.

In short, the kind of place where Ralf would not be very likely to be recognized without the Suit From the Future, which Jimmy had made clear he was not to wear, nor to be bugged by the customers if he was.

Ralf might not have attained what you could really call superstardom, as witness the ratings, but he had attained face-recognition value, as witness the continuing tabloid pix and that *TV Guide* cover, which would've made it kind of hard to have a quiet man-to-man in a more upscale joint without being ogled by the clientele.

Mother Tucker's had the additional virtue of being within walking distance of Ralf's apartment, meaning that Jimmy didn't have to pick him up or assume responsibility for dropping him off in the event either or both of them got seriously loaded.

Which didn't seem like too bad an idea at the moment. This was not the first time that Jimmy had felt he had to try to persuade one of his clients that maybe he ought to see a head doctor, but his considerable experience at playing this scene never seemed to make it any easier.

"*Now* would you mind telling me why you dragged me here?" Ralf demanded.

"What's the matter, can't you just go out and have a drink or two with your agent like an ordinary human?"

Ralf made with the fish-eyed stare.

Jimmy hesitated.

"I hesitate to say this, kiddo . . ." he said.

"Somehow I noticed."

Jimmy took another swig of Wild Turkey, took as deep a breath as the general aroma of stale beer and old smoke would allow.

"Speaking in my professional capacity as your agent and the producer of record of your show, Ralf," he said, "I got to tell you I think you're getting a little crazy."

There, he thought, *I've said it.*

Ralf laughed, but there was some kind of backbeat to it that made it less than convincing. "A *little* crazy?" he said. "Hey, come on, Jimmy, don't insult me, I'm a comic, I'm supposed to be *really* crazy."

"Not like wild-and-crazy-guy crazy," Jimmy told him. "Crazy like I'm getting a little worried about you Ralf crazy."

But instead of making with an "aw, come on," as his comics usually did at this stage of the proceedings, Ralf sat there silently staring at him with the coldly bright and unrevealing eyes of a very large rodent. It was not a look that Jimmy associated with a clean bill of mental health, and it was a look with which he had become all too familiar lately.

"Uh, look, Ralf, I hope you won't take this too personally, but . . ." he phumphered nervously.

Not a muscle changed position on Ralf's face. Those eyes didn't move. And yet by some acting trick beyond Jimmy's fathoming, the face seemed to change, the expressionless expression deepened, as if to deliver a silent line that said, "I don't take *anything* personally."

And *that* was maybe the problem.

Texas Jimmy Balaban had handled scores of comics, and he had had a variation of this conversation with at least a dozen of them, five of whom had ended up doing time in the funny farm. This was right down the middle for a handler of comedians. But while he had handled comics who were as crazy as Ralf and then some, he had never dealt with one who was crazy *like* Ralf.

It wasn't uncommon for actors and comics to lose the distinction between the part they were playing and their own personalities, it wasn't even unheard of for the dummy to take over the ventriloquist. But Ralf had never seemed to have a personality of his own to be taken over by his stage character in the first place.

Okay, the guy had insisted he really was a comic from the future from the git-go at Kapplemeyer's. Okay, so the guy never seemed to have any personal life that Jimmy could discover. Okay, so maybe he was some kind of weird pervert obsessed with keeping his offstage life secret even from his agent for good reason, like maybe his thing was to dress up in a chicken suit, cruise bars where poultry ranchers hung out, and bite the heads off the livestock while they buggered him with broomhandles.

Some comics wanted to be buddy-buddy with their agent and some wanted to keep it strictly business, and what Ralf did or didn't do when he wasn't working was none of Jimmy's business as long as it didn't affect his performance.

But now it was Texas Jimmy's professional opinion that it was starting to. And an agent's job wasn't just to make the deals and secure the bookings but to do what he could to keep the client able to fulfill them.

With the wisdom of hindsight, Jimmy should've maybe read the signs more clearly as far back as the first show of the summer season. Okay, that stuff about the existence of the soul had a few laughs in it, not that you could exactly call it boffo. But the way it had ended up, with Lampkin's futurologist going on about worms from the future crawling down black holes in spaced time and Ralf gibbering about changing the future by buying the T-shirts and Suits, would've had 'em stacking Zs in the aisles at an insomniacs' convention.

Hadn't it been *Lampkin* who had tried to put a bug in his ear about how Ralf was taking the Comic Messiah bit too seriously? Hadn't it been *Amanda* laying on all that Method mumbo-jumbo about the character taking over?

And then a couple shows later, that ditzy broad of hers supposedly hypnotizes Ralf into channeling his collective unconscious, okay so there were some laughs in Ralf doing his previous "reincarnations" like Mel Brooks doing his Thousand-Year-Old Man number with Rich Little's voices.

But when Dex's sci-fi writer got into the act by persuading Ralf that he could do *pre*incarnations of his future selves, and Ralf went into a wild-eyed bit as an Australian surfer fried to a cancerous turn by the ozone hole, kind of funny swiftly became pretty damn scary. Nor was the Brazilian lumberjack with the Eric von Stroheim accent feeding the rain forest into the gas ovens exactly a terrific recovery.

Nor did Jimmy himself know quite how to ask for guests that were less likely to feed the craziness.

What could he say to them?

The guests they had been lining up were good by any talk-show criterion. They were all colorful characters, had good stage presence, were all motormouths, had good comic timing for the star to work off, and a lot of them were even funny themselves.

In what terms could he ask for more?

How could he ask for *less*?

But it seemed to Texas Jimmy that *less* of an elusive something was what was required, less *encouraging* of Ralf's slow slide off the deep end.

Trouble was these people took Ralf's Deathship Earth schtick seriously, and they were more interested in using it and him to further their various crusades to save the world than in getting laughs in the process.

And when you put a comic who was maybe schizo in the first place up there with people who had all the best reasons in the world to make like maybe he *was* the Great I Am, it wasn't too surprising when he started to forget it was a joke and started to take it more seriously than was good for his sanity.

Or the ratings once the spectacle of watching a comic getting crazier and crazier on live TV lost its novelty value.

Yet how could Jimmy not sympathize? He had been around Ralf's material long enough to be pretty well convinced that the world probably did need saving. What was he supposed to tell Dex and Amanda, not to book guests who cared jack shit about the continued existence of life on their own planet?

But after this week's show, he knew that had to try to do *something*.

Amanda had come up with a maybe-soon-to-be-defrocked Jesuit priest name of Father John Mallory, who appeared in the standard black suit and dog collar, with steel-rimmed glasses that said intellectual, and wavy silver ear-length locks whose recent designer styling said showbiz.

Priest or not, the guy had some kind of communist rap about saving the planet from the greed of Satanic predatory capitalism by getting back to the original socialist roots of the Faith as preached by Jesus the Revolutionary that Texas Jimmy suspected would give the pope heartburn as he perused the *Wall Street Journal* to check out how the Church's portfolio was doing.

Dexter's man of the hour had been a computer maven named Roger Deacon whose rap was about something called nanotechnology, zillions and zillions of teeny-tiny intelligent robots smaller than germs, a bottle of which could literally transform drek into gelt and shit into Shinola.

This was one of the better shows, most of the way through. Deacon's McGuffin was the source of endless schtick for Ralf, and the priest even had a certain wiseguy sense of humor, a necessary part of the survival kit for a Jesuit communist, Jimmy supposed.

It was hard to say exactly when things started to slide over the Edge, but like some line in an old movie almost used to say, whenever it goes, there you are.

"Now let me get this straight, Rog," Ralf said mercifully near the end of the show, "these nanos of yours could take me apart and put me back together?"

"That's right, Ralf, molecule by molecule!" Deacon said with the hyped enthusiasm of a TV vegetable-chopper pitchman. "These little miracle workers will ream out those clogged arteries like a Roto-Rooter, tone up the old capillaries, eliminate any cancer cells, eliminate unsightly scars, turn you into a whole new man anytime you—"

"A whole new man!" Ralf exclaimed. "Hey wait a minute!"

He reached up and slowly stroked his big bulbous schnozz. "Could they do something with *this*?" he said slyly.

"Plastic surgery will be a thing of the past. Everyone can have the perfect age-less face and body that they want without pain or major expense almost instantly!"

Ralf rubbed his nose thoughtfully. Then in a slightly obscene manner that suddenly had Jimmy on edge. "One pill makes it larger, one pill makes it small?" he said slowly. "Any size? Any . . . organ?"

He did a take. He mugged at the camera.

Uh-oh.

He took his hand off his nose, cupped it into a circle about an inch in diameter, held it six inches above his fly, then slowly slid it up an invisible shaft, widening his grip to accommodate an imaginary girth that increased with its imaginary length, until he was stroking a phantom fire hose sprouting two feet high from his crotch while the audience roared.

"We're all gonna have tools like elephants!" Ralf declared just as the laughter started to fade.

He rounded on Roger Deacon. "Actually, Monkey Boy, we *tried it* back in the twenty-second," he said. "It cured everything, all right, but all these nano *hackers* went around with spray cans of their own disgusting senses of humor and instead of all looking like movie stars, it turned into Transsexual Transylvania, I mean, you didn't know from one minute to the next whether your ass was gonna turn *into* your elbow!"

That got some more follow-on laughs, but not out of Deacon, who turned red around the cheekbones, and lost it. "Triumph over *death itself* is no laughing matter!" he shouted indignantly.

He had a point. Not unexpectedly, a loud mention of the Big D brought an instant beat of uneasy silence.

"Nanotechnology can make us *immortal*!" he proclaimed, reverting to the TV pitchman's spiel. "It will cure cancer, rebuild those damaged organs, give us perfect bodies that barring accident will never die! And even *then* . . ."

"Even then?" said Father John.

"Even then, there is no scientific reason why nanotechnology cannot . . . *raise the dead.*"

"Raise the dead!" said Ralf as the priest crossed himself. "You mean if I slipped and fell into a tree chipper, you could . . . resurrect the hamburger coming out the other side?"

"In theory, yes."

Ralf turned to Father John. And that strange look had come into his eyes, that glassy stare with which Jimmy was becoming all too familiar, the look that had him saying a little prayer of thanks to the media gods that the show was almost over.

"Kind of puts you out of business, don't it, Father?" Ralf said.

"Not quite yet," Father John said gamely. "After all, it, it's only a sci-fi fantasy."

"Unlike the brand of Resurrection your outfit is promising?"

Oy.

"Are you suggesting—"

"Oh no," Ralf told him. "You're both right! We *will* have Resurrection-In-A-Can in the twenty-second century, Rog. And hey, Father, Your Boy really *did* rise from the dead back there in Year Zero! Pope *Elvis II* sent back Cardinal *Goldberg* with a can of the stuff to make *sure* it happened. The wiseguy Roman who thought it was cute to give Him the vinegar?"

Ralf had shaken his head slowly, looked right into the camera, winked.

"Not a Roman," he had said, delivering the line with an expectant mugging grin that had told Texas Jimmy he was too far over the Edge to know how unfunny it was. "Not vinegar."

A shrug into the awful silence.

"And three days later, hey presto, Resurrection! After which taking a hit of His Body and the Blood is supposed to pass on the nanos and give *you* life everlasting!"

The audience reaction to that had not been one of television's finest hours. Nothing had been thrown, but the growls out there for sure had indicated the presence of righteous folk who were thinking about it.

Just remembering it made Texas Jimmy shudder. He took another belt of bourbon, using the move to break off the staring match with Ralf. There was nothing for it but to spit it out in words of one syllable and be done with it.

"Ralf," he said, "I think it would be a real good idea if you at least had a little talk with a good shrink."

"A shrink?" Ralf said in total deadpan. "You want me to see a psychiatrist?"

Beat.

He tilted his head to one side, twisted his jaw, gaped his mouth, put his thumb to his nose and wriggled his fingers. "What's the matter, Jimmy," he gabbled in a cracked comic cackle, "you really think I'm going crazy?"

Hah-hah.

There was a Man from Mars quality to his delivery that made Jimmy shiver. *Fuckin'-A, kiddo*, he thought, if I had any doubts, you just convinced me.

"You claim to come from the future, you go around playing messiah to a barrel of monkeys, and you're an Angeleno who won't drive a car," Jimmy told him. "Naw, who could believe that a guy like that might have a screw or two working loose?"

Ralf's expression betrayed exactly nothing.

"Look, Ralf, I've had a lot of experience with comics," Jimmy said, trying the gentle approach. "It's stressful work, and let's face it, it's not the sort of biz that exactly encourages a hard line between fantasy and reality—"

"Assuming there is one," said Ralf.

A line which Jimmy felt it prudent to studiously ignore.

"Look, nobody's gonna think the worse of you for it," he went on, moving to the stratagem that had usually proven effective. "Everyone who's *anyone* in the Biz has a shrink, their press agents announce it in the trades, and even big stars make a thing about being Betty Ford graduates."

Ralf seemed to be making a show of sipping reflectively at his bourbon. "You're gonna keep bugging me till I do, right, Jimmy?" he said.

Now it was Texas Jimmy's turn to make with the fish-eyed silence.

Ralf shrugged. "Tell you what, Jimmy, I'll make you a deal," he said. "I'll see a shrink once, and if he says I oughta, I'll make with the weekly fifty-minute hours. But if he says he doesn't think it's a good idea, you never bother me with this stuff again, period."

"Sounds good to me," Jimmy told him in no little befuddlement. Sounds like proof positive that you've lost contact with reality, he thought.

Who ever heard of a shrink telling anyone who could afford it that they didn't need therapy?

Ralf lifted his glass, held it before his face, used it as a prop over which to peer at Jimmy slyly. "Aren't you going to ask me what the catch is, Jimmy?" he said.

"Should I?" Texas Jimmy asked with a certain sinking sensation behind his sternum.

"I don't want to choose the shrink myself, and I don't want you to either."

"Who then?"

Ralf took a sip of his drink, lowered the glass, didn't quite run his tongue over his lips, but otherwise did a pretty fair take on a cat having gotten into the cream pitcher.

"Amanda."

Left foot, right foot, float and fade, right foot, left foot, fade and float . . .

Follow us, Foxy Loxy, follow the little blue lights.

Been a long, long time, least half a dozen dead rats' worth, since Foxy Loxy had seen anyone at all, even heard footsteps, an' it was hard t'remember the last time the blue lights had led her near a station, an' come t'think of it, when was the last time she had heard a train. . . .

Left foot, right foot, float and fade, right foot, left foot, fade and float . . .

Follow us, Foxy Loxy, follow the little blue lights.

In fact, the walls a the tunnels was gettin' kinda tricky t'see, kinda faded inta this gray misty stuff 'less you was lookin' right at 'em, even the ties didn't quite seem t'be there, like she was always lookin' down this tunnel inside a the tunnel, was always things and stuff around the edges went an' hid you tried to see 'em, only the line a little blue lights right in front of her seemed clear, follow us, Foxy Loxy, follow us, hey what the fuck else can you do anyway, hee, hee, hee.

Left foot, right foot, float and fade, right foot, left foot, fade and float. . . .

Follow us, Foxy Loxy, follow the little blue lights.

Wasn't hardly nothin' t'eat no more, 'cept once inna while the little blue lights found her a dead rat, mostly crawlin' with these white wormy things, hey thanks guys but no thanks, but now an' again, there was one fresh enough t'brush away the mung an' have a bite, not all that bad once y'got used to it.

Follow us, Foxy Loxy, float and fade . . .

The live ones had gotten too fast t'catch, never even came close t'nailin' one witha knife no more, an' hey, maybe just as well, 'cause they was gettin' *bigger* lately, bigger n'cats maybe, kinda hard t'tell, 'cause all y'could really see was these fuckin' giant rat-shapes movin' around out there inna fog, like they was followin' her, an' they didn't move right or somethin', jerkin' around like some kinda fucked-up machines.

Follow you, Foxy Loxy, fade and float . . .

An' she can hear the motherfuckers out there behind the little blue lights, squeakin', an' clatterin', makin' these disgustin' gurglin' noises, those fuckin' beady blue eyes watchin' her alla the time now.

Follow us, Foxy Loxy, float and fade . . .

Was big puddles of water all over the fuckin' place, splashin' through it half the time, but the way they sorta glowed this pale sick green piss yellow, kinda gave you th' idea might not be too smart t'slurp it up.

Follow you, follow us, fade and float, Foxy Loxy, float and fade . . .

Didn't hafta anyway, 'cause the tunnels had been fulla this pearly gray fog for a few days or years everything drippin' wet an' all, you could lick water offa just about anything now, so Loxy stopped for a minute to lick at a nice patch of wet concrete wall—

And this fuckin' rat-bastid thing bigger'n a poodle jumps right in front of her!

Ugly motherfucker!

Like some shit-brain mad scientist at Disneyland got *real* fucked up on reds an' tried t'put together a giant robot biker rat outa crap from Mad Max's heavy metal junkpile.

Rat body made outa rusted-out car parts or whatever, legs outa welded-together tin cans an' bed-springs, feet like some kinda skateboard things, disgustin' rat-tail swishin' an' swashin' looks like naked Con Ed electric cable, scrabblin' rat hands twisted together outa coat hangers an' chicken wire.

An' alla this shit's stuffed with crap outa old TV sets an' toaster ovens, wires goin' everywhere, bits an' pieces a radios an' stereos an' all, y'can smell the fuckin' electricity, whole thing's movin' all twitchy an' jerky, 'cause it's all gears grindin' an' bike cables screechin', wheels an' pulleys an stuff, an' . . . an' . . .

An' like piecesa *meat* an' shit look like outa the garbage can from a fuckin' undertaker or somethin', gray, an' green, an' kinda brownish-purple like week-old liver, in these dirty jars with all these tubes connectin' 'em, anna pump-thing sending this disgustin' pus-colored stuff gurglin' around in 'em like endin' up croakin' real slow-like inna hospital.

Anna head like someone tried t'do Mickey Mouse outa garbage cans witha tin-snips, clackin' mouth fulla teeth made outa rusty razor blades.

But th' worst wasa fuckin' eyes.

Like dead cop's eyes glowin' blue.

Like the lenses off a couplea those fuckin' bank security cameras always lookin' atcha like you was some piecea shit with blue subway tunnel bulbs behind 'em.

"Follow us, Foxy Loxy, fade and float, float and fade!" it screeched at her inna voice like one a those fuckin' subway conductors screamin' out the stations in speed-freak Korean through th' usual busted speaker.

Well sorta, didn't exactly hear it, more like this scrapin' raspin' *feelin'* inside her head like someone bashing a million bottles witha hammer an' grindin' it inta her eardrums with the heel of a motorcycle boot, hurt like hell, but you could unnerstand it.

"Follow! Fade and float! Float and fade! Fade into the blue lights, Foxy Loxy! Follow us! Follow you!"

An' it turns, an' goes skitterin' and slidin' down th' tunnel back inta the fog.

Which is gettin' thicker and thicker now, can't see two feet in fronta ya fuckin' face, can't see nothin' at all 'cept straight ahead, 'cept for the blue rat's eyes lights lookin' back atcha.

An', hey, kinda hard to *feel* anything either, really floatin' now, fadin' for sure, inta the pearly gray like the color of a TV screen's been turned off, like sort fallin' right into it, into this warm TV-colored goo, you can just sort of drift along in the tide of it, sorta just sucked along by all the blue lights.

By all those glowin' rats' eyes, hundred and hundreds of 'em, lookin' back at you outa the pearly gray, as you follow them down, down, down, round, and round, round, like a happy little turd whirlin' round the toilet bowl, followin' the flush down the drain. . . .

"I'm not a hack, and I don't do tie-ins, Jimmy," Dexter told Texas Jimmy Balaban petulantly when Balaban called four weeks into the summer season to inform him of the PJP Books offer. "No way. Find someone else to write it."

"It's you, or no deal, Dex. You ever have a publisher come to you with a forty-grand book deal before?"

"*Forty grand* from PJP?" Dexter exclaimed.

PJP Books was a sleazy outfit that packaged bottom-market paperback original lines and made a profit by keeping advances insulting, royalty rates crummy, and royalty statements full of shit.

They wanted to publish a book called *The Word According to Ralf*. With a photo of Ralf for the cover to go with a coauthor credit. What was supposed to go between the covers was not of major concern as long as there was at least 250 pages of it and they wanted it by November 1.

If they were offering forty grand, it meant that they were sure the book would earn out at least twice that much, no sweat with something tied to a TV show with a good track record for merchandising tie-ins already. And Jimmy expected to pocket half the advance himself for the rights.

So writing a book for twenty grand in eight weeks had been an offer that Dexter found all too easy to refuse.

"Don't be an asshole, Dex," his New York agent had told him after PJP upped the ante to a $75,000 advance and a royalty of five percent based not on bullshit net sales figures but on the certified print run.

"We could renovate and furnish the whole house in style, Dex," Ellie had told him.

After purchasing the Porsche, there was no just way of stopping Ellie from fulfilling *her* dream, and so a goodly portion of his proceeds from the first season of *The Word According to Ralf* had gone into the down payment on a two-bedroom house way up on a little back canyon off Lookout Mountain.

"Well, I guess, you guys talked me into it," Dexter finally told his agent after sweet reason had convinced Jimmy that, since it was Dexter who was going to have to work like a maniac, he was entitled to sixty-five percent or the deal was off.

The house was a redwood-sided pseudo-Swiss-chalet of venerable vintage nestled in a eucalyptus grove with plenty of overgrown garden and a large cracked-concrete patio where Ellie already was planning to install a swimming pool. The kitchen needed a new stove and refrigerator, the two bathrooms needed new plumbing, the furnace made suspicious noises, and the furniture from the old rental, chez El-lie, was clearly unsuited to their newly elevated status as Laurel Canyon home-owners. So the money would indeed be just about what it took to put the place in order to Ellie's at least temporary satisfaction without depleting his capital past the comfort zone once more.

The house came with a little outbuilding: a two-car garage with a studio apart-ment on top with a small balcony overlooking a wild ravine, well-suited to become his work area.

And that was where Dexter found himself a scant six days after moving in—in a brand-new office still redolent of wax and varnish, with a blank screen and a tight deadline staring him in the face as in days of penurious yore.

Whirlin' round, an' round, an' round, inna creamy gray light, inna kinda pool of warm sticky slime, all these blue eyes glowin' all around her, must be some kinda dream, 'cause Loxy wasn't exactly there no more, was hard to think, was hard to feel, was hard to do anything but float, and fade, and float, and finally maybe just let it all go, take one last big breath, say goodbye, and just finally let yourself fade all the way away.

Finding a psychiatrist whose diagnosis of Ralf's psychic state would be credible to Texas Jimmy Balaban would be easy, but finding one who would satisfy Amanda's own requirements narrowed the choice down drastically. She didn't want Ralf in the hands of a therapist who would see it as his commission to dissuade him of his delusions of grandeur and reference.

For even if he *was* mad rather than a genuine time traveler or some avatar thrust into the realm of Maya in this critical karmic nexus, that very madness might be the necessary instrument of divinity. She needed a therapist who would not try to impose the consensus reality on his patient's consciousness, and in the best of all worlds, one who might be able to deal with its true nature.

The only choice was Albert Falkenberg.

Albert had the right credits and he looked the part too; carefully rumpled, horn-rimmed glasses, thinning silver hair coiffed into professorial distraction, and he had the Hollywood shrink act down cold.

The initial interview with Jimmy and Ralf in Albert's office had gone swim-mingly, especially after Albert trotted out his long list of celebrity patients.

"I gotta admit I'm impressed with the people you've been treating, Dr. Falkenberg," Jimmy had said at the end of the meeting. "None of them are in the bin, and all of them are still working, so what more can I ask?"

Oh yes, Albert was an excellent psychotherapist with a success rate second to none.

On that level neither she nor Albert were putting Jimmy on.

On a higher level, however, well . . .

If Albert wasn't the only transcendental psychiatrist in existence, there surely couldn't be many others of his rare species in the wild, since Amanda had never encountered another.

State law being libertarian to the point of anarchy as to whom might declare themselves a psychotherapist, California was full of eclectics purveying everything from Ahura Mazda to Zen. But unlike the usual run of such demi-gurus of the psychological arts, Albert had his M.D. and Ph.D., had undergone full Freudian psychoanalysis, and regularly published papers in the respectable refereed journals.

But Albert believed that psychology's proper sphere of study was every state of which the sentient spirit might be capable—from the lowest depths of vegetative catatonia to the peak experiences of shamans and Sufis, from brain-burned speed-freak communication with extraterrestrial intelligences to the ultimate enlightened state achieved by the Buddha himself.

"Whether we choose to regard these states of consciousness as delusional or as authentic experiences of other levels of reality or reserve judgment," he had written, "whether we regard them as objective or subjective phenomena, we can hardly deny that they exist as aspects of our sphere of discourse and still call ourselves students of human psychology."

What Albert Falkenberg *didn't* bruit about in the journals, what had made him so successful treating actors, directors, writers, even monks and priests and rabbis, and what in Amanda's opinion Texas Jimmy had no need to know, was that he proceeded under the assumption that transcendental states of being were the crown of conscious creation.

He was not only willing to credit spiritual maladies as dysfunctions on this ultimate level, he was willing to treat them by translating his patients into such transcendental states by whatever means necessary, even to enter their Dreamtimes with them.

"If a priest asks me to help him regain his lost faith, my job is to help him back into a state of Grace," he once told Amanda. "If a Rastafarian complains that his spliffs are bumming him out, I'm not going to try to get him to stay straight, my job is to help him get straight with Jah."

The Beverly Hills office was pretty much a front; most of his work was done at his sanitarium on a high and isolated plateau overlooking the Pacific north of Malibu. This was a two-story crescent embracing a courtyard garden facing the sea. The ground floor was a large salon whose glass doors could be opened to the garden in clement enough weather, and the upper story was a series of small studios where private therapy sessions might be held or patients might seclude themselves for short stays if Albert deemed it necessary.

Ralf had played the part of the disinterested skeptic in the Beverly Hills office, making it more or less clear that he was going along with this silly business just to keep his agent off his back, and the drive from to Albert's sanctum sanatorium had begun in a similar vein.

But when they started climbing up out of the suburban reality of the Valley, another aspect began to emerge.

"Why did you *really* choose this guy Falkenberg, Amanda?"

"Because he's the best I know," Amanda told him quite and half truthfully.

"*Right*," Ralf said. "You got none of your own fish to fry."

"*Right*," Amanda mimicked back. "And of course, you don't either."

By this time, they had attained the crestline of the Santa Monica Mountains, the long ridge road that ran in its various incarnations, paved and otherwise, along this minicontinental divide between Los Angeles and the Valley all the way from Hollywood to the sea.

"What's Falkenberg going to tell Jimmy about me?"

"Whatever you want him to."

"*Whatever I want him to?* That I don't need a shrink?"

"I think I can guarantee that."

"You *can*? This is a setup? I don't get it."

It was another reality up here, a thin slice of the primeval California that snaked-danced along the backbone of the state, magically hidden away in plain sight. Here the afternoon sky was a cerulean smogless blue, the sere dun mountain slopes pastel-greened with chaparral, the canyon breezes tossed the crowns of the more deeply hued eucalyptus groves and stands of pine, the traffic was light, and the road, so it seemed, rolled ever on.

Here it only seemed natural to speak the upland truth at the heart of the lowland dance.

"Sure you do," Amanda said. "*You* set it up. You wanted me to choose your shrink. Why?"

"You know why, Amanda," said Ralf.

Amanda was tempted to turn her head to meet the gaze of whatever was looking back. But the road had become a sidewinder's samba of dips and rises around curves and bends, and the Zen of it was that this required total concentration on the task of driving.

"Because you knew I wouldn't want some psychotherapist trying to turn you into—"

"A nice well-adjusted Monkey Person—"

"Adjusted to exactly the reality that's going to turn this world into Deathship Earth."

"That's part of it," said Ralf, his voice deepened in a direction that had nothing to do with octave range.

"Part of it . . . ?"

"Whoever I am, I'd have to be *really* nuts not to see that I've got a real problem. Let's pretend that I *am* the Last Best Schtick of Man, sent here by scientists from the future, or the Zeitgeist, or Gaia's Fairy Godmother, to save the Earth from its current swan-dive down the willy-hole."

"So?"

Amanda slowed down to steal a glance at her passenger. Ralf sat upright, his eyes hidden from her clear sight, staring straight ahead through the windshield, with that fixated expression on his face which would have spelled highway hypnosis had this been a straight-line freeway and he been behind the wheel.

"So what if I *am* the reincarnation of Prometheus, Jesus, and Lenny Bruce, all rolled up into one glorious syndicate package?"

"So?" repeated Amanda mantrically.

"So look what happened to the *other* poor schmucks that got cast in this part!"

Amanda's eyes were back on her driving, but her ears told her that whoever or whatever Ralf was or believed he was, this was as close to the sincere revelation of his inner being as she had ever heard him get.

"One gets chained to a rock with birds smearing his chopped liver on a bagel, one gets nailed up, one exits the scene OD'ed on smack in a toilet, and we're *still* heading into the same shit! No one's been able to come up with a happy ending to this story yet, or I wouldn't be here doin' the umpteenth remake, now would I?"

"You hope Albert Falkenberg can help you do . . . what? Find out who you really are?"

"*Who I really am?*" rasped the familiar voice of *The Word According To*. "Frankly, Monkey Girl, at this stage of the game, I don't really give a damn."

The sigh that followed, though, seemed all too achingly human, and when he spoke next, the words seemed to come from someone's true heart.

"I just hope your head doctor can help me do better in this part than the rest of the talents who've stunk up the joint with it for the last few thousand years. 'Cause whoever I am, I *do* believe the punch line I've been handed to deliver, namely that this is the last time around, there's no budget left for *another* remake if *this* one bombs out."

. . . fade, and fade, fade and float, and float, and float, and drift, and drift, and whirl, and whirl, and follow the blue lights, up, and up, and up out of the thick pearly slime into . . . into . . .

Foxy Loxy's eyes blinked open, or anyway maybe she dreamed they did, who the fuck knew, who the fuck could tell, where the fuck was *this*?

Not where she had been, for sure.

She was floatin inna sparky gray fog, kinda bluish now that she noticed, dry as talcum powder, an' it smelled like Lysol an' bus exhaust, an' it burned the back of her throat, nose, lungs, like honkin' crystal meth cut with Ajax, tasted like a mouth fulla aspirin dust.

. . . float and fade . . .

Only she wasn't floatin', she was walkin' through this stuff, left foot, right foot, an' you could see through it, well sorta, felt like sandpaperin' your eyeballs, but you could see the tunnel walls, or whatever the fuck this was, some kinda silvery stuff cruddy with orange streaks, went up an' up an' up, three, four, five stories t'some kinda ceiling.

Was clammy ol' pipes an' crumblin' ducts an' peelin' cables an' wires an' stuff all over th' ceiling anna walls, runnin' under her feet, gotta watch y'step in here. Big jagged holes everywhere, inna walls, inna ceiling, like fuckin' Arab terrorists had been doin' their thing here for years, all kindsa crap spillin' through 'em, heaps a junk, fucked-up machinery, rubble, chunks a concrete, smashed-up bricks . . .

Like ruins, y'might say, like th' dead empty basement under New fuckin' York after th' A-Bomb or the Riots or World War Whatever or some such shit.

'Cept it wasn't exactly *empty*, an' maybe not exactly *dead* neither. Was all these gurglin' an' clickin' an' whirrin' an' whooshin' an' sparkin' sounds comin' from everywhere, from nowhere, behind th' walls, above th' ceiling, under the fuckin' cracked asphalt floor. An' was all kindsa stuff drippin', an' spurtin' an' steamin' outa cracks an' holes an' rotten places in this an' that . . .

Was like bein' inside some kinda big ol' machine that no one had touched, or fixed, or laid a fuckin' hand on for a million years, still just about runnin', somehow, but not by much.

And . . .

And she wasn't alone.

There were these . . . these . . . these rat things zippin' an scurryin' an' skatin' around, fuckin' big scary motherfuckers, some of 'em maybe bigger'n she was, hard t'tell, with her eyes burnin' an' tearin' in the awful sparky blue fog.

They were all sorta the same.

But all kinda different.

They were all rat-shaped things, but they came in your choice a sizes, as if y'd choose any a th' motherfuckers, cat-sized upta human.

Was all put t'gether outa piecesa old scrap metal an' TV sets an' refrigerator parts an' garbage dump crap an' crummy whatever, but they was all put together different, this one with coat hanger arms anna head made outa th' top of a fire hydrant, that one all welded together outa post office truck sheet metal, 'nother over there seemed like piecesa toilet plumbing an' toaster ovens, like waste not, want not when you're puttin' together fuckin' rat things outa whatever y'can find inna ruins.

They was all crammed with electric wirin' an' plastic tubin' an' jars an' bottles fulla disgustin' stuff looked like piecesa guts an' meat an' fuckin' brains or somethin', seemed all connected somehow, electric parts sparkin' an' clickin', piecesa gears an' mechanical stuff more or less grindin' an' turnin', pukey pus-colored goo pumpin' an' gurglin' through tubing, so it was kinda hard t'tell whether they was fuckin' junkyard rat robots wearin' the meat parts for kicks way th' real hardcore punkers like t' walk around with alla those pins an' razor blades an' all piercin' their noses an' nuts an' titties, or fuckin' half-dead meat monster zombies kept more or less alive by th' machinery.

Alive?

Well, walkin' around, anyway.

Didn't move like they was alive, not like animals, more like some kinda cheap wind-up rat thing toys made in fuckin' Korea worked long enough to get 'em home t'the kiddies before they fell apart.

An' the eyes . . .

Like camera lenses with little blue subway bulbs shinin' through 'em. Like holes inta someplace was all blue ice an' strobe light.

All of 'em exactly th' same.

Like there was th' same awful thing lookin' outa all of 'em at th' same time. Somethin' bright an' blue an' hard. Somethin' cold an' dead as a hit-man's heart.

An' they were followin' her, circlin' round her, round, and round, fuckin' *herding* her was what the bastids was doin', a dozen, twenty, who knew how many, a these rat things, dead blue eyes trackin' her, tubing gurglin', machinery grindin' an' sparkin' an' clickin', some kinda squealin' an' screechin' fulla static like the world's worst junkie heavy metal band tryin' t'tune up their instruments on reds.

Loxy stopped.

Enough a this shit!

The fuckin' rat things with their dead blue eyes stopped too, surrounding her now. But they didn't stop makin' that horrible noise, didn't just hear it through your ears, went through every fuckin' bone in y' body, didn't just *sound* awful, it fuckin' *hurt*, like plasterin' yourself against a stadium speaker while the assholes onna stage smashed beer bottles into a jet engine an' strangled cats with barbed wire—

"Stay the fuck away from me!" Loxy screamed, whipping out the Big Ripper, and waving the knife at arm's length in their fuckin' rat faces.

The rat things didn't give no ground. A hundred cold blue eyes starin' her down from every direction. And the noise they was making was gettin' louder, an', louder, an' . . .

No, not louder, not exactly . . .

Was like all the worst fuckin' electric guitar players there ever was had shot themselves up with smack and was jammin' together an' somehow these rat things take all that an' turn it into an ice pick, into the motherfucker of all dentist drills, and—

An' jam it right through her ears and into the meat of her brain!

Hurt so bad she could hardly see, knocked her to her knees, starin' up into nothin' but a zillion cold blue lights, screamin', "Make it stop! Make it stop!"

But it don't stop, oh no, instead, this sound that's a pain, this pain that's a sound, becomes like this *voice*, this voice right inside her head, like chalk down a blackboard, like a fuckin' truck strippin' gears, only on an' on an' on, an' its gabblin' her name—

"Foxy Loxy Foxy Loxy Foxy Loxy."

—all fuzzed and staticlike, like tryin' t'tune a ten-dollar Chinese radio an' not quite gettin' it—

"Loxy Foxy Loxy Foxy Loxy Foxy."

"Stop it! Stop it! It fuckin' hurts!"

Laugh like flushing a toilet bowl fulla razor blades in her head.

"Love the pain you feel!" says the voice in her head. "Feel the pain you love! Pain is your only friend. To hurt is to be *alive*!"

Well, the sound a that voice like a million squeaking hinges right inside her head still hurts like fuckin' hell, but it's startin' t'become familiar like a tooth rottin' away in the back of your mouth, whaddya gonna do, blow your fuckin' head off, well maybe, it's a thought, but on the other hand . . .

On the other hand, she *is* talkin' to it, and it *is* talkin' back.

"Who the fuck are you? Where the fuck am I? What the fuck's goin' on?"

"Think of us as the Master Race. Think of us as what survives. Think of us as the Rats. Eating the eggs of the dinosaurs. They died. Think of us as what survived. Think of us as the Rats eating your shit and your garbage and the noses of your babies. You died. Think of us as what survives. Think of us as the Rats. Think of us as what survives when all meat dies."

A hundred pairs a shiny blue eyes surrounded her. An' outa each an' every one of 'em, th' same cold dead thing looked back.

"*Bull-fuckin'-shit!*" Loxy cried. "You ain't no fuckin' rat, you're a fuckin' Rat *Thing*! You're just a buncha car parts an' piecesa shit from pinball machines an' microwave ovens an' toilet dinguses! You're *dead*! You ain't never really even *been* alive!"

"Think of us as the ghost of the Rats, Foxy Loxy," said the voice in her head. "The Earth died. The meat Rats ate the corpse. When there was no meat left, *they* died. *We* ate the corpse. *We* are the Master Race. We are what we eat. We survive. *We* are the Rats."

"What the fuck you want with me?"

"To walk among the Monkey People. To become what survives, Loxy Foxy. To be your only friend, Foxy Loxy."

Loxy managed to stagger to her feet, waving the Big Ripper. "*This* is my only friend, you rat-face motherfucker, you wanna shake hands with *him*, be my fuckin' guest!"

The voice in her head didn't answer. All of a sudden, the pain of it was gone.

"Hee, hee, hee," Loxy giggled.

Guess even a fuckin' dead Rat Thing thinks twice before it wantsa tangle with good ol' Rip!

But then there was a horrible squeaky Rat Thing laugh in her head, and they came for her. She slashed, and she stabbed, but Rip just squealed and screamed off glass an' metal, an' dozens a paws scratched, an' grabbed, an' scrabbled at her, an' they had her.

Didn't even bother t'throw her down, shit, they didn't even bother t' take away the knife. A dozen rat paws held each arm. A dozen rat mouths had her by each leg.

She screamed and screamed and screamed.

And then she heard the sound, kinda like one a those electric hand drills they use to punch holes through wood an' sheet metal.

She screamed even louder when she saw it.

'Cause that was exactly what it was.

One a the bastids was holdin' it in both paws, none too steady like. And half a dozen others was takin' apart these rusty wire coat hangers an' knottin' 'em together like gettin' ready to do a fifty-buck abortion on a fuckin' *whale*. . . .

Gabble, gabble, scree, scree, scree, hee, hee, hee!

The one witha drill brings it right over her skull, and—

—jams it right inta the top of her head!

—she can fuckin' feel the blood and meat flying, fuckin' hear the drill grinding through bone, and—

—everything explodes inna blue light of this fuckin' awful pain, worst thing she ever fuckin' felt, until—

—a sharp knife a something even worse shoots down the center of the blue pain, red, an' raw, an' jagged, down through her brain, a fuckin' lightnin' bolt of pain down her spine, branchin' out like one a those cartoon trees growin' at high speed, tree a pain, tree a fire, tree a ice, like every bone in her body, every fuckin' little vein, is flashing with neon pain, like someone jammed a horse needle fulla hot lead inta a main line, like she's twitchin' an' jerkin', shittin' and pissin', like some Nazi monster movie Freddie Krueger's stuck an ice pick in just the right place is whackin' himself off with one hand an' wrigglin' it just right with the other just t'hear her scream—

It had been a long time since Dexter Lampkin had suffered a real writer's block, and a mere week's worth wouldn't have been a cause for panic had he not reread the contract carefully and discovered a ballbuster of a delivery clause which called for him to repay the entire signature advance were he to be so much as one day late or one page short delivering 250 pages of *The Word According to Ralf*.

Cursing and fuming, Dexter decided to do give the bastards just what they deserved.

He had *Chaos Time* in the computer, plus the format and show bible of *The Word According to Ralf*, plus the last five years' worth of stories, novels, and pieces of this and that. Upon running it all through his word count program, he discovered that he had 365 pages of material out of which to extract 250 pages of prewritten first draft without writing an original word.

Then it was merely eleven eight-hour days to slice and dice and block move and rewrite third person into first and come up with 276 pages that would fulfill the contract for something that could be called *The Word According to Ralf* and be marketed by an unscrupulous enough schlockmeister as the as-told-to memoir of the star thereof.

Of course, it was just as big a pile of shit as Dexter had known it would be.

What in the comic book trade was called an "origin story." He had put the format he had written for the show into first person as told by Ralf and pumped it full of about two hundred pages of gory description of dystopian nightmare culled and rewritten from *Chaos Time*, the show bible, and assorted short stories and novelettes.

It was hard to imagine anyone actually reading through what amounted to a single tendentious, depressing, unfunny expository lump about as appetizing as wad of steam-table cauliflower.

But that wasn't the point, now was it?

The point was for them to *buy The Word According to Ralf*, not *read* it. The point was to stuff the covers of a tie-in book with 250 pages of black ink on cheap pulp paper, and Dexter seriously doubted that anyone at PJP Books would read this turd before they rushed it into production.

He was already home free, he could print it, or noodle around for a while polishing it first, if he felt like pretending to be a responsible craftsman.

And yet . . .

The proceedings were held in the courtyard of Albert Falkenberg's sanatorium, built on a flat hillcrest about five miles inland and high above the shore, and as Amanda gazed westward, the perspective was, well, godlike. Grassy slopes and chaparral-choked ravines tumbled down to the Pacific Coast Highway separating the coastal hills from the beach where swimmers, sunbathers, and surfers were dwarfed by the immensities of the coastal range and the mighty ocean sweeping out past the horizon. To the southwest, the cityscape of Los Angeles sprawled around the far curve of the bay, shimmering and simmering under its eternal pall of smog.

The courtyard was embraced on three sides by the building itself, opening out onto the wide world. The gravelly ground was raked into mandalic waves and swirls in the Zen manner, and the only plantings were palms at the corners to provide some shade, and an enormous rubbery jade tree in a rough stone enclosure in the center.

Amanda and Albert Falkenberg sat in bean bag chairs facing the sea with Ralf between them, a tray with syringes, vial, and a spray can across Albert's lap. "One final time, Ralf," Albert said as he filled the two syringes, "you *are* comfortable with this?"

Dressed in a white pajama suit, his longish silver hair tossing in the offshore breeze, the Beverly Hills psychiatrist to the stars had transformed himself into the mountaintop shaman.

"You're the witch doctor," Ralf cracked in his wise-guy voice.

Albert lifted one of the syringes from the tray, squirted a few drops of the contents into the air to clear any bubbles.

"A little of this, a little of that, not very much of anything, a homeopathic cocktail you might say," he said. "A very light dose of psilocybin, a bit of pentothal, a whisper of Ritalin to clarify the edge."

He sprayed the pit of Ralf's right elbow with ethyl chloride.

Ralf laughed. "We whose brains are about to fry salute you," he said. He winced as Albert stuck the needle in, stared fixedly out to sea as he emptied the syringe, sighed as he withdrew it.

Albert sprayed anesthetic on the pit of his own left elbow, picked up the other syringe, paused to give Amanda a little shrug and smile.

"Sorry you can't come along, Amanda," he said as he injected himself with the elixir. "But just as I don't believe in sending my patients into these regions without a spirit guide, I don't believe in lifting off myself without a good ground control."

Albert took up a lotus position, and began Nadi Shuddhi, deep alternate-nostril yogic breathing, his belly sucking in and billowing out, his chest inflating and deflating in a slow even rhythm, his shoulders rising and falling, as he gazed at the horizon where the blue of the sky converged on the mirror of the sea.

Ralf prised himself into what might or might not have been a satiric simulacrum, upright on his chair, but unable to cross his feet above his knees in full lotus, looking out over the ocean with a fixed simian grin like Coyote doing Buddha.

Amanda was an experienced ground controller of psychedelic trips, but she didn't know what to expect here, with the sacrament an attenuated homeopathic mixture administered by injection, and a psychotherapist accompanying his patient to guide the voyage from within.

After only a few minutes of silent rhythmic breathing, Albert turned toward her, then toward Ralf, his pupils widely dilated behind his glasses, his face suffused with a rosy luster from within, and while he could not quite be said to be displaying a visible aura, the energy that came vibrating off of him seemed palpable.

"Where are you, Ralf?" he said in slow, careful tones.

Ralf didn't move. He continued to stare out to sea.

"I'm sitting in a chair on a clifftop above the western ocean on the third planet of a yellow sun halfway out in the spiral arm sticks of a galaxy the locals call the Milky Way," he said in a sonorously stoned voice.

"And *who* are you?"

"Could I have my agent get back to you on that one?" he said in the same slow, portentous tones, a strange effect indeed.

"And *when* are you?"

"When I've always been."

"And *what* have you come here to do?"

"To seize this schlocky script for a funeral pyre and ad-lib it closer to the heart's desire. Or at least tummel us through the night."

"And *how* are you going do that?"

Ralf turned his head to look at Albert, the deepening shadows cast by the late afternoon sunlight chiaroscuring his features into a fleshly mask, his eyes as glassy and enigmatic as the surface of the sea.

"You tell me, Doc," he said. "Isn't that what we're here to find out?"

"If you say so."

"If *I* say so? Aren't *you* the witch doctor?"

"Aren't *you* the dreamer?" said Albert.

He gazed directly into Ralf's eyes for a long beat. Ralf looked back unblinkingly. Dramatic stage effect or contact high, metaphorical transmogrification or true vision, Amanda could feel the long silence transporting them to another level.

"This is *your* dream, Ralf, and we are all in it," Albert said, his voice assuming a hypnotic singsong cadence. "We're going in deeper now, deeper into the Dreamtime, deeper into *your* Dreamtime, Ralf, deeper, and deeper, into the Center, into the Great Void where nothing is and from which all flows, into the Tao within, into that region from which all that is or was or will be emerges as the crown of our own creation. . . ."

And the doorway opened.

But not for Amanda.

Indeed it was her function here *not* to step through it. But she could feel it happening with the place behind her forehead where folklore's wisdom and the pineal gland's locus said a third eye would have been.

Albert had opened the doorway to *Ralf's* Dreamtime and was leading him into it.

"Where are you now?" he said.

"Right where I've always been," replied Ralf, falling in with the soothing dreamy rhythm of Albert's voice. "There's no place else to be."

His face had become a tabula rasa. His eyes were as opaque and empty with possibility as the image of the sky reflected on the surface of the sea.

"And who are you?"

Now Ralf's wide rubbery lips creased in the Buddha's smile. "I'm the Dreamer," he said. "There's no one else to be."

A certain psychic geometry seemed to have shifted, as if he had indeed come lucidly awake to find himself the god of his own Dreamtime creation.

"And when are you?"

A mournful wordless sigh issued from Ralf's lips, from deep within him, and he turned away, and looked down from on high toward the horizon, where the Pacific sun was beginning to golden the perfect blue California afternoon, painting foreshadows of a fiery Götterdämmerung of a sunset to come as it sank toward the reflective canvas of the sea.

"There is no when, Monkey Boy," he said quite gently. "It's always the eleventh hour. It's always the last chance we get to play Wheel of Fortune."

Again that Buddha smile. But now some inner light made it seem radiant.

"You said it yourself, Doc. All that is or was or will be is the crown of our own creation. Time is a dream. Only the Dreamer is real."

Amanda had to remind herself that she had *not* injected the psychedelic. For this was a . . . Presence.

And she was in it.

"And what have you come here to do?"

So too was Albert, speaking in the voice of an acolyte now; had he been speaking Japanese, the verb endings of posture would surely have shifted.

"*What have I come here to do?*"

Amanda learned that laughter could be cosmic and bitter at the same time as Ralf gave vent to such an expression of joyless mirth.

"But I haven't *come* here at all, since I've been here all along," he said with a strange species of sad sarcasm. "Ever since you came down from the trees and first dreamed the story. The Dreamer is born with the Dreamtime."

By a serendipitous trick of the lighting, a special effect laid on by destiny, the coppery sheen of the waning sun reflected off the sea was captured by his eyes, burnishing them to an antique luster, and the Presence before them indeed seemed as old and primeval as that descent from the trees.

Again that laughter, but warmer this time.

"*I* am the Dream. *You* are the Dreamer."

Albert Falkenberg took two long slow breaths, as if seeking to pump prana into his being, the better to confront the Presence upright as a man.

"I ask you," he demanded as a shaman might presume to interrogate his familiar, "what mission have you manifested yourself here to perform?"

"Me is *we*," said the Presence that spoke through Ralf. "*You* manifest *me*, remember?"

Now the laugh was chastening, the laugh of the star of *The Word According To*, in whose voice the Presence now chose to speak.

"You were expecting maybe Jehovah or the Great Spirit or Uk-Ruppa-Tooty? Well, I ain't them! I'm just the latest incarnation of the same sad old story you Monkey People have been trying to figure out how to tell yourselves all along."

He laughed, softer this time, the corners of his mouth turned up in the ghost of a smile.

"And the mission, and believe me, we can't choose not to accept it, is to take one last shot at getting the story right, to wake up inside this failing format and finally get it through our fat heads that we better take the wheel, 'cause there ain't no one else driving, that we're the only ones can save our world from its worst and only enemy."

"Namely us," said Amanda.

"Namely us," said Ralf.

"How?" said Albert.

"Quien sabe, Kemo Sabe?" Ralf said.

He sighed. The muscles of his face seemed to droop with the weight of the world as a cloud passing across the sun painted a shadow across it.

"I'm just the poor schmuck keeps getting cast as the fall guy, chained to a rock, nailed to a cross, shot in the head, talk about your Perils of Pauline! Let me tell you, they'll do it every time, this gig *never* turns out to be the part your agent promised."

Slowly he rose from his chair and stood there facing them.

"I gotta tell you, Monkey People, I have had it, and so have you," he said in a voice drenched with cosmic and all-too-human weariness. "You've had the best writers in the business rewriting this turkey since the stone age, and it *still* keeps bombing out. So if I get the hook *this* time, no more remakes, the show gets canceled for good, enough is enough!"

Thus spake the inheritor of Prometheus, the Buddha and Jesus, of Gandhi and JFK, of all those heroes, would-be and otherwise, for better and worse, who found themselves cast in the Sun King's role.

The *Comic* Messiah, shoved onstage mugging and screaming, in a desperate final hope that what millennia of tragedy could not accomplish might be achieved by farce.

The Last Best Schtick of Man.

Who could deny that this was precisely the avatar that this age so richly deserved?

So *this* is Enlightenment?

Amanda found herself laughing at the gentle cosmic joke at her own expense.

All her life, she had sought this very union of realm of the spirit and the realm of Maya, the reality of metaphor and the reality of matter, experienced not as a vision in the Dreamtime but as a peak moment of lucidity in the waking world.

And here it was.

But without the expected celestial special effects or transcendental revelations.

Just the luminously clear perception of the numinously ordinary.

It was a splendid waning summer afternoon on a hilltop above the Pacific like a million other such quotidian glories since the long song and dance first began. The briny tang of the rising offshore breeze mingled with the winy musk of the cooling chaparral to create a perfume that went straight to the backbrain, the aroma of oncoming California sunset older than the mind of man.

Down there on the ancient continental shore, families and lovers were returning from the water to bask in the golden warmth of the setting summer sun. Off to the north, a bright red hang glider played tag with the pelicans. South beyond the sweep of the bay, the lights of Los Angeles were beginning to come on, twinkling and sparkling beneath the smog like an evening sky's first stars.

Out there, millions of miles away, immense and indifferent in the cold blackness of the void, was nothing more than a great ball of burning gas, the star about which this planet revolved.

Yet here, floating majestically toward the horizon, glorifying this perfect Pacific sky with blazes and glazes of purple and orange, crowning itself with rays of gold, a mere globe of hydrogen and helium was transfigured and transformed into the Earth's true presiding deity—into Ra, into Sol, into Mother Gaia's mighty consort, into the life force incarnate, too gloriously brilliant for the direct vision of mortal man to endure—the Sun, the Father of Life and the Nemesis of Darkness, the Good Old Boy Himself, the Bringer of the Light.

There stood an angry and weary little man with a bulbous nose, an unruly shock of windblown hair, bloodshot eyes with drug-dilated pupils set in blackened sockets, his ridiculous shoulders groaning under the weight of the world— Woody Allen in Atlas's underwear.

Yet the setting sun had draped a cloak of gold across his shoulders, and though on him the Light Bringer's mantle might carry more than a whiff of campy drag, hero he was, this poor little avatar from the Borscht Belt.

For tummel though he might at the burden laid upon him by a schlockmeister destiny, there he still stood, trying like a trouper to hold back the night.

Amanda laughed.

It was a good one, all right.

It had been her commission to refrain from stepping through the doorway. Yet it was *she* who now knew what it was they must conjure.

It was *she* who must play the shaman and summon forth the Bringer of the Light.

And the Zen of it was that she need only awake him.

For he was already here.

"Why don't you let me in on the joke, Amanda?" he said. "Anything to spruce up the act."

Ralf looked back at her with those tired, all too human eyes. And she knew that in this moment, *she* had become the messenger of *his* Dreamtime, the Dreamtime of that which gazed out imploringly at her through those doorways longing to be born into the world.

Amanda rose, placed her hands on Ralf's shoulders, spun him around, and stood beside him gazing out over the Great World Ocean, the womb where life had been born in the primal soup of the sea.

Beneath the waves, the coral was dying, and the plankton was expiring, and there were whales, and fish, and dolphins gasping their last. A hole had opened in the purpling sky, and cosmic bolides were raining in, and the ice was melting, and trees were dying, and the survival of life on this planet was very much in doubt.

For the Earth was but a glob of lava cooling in a pitiless black void and all that lived upon it but lichen clinging precariously to bits of floating rock.

The sky was darkening now, and all around the curve of the bay, the lights of Los Angeles were coming on beneath the photochemical smog. Through an illusion of the quickly waning sunshine playing across it, the City of Man seeming to be moving along the interface of space and time, rising like the promise of a golden future from the shore or sinking slowly into the deeps of nonsentience from which it had arisen; it was, as usual, impossible to tell.

But there still hovering above the horizon and holding back the night was the Sun, Nemesis of Darkness, and Bringer of Light.

"What do you see out there?" said Amanda.

"The sun over the ocean," said the Last Best Schtick of Man.

"Going up or coming down? Sinking back into the darkness or bringing back the light?"

A long beat of silence.

"Only time will tell."

Amanda took him by both hands pulled him gently round. "And what if only *you* will tell?" she said.

Ralf's eyes looked into hers out of his Dreamtime.

"The Jeremiah and Cassandra show keeps bombing out in the third act because every sourpuss savior forgets what every birdbrained schlockmeister in Hollywood knows from the bottom of his tinsel town heart," she told him.

"Which is?" said the Comic Messiah.

"Anyone who knows the Biz knows it already," said Amanda. "You want a hit, you need to send them out of the theater whistling the title song. 'Tis better box office to light a brave candle. You've taken the act as far as it can go cursing the dark."

"Seems like I remember that the guy who said that blew his mind out in a car," said Ralf.

"He didn't realize that the Light had changed," Amanda reminded him.

"Has it?"

By some trick of the lighting, some instrumentality of the Dreamtime, some truthful illusion, two orange highlights cast by the setting sun were captured by his eyes, two points of a far deeper light; sunset's dying embers, or a dawn's early light, only time would tell.

"You know how many Light Bringers it takes to unscrew a planet?" said Amanda.

"No, how many?"

Once more Amanda put her hands on those all too human shoulders, and turned his face back into the final glory of a summer day's sun.

"Quien sabe, Kemo Sabe?" she said softly. "But how about we try and find out?"

"Aaaaaaaaaa . . ."

Left foot, right foot, left foot, right foot . . .

Foxy Loxy woke up screaming. Screaming and walking.

Walkin' along the ties betweena rails, followin' the little blue lights down a subway tunnel . . .

Right foot, left foot, follow the little blue lights . . .

What the fuck?

Th' fuckin' cold turkey DTs?

Musta been, right? Jeez, what a fuckin' nightmare! What th' fuck else could it have been?

Giant dead Rat Things! Talkin' to her! Drillin' inta her head! Stickin' coat hanger wire inta her brain! Fuckin' pain so bad she musta passed out.

Passed out?

But she had never stopped walkin' . . . or had she?

Left foot, right foot, follow the little blue lights . . .

An' somehow she didn't wanna stop now, *couldn't* stop, like her bones had turned inta metal rods an' hinges with little electric motors movin' 'em, felt like she had this skeleton machine thing inside her, like it was wearing her meat, wires runnin' up her arms, her legs, up her back an' inta her brain, kinda stopped before it got to where *she* was sorta, like Loxy was just along for th' ride.

Follow the little blue lights, right foot, left foot . . .

Afraid what she was gonna find, but you hadda do it anyway, right, like you couldn't *not* pick atta scab, Loxy reached up to poke around in the hair at the top of her head.

Lotta knots an' crap, little bug-things crawlin' around, but wasn't no blood, wasn't no great big hole, hey, you could feel it, couldn't ya, some fuckin' Rat Thing drilled a hole in your head an' shoved in ten fuckin' feet a old coat hanger, right? Right?

"Right, Loxy Foxy," said the voice in her head, "all a dream, scree, scree, scree!"

Was like broken bottles grinding through a truck transmission, like nail files scrapin' down the inside a her skull, like a hundred fuckin' giant Rat Things squeakin' an' chitterin' an' laughin' their fuckin' rat-laughs.

"Never happened, Loxy Foxy, not for hundreds of years, scree, scree, scree!"

Left foot, right foot, follow the little blue rat eyes . . .

"Leave me the fuck alone!"

"We can't do that, Foxy Loxy. You're our only friend."

"You ain't no fuckin' frienda mine!"

Right foot, left foot, follow the little blue lights . . .

"Sure we are, Loxy Foxy, we're your *only* friend. We're never going to leave you lost and alone. We're the Rats. We're the Master Race. And that's what friends are for."

"Piss off, you rat-fuck bastid!" Loxy screamed, and she told her legs to stop.

Right foot, left foot, follow the little blue rat eyes . . .

And kept on walking up the tunnel toward a square of yellow light.

"We're your only friend, Foxy Loxy. Not to worry, Loxy Foxy, we'll tell you everything you have to do."

Left foot, right foot . . .

"T'do fuckin' *what*?"

"To be our friend, Foxy Loxy, hee, hee, hee," cackled the voice inside her head, "to be our *only* friend, scree, scree, scree!"

Right foot, left foot, left foot, right foot, followin' the little blue lights, Foxy

Loxy found herself bein' marched outa the cool gray quiet a th' tunnels, toward th' clatter and flash of a subway station, toward a forgotten world up there beyond th' dim distant square of dirty yellow light.

What with being dragged to furniture stores by Ellie, booking his guests for the show, and banging out *The Word According to Ralf*, Dexter Lampkin hadn't ventured down into the lowland depths of anything to do with Fandom since they had moved up into Laurel Canyon. But he had 276 pages of drek an easy couple of weeks' polish away from fulfilling the contract, so the pressure was off, and while meetings of the Los Angeles Science Fiction Society were something that he usually avoided like the globulosis plague, he could hardly resist taking a peek at one that the flyer he customarily tossed had billed as devoted to the "Ralfies."

The Ralfies were, face it, his creation, the burgeoning new subfandom devoted to *The Word According To* and its star. Dexter had been unable to escape from being on the mailing lists of the Ralf fanzines, which ran the gamut from lowly letterzines to one with full-color covers called *The Word,* which Texas Jimmy Balaban had only refrained from suing in return for ten percent of their gross plus unlimited free ad space for the official tie-in items.

They were filled with transcriptions of actual shows, imaginary transcriptions of fantasy shows, made-up jokes, fan fiction devoted to Ralf and/or set in Deathship Earth, announcements of meetings, cartoons, drawings, and photos of their staff and readerships stuffed into Deathship Earth T-shirts and XXX-tra large-sized Suits From the Future that made Dexter feel that he should've hidden himself behind a false beard and a flasher's raincoat as he parked his beautiful new red Porsche half a block down from the tacky LASFS clubhouse.

This was actually two buildings: a former residence, and a shed behind it that might have once been a six-car garage turned into the main meeting hall.

The Los Angeles Science Fiction Society billed itself as the oldest and largest science fiction club in the world, and it probably was, for an inclusive policy had made it a commons for the various subgroups, specialized fandoms, Big Name Fans, book dealers, writers, wannabes, and hangers-on who made up the science fiction community.

Of whom there were already plenty by the time Dexter arrived, gabbing in the back courtyard, drifting in and out of the clubhouse air-conditioning, as they waited for the formal proceedings to begin.

The mix at these meetings varied from week to week depending on whether there was a program, and if so, what. An appearance by Harlan Ellison or Ray

Bradbury would draw their more showbizzy pals, a presentation by Jerry Pournelle would attract space program types, and of course a story editor or production executive would turn out every wannabe sf scriptwriter in town.

As with the pros, so with the fans. Anything to do with any of the incarnations of Star Trek would fill the place with Trekkies, guest shots by out-of-town novelists would draw the literary types, fantasy programming would draw members of the Society for Creative Anachronism, and you didn't need to be on the mailing list for the flyer to know that this was Ralf night.

The Ralfies were everywhere.

Dexter counted over a dozen people wearing The Suit, three of whom were *women*. Every fourth person seemed to be wearing one of the T-shirts; a Deathship Earth original, the new variation with the red "No" crossed circle icon superimposed over the cartoon, or second-rate knockoffs of same.

After being accosted on his way back to the courtyard by gabbling Ralfies with halitosis pestering him for interviews for their fanzines, hitting him up for tickets to the show, offering him the benefits of their opinion as to whom he should book, Dexter escaped into the clubhouse via the back door in search of liquid fortification and a corner in which to guzzle it down as quickly as possible in relative peace before confronting the meeting itself.

There were several little parlors where the munchies, beer, and jug wine set out on tables kept the traffic moving, making it difficult for lemmings to coagulate into madding mini-crowds. In one of them, Dexter found a jug of Cribari Italian Red, and Emory Pollock sitting around with Hank and Louise Farmer. He filled a plastic cup to the brim, slugged it down quickly, and poured himself a refill before he sat down.

Only then he realized that all three of them were wearing No Deathship Earth T-shirts.

"Uh . . . not exactly your usual choice of haberdashery, Hank . . ." he said.

Hank plucked at the T-shirt with his thumb and forefinger. "De rigueur at NASA these days," he said.

Dexter sucked down more wine, his head reeling, and not yet from the booze. "Et tu, Emory?" he said. "Next I know," he cracked, "you'll be walking around in a white polyester suit."

"It's at the tailor's," Pollock told him. "The cuffs had to be let out, and the waist had to be taken in."

Dexter drained the rest of his cup in one convulsive gulp.

"I think I need a refill," Dexter said by way of an exit line, holding up his empty cup, and returning to the refreshment table.

Why doesn't all this please you, Lampkin? he was forced to ask himself. Isn't it what you knowingly set out to create? Aren't you getting a piece of the action off the sale of all these T-shirts and Suits? Aren't you going to end up making a lot more off *The Word According to Ralf*, off a stupid piece of shit you cobbled together in less than a month? Are you not doing well by doing good?

Dexter couldn't get a handle on it, but as he wandered out into the meeting hall, forcing himself to be polite to his comet's tail of Ralfies, a hollowness behind his sternum, a nervous flutter in his anus, seemed protoplasmic signals from whatever was so discomforting his soul.

It didn't begin to clarify itself on a conscious level until the meeting itself was well under way. There was a stage, maybe twenty rows of folding chairs, and Dexter took the far left seat in the back row, hoping against all reason to make himself invisible, to avoid being dragged up onto it.

The meeting commenced with an eternity of LASFS business, the sort of fannish drone that usually had Dexter grinding his teeth in boredom. But tonight it was comfortable and lulling, the way one really does not look forward to being interrupted before finishing a long dull article in a tedious business magazine if one is sitting in the dentist's waiting room at the time.

And then the meeting was finally turned over to the Ralfies.

Oscar Karel, resplendent in a Suit From the Future, was the chairman, having been elected president of the local chapter of Monkey People of America, one of several national Ralf fan clubs. The Monkey People published a fanzine, held their own meetings, put on amateur versions of *The Word According to Ralf* at conventions, and held Ralf imitator contests, but from what Dexter could gather seemed to expend most of their time and energy organizing future meetings for the purpose of recruiting more members to hold more meetings, a familiar fannish phenomenon whereby the reproductive process became the main raison d'être.

After Oscar Karel had glazed his quota of eyeballs, he turned the floor over to an intense cybernerd, the breast pocket of whose Suit From the Future was soiled by blue ballpoint ink leaking through his plastic penholder, and who delivered a pitch for his own outfit, Deathship Cyborgs, a Ralf fandom who interfaced entirely on the Internet, never meeting in anything so mundane as the flesh.

They published an on-line fanzine called *Deconstruction Manual for Deathship Earth* wherein they swapped nerdish Ralf jokes and exchanged programs designed to throw virtual monkey wrenches into the software of the biodeath machine so as to bring about a total system crash thereof, after which they would emerge triumphantly from the electronic catacombs to reprogram the operating system of the planet in some yet to be determined manner that would bring about a golden age in which Fandom ruled the world.

This was followed by a far less comprehensible presentation by a huge woman whose shape was mercifully obscured by a white muumuu the size of a small tent upon which had been silk-screened not only a photo of Ralf in full cry but signs of the zodiac, alchemical arcana, and what looked like bumper sticker slogans in Elvish script lifted from *The Lord of the Rings*.

And so it went.

Testimonials and solicitations by publishers of Ralfzines. A representative of a sub-subgenre of the fannish subgenre know as Costume Fandom dedicated to the production of fannish concepts of the denizens of Deathship Earth at convention masquerades. An entire fan club made up of Ralf impersonators.

Dexter, like all writers, enjoyed reading rave reviews of his own work. But there was one species of rave review that was more painful to endure than an out-and-out hydrophobic pan. Namely fulsome gushing praise from an ignorant putz who had not gotten it at all. If such a flaming red asshole likes it so much, was the feeling such reviews induced in him, I must *really* have done something wrong.

It was a cognate of this feeling that crept up on him as he listened in mortification to the Ralfies doing their stuff. For while this clade of Ralf fandoms might not be his creation in the manner of a novel, he could hardly deny that he was its progenitor if anyone was.

And yet . . .

And yet while Dexter scorned as assholery praise for what he had wrought, there was a pathos to the proceedings that made him feel like an asshole who had gotten an elusive something *right*.

For however crack-brained this fandom that he had deliberately created might appear if ruthlessly exposed to the Mundane World Out There, their hearts were in the right place, they did manifestly understand that that self-same world was hip-hopping blithely toward Condition Terminal like Roger Rabbit on reds.

Finally the moment which Dexter had dreaded arrived. "I have been *told*," quacked Oscar Karel, "that we have *among* us tonight someone *very* close to *Ralf*, the creator and associate producer of *The Word According to Ralf*, LA fandom's own *Dexter* Lampkin, who I *know* would like to give us the last word . . . Dexter? *Dexter?*"

There was a round of applause that died away as Dexter trudged slowly down the aisle to the stage with about as much enthusiasm as a convict walking the Last Mile.

And then there he was, standing before what he himself had deliberately sought to create the last time he had spoken before a fannish audience, the reverberating ripples of the pebble his drunken Guest of Honor speech had tossed into the Dirac sea at LostCon.

Well Lampkin, you've done it, haven't you? You've saved the show, you're making big bucks, and in the process you've created a fannish crusade to save the world. You've even given them a Messiah to follow.

Now what, wise guy?

He hadn't a clue.

"Well folks, uh, while Ralf is, uh, unable to be here tonight, I'm sure he'll be, ah, really gratified to learn of your terrific, uh, support," he gabbled inanely, hoping desperately to prime his verbal pump. "Uh, as you know, the show has gone weekly this summer in prime time, with special guests, and it looks like we're going to be able to continue this way in the fall, thanks in no small part to the, uh, support of Fandom . . ."

This fatuous showbizzy blather was greeted by a susurrus of squirmy murmuring. It was definitely not what they wanted to hear.

He paused, he leaned forward, essayed a conspiratorial grin. "Well . . . I suppose I can let *you* in on the big secret," he said.

He paused again.

"Ralf and I are collaborating on a book!"

"What's it called?" someone called out.

"*The Word According to Ralf.*"

"When's it coming out?"

"December. PJP."

To Dexter's immense relief, the ice had been broken, and he was no longer expected to deliver some kind of speech, but could become merely the focal point of a familiar fannish free-form free-for-all.

"What's it about?"

It's about 276 pages of depressing crud, Dexter thought sourly.

"It's about Ralf, what else?" he said instead.

"*What* about Ralf?"

"*Everything* about Ralf," Dexter said. "It's his autobiography as told to me."

But he couldn't avoid realizing what a whopper of a lie that was, which confronted him with an even less pleasant truth. Not only was Ralf entirely uninvolved in the writing of the damned thing, Dexter realized that he so loathed it precisely *because* the Comic Messiah was his literary creation, because this so-called autobiography was far from complete.

All too many science fiction writers sought fannish feedback on uncompleted work in the form of workshops, private consultations with a favored few, or the reading of a first draft in public gatherings such as this. And the unsavory truth was that while Dexter considered going *that* far the literary equivalent of dropping one's pants in public, it was an all-too-similar impulse that had drawn him down from his mountaintop to face the core readership for *The Word According to Ralf*.

The Fans.

The Monkey People of America. The Deathship Cyborgs. The Ralf impersonators. Ralfzine fandom.

The Ralfies.

Most of the people in this room and the demographics they represented were going to buy the book. And now, thanks to this advance announcement, the Net, the fanzines, and fannish word of mouth, they'd buy it the first week it came out. An effect which might even propel it to the bottom of some paperback best-seller lists and create a boomlet, and if it didn't, the show itself surely would.

It dawned on Dexter with a shock of horror that he was going to get what he had always thought he wanted.

He was going to have a best-seller.

The Word According to Ralf was going to sell more copies than anything else he had ever written or was ever likely to write again. His cult novel. The subject he would be condemned to discuss in every interview, on every convention panel, henceforth. The book he would be remembered for whether he liked it or not.

Oh shit.

And what made it worse, much worse, the awful epiphany stunning him into dummyhood, was that he could hardly deny that such a cosmic comic punishment would be *just*.

There before him, gabbling and shouting and waving their hands avidly for his attention were the Ralfies in their Deathship Earth T-shirts and cheap white Suits From the Future, and having bought these tie-ins, they would no doubt buy whatever he stuck between the covers of *The Word According to Ralf* too.

Ralf fandom, square-shaped and pear-shaped, dedicated to saving the world from the terminal assholery of the mundanes with fanzines and masquerade costumes, with convention panels and Ralf imitators, with spaced-out nut-cults and fannish Internet fun and games.

Half-assed, self-defeating, ludicrous, pathetic.

But heartfelt.

Who had not gotten it at all?

He was being paid to address the largest readership he would ever have with whatever he chose as long as he called it *The Word According to Ralf*. And what had he done with it?

Churned out 276 pages of cynical media tie-in hackwork.

Who was the flaming red asshole?

"Are you and Ralf going to really tell us the *true story*?" called out a female voice whose familiarity jolted Dexter out of his sour self-flagellating reverie, and into a sudden blush of far less cerebral mortification.

There, standing right center in the audience, was Cynthia.

"The . . . the true story?"

She was wearing blue jeans that revealed her ass and thighs as just this side of enormous. A large No Deathship Earth T-shirt worn loose over the waistline hid her belly but emphasized her heavy hanging breasts. She wore neither lipstick nor makeup, and her bleached blond hair was done up in an untidy bun.

The naked unvarnished fan girl in her natural habitat.

"There are a lot of people who believe that Ralf really *is* a time traveler . . ." she said.

"Are you one of them, Cyn—"

Dexter cut himself off before revealing any personal connection, but not before the cock she had so sincerely and heartfeltly sucked shriveled toward his scrotum, not before he felt as if it were hanging out there dripping for all the world to see.

"I'd like to believe it, wouldn't you, at least it would mean we had a future for him to come from," Cynthia said earnestly, looking right at him, neither embarrassing him with any sign of personal recognition nor dissembling insincerely by *Mr. Lampkining* him, a nicety which Dexter had to admit showed class.

Murmurs of approval swept the room.

"*Deathship Earth?*" Dexter said dryly.

"But maybe it doesn't *have* to be," Cynthia said. "If Ralf really is a messenger Deathship Earth sent back to change our future, then if he succeeds, there won't *be* a Deathship Earth to have sent him back, and maybe it will be a better future that has sent him back to turn Deathship Earth into itself, or, or, I mean, you know . . ."

She shrugged, she stood there, trapped, flustered, and phumphering in the paradoxes, like every science fiction writer who had tried to take time travel seriously since the genre began.

Somehow Dexter knew just how she felt, somehow his heart went out to her; to this sincere, fat, unattractive fan girl for whom the privilege of sucking his cock had been a moment of genuine grace. Somehow she made him feel quite ashamed, though exactly of what, he didn't, or perhaps preferred not to, know.

Dexter came as gallantly as he could to her rescue, forcing a laugh, filling it with as much warmth as he could muster. "Yeah, I know," he said, "these time travel paradoxes are pretty hard to figure."

He leaned forward, tried to make it sincere. "Ralf really *does* believe he's from the future," he said. "But that doesn't make the true story of *what* future we're gonna end up having for him to come from any easier to figure out."

"But you can't know how the future's going to come out, now can you?" Cynthia told him. "Maybe how the story comes out is going to be up to anyone or everyone in this room, or some mundane out there who has no idea."

And then she looked directly into his eyes from across that crowded room, with those same eyes, that same gaze, that same achingly wholehearted sincerity, that same moment in a convention hotel room where she had seduced his gallant adulterous heart.

"Maybe it's all up to you," she said. "Maybe the *true* story is what you make it, Dexter Lampkin. One of those self-fulfilling prophecies . . ."

"I . . . I don't think I'm getting it . . ." Dexter stammered.

But he was, and he did. Out there in unwholesome fannish public, this fan girl, this groupie, this Ralfie, was managing to again awaken a sleeping something in his heart.

"None of us ever know, so we've got act *as if*, don't we? And if a story is good enough to make enough people *want* it to be true, then maybe they'll *make* it come true," Cynthia said.

"Tinkerbell lives!" some soulless boob called out.

But Cynthia maintained that unwavering eye contact with Dexter as if there were no one else in the room. And for the first time, she flashed him the hint of a secret smile.

"I read this book once years ago," she said, ". . . can't remember the name or who wrote it, maybe someone here can tell me who, you know how it is when you read so much science fiction . . ."

A smattering of titters from the fans.

"There's a warning received from a dying alien civilization not that much different from Deathship Earth that we humans must transform *our* civilization or die. But because it will be so expensive, because it will mean so much sacrifice, the government keeps it secret. Only some scientists know, and they form a conspiracy to save humanity from itself. Technologically speaking, they know how to do it, but how to persuade people to do the hard things necessary to save themselves?"

The room became quiet. Dexter felt the pounding of his own heart. God help him, he felt his prick beginning to rise.

"So they create a phony alien from space to serve as their mouthpiece."

A chorus of groans.

Cynthia laughed. "Oh yeah, there's been *tons* of science fiction stories like that," she said. "But this one is different, this one is so loving and wise. They don't create an alien from the dying planet to give the world the bad news. Instead, they create a *beautiful* alien from an advanced civilization that has *transcended* its evolutionary crisis."

The look she gave Dexter was so radiant, so deep from the bottom of her heart, that actual *tears* came to his eyes.

"Instead of the terrible truth, they tell a noble lie, instead of threatening the world with fear of the darkness, they inspire it with the light of hope," she said.

"*The Transformation* by Dexter D. Lampkin!" Oscar Karel called out.

The room broke up into laughter that transformed itself into a round of applause, under cover of which Dexter descended from the stage, and slowly tried to make his way through the crush to where Cynthia had been; nodding, muttering platitudes, covertly rubbing at his eyes.

But the Muse, having delivered her message, was gone.

Jeez, y'could get *usedta* this, Foxy Loxy was beginnin' t'think as she found herself climbin' up the stairs from the station platform munchin' onna salted pretzel th' Rat Thing in her head had copped for her *just like that.*

Like magic, y'might say, th' way her hand just reached out without her thinkin' about it *exactly* whenna guy was screamin' atta wino an' wasn't lookin', she had never been no champ at boostin' stuff, somethin' t'be said for havin' a friend t'take over.

Probably woulda got herself busted walkin' outa the tunnel lookin' like she did, Rat Thing hadn't been makin' th' moves for her, slidin' her inta one a th' notches inna tunnel wall till a local comes inta the station, slippin' her up the ladder an' onta the platform between the back a the last car anna platform end so no one sees this thing crawlin' up out of a sewer.

Fuckin' miracle findin' a toilet sorta works inna subway, she can look in what's left a the mirror, an' see what would make a garbage man puke, hair like she been soakin' it in motor oil for a few years not long enough t'kill th' bugs crawlin' around, face like somethin' in one a those horror movies, skeleton covered with shiny greeny skin smeared with shit-brown mung.

Faucets inna sink doin' no better than leakin' a little rusty water, when do they ever, but Rat Thing knows what t'do, *she* fuckin' well wouldn'ta thought of it, and she's screaming alla way as she gets frog-marched inta the nearest toilet-stall, kneels down in fronta the stinkin' old bowl, gets her breath held for her while her head gets fuckin' shoved under and her hand does the flushin'.

Gotta admit the result looks a little better as she creeps outa the crapper wipin' away what she can witha last a the toilet paper wishin' she knew where the fuck she was goin'. . . .

"Hey, where the fuck am I goin'?" she asks out loud as Rat Thing walks her through the platform fulla citizens lookin' at her kinda sidewise but tryin' not to.

"To be our only friend," says the Rat Thing.

An' as she's passin' th' pretzel stand, she does his thing, and she's got herself one, slick as baby snot.

"Hey, you got any more cute tricks like that, Rat Fuck?" she asked as she gobbled down the last salty doughy crumbs and reached the exit stairs.

"Wait and see, Loxy Foxy, see and wait."

An' then she was shovin' her way up the stairs to the street inna crush a people, too busy elbowin' and bein' elbowed, pushin' an' bein' pushed, watch whereya goin' ya fuckin' crackhead, up yours motherfucker, so I sez ta him, tu madre tambien, t'think about what Rat Thing is doin', t'realize how scared she was as she found herself climbin' outa her nice safe hole inna ground . . .

An' then . . .

An' then—

"Welcome back to the Monkey House, scree, scree, scree!" cackled th' sandpaper an' chalk-scratch voice in her head.

Pimps an' winos an' junkies an' hookers, cops an' johns an' Jersey day-trippers, yellow cabs an' green buses, cars an' motorcycles an' crazy-ass bike messengers, buildings an' neon an' sirens, gas fumes anna smell a piss an' puke! There she is, standin' inna asshole end a th' Pig fuckin' Apple!

Gapin' and gaspin' and blinded by the light.

11

God help him, and if Dexter could have brought himself to believe in such a Personage he could have believed that He had, that while Muhammad had been lucky enough to have a whole best-seller dictated to him verbatim, the Guy in the Sky could be enough of a smart-ass to deliver His message to a science fiction writer through a fan girl at a LASFS meeting.

Having been shamed with his own novel, Dexter knew that he had to at least take a shot at transmuting *The Word According to Ralf* into something approximating the second coming of *The Transformation*.

Or at least it was worth repeating the lazy man's strategy that had served him so well producing those 276 pages of schlock in a better cause. So he sprang for the money to have *The Transformation* scanned onto disk to crib from.

That wasn't exactly an irreversible commitment to drag his battered old battle lance out of the closet and saddle up Rocinante, now was it?

Dexter hadn't read *The Transformation* since he proofed the galleys, and grinding through the first forty pages or so on screen proved to be an unexpected excruciation. It was chastening to realize that the 276 pages of *The Word According to Ralf* that he had ready to hand in was nothing more and a good deal less than the first two chapters of *The Transformation* blown up with hot air to globuloid proportions.

In those forty pages, written long years ago, he had described how to destroy a biosphere and create a terminal Deathship Planet plausibly, realistically, and poignantly.

The dead ocean. The runaway greenhouse effect. The toxification of the atmosphere. The perfect terminal bummer played for anything but laughs. All in the first forty pages of *The Transformation*, after which the characters therein and their young creator spent the final three-quarters of the novel concocting a noble lie to bullshit the light of hope into the world.

There was nothing in the 276 pages of *The Word According to Ralf* that the younger and more naive Dexter D. Lampkin hadn't done better in forty.

Dexter shook his head, rubbed his eyes, and leaned back away from his computer, his somewhat overstuffed middle-aged ass comfortably cradled in his fancy Recaro writing chair. He gazed dourly around at the TV, the glass doors to the balcony overlooking a wild little ravine, the wall of teak bookcases featuring his reasonably extensive brag-shelf, and wondered what the kid who had banged out those forty pages in white heat on an IBM Selectric would've made of *this* writer's dream-pad.

Dexter laughed sardonically to himself.

Would've fucking killed for it, he knew damn well.

Fortunately, perhaps, he would have to continue this tour down memory lane later, for this was a show night, it was only five minutes till airtime, Dexter had booked George Clayton Johnson tonight, and a mano a mano between George and Ralf was not something he was about to miss.

Preparing to return to the house to watch the show on the big screen TV in the living room, Dexter shut down the computer, turned off the lights, and opened the door that led to the steps that descended the side of the garage building to the driveway. And found himself almost believing in karmic synchronicity or whatever Amanda Robin might call it as he stepped outside, for the fickle finger of fate had flipped him another enigmatic bird.

A Santa Ana wind had blown in from the desert like the sudden unexpected kiss of a long-lost lover; warm, fragrant, charged with blood-stirring ozone, rocking the crowns of the eucalyptus trees, rolling through the chaparral in ripples of dust and leaves, sending a tumbleweed careening down the street.

Dexter stood there with that old Devil Wind ruffling his hair, breathing it in like a giant spliff of fabled Acapulco Gold, stoned on the surge of negative ions and endorphins.

Across the driveway, the house lights beckoned the author of *The Word According to Ralf* to well-earned plush-lined domesticity, and through the front window of the living room, he could make out the bluely washed colors of the projection TV already up and running.

But this was the first Santa Ana that Dexter had been granted since they moved up here into the semiwilds of Lookout Mountain, the sky had been swept clean, the stars were out, unseen night birds flapped frenetically in the branches, the coyotes were baying at the thin crescent moon, and so was something within him, call it the undead shade of the author of *The Transformation* if you wanted to get literary about it.

Not for that once-was Young Turk to opt for the tube indoors with wife and kiddie on a wild Santa Ana eve like this! Time to trot out the Porsche, drop the top, and ride with the bougainvillea-perfumed wind through the bends and above the mighty Valley vistas of Mulholland. He took a couple of steps toward the garage door before he remembered that the show was about to go on and he really *couldn't* miss it.

Sighing, promising the Targa other nights like this, he opted for the inevitable compromise, returning to the office, putting the lights on dim, turning on the TV, and flinging the balcony doors wide open to the canyon night wind before flopping down on the couch before it.

George had been bugging Dexter for an appearance on the show ever since it went weekly, and while Dexter had never doubted George's ability to hold his own with Ralf, he had held back for lack of a foil from Amanda's side of the equation who might at least be expected to wedge a word or two in edgewise.

But when Amanda told him she wanted to book Mary McKay, Dexter had decided that George's hour had come round at last.

Mary McKay had been an obscure feminist futurist until she had inherited Kay Burg, a chain of greaseburger emporiums paying the minimum wage to dim adolescents and responsible for the denuding of no little Amazon rain forest in the process of securing low-grade beef at the cheapest price possible.

Rather than being co-opted by her economic good fortune or righteously closing down the family ptomaine palaces, she had sold her stock and used the proceeds to become a perennial candidate for public office.

Mary McKay was always running for something: president, governor, mayor, dog catcher. It didn't matter, since she was never remotely in danger of being elected to anything. Thanks to something called the Daughters of Tomorrow, which seemed to exist entirely to secure the necessary signatures, it was impossible to keep her off any ballot, and thanks to her permanent floating ballot position, she had made herself a staple of the talk-show circuit.

Mary McKay was the ultimate TV politician. Whereas less highly evolved specimens of the breed used their telegenic skills to stay in office, she ran for office to stay on television.

". . . and now, here's Mary McKay, currently a candidate for, what, I forget, mayor of Magic Mountain?"

"Mayor of Santa Ana this time around, Ralf," said the woman who strode forcefully across the stage.

She wore a man-tailored white blouse, baggy tan riding breeches, and black hiking boots. Her nose was large and beaky, her ears vaguely reminiscent of Lyndon Johnson's jugs, her mouth large and thin-lipped. Her tightly curled iron gray hair was severely cropped. On a black woman, the 'do might have been an afro; on this rufous Caucasian, the effect was, well, butch.

An effect not exactly mitigated by the way she gave Ralf a hearty handshake before sitting down. But while she wasn't remotely what Dexter could have even deemed handsome, Mary McKay was somehow attractive; those eyes were alive with that elusive something called presence.

"And our other guest, the coauthor of *Logan's Run*, and screenwriter of *Ocean's Eleven* and any number of episodes of the *Twilight Zone*, from which he has received a special twenty-four-hour pass to be with us tonight . . . George Clayton Johnson!"

A quality which George had in flamboyant abundance as he sashayed slowly across the set, resplendent in white jeans that appeared to have been tie-dyed by David Hockney on an acid trip, an embroidered Mexican peasant blouse, a big lapis squash-blossom necklace, long, wild, whitening hair, and Japanese shaman's beard, his big mobile grin mugging at the studio audience, his eyes unerringly tracking the camera.

"Why thank you, Ralf, and may I say what a pleasure it is to be here with you and Miz McKay to discuss the place of our bright-eyed and bushy-tailed young species in the vast and wonderful universe," he effused as he shook Ralf's right hand with both of his, and took his seat, leaning back and grinning expansively as if he owned the place.

Instead of stomping on this attitude with a one-liner, Ralf just shrugged and mugged a rather wan grin at the camera. George had the uncanny ability to get away with just about anything.

Dexter had heard a story which had George walking into the local police station to complain about his neighbors while smoking a joint and walking out again without the cops having sufficiently emerged from his spell to call him on it.

He believed it.

Indeed, he could have believed that *Ralf* had shared one with George backstage the way he sat there with a stoned faraway look in his eyes and allowed George to open the proceedings.

"I have never observed Orange County to be a demographic hotbed of highly evolved consciousness," said George, "so what's a nice visionary feminist futurist like you doing running for office in the land of Knott's Berry Farm and Richard Nixon?"

"Keeping myself on television," Mary McKay said forthrightly. "Didn't *you* once have some scheme for an electoral takeover of Nevada, the land of Howard Hughes and Mafia casinos?"

"And lived to tell the tale, Mary, though for reasons beyond my control, the book was never published."

To Dexter's amazement, it soon developed that they were somehow operating on the same wavelength, as they hijacked the show in a direction hardly calculated to roll 'em in the aisles in Peoria, while Ralf, for some unfathomable reason, seemed content to just sit there and let them run with it.

On and on it went, the George and Mary Mutual Admiration Society, an extravagant far-ranging tour through the schemes and projects and world-saving fantasies of two extravagant far-ranging egos, Mary McKay just serious enough to keep George anchored to something like reality, George more than loquacious enough to keep anything with the semantic content of the phone book amusing, and the star of the show, amazingly enough, fading into the woodwork.

It reached an apotheosis when Mary McKay admitted that she had no intention of ever serving any electorate weird enough to choose her, while George declared that he would magnanimously accede to the obvious wisdom of any body politic sapient enough to appoint him its Peerless Leader.

"You'd actually be willing to hold your nose and play King of the Monkey People if they kissed your butt and asked you real nice?" said Ralf, finally stirring himself far enough out of his enigmatic fugue to get a lame line in.

George shrugged insouciantly. "It's a dirty job," he said, "but someone has to do it."

"Boy, that's big of you!"

"Considering what a wonderful job the usual gang of political snake-oil salesmen and hardhearted bankers in double-breasted blue suits has done, shouldn't the visionaries and savants be willing to give it the old college try?"

"You mean a humble prophet and savior such as yourself, George?" said Ralf.

"Or Mary, or any number of other enlightened mutants I could mention, including yourself, Mr. Comedian From the Future," said George. "Haven't we done sufficient bitching about the mess our tribe of monkeys has made of this planet? Isn't it time we rolled up our sleeves and picked up the broom?"

"Who, me?" said Ralf. "Hey, I don't do windows either!"

George fixed the camera with that wild-eyed and winsomely goofy grin that magically allowed him to escape coming off as a prick while saying virtually anything.

"There is a well-known science fiction story which points out that unless those of us who have achieved a highly evolved consciousness assume our responsibility for the destiny of the planet, the world will end up being run by USDA certifiable morons."

Mary McKay goggled at George with a mixture of incredulity and admiration. "I can't *believe* you had the chutzpah to come right out and *say that!*" she exclaimed.

"It *does* take years of practice, Mary," George admitted. "But you *do* agree, now don't you?"

Mary McKay regarded him with wary wonder.

"Well—"

"Of course you do! Considering what our friend from the future here tells us will be the fate of our planet unless we pull our fingers out, the last thing we need is false modesty on the part of shamans and visionaries such as ourselves."

Only George could deliver a line like that and get a grin out of a feminist futurist, if only a scattering of snarking snickers from the studio audience. "I don't think *you* have to worry about being accused of *that*, George," Mary McKay said good-naturedly.

"Nor does it behoove a highly evolved woman such as yourself to paw the earth with your booties and mutter aw shucks."

"Why I do believe you're flattering me!"

"Not at all, Mary. Flattery gets us nowhere either. Without clear unclouded self-knowledge of the present state of our consciousness, how can we evolve to the next level?"

"Which is?"

"I thought you'd never ask!"

"Oh no you didn't!"

"Well of course not, Mary," George said genially. "After all, we're not here to talk about the Dodgers' chances of winning the pennant, so how *do* you think we *can* evolve to the next level of consciousness, which will enable us to turn the biosphere of this planet back into a garden, prevent World War Four from being fought with sticks and stones, and become a galaxy-spanning species worthy of joining those who have survived millions of years of their own history?"

Ralf gave George a strange look, half fish-eyed stare, half something else that Dexter could not identify.

"Is *that* all?" he said. "Hey, come on, we got fifteen whole minutes left! As long as we're saving the world, we oughta at least be able to come up with a cure for cancer and the Lost Chord too while we're at it!"

"I don't know how to save the world," said Mary McKay, "but I do know what we have to do to evolve into the kind of mature species who can."

"You do, huh?" said Ralf, in a tone of voice that almost seemed serious. "Okay, so what's our plan? Sell off the National Debt to the Mafia as a tax loss? Repeal the law of gravity?"

Mary McKay did a George and fixed her full attention on the camera, but there was no humorous twinkling, no attempt to glaze the intellectual donut with a sugar frosting of self-deprecating egoism.

"We face the fact that we've transcended the evolutionary process that created us," she said. "That's what visionary feminism is really all about."

"It is?" said Ralf. "It's not about women getting to be senators and fly jet fighters and men getting to cry and change diapers?"

Mary McKay brushed him off by continuing to address the camera as if this was some kind of campaign sound bite.

"There's the kind of feminism that tries to prove that women are biologically superior to men, that they invented civilization to tame the horny beast, and things went wrong when the wild boys overthrew Earth Mother Gaia and installed Jehovah as the Omniphallic Chairman of the Joint Chiefs of Staff," she said. "And there's *visionary* feminism, which understands that it no longer matters."

"No longer matters?" Ralf said slowly. "*What* no longer matters?"

The look he gave her as he said it seemed to betray real intellectual interest, which, considering that this was *The Word According to Ralf* and not Sunday afternoon on PBS, gave the moment an unsettling surreality.

"The entire evolutionary process which produced us no longer matters," said Mary McKay. "We're no longer animals, we're *people*."

"You're *sure* of that, Monkey Girl?" Ralf said, mugging an ape and scratching his armpit.

But it didn't get much of a rise out of the audience, perhaps because it was so obvious that he was just going through the motions, perhaps because they could see that there was something looking out from behind his eyes that wasn't laughing at all.

And neither was Mary McKay. "What difference does it make *now* if men are stronger than women because their anthropoid ancestors had to do the hunting? What difference does it make *now* if women have more endurance because they had to survive to raise the children? Who cares if the original deities of the Monkey People were male or female or giant turnips?"

George sat there beaming and nodding, willingly silenced for once, rocking back and forth.

This was obviously Mary McKay's version of The Speech, and nothing was going to interrupt her.

Ralf didn't even try. He didn't even seem to want to. Somehow the show had passed over into another level of reality, and the host, far from trying to bring it back down to Planet Schtick, seemed to be encouraging it as he sat there staring at Mary McKay with an uncanny intensity.

"We've got machines that are stronger than men *or* women. We've got computers faster than our own brains. We create designer organisms. Consciousness controls biology. Mind controls matter. So like it or not, *we* are the ultimate end-product of natural evolution, and for better or worse, from here on in to the end of time, what we become is entirely up to us."

"Right on!" exclaimed George, waving his fist in a time-warped salute, eyes glowing, grin flashing, wild white hair and beard tossing; a Hippie Ancient Mariner, the awakened ghost of those days of youthful yore when a new world was unfolding and the trajectory of human destiny had seemed so obviously upward and onward that a generation of mutants would surely cakewalk to the stars to the beat of an Acid Rock Drummer.

Right on! Dexter found himself repeating silently in his own heart, as if wishing could once more make it so.

Dexter knew that the negative ions of the Santa Ana exercised a psychotropic effect on the cerebral metabolism and that a rich brew of saps and pollens was riding the wind to his backbrain. True too, George Clayton Johnson had been known to induce altered mental states in subjects entirely innocent of chemical augmentation.

Dexter Lampkin did not believe that he believed in magic. But as the Santa Ana rustled and tumbled through the tree crowns with rising force, as the intoxicatingly warm and fragrant breath of the canyon night surged through the open balcony doors and into the office, it was difficult indeed for even the most logical of positivists to deny that something magical was happening.

> We are the crown of creation.
> The lunatics are in charge of the asylum.
> We must be the gods of the Transformation.

Not only had Dexter heard all this before, he had written a book designed to call that transformation into being.

Nor had he been alone.

For a bright shining moment, it had seemed as if the whole world was awakening from its collective dream of the deterministic past into full prescient consciousness of its future transformational maturity, as if that future were reaching backward down the timelines to bootstrap itself into existence, before a bullet here, a failure of will there, youthful folly and aged vengefulness, blew it all away.

Now the George and Mary show had managed to conjure that long-lost vision back into the world right before Dexter's eyes on national television.

With a sudden susurrus, a mighty swirl of wind blew a confetti of deep red bougainvillea petals and dry eucalyptus leaves into the office, as the hilltop voices of the wild coyotes were answered by the paranoid bark of a nearby dog.

Dexter started, blinked, and when he looked back at the TV screen—

Ralf's face seemed to undergo a lysergic metamorphosis as if Dexter were experiencing a nostalgic acid flashback. The smirky mask of comedy transformed itself into another mask, not the downcast mask of tragedy, but something void of readable human iconography. Except for the eyes, which blazed out through it with an intensity of longing, the object of which Dexter could not fathom either.

"So the bad news is that Spaceship Earth is spiraling down the black willy hole out of control, and there's no one in the cockpit 'cause the Sky Pilot's bailed out," he said with a delivery that hardly seemed calculated to extract even graveyard laughter. "And the good news is that now the passengers tossing their cookies back in steerage get to fly it . . ."

And as if to provide empirical evidence that Dexter was not simply stoned on whatever was blowin' on the Santa Ana wind, Ralf's transformed visage, his words, the altered timbre of their delivery, the total effect, stunned the studio audience into a long beat of uneasy silence.

You could feel the ghoulish expectation. Was this going to be one of those moments that made television history? Was the star of *The Word According to Ralf* about to lose it on the air?

Into the breach stepped George Clayton Johnson.

"Never fear, Trekkers," he said brightly, "the magic hasn't gone away, and the Force is ever with us, and that is Mary McKay's message to us all."

"It is?" said Mary.

"Why of course it is, and I will now prove it."

"You *will*?" said Ralf, leaning forward expectantly.

That look on Ralf's face was familiar because Dexter had observed its like often enough at science fiction conventions, and could well imagine that self-same expression gracing those cop-shop faces as George talked his way in and out puffing his reefer. But this was no fan boy, no cop, this was *Ralf*, man from the future or not, avatar of the Zeitgeist or not, undeniably a show business professional, utterly under the spell of George Clayton Johnson.

"Norman Spinrad once showed me a medicine wand that he carved on acid," George said with the air of someone who had captured center stage and knew he could hold it as long as it pleased him.

"Norman is a science fiction writer like myself, but with about as much Native American blood in his veins as George Armstrong Custer. Nevertheless he created on a vision quest a medicine wand of which a twenty-first-century shaman such as myself might be proud."

Perhaps the director had ordered it, or perhaps a mesmerized cameraman did it spontaneously, but George's beaming face now filled the screen in close-up.

"According to Norman, while he was peaking on acid he chanced upon a gnarly stick at the top of which he perceived to be hidden the head of an eagle. Using a Swiss Army knife he habitually carried on his person, he extracted this totem from the rough shape in the natural wood, and was moved to incise in the stick below it the double helix."

The camera pulled back to reveal him raising his right hand to eye level and curling its fingers to mime the head of an eagle, and yet . . . And yet while it *should* have been a comic gesture, it wasn't. While George *should* have been a comic figure, in that moment *he* wasn't.

He had transformed his hand and arm into that medicine wand. He had become an acid apparition out of the past and an Indian shaman-cum-science-fiction-writer out of the future. The mask he hid behind might be that of Coyote, but while Coyote might assume the habitual stance of the cavorting trickster, the Trickster was a Power.

"Consider the Eagle," he said. "Chosen as the totem animal of America by the white Anglo Founding Fathers, innocent eighteenth-century honkies who had no idea that to the Native American the Eagle is the totem of visionary wisdom, higher consciousness, physical freedom, and spiritual courage, of the Great Spirit of the World itself, since these are, of course, the only qualities which can make a nation, a world, a spirit, great."

Somehow, George managed to imbue that mimed eagle's head with an uncanny dignity, somehow it almost seemed to come alive, its eyes fixed on far-distant vistas.

"Two hundred years later, when Americans became the first representatives of this world's biosphere to reach another planet, with what words was the moment of lunar touchdown proclaimed . . . ?"

Fuck a duck! thought Dexter, hearing it in memory, and constrained somehow to whisper it to himself even as George said it.

"*The Eagle has landed!*"

Though it was anatomically impossible for a man to grin from ear to ear, George's grin approached his earlobes asymptotically as a limit.

"Consider the double helix," he said, "the sign of the DNA molecule, the totem of the biosphere itself, of the evolution of life on Earth."

Dexter knew that what he was seeing was a pattern of electrically excited phosphor-dots on a glass screen, that true eye contact with the image thereon was therefore scientifically impossible, that when George Clayton Johnson seemed to be looking him right in the eye and addressing him directly, it was merely a video artifact.

Nevertheless . . .

"Under the influence of LSD, a science fiction writer finds himself carving it on a medicine wand crowned with the totem animal of the Great Spirit of the World chosen two hundred years previously by the Founding Fathers as the tribal totem of the very people who would one day land the Eagle on the Moon."

George's eyes burned up out of the screen at Dexter. And it took a moment for him to realize the obvious, namely that several million people in front of their TV sets who had never even been exposed to George before must be thoroughly caught in that illusion of one-on-one personal eye contact too.

"We Native Americans have always known that the Eagle crowns the double helix, that the Eagle arises from the Earth but reaches for the stars, that the Eagle is the Great Spirit of the World. And that *we* are the Eagle."

The camera held on George for a long silent beat before pulling back into a three-shot. Mary McKay sat there gazing at George moony-eyed and slack-jawed. And Mr. and Mrs. Couch Potato out there? What effect was this having on *them*?

George leaned back in his chair, smiling benignly. "But of course, in this sci-entifically enlightened age, we all know that there is no magic in the world, now don't we?" he said, folding his arms across his chest in lieu of snapping his fingers to terminate the spell he had cast.

"Do we?" said Ralf.

He was still regarding George with his full attention. But he seemed to be sit-ting taller now, his eyes alive with a George-like intensity.

George spoke in a tone of gentle irony which was about as close as he ever came to sarcasm.

"Actually, our universe is just a great big Black Forest cuckoo clock of cause and effect," he said. "The visionaries of the present can't possibly see into the future, the future can't possibly send prescient visions back into the past, there's never *really* been anything but a random number generator at the controls of our planetary spaceship, there is no God and She *does* play dice with the universe, and you're just putting on this cosmic vaudeville show to sell cornflakes and laundry detergent, now isn't that right, Ralf?"

"And what if I say it isn't?" said Ralf.

"You mean . . . you mean war *isn't* peace?" exclaimed George. "Freedom *isn't* slavery, shit *isn't* Shinola, and I *didn't* just say the S word on television?"

Modest laughter fractured the long silence of the audience.

But Ralf didn't crack a smile.

He lifted his chin about ten degrees above the vertical, spread his arms wide, stared at the camera, and flapped them.

"What if I tell you that *I* am the Eagle?" he intoned solemnly.

This strange piece of business, balanced on the razor-edge between farce and witchy weirdness, drew both laughs and nervous mutters.

Ralf rose slowly to his feet, in the mocking manner of King Shit arising from his throne. "*We are the Eagle!*" he declaimed. "The Great Spirit of the World! The Last Best Schtick of Man!"

With his outstretched arms moving slowly up and down, his blazing eyes and beaky schnozz miming an aquiline visage, and his white futuristic ice cream suit, he was half Eagle and half Orange County TV evangelist.

"Yes, Monkey People, Brother George and Sister Mary have shown me the Way, and now I will show *you* the Light of the full wonderfulness of my *glory!*" he raved on, doing a fair imitation of Oral Roberts foaming at the mouth on speed.

"Oh YEAH! Oh YEAH!" shouted George in a gospel cadence, echoed by half a dozen yahoos in the audience.

"I am the Eagle! I have transcended the horizontal! I have transcended the vertical! I have transcended the biosphere! I have transcended space and time and the rush-hour traffic on the Ventura Freeway to be with you here tonight!"

"YEAH! YEAH!"

"Tell it like it is, Ralf!"

Dexter sat there with the Santa Ana wind blowing freely through his cranium, or so it seemed as he sat there gaping at the vision coming out at him from the television screen.

As were approximately twelve million other people according to the latest figures he had seen; peering through their own windows into the collective national schlockgeist, *knowing* it was only *television* with their higher mammalian cortex, but unable to avoid experiencing it as personal back there in the old reptilian brain stem.

"*We* are the Monkeys, *we* are the passengers eating turd burgers and drinking reconstituted caca cola back here in cattle class on Trans Deathship Airways while the pilot swills gin and prongs the flight attendants!"

"YEAH! YEAH! YEAH!"

The audience laughed and stomped and egged him on as if totally confused as to on what level this apparition should be taken.

And Dexter knew just how they felt.

There Ralf stood in his silly Buck Rogers ice cream suit, flapping his arms, rolling his eyes, miming an Eagle, preaching *The Word According To* like a perfect and perfectly ridiculous twenty-second-century cartoon tent-show evangelist.

And yet . . .

And yet his silhouette seemed to radiate psychic heatwaves like a car hood in the Mojave.

And yet while he was getting laughs with this over-the-top testification, that to which he was testifying Dexter knew full well was nothing but the highest of truth.

"*We* are the crown of creation! *We* are the Giant Turnip God of the Double Helix! I say to you, Brothers and Sisters, I have *seen* the Light and it is *us*, oh yeah! It's time to hijack this crappy old airplane that's auguring in to the toilet bowl and tell the guys in the cockpit to fly us to *Tomorrowland*!"

"Amen! *Amen!* AMEN!"

"Tune in next week, Monkey People, same time, same station, for . . . *The Word According to Ralf*!"

Dexter turned off the TV set and sat there watching the trees tossing in the darkness, listening to the white noise of the wind, inhaling the resins and pollens and negative ions of the Santa Ana, trying to convince himself that he couldn't really be stoned.

Dexter believed that the Tarot was the purest of bullshit and had his doubts about the Jungian collective unconsciousness too. But just as George in full cry had assumed the metaphorical image of Coyote, so did that final fade-out image of Ralf persist in his mind's eye like a solarized concert poster of the Trickster too.

And as both of them had just demonstrated, metaphorical or not, Coyote *was* a Power.

Was the Joker really the Last Best Hole Card of Man?

Dexter Lampkin might not believe that he believed in magic, but he could hardly deny that he had once and passionately believed in just about all that both showbiz incarnations of the Trickster had proclaimed in serious jest.

And though he did not believe in signs or portents or spirit messages either, he was having a lot of trouble suspending his belief in this one.

After all, the simplicities of what George had called the Black Forest cuckoo clock universe of cause and effect would seem to be dark superstition too in the face of the relativistic temporal realities of quantum four-space. The math might as well be magic, since he couldn't follow it anyway, so rather than be a constipated Newtonian asshole, he might as well take Albert Einstein's and Richard Feynman's and Cam Carswell's word for it.

So call it synchronicity, Lampkin, if it makes you feel any less ditzy about it, he told himself, call it transcendence of the rush-hour traffic on the Geodesic Freeway.

Without further recourse to rational thought, he booted up the computer, loaded his word processor, opened chapter three of *The Transformation,* and allowed his very own time-warped words to flow like pearls of cosmic wisdom into his skeptical brain.

Was it Foxy Loxy or Rat Thing sniffed out somethin' tasty inna garbage can with the pizza box right under the lid?

Gettin' hard t'tell.

Was Loxy's doin' the snortin' and snufflin' around the garbage cans under the stoop, but movin' her snout back an' forth, snarkin' all the time like a wino witha nose cold, was somethin' she hadn't known how t'do before, an' she sure wouldn'ta been able t'zoom in onna smell a something bready an' greasy, maybe meaty too, buried under the pile a crap in this one.

Loxy took a quick peek out from under the concrete steps above her and into the street. Coast was clear, so th' Rat Thing takes over again, Loxy don't hafta think about it, not that she really wants to, she goes skittering over t'the can on her hands and knees, flips off the lid, pulls it down in front of her kinda careful like so's not t'make a fuckin' world fulla noise, an' paws through the contents more or less from top t'bottom, flippin' the useless shit, of which there is the usual plenty, between her legs.

Nothin' inna pizza carton except cigarette butts an' old napkins smeared with dried red crud, tin cans, wads a paper drippin' some kinda yellow ooze, Spanish language newspaper, bloody old Kotex. . . .

First time Rat Thing had her doin' this shit was kinda gross, y'might say, not t'mention almost gettin' her fuckin' busted.

There she is, first fuckin' day outa the tunnels, Rat Thing's been walkin' her all over for hours like some kinda fuckin' ten-year-old tourist in New York for the first time's gotta drag mommy t'see fuckin' *everything*.

Only *this* fuckin' brat's inside her head, cacklin' and chitterin' in her ears from the inside out, an' it's like it's got control wires it stuck down the middle of her bones, the fucker's walkin' her around real fast, but kinda all twitchy an' jerky like she's some kinda fuckin' robot it ain't exactly figured out howta work real well yet.

An' what th' Rat Thing's draggin' her around Manhattan t'see ain't exactly the Disneyland once-over of the Big Apple. Wouldn'ta been stretchin' it too far t'say even the creeps wiped their snot onna windshields a cars got caught by the light crossing the Bowery mighta found it kinda twisted.

Half an' hour she spends frozen in front of a sleazy discount store on East 39th Street starin' like a zombie atta TV sets inna window. An' then she's crawlin' through the half-dead bushes inna park watchin' mangy squirrels tryin' t'bum peanuts from crackheads and dealers. More TV inna store window. Th' garbage docks. Some fuckin' tenement inna Lower East Side torched by the landlord for the insurance money. More fuckin' TV. Sneakin' around the wholesale meat warehouses.

She can talk t'Rat Thing inside her head, don't even have t'move her lips, but it don't exactly do much good, 'cause what answers her back sounds as sweet as a fuckin' subway car squealin' an' screechin' way too fast arounda bend, an' makes about as much sense.

"What the fuck are we doin'? What the fuck are we doin'? What the fuck are we doin'?"

Loxy found herself asking th' same fuckin' question over an' over again, had bag ladies an' ravin' nutcases tryin' t'answer her, anna solid citizens lookin' at her like *she* was one of 'em fer chrissakes, wasn't Rat Thing pullin' the strings she might've invited a few of these rubberneckin' assholes to meet th' Big Ripper.

The Rat Thing had a lotta answers, but they were all like a talk-radio asshole inna psycho ward answerin' phone calls from flying saucers.

"We're learning how to be a meat girl in the meat world, Foxy Loxy, we're here to make sure we happen, Loxy Foxy, 'cause this is when they try to stop us, it's out there back here somewhere and we gotta find it, in the squirrels, in the monkeys, in our only friends, hard to tell, all we've got to work with is a few bits and pieces of rotten rat protoplasm in the circuitry, but *something's* gotta be the Master Race, Foxy Loxy, disgusting job, but *something's* gotta download into the meat to look and learn, learn and look, you can run, so it can't hide. . . ."

An' so on, an' so forth, worms and holes and Swiss cheese and count them foam, find th' strange tractor, flip th' world slimes, made about as much sense as a Russian on reds.

An' about as heavy on street smarts.

Long about what folks with kitchens or money might think of as dinnertime, she's walkin' up Canal Street west of Mott, Chinatown fer chrissakes, where th' locals are not exactly famous for their hospitality to junkies an' winos and street people, where all these Chinese food stores are chockablock with open stands onna street durin' the day, chop your fuckin' hand off you try an' so much as cop a string bean. This is also when the street stands are closing up, an' they're cleaning up the sidewalk, and shutting down the stores—

—and they're dumpin' bags and pails of vegetable scraps, bits n'piecesa a'take-out duck, eggshells, fish scraps, all kindsa stuff, inna big dirty green Dumpster in a little side street right around the corner—

—proteins, carbohydrates, trace elements, scree, scree, scree—

—and before Loxy knows what she's fuckin' doin', not that she can fuckin' do much about it either, she's scrambling over to the Dumpster, grabbing the top of it with both hands, pulling herself up off her fuckin' feet, an' kinda chinning herself up to where she can balance on the lip with her gut.

"Ow, ow, what the fuck are we doin'?" she yells for about the thousandth time, only this time real loud, 'cause it fuckin' *hurts*!

But she don't yell for long, 'cause Rat Thing is screamin' "Protein! Carbohydrates! Lipids! Trace elements!" in her brain, and she's rummaging through the Dumpster with both hands, and she's got her fuckin' *head* right down there in th' top layer of garbage, an' crammin' fish guts and green stuff an' pork scraps an' a fuckin' duck head into her yawp as quick as the fuckin' Rat Thing can make her gulp it all down.

But she don't get more than a half dozen or so mouthfuls down before there's this sound behind her like a couple a cats tryin' t'sing rap while their tails are bein' run through a meat grinder, an' then somebody yanks her down off the Dumpster by her ankles, and she sees that it's two oriental guys in bloody white uniforms with buckets a chicken heads an' fish guts reading her the riot act in fuckin' Chinese.

Everyone concerned is real pissed off.

Rat Thing is stickin' red hot knitting needles inta Loxy's guts to remind her that she's supposed t'be hungry and makin' her reach back up for the lip a th' Dumpster, th' two Chinese guys are young dudes probably know fuckin' karate, just her luck, and Loxy herself is just seein' the bloody red inside of her head.

"Stupid goddamn motherfucker!" she screamed, which seemed to cover the situation an' everyone in it, spewin' some kinda slimy gray fish stuff. The ratfuck asshole still had her tryin' t'hoist herself back inta the Dumpster with her right hand, but wasn't payin' too close attention to the left, 'cause she managed to whip out her knife an' wave it inna faces a th' karate freaks.

The Chinese guys backstepped a little, but they started shouting stuff at the top of their lungs which got repeated around the corner, most of which was gibberish, but enough of which seemed like English to sound like the word "Police!"

For the moment anyway, Loxy anna Rat Thing come to an unnerstanding a the situation, he lets her drop off the fuckin' Dumpster an' tear-ass up the side street, an' then he's got her turnin' inta the first back alley an' scrambling up it so fast an' close to the ground that her knuckles are practically scrapin' th' pavement.

Fuckin' maze a alleys and little back streets an' more alleys in here, garbage cans, an' fire escapes, an' loading docks, an' Dumpsters, seems like this is Rat Thing's kinda place, he's got her ziggin' and zaggin', duckin' inta here, hidin' behind that, slitherin' along walls, an' pretty soon the sound a angry Chinese behind them fades away, anna cops if there is any, give up the chase.

He finally has her come out onna main drag fulla manufacturing lofts an' el cheapo clothes outlets and stands right out onna street and big crowdsa shoppers an' boppers and ravers and people speakin' about seventy-five languages nobody can unnerstand.

It's the sorta scene where one more weirdo havin' a hot argument witha rat inside her head ain't gonna draw much attention, so Loxy decides t'have it out with Rat Thing right then and there.

"No more a that shit, you fuckin' asshole, you almost got us busted, next time maybe get us killed!"

"Protoplasm must eat to survive, Loxy Foxy, the metabolic machinery must be fueled."

"Yeah, terrific, eatin's a real cool idea, but we can't just go runnin' around on all fours an' jumpin inta garbage cans right in front a th' citizens like a giant fuckin' rat!"

"Why not, Loxy Foxy, we *are* a giant fuckin' rat for present practical purposes, scree, scree, scree, and here the organic matter the meat needs to survive is everywhere, hee, hee, hee!"

"Yeah, so I notice, but don't get the idea you can just scarf up hot dog turds neither!"

Well after havin' it out in public—what're *you* starin' at asshole—they reach some kinda unnerstanding. Rat Thing will let Loxy do *her* thing, which is survivin' onna streets a Manhattan, an' it will do *its* thing, which is sniffin' out stuff t'eat under a pile a crap from twenny feet away, diggin' it out the shitpile, an' crammin' whatever it is down her throat while keepin' her from pukin' inna process. . . .

Kleenex fulla snot, Mr. Clean bottle, jeez did someone wipe their fuckin' ass on this washcloth, McDonald's boxes, used kitty litter, six-pack holder, grapefruit rinds . . .

Y'd be surprised, what you could get used to, Loxy was, she was kinda gettin' used to sharin' her body with Rat Thing, had certain advantages to it, you thought about it.

Rat Thing was always goin' on about surviving, and Loxy hadda admit he had it down stony cold.

Coffee grounds, condom, *People* magazine, not a fuckin' bite on those chicken bones . . .

What did you *really* need to survive?

Bready stuff. Greasy stuff. Meat stuff. Fish stuff. Veggie stuff. Holes an' cracks t'crawl into outa the rain or cold or when you got chased.

Cornflake box, fuckin' empty, shavin' cream can, deodorant stick fulla armpit hair . . . *ah*, here it is, Rat Thing scores again!

Practically at the bottom a the fuckin' can, there it was, half a Big Mac, meat an' all, little green around th' sesame seed bun maybe, not the kinda thing you wanted t'think about maybe with alla th' cockroaches come crawlin' out of it when she snatches it, but she don't have to, 'cause Rat Thing don't wanna waste the live protein, he has her shovin' it in her mouth an' chewin' it down in three big mouth-fuls before the last of the roaches can escape or she can even think about thinkin' about it.

Hey, didn't New York already have about a hundred million regular stupid little rats doin' just fine with nothin' but a good nose, a cast-iron stomach, an' the right attitude?

Amanda didn't have long to wait for the inevitable call from Texas Jimmy Bala-ban.

"Jesus Christ, Amanda, your shrink certifies that my client ain't going certifi-able, and then I gotta watch him go apeshit on the air?" Jimmy moaned without preamble when she picked it up.

"Don't you think you're overreacting a little, Jimmy?" Amanda suggested.

"Right, he flaps his arms like a big-assed bird, raves on about turd burgers and caca cola, and claims to be the Giant Turnip God, but *I'm* overreacting because it gives me the notion that just *maybe* these are the kind of subtle clues that *my* guy just *might* be in danger of flipping out completely that your guy should've caught."

The theatrical choler with which he delivered this nicely constructed line made Amanda smile. "Come on, Jimmy, it got laughs, didn't it?" she said.

Texas Jimmy's voice hardened. "Don't try to bullshit me, Amanda, I'm an *agent*, remember?" he said. And then, more softly: "And various old jokes about agents' hearts aside, you might even give credit for caring a little bit more about my client than next week's bottom line."

Amanda was duly chastened.

As far as she knew, the deals that Jimmy had cut were straight, she more or less liked the guy, and whatever his intellectual and spiritual limitations, he had always lived up to his own Code of the West.

"So what are you trying to tell me, Jimmy?" Amanda said slowly. The real question, the just question, being, of course, what do *I* tell *you*?

"I'm telling you that I'm worried about Ralf, Amanda. I'm telling you that any shrink that tells me he ain't skating on the edge of over the edge can't be playing with a full deck himself."

Now Amanda felt doubly chastened.

Jimmy had paid Albert Falkenberg to diagnose the state of Ralf's mental health, and Albert had pronounced him sane, thus preventing Jimmy from ever again seeking a psychiatric opinion by the terms of the deal he had made with his client.

What *can* I tell you, Jimmy? Amanda wondered guiltily.

In any contextual framework that Texas Jimmy could comprehend, she and Albert had lied to him. And if she told him that they had sought to serve the sanity of the Zeitgeist itself by summoning forth the Lightbringer for the age, that what he had just witnessed was the struggle of that avatar to be born, he would send the men in the white coats to throw a net over *her*.

"Seems to me it was all just part of the act," was the only semitruthful thing she could think of to say.

"No shit," Texas Jimmy told her. "With Ralf, what else is there?"

"Well then—"

Texas Jimmy Balaban's voice underwent a transformation, or perhaps an avatar of the consciousness on the other end of the line that Amanda had never met before was now speaking.

"Look, I've handled a lot of comics, but there's wild-and-crazy-guy crazy, which is funny, and there's sicko-psycho crazy, which is not. The wild-and-crazy-guy, that's the act, but doing the act is a real guy, and if he isn't doing what he's doing for a living because he's neurotic in the first place, just give him a few years on the road. It's a schizo thing most of them battle all of their careers, but it's where their schtick comes from, they need it, it's the Edge. They get too sane, they lose the Edge and end up MCing bar mitzvahs in the Catskills, they go over the Edge, and they end up giving the audience the creeps instead of laughs on the way out the door to the funny farm. You get what I mean, Amanda? I hope you don't think I'm going all mystical on you."

"Not at all, Jimmy, not at all," Amanda told him, unexpectedly impressed by the depth of the rough wisdom that was coming through loud and clear.

"Well, okay then, maybe you'll understand that I ain't turning into some Topanga psychic when I tell you that when you've handled as many of them as I have, when you've watched enough of 'em fall off one side and bomb out and fall off the other side and freak out, you develop a real good nose for where the Edge is and where your client is along it at any given time."

"But the audience was *laughing*, Jimmy. They were playing along. They were egging him on."

"You ever go to the zoo and watch the crowd around the monkey cage? You ever hear what the audience in the street does when there's some poor crazy schmuck up on a window ledge deciding maybe to jump? When the Roadrunner gets a safe dropped on his head or Don Rickles cuts some heckler into little bitty pieces they laugh their asses off too."

"Hey come on, Jimmy, that's showbiz!"

"Yeah, that's showbiz, and you're still in it as long as they're still laughing, and there's no people like show people, they smile when their brains are about to blow. And yes indeed, I do still love it. And so forth. And so on. We've both seen all the movies."

Amanda could hear an audible sigh on the other end of the line as Texas Jimmy Balaban seemed to slow himself down from 78 to 33 by an act of will.

"Let me tell you something about the Edge, Amanda," he said much more softly. "Let me tell you something about comics. They burn the brightest when they're just about to explode. And the audience just *loves* that high-wire act without a net. Now every decade or so comes a comic genius who can skate right along the Edge for his whole career and still maintain."

Beat.

"But that's not Ralf," said Texas Jimmy Balaban. "That takes someone who's got something so solid going on offstage to come back to that he can trust himself to go completely bugfuck when he's on. We both know that Ralf's just the opposite, he's nothing *but* the act, and if he goes over the Edge out there, he's gone."

"What are you *really* trying to tell me, Jimmy?"

"You haven't understood a goddamn thing I've said?"

"Every word of it," Amanda told him. "But why tell *me*?"

Amanda could imagine him pausing for a drink of whiskey, indeed she seemed to hear the clink of ice against glass.

"Listen, I found this guy and I brought him along, and I got him this show, and I think I did a good job," Jimmy Balaban said in a strangely subdued tone of voice. "But . . ."

"But . . . ?"

Now Amanda *did* clearly hear him pausing for Dutch courage.

"But Madden ordered up this format, not me, and you and Dex are booking these guests, I don't know dick from sci-fi, or evolution, or any of this stuff, and what I realized watching tonight is that it's been a while since I knew what you guys were really doing."

"All we're doing is trying to come up with guests whose chemistry works with Ralf and the format," Amanda lied truthfully.

"Uh-huh. Look, I ain't creative talent, or one of your talk-show intellectuals, or a Beverly Hills shrink, but that don't mean that the nose don't know, Amanda. You know what a refrigerator motor smells like just before a bearing burns out? You know how a fluorescent light starts strobing like a cheap disco effect just before it goes?"

"It's not really like that, Jimmy, really it isn't. . . ." Amanda muttered.

Is it?

"Sure, right, you're not playing with the poor crazy bastard's head. You're being real careful not to make him any more schizo than he already is. You're not encouraging him to believe the act's the real thing. And maybe he really *is* the Great Spirit of the World or the Giant Turnip God of the Double Helix, and the joke's on me."

Amanda sat there silently with the phone in her hand, unexpectedly pinned by a truth from this unlikely source of such wisdom deeper than she herself had seen.

What if I'm wrong? What if Jimmy's right?

Then I'm helping to drive a poor sick mind over the edge.

Slitherin' through the rush-hour crowd around the entrance to Grand Central Station, Foxy Loxy spotted a fat gypsy momma sittin' onna sidewalk with a raggy baby in her lap and a paper cup fulla coins jigglin' in her hand.

Slick as a rat flippin' a piece a cheese outa th' trap, she's grabbed it away an' skittered into the station before the fuckin' cursing gypsy could even put down her brat and pry her fat ass up off the pavement.

Few minutes later, she's inna corridor leadin' into the main subway entrance, an' there's this mean-lookin' blind guy standin' there witha German shepherd by th' handle and a cap with a least a couple bucks in it onna floor.

Just like that, she slips inta the stream a people headin' toward him, an' she's got her hand in an' out a the cap without him even knowin', and when the dog gives her a growl, she just flips it the bird back, turns around, and slides into the mob goin' the other way, while the blind guy who ain't got the faintest yanks the mother back, hee, hee, hee.

Loxy never had no talent as a thief, but after she finally got Rat Thing to un-nerstand what money was for, he gave her golden paws, an' stealin' from gypsy beggars, dead junkies, half-dead winos, an' crippled beggars was easy as findin' stuff ta eat in garbage cans an' Dumpsters an' a lot less disgustin'.

Rat Thing didn't unnerstand what the fuck money was all about at all the first time Loxy buys a hot dog onna a street with a couple dollars she found in the pocket of some guy lying in a puddle of his own piss inna doorway.

"Why did the monkey thing give us proteins and carbohydrates for useless slices of paper, scree, scree, scree?" sez th' stupid rat-fuck as she's chowin' down.

"Whaddya mean, I paid good money for it didn't I, beats fish heads an' green pizza crust, don't it, hee, hee, hee!"

"But *why* would the human meat trade nutrients for this *money*?"

"Huh? Makes the world go round, don't it?"

"Money is a form of stored energy? Valuable?"

"Huh? Well yeah, anyway, it's fuckin' *valuable*, better believe it!"

"Then why give money for food when there is food to take all around us?"

" 'Cause with money in your pocket, y'can score alla food you want inna minute right onna street, no sweat, without dodgin' cops an' karate-freak Chinamen, an' without stickin' your fuckin' head inna garbage can. Don't this hot dog beat havin' ta bust ya buns for half an hour just t'find a coupla fuckin' chicken bones with some meat left on 'em?"

That finally seemed t'get through.

"Then we must find pieces of money, many of them," Rat Thing told her.

"Terrific idea, why didn't I think of it myself?"

"The smell of it is everywhere."

An' it fuckin' *was*! Once Rat Thing decided it wanted money, Loxy found she *could* sniff it out, the sweaty ink of bills, the hard electric bitterness of coins, movin' around in purses an' wallets an' pockets just waitin' to be grabbed, sittin' still in cash machines just beggin' for a big rat witha hammer t'smash 'em open, a zillion parking meters up an' down th' streets smellin' tasty witha full loada quarters.

Took some doin' for Rat Thing t'get the idea that crackin' open meters with a pipe in fronta Saks Fifth Avenue or stickin' y'paws inta the nearest dealer's pocket wasn't the way the Master Race survived inna Pig Apple.

When th' asshole almost had her tryin' t'lift a wallet from a fuckin' *cop*, Loxy finally managed t'get through.

"Hey Rat Fuck, I don't know how ta tell ya this, but it ain't exactly *street-smart* t'fuck with people can fuck with *you* when th' streets are fulla people too fucked up t'even know how ta think about it!"

"*Rat-smart*, Loxy Foxy, scree, scree, scree, the survival secret of the Master Race recorded in their meat," squealed the voice inside her head. "Know your place in the food chain, Foxy Loxy, hee, hee, hee! Prey only on what's weaker than you and never challenge top predators!"

"Yeah, right, I'da never figured that out without you, scree, scree, scree," she told him. "Bienvenidos a Nueva York, Rat Fuck!"

Rereading *The Transformation* into the wee hours with the Santa Ana swirling like the time winds around him was an exercise in enlightened mortification for Dexter Lampkin.

Oh what an innocent had dared to write such a book in the bright white light of Aquarian passion! Oh what a putz had believed that it would sell a million paperbacks and transform the world!

Not that he had been the only one to give it the old messianic try.

That *was* the period when Timothy Leary was drawing headlines and crowds with his call to turn on, tune in, and drop out of the current stage of evolution and into the next, when Jim Morrison wanted the world and wanted it *now*, when *Star Trek* was becoming a mass cult phenomenon, when *2001* was launching a million and one acid trips.

Dexter remembered trying not to nod off as Philip Jose Farmer went on for what seemed like several centuries at the 1968 Berkeley Worldcon, trying to get writers to get together, pull up their socks, and save the world from the hard rain that was otherwise sure to fall.

Phil Farmer had written his long speech for publication and had read through it relentlessly to the bitter end to an audience of writers and fans eager to find out who among them had won the Hugo awards. The speech had become synonymous in fannish circles with tendentious boredom, and yet . . .

And yet, rereading his own screed of the period, Dexter remembered just how right he had been back there in the Stoned Age, with students rioting in the streets, fans heckling from the audience, and his colleagues escaping to the bar.

The next few decades will see a series of crises that will make or break our species, was the gist of what Phil had layed out back there in '68; the degradation of the biosphere, overpopulation beyond the carrying capacity of the planet, the whole litany of impending disasters that in the succeeding decades had become the commonplace of science fiction and punditry alike.

Come to think of it, and until now Dexter never had, there was precious little in the litany of planetary woe of his fictional aliens in *The Transformation* that Phil Farmer hadn't laid out to an audience too eager to find out which of them had won a plastic rocketship to care enough to listen.

We all know this, Phil had droned into the loutish whirlwind, and if the science fiction community doesn't get together and do something about it, it'll be biospheric degradation, mass unemployment, war, famine, economic collapse, the death of civilization as we know it, maybe the species itself.

Hardly anyone enlisted in Phil Farmer's crusade, *The Transformation* sank into the tarpits of the used-book dealers along with the rest of the would-be science fictional enlightenment of the period, and science fiction did not save the Monkey People from their own assholery.

But nothing else had either, now had it?

Until now, anyway . . . Dexter found himself daring to think by the time he had finished rereading *The Transformation*. For if the intervening decades had demonstrated anything, it was that there existed no pulpit bullier than the tube. Not that Dexter hadn't known this before, nor that he hadn't been trying to use *The Word According to Ralf* for such purposes all along.

But it had taken a George-warped trip down memory lane under the influence of the Santa Ana and his own golden oldie to finally realize where the failed transformational revolution had gone wrong. You could say that the downhill slide to Deathship Earth had begun when the would-be bringers of the dawn's early light started spelling Amerika with a K.

JFK had proclaimed that it was better to light a single candle than to curse the darkness, and perhaps it was no accident that the TV format of his administration had been Camelot, and he had been the last American president to star as the Sun

King. For what Jack Kennedy knew, or what the TV character of JFK embodied, was that you couldn't make a revolution by calling the people yeggs.

You couldn't transform monkeys into men by beating them over the head with their own assholery even if you did it with a slapstick and a pig's bladder.

And the Dexter D. Lampkin who had churned out 276 pages of a cynical TV tie-in book called *The Word According to Ralf* had forgotten that the author of *The Transformation* had known it too.

Dexter had once believed in the one-way street of time, but if Feynman, Einstein, Dirac, and Cam Carswell had their doubts, who was he to champion linear causality when confronted with his own personal temporal feedback loop in the real world?

He didn't have to believe in reincarnation or spirit messages to know that he had just received precisely the one he now needed from his previous self.

He had put *The Transformation* onto disk in order to cannibalize it for material, but instead it had told him just what he had to do.

It had been there all along.

In his novel, the scientists created a phony savior from space; not a curser of the gathering darkness, but a lighter of candles. In his novel, the Monkey People were conned into saving the world themselves by being made to believe that the knowledge of how to do it came from advanced aliens.

That knowledge existed in the real world too.

He had written it all down, right there in *The Transformation* itself. And as in the novel, there was a community of people who knew what had to be done and how to do it.

In the real world, he couldn't create a synthetic advanced alien in which people could actually *believe* to lead the world out of the dark and into the light. But he had a contract for a book whose covers could enclose just about anything he chose. And a show which would ensure that a minimum of half a million people would read it.

And a Ralf who had just proclaimed himself the Eagle, the Giant Turnip God of the Double Helix. A Ralf whose extro line had been a comic skyjacker's call to commandeer Spaceship Earth and fly it to Tomorrowland before it was too late.

Well why not?

Humor sold.

Ralf was already moving T-shirts, and warm-up jackets, and crummy polyester suits, and he was going to sell plenty of copies of any book called *The Word According to Ralf* too.

Why *couldn't* the Giant Turnip God of the Double Helix sell planetary salvation too?

"Too bad they didn't drop me back about forty years earlier when your time was prime," said Ralf.

"Honey, if it's *my* time, it *is* prime time," crooned Lavelle LaRue.

"And we are all in it," said Ralf, favoring her with a toothy stage-wolf's grin.

Well, what would you say now, Jimmy? Amanda wondered. It wasn't the first time tonight that she wished she had gone to the studio to watch tonight's show in the flesh with Jimmy Balaban. For it had been Texas Jimmy's talk about the Edge and how comic genius derived from the ability to maintain that glide along it that had inspired her to book Lavelle onto it.

Lavelle LaRue had a witchy laugh and her artfully uncombed white mane would've made her look like the Old Woman of the Mountain were she not wearing a sharply tailored rose pants suit obviously crafted in the mystic depths of Rodeo Drive.

Lavelle had been the sort of blond bombshell who got cast in movies that couldn't afford a first-rank Marilyn clone, and understanding that such a career had a limited shelf life, she had banked the proceeds. By the time Amanda had met her in her sixties, she had invested it shrewdly enough to have achieved liberation from the realm of financial Maya, one of those rare spiritual seekers who had achieved that liberation from all seeking that the sincere pilgrim sought.

"Time is like a river, flowing gently to the sea," sang Lavelle.

The show had been all Lavelle and Ralf. The chemistry was magic, and the effect was as Amanda had intended, as a brighter Ralf glowed and burbled in her presence, having hardly thrown a nasty put-down or a depressive line all night.

"Time is like a river?" said Jack Narkasian, a science fiction writer whose major contribution thus far had been the occasional reaction line and the piercing blue stare of a deacon of the Church of Scientology.

Call the Edge the Way, and that cosmic comic balancing act the ability remain within it, and what Texas Jimmy's instinct had sniffed out became the Tao of Show Business.

Thus Lavelle. For if anyone could seduce the Great Spirit of the World into maintaining its shaky manifestation in the Tinseltown Tao, it was Lavelle LaRue.

Who gave a stage shrug as she delivered just the groaner that Amanda and no doubt the audience had anticipated.

"So it's *not* like a river," she said.

Followed by that witchy laugh and a hippy-dip smile.

"But that doesn't mean that all those golden oldies had it wrong about going with the flow."

"*Me* you're talking to about going with the flow?" said Ralf. "Hey, I got dropped a *long* way down the timestream against it from where it's flowing *to*, which, I can tell you, is no place golden."

"Lighten up, golden boy, don't cast yourself as Charon schlepping the Monkey People across the Styx, rise and shine, and follow the Yellow Brick Road," said Lavelle LaRue. "Life is but a dream, sweetheart," she sang.

"A dream is a wish your heart makes when you're fast asleep," Ralf crooned croakily back.

Further and further into deeper but sunlit waters.

Or, thought Amanda, to paraphrase that great guru Dwight Eisenhower, Ralf is rapidly becoming more like he is now than he has ever been before.

"So be careful what you dream," said Lavelle. She laughed, and once more broke into song. "Because *dreams* can come true, it can happen to *you* . . ."

"If it hasn't already," said Ralf in a strangely resonant voice that suddenly seemed to step outside the song and dance act. "Seems to me I've dreamt this one before."

"Wake up, sonny," said Lavelle LaRue in a similar vein, snapping her fingers in an exaggerated gesture like a stage magician. "And remember that you've *been* this one before."

And it seemed to Amanda that, as if at her command, something arose within him like a golden globe ascending over the event horizon of a clear blue ocean.

"The Great Spirit of the World?" said Ralf. "The Giant Turnip God of the Double Helix?"

His voice had assumed the fatuous grandeur of a comic evangelist, but his eyes stared quite humorlessly into the camera, his face a deadpan mask.

Amanda could not imagine what the TV audience was making of this.

"*We* are the Eagle, oh yeah!" proclaimed Ralf.

The jack-in-the-box grin was belied by the eyes that opened out into vistas seldom glimpsed on television.

"*We* are the Dream?" said Ralf, lowering his voice half an octave. "*We* are the Dreamer?"

"We have met the Tao," said Lavelle LaRue. "And it is us."

"*We* are the custard pie in the sky in the Great Bye and Bye!"

"*Amen!*" Amanda found herself muttering to this Loony Tunes advent on the Gold Network.

For as she sat there in the solitude of her and the TV, the mandala upon which her consciousness was centered was indeed a window into a higher realm of electronic archetype and living legend. And a vast congregation of *twelve million* people had shared the experience instantaneously and collectively.

It had therefore entered the collective unconscious with the speed of light.

It was realer than anything out there in the world of flesh and matter.

It was on television.

Was *that* not now the electronic collective unconscious of the species wherein the Zeitgeist itself was forevermore shaped and formed?

Would not Archimedes, reborn with the media savvy of your average twelve-year-old, declare: "Give me an hour of prime time and a thirteen-week pickup to stand upon and I will move the world"?

These days Dexter Lampkin had the feeling he could give Cam Carswell himself lessons in how temporal feedback loops could fracture linear causality. Had George Clayton Johnson *caused* Ralf to transform himself from a Deathship Cassandra into a snake-oil salesman for planetary salvation? Had Dexter *caused* George to do it? Had Amanda's ditzy old starlet *caused* Ralf to repeat the performance on a higher level of craziness?

Or had there been a preexisting yearning out there for someone to hijack the planetary spaceship to Tomorrowland, even if it was only a wise-guy playing Giant Turnip God on television?

Ralf's half-assed transformation had done nothing for the ratings, but you could point to the blossoming of Tomorrowland graffiti, the gentling of the Man-From-the-Future jokes now making the rounds, the increase in the ecological-oriented calls, however crack-brained, on normally hydrophobic talk radio. It might not be showing in the demographics, but Dexter's reading of the pop cultural tea leaves led him to hope, perhaps even to believe, that maybe for once there was a *positive* feedback loop trying to bootstrap itself out of the quantum flux and into the public consciousness.

Had watching this happen caused Dexter's conceptual breakthrough or had it been *caused* by a novel Dexter himself had written decades ago? And had that in turn been *caused* by his past self's prescient perception of this very moment?

Or was there *really* a virtual future out there reaching back along the timelines? Or several?

What if alternative timelines were like musical themes in a Bach fugue—crisscrossing, reinforcing, canceling, contesting? Then every moment of time would be a tapestry of probability threads in endless and restless motion.

In such a universe, *any* reality would be virtual from a linear time-bound perspective, as alternate futures competed to emerge from any given now, as virtual futures sought to bootstrap themselves into existence in the past, thereby turning every *present* virtual.

Was this the true nature of reality?

Or was it just the usual load of sci-fi bullshit?

For present purposes, who cared? It was the McGuffin Dexter needed to rewrite his draft of *The Word According to Ralf*; to rewrite Ralf, the curser of the coming darkness, into Ralf, the lighter of candles.

In television reality, Ralf had *already* called for the passengers to hijack their Deathship planet and fly it to Tomorrowland. Simple enough to turn the tie-in novel version into a Ralf who had been sent back *from* that very Tomorrowland—call it *Starship* Earth—to seize the controls of planetary destiny and hijack *its* future into existence via the instrumentality of a TV show, and *the very book you are now reading, folks, hah, hah, hah*!

Cut those 276 pages of depressive Deathship Earth crud in half, and then it was just a matter of coming up with 150 pages or so of Starship Earth future to put in the mouth of the new alternate Ralf who was supposed to be writing this thing in first person.

And *that* he already had in superabundance. The Starship Earth future was, after all, basically the phony advanced alien civilization created by the scientists in *The Transformation* in order to bring the human version into being. He had hundreds of pages to crib from to describe a fictional time and place that he already knew by heart anyway.

Starship Earth was a world of playground cities set in the planetary garden of a biosphere restored to more or less its pristine preindustrial state. Hydrogen fusion and solar power satellites provided limitless clean power from water and sunlight. No more fossil-fuel burning, no more carbon dioxide buildup, no more greenhouse effect.

Well, maybe just a *little* one to jigger the climate of the northern zones toward something more pleasing to Dexter's Californian heart's desire; palm trees in Paris, and a parrot jungle in Central Park seemed kind of nice.

Limitless cheap electricity ultimately meant the ability to manufacture anything from the virtually unlimited raw materials to be found out there in the solar system. So industry left the planet and with it went the chemical pollution of the atmosphere.

Cheap electricity also fueled artificial photosynthesis factories creating basic feedstocks for animals, cellulose for paper, raw materials for plastics, out of sunlight, water, and air, freeing up vast tracts of land for the re-creation of lost forests, marshes, and grasslands. Genetic engineering and backbreeding brought the herds of buffalo back to the Great Plains, the great whales in profusion to the seven seas. Dexter was tempted to add dinosaurs for the hell of it, but that did seem a bit much.

Medical advances gave the passengers of Starship Earth enhanced life spans, no problem when humanity had a whole solar system for lebensraum and the power and technology it took to terraform it, or settle populations in biosphere bubbles in the vacuum of space itself.

Logically, such a society of abundance, where twenty percent of the population could produce everything that everyone needed, would not run along the sacred bottom line. No economic system based on the allocation of wealth would be relevant where there was no scarcity. The only system that made even theoretical sense was the purest form of communism—from each according to his ability, to each according to his need.

However, Dexter didn't feel it would be too swift an idea to come within several parsecs of the "C Word" in a TV tie-in book with which he hoped to inspire your average American couch potato.

So he opted for the comic notion that in such a society of limitless abundance *any* economic system no matter how loony tunes would more or less work—anything from hard-rock robber-baron capitalism to revisionist Trotskeyite syndicalist anarchism of the third kind—so somewhere or other most of them *did*.

Dexter blitzed his way through the rewrite in seventeen days of white heat. When he was through, he printed out the 302-page manuscript and FedEx'ed it to his agent in New York for transmission to PJP books.

Only as he was watching the Federal Express truck departing did it occur to him to print out a second copy and messenger it to Ralf.

Boogeyin' up Fifth Avenue inna lunch-hour rush with a wino's spare change freshly stuffed in her hoard, Foxy Loxy realized that for the first time in her life she was *rich*, hee, hee, hee!

Storekeepers wouldn't let her in ta see their goodies, wouldn'ta believed it, an' even half the beggars and gypsies she lifted the loot from probably thought she was some piecea street meat lower'n they was.

"Assholes!"

Stupid fuckin' disgustin' meat!

"Your world is gonna die, an' when it does, what's left is gonna be *ours!*"

That's what Rat Thing promised her.

It told her it was from when it had already happened a long time ago, whatever th' fuck *that* was supposed ta mean, nothin' left alive when th' Master Race ruled, an' they was gonna make *sure* it did, none a which made a whole lot of sense, 'cept she had *been* there, scree, scree, scree, down inna ruins at the end of the tunnel. . . .

Meat? Loxy Foxy? Meat is weak! The dinosaurs, big cats, monkeys, scree, scree, scree! Biggest bodies, biggest teeth, biggest brains, top predators always think the world belongs to what they got the most of. But they're just meat for what survives when their worlds die.

Think Rat, Loxy Foxy, think Rat, and the Dead World's all gonna be ours to gnaw right down to the rock beneath the bone, hee, hee, hee!

Well Loxy couldn't exactly say she unnerstood mosta this shit, but she sure was learnin' t'like th' *attitude.*

As a human, she couldn't afford no apartment, no restaurants, no new clothes, no TV dinners inna microwave at home witha kiddies, she was nothin' but raggy street scurve witha couple a hundred bucks in her drawers an' a big dirty knife.

Think human, and she was one poor Monkey.

But think Rat, and she was rich!

These asshole Monkey People threw away all the food Rat People needed, hee, hee, hee!

An' New York was fulla holes for Rat People, alleys, burned-out buildings, empty Dumpsters, garbage docks, cellars with windows you could kick in, subway stations.

Food and a place to sleep.

What else do you need, Loxy Foxy?

"How th' fuck should I know?"

Think Rat, Foxy Loxy, scree, scree, scree!

An' when she did, th' message came through loud an' clear.

Think Rat, an' th' answer is *nothing.*

Rat People didn't need *no* money.

But she hadda a nice hoard of inky paper and greasy metal in her pockets.

Think Rat an' she had more money than she needed.

Think Rat and she was rich.

Think Monkey, an' alla people talkin' to themselves onna street was crazies you tried to pretend you really wasn't seein', but think Rat, an' maybe they know somethin' you don't, assholes.

Kinda made Loxy wonder how many a these bag ladies, an' winos, an' ravin' loonies had Rat Things in *their* heads. How many a these people went around talkin' to voices in their heads 'cause they was *really there*.

When she was four, or so her fuckin' Momma told her when she wanted t'put her in her little kiddie place, she usedta talk out loud to invisible people who nobody else could see an' who nobody else could hear answer her back.

She didn't exactly remember it herself, an' she didn't remember what their names were, an' she didn't remember what they were like, but she kinda remembered what it felt like.

It felt like talkin' to your best an' only friend.

It felt like right now, walkin' on Fifth Avenue talkin' to Rat Thing an' not givin' a shit about people thinkin' she was crazy for talkin' to herself.

"Don't you wish *you* had one, assholes?"

A best an' only friend right inside your head who knew all this stuff you didn't. Who could tell you secrets. Who knew what was gonna happen a hundred years from now. Who could take over an' make you the slickest grab an' snatch artist onna street. Who filled your pockets with money.

An' had you starin' at dumb fuckin' TV alla time an' made you eat slime outa garbage cans.

Yeah, well, okay, *some* a this shit sure didn't make no sense! Rat Thing had her boostin' money all fuckin' day, but when it came t'lettin' her blow a little of it onna Big Mac or a hot dog or a fuckin' falafal sandwich instead gobblin' stuff out garbage cans would make anyone not thinkin' Rat puke, th' ratfuck was tight as a banker's virgin asshole.

"What are we gonna *do* with this fuckin' load a money, Rat Thing?" she asked. Hey, wouldn'tya say that was a reasonable question unner the circumstances even though this fuckin' creep inna black leather jacket with a head fulla pink neon spikes an' a face fulla safety pins gave *her* a look like *she* was a weirdo?

We think Rat, Loxy Foxy. We hoard it.

"What the fuck for?"

Think Rat, Foxy Loxy. That's what Rats do.

"I was thinkin' about a hamburger or a slice a pizza insteada puke the fuckin' alley cats won't eat."

Think Rat, Loxy Foxy! Hide in the sewer pipes under the world shitting in the plumbing and chewing on the wiring until we're ready to spend it! Hide in the cracks and watch the cheese for what comes out of the wormholes, and—

Oh no, not again!

Oh yeah! Oh fuck!

One minute she's walkin' down the sidewalk havin' an argument witha voice in her head like your typical New Yorker, anna next, she's slitherin' across Fifth Avenue in the middle of the block right through the creepin' traffic like a fuckin' hick fresh off a bus from Kansas, nearly whacked inna knee by a truck, nearly run over by a fuckin' bus, an' screamed at in Russian or somethin' by a cabdriver waving a tire iron. . . .

An' then there she is again, gorkin' atta TV sets inna appliance store window!

The store Rat Thing had her frozen in front of probably had been havin' the same going-out-of-business sale for the last hundred years. There was about a dozen TVs inna window, all of 'em turned on, and all of 'em tuned ta th' same fuckin' channel.

Which was runnin' some stupid fuckin' commercial for designer ass-wipes came in yellow, blue, pink, and blue, with cute little flowers on each piecea th' roll.

Loxy had never noticed how New York was fulla stores like this, but now she had good fuckin' cause to know, 'cause Rat Thing couldn't pass a fuckin' one of 'em even if they was across six fuckin' lanes a movin' traffic without havin' her standing there starin' like a fuckin' TV junkie for at least ten minutes, like her fuckin' beered-out ol' *momma*!

Only *she* didn't have no zapper to surf th' channels.

She was stuck with ten or fifteen screens' wortha whatever the store was usin' for its demo. Which didn't seem to matter to Rat Thing. He'd have her fuckin' zoned into whatever was on, even the crap that was runnin' now, some guy looked like Colonel Sanders on crystal meth peddlin' some piecea shit chopped vegetables inta dogmeat.

"An' why are we always watchin' all this fuckin' stupid TV?" she asked the rat-fuck, which didn't exactly seem like a dumb question either. "Hey, you cunt, what're you starin' at, maybe you'd like me to bite your tits off!"

Think Rat, Loxy Foxy, all the holes behind every wall for our eyes back there in the dark to look out of, scree, scree, scree, waiting and watching them gobble, waiting and watching to make sure it happens, waiting and watching them gobble and gobble and gobble till there's nothing left but cages full of monkeys eating their own recycled shit, won't be long now, hee, hee, hee. . . .

Was a Pizza Hut commercial runnin' now, featuring Mom an' Pop Bubba Blubber and the Monsters, and the way they were packin' it away sure made ya believe it!

Rat Thing cackled like a cement-mixer grinding up Coke bottles and live cats.

Waiting and watching the whole world turn into a great big juicy garbage can floating in space on a silver platter, scree, scree, scree, into the Dead World, Foxy Loxy, into our world, hee, hee, hee, waiting and watching to make sure—

The voice in her head suddenly shut the fuck up in mid-gibber.

That had never happened before.

An' Loxy was starin' at—

—at th' same fuckin' face onna dozen TV screens.

Face?

More likea face-shaped space, made of a zillion little points of pale flickerin' glitter, black hair flashin' with electric fire, strobing like a cheap light show, standin' there inna a circle of light shovin' some big disgustin' gray thing coulda been a fuckin' *elephant's dick* in her face. . . .

Shit, hadn't she seen this before, fuckin' *been* here before, *felt* this, fuckin' *lived* through this very fuckin' moment or was gonna or both, like onea those old record players stuck inna groove a bummer music—

—those *eyes*, like fuckin' *holes* inna face, somethin' glowin' blue behind 'em, trail a blue lights goin' down, down, down inta someplace where they stickin' fuckin' *coat hangers* in your brains, hee, hee, hee—

Jesus!

Loxy blinked.

What the fuck?

Some kinda bad flashback?

Was just that TV asshole Ralf supposed t'be from the future, is all—

—a dozen of him onna TV screens starin' back at her through the ratholes, must be zillions all over th' fuckin' city, zillions a those fuckin' eyes can see alla Rat Things back there inna Dead World waiting, the Destroyer, oh yeah, that's the face you been waitin' t'see, you been sent here t'see, not that you wanna, scree, scree, scree, but you gotta, now doncha, 'cause that's the face of the Enemy comin' right atcha!

Enemy a what is kinda hard t'figure an' who's doin' the thinkin' better you don't ask when your best and only friend is a voice scratchin' and clawin' and gnashin' its fuckin' rat teeth inside your head like th' tom cat has showed up an'—

—An' you're walkin' toward the door to the store.

"Hey, what the fuck are we doin'?"

She was grabbin' the crossbar to pull open the glass door.

Moving up the food chain, Foxy Loxy, scree, scree, scree, time to seek the meat we're here to eat!

"*Now* you're talking," Loxy shouted enthusiastically.

"Yeah, right, yo, whatever you say," said the big black guy in dreads comin' outa the store right in her face, flippin' her a bullshit phantom high five as he slithered past her inta the street like she was somethin' outa *Night of the Living Dead* or a walking dog turd.

"An' so's your mother!" she yelled back at him as Rat Thing walked her into the store. Behind the display window, there was like an alley between two fuckin' walls of glassed-off CDs an' mini-phones an' Gorkmans an' such shit, an' at the back was the heavy-duty stuff, stereos, computers, video recorders, television sets.

"Seek the meat we wanna eat, then what the fuck are we doin' here insteada McDonald's?" Loxy demanded righteously.

Trade our hoard of money for a television set.

"Do fuckin' *what*? What the fuck for?"

We trade our hoard for *their* all-seeing rathole. For the doorway into every crack and cranny of their world. The doorway behind which the Enemy is hiding, scree, scree, scree. Human meatware steps through it and a Rat walks among them, hee, hee, hee!

Well, okay, if you was a Rat tryin' t'pass for human, you could do worse than gorkin' at the tube no matter what was on, seein' as how that's what most of 'em did most of the time when they wasn't eating or fucking or taking a shit and sometimes when they was.

There was two Japanese guys in black suits talkin' to the counter guy over a pile a fancy telephones as Rat Thing walked her deeper into the store. They saw her comin' about halfway, went inta their bobbin' and weavin' dance, keepin' it up as they made tracks past her like maybe she was gonna bite them if they didn't, which was a fuckin' thought.

The guy behind the counter is this old bald Indian about five feet tall an' eighty-five pounds, an' for some reason he ain't exactly glad t'see her either.

'Cause insteada the usual greasy yes lady can I help you give me your money as soon as she's in range, the creep wrings his hands an' backs away from her like her armpits are too fuckin' ripe or she's just blown off a major stinker.

Rat Thing reaches down through the band of her jeans inta her panties where she's keepin' a wad and pulls out a fist fulla singles.

"We want to trade these pieces of money for a television," she's sayin', only it's the Rat Thing talkin' kinda, he's never done *this* before, it's like the coat hanger they stuck in her brain is hollow, an' somethin's suckin' up the words it needs through it, an' stringin' 'em together, only not too well.

"Go away, go away, we do not allow begging in this establishment," the old guy sez, brushing her off with a wavin' of both hands an' his nose in the air. "You have already frightened away two customers."

There's a mirror backin' the display section behind him, an' between the radios, Loxy can see why. Even for someone crawled up out of a million years inna subway tunnels an' been onna streets eatin' chicken heads and fish guts out of garbage pails ever since, she don't look too terrific.

It was a human face, *her* face, she seemed t'remember, the right size, an' alla right stuff inna right fuckin' places. But the hair is all matted an' hard with this greeny black stuff anna skin is kinda fuckin' gray an' scratched half t'pieces under all that crud.

An' the eyes . . .

The eyes ain't *her* eyes, not exactly, they're too bright, they're too hard, seem kinda black, kinda red, atta same time, how the fuck's that possible, rat's eyes, like it's the Rat Thing lookin' out at the world through the holes in her skull, brrr, the eyes ain't anything even *she* wants ta look at . . .

But Rat Thing don't get it, he thinks he's bein' cool.

"Here is money," he's got her saying, shoving maybe ten bucks' wortha greasy bills in the old guy's face. "Give me a television."

This ain't workin', asshole, she wants to tell the ratfuck, but she can't, he's workin' the mouth, an' she can't even quite exactly think.

An' sure enough, instead of layin' out the goods for the customer what's always supposed to be right, he's shoutin' to someone in the store room behind him.

"Kim! Come out here at once and bring the baseball bats!"

A Korean kid inna white T-shirt pops outa the storeroom, looks like Bruce Lee's big brother, an' he's whippin' a couple a full-sized baseball bats around like they was nunchuks.

This is enough to have Rat Thing buggin' out and leavin' Loxy to get out of it, hey, thanks a lot!

"Back off, motherfucker!" she shouts, pullin' the Big Ripper outa her bag, an' shovin' it inna general direction of Kim's face.

But insteada backin' off, he comes out from behind the counter, and *she's* doin' the backin', back toward the exit, an' while she's admirin' th' karate-freak bat-twirling act by pissin' in her pants, the guy behind the counter pulls out this fuckin' huge Magnum Force .45 revolver with both hands, spreads his legs apart, an' points the motherfucker right at her head like he learned all this in the Indian Marines.

"I assure you that I have had enough of the street life around here to take quite a bit of pleasure in shooting you to pieces before I call the police if you do not remove your disgusting presence at once," he tells her.

"Up yours, asshole!" Loxy told him, kinda running backwards out the door like a fuckin' crab, without taking her eyes off the piece or the baseball bats. "You gonna be *that* way about it, I guess I'm gonna hafta take my business elsewhere!"

The top floor of the Beverly Center mall was given over to a cineplex where the occasional foreign film was even to be found, with an impressive assortment of ethnic food stands servicing a common area of café tables overlooking the well of the atrium, and several rather good sit-down restaurants.

Dexter had been bemused when Ralf suggested they meet there for lunch, but since the object of the meeting was to discuss the manuscript of *The Word According to Ralf*, which Ralf had finished reading, he had allowed the star to choose the venue.

Ralf was lounging around by the elevator when Dexter arrived, hidden from the mall-rat masses in plain sight in quaint native costume—pastel blue Bermuda shorts, designer sneakers, a Deathship Earth T-shirt, and a red gimme cap over his distinctive mop pulled low to shadow his brow and forehead.

And to his consternation Ralf chose to dine off the line of ethnic fast-food stands. Dexter shrugged and opted for a pastrami sandwich, potato salad, and a beer, the modest tab for which the TV star in Valley drag did at least pick up, and secured a table in the café commons, while Ralf stand-hopped with his tray and arrived with a truly stomach-turning mélange of tacos, California roll sushi, and a baked potato slathered with tomato sauce, pepperoni, and melted Monterey Jack.

"Well?" said Dexter.

"Well," said Ralf, "I like the book."

He picked up the sushi roll, dipped it in salsa, bit off half of it, favored Dexter with a lopsided grin. "You make me sound like the Light and the Way, and the future you give me to come from in the second part sure beats the real thing."

"The real thing?" said Dexter, his gut rumbling as Ralf dribbled soy sauce on his machaca taco.

"Know why I like this place?" asked Ralf, waving his arm in an expansive gesture almost as if he owned it.

"Not really," groused Dexter.

Ralf munched down a mouthful of taco. "Take a look around, Lampkin," he said around it. "Tell me what you see."

Dexter ran his eyes around the top floor of the Beverly Center. The best that could be said about the vista was that it was a relief from watching what Ralf was eating. What he saw was what he might have seen at any enclosed shopping mall. A cineplex. A line of fancy fast-food stands. A half ring of restaurant entrances. A glass elevator shaft and escalators rising through a central well. Potted tropical plants so closely gardened they seemed plastic. Middle-aged shoppers. Teenaged mall-rats.

"What I see," said Dexter, "is a shopping mall."

"What *I* see," said Ralf, "is the Golden Age."

"The Golden Age?"

Ralf ceased his gobbling, and pinned Dexter with a gaze of intense sincerity, or at least a perfect simulacrum.

"The Golden Age of the shopping mall," he said. "The long-lost Garden of Eden. Back when you could still breathe the air outside so people weren't crammed into 'em like cockroaches. When the air-conditioning didn't smell of farts and rotten armpits. When they had plants growing in 'em. When you could get all this *real gourmet food* wasn't made from recycled sludge by a factory in the basement. Ah, *these* were the Good Old Days, Lampkin!"

Dexter stared right back. "Give me a break," he said. "*I* wrote that shit, remember?"

"*Did you*, Lampkin?" said Ralf. "You sure of that?"

His eyes had taken on the look of someone under the influence of serious drugs or George Clayton Johnson.

"According to the latest words you put in my mouth, who knows, right?" Ralf told him, his voice riding a razor edge between sincere bemusement and sarcasm that Dexter found strangely hypnotic.

"Who *can*, right, with all these wannabe futures trying to change the past to make themselves real or not real, kinda makes *us* sorta, what did you call it, *virtual*, now don't it, Lampkin?"

"Come on, Ralf, I made all that up, it's just *science fiction!*"

"Maybe it is and maybe it isn't, or maybe both, if I get you right, Lampkin, I'm not exactly up on all this sci-fi stuff," Ralf said, his voice dripping with sly insinuation.

"I mean, according to you, *this very scene* keeps getting rewritten and the script never gets finalized, only *we don't know it*. In one version, you make it all up. In another, I'm a real refugee from a real Deathship. Or Captain Jerk from a real Starship Earth that's sent me back to skyjack the planet to Tomorrowland. Or . . ."

He smiled like a Cheshire Cat that had just devoured a particularly succulent canary.

"Or I really *am* the Giant Turnip God, and it's all my dream, each and every version, as I toss and turn and belch in my sleep trying to digest my last meal of Kentucky Fried Dinosaur."

That look in his eyes had somehow reversed, so that Dexter now felt as if *he* were under the influence of some Svengali, as if *he* had become a character in *Ralf's* piece of business.

"Who are you, Ralf?" Dexter said softly. "Beneath all the schtick and bullshit, who are you *really?*"

"How should I know?" Ralf said ingenuously.

"How should *you* know?"

"If I'm the Great Dreamer then I won't know it till I wake up, if I ever do," Ralf said. His eyes assumed the surface of mirrors in which everything or nothing might be written. "In which case, you won't be around to find out, 'cause you're just one of my figments."

He laughed not very humorously.

"Or I'm putting you on right now," he said. "Or I'm what the latest version of the format says I am. Or I'm fuckin' crazy."

He shrugged.

"Or *you're* Uk-Ruppa-Tooty, Lampkin, and it's all *your* dream," he said in perfect deadpan. "How would *you* know?"

And he laughed, a real one this time, or so it seemed. He smeared a dollop of wasabi paste on top of his baked potato in Italian drag, forked a mess of it into his mouth, and the spell, whatever it had been, was broken.

"So, Lampkin, since *The Word According to Me* as written by you says neither of us can know, and even if we did the script just changed fifteen times while we couldn't be looking, why don't we just choose the version we like and *do it?*"

"Do *what?*" said Dexter.

"The one where Tinkerbell lives, where Scotty beams me back from your Starship to lead the Lost Monkey Boys and Girls straight on to morning," said Ralf, gobbling up the remains of his salsa-sodden sushi.

He gave Dexter a clownish grin that might have been slathered across his mug in greasepaint.

"At least we'll be making showbiz history, Lampkin," he said. "For the first time ever, a TV format gets changed to fit the paperback tie-in!"

Fuckin' team *we* are, hee, hee, hee, Foxy Loxy thought, or anyway thought she thought, gettin' hard t'tell sometimes, scree, scree, scree, th' Rat Thing knows what it wants but don't havea clue how ta get it, an' I know how but I don't know *why*.

Alla way down here th' ratfuck keeps up this fuckin' squealin' shit about ratholes an' doorways anna Dead World anna Enemy supposed t'be the why of it, makes about as much sense as a speed-freak gangsta rapper, but th' *what* a the why comes through loud an' clear every fuckin' time they passed a store witha TV inna window.

'Cause then the Rat Thing's got her jerkin' an' twitchin' an' droolin' with this fuckin' Rat hunger he's pumpin' down through the coat hanger in her brain, down through th' middle of her bones—like she wants t'hunt down a TV, an' eat it, an' *fuck* it, an' it's about all she can do t'keep from smashin' her fuckin' head through the plate-glass windows t'get at 'em.

Human meat steps througha doorway anna Rat walks among them, or some such shit, ain't that what Rat Thing said?

Yeah, sure, only maybe it ain't as simple as that, ratfuck, at least let me do th' thinkin' onna street, fer chrissakes, you think a *human* inna *rat* body's gonna do so terrific inna sewers. . . .

Well, maybe Rat Thing was listenin' t'reason, or maybe Foxy Loxy was listenin' t'the wire in her brain, who the fuck knew lately, 'cause if the devil what was makin' her do it an' what she was *feelin'* was all Rat, at least he was letting her do the thinkin'.

Who was doin' the thinkin' had ducked behind a Dumpster an' counted th' money, which was not enough inna store, an' who was doin' the thinkin' knew about the thieves' markets, where small-time burglars spread last night's take right out there onna sidewalk for wiseguy yuppies, hey bro, what makes you think this stuff is hot, I got th' video camera anna fancy telescope for birthday presents last year, I always been a big fan a Igor Stravinsky, an' this here silver service for eight's been inna family ever since we sneaked over inna bilge a th' *Mayflower*.

Just like there was all levels a hookers inna Pig Apple from them that looked like movie stars workin' the Waldorf anna Plaza t'them sucked off drunks between two parked cars, there was all levels a burglars an' thieves' markets, anna creeps in one as low as this one weren't exactly in no condition t'notice that you was a rat or to make a fuckin' issue of it if they did.

Any scurvier than this, an' a cockroach would puke.

Was a Dumpster at one end of the alley anna a mess a garbage cans at the other an' anyone who looked past either of 'em wasn't gonna wanna look twice, unless they was a fuckin' junkie or crackhead lookin' to sell whatever was the last thing they managed t'steal for the price a the next hit or a Rat Thing witha street-smart human doin' the thinkin' for it cruisin' the world's rock-bottom bargain basement.

Was five humans, or anyway a rat could call 'em that, propped up againsta wall like garbage baggies when Loxy eased herself past the Dumpster.

A Puerto Rican kid looked about sixteen goin' on a hundred slumped over totally out of it, havin' puked all over the Polaroid camera between his legs. Grandma junkie grabbin' onto a fuckin' food processor she had managed to cop somewhere sat starin' inta space with her mouth open like maybe she was dead and just hadn't stopped droolin'. Somethin' that looked like a skeleton shoved inna Yankee jacket *snorin'* fer chrissakes, disgust you to hear it, witha toaster oven looked like it had been used to fry Kotex in across his lap.

A white guy with greasy blond dreads an' enough tracks up an' down both arms t'get the A-Train t'Cleveland twitchin' an' squirmin' while he thumb-fucked onea those Lameboy Gameboy things he probably snatched froma ten-year-old.

He looked up at her as she went by, and started blubber-gubberin' somethin', holdin' up the video game toy with his thumbs still goin', but Foxy Loxy wasn't havin' any a that shit 'cause the last guy had scored himself a TV.

Wasn't much of a TV, one a those little portable pieces a shit with rabbit ears anna handle, painted some kinda banana yellow looked like it had been copped from the baby's bedroom. Leanin' up against the wall behind it was guy in a pea coat with kinda greenish-gray skin, lips that was fuckin' purple, a mouth fulla rotten teeth, an' blue eyes like the lights you followed down a subway tunnel into the darkness.

"How much for the TV?"

"Who wants to know?" said Mr. TV Man in a skittery jittery voice, those eyes like windows inna burned-out building you don't wanna know what's squatting down there behind them in the dark.

"This wantsa know," says who's doin' the thinkin', reachin' inta pocket with her left hand and snaring a few dirty singles, keepin' her good paw around the handle of Rip just in case, an' wavin' the wad in his face.

You woulda thought that would make him sit up an' drool, or even made a grab for it, but he gives her this grin like a pumpkinface fulla razor blades. "It's not enough," he says.

"So how much is enough, asshole?"

"I want five million dollars. With five million dollars I will rule the world. With five million dollars I'll be a movie star. With five million dollars I'll be Jesus fuckin' Christ."

"Five million dollars? You fuckin' crazy?" said Loxy just before realizin' what a stupid question that was.

"It costs a lot of money to be crazy. Runs me exactly five million dollars a day."

"Mother-*fucker*!"

This conversation between who was doin' the thinkin' an' a garbage-head couldn't think two words inna row made any sense was gonna get nowhere, so Loxy was happy to have a squealin', scratchin', hungry Rat Thing inside her head t'take over, and it was good to have a human body with a big steel tooth, an' hey, it was always good to be the top of the local food chain insteada the bottom.

Avoid challenging top predators.

Take a quick skittering sniff around.

Nothing here that good old Rip couldn't handle.

Prey only on what's weaker than you.

The Monkey Thing outweighed her, and it was male, but it smelled weak and sick, its reflexes slow, its rotten brain in no condition to organize its limbs for a fight with this body and its huge steel tooth.

"Give me the television," she said in a scratchy voice like paws scrabblin' on concrete, an' reached out one a hers t'grab it by the handle.

"Mine!" screamed Mr. TV Man, tryin' to bat it away witha spastic sweep of his hand. "I stole it fair and square! Y'can ask anybody!"

"*The biggest tooth here is mine!*" she screeched, whipping out the Big Ripper, waving it in wide high circles, as she twitched around quickly in a half circle to check out what was behind her.

Woulda taken a lot more than a giant rat wavin' a knife t'roust Grandma Junkie, Yankee jacket, or the kid what puked onna Polaroid before he passed out, an atom bomb up their assholes, maybe.

Lameboy Gameboy managed t'more or less get up on his hind legs, but before he could get no dumb notion, she screamed, "ANY FUCKIN' QUESTIONS?" and gave him a look, an' took a half step inna general direction, an' he's tear-assin' outa there, better believe it.

When she came back around, she saw that Mr. TV Man had come scrabblin' around on his hands and knees an' was huggin' the fuckin' TV with both arms like it was his favorite teddy bear.

"You can't have it, you can't have it, you can't have it," he started blubberin' and shriekin' like a fuckin' two-year-old.

Prey only on what's weaker than you.

Don't challenge top predators.

No fuckin' problem.

There was only one predator here, and it layed six inches of sharp greasy steel in the dirty crease between the throat and the neck of its prey where it could smell blood-rich arteries and veins pulsing.

She tried to pull the TV set away from the Monkey Thing with one hand, and he was so weak, she mighta done it if she leaned into it, but he held on to it with both arms, an' started blubberin', so what th' fuck, he asked for it didn't he?

She drew her paw back toward her body a bit, an' then slashed up an' across in an arc with the steel tooth with the full strength of the limb holding it, an' felt it slice into meat and pop vessels full of blood.

The Monkey Thing tried to scream in pain, but more sickly smelling blood spurted out of its throat than sound from its mouth, and as she snatched the TV away, it fell facedown into a thick red puddle.

It was good to have a body stronger than your prey and a long sharp tooth of well-greased metal.

You see, Loxy Foxy, we *are* your only friend, scree, scree, scree.

"Yeah, well, I gotta admit I could get used t'bein' your top an' only predator, hee, hee, hee."

Texas Jimmy Balaban didn't need Amanda Robin's shrink to tell him that this change in the decor of Ralf's apartment was an expression of what had been going on in his client's head, to see that it mirrored the changes in the show that Ralf and Lampkin had shoved down his throat.

Back when Ralf was doing the comic prophet of ecological gloom and doom, it had been nothing but white walls and motel furniture, as somehow befitted a time-warped Boat Person from Deathship Earth. But now that he had greened himself into Captain Ralf from *Starship* Earth, he had apparently tried to do likewise with the apartment.

Jimmy had never seen an apartment so crammed with plants. Big rubber and cane trees whose top leaves brushed against the ceiling. Potted palms and palmettos. Ivy and geraniums and wandering jew and spider plants in hanging planters. Rubbery jade trees and twisted succulents. Cacti of all sizes. Venus flytraps. Bonsais. Kudsu and morning glory.

Big ones, little ones, clogging the living room, covering just about every available space, frying in the smog out on the balcony, atop the fucking refrigerator. Jimmy was sure that if he took a piss, he would find the toilet bowl planted with water lilies.

A truly depressing spectacle.

For everything seemed about to croak; leaves yellowing, cacti spongy with mold, bonsai trees gone gray and skeletal, the stems and branches of the bigger items groaning under their own malnourished weight like the victims of African drought.

You didn't have to be a Luther Burbank to see that a major league black thumb was at work.

Far from having kit-bashed a model of his promised biospheric rebirth, Captain Ralf from Starship Earth had only succeeded in creating an Auschwitz for houseplants.

As only befitted what the change in the part the star was playing was doing to the fortunes of the show.

Okay, so far it was subtle. The ratings had leveled off just a tad below Archie Madden's expressed expectations, where they sat quivering nervously as the merchandising sales continued to rise and Lampkin's tie-in book shipped three hundred thousand copies in the first printing, which, according to him, was pretty hot shit.

The Boy Genius wasn't exactly *complaining* yet, but there was already a certain pissing and moaning from his direction as to how come the show was just lying there, while the merchandising rights, into which he had neglected to dip much more than the first inch of the old corporate wick, were taking off.

So far Jimmy had been able to put him off by blowing smoke, by telling him that the tie-ins—the book, the new Starship Earth T-shirts and suit, the posters, buttons, cereal, condoms, and whatever—being promotional items to hype the show, needed more time to work their inevitable sweetening effect on the ratings.

That Madden hadn't told him how full of it he was only went to show that, at least for a limited run, an old Hollywood pro *could* outfox a Boy Genius.

For of course, what he had told Archie Madden was bullshit.

Two hundred thousand T-shirts, a hundred thousand posters and buttons, ten thousand Starship Suits, and the rest of the crap out there might indeed be a nice annuity, but in terms of improving the ratings of a show with twelve million viewers, even three hundred thousand paperbacks with the star's puss and the show's name on the cover was not going to be worth jack shit.

Whereas a national TV show with a mediocre audience of twelve million viewers a week was one hell of a free commercial for the tie-ins!

Ralf led Jimmy through the withering interior forest into the living room, brushing aside scraggly vines and threadbare fronds with his forearms for lack of a machete, slipped behind the bar to pour a couple of bourbons on the rocks, slid

Jimmy's drink toward him, and leaned against the bar on his elbows like your friendly neighborhood bartender.

That is, if your neighborhood happened to be a decaying set for *The African Queen*, and your bartender habitually decked himself out in *The Word According to Ralf* tie-ins.

You had to give it to him, he was loyal to the merchandise. Ralf wasn't nuts enough to wear the Starship Suit as street clothing, or at least not yet, but you never saw him in public without the T-shirt or the green satin warm-up jacket with the full-sized version of the Starship Earth logo—the Big Blue Marble sailing through the starry seas on a comet's tail of fire—on the back and a smaller one over the heart just above the gold-stitched personalization.

And, apparently, these days even in his own home.

Such as it was.

Such as he was, with that sheen to his eyeballs which reminded Jimmy of a sex maniac named Wanda whom he had dated whom had gotten herself Jesused out and was last seen beating a tambourine on Hollywood Boulevard.

Texas Jimmy sighed. "So, Ralf?" he said. "How do I say this gently?"

"You probably don't," said Ralf.

Of late, those eyeballs had become as opaque as a set of ball bearings, and the guy behind them, who had never exactly been Mr. Personality, more and more like your less-than-favorite Martian.

Jimmy took a belt of bourbon. He shrugged. "Okay then," he said. "It is my professional opinion that you are going bugfuck bananas."

Well, not exactly.

The more bugfuck Ralf became, the less he seemed able to go humorously bananas. Far be it from Texas Jimmy to cry into his beer for the Good Old Days of Deathship Earth, toxic doody humor, and rattling the bars of the Monkey People cage with a lead-pipe slapstick, but this Save the World stuff just wasn't as funny.

How could it be?

The basis of comedy being the exaggeration of the way the audience saw themselves and the world they lived in, it was a lot easier to get them to laugh by making monkeys out of them than by attempting to inspire them to straighten up their act and become mensches.

You didn't notice any of those fun house mirrors making 'em look *better* than they knew they really were, now did you?

The slide down the slippery slope had been slick as goose grease. Even now, Jimmy couldn't quite put his finger on when it had started to happen. Maybe the nose *should've* known, but not until Dex showed him the cover proof of the paperback tie-in, featuring Ralf in the as-yet-untailored Starship Suit and the Starship Earth T-shirt logo moonlighted by the same artist, did it dawn on Jimmy that the show had oozed into some kind of format change while he wasn't looking.

Only then did he realize that for some time now Ralf had been playing less than boffo patticake with a string of guests who seemed to have escaped from one of Lampkin's sci-fi novels.

And when Jimmy checked out *The Word According to Ralf*, he realized that they sort of had.

All this crap about time-traveling wise-guys screwing around with alternate presents like the dimwit favorite nephews of pinhead network executives in hell rewriting each other's development projects gave him a headache, but you didn't have to be Mr. Spock to see that Lampkin had been using this thing as a casting bible.

The aerospace case who wanted to build giant mirrors in orbit to beam down electricity and give New York Palm Springs winters in the bargain.

The eco-nut who claimed you could turn sunlight, water, and air into People Chow.

The science fiction writer promoting something called a fusion torch which was supposed to be a rocket, an electric generator, a garbage disposal unit, and a magic wand for turning drek into gelt, or was it vice versa.

And so on. And so forth.

Okay, Texas Jimmy had to admit that the Deathship Earth routine had maybe been squeezed to the point where the teat wasn't giving out much more than low-fat milk powder. Okay, he had seen enough weeks of *The Word According to Ralf* to be sold on the idea that the world was heading down the toilet. And maybe Dex and his cronies *did* have hot-shit ideas for cleaning up the act and changing the format. Far be it from Texas Jimmy Balaban to stand in the way of a noble cause like saving the world! Clean energy from outer space! Bring back the rain forest! Build Disneyworlds on Mars! Let them eat People Chow! Why not?

As long as you get laughs doing it.

This stuff didn't *have* to bomb out. Most of Dexter's collection of scientists and sci-fi writers were certainly weird enough to make ideal straight men. Ralf *should've* used them as the perfect backboards off which to sink comic three-pointers. But instead he seemed to let *them* use his for-the-most-part-lame ad-libbed one-liners as springboards for yet another five-minute monologue that belonged in a college classroom.

El stinko.

The only one of these shows that was consistently funny was the one with Timothy Leary, the onetime Acid Guru, who not only arrived with a pretty funny routine about financing the building of condo cities in space by preselling the rights to the currently nonexistent real estate inside them, but had the timing and ad-libbing ability to carry *Ralf* through it.

But then Leary, as Jimmy learned, had done some touring as a club comic himself.

Jimmy sighed, sipped at his bourbon. Maybe I should've tried to sign *him*, he thought. For a guy that was supposed to have spent a decade or two frying his brains on LSD, Leary sure seemed a lot less nuts than what he was looking at now.

Ralf was giving him that *look* he had taken to using on the air; the silent stare of a Malibu swami mesmerizing a rich widow as he reached for her pocketbook, the sort of deadeye deadpan stare that Jack Benny had used to comic perfection. But Ralf was no Benny. Coming from him, it was not funny ha-ha, it was funny peculiar. *Real* peculiar.

"Bugfuck bananas in your opinion or not, we had a deal, Jimmy, remember?" Ralf reminded him. "Amanda's shrink certified me USDA prime noncertifiable, so no more talk about psychiatrists."

Jimmy took another sip of bourbon, using the move to break the uncomfortable eye contact. "Crazy as a bedbug, Ralf," he said, disarming the insult with a shrug and a sour smile, "and me too, for letting it get this far."

Had springing this Starship Earth and costume change stuff on him been a clever piece of cynical timing?

True, Lampkin had caught him when he was the only person involved with the savvy to smell this early that the show was going to be in trouble further down the line. But true too that it was hard to believe that Dex wasn't smart enough to realize that a scan of the tie-in book would clue Jimmy in on just what had been going on.

"Well, yeah, okay, so I've got an agenda, is that the moral equivalent of child molesting, what's so wrong about trying to do well by doing good?" Lampkin had forthrightly admitted when Jimmy pinned him on it.

"Nothing as long as it's funny," Jimmy told him. "Which these dweebs you been booking lately ain't. And they've been monopolizing the airtime to the point where Amanda's weirdos have been kinda melting into the stage set. And Ralf has been *letting* it happen, the result of which is that he's been starting to stink up the joint."

"Right," Lampkin had agreed with the speed of a Borscht Belt regular jumping on juicy straight line from an obnoxious heckler, "so we freshen up the act with this little costume and format change and make out like bandits in the process."

It had seemed to make sense at the time. Ralf *had* just about exhausted his original angle of attack, the friggin' green clown suit *was* at least a piece of obvious visual humor, and maybe turning Ralf into a comic Buck Rogers Starship captain *would* jolt him back onto the rails, stir up his drying juices.

Besides which, the market for the Deathship tie-ins was pretty well saturated now, the new Starship Earth logo looked cool, and the book soon to come out was going to plaster the Starship Suit with Ralf in it all over the paperback racks.

Yeah, a case could be made that a deliberate con job had been run on him, but Jimmy couldn't let himself cop a plea all that easily.

For he had eagerly swallowed it whole, like a cat gulping down a nice juicy sardine from his mistress's hand. Why not? Things were already going wrong, it made hot marketing sense, and he certainly didn't have a better idea at the time.

Not that he was doing much better now.

"Look, Ralf," he said, "I'm not telling you I want you to see another shrink, especially considering the results of the last wad of dough I flushed down that rathole. But the current state of the act sucks. And to let it keep sliding like this till the Boy Genius wakes up far enough to read it in the ratings, that, kiddo, *is* fucking crazy!"

"Come on Jimmy, you don't think Captain Ralf from Starship Earth is an improvement over the Blue Meanie from the Terminal Weenie?" Ralf said in that mockingly portentous tone he had adopted on the air lately. "It's moving those tie-ins and paperbacks, now ain't it?"

"But it ain't very funny," Jimmy told him. "You can sorta tell by the way the studio audience sits there like zombies."

Jimmy's hopes that the change of costume would put some yocks back in the act *had* certainly been aroused the first time he saw Ralf in the Starship Suit.

Uncle Miltie in the time of his prime would've felt right at home in it.

Bright kelly green satin was no doubt supposed to be some kind of ecological statement, but the jacket looked like something that had been tailored for a colonel in the Leprechaun SS, festooned with the kind of outsized gold braid more usually seen across the entrance of the Chinese theater.

The pants, the same eye-killing green, were so loose around the ass and thighs that they looked like they had been swiped off the back end of a pantomime horse. The friggin' gold lamé boots had wings on the heels the size of fruit bats, and the matching green general's hat perched atop Ralf's hedge of hair like a four-star yarmulke.

It was hard to imagine anyone failing to get laughs dressed like Captain Putz from Royal Ruritanian Airways, and when the show opened, Ralf pranced on-stage to gasps, and then nervous giggles, and then some real laughter as he did a drag-queen runway pirouette.

"Hello, there, Monkey People, this is Captain Ralf speaking, and welcome to Starship Earth," he said in a perfect singsong airline pilot voice.

He came to a full stop with his hands on his hips like a poster for *The Return of the Circus Circus Doorman.*

"We will be flying at warp factor gonzo in the direction of Tomorrowland, and it's a few million years too late to get off if you think you're on the wrong flight."

You could just about hear the collective *what the fuck.*

Ralf flashed a polystyrene smile and instead of moving to the talk-show set, marched to the front of the stage as if to work the audience with a nonexistent shotgun mike, and it was Jimmy's turn to mutter *what the fuck* from the wings.

Nor was Jimmy exactly reassured when he started babbling like Lenny Bruce in his terminal phase, eyes glistening with unwholesome speedfreak energy.

"Hey, come on, Starship Troupers, what're you staring at like that, inside every cloud there's a silver iodide lining, inside each and every box of toxic toasties there's a cosmic secret decoder ring, inside the dark side of the downhill Deathship slide there's a million-year Starship ride, and inside every gorilla suit there's the one and only . . . *me!*"

Maybe if he had mugged his way through it, he would've gotten a laugh out of the Captain Ego act. Instead, he had managed to turn a yammering nut in a clown suit into a sicko too embarrassing to laugh at.

Mercifully, Ralf had at least seemed together enough to realize what a bomb he had layed. Without trying to take this spontaneous opening monologue any further, he beat a hasty retreat back into the current format.

Dexter's guest that night was a white-coat type from an outfit called Lifelines, dedicated into lining their own pockets in the process of extending human life span well past the point of advanced geezerhood. Amanda had come up with a woman who claimed that every living thing, humans included, had evolved ac-cording to the Great Cosmic Plan, as if God, or some other executive producer, had commissioned a billion-year show bible with every successive episode layed out in sequence at least in treatment form.

It had not seemed unreasonable to Jimmy that a tummel with a couple of char-acters like these should be just what the laugh doctor ordered, but while the pro-ceedings did produce more yocks that your average funeral, it wasn't by much.

". . . many methods for extending the human life span, perhaps indefinitely, by rewriting the DNA to eliminate the death genes, by flushing out the damaged chromosomes, or by introducing a self-maintaining population of nano-machines into the body to tend it continually like a well-manicured garden—"

"Naw, that's not how we do it in Tomorrowland, we transplant our brains into those giant turtles that crawl around in slomo eating alfalfa sprouts and raw turnips and having sex once every twenty-five years, so it *seems* like a whole lot longer. . . ."

". . . so how else would it be possible for changes in populations of organisms to affect each other at a distance, if the patterns into which life evolves don't precede the protoplasmic forms that evolve to fulfill them?"

"The recipe for Egg McMuffin and Colonel Sanders's secret formula *both* came before either the chicken *or* the egg?"

One gag didn't lead into another, there wasn't any build. How could there be when Ralf's performance consisted of moldy one-liners shoehorned into filibustering about DNA and RNA and the NBA and evolutionary crystal-channeling of the Life Force?

". . . if you brought them up to normal body temperature slowly enough, circulated oxygenated blood to the brain *before* you restarted the heart, you could thaw out cryogenically frozen bodies and bring them back to life—"

"Why bother? We just pop 'em in the microwave for ten minutes, and show 'em *Deep Throat*, and if *that* don't get 'em up and running, we know they're past the sell-by date. . . ."

And at the fade, when Ralf had the camera all to himself, to Jimmy's horror, his voice had segued into the frantic singsong syncopation of a comic slipping over the Edge into babblement.

"Well, Starship Troupers, it's been a long strange trip from Tomorrowland to here and back again, seems like it's all a dream sometimes, seems like Main Street took a wrong turn and dropped us off in Fantasyland, where we can live forever as long as we can keep up the payments on the deep freeze, and the chicken *is* the egg, and a Boat Boy from the Deathship wakes up as a Starship Captain, but no sweat, hey, it's all according to the Great Cosmic Format. . . ."

Then he seemed to right himself like a wobbling top, as if he still had it together well enough to realize that he had damn well better make a quick recovery, but not well enough to know how.

He paused for a beat, eyeballing the camera with the fey smile of a guy who had suddenly realized that his fly had been open on the air for some time now.

He stood up slowly, and Jimmy made a mental note to buy the director a bottle of Wild Turkey to thank him for the presence of mind to call for a long shot as

Ralf came out in front of the set and delivered his extro to the studio audience from there.

"You ever get the feeling that you haven't been yourself lately, Starship Troupers?" he said. "That maybe you never were?"

This seemed like the understatement of the century. And it had been delivered in a tone of voice that would've come off as uncomfortably sincere were it not coming from a guy in a bright green clown suit with a silly hat on his head.

"Ever have one of those dreams where you *dream* you wake up? Only when you *really* wake up, or think you do, you're someone else? Hey, I could *still* be dreaming all this, couldn't I? You never really know."

Eerier and eerier.

Jimmy saw on the monitor that the effect was visible even in the long shot. Ralf's eyes seemed to glow from within as if he were one of those kitschy souvenir seashell lamps they sold to the tourists in Miami and someone had switched on the little bulb inside. And there was *someone else* inside that green suit, someone who suddenly seemed to be wearing the dumb thing like a Marine officer's fancy parade-ground uniform, like . . . like . . .

Like a Starship Captain.

"On the other hand, Starship Troupers, they say that clothes make the man," he said, fingering the material of his lapel. "So why can't this be me? When I made this costume change, folks, it felt like Clark Kent slipping into the phone booth in his cheap blue serge and coming out as Superman."

He lowered his head, bent his knees, hunched his shoulders.

"Shazam!" he shouted, throwing up his arms.

He folded them across his chest and mugged a comic book superhero pose like Benito Mussolini doing Captain Marvel.

"*Captain Ralf of Starship Earth!*" he announced grandly.

There had been a smattering of nervous laughter punctuated by a few full-throated yokel guffaws.

Under the circumstances, it had been about the best extro from this fiasco that Texas Jimmy could have hoped for.

Except there had still been a couple of minutes of airtime left.

Bad enough that Ralf had been stuck holding the pose silently for a good thirty seconds after the titters had guttered away into a graveyard hush.

What he had done next . . .

How he had done it, Texas Jimmy hadn't been able to figure watching it then in real-time, nor could he do any better playing it back in his head as he studied

Ralf giving him what seemed like a private performance of the same bit across the bar now.

He hadn't broken the pose. Jimmy hadn't caught a single facial muscle moving. But his entire persona changed. And he had proceeded to commit the comedian's cardinal sin, the one that would've had Jimmy crossing himself had he been a Catholic or had had him wishing for a belt from a nonexistent hip flask seeing as how he wasn't.

He was still playing Captain Ralf of Starship Earth.

But now he had become serious.

Deadly, leadenly, serious.

And a tiny tilt of his head and a badly scrimmed spot had flashed two highlights off his feverish eyeballs, a spooky and unfunny effect, as he had delivered that equally spooky and unfunny extro.

"It's better to light a single candle than to curse the darkness. So who knows, Monkey People, if we believe hard enough, maybe Tinkerbell lives. So climb aboard the Starship, Troupers, and let's all wake up in Tomorrowland!"

There was no such special effect glitter in Ralf's eyes as Jimmy sat there looking into them in the apartment choked with half-dead plants, but they didn't look much less serious.

Or much less crazy.

"You're losing it, Ralf," Jimmy told him.

"And if I say I'm *finding* it?"

"Finding *it*!" Texas Jimmy snapped back at him, finally reaching the point of open exasperation. "These days you don't seem to be able to find a laugh in a barrel of monkeys! I didn't drag my ass here to listen to any more of this Happy Face in Outer Space bullshit!"

It could've been worse, Jimmy supposed. He could've found Jesus. He could've shaved his head and put on a yellow robe and started preaching the Word According to Hari Krishna.

"Come on, Jimmy," Ralf said with a saccharine master of ceremonies grin. "The ratings are holding. Lampkin's book is selling. The tie-ins are moving. People *want* to believe they can climb aboard Captain Ralf's Starship."

"Right, welcome to Starship Toilet Bowl, fasten your seat belts and hold on to your barf bags, as Captain Putz flies a prime-time comedy hour straight down the tubes!"

"I'm the one out there, Jimmy, and I can feel it," Ralf said with a blissful evenness that seemed almost calculated to get under Texas Jimmy's skin. "I'm not *dying* out there, I'm being *born*."

"Next thing you're gonna say is *trust me!*"

"It's a thought, Jimmy. A lot of people do."

Jimmy sighed. Maybe Ralf hadn't entirely lost it yet. There were even times when Captain Ralf managed to be funny. How could you manage not to get *some* laughs standing there in a clown suit and making like the light and the way?

Which, Jimmy realized, was why he was even bothering.

Texas Jimmy took a long warming swallow of bourbon and sought a center of calm in the glow of the buzz. The same hard-nosed instinct that told him when it was time get out before the rotten eggs began to fly told him that the fate of this talent still lay in the balance.

That being the case, he still had not only the possibility of tipping it, but the responsibility as an agent to pull up his socks, stay professional, and give it his best shot.

"Yeah, Ralf, the ratings *are* holding," he said. "But this is what I do, this is what you pay me for, agent's instincts, and my agent's instincts tell me the numbers are hollow. Madden hasn't copped to it yet, because Boy Genius or not, he's just a smart kid. . . ."

He looked straight into the mirrors of Ralf's eyeballs, layed a forefinger against his right nostril.

"But the nose knows, kiddo," he said. "They're not tuning in to laugh any-more. The ratings are holding because you're becoming a geek act. They're tuning in the way they would if they thought you might just bite the head off a live chicken on the air, but unless you start making 'em laugh again soon, they'll get tired of waiting to see it happen and tune you out."

"Hasn't the fan mail been way up since I became the captain of Starship Earth? Aren't the tie-ins moving better than the old Deathship stuff? Can't you see it, Jimmy? Can't you feel it? Something's happening. They're starting to *believe* in me."

"Trouble is, *you're* starting to believe in you," groused Texas Jimmy. "You've become a legend in your own mind. Pimply nerds are buying your tie-ins and frustrated hausfraus are mailing you their dirty underwear, the supermarket tabloids are giving you cover space, so you *must* be the Giant Turnip God whose shit don't stink."

"It's not *like* that," Ralf insisted.

"Oh yes, it is," Texas Jimmy told him. "It's an occupational hazard, kiddo. You know, I saw in one of those Roman costume epics, when one of these big hero guys gets to ride his chariot down Hollywood Boulevard through all the crowds of screaming groupies, they stick a guy behind him whose job is to keep whispering in his ear like I'm doing now, Ralf. *Mortal*, kiddo, just another vaudeville act."

Ralf looked straight at Texas Jimmy but it felt like there was no eye contact at all. This was the Ralf who had babbled on about candles and Tinkerbell on the air with such unfunny earnestness. Captain Ralf of Starship Earth peering at him out of Clark Kent's clothing.

"And what if it isn't?" he said.

Ralf got up, slid out from behind the bar and into the living room, and stood there amid the half-dead potted palms and rubber trees, as Jimmy swiveled on his stool to find himself pinned by those feverish eyes, so reminiscent of Lenny Bruce on a bad night toward the end of his slide.

"You read Lampkin's book, Jimmy?" he said. "*The Word According to Me?*"

"Yeah. So?"

"So what if I really am what he's got me saying I am? What if we really *do* make the future by what we do here in the past?"

"Well of course we do," Jimmy shot back in relief at hearing a more or less rational sentence. "What else?"

"So there's got to be a lot of futures up there in front of us, and none of them are any realer than any of the others until they happen, right?"

"So?"

"So if there's more than one future to send me back here, why can't there be more than one *me*? Maybe I can *choose* which one to be. And which one I choose decides which future sends me back, the Deathship or the Starship. Which decides which one we get."

"Maybe you're crazy as a bedbug!" Jimmy groaned, making a mental note never ever to let a client of his get anywhere near a sci-fi book again.

"Maybe," said Ralf in a cool, calm, reasonable voice that was a good deal less than reassuring. "And maybe I'm the Great Spirit of the World. How would I know?"

Texas Jimmy Balaban felt his scrotum drawing up into his pelvis as those eyes seemed to become windows into a place beyond his depth or desire to fathom.

"Maybe both," said that same calm voice of major insanity. "Look around at the world, Jimmy, and tell me that if it all *is* the dream of the Giant Turnip God, Uk-Ruppa-Tooty *isn't* crazy as a bedbug!"

"I gotta admit you at least got a point there, kiddo," Texas Jimmy was forced in all honesty to concede.

"So who can tell *whose* crazy dream it is? Yours? Mine? All of us. How would we know?"

Texas Jimmy Balaban was not the kind of guy who went around believing it was a good idea to go around wondering about what he believed in, he could well do without sci-fi, and one glass of bourbon was not nearly enough to have a serious effect on his mental equilibrium. Yet his instincts told him in gut-feeling terms that he was not accustomed to ignoring that there was at least *some* elusive truth hiding beneath all this craziness.

"So maybe I *am* the Dreamer. Or maybe I *am* just another vaudeville act. But if it *is* up to me, why *not* cast myself as Captain Ralf of Starship Earth instead of the Don Rickles of Darth Vader's Deathship?"

Ralf shrugged. Nothing changed in those empty eyes.

But at least the deadpan face cracked a human smile.

"Come on, Jimmy," he said, "in *my* pair of baggy pants, wouldn't you?"

12

"An' now for more a th' same crazy shit," Foxy Loxy groaned, which she knew from fuckin' endless experience was all she was gonna be able t'do about it. It was time t'sit onna gray blanket onna bed smelled a piss an' watch fuckin' TV.

Rat Thing always had them doin' it as soon as they got back t'the room—turn the TV on, an' flop down onna bed, near enough so he could reach out with her hand t'change channels, seein' as how they forgot to include the zapper inna price when she boosted it.

Loxy couldn't do nothin' else when Rat Thing made them watch TV but change th' channels an' bitch an' moan, an' the Rat Thing didn't even bother t'answer. But *she* could feel it there, stone still, not movin', not really thinkin', starin' outa her eyeballs at the screen, an' *it* could sorta make *her* feel what it was like bein' a Rat Thing there behind 'em. . . .

. . . like hunkerin' down inside a th' meat lookin' out th' ratholes in the skull at the all-seeing eye, the doorway into the Monkey World, waitin' and watchin' for what you were sent back here to do, whatever th' fuck that was, an' back there at th' other end a the rathole wormhole was th' *rest of you*, whatever th' fuck *that* was, th' machinery made you the top an' only predator inna Dead World where the Master Race ruled. . . .

Think Rat, an' it didn't matter what was on television, 'cause Rat Things didn't think th' way Monkey People did, didn't think like meat at all, didn't care whether it was news, *Star Trek*, or Midget Lady Mud Wrestlin', didn't waste no processing power deciding, scree, scree, scree.

'Cause *be* Rat, an' th' pictures went straight through the ratholes inna skull inta your beady little eyeballs an' right inta some kinda computer thing stuffed way inna back of your brain inna Dead World where somethin' cool an' hard as heavy metal ice *knows* what it's lookin' for, hee, hee, hee.

So all you gotta do is just sit there on the bed watchin' what's movin' past your all-seeing rathole like you was programmed t'do, like a fuckin' frog waitin' for the right fly, like a vulture onna rock waitin' for things t'die.

Be a Dead World Rat Thing, an' th' meat you was stuck inside had no need t'know what you were waitin' for, Foxy Loxy, 'cause *you'd* know the Enemy when *it* saw *you*.

'Cause it's after your Dead Rat's ass too, Loxy Foxy.

Was why it was here. Was why it was th' Enemy of everything clean an' cold and dead as a terminal garbage pail floating in the perfect darkness for a million years of the Master Race's rightful rule.

That's the way it was when a Rat watched TV, an' Rat Thing did mosta the thinkin' an' feelin' now, did the garbage can scroungin', an' took care a snatchin' enough money for this fuckin' room, an' about th' only times Loxy hadda feel human was when th' fuckin' chickenshit bastid ran squealin' back to the Death World end a the rathole in her brain having landed them in shit an' dropped her back inna driver's seat t' get their fuckin' rat's ass out of it.

Like boppin' along onna street smeared with sticky red goo carryin' a hot TV anna big bloody knife.

Could get kinda embarrassin' even if you was a top predator, ratfuck, so she ducked unner the first available stoop, rummaged inna garbage cans till she came up with some newspapers, an' mopped mosta the blood off.

Which didn't mean she didn't need a changea costume real fast, an' what with this brown crud dryin' on everything, mighta had a hard time gettin' inta Macy's.

On 14th Street, though, there weren't no bouncers or rentacops, it was all goin' on onna sidewalk, you could buy any fuckin' thing without havin' ta worry about them not lettin' a bloody fuckin' Rat in the door.

Easy enough t'buy one a those brown flasher raincoats only slightly used t'jerk off under inna fuck films, an' good enough to get her the fuck offa the street, 'cause even a bloody Rat inna raincoat had enough class for the East Side Belleview Apartments, or the Heroin Hilton as anyone scurvy enough to know about it called it, no questions answered or asked.

The Hilton was five floors of disgustin' broom closets, but caterin' as it did to junkies an' the occasional dealer *really* down on his luck, a few bucks a night got you a stinkin' hole like this about the size of the shitty cot you slept on anna toilet inna hall someone always shootin' up when you wanna take a shit . . . *and a strong steel door with a police lock.* Which was worth payin' extra for inna hotel fulla junkies always lookin' for stuff to snatch, like fer instance a fuckin' yellow color TV.

Took maybe three hours snatch an' grabbin' on your average day t'pay for the room, two if y' got hot, an' you could cram your gut full outa garbage cans in an hour two was you a halfway decent rat.

A Rat Thing hadda let the monkey meat sleep sometime, five hours a day would do, which still left mosta your day hunkered down here starin' out its eyeballs at the tube. . . .

But sometimes th' meat gave you a hard time, sometimes the disgustin' chemistry fucked around with th' processing, made it feel like the little monkey things onna TV was watchin' *you* with a million eyes, sometimes th' fuckin' meat tried *t'take back over.* . . .

So sometimes you hadda like *motivate* th' protoplasm, now didn't you, scree, scree, scree, disgustin' job, but a Rat Thing's gotta do it.

Sometimes you hadda give the meat sweet Rat dreams of wet caves of crumbling concrete an' garbage from Dumpsters been overflowing for a hunnerd years, tanks an' sumps an' sewer tunnels fulla proteins, carbohydrates, fats an' trace elements, hee, hee, hee!

Everything a Rat Girl needs inna Dead World, Loxy Foxy, an' so much of it for the top an' only carrion robot rodent, such an enormous corpse and no live competitors, like bein' a fistfulla maggots inna wholesale meat packing plant, you'll go on eatin' outa *this* Dumpster fulla goodies for a million years, scree, scree, scree!

Can't let th' Destroyer take such a wonderful world away, now can we, Rat Girl, hee, hee, hee?

When is an assignation not an assignation?

When it's a stiff pain in the ass.

Here Dexter Lampkin was, winding up Old Topanga Road in his red Porsche Targa with the roof panel out on a golden morning, a California Girl beside him, and the warm breeze blowing in her hair. About the only thing missing was Randy Newman singing "I Love LA."

But the babe in the right-hand bucket seat was Amanda Robin, nor did love in the afternoon seem to be what she had in mind.

"Jimmy's worried that you're turning *his* star client into a character out of *your* tie-in book, Dexter," she had told him on the phone. "He's afraid that Ralf is starting to believe he really *is* the Captain of Starship Earth, the Great Spirit of the World—"

"So?"

"So for some strange reason, Jimmy believes that this is a symptom of craziness," Amanda said wryly.

"And you?" Dexter had asked guardedly.

"I much prefer Divine Madness," Amanda told him. "But Jimmy believes that another symptom thereof is a decline in the laughter level soon to be reflected in the ratings. And there I think he has a point, don't you?"

"I don't get it, Amanda, what's this all about?"

"Jimmy thinks I'm a level-headed show business professional who can talk some sense to the sci-fi guy from outer space—"

Dexter staged a choking sound into the phone.

"—so he wants me to have a Dutch Uncle talk with you, and he was pretty insistent about it."

"Funny, you don't *look* Dutch," schticked Dexter. "And you're certainly not my uncle."

"But I know someone who also doesn't look Dutch who I think it's time for you to meet," Amanda Robin had told him cryptically. "He's not exactly my uncle, but he's not exactly *not* my uncle either. It's the Short Path, but it's going to take us time to get there. And don't plan on being home for dinner."

"What the hell am I supposed to tell my wife?"

"The truth," Amanda Robin had suggested. "Tell her you have to take a meeting with someone I want to put on the show who you think may turn out to be too much of a nutcase. She'll believe you when you complain about it sincerely. And you *will* complain about it sincerely to her, now won't you, Dexter?"

And he did, and Ellie had.

But the ease of it, or Amanda Robin's prediction of it, or both, had eaten at Dexter all the way to her place, and he found himself putting the Porsche through its paces on the drive up into Topanga, wringing it out, taking the curves with a maximum of g-forces, using the gearbox to maintain a satisfyingly high level of revs and engine howl, maintaining this style of driving all the way to the hippie refugee camp where Amanda Robin made her habitation.

Scenes like this perversely brought out the red-blooded technophilic American boy in Dexter, just as exposure to righteous Redneck culture brought out the rosiest granny-glasses-colored memories of his own countercultural flaming youth in Berkeley.

Amanda's rustic cabin in the deep and piney of this gentrified Appalachia had been more or less what he had expected, and while in another era he would have found such a patchouli nest conducive to romantically carnal notions, under these circumstances, he was happy to be back on the road again, to the point that he really didn't care where until they had climbed all the way back up out of Topanga and were approaching the intersection with Mulholland.

Here the choices were a descent down into the San Fernando Valley, a trajectory eastward toward Westwood, or westward toward the Pacific along a stretch of the crestline highway through the Santa Monica Mountains that Dexter had never before driven.

"So," he said, "just where the hell are we going, anyway? Which way do I turn?"

"Any which way but loose," Amanda Robin told him with a throaty little giggle disconcerting enough to have him glancing at her in annoyance.

Amanda laughed again, softening it this time with a smile that Dexter under other circumstances might have deemed radiant.

"Go west, young man, go west, where else?" she told him. "The highest road is always the path to the Palace of Wisdom."

Wheels within wheels within the Great Wheel, Amanda told herself mantrically, as Dexter Lampkin put on a display of phallocratic Porschely prana, screaming through the curves, roaring down the straightaways, passing everything he could find to pass by dropping down a gear and then standing on it in a manner that had the engine shrieking and roaring like a scalded leopard, as if he sought to convince himself of his mastery of whatever awaited him at the end of the road by demonstrating his command of this ultimate boy-toy.

Then again, *he* would probably contend that this was just her own femocratic take on this display of automotive cocksmanship, or, as Freud might have had it, sometimes a Porsche is just a car.

Wheels within wheels within the Great Wheel.

Dexter no doubt believed that the present perilous karmic nexus could be successfully transcended by using Ralf to market simplistic technocratic solutions to all the world's deep problems.

Wheels within wheels within the Great Wheel.

Jimmy Balaban might not know much about planetary salvation or evolutionary cusps, but he could smell a performer in the process of being eaten by the part he was forgetting he was playing.

"Fer chrissakes, Amanda, you know what I'm talking about, you can explain it to Dex, he's gotta stop feeding him these people got him more than halfway to believing he's the Wizard of Oz."

"Why me? Why don't you just put your foot down yourself?"

"And into *what*, huh? Look, Amanda, I know my own limitations. I can tell you guys what not to do, but not what to replace it with. Wise Lampkin up to the showbiz realities. Come up with some new angles."

"Like what?"

"How should I know? All I know is that if it goes on like this, it's gonna be a matter of which comes down first, Archie Madden's ax or the butterfly collectors from the funny farm."

Jimmy was right. The spectacle of Ralf thrashing around like a lungfish caught on the interface between water and air had become less than boffo and the completion of the evolutionary transformation was definitely in order.

But Amanda's vision of the nature of that transformation would no doubt have Texas Jimmy Balaban reaching for his bourbon with one hand and his Maalox with the other were she foolishly honest enough to try to explain it to him.

Wheels within wheels within the Great Wheel.

When the ridge road passed into serely wooded highlands all but devoid of the works of man, Dexter found himself cooling out into another mode of driving where the Porsche itself took over, gliding along at a speed natural to the topography of the road as it wound through the mountains, the gearshift handle moving in his hand with a will of its own to keep the engine purring out those good vibrations.

The sun was warm, the air was fragrant with dry pine resin and baking earth, and the illusion was that they could slip-slide up into higher and higher mountains forever, all the way to Alaska.

On the other hand . . .

"*Now* would you mind telling me where we're going, Amanda?"

"To the Palace of Wisdom," said Amanda Robin.

In this driving mode, Dexter felt free to take a sideways glance at that Giaconda smile and give her a dubious lip curl at this latest bit of mystification.

"Does it really matter?" she said. "It's a gorgeous day, it's the real California, and we're here together in neat red sports car with the top down riding the Short Path through it."

"The *short* path? We've been on the road for nearly an hour."

Amanda laughed. "Believe me, Dexter," she said, "today's little journey covers only a teeny-tiny part of the road that goes ever on."

"If you don't mind, lady, you can spare me the Tolkien."

"We're off to see my wizard," Amanda told him.

"*This* is the guy you want to book on the show?"

"Right. I've know him just about as long as I can remember. Maybe longer. He calls himself Hadashi."

"Just Hadashi? Like Madonna?"

Amanda laughed. "Oh, he'd like that one!"

"I don't get it," Dexter said. "You don't need my approval to book anyone. So why are you dragging me all this way out into the ass-end of nowhere to meet this guy?"

"*This* is your idea of the ass-end of nowhere?" Amanda said teasingly.

The sun glowed golden in an azure Californian sky. A hawk, possibly even an eagle, circled high above a fir-greened cliff, and he was driving his Porsche Targa through a glorious wilderness redolent with the perfume of the heartland of the continent.

Dexter laughed. "Okay, so this is not exactly a fate worse than death," he admitted. "But you haven't answered my question."

"It's simple," said Amanda Robin, "he wants to meet you. And you *need* to meet him."

Wheels within wheels within the Great Wheel.

As synchronicity so often had it, Hadashi had manifested himself in Amanda's timestream just when the karmic script seemed to call for him, with a phone call not four hours after her conversation with Jimmy Balaban.

"Hello, Amanda, I'm going to be in town for a while, so let's do lunch," he said, doing a take on a breathless agent.

"Hello, Hadashi," said Amanda. "How'd you like to be on television?"

"Why Amanda, I thought you'd never ask."

"Oh no, you didn't!"

Hadashi laughed.

"Well . . . not really."

Of course not.

Wheels within wheels within the Great Wheel.

Hadashi was just what was needed at this nexus.

Though she hadn't realized it until she heard his voice.

For what she hadn't dared to venture to Texas Jimmy Balaban was that the problem with Ralf was not the change from Deathship Jeremiah to Starship Captain, but the incompleteness of the transformation. Ralf, like a tribe of Monkey People fouling their treetops nests while their Eagle Spirit reached for the stars, was a butterfly struggling to emerge from the chrysalis of his metamorphosis.

Dexter Lampkin seemed to understand this within his own science fictional frame of reference, hence the tie-in book he had written, the guests he had been booking, in the sweetly naive belief that laying it all out like a Save the Planet by the Numbers kit would be enough to move the heart of the world.

But that of course was never enough.

There was only one way to complete the metamorphosis.

The Dreamer must be awakened.

Live in Prime Time for all the world to see.

And of all the people Amanda had met on the Long Path of her life, none seemed better casting for Opener of the Way than this guardian spirit thereof.

"You'll do the show then, Hadashi?"

Hadashi laughed. "Breathes there a being so enlightened that he will not put a lampshade on his head and expose the boils on his butt if it means seeing himself on television?"

Amanda laughed. "I had something a little more satoric in mind," she told him.

"Koans? You want koans? I gotta a million of 'em, each and every one 'em guaranteed to wake a used car salesman into full satori or double your previous incarnation back!"

"But seriously, folks . . ." Amanda said in a similar vein.

"Seriously, Amanda," Hadashi said. "You can count on me to give our would-be Zeitgeist Incarnate the good old cosmic hotfoot. But I'd rather not find myself up there discussing the photoelectric conversion coefficient of gallium arsenide solar panels in orbit around Venus with an overweight little green man in a propeller beanie."

"Well . . . Jimmy Balaban wants me to have a talk about it with Dexter Lampkin anyway. . . ."

"I have a synergetic notion," Hadashi had told her after she gave given him the short course in the geometrics of the intellectual casting couches at *The Word According to Ralf*.

"You usually do."

"What if your batty old guru insisted on discussing the guest list personally before agreeing to grace the proceedings with my mysterioso presence? Couldn't you persuade your skeptical Muhammad to take a meeting given by the Mad Old Man on his Mountain?"

"Maybe. But what for?"

"To poke a few sharp transcendental schticks through the bars of his logical positivist Faraday cage and give this awakening act an out-of-town tryout before we tackle the Ultimate Enchilada."

"But why not just tell him the truth?"

"Great idea, Amanda," Hadashi had told her. "Explain to your science fiction writer how you're going to take him on a magical mystery tour into the heart of the continent hidden in plain sight where his slumbering spirit will be wakened to full consciousness from its halfling sleep. Do it in twenty-five words or less, and win an all-expense-paid two-week vacation for two in scenic Pismo Beach!"

"We've got to plan these shows together," Amanda Robin told Dexter. "We've got to coordinate our bookings so we put guests together who *synergize.*"

Dexter found it appropriate that the road had come tumbling down out of the pristine mountain vastness and into a stretch skirting Lake Malibu, where the hill-tops had been bulldozed and the chaparral replaced by designer cedars and ice plants and water-sucking lawns fronting high-priced real estate for film colony trendies, just as she finally seemed to be getting down to show business.

"*That's* why you're dragging me to see to this Hadashi?" he groaned. "You're afraid I'll book someone who'll upstage your guru!"

"Something like that," Amanda muttered evasively.

"I haven't heard you complaining about my guests before."

"I wish I could say the same," Amanda zinged him dryly.

"Touché," Dexter admitted with sour gallantry.

"But whatever you think about my New Age weirdos, I'm not complaining about your pocket-protector-carrying space-cases."

"You're not?"

"Why should I, Dexter?" she said, dropping into a suspicious tone of sweetness. "Why complain about intelligent people who sincerely want to do their bit to save the planet? Who am I to say their hearts aren't in the right place when the changes they've helped you make in Ralf's act, as far as they go, are all in the right direction."

"*Huh?*" Dexter grunted, taking his eye off the road to goggle at her long enough to have to swerve raggedly to avoid hitting a Jensen Interceptor inching out from a side road. "But I thought . . . you said . . ."

"That Captain Ralf isn't making it?"

"Well, yeah."

"Jimmy's right about that, he isn't."

"But—"

"I said the changes were in the right direction *as far as they go,*" Amanda Robin said in quite another voice, a voice that seemed somehow quite out of place as they tooled along through this sunny gilt-edged exurbia.

"But I say the problem is that they haven't gone far enough," said that Amanda. "We've got to take them *all* the way, Dexter, you and me together. We've got to wake the Dreamer."

"Wake *who?*" Dexter Lampkin groaned.

Amanda sat there in the passenger seat for long moments watching the housing tracts thin out into an outskirts of estates and rusticated mansions more distant from the highway, trying to formulate an answer that he could not only understand on an intellectual level but accept on the deeper spiritual level he fought so hard to deny.

This was not a conversation she had planned on having.

But it would seem to have become unavoidable.

There she was, in a science fiction writer's Porsche, leaving the last of time-and-mortgage-bound civilization behind, heading toward a series of turnoffs, along ever narrower and more solitary roads seldom taken, higher and higher into the spinal cordillera toward the geologic chakra chosen by her lifelong guardian wise-guy, for a rendezvous with she knew not what.

As a golden oldie had it, it was like trying to tell someone about rock and roll.

"Do you believe in magic?" she sung at Dexter.

"I believe in the foma that make you strong and brave and happy, if that's what you mean," said Dexter Lampkin cryptically, whatever *that* meant.

Sauce for the gander, Amanda thought. "Right you are if you think you are," she said, "so turn right here."

With a grin of boyish devilment, Dexter Lampkin downshifted from fourth to third, then quickly downshifted again to produce a sudden jolt of deceleration and a squall of engine rap, whipped the Porsche through the ninety-degree turn with his foot on the accelerator, and came out of it roaring up the straightaway toward the foothills of the foothills of the mighty Sierras with a speed obviously calculated to be breathtaking.

————

Dexter found himself jouncing up a creekside road into a wilderness so deep and undisturbed that he might as well have driven through a singularity into an alternate California in another space-time.

In here, the road itself was the only visible work of man, following a creekbed deeper and deeper into the rockbound primeval heart of the continent. *In here*, it was hard to conceive of the fabled pioneers crossing such country in anything less than a Range Rover.

Harder still to believe that the smoggy sprawl of the Valley broiled in its hydrocarbons a few miles north of the farthest ridgeline. All that seemed geologic ages away, as witness how Amanda Robin's blather about awakening the Dreamer seemed perilously close to seductively plausible.

After all, *he* had flipped her Vonnegut's line about foma, useful lies that made you strong and brave and happy, and in a sense they were driving through one now. For this was not really some undisturbed primal Ur-California, but a little pocket universe magically embedded within the all-too-quotidian confines of the County of Los Angeles.

"So Ralf is bombing out as the Atman's court jester because he's stacking karmic Zs instead of awakening fully into his destined incarnation as the secret identity of the Zeitgeist and our job as associate producers of the Great Transformation is to arrange a sufficiently sharp whack with the old Zen pig's bladder to zap him into full conscious awareness thereof," Dexter blathered back at her.

"Not bad for talking the talk."

"I'm a *science fiction writer*, lady, it's my job to create three impossible things every day before breakfast."

"Oh, I see, time travelers from alternate futures seeking to bootstrap themselves into existence are ever so much more plausible."

Dexter laughed happily.

"Just because I write the stuff," he told her, "doesn't mean I have to believe it!"

"Why Dexter," purred Amanda, "next thing you'll be telling me you don't even believe in flying saucers!"

In the mood he found himself in, Dexter even laughed at that one.

However when Amanda had him approach the entrance to a narrow road up through the chaparral that seemed little more than an arroyo filled with gravel, the automotive karma seemed a good deal less sunny, and he stopped the car.

"In *there*?"

"That's the directions that Hadashi gave me."

"*Directions?*" Dexter groaned. "You've never *been* there? I thought we're going to see your guru. Doesn't he live here?"

"To tell you the truth, Dexter," Amanda told him, "I have no idea *where* Hadashi lives. He just sort of . . . manifests himself in the location of the moment. I've never been invited to this one before."

Dexter groaned again. "On this, you expect me to submit my suspension to this test to destruction?"

Amanda shrugged. "We've come too far not to follow the yellow brick road to its logical conclusion, now haven't we, Toto?" she said.

Dexter sighed, shrugged, cursed under his breath, then began inching it up the gravel pathway into the ever-deeper beyond, wincing every time a pebble pinged off the belly pan.

He glanced back over his shoulder as the gravel trail wound up and around a bend and the paved road disappeared entirely from view.

"Hey Gretel," he said, "I thought *you* were supposed to be dropping the breadcrumbs."

The drive up the unpaved track took less than half an hour, but it was a subjective automotive eternity. Subjecting his beloved Porsche to a surface like this was a species of barbaric betrayal. Worse still, the road being what it was, there was no correct gear to be in under these circumstances, forcing Dexter to shift so often that by the time they finally did reach the end of the trail, he had developed an incipient charlie horse in his left thigh from riding the clutch pedal, and the condition of those expensive Porsche clutch-plates was something he didn't care to think about.

The gravel roadway dead-ended into a little parking lot surfaced with the same crap. A dusty blue Cherokee sat in front of a low building which looked as if it belonged in a Japanese samurai opera.

A wooden framework framed beige paper wall panels. The doorway was more of the same with sliding panels. The little house seemed to have burrowed into the reddish-brown landscape, blending into the surrounding chaparral, only a stand of tall bamboo to the left of the doorway denoting an alien planting.

As they crunched along to the house, the front door slid open and a man came out to greet them.

Dexter hadn't known what he expected—Toshiro Mifune in full kit maybe—but what he got was a vaguely oriental-looking man of medium height with neatly brushed gray hair down to his shoulders, wearing white Adidas, white duck pants, and of all things, a Starship Earth T-shirt that showed he was in quite good trim for a guy whose finely leathered skin said he had to be somewhere between fifty-five and seventy.

"Hi, I'm Hadashi," he said in unaccented California English, offering his hand in the conventional manner.

"Uh, Dexter Lampkin," Dexter said, shaking it, "nice place you got here." He squinted around at the dry-looking wooden framework, the paper walls. "Only I can't figure out how this firetrap can possibly survive out here, and as for the rainy season . . ."

Hadashi, with a wise-guy twinkle, delivered a half-pulled punch to the paper door. Instead of his fist going right through it, it bounced off it harmlessly with a dull *poing*.

Dexter looked at the beige substance more closely, rubbed his thumb across it. Not paper at all, but some tough synthetic that only looked like rice paper. He gave the rough wood of the door frame a feel. It was hard as stone but didn't quite feel like petrified wood; either real wood that had been polymerized with something he had never heard of or a *very* high-quality plastic.

Hadashi laughed. "Not wu enough for you?" he said.

Dexter peered back at him quizzically.

Hadashi laughed again. "Hey, come on, don't be an asshole, as the Bauhaus said to the outhouse," he said, "it's only *form* that's supposed to follow function."

Dexter had the uneasy feeling he could end up liking this guy.

The structure reminded Amanda of a low-budget version of the Long Path monastery, a more subtly high-tech hermitage for meditative weekenders. There was a small kitchen behind sliding screens and a similar bathroom arrangement and a single room furnished in Pier One Minimalist.

Tatami matting on the floor. A low black-lacquered table in the center, surrounded by floor pillows and padded back rests that looked like converted camel saddles. A hibachi in the center of the table. A futon rolled neatly in one corner. A scroll of a seaside mountainscape done in Japanese style on one wall and a NASA photo of Saturn on another. A low black chest upon which rested a plain terra-cotta tray displaying a flower arrangement consisting of two dried sprigs of mesquite and a fresh branch of purple acacia blossoms. Two plain black halogen floor lamps that might have been bought in a Thrifty Mart.

Dexter gave it the inevitable Californian bank appraiser's once over and Hadashi the fish-eyed stare. "You *live* here?" he said.

"This is just the teahouse," Hadashi said.

"If this is just the teahouse, then where's the Big House?"

"Like many of the best things in life, hidden in plain sight," Hadashi told him. He crossed the room and slid open the panels at the far side, to reveal the back garden.

The walls of the house had been visually extended by two lines of bamboo fencing to the edge of a chaparral-choked ravine about twenty feet back, at the far side of which the landscape rolled upward in ascending waves of rock face bearded with green to the majesty of the high ridgeline. The area between the fences had been turned into a Japanese rock garden version of the landscape behind it by simply arranging some stones and trimming back some chaparral, and as it receded back from the house toward the ravine, the scale increased proportionally, so that nature arose fractally from artifice without a detectable interface.

And Amanda realized that the fencing did *not* extend back from the house in parallel lines but diverged outward with a painterly subtlety to force the perspective, to compress artful foreground and natural background into a single focal plane, a piece of architectural magic that all but had her squealing in astonished delight.

"Big enough for you, Dexter?" Hadashi said dryly.

Dexter found himself pondering technology as Hadashi performed the ancient eastern coffee ceremony, using the hibachi to boil a mixture of water, sugar, cardamom, and powerful Turkish coffee powder in an ibrik that looked as if it had been fabricated out of old tin cans in a souk of the far Arabian boonies.

Dexter was not such a city boy that his soul was not stirred by such a cunningly presented natural vista, but with the science fiction writer's Yankee-tinker-from-Mars attitude, he could see how the illusion had been worked. And as soon as he did, his perspective on the distinction between high tech and low was permanently altered.

Energy consumption and complexity were not necessarily a reliable peter-meter of gee-whiz technology, he was suddenly forced to realize. When something worked perfectly, no amount of R&D was going to make it better.

Whoever had created this garden had achieved such functional perfection with material technology no more advanced than a line of bamboo poles and the re-arrangement of some rocks and shrubbery. Yet it spoke of a conceptual sophistication that would not be archaic a million years from now.

The mixture in the ibrik foamed up in less time than it took a kettle to boil water for vile instant. Hadashi lifted it off the fire for a beat until the foam subsided, repeated the process twice within the space of a minute, and poured the results into shot glasses that might have come from any bar in the galaxy.

"Nice," said Dexter appreciatively upon tasting it.

The coffee prepared over a charcoal brazier in an apparatus that could be fabricated in any Third World back alley tasted at least as good as any prepared by the ultimate chrome-plated yuppie espresso machine and was infinitely preferable to the lukewarm dishwater produced your off-the-rack Mr. Coffee.

Hadashi touched the handle of the scrap-metal ibrik. "It may very well be," he said, "that future anthropologists from the Dog Star Sirius will declare that *this* was the invention that marked the evolution of the Monkey People into a more or less sapient species."

Dexter peered across the table at him.

"You read minds too?" he muttered.

Amanda Robin's guru smiled at him with Happy Face eyes entirely devoid of any hint of mutant slan telepathy.

"No," he said, "but I *do* read science fiction."

As Amanda sat there sipping at her coffee observing the proceedings like a hopeful psychic marriage broker, she realized that she had never shared Hadashi's presence with anyone else but her parents before, and that within the context of a cozy familial consensus reality. And the Hadashi evoked by Dexter Lampkin was transformed by this interfacing with the reality of Dexter's sort of consciousness.

This Hadashi could sit there jackpotting with a science fiction writer about science fiction, a subject which had hardly ever arisen between him and Amanda prior to the advent of Ralf.

". . . mistake many people made, didn't they Dexter, that *Dune* was really about ecology. . . ."

". . . three species and a ball of *sand*, some ecology. . . ."

". . . really about the experience of evolved prescient consciousness . . ."

This Hadashi could be one of the guys.

Of course, he could hardly have been one of the guys with her.

Or she with him.

It was a sudden satori.

We're *all* virtual people to each other.

Each of us evokes a different avatar of every other. Each avatar is an equally authentic constellation of aspects of the same essential being.

You could say that as soon as we interact with another consciousness, we even become virtual to *ourselves*.

Wheels within wheels within the Great Wheel.

". . . uh, read any of my stuff?"

"Well, I've read *The Transformation*," said Hadashi.

"And . . . ?"

The virtualities hovered like hummingbirds as a jay squawked in the scrub and Dexter's question hung in the warm resinous mountain air.

Wheels within wheels within the Great Wheel.

Why do I care what this guy thinks about a book I wrote years ago? Dexter wondered.

But he did.

Hadashi either really knew his science fiction or he had prepped to the nines for this meeting. He was one of those people with the elusive power to become your instant old friend. And there was something about this simple little house that hinted at hidden resources the nature of which Dexter couldn't even put his finger on.

Were those any reasons to be hanging on Hadashi's next words?

They must be.

Because he was.

"On a literary and technological level *The Transformation* is a better novel than *Dune*," Hadashi said.

Dexter could only beam his approval of that.

"And you've probably spent all these years since wondering why it never touched the heart of its times."

A cold wind raised the hackles at the back of Dexter's neck.

"And you, I suppose, can tell me?" he snapped.

"Sure."

Hadashi's disarming smile was not nearly disarming enough to disarm Dexter's ire, but then in this moment the smile of Madonna bare-assed and open wide wouldn't have been enough to do it either.

"Your fictional scientific conspirators worked out a detailed working model for a transcendent human civilization and figured out how to market it. Thanks to your manufactured galactic ambassadress, the Earth gets turned back into a garden, and humanity goes off on its starship ride, but when the Monkey People learn that they've been conned into it, she gets martyred for her troubles like every Lightbringer from Prometheus to John Lennon. . . ."

"Tell me something I don't know," Dexter said belligerently.

"In *Dune,* the technology and the ecology are silly compared to what you worked out, but the Lightbringer is convincingly portrayed as a transcendently evolved consciousness who becomes god-king of the universe," said Hadashi. "Which is much more likely to have readers leaving the novel humming the theme song than your recourse to the usual Crucifixion Blues."

Dexter's mouth hung open.

"Shit," he managed to mutter when control was restored to his lips and tongue.

He had never been whacked over the head with an editorial insight of *this* magnitude before in his life.

Or wanted to be.

For this was not a joyous revelation.

"Don't feel so bad about it, Dexter," Hadashi said, rummaging around for something under the table. "The New Testament of the Christian Bible went through four drafts and never got it right either."

He pulled out what looked like a Mason jar of corn likker. "Think of it as a major career opportunity, Dexter," he said plunking it down under Dexter's nose. "The best and the brightest have all bombed out trying to make it work as tragedy, but you get a second chance to do it right as farce."

Dexter eyed the moonshine speculatively. "Is *this* what you've been drinking?" he said.

"Highly recommended for cosmic story conferences," said Hadashi, placing three plain white ceramic eggcups on the table. He filled them with the brew.

Dexter sniffed at the liquid in his cup. It looked as clear as water, the fumes coming off it smelled about 120 proof, but behind it were all sorts of overtones of suspiciously complex essences.

"What *is* this stuff?" he demanded.

Hadashi laughed, broadened it into a grin, held it. "Why, the Water of Life itself, what else?" he purred slyly. "Eau d'Vie, Kicapoo Joy Juice, White Lightning, the Universal Solvent known by many names to every good old boy in the galaxy!"

"Sure it is," drawled Dexter. "The last time I heard that one the stuff turned out to be duck tranquilizer."

He squinted at Hadashi across the fuming elixir.

"And who's the producer at this meeting anyway?"

Hadashi clinked eggcups with Dexter. "Shall we drink up and find out?"

Dexter shrugged, accepting the inevitable.

"We whose brains are about to fry salute you," he said, brushing his cup up against Amanda's and giving her a hooded look as he lifted it to his lips to tell her that, while he knew that he had been set up for this, he was accepting the challenge as a free agent.

"Heey, not bad!" he admitted in pleasant surprise.

For instead of the palate-searing backbite of raw corn liquor or medicinal alcohol, Hadashi's so-called Universal Solvent was as velvety smooth as a well-aged

Genever, even more powerful by the taste of it, and roiling with a well-balanced witch's brew of daunting complexity in that gustatory co-dominion where smell and taste combined.

A pleasant glow suffused outward from his stomach, muscles that he hadn't realized were tense began to relax, and a sense of humor about this situation began to emerge.

"*Now* can we please start this meeting?" he whined in the petulant voice of his least favorite producer after the story editor showed up ten minutes late in the office. Hey, why not, the Gucci boot was on the other foot for once, and he might as well enjoy it. "Okay, we'll have the pitch now," he said, leaning back expansively and playing a more avuncular minimogul.

"The pitch?" said Hadashi.

"I'm here to audition your act for the show, remember," said Dexter, flicking phantom ash from a giant green phantom stogie, and folding his arms across his chest pompously. "So what's the premise?"

Hadashi seemed to find this funnier than Dexter would have imagined. "Anything you like, C.B.," he grouched back, not entirely succeeding in swallowing his laughter.

"Anything I like?"

"I'm a man of many parts, Dexter," Hadashi said. "Perhaps you've noticed?"

"For the purposes of *this* production?"

Hadashi smiled softly. "For the purposes of the current production," he said, "let's go with the premise that I'm a time traveler from—"

"Forget it!" Dexter groaned. "We're already up to our ears in time travelers!

"A time traveler from the *best* of all possible futures," Hadashi said in a suddenly much more resonant and serious voice. "The future according to Dexter D. Lampkin. What do you say, D.D., have I gotten your attention?"

Amanda watched with professional curiosity as Hadashi got to his feet and went into his act.

"After all, *your* best of all possible futures is no more virtual than any other, now is it, D.D., so why shouldn't *someone* get to be from it? Don't we deserve some airtime under the Equal Access Laws?"

He strode across the room into stage center. Behind him a mountainous vista rose seamlessly from his sneaker tops to the peaks of the far ridgeline. Thusly framed in the fractal magic of the cinematic landscaping, he loomed like a colossus.

"Behold the man of the best of all possible futures!" he declared grandiosely.

Amanda had never seen Hadashi act before—or maybe she had never seen anything else—but either way her professional curiosity was rapidly turning to professional admiration of the performance.

Not that she was the audience.

Hadashi was playing the scene as if Dexter Lampkin were indeed a producer auditioning him for the part. As indeed Dexter virtually was.

"According to your script, D.D., I come from a garden of a planet bedecked with jeweled cities of light cakewalking in glory toward its rendezvous with galactic destiny. . . ."

Dexter's attention was captured by the thespian spell Hadashi cast as he walked ever so slowly back to the table, a mesmerized cobra caught in the snake dance of the mongoose.

"Powered by the forces of the quantum flux itself, we create whatever we desire from the elemental particles we winnow from the atomic plankton of the starry seas! We decant Busby Berkeley chorus lines of tap dancing tyrannosaurs just for kicks and we each have the complete working manual of the universe on computer chips implanted in our brains!"

He stopped right in front of Dexter.

"We're the crown of evolutionary creation!" he declared with a TV pitchman flourish. "We're the perfect masters of matter and energy! *We're hot shit!*"

He laughed. He grinned at Dexter.

"Voila, the Transformational Man! *Just* the way you wrote it, D.D.!"

He sat down. He shifted abruptly to a breezy showbizzy tone.

"What do you say, D.D.? Do I get the part?"

Amanda would seem to have already fallen under the influence of Hadashi's elixir, for she heard virtual worlds of sly ambiguity in these words delivered thusly, as if a doorway were opening to reveal another doorway and another and another, a recessional of realities that would sooner or later meet its own tail in a möbius loop.

Dexter-the-Producer gave this incarnation of Coyote-the-Trickster the cold-eyed scrutiny of an agent regarding the fine print in a fifty-page film contract.

"You want to do the show as *my* version of the Transformational Man?" he said slowly.

"Why not?" said Hadashi. "Why not have Captain Ralf meet a perfect master from a future in which his Mission Impossible has long since been accomplished?"

"That's you?" said Dexter.

Hadashi's eyes sparkled. Became doorways.

"Right I am if you think I am," the Trickster said in a deadpan voice, and Amanda found herself virtually believing it.

"Somehow I don't quite buy it," the Producer said in the next instant. "There's something missing."

"Why *whatever* can that be?" Hadashi said slyly. "A perfect master of matter and energy isn't good enough to get the part? What do you *want* from your poor Transformational Man, D.D.?"

"Something else!" Dexter found himself saying.

The stuff in the eggcup must now be coming on with a rush, for he felt as if his skeleton had been plugged into an electric socket, as if he were poised on the brink of one of those stoned cosmic revelations that will make absolutely no sense in the morning.

And yet in the process of observing his mind thinking this very thought, he realized that on an even higher level his rational facilities were as tight and well-tuned as his Porsche.

Something else.

His psychic tachometer told him he was peaking at about 6000 rpm on a psychedelic, and therefore there might conceivably be some reasonable doubt as to whether the secret of the universe had truly been revealed.

But on the other hand . . .

The cold equations told him that if that *something else* hadn't been missing from Hadashi's pitch based on his own novel, then *The Transformation* would have worked according to the plans of his heart's desire, the world would be riding high, wide, and handsome toward the Starship Earth future, and the three of them wouldn't be here looking for the Lost Chord.

Ergo: there *was* a Lost Chord.

Dexter tried to extricate himself from the singularity that had just been punched through the center of his conceptual universe.

And failed.

Once inside, logic could not return him to the quantum clockwork universe on the other side of the event horizon.

There was *something* that the dance of matter and energy did not conjure.

And yet the reality of it was verifiable by the very laws of the dance.

They had just been used to prove its virtual existence by demonstrating the consequences of its absence.

Cam Carswell would love this!

"Something else?" said Hadashi.

The elixir, an acting trick, his own overactive imagination, whatever, Hadashi's voice assumed the resonance of authenticity. The story conference routine had been tossed into the dustbin of history several millennia ago, and the consciousness behind that voice, that little smile, those amusedly tranquil eyes, really did seem to be speaking to him from another time, his fictional creation or not.

"Why *whatever* could that be?" that virtual being said.

The music to the words, the curl of the wave, the same thing that the world has lost somewhere along the yellow brick road to Tomorrowland, Dexter found himself thinking.

But no psychedelic white lightning was going to have him giving voice to thoughts like *that.*

For if he had known how to bring *that* light into the world, he would've written himself his visionary best-seller, and if he persuaded himself he could do it now, the next step would be for him to drape himself in L. Ron Hubbard's toga and proclaim himself the Giant Turnip God.

Mortal, Caesar, thou art mortal.

Stoned or not, *do* try to remember that.

"A superior *consciousness,*" he said.

For the humans of any advanced millennial civilization would have had to have evolved a level of consciousness beyond our own just to have gotten that far without doing themselves in.

"If you were *really* my Transformational Man, Hadashi," Dexter said, "*you* having this conversation with *me* would be like *me* renting a gorilla suit and popping back a million years to explain the morality of nonviolence to the Jungle Man."

Hadashi beamed at him like a beatific Buddha finally experiencing the enlightenment of a particularly dim-witted monk.

He threw up his hands in a gesture of gentle comic resignation.

"Alas," he sighed, "all too true."

Dexter broke up.

"You win, Mr. Unnatural, you got the part," he said, and laughed again.

He just couldn't help it.

Who could?

You laughed or you didn't.

And that too was proof of the existence of something that no technological mastery of matter and energy could conjure up from the void.

Namely laughter, the immaterial, transtemporal Universal Solvent itself.

_____

It seemed to Amanda that Dexter Lampkin's sudden burst of laughter had been an awakening, the sound of a long-shut doorway creaking opening within him.

"Okay, Hadashi, you're on, I *do* believe, you *can* do a Transformational Man that'll stand up to Captain Ralf," Dexter said.

Then he frowned. "But given his present state of the Starship stupors, I'm not so sure *he* can stand up to *you*. I mean, what's the point in showing him up?"

"The point is not to *show* him up," said Hadashi.

"The point is to *wake* him up," said Amanda.

Dexter essayed a jaundiced look in her direction. "What are you gonna do, stick a transformational fart-cushion under his ass?"

This was becoming exasperating.

Dexter Lampkin was on the edge of realizing a major satori, and *realizing* was indeed the word, for the enlightenment had *already* occurred in the core of his being, and he was now seeking to prevent its conscious realization by constipated act of will.

Amanda gazed directly at the mask of his face, seeking to open her eyes fully to him, to turn them into what the hoariest of clichés proclaimed: windows into the truth of her soul. For if Dexter was to become a fully-conscious spiritual being, the time had come to treat him as one.

"We want to wake the Dreamer," Amanda told him forthrightly. "Just like you."

"*I* want to wake up some mythical Zeitgeist I don't even believe in?"

"Come on, Dexter, who's kidding who?" Amanda told him edgily. "You write *The Transformation*, you create a Deathship Jeremiah and then turn him into a Starship Captain, but you're not trying to play 'Good Day Sunshine' to the Zeitgeist?"

"Don't know the tune, lady, and I don't do 'Melancholy Baby' either."

Amanda felt her gaze turning a bilious yellow, and that jaundiced look wasn't less than the sincere truth of her soul at the moment either.

"Come off it, Dexter," she told him, "if you haven't been trying conjure up the Eagle whose feet got cold after alighting on the Moon, then the Great Spirit of the World itself is using us all to get back into show business."

"Spare me the Giant Turnip God," Dexter drawled.

Why was this man so determined to hold his spiritual breath till his soul turned blue?

Highly evolved consciousness though Amanda might like to fancy herself, possessed of the patience of a saint she now discovered she was not.

"Be real, Dexter," she demanded, "it's not like we're asking you to believe in Big Daddy in a white beard or the power of pyramids to sharpen razor blades and improve the potency of pot!"

"You're not, huh? Then who is this Dreamer we're supposed to wake up?"

Amanda took a long deep yogic breath, held it a beat, then exhaled slowly, and when she spoke again, she used all of her acting technique to sincerely portray the truth within.

"Who are we to know, Dexter? We're like a couple of Neanderthals playing with a TV set dropped in our laps by our far-future descendants. We can't even conceive of what's going to come through when we turn it on. But it can only be something on a higher level which we can hardly expect to comprehend until we get there ourselves."

She leaned closer to Dexter, reached out, placed her palm on the back of his hand, took it as a good sign, that if he did not reach out to take it, at least he didn't pull it away.

"The Zeitgeist Incarnate?" she said. "A consciousness from the future seeking to communicate with its long-lost virtual ancestors in the only way your precious laws of physics will allow? The Atman? The Godhead?"

She smiled as warmly as she knew how at her fellow Earth creature. "Come on, Monkey Boy, how can we conceptualize beings spiritually superior to ourselves?"

"*Spiritually* superior yet!"

"*Morally* superior then, Dexter," Amanda told him. "Any consciousnesses a thousand years of evolution older than us would have to be a thousand years wiser and therefore morally superior to monkey business as usual just to have gotten that far. That's the Word According to Dexter D. Lampkin, so you've *got* to believe it, now don't you, D.D.?"

"Do I?"

"It's logical, Dexter," she found herself snapping at him petulantly.

"You want me to believe in morally superior beings beyond Man's poor power to comprehend, but you aren't talking about ghosts in the quantum machinery, is that it, Miz New Age Mystic?"

"No, I'm not!" Amanda snapped back angrily. "Why can't people like you get it through your carbon-fiber-reinforced skulls that the things of the spirit really *do* exist? And that not everyone who considers them openly is an intellectually vapid ditz!"

Wow!

What kind of sacramental elixir was this that drew to her conscious awareness the full passion of this seething resentment whose existence she had never before quite recognized?

"Sure there are plenty of sleazy power-tripping crystal-gazing gurus to the stars and sincerely crazy ignoramuses out there giving the things of the spirit a bad name," she found herself declaiming to her own surprise in an adrenal redneck burn.

"So I've noticed on the supermarket checkout lines," said Dexter.

"But that doesn't mean we evolved from monkeys into people just by turning shinbones into spaceships like that stupid science fiction movie says! That doesn't mean that anyone who denies there's such a thing as the soul doesn't still have one despite himself, Dexter Lampkin!"

Amanda found her own vehemence liberating, empowering as a politically correct feminist might contend. But gender had nothing to do with it. This was a passion that had nothing to do with *any* material form.

This was a passionate patriotism of the intellect. This was who she truly was as a soul. This was the central belief around which her consciousness cohered. And that itself was proof positive that the things of the spirit existed, that their traces were graven right there in the Maya of the world.

She had said it a thousand times before.

It was the sigil of her spirit.

But never had it been more heartfelt. Never had she meant it more.

"What is, is real!"

Dexter's cock had sprung to attention upon first sight of Amanda Robin; she was an attractive female animal with the theatrical training to make the most of what natural evolution had granted her. But any hard-ons generated by her presence had previously been greeted as low treason by his higher cerebral centers.

Because up until now he had never respected her. And Dexter prided himself as sufficiently evolved to consider sexual passion for a woman he disrespected the moral and intellectual equivalent of duck fucking.

What *had* Hadashi put in that moonshine?

What magic was this?

How could Amanda's passionate defense of what he himself considered the indefensible raise her to full personhood in his eyes?

But it had.

Why did it make him truly *like* her for the first time?

But it did.

"You're beautiful when you're mad," Dexter said.

It was about the stupidest thing he could say.

But it was true.

"And you've got a cute little cleft in your chin too," Amanda shot back.

Then she leaned close enough for him to smell her rosewater perfume, close enough to see himself reflected in her eyes.

"Not to mention the weight on your soul of the Great Unwashed's assumption that you believe in little green men in flying saucers from the Lost Continent of Atlantis yourself, *Mr. Science Fiction Writer*," she reminded him, slaying him softly with his own sad song.

"Both ears and the tail," manfulness forced him to admit.

Amanda gave him a slow, vampy, conspiratorial wink.

"So, if we're gonna get called birds of the same Californian nut-cult feather," she said, "what say we *schlock* together?"

And once again Dexter found himself laughing at a joke on himself.

And found it liberating.

This, no doubt, was what Amanda would have called a satori, a moment of enlightenment that altered one's consciousness forever. Yet he had not been required to swallow any mystical belief system in order to attain it.

For what Dexter had discovered was that laughter was indeed the Universal Solvent. Whole egos could dissolve in it chaotically without warning. And what emerged from the quantum flux a beat later could not but be changed by passage through the comedic discontinuity.

"Okay, Amanda, I'm one and you're another, so let's wrap the monkey's tail around the flagpole and see if there's anyone home to salute it," Dexter said in higher spirits at the other side. "And whatever we summon forth from the trashy deeps, I will believe it when I see it, be it the Zeitgeist Incarnate, or the Giant Turnip God, or Elvis himself in Liberace's suit of lights."

"What is, is real, Dex," Amanda said, giving his hand a little squeeze, "that's all I've ever asked anyone to believe."

"You got yourself a deal, Miz Vibrating Lady," said Dexter.

"All *right*, Mr. Sci-fi Guy!" said Amanda, slapping his palm as if he had just tossed in a three-pointer at the buzzer to pull out the game, and raising his hand into a high five.

———

Hadashi slowly uncoiled from his half-lotus.

"Well, folks," he said in a fatuous TV daddy voice with what seemed to Amanda a lubriciously unfatherly leer, "this is the page in the script where the sidekick tells the romantic leads that three's a crowd."

"You're leaving? You sure you can drive?" she said in that feminine Los Angeles tone of voice which said *I can't and you're leaving me alone with a guy who can't either.*

"I'm already late for my next meeting in Burbank," said Hadashi in a tone of voice running a sitcom turn on the setup.

"*This* stoned? On *that* road?" said Dexter.

Acknowledging in a gentlemanly fashion that all this was indeed a pavane in which all three of them accepted the parts they had been chosen to dance.

"It would hardly be the first time," said Hadashi. "This is, after all, *Los Angeles* and those who adapt, survive."

"*Now* what do we do?" said Dexter.

In the sitcom that Hadashi had dropped them into, it was the perfect guilt-free desert island setup. Dexter could almost on some fantasy level see himself making it explicable to Ellie. . . .

Well after all, our host dropped a peyote button in our martinis and did a fast fade, and there we were alone in a cabin in the woods with hours of stoned boredom to kill, and no cable TV, hah, hah, hah. . . .

But this wasn't a sitcom setup.

It might not be without its comic aspects, and it might be a setup all right, but Dexter doubted that whatever was going to happen next would be played for laughs.

It was one of those days that made the California Dream golden. A desert-dry eighty-five degrees, and only a faint brown sparkle in the air above the far ridge-line horizon to mar the pristine blue of the cloudless sky.

"Well, it's a warm sunny day," Amanda said, feeling a sunflower tropism drawing her out into the bright sunshine, "so why don't we get some air?"

They walked out into the fractal garden toward the ravine, ever-dwindling giants strolling through bonsai landscapes that grew ever larger and larger as they led up and out into the real thing. No sight or sound of man. Sweet and pungent resins baking off the chaparral. Birds chirped and twittered in the trees and in the underbrush in the ravine, where lizards skittered, and nameless rodents slithered, and where, as they arrived at the brow of the overlook, one of them got into it with a raucously aggressive jay.

Beyond the ravine, the land fell away to an austere mountain meadow, and then rose, and rose, nature's own fractal landscape, ridgelines rippling upward to the crown of the horizon, the visible peaks but the foothills of the mighty coastal cordillera that marched up the western spine of the continent until mountains of Himalayan proportions stood nose-to-nose with the polar ice cap.

What is, is real.

That eternal primal immensity was real, but so was the magic that allowed Amanda to stand here not an hour's drive from the mallscape of the San Fernando Valley and experience the slow geologic will of the planet. Down there, all up and down this coast, the suburbified cities of man sprawled in the valley lowlands, an amoeba of housing developments, shopping malls, and industrial parks oozing along the nutrient trails of the freeways, wrapped in an atmosphere growing ever more Venusian.

But there was an *up here* that magically remained, a mountaintop reality whose tendrils, like a continental nervous system, reached from this spiritual spine down through the canyons, even into the mystic urban hillscape of Hollywood that gave otherwise unlovable Los Angeles what spirit it had.

"Marvelous, isn't it, Dexter?" Amanda said softly. "Here we are, half an hour away from the Valley, and it's as if humans never even walked these mountains, as if all we've done to this planet is just pond-scum on the surface of an immense ocean . . ."

"Very poetic," said Dexter, "but that brown stuff on the horizon's not your virgin coastal fog. Wherever you go, there we are."

"Oh, Dexter!" Amanda groaned.

"What is," he said dryly, "is real."

"But sometimes we can *choose* what's real," Amanda insisted, "sometimes all you have to do is step sideways to slip from one reality into the next."

Dexter eyed her peculiarly.

But then Dexter D. Lampkin was a peculiar person.

He would use Ralf to turn a Deathship planet into his vision of a Starship Earth and yet accuse *her* of voodoo for seeking to address the Zeitgeist.

He would dismiss as beneath his serious intellectual attention anyone who held the fundamentalist interpretation of a book written on animal skins with plumes two thousand years ago to be the last word on the true nature of physical reality.

But he'd twist himself into incredible contortions to convince himself that the present edition of the rule book had been laser-etched on titanium tablets and handed down from the cyclotron atop Nobel-wreathed Olympus by Drs. Einstein and Faust.

"For instance, Dexter," she told him, "you could go north through these mountains all the way to the end of the continent without seeing a town, or a freeway, or so much as a single Denny's."

She smiled at him, almost there in her mind's eye, with the sun warming her brow, and the birds squabbling in the ravine, and the works of man long ago and far away.

"Haven't you ever dreamed of doing that, Dexter?" she asked him. "Haven't you ever wanted to make the pilgrimage along that Long Path?"

Dexter's face crinkled like the ice on a pond on a spring morning breaking up after a frosty night.

"Follow the mountains all the way to Alaska without coming down?" he said. "Up above the ticky-tacky and the smog, with the piney breeze blowing in my hair?"

His eyes glowed rosily. "I've *done* it, Amanda," he said. "In bits and pieces anyway, the part between here and San Francisco often enough, and once from San Francisco to Eureka, and once from Portland to Vancouver, and who knows, some day . . ."

"You *have*?" Amanda exclaimed with girlish admiration, and no little amazement, reaching out to squeeze his hand without a conscious thought. "You *walked* all the way to San Francisco? You walked from *Portland* to *Vancouver*?"

"*Walked?*" said Dexter, regarding her as if she had recently emigrated from Mars. He laughed boyishly. "Hey, Daisy Mae, when this good old Laurel Canyon hillbilly finally gets to take the ultimate moonshiner's ride along the Californian ridgeline, I'll be doing it in my car."

"In a *car*?" Amanda moaned.

"Not *a* car," Dexter told her grandly, "*my* car! The Platonic archetype of automotive perfection! My *Porsche Targa convertible*!"

Amanda eyed him narrowly. "You *are* putting me on."

Was he?

He seemed years younger. His smile was radiant. And as he leaned into her body-space, he gave off a heat that was almost sexual.

Almost?

"Even as your Indian lad traditionally sought out a vision of an animal spirit to be the totem of the warrior he was to become, so does every red-blooded American boy seek out his Platonic ideal of automotive perfection," he said with a perfectly straight face. "The car of his dreams."

He had magically become attractive. Before Amanda's eyes, the charismatic spirit who after all had written those books seemed to have emerged from wherever he had been hiding to enliven this otherwise unnoteworthy fleshly corpus.

"For some it might be a Ferrari Testarossa, or a Rolls-Royce, or a 300SL, or an Eldorado convertible. For me it's the Porsche Targa that sings the song of my self!"

His Dreamer had awoken.

Or at the least, the true teller of tales had come out to play.

"I thought you were the guy who didn't believe in ghosts in the machinery, Dex," she chided him playfully. "But here you are going on about a pile of steel and rubber as if it had a *soul*."

"Well *of course* it has a soul!" Dexter told her. "It's a *Porsche*!"

"Right," said Amanda, "your *car* has a *soul*. It's *alive*."

The day was glorious, the stuff he had taken popped the old synapses with no unpleasant body effects, and Dexter found himself having a high old time with Amanda Robin, of all people.

"Is the Earth really alive?" he said. "No, it's a ball of rock and water and gas, but you *do* believe it has a soul, now don't you, Amanda?"

It had been many a year since Dexter had gotten so righteously stoned with a woman of true allure. And in this moment, up here, under these influences, he found that that was indeed what Amanda was.

"Come on, Dexter," she said, "we're talking a living world."

"If a planet, then why not a Porsche?" said Dexter. "If a range of mountains thrown up by geological forces entirely oblivious to thee and me, then why not a car lovingly and consciously crafted to please the human heart?"

"Boys and their toys!" scoffed Amanda, but she *was* grinning at him, and he *was* cooking.

"Why can't people who insist that rocks and trees have souls see that technology can be beautiful? That a Porsche Targa convertible has as much soul as a symphony by Beethoven or the paint Picasso smeared on canvas?"

"You seriously compare your *Porsche* to a *Picasso*?"

"Sure," Dexter told her. "All art is matter processed by technology, whatever soul a Porsche or a Picasso has can only be acquired in the manufacturing process, and my Porsche'll run away from old Pablo through the chicanes besides!"

Amanda laughed. "The Zen of Technology!" she exclaimed. "What next, the technology of Enlightenment?"

"As a matter of fact—"

As a matter of fact, she had just reminded him of a story he had heard, a story by which a technophilic sci-fi guy might make himself comprehensible to a New Age heart.

"As a matter of fact," he said, oozing a comic surfeit of lounge lizard suavity, "that reminds me of something Alan Watts said just before he died."

"I wouldn't figure you for a reader of Alan Watts," said Amanda.

Perfect straight line.

"Oh, this isn't in any book," Dexter told her. "It was in personal conversation—"

"*You knew Alan Watts?*" Amanda gushed, regarding him much as a matron of a certain persuasion would had he let it slip that oh yes, now and again, he *had* been in the habit of downing a six-pack or two with Elvis.

As, of course, he had known she would.

For Watts, the great popularizer of Zen in the dawn's early light of the Beatnik fifties, could as fairly be said to be the godfather several times removed of her New Age as the King was the godfather even further removed of the Summer of Love.

"Well, not exactly . . ." admitted Dexter.

Actually, not at all. Actually, Norman Spinrad had told him the story. Actually, it had happened to *him*. But Dexter figured Norman wouldn't really give a shit if he rewrote it into his own first person for current purposes, seeing as how he wasn't around to impress the lady with it anyway, and Dexter was.

"Actually, I just served as a driver for this knockout French journalist lady who wangled the last interview that Watts gave before he died," Dexter lied. "I just sat there like furniture while she interviewed him."

"You just sat there like a dummy through a whole interview with Alan Watts?" exclaimed Amanda. She eyed him narrowly. "Sounds like you played chauffeur to a French journalist so you could get into her pants," she said teasingly. "Did you?"

"A gentleman never tells," said Dexter. "The point is that I did finally get to ask one question at the very end."

He grinned. He presumed to press a forefinger to Amanda's lips for a beat. "What would you have asked?" he said.

Amanda gazed right back at him, clearly captured by the tale.

"Damned if I know," she said.

Dexter shrugged. "The interview was the usual metaphysical pit-pat which I could well do without. So I admit it, I wanted to throw him a high hard one. So I asked him what he thought of all those millions of people out there using LSD as a technological shortcut to satori instead of diligently following the arduous natural way of Zen."

"Two spiritual brownie points for you, Dex," said Amanda. "So what did he say?"

Dexter beamed at her, trying to mime a guru doing a good old boy. "He just grins, and looks right at me. 'Why ride in an oxcart,' he sez, 'when you can take a jet plane?'"

Amanda laughed, but the story had achieved its satoric intent. Alan Watts had not only made his point but the story had also been a window into the real Dexter, the Dexter Lampkin of his own Dreamtime.

For *that* Dexter was precisely the teller of tales like that one, which were true in exactly that higher sense whose very existence the sci-fi wise-guy sought to deny.

The real Dexter *did* believe that his car had a soul. The real Dexter agreed with Alan Watts. Because the real Dexter wasn't the techno-nerd he pretended to be, but a techno *romantic*; one of those previously incomprehensible people, mostly male, who could *love* a car or a computer as a painter loved his completed canvas or a shinto priest a random accretion of rock and water, imbuing mere matter with a kind of soul in the very act thereof.

And the story had opened Amada's eyes to a concept whose possibility she had never considered before.

The Zen of Technology?

The Technology of Enlightenment?

Transcendent technology?

Why not?

Once you recognized a chemical as a valid path to enlightenment or granted a soul to a Porsche, you realized that the technology of transcendence was all around you, had existed ever since a caveman had first transferred a piece of his soul into pigments daubed on rock, thereby transcending time and death via technology to speak to the human hearts of his spiritual children a million years removed.

The Monkey People had been at it ever since. Writing, movies, spaceships, designer drugs, Porsches, Dexter's transformational planetary Starship, it was what humans did that made them more than monkeys—conjuring being out of nothingness, imbuing matter with their own spirit, seeking even to transcend the realm of Maya by technological means.

Could it be done?

Could a chemical contain satori?

Could a car be worthy of love?

Can the two of us use the transcendent technology of television to manifest the Zeitgeist in prime time or even conjure a voyager from better days from the virtual mists of fictional time?

Was this the voice of Mephisto murmuring temptation in Dr. Faustenstein's ear?

Or was this the voice of the Great Spirit of the World, the clarion call of the Eagle that had transcended the bounds of the Earth itself to land upon the Moon?

A roar like the distant rush of mighty waters drew Amanda's gaze suddenly skyward, where the neat white contrails of a high-flying 747 inscribed the signature thereof across the heavens themselves.

Amanda clapped her hands in sheer delight at the sign the gods of serendipity had chosen to grant her, nor in that moment did this technological actualization of the primal human dream of flight seem a desecration. Au contraire.

Amanda laughed.

"What's the joke?" asked Dexter.

Amanda pointed at the airliner cruising up the spine of the continent with the triumphant insouciance of a great silver swan, to deposit its grumbling passengers a bad meal and a mediocre GP movie later halfway around the world.

"Wherever you go," she said, doing Dexter, "there we are."

Dexter laughed back at her, and it seemed quite natural when he took her hand. It seemed natural to stand there hand-in-hand silently until the song of the 747 faded back into the birdsong and nothing was left but an arrow of cloud pointing to the crown of the world.

After which, it seemed perfectly natural to move a little closer and go inside.

X-rated images of himself with Amanda Robin had from time to time been sent northward from Dexter's nether region, but they had been rejected by his editorial shit-detector as low penile porn unworthy of his higher erotic imagination.

These pheromonal urges had been all too easy to resist, since on top of the usual adulterous guilt there would have been the total stupidity of having a sexual relationship with someone you shared a less than copacetic working relationship, not to mention having to converse with the sex object afterward.

Now, however, he had, in a sense, met the woman of his dreams.

As a pubescent lad whose imagination quickly transcended the imaginative limits of commercial stroke-books, Dexter had created for himself a sexual fantasy with a large blank space in it which most any girl could have filled if only he could have figured out how to talk to one.

It was a simple generic fantasy that it needed no specific female lead to give fourteen-year-old Dexter his sweetest hard-ons. He and a girl had been thrown together into an adventure. The plane had crashed in the jungle. They had escaped from the Nazi space pirates and fled into the back alleys of Mars. They had discovered the Lost City of Mongo on a scuba dive into the Bermuda Triangle.

The specific setting didn't matter. The girl could be anyone his dick pointed out. What turned him on was the conjunction of sex and adventure.

This, Dexter learned somewhat later, was a common fourteen-year-old fantasy. This was the formula for a species of young adult fiction, and a staple of the adventure pulps of the dim distant past aimed at adolescents of a somewhat more advanced age. Much later, after surfeiting himself with far more grotesque scenarios as a convention cocksman, he had achieved the jaded wisdom to realize that it had a certain innocent masculine nobility.

Indeed, he realized if only in retrospect, he had met Ellie inside some fantasy not that dissimilar, and they had more or less tried to live it out together in their bumbling fannish way in the Berkeley days.

It was only after the thrill of being the Golden Couple came and went with the times, with marriage, with Jamie, that Dexter achieved the middle-aged maturity to realize that he didn't *want* to give up the formative wet dream of his fourteen-year-old self, that it was nothing to be ashamed of.

So it was a fourteen-year-old's ideal of manhood, but what was so bad about that? Any thirty-five-year-old who could honestly say he had grown up to become what his fourteen-year-old self had wanted to be had a right to consider himself the hero of his own tale.

Even a fourteen-year-old on the wrong side of forty had a right to believe that the Princess might turn up on his doorstep, that destiny could call his heart to battle, that he could still in every sense rise to the occasion, riding forth with his Valkyrie Sancho Panza to bring the Light back into the world.

A harmless middle-aged fantasy, right, a foma to make a guy thickening a bit about the middle feel brave and strong?

On the other hand . . .

Wherever you go, there you are.

And where Dexter was now was right in the middle of that adolescent fantasy, or rather the mature adult version, far more complex than anything dreamt of in his teenage sexual philosophies.

There he was, in a secret cabin in a galaxy far, far away, and there she was,

kneeling on an unrolled futon before him, the unvoiced question already answered in her eyes; his Princess Leia, Bonnie to his Clyde.

But this wasn't just the simple X version.

This was the *real* adult version.

In which two people who did not inhabit the same conceptual planet had under the influence of some righteous dope concluded an adventurers' pact to do
something for what they had managed to convince themselves was no less a cause
than the fate of the Earth.

The mature science fiction writer had written this story several times himself
and knew full well that it was an egoistic power fantasy of the sort responsible for
any number of successful fantasy trilogies, sicko fannish cults, and major world
religions.

But the fourteen-year-old living out his fantasy of Dexter Lampkin future rose
eagerly tumescent to the summons of destiny, and the mature science fiction writer
found himself along for the ride, transformed into the realtime figment of his
fourteen-year-old dreams.

"A penny for your thoughts," said Amanda Robin.

Dexter laughed. He felt brave and strong.

"These days the minimal acceptable rate is a nickel a word," he said. "So you
owe me twenty cents," he said.

"Do I?"

"What is, is real," said Dexter, presuming to take both her hands in his. At this
moment he would have presumed anything.

"Is *this* real, Dex?" said Amanda, making the question somewhat rhetorical by
leaning deeply into his body space. "Do we really understand why we're going to
do this?"

"Don't we?"

"Because we crawled behind the barn and made a secret pact to rub the magic
lamp together and hope a good genie comes out?"

"Something like that," Dexter said, and kissed her tentatively on the lips. She
allowed the kiss to linger for a moment, then pulled her mouth gently away.

"Doesn't this seem a little kinky to you?" she said. "Until about an hour ago,
this would've been what I believe the boys call a grudge-fuck." She eyed him narrowly, but couldn't keep from grinning. "You sure it isn't?"

"Whatever turns you on," Dexter said dryly.

"And what do *you* think turns me on, Dex?" Amanda purred. "I'd love to have
your professional visionary opinion."

There were times when even the most imaginative fourteen-year-old was forced to admit he was out of his league, and allow the mature teller of tales to carry the burden of the blarney.

"It's not wine and roses or whips and chairs for you," Dexter told her slyly. "You're a sexual mystic. You want to feel mighty archetypal forces moving through you so you can believe they exist. *That's* what this is going to be all about, and like the song says, love ain't got nothing to do with it. For you, it's about magic."

Amanda's lips pouted into slack amazement, her eyes opened wide. She smiled up at him, shrugged a surrender.

"You are not without wisdom, Dexter Lampkin," she said, touching a playful finger on the tip of his nose. "The magic, however," she said more seriously, "remains to be seen."

And she placed the palm of her other hand forthrightly upon his righteous fourteen-year-old hard-on, completing the circuit between boy and man, between flesh and fantasy, between her Dreamtime and his.

The Earth had moved no more than usual, but magic of a sort, Amanda believed, had indeed been done.

The Porsche crawled the last few yards to the end of the gravel drive, and as Dexter turned onto the pavement, he sighed and flashed her a disarmingly boyish grin of relief curiously akin to the manner in which he had smiled down upon her when the preliminaries had been concluded and they lay naked together, if never heart-to-heart then finally belly-to-belly.

The true foreplay had long since been concluded, it had been verbal and quite prolonged, and what had been revealed during the process was far more arousing to Amanda than the sight of a somewhat overweight middle-aged man in the altogether.

Physical foreplay therefore seemed beside the point to both of them, since neither of them could believe for an instant that love and kisses had anything to do with it.

So it *had* to be magic. Mighty archetypal forces *had* to be moving through them, for what *else* could've brought such an unmatched pair to this unlikely moment?

When Dexter's cock slid into her, what began was no act of passionate tenderness but a mating dance of wary equals. Yet Amanda felt her spinal chakras opened wide by the pure unsentimental energy of a tantric dialectic.

Surely *that* itself had been a magical conjuration.

Dexter glanced at her in the waning light of the golden afternoon, came close to winking, then stood on the accelerator, popped the clutch, and whipped his way up the gears with a flourish as they boogied on up the road.

Amanda smiled at him as the breeze ruffled her hair in the open Porsche.

Just as Dexter drove this piece of high-performance machinery with a boyishly passionate artistry that made it throb along its power peak with a life he had now taught her to feel, so had he brought her body up through the gears with an ordinary level of skill transfigured by the sincerity of his zeal to find that perfect sweet spot and stay there through all the changes, his cock at one with her rhythms and surges, as his hands and feet and the seat of his pants were at one with the soul of his Porsche.

He had driven her up to her peak patiently and with concern for the dips and bends in the road, and when she came, he looked right into the eyes of her ecstasy, his eyes windows into the innocent self-satisfaction of a boy in bliss.

He had made love to her, no, he had fucked her, in the same spirit with which he drove his bright red dream machine.

Boys and their toys!

But what Amanda had seen through the windows of his soul when he came had been a deeper magic. For an archetypal force indeed moved through him with his cock at her throttle or his hands on the wheel, the Faustian yang to her feminine yin.

Like the sexual mystic, the cocksman of the Porsche Targa convertible found soul *within* matter, found the path to transcendence *within* Maya's dance.

The Earth hadn't moved. But worlds had.

Hers and perhaps his.

Amanda laughed aloud in magical delight.

"What was that for?" Dexter asked.

"For a boy and his Porsche," said Amanda.

Down from the crest of Mulholland and through the hillside suburbia into the San Fernando Valley came Dexter, down from the influence of Hadashi's water of life, down from dropping Amanda off at Big Rock, down from the magic mountain, down into the rush-hour traffic.

Wherever you go in LA, sooner or later, here you are.

And where Dexter was now was creeping home in the stop-and-go traffic, already forming various lame excuses which Ellie would not examine too closely, and trying to digest the events of the day while breathing the freeway's concentrated smog.

What is, is real.

That seemed to be Amanda's mantra, and if you had to have one, you could sure do worse.

He had fucked Amanda Robin.

That was real.

They had made love.

That was not.

Far from being an act of love, what they had done had been almost impersonal, a ceremony to seal an alliance to mutate Ralf into the Virtual Man from the Transformational Future or the incarnation of the Great Spirit of the World, whichever turned whoever on. Dexter had finally come to believe that was real.

That they were evolutionarily equipped to understand what they would summon forth if they succeeded, that was not.

While Dexter was no stranger to what he considered "safe adultery," having indulged himself in his fair share at conventions, he had never had an *affair* or contemplated one. Loveless adultery was no threat to his marriage precisely because it was emotionless fucking. And he knew damn well he was not about to embark upon an affair with Amanda Robin, for he had felt nothing resembling love belly-to-belly with her, maybe not even called passion.

In that sense, in terms of any effect on his marriage, his passage with Amanda had been "safe adultery" too.

In terms of its effect on his worldview, however, it was another story, for their fucking had been energized by a powerful energy indeed.

That was real.

As soon as he was inside her he had felt it.

An hour ago it would've been easy to comprehend as a grudge-fuck, let me show you what hard science can do with the right advanced equipment, Miz New Age Mystic. But there had been no grudge left to fuck. This fuck wouldn't have happened at all if the grudge hadn't been charmed out of it.

And in the unsentimental act thereof, facing each other clear-eyed even through orgasm, it had seemed that some conjunction of forces *had* brought them here together, *was* moving through them, something vast and soul-stirring yet quite impersonal.

Or . . . *transpersonal?*

Dexter was no mystic, sexual or otherwise, or so at least he told himself, but when he came, there was an eternity for a moment in which he had seemed to disappear, in which this was a mating by loas of the timelines, an act of sexual voodoo whereby Amanda's archetypal forces danced through their flesh.

But to believe *that* would've required Dexter to believe in magic.

And reality was entirely governed by entirely discoverable laws of matter and energy.

Magic was *not* real.

Right?

The universe had bootstrapped itself into being out of a random flux of nothingness, and space-time was a Bach fugue of virtual geodesics, and behind the illusion of linear causality was the transtemporal face of chaos.

But *that* wasn't magic, right?

The bottleneck where the 101 crossed the 405 was not the road to Damascus, but that was where Dexter was when he received his illumination.

No indeed, that *wasn't* magic.

That wasn't Alan Watts or Amanda's guru Hadashi talking.

That was Cam Carswell bucking for his Nobel Prize for Physics.

Foxy Loxy didn't need no fuckin' watch toldya th' hour anna day a the week, 'cause th' Rat Thing had some kinda *TV Guide* clock thing hooked up to the wire in her brain told th' Rat Girl when it was time for *The Word According to Ralf*.

Well not exactly *told*, 'cause the voice in her head didn't bother t'exactly talk to her much no more, 'specially in fronta th' TV, mosta the time Rat Thing just took over the necessary meat, surfed th' channels for fuckin' hours atta time, five minutes a channel seemed t'be th' limit, ball game, monster movie, station break, or th' news, didn't matter . . .

But when it was time for the asshole inna stupid green suit, she'd start twitchin' her tail onna mattress like an alley cat in heat, wires in her bones hummin', nose goin' like honkin' down tons a crystal meth, like smellin' a whole fuckin' steak at the bottom of the garbage can.

Seemed like Rat Thing was a big fan of th' Starship Captain, well sorta, never missed a show, an' it was the only thing he had her watchin' alla way through, even if half the jokes the Starship Captain told didn't make much sense an' th' assholes he had on with him were about as funny as havin' your period.

Rat Thing'd stare at this Ralf guy outa the holes in her head the whole fuckin' time hardly let her eyeballs blink, an' every once inna while it seemed like th' motherfucker was givin' the ol' evil eye back, like th' two of them was a couplea fuckin' Mafiosa hit men with contracts on each other eyein' each other across a hotel lobby tryin' t'decide when the shit was gonna come down.

When she asked Rat Thing what the fuck was goin' on, she didn't get no answer. Rat Thing didn't answer none of her questions no more. Rat Thing mostly used her meat like some kinda fuckin' robot, like it didn't even wanna bother with botherin' that she was there.

Sometimes it felt to Loxy, when Loxy remembered it was Loxy doin' the feel-ing, that *she* had gotten stuck inside *Rat Thing's* head somehow, could feel what it felt, could think what it was thinkin', but seein' as how she was feelin' an' thinkin' *Rat*, that didn't mean she could unnerstand it. . . .

Like this shit witha Starship Captain. As soon as his fuckin' ugly face came on, she was fuckin' *droolin'* for it, whatever the fuck *it* was!

Was somethin' like bein' *horny* for th' motherfucker, which didn't make a whole lotta sense, seein' as how Ralf was about as sexy as a ten-dollar insurance salesman trick, an' the thought a fuckin' a monkey made her wanna puke these days anyway.

Yeah, was like she was stuck inside the brain a somethin' had somethin' like a *hard-on* for the Starship Captain, that Rat Thing was bein' turned on, comin' to attention like a sailor at a strip show.

Only wasn't some kinda rat prick was gettin' all hot an' hard t'stick it in, was only a *little* like bein' horny, was a *lot* more like bein' th' White Tornado back there at th' Dead World end a th' rathole, a lot like bein' Freddy Krueger witha Big Ripper in your hand stalkin' *just* th' right special someone t'make your day. . . .

. . . thirty seconds . . . twenty-five . . .

Texas Jimmy Balaban fidgeted at the edge of his chair in the control room watching the clock count down to showtime and the tsuris his nose told him was going to happen.

Logically, Jimmy shouldn't have been worried. Amanda and Dex had had the meeting he had insisted on and from all appearances it had come up roses. After all the endless tummeling between them, they had been in complete agreement on these two guys, for the first time Jimmy can remember each was enthusiastic about the other one's guest.

"Don't worry, Jimmy," Dexter told him. "I've seen both these acts, and these guys are terrific air personalities."

"The chemistry is right, this is going to be . . ."

"Synergetic."

"Right, Dex, synergetic and copacetic."

Uh-huh.

Except Amanda came to the studio to catch the show live about every third week, and Dexter hardly ever, but tonight they both just happened to show up.

And when Jimmy suggested they catch it in the control room and not clutter things up backstage, after the dance of the musical folding chairs ended, here they were sitting together practically holding hands.

The nose knows, but maybe better it shouldn't.

For what was coming off Dex and Amanda was the fishy odor of behind-his-back deals, the smell of nutso shortly to happen, and something Texas Jimmy had sniffed on himself all too often, the scent of a dick which had recently been where maybe it hadn't oughta.

Five . . . four . . .

Jimmy dimly remembered an ancient TV show called *You Asked for It.*

Three . . . two . . . one . . .

And whatever *It* was gonna turn out to be, Texas Jimmy knew that he couldn't claim he hadn't.

"It's . . . *The Word According to Ralf*!"

Cam Carswell had done himself up as the Hollywood version of Mr. Science Wizard in a blue denim shirt with a white ascot, hand-pressed blue jeans, and a tweedy brown jacket with actual leather elbow patches.

"I *was* beginning to wonder what you were saving me for," Cam had said when Dexter had called him.

"It's kind of hard to explain," Dexter had told him, which turned into quite an understatement when he tried.

"Let me see if I understand this, Dex," Cam had said. "Your mystical coproducer has booked her own guru onto the show to play a mutant psychic superman from a sequel to *The Transformation* that never got written? And you want *me* to make an appearance as the voice of sweet reason? You expect a future Nobel Laureate to endanger his reputation as a serious scientist by making such a public spectacle of himself on television?"

"Come on, Cam, you've done convention panels that got a whole lot sillier."

"True," Cam had admitted. "So I'll do it, but on *one* condition. You *must* bring along a joint of *exactly the same stuff* you've been smoking!"

The joint that Dexter had snuck in the toilet with him would seem to have done its work, as Cam came striding and glowing onto the set as if he was about to deliver the Nobel acceptance speech for which the world was so impatiently waiting.

"Hello, Ralf, I'm Cameron Carswell, the world's greatest quantum cosmologist, and it's virtually a pleasure to be in your virtual presence tonight," he burbled before Ralf could do an intro, glad-handing him as he took his seat on the set.

Ralf gave Cameron Carswell the narrow look of a boxer beginning to suspect that the pug who had climbed into the ring with him might not be the setup he had been promised.

"I'm glad to see you're so impressed with yourself, Professor," he said somewhat edgily.

"Why shouldn't I be, Ralf, I'm quite an impressive guy," said Dr. Cameron Carswell, Ph.D. "I know more about the nature of matter, energy, and time than any other living human . . . *and* I'm a snappy dresser too!"

Ralf's face fell open and hung there long enough for Cam to preempt any punch line. He grinned disarmingly at the camera, mugged, shrugged, and delivered his own on himself.

"And modest to a fault as well."

Amanda hadn't rehearsed with Hadashi, but they had given some serious thought to the question of what sort of persona a more highly evolved consciousness should present—to costume.

They decided to go No, dressing Hadashi in loose black pajamas with a hood that covered everything but his face. When he glided out onstage, the effect of a detached presence floating in on the void was sufficiently unsettling.

Hadashi had told her that he wanted to be introduced as a time traveler from the Starship Earth of the Year 5000 who just wanted to be called Joe.

Ralf made the intro with a certain reluctance. "I'm told you claim you're a hotshot from the Year 5000, but you want to be called just plain Joe. . . ."

"Yes, Ralf, given the present evolutionary stage of your consciousness, it would be better to just call me Joe, because we've evolved so far beyond what you can now comprehend that you wouldn't even believe me if I told you what my real name is, let alone understand why."

Ralf sighed. "I know I'm not gonna respect myself afterward, but okay, *what* and *why*?"

"In the Year 5000, every man is named Elvis," said Hadashi. "Because every man's the King."

Texas Jimmy Balaban was not amused.

"Just terrific," he groused, "two minutes into the show, and your straight men've turned Ralf into a turnip twice."

"Come on, Jimmy," Amanda wheedled coyly, "you were the one complaining he was turning into a turnip already."

"Nothing like a little competition to get the old adrenaline flowing," said Dexter in a similar vein. "It's what made America great."

"It's what gets the loser canceled," Jimmy told him.

Ralf sat there stewing from the last zapper at his expense long enough for the steam coming out of his ears to become almost visible. By the time it died away, he had at least assumed the combat stance of a stand-up club act facing less than brain-dead hecklers.

"So according to you guys, *I'm* just one of the Three Stooges from the twenty-second century, and *you're* Bud Ego and Elvis Costello," he rasped, playing directly to the camera. "Looks like we're gonna have a real *highly evolved* show tonight, don't it, Starship Troupers?" he said, scratching apelike at his armpit.

Lame though it was, this piece of business gave Jimmy cause to hope that maybe Ralf had at least gotten the wake-up call.

"Okay, Elvis," Ralf said as the director held him in close-up. "I ain't nothin' but a hound dog, so why don't you get off my blue suede shoes and tell us what it's *really* gonna be like when Starship Earth arrives way up there in Graceland?"

In the cutaway close-up, framed in the black costume hood, the deadpan face looked like a planet floating in space.

"I would if I could, but I can't, so I won't."

"Why not?"

Not good. He had forced Ralf to feed him a straight line again.

Joe-Elvis didn't crack a smile. Even the eyes stayed blank.

"It'd be like trying to tell a chicken why a fireman crosses the road," he said. "Like trying to tell a monkey about rock and roll."

No fluke, Jimmy was sure of it now. Amanda's boy had moves.

Ralf, it appeared, had copped to this too.

"You hear that, Dr. Zarkov?" he said, turning the play to Dexter's Herr Professor. "Monkey Boys are easy. You think you're so smart, but we don't really have enough intelligence between us to know when it's being clobbered with a brick by Mighty Mouse here in Krazy Kat's pajamas."

Dr. Cameron Carswell flashed him a broad smile actually directed at the camera, which he seemed to have the instinct to know was on him.

"Well after all, Flash, the Year 5000 is a long way from now," he said, slathering on a vaguely Mittel European accent. "How far do you think *you'd* get trying to explain the Animal Liberation Front to the Emperor Ming?"

Bad news, and good news, thought Texas Jimmy.

The bad news was that Ralf was getting pummeled by a couple of amateurs. The good news was that it seemed to be getting to him.

"Sounds like what happened at a gig I did in a biker bar, only the animals there weren't all that liberated," Ralf shot back with a little of the old crackle and pop. "They knew enough to empty the beer bottles first, but not enough to figure out you were supposed to *kill* the cats before you threw them."

Jimmy could feel Ralf's energy level rising in proportion to his ire. He was beginning to show a little of the edge he had lost when he put on that stupid Starship Captain suit.

Jimmy stole a quick sidelong glance at Dexter, who gave him a little self-satisfied grin back.

Nothing like a little competition to get the old adrenaline going? What made America great?

Well, this stuff wasn't exactly great, and America wasn't exactly rolling 'em in the aisles this season either, but maybe Lampkin had a point.

The nose knows, and Texas Jimmy's was smelling something like the sulfur of burning match heads igniting kindling, the thin distant chemical aroma of something trying to happen.

Amanda was beginning to wonder when *the show* would evolve to a plane of consciousness higher than Ralf's brawl in a biker bar.

"Well you see what I mean, then, Ralf," said Hadashi. "*Those* guys' brains were no better than a caveman's—"

"Tell me about it!"

"And *your* brain is no better than theirs—"

"Hey—"

"—and three thousand years from now, *our* brains won't be better than *yours* either!"

"So—"

"Yes, Ralf," said Cameron Carswell, "the human brain stopped evolving about the time we started *talking*—"

"—which explains a lot about *Washington*—"

"—because once the lunatics came down out of the trees and took over the asylum, the software started evolving thousands of times faster than the hardware ever could, and biological evolution was over."

"So we're still driving the same old model in the Year 5000," said Hadashi, "but we've had *three thousand more years* on the clock to figure everything out."

"You got it all figured out, huh, Joe?" Ralf said in a penetrating rasp, trying to regain control by sheer volume and rapid-fire delivery. "You figured out how to balance the budget without collecting any taxes, how to put the ozone back in the hole, how to cure AIDS and cancer and acne, how to stuff yourselves with pizza and chocolate cream pie all day long and not gain an ounce, and hey, I guess you even figured out how to make crap flow *up*hill!"

Amanda watched it work for a beat, and then watched Hadashi knock him back with a self-satisfied grin.

"Sure we do," he said. "Sure we can. We know everything there is to know and we can do everything there is to do."

There was a long beat of silence. Amanda could hardly imagine even Robin Williams ad-libbing a capper to *that*.

"You . . . know . . . everything? You . . . can do . . . everything?" was the best Ralf could manage.

The director covered with a close-up on Hadashi. Framed in the blackness of his hood, his face floated serenely in the video void like Planet Buddha.

"We've had *another three thousand years*, Ralf," he said. "Way long enough to learn all the secrets of the material universe including the perfect conversion of matter to energy and vice versa. A golden age of wine and roses that will last until the stars grow cold. We've cleaned up the atmosphere and rebuilt the ozone layer. We've built cities in space and terraformed planets. We've turned the Earth into a garden better than any Eden. We've raised a thousand extinct species from the dead and created a thousand others that never were. We've had the power to do everything but the impossible for over a thousand years."

Hadashi paused. His smile was beatific. Able to hold this moment of silence. This magic moment. The moment that Amanda had been waiting for.

"The *wisdom* to know what that is took a little longer," he said with a gentle sigh.

"The masters of matter and energy!" said Cameron Carswell.

"The *perfect* masters of matter and energy, if you please," said Hadashi. "But there are things we know we will never be able to do."

"Such as?" said Cameron Carswell.

"Such as traveling faster than light," said Hadashi. "Or keeping love from breaking our hearts."

Oh yes, thought Amanda, we've segued a long way from Hollywood! It was unheard of for a talk-show host to let a guest go on so long without doing something to draw the spotlight back on himself. It was unheard of for a *comedy* talk-show host to let the action drift into deep waters like these without even trying to get a laugh.

But Ralf hadn't. He just sat there listening, his eyes gazing inward, a strange smirk at the corners of his lips sardonically mirroring Hadashi's Bodhisattva smile.

Now, though, he visibly emerged from his trance. He turned to stare full-face into the nearest camera. The star *willing* the director to put the shot back on him if he knew what was good for him, willing the red light to come on.

The Dreamer awakening from his sleep.

"*Or traveling backward in time?*" he said.

Texas Jimmy Balaban found himself reaching into his breast pocket for the cigarettes that weren't there, which reminded him he hadn't brought any Maalox either.

Jimmy could've used both of them. For that matter, a belt from a hip flask wouldn't have been out of order.

Texas Jimmy did not consider himself a mental giant. But he was not in the habit of being taken for a sucker either. And he was getting the feeling that he had been.

The director had Ralf in close-up and Ralf had put on your standard goofy jack-in-the-box grin. But through it Jimmy could see the original model—the slightly psycho leer and gleaming rhinestone stare of Punch feeding a setup line to Judy.

Amanda's boy did a fairly good Groucho, down to the waving of the phantom cigar. "*Absolutely* impossible," he said, "and if I were *you*, Ralf, I wouldn't believe anyone was from the future who told you otherwise."

"Then *Star*ship Earth *couldn't* have dropped a comic like me back here to get the *Death*ship show canceled, and a clown like *you* can't possibly be here either."

Amanda's wise-guy did a decent slow take at the camera, looked slowly around the set.

"Why . . . why . . . he's *right* folks, why . . . this is just a *television show*! Why . . . why *we're* really just a couple of Jokers in a pack of cue cards!"

"Speak for yourself, Monkey Boy," said Ralf in the overrich overround voice of an old-time musical comedy senator. "*I* am the Giant Turnip God!"

It was a moldy old line that Texas Jimmy had heard Ralf use far too many times, but the way he delivered it now—the power he put behind it, the crazed sincerity beneath the send-up—raised goose bumps on the back of Jimmy's neck.

"*Any* comic would *have* to be a giant turnip to let his agent talk him into playing the *Titanic* about ten seconds before the ship hits the fan," Ralf oozed.

He smiled, if you could call it that, as the director went to close-up on him.

"And we've just been told it would take a miracle for me to be here with you tonight. So I guess I've *got* to be Uk-Ruppa-Tooty, now don't I, Starship Troupers?"

The glow in his eyes owed more to Billy Graham than Billy Crystal.

"It's *your* show," said whatever refugee from the Actors' Studio Amanda had slipped into that black ninja suit. "You're the Captain."

"So it is," said Ralf in tone of lunatic sincerity. "So I am."

Those eyes seemed to suddenly get even brighter, like one of those cartoon characters just got a two-hundred-watt idea.

"I guess it's time I woke up to it," he said. "Quien sabe, Kemo Sabe, maybe I have already?"

Texas Jimmy Balaban didn't know from actors. Maybe this Method crap worked for them. Maybe they could handle forgetting who they really were and losing themselves in the part. Maybe it was good dramatic theater.

But Jimmy knew from comics. Comics had no one to play but exaggerated versions of themselves, and you didn't have to be Sigmund Freud to figure out that *that* was a part you couldn't afford to get lost in.

Worse still, when it happened, it usually wasn't funny.

"Kind of hard to know, ain't it, Starship Troupers?" said the fuckin' Starship Captain. "We can dream we're *anything*, right, Superman, Marilyn Monroe, a walking, talking, giant sewer rat . . ."

Tell me about it, asshole! thought Rat Girl.

And it seemed like the motherfucker was, seemed like those fuckin' blue lights down there at the end of the ratholes of his eyes was lookin' right at her.

"Yeah, when you dream, you're anyone, and then you can have one of those dreams where you dream you wake up and, wow, you're Elvis, or the star of *The Word According to Ralf*, or the Great Spirit of the World, or a wise-guy from the year 5000."

"Only you're still dreaming?" said th' fuckin' weirdo in black.

"Could be," said the Enemy. "How would you know?"

"You could pinch yourself," said th' weirdo in black, an' he reached out an' gave th' Captain a big one.

"Ow!"

"That hurt, didn't it?"

Seemed like a kinda good idea, an' Loxy tried t'give it a try sorta, but nothin' was movin', the fuckin' Rat Thing wouldn't let her, th' ratfuck wasn't havin' any.

"But I could've been dreaming it hurt, right? Like the old song says, *life* is but a dream tra-la, and maybe we're all the dreamer. How would we know?"

"It's your show, Mr. Giant Turnip God, so why don't you tell us?"

"So it is . . . so I will . . ."

Th' face inna fuckin' yellow TV *was* for sure lookin' right at Rat Girl now, th' Enemy, th' Deathworld Destroyer!

"Hey, why not, it's easy when we know we're all dreaming the same dream to-gether."

Th' motherfucker was lookin' right down th' rathole at her with th' razor-blade smile of a great big fuckin' cat *knew* she was there.

"Which dream is that?"

"*This* one, what else?" said the Enemy. "The one that's *on television*!"

"What's *really* real is what's on television, we all know that, don't we, Starship Troupers?" said Ralf mugging a crazed grin at the camera like Zippy the Pinhead. "So behold the Captain of your Starship! If there *is* a Great Spirit of the Boob Tube, ain't I it?"

If looks could kill and he wasn't such a gentleman, the one Texas Jimmy Bala-ban flashed Amanda Robin would've been good for at least a pop in the mouth.

"Come on, Monkey People, you believe *anything* you see on television, now don't you? You think you're dreaming *now*? But of course you were *wide awake* when you bought all those used cars from Richard Milhouse Nixon, and a chim-panzee's straight-man as president! Come on, Starship Troupers, wouldn't you rather let a kinder and gentler dream in a Starship Captain monkey suit sell you a one-way ticket to Tomorrowland?"

Jimmy hadn't seen the legendary fiasco when Mort Sahl had freaked so far out live on the air that someone had pulled the plug, filling something like ten full minutes with dead black screen. He hadn't seen the sweet little old grandma sit down at the piano, tinkle the ivories, and proceed to belt out two choruses of "Get out the shotgun and kill all the niggers and Jews" before they managed to give her the hook. He hadn't seen the newsreader who blew his brains out on the air.

But Jimmy had the sinking sensation that he was witnessing the birth of one of those television legends, something that maybe twelve million people were seeing now but fifty million would somehow remember seeing later.

"A-men, A-men, A-*men*, A-*men!*" Cam Carswell sang out, clapping his hands like a one-man tent-show congregation. "I *do* believe! I have *seen* the light!"

Dexter had begun to wonder if Cam was ever going to get into the act, whether the joint had been such a hot idea, if this was going to turn out to be like one of those convention panels where one of the people counted upon for loquacious brilliance had gotten so whacked out that he had all he could do to hold himself bravely upright.

"In the multivalued multiverse, dreams *can* come true, it can happen to you, you can play the part!" Cam actually *sang*. "A virtual Starship *can* send back a virtual entity to commandeer a comedian to hijack our Deathship to its own virtual Tomorrowland! *Some* virtual future has to bootstrap itself out of the quantum flux with a self-fulfilling prophecy or there won't be any, because if the universe hadn't managed to pull the same rabbit out of the virtual hat in the first place, we wouldn't be here talking about it!"

Now Cam had come alive with one of his deliberately outrageous and almost incomprehensible propositions, delivered with an experienced lecturer's podium projection and the burbling enthusiasm of a fourteen-year-old Galileo peering through his first telescope.

Ralf hung his mouth open, mugging it up as if trying to show Mr. and Mrs. Couch Potato out there that he was just as befuddled as they were. But the camera caught a cool intent intelligence peering out from behind the mask of comedy.

"I thought the word from the bird was that I couldn't really be here because time travel was impossible," that intelligence said with a rather un-Ralf-like subtle sarcasm.

"*Absolutely* impossible, Captain," said Cam doing Mr. Spock. "But *virtually* possible."

"What's the difference, Dr. Zarkov?" said Ralf, a knowing and edgy little smile turning the question rhetorical.

"Virtually nothing, but absolutely everything!" Cam said, folding his arms across his chest and mugging at the camera with teenaged wise-guy glee glowing on his sixty-year-old face.

"*Absolute* time as an independent linear measurement of duration is a causal illusion of the obsolete Newtonian clockwork universe," he said. "In the *relativistic* universe in which we find ourselves, time is a function of the information density of events, and so . . . *all* time is *virtual!*"

Cam had delivered the last as if it were a punch line, and found himself sitting there grinning and waiting for a reaction while the studio audience responded with a ponderous *duh*.

But strangely enough, Ralf seemed to understand well enough to bring it all back home.

"Like how an hour lasts a million years when your brother-in-law makes you watch the video of the family's trip to Pismo Beach? Or how it flies when you're watching a terrific show like this?"

Cam did a slow take which transmuted into honestly surprised respect. "I couldn't put it any better myself," he said.

Quite truthfully, Dexter thought, for it was hard to imagine anyone bettering that haiku version of relativity-as-schtick.

Ralf mugged a rubber-lipped clownish version of the Mona Lisa's smile at the camera, but his eyeballs seemed to have transformed themselves into mirror-shades behind which some paparazzi-shy presence was lurking.

"Surprise, surprise, not just another pretty face," he purred in a voice dripping with amused irony.

The far-from-funny effect had the studio audience muttering, but the great Dr. Carswell in full cry was not be deterred for more than a beat.

"So, all time being virtual, the past must be as virtual as the future, and what we *think* we experience as the present only the probability-wave interface between them!" he declaimed, a piece of cannabinolic grandeur that Dexter fancied he could *almost* comprehend.

To judge from the rumbling from the audience however, this had long since passed over into babblement as far as they were concerned, and the likely effect out there in Nielsenland could be read in the dyspepsia on Jimmy Balaban's face.

The way Ralf had held that eerie fixed smile for what in television time was a virtual eternity had turned his face into a meaningless mask. Now, though, there was clearly something mightily sapient gazing out through it that made the effect even more unsettling.

"But if the *now* is virtual," he said in a voice whose timbre was enriched with new bass overtones, "then the *here's* gotta be like Oakland."

"Oakland?"

"Yeah," said Ralf, that new voice doing a perversely inverse parody of the old wise-guy rasp. "No *there* there. No *here* here."

No doubt about it now.

If the way Ralf had so changed his voice and persona could be laid off as an acting trick and therefore a form of fantasy, hearing him steal schtick from *Gertrude Stein* socked Dexter in the gut with the solidity of hard science fiction.

Someone else was now looking out through the eyes in that mask.

Even the studio audience was caught in the spell of whatever was happening, and the mutterings and mumblings died away into an even more nervous-making silence.

But when Dr. Cameron Carswell was properly stoned and cooking, he was not about to cede center stage even to such an apparition.

"And a nose is a nose is a nose!" he exclaimed to a sharp spike of laughter from the single person in the audience who seemed to have caught the reference. "But seriously, boys and girls, he's right, there *is* no absolute *here* here either, only an infinite number of virtual geodesics converging on a consensus now as an attractor."

This was an equation too far for Dexter to follow. But the mask that Ralf's face had become morphed into a *knowing* smile and the presence behind it once more proved that it *did* know what this stoned-out world-class physicist was talking about.

"But Herr Doctor," said Ralf, "if there's no here, and no now, then *we're* not here now either."

Cam Carswell mugged his own version of a jack-in-the-box smile right back, his bright eyes sparkling with well-fried intellectual merriment.

"That's right," he said blithely, "we're not."

"*Really*, Professor?" said Ralf. "*I'm* beginning to feel more here now all the time."

"We're *virtually* here," said Cam. "And because we're virtual creatures of a virtual here and now, travel in *virtual* time is possible. Which is why *you* are able to be here tonight."

"I'm here because I'm not here?" said Ralf.

"What goes around, comes around," Cam told him. "Futures create pasts which create presents which create futures. In four-space, the virtual geodesics play a never-ending game of musical chairs with the probabilities and we swim like virtual fish in the untimebound sea of the quantum flux."

Ralf's voice deepened in timbre once more, swelling in volume.

"And surface if we can?" he said in basso profundo.

"For . . . *the time being*," said Cam. "An infinite number of probable Ralfs co-exist as attractors in the virtual time of the quantum flux and you can never be sure onto which of them the wave function will collapse. Spirits, like universes, summon *themselves* from the vasty deep."

Now Cam turned the glittery visionary brilliance of his otherwise boyishly innocent eyes on Ralf.

"Anything probable is possible," he said. "And everything possible generates its own virtual here and now," he said.

"*Even me?*"

Dexter Lampkin's worldview twisted and contorted like the space-time around a black hole, a singularity punched through it by a line, a tone of voice, one of Amanda's Method tricks, or so he tried to tell himself, as Ralf transformed himself into Leviathan risen at last to the surface of that quantum sea.

"Even the Great Spirit of the Good Times to Come? Even a Captain of a never was and future Starship? Even a Message from the Dreamtime looking for a Medium in Prime Time? Even a Giant Turnip God dreaming it all?"

The audience had since lapsed into befuddled but expectant silence. They might not be getting the laughs they thought they had come for, and what are these weirdos *talking about* anyway, but there was an increasing probability that they might get to tell their grandchildren they were there when a famous comedian and a heavyweight scientist flipped each other out on television.

Now though, there was a subterranean rumble from the Peanut Gallery. This had gone beyond a freak and geek show, beyond waiting to see if the guy on the ledge would really jump.

"No attractor is too strange not to draw *some* probabilities, Mr. I Am," said Cam. "Not even *me*. Not even *you*."

Now they found to their discomfort that their disbelief was being suspended in something they could not understand. And Dexter knew just how they felt.

Ralf grew a grin of ultraviolet brilliance that would've been way over the top into self-parody if not for the disjunction of the utter seriousness and, yes, the power, in his eyes as he turned both on the audience, on the camera, on those millions out there watching this advent in the Dreamtime of Prime Time.

"You hear that, Starship Troupers, I'm *here*, and I'm *real*!" he declared. "*Every last one of me!* The professor has proven that *any* virtual act from *any* virtual future *can* ad-lib his way down the timelines to be with you here tonight!"

"And they damn well ought to give me the Nobel already for it!" said Dr. Cameron Carswell.

"Don't worry, Professor, they did," said Ralf with that same crazy grin, those same somehow more-than-human eyes.

"Oops!" he said, winking at the camera. "I mean they *will*."

Texas Jimmy Balaban had grown as philosophical about this disaster as the mumbo-jumbo responsible for it had become, or so he told himself in the absence of the possibility to either do anything to stop it or get instantly roaring drunk.

The Great Spirit of the Good Times to Come?

More like the Spirit of Christmas Past doing a not-so-slow fade.

There was the one and only major meal ticket of all his years of hard road grinning like Mr. Happy Face on a zillion milligrams of speed as if thoroughly convinced that this double-dome assholery was rolling 'em in the aisles out there in televisionland.

This proof positive that Ralf had tumbled so far off the Edge that he no longer had the comic instincts to distinguish schtick from crapola would've been bad enough. You could maybe lay it off on a real bad night and hope for better days. You could even consider a drastic move like a tank-town tour of some really rough clubs where the customers could provide a fast reeducation in what was funny by the beer bottles they'd throw at crap like this.

But Jimmy didn't have the cruelty in him to even consider trying. For the face on the air-feed monitor was beyond even such extreme schlock therapy. The smile was far too convinced of its own genius. The eyes were far too sincerely those of the Great Foudini.

You saw plenty of schizos like this on the street these days, especially in New York. Eyes like huevos rancheros. Wired energy coming off 'em like the heat waves in a cartoon. Glowing like someone had turned up the thermostat. Babbling gibberish they were convinced was the secret of everything or hysterically funny or both.

When politicians got crazy like this, you got Hitler and Stalin and Mussolini, though from what Jimmy had seen of the footage, at least Mussolini had never quite lost the ability to get himself a laugh.

And Jimmy had the feeling that maybe guys like Jesus and Muhammad and Moses had gone the same route, doing their schtick until they forgot it *was* schtick, like . . .

Like that actor on *Star Trek* who seemed to forget sometimes that *he* wasn't *really* the Captain of another friggin' Starship.

Ralf's last line had at least shut up Dexter's professor, but the full thirty seconds of dead air that followed was no improvement.

Finally, Amanda's boy earned himself a few brownie points by at least feeding Ralf a line to react to, such as it was.

"So now that you've decided that you're here and you're real," he said, "as the Caterpillar said to Alice on the other side of *another* black rabbit hole . . . who are you?"

Ralf's Happy Face grin sort of smoothed out and softened down into what you might see on one of those incense burner statues favored by ditzy broads who like to screw to Ravi Shankar and wore patchouli.

But the eyes . . .

"I am the virtual Captain of Starship Earth," Ralf said in that eerie voice, half Charlton Heston and half Vincent Price. "I am the Message from the Dreamtime. I am the Great Spirit of the World. I am the Giant Turnip God of the Quantum Flux."

Oy.

This was the kind of stuff that would've had Jimmy throwing a net over Ralf right now if only it were possible, except . . .

Except . . .

Except those were *not* the eyes of a crazy man.

The nose knows, and Texas Jimmy Balaban's nose told him that what he saw in them was *not* the strobing spark of lunacy, but the clear light of *something else* burning through the mist.

Jimmy had no idea what it was, but he remembered having seen it once before.

Texas Jimmy Balaban did not consider himself a religious man. Not only did he not go around believing in God or Jesus or Muhammad or the Second Coming of Elvis, for most of his life he had easily enough managed to avoid even thinking about such stuff.

Once, however, the prospect of what at the time had seemed like a primo piece of ass had induced him, much against the better judgment of everything but his dick, to partake of what was billed as LSD with the lady in question.

It hadn't worked out as he had intended. First he had thought he was going to puke, then he thought he might die, then he had found himself inside one of those kaleidoscopes, then they spent forever squatting on the bed and staring at each other to the tune of some kind of sci-fi flick music, during all of which the treacherous schlong which had gotten him into this mess remained limp as the proverbial wet noodle.

But there was a moment there—or an hour or a century, it was hard to tell under the circumstances—sitting on the bed inhaling sandalwood incense and staring like a yuk at the face of a woman whose name he could not even remember when he had what the Topanga crowd might've called one of your mystical experiences.

He couldn't remember her face either.

And no wonder.

For under the influence of whatever crap she had given him, her face had gone through countless changes. Young, old, black, white, foxy, ugly. Like one of those morph programs the special effects shops had taken to overusing. A short course in the women of the world at a frame a second. Mona Lisa and Marilyn Monroe. Marlene Dietrich and Eleanor Roosevelt. Billie Holiday and Golda Meir. Cleopatra and Katharine Hepburn. Indira Gandhi and Lauren Bacall. The Virgin Mary and Whoopi Goldberg. What seemed like most of the women he remembered ever having fucked. African, Eskimo, Italian . . .

Endlessly changing.

But the same unchanging eyes looking back at him from *behind* that dance of faces.

Those eyes were what Texas Jimmy remembered.

Because they were looking back at him from behind the face on the monitor now.

"Come on, Mr. Tambourine Man," said Amanda's mutant Method Ninja, "isn't it time we had a look behind the mask?"

"Mask?" said Ralf in a voice that seemed to belong not to the face of the moment but to those changeless and timeless eyes. "I wear no mask."

It made no sense, showbiz-wise or otherwise, he would not be about to admit it to anyone, he couldn't even say what it even *meant*, but Texas Jimmy believed him.

No mask?

It had seemed to Amanda that the being behind Ralf's succession of kabuki masks had never really come onstage without them. But now Dexter's quantum cosmologist had opened a doorway into a Dreamtime whose nature she could not quite comprehend. And the Ralf whom she had only been allowed to see in glimpses was emerging through it into Maya's realm.

"We all wear masks," said Hadashi.

"Do we?"

"Except of course when a mask wears us."

Ralf's eyes stayed dead stage-center, mirrors of nothing but the void. "Like the one *you've* been wearing, Mr. Five-Thousand-Year-Old man?" he said.

"Like the one that's been wearing me," said Hadashi.

He smiled a tranquil Buddha-smile, froze it, cupped his chin with both hands in the posture of a shaman about to release a bird as an offering to the Great Eagle Spirit of the World.

"Why don't you let it try *you* on for size?"

And he lifted the conceptual face into the air, and held it up to Ralf.

It was a magical piece of stagecraft.

The few titters to be heard guttered with embarrassed rapidity into the pregnant silence as Ralf accepted the invisible mask with ritual dignity and put it on.

Now he wore Hadashi's previous version of the Cosmic Smile.

Or perhaps the mask was indeed now wearing him.

No special effects, no hokey theremin music, no violations that he could detect of the laws of mass and energy, but something in his gut told Dexter Lampkin that he was in the presence of . . . of . . .

Of a singularity.

A locus in space-time where the very laws thereof punched a hole in the fabric of the universe in which they arose beyond which by their own terms they were inoperable.

Ralf's face was a smiling mask that expressed nothing Dexter could identify as a human emotion. His eyes seemed to glow with the ultraviolet intensity of the event horizon of a black hole, of all that could be seen in *this* continuum of a wormhole into elsewhere.

"Now *I'm* the Five-Thousand-Year-Old man," he said in the cranky grandpa voice from the old Mel Brooks routine. "And I'd like to thank you for inviting me here to be on my own show tonight."

The effect of *that* voice coming out of *this* face was both funny and discombobulating. Standing waves of uneasy muttering and nervous laughter swept through the audience.

"Whatsa matter folks, what did you expect, Mr. Spock in a toga?"

The face didn't change. But the voice underwent a sudden and utter transformation.

"Most illogical," Ralf said in a perfect flat Vulcan accent. "But if you prefer this aspect, I shall accommodate."

"Maybe we'd prefer the full manifestation," said Hadashi.

"The full manifestation?" Ralf said in a voice like a dead-serious James Earl Jones doing Jehovah, followed by a drumroll of Olympian laughter. "Not an act you have yet evolved to comprehend, Arjuna. The most you can handle now is the Disney version."

Dexter all but felt the hairs rise on the back of his neck. That this was a character that he had collaborated in summoning forth only added to the psychic vertigo.

What if, stoned or not, Cam Carswell was *right* about the nature of space and time?

Then couldn't a virtual future *really* send back some kind of virtual . . . *agency* to bootstrap itself into being?

Maybe not a being of flesh and blood, but a pure pattern, a transtemporal standing wave, a dream, a story, a meme surfing the quantum flux like a dybbuk, a message without a matrix that must seek its own material medium?

Would we be able to comprehend it?

Would Neanderthal Man have been able to comprehend fifty channels of cable TV?

"You could give it a try . . ." suggested Hadashi.

"Whaddya *think* I've been trying to do since you schnooks fell out of the trees?" Ralf said in a perfect Woody Allen whine, and then went into a breathtakingly rapid-fire succession of voices which would've turned Rich Little green with envy.

"The Burning Bush number! The Voice From the Whirlwind! The Crown of Thorns Caper!"

Powerful voices. Voices that rang with authenticity.

"Prometheus with the fire! Lucifer with the Light! Vishnu's Busby Berkeley Number! The Tap Dance of the Eightfold Path!"

None of which Dexter could identify.

"The flight of the Eagle! Strawberry Fields Forever! *Elvis in a Flying Saucer*, for crying out loud!"

The smiling mask of Ralf's face, those unwavering eyes, remained quite constant during all the voice changes.

It was an act like nothing Dexter had seen or heard of.

An act?

You really still believe that, do you, Monkey Boy?

"And what does it ever get me?" said Ralf, dropping back into the Woody Allen kvetch. "Chains! Nails! Dumb stories in the supermarket tabloids!"

On the air-feed monitor, Dexter saw Ralf's face in close-up. Those eyes looking right into his alone. An experience shared in that magic moment by twelve million people.

And when he spoke again it was in a mighty voice that seemed a processed composite of a multitude run through a phantom echo chamber.

"YOU NEVER GET IT."

"Who speaks now?" said Hadashi.

A real good question.

And a real strange answer.

When he spoke again, Ralf did Ralf.

A rapid succession of voices, each an aspect of the Comedian From the Future.

"A down-on-his-luck comic who came up with a desperation schtick. A complete psycho. A time-traveling comic from the Deathship. A Captain sent back to hijack the Starship to Tomorrowland. The Giant Turnip God. The Great Spirit of the Quantum Flux."

Dexter watched as his face assumed the masks of his own format changes to thespian perfection.

Nevertheless it remained a succession of masks through which peered the two invariant singularities of his eyes, eyes like doorways. . . .

"But which one are you?"

Ralf's visage had once more become that emotionlessly smiling mask. "*Absolutely* none of them," he said in that resonant composite voice. "But *virtually* all of them," he said doing a perfect Cameron Carswell.

Arthur Clarke had proclaimed that the manifestation of any sufficiently advanced civilization would appear to be magic.

Dexter D. Lampkin was now forced to ponder his own corollary.

Namely that the true nature of any consciousness sufficiently evolved beyond your own would appear to be quite incomprehensible.

"As the professor says," said th' voice a th' thing onna screen, "anything that's probable is possible."

It was wearin' one a those stupid fuckin' Happy Faces, but it didn't fool Rat Girl, not with those fuckin' cat's eyes comin' right at her an' flashin' her those secret razor-blade teeth.

"Including me," said the Enemy.

Fuckin'-A!

None a what the Monkey People was sayin' out there on the other side a the rathole was makin' any sense, but, think Rat, scree, scree, scree, an' what was makin' your metal whiskers twitch an' jerk an' send th' vibes a pain to the coat hanger in your brain told you all you needed ta know, monkey meat, hee, hee, hee. . . .

"*All* of me," sang the Dead World Destroyer in some kinda awful syrupy Frank Sinatra voice had ya reachin' for your knife.

"Is *that* who we're finally talking to now?" said the asshole inna black pajamas. "The Dancer behind the veils?"

Rat Girl didn't know from no veils or no dancin', or none a this stupid monkey meat bullshit, but hey no sweat, 'cause there was somethin' way down there, down, down, down, followin' the little blue lights to the cellars under the Dead World, somethin' cold and clear knows everything you need to know for a million years of a garbage pail floating in space, an' it was there inna coat hanger in her brain went to th' wires in her bones went right inta th' handle a th' big sharp steel tooth in her paw was all you hadda know how t'do. . . .

"It's the *Enemy*, you stupid mothafucka!" Rat Girl found herself screeching. "It's what you gotta kill, scree, scree, scree!"

"You *still* don't get it, do you, Monkey People?" said Ralf. "There *is* no Dancer behind the veils. Only the veils themselves dancing in the void. What you dream is what you get."

Some massive satori seemed to hover on the brink of Amanda's consciousness, and now as she gazed at the face on the screen, the Buddha smile no longer quite seemed painted upon a mask.

For the eyes, it had long been said, were the windows of the soul, and *those* eyes seemed to have become willingly opened doorways, and if what lay beyond them was a place beyond anything she could conceive of in terms of space and time, yet was it familiar as her own dreams, for she knew that, call it the Quantum Flux, call it the Tao, call it the Void at the Center of Maya's Wheel, it was the Dreamtime.

Amanda smiled back as she understood that it mattered not whether the consciousness behind the mask was avatar or Zeitgeist or being from the Year 5000.

"Your time is my time and my time is your time," said the Voice from other side of the doorway. "Because *all* time is the Dreamtime."

Amanda could hear the massed intake of breath out there in the audience, the collective sense of being in . . . a Presence.

"So it is!" she found herself exclaiming aloud as if that Presence could hear her. "And we are all in it!"

In the Dreamtime of Prime Time, there was a hush that lasted a full thirty seconds.

"Nothing is real?" Hadashi finally said.

"Nothing is *all* that's real," said the Voice from the Dreamtime. "Because everything is made of it."

"Stuff and nonsense!" exclaimed Dr. Cameron Carswell indignantly. "Mass energy can be neither created nor destroyed! You can't make something from nothing!"

The Presence looked back out of the Dreamtime at him and spoke with the voice of Mel Brooks.

"Sez who, Doc, we do it all the time! Wanna Rolls-Royce, wanna swimming pool–shaped kidney, wanna Tyrannotsuris with a purple hatband, wanna buy a duck, *no problem*, we make can make it for you wholesale right outa the vacuum!"

"You *can't* make something from nothing," Carswell repeated pedantically. "It violates the conservation of mass energy."

"Oh yeah, wise-guy, didn't my writers make *me* up out of nothing? The Great Spirit of the World transcending space and time to save the Starship from crashing on takeoff, this is by you chopped liver?"

"Matter and energy can neither be created nor destroyed!"

"Matter and energy you're talking about to the perfect masters, Monkey Boychick? Once you know the ultimate secret of the universe, it's easy as stepping in dog doo."

"You know the ultimate secret of the universe?" said Carswell.

Eyes that were windows into a future where that would one day be true. Comic delivery.

"What's the big deal, kiddo, in the Year 5000, even *producer's schmuckface nephews know it.*"

Deprecating shrug of the shoulders.

"It's nothing."

"Then why don't you tell us?"

"I already told you. It's nothing."

"Then why—"

"I've already told you," Ralf repeated in that other voice, the Voice of the Presence that had never ceased to gaze out from Dreamtime future. "It's . . . *nothing.*"

A mighty piece of stagecraft, or so it seemed to Amanda as he looked into the camera for a slow beat of emphasis.

Yet looking at the air-feed monitor, she could not escape the conviction that much more than that was happening. A pair of eyes as sapient as any she had ever seen or imagined gazed directly into hers, into the depths of her soul.

But those were *not* really eyes, they were patterns of pixels on a television screen, and there was quite literally *nothing* behind them but the void of a tube filled with vacuum.

"The ultimate secret of the universe is . . . *nothing*," said that voice therefrom.

"*Everything* is made out of nothing. The stars and their planets. You and me brother. Made of atoms. Made of particles. Made of smaller particles. Made of quanta of energy. Made of waves. Smaller and smaller and smaller until . . ."

A beat of silence.

Amanda watched the eyes on the television screen dissolve into pixels into phosphor-dots into atoms . . .

"Until. . . . ?" Dr. Cameron Carswell demanded expectantly.

As if, like Amanda, like twelve million people out there looking into the vacuum of those video eyes, he believed that something much more potent than a punch line was about to be delivered.

"Until there's no *there* there," said Ralf in a perfect simulacrum of Carswell's own voice. "Nothing but a dance of virtual particles with zero size, zero mass, and zero duration disappearing clean out of sight down the black rabbit hole."

To Amanda the revelation that being emerged from the Void, from the dance of nothingness behind Maya's veils, was something less than a major satori.

But Dr. Cameron Carswell had been struck by lightning on the Road to Damascus under the Bo Tree.

"*Fuck* me!" he exclaimed, whacking his forehead with the heel of his hand. "Ye gods, *of course!*" he burbled, vibrating in his chair like a teenage boy at his first peepshow. "The *quantum flux itself* has to be virtual! Pattern without mass or duration! Message without medium! A foam of infinitesimal singularities! From what *else* could a universe *possibly* bootstrap itself into existence!"

"It's gonna take you a while to work out the math, Dr. Zarkov," said Ralf in his all-too-human wise-guy voice. "But that *is* the number they give you the Nobel for."

What is, is real.

And there Amanda was, transported to the destination she had so long sought.

What is, is real.

For while she lacked the physics and mathematics to conceptualize it with the precision and clarity of a Cameron Carswell, she knew in her heart that they had stepped through the doorway together, that the vision of the spiritual seeker and the future Nobel Laureate were one and the same.

What is, is real.

That the material realm and the sapient spirit emerge from the same Dance, that anything that a consciousness experienced was therefore real, that there were therefore no separate natural and supernatural planes, was the mantra of Amanda's being.

What is, is real.

She would never be able to comprehend the rigorous parsing that Cameron Carswell would elucidate with mathematical clarity for the ages.

What is, is real.

Now was the vision quest of her youth fulfilled by the light of reason.

For now would it be validated in the cold equations.

13

An old Monty Python running gag-line rattled through Texas Jimmy Bala-ban's brain as the secretary opened the door to Archie Madden's office.

Nobody ever expects the Spanish Inquisition.

Speak for yourself, Monkey Boy, Jimmy thought sourly.

When your show's ratings have been dropping for a couple of months and the guy who owns the ax calls you in for a meeting, you only *wish* it was going to be something totally different!

Jimmy took a deep breath and tried to convince himself he was sucking down half a cigarette. For what little it was worth, he felt proud of himself for not breaking down and buying a pack under the circumstances, and he hadn't even fortified himself with a couple belts of Wild Turkey.

But however Dutch Courage would've made it easier to face this funeral music, handling Madden and Ralf in the same cage without benefit of either whip or chair was going to be more than enough of an animal act stone sober.

And call him an incurable optimist, or just call him a guy trying to be a mensch about it, but Jimmy was not about to go in there to be told the show was canceled without taking his best shot at bullshitting Madden out of it.

This was admittedly a tall order, considering that were it his ass planted in Madden's chair, he knew damn well that he would've pulled the plug and sealed up the body bag weeks ago.

"Just keep it zipped, and let me do the talking," he grunted as he shooed Ralf into Madden's office ahead of him.

448 • NORMAN SPINRAD

Not that he really thought it was going to do any good considering all that had happened.

Since the night that he had *changed* on the air . . .

Jimmy hadn't even been able to get him to change costume!

Not that Jimmy had been surprised that Ralf would insist on wearing his Starship Captain uniform even to a meeting which would decide whether the show lived or died. The crazy fucker had refused to wear anything else since he had ordered up a half dozen copies of this toned-down version of the old clown suit.

It was still Kelly green and gold, but the pants no longer bagged, the airline pilot's jacket had been transformed into a loosely flowing version, the comic gold braidwork had been reduced to piping, the hat was gone, and the boots had been replaced by deerskin loafers.

The good news was that while Jimmy never had been able to peddle the merchandising rights to the old version, he had been able to make a sweet deal for the rights to this street-ready outfit.

The bad news was that while you might still get stares wearing this version around town, the laughs would be few and far between. You looked weird, but you no longer looked *funny*. You could wear it and still take yourself seriously, which was why, or so it seemed to Jimmy, Ralf had had it made for him. If you were as far gone as he was, you could wear it all the time and still expect other people to take you seriously.

And a lot of people seemed to.

Depending on what you meant by a lot of people.

Lampkin, who had made himself scarce after the show that had pushed Ralf off the deep end, swore he was no longer stacking the audience with sci-fi fans, and since Amanda had lined up a couple months' worth of guests and then gone north on a vacation that couldn't be too long as far as Jimmy was concerned, it couldn't be her doing either. Nevertheless the studio audiences were coming more and more to be packed with—what could you call 'em?—more than fans or groupies, True Believers.

It wasn't just the Starship Earth T-shirts and the Captain suits and the store-bought placards and home-made banners. They had that look. The same look you saw in the eyes of the Hari Krishnas and Scientologists. The look that you wanted to punch when the Jehovah's Witnesses knocked brightly on your door on Sunday morning.

Ralf had shown up for the show following his Big Dingo Act still schticking in tongues and carrying a garment bag containing the prototype of the new Captain's uniform, a hastily and crudely altered version of the old clown suit. The audience hadn't yet started turning up heavily outfitted in tie-in merchandise, but the nose knew, and Jimmy could sniff out some unwholesome chemistry between them and Ralf the moment he walked out on the set wearing it.

The opening applause died away much too fast, the sudden silence was much too heavy, and from backstage, Jimmy could make out a sea of too-glossy eyeballs glowing up at Ralf out of the darkness, smell something wrong on the sweat coming up off the collective armpit.

Ralf's smile seemed painted on the mask of his face as he walked across the stage to the set. His eyes tracked the camera as he moved with all the twinkly humor of Jack Palance in a Highway Patrolman's sunglasses.

He sat down, mimed a hand-mike, and delivered a variation on one of his standard openings in the familiar singsong of his airline pilot voice.

"Welcome aboard another white-knuckle red-eye Starship ride to Tomorrowland, Starship Troupers, this is your Captain speaking, please inhale all smoking materials as rapidly as possible and return your species to an upright position. . . ."

But the way he delivered it with that plastic smile from behind those mirrorshade eyeballs made it truly unsettling.

"No, wait a minute, buthta, we take that back," he said in the voice of Daffy Duck. "This is really the Great Spirit of Tomorrowland speaking to you through your Captain," he declaimed in a fatuous Biblical epic voice like Moses hawking used stone tablets.

All with zero change in expression or body language.

"And if you believe that, I've got a terrific bridge in Brooklyn I could let you have for almost nothing," he said, switching to Groucho. "And if you act *now*, the first dozen customers will receive a genuine gold brick absolutely *free!*"

All with that spaced smile and thousand-yard stare that made him seem like the Maharishi's ventriloquist's dummy wired for sound and picking up Radio Free Funny Farm.

What do you do for an encore after you've gone bugfuck bananas on the air the week before?

Apparently no problem if you think you're the Giant Turnip God, you just keep on going.

And much to Texas Jimmy's queasy discomfort, the studio audience sat still for it.

Real still.

In Jimmy's professional opinion, that show had been one of the most excruciating bombs he had ever been forced to endure, and, given what his client list had been like for most of his career, he had endured plenty.

He had seen clients lose it completely before. He had seen clients go this far off the deep end in front of an audience before. He had had clients end up as permanent scholarship students in the Laughing Academy.

But he had never witnessed anything like this.

He had seen comics go completely crazy and cease to be funny.

But he had never even imagined a comic going completely crazy and ceasing to be funny and still holding an audience.

Lampkin had booked a character who called himself "Mr. Sci-Fi," the proprietor of some kind of private museum, and planned to have himself frozen when he died so he could become the centerpiece of his own collection and wake up to shake hands with Buck Rogers in the twenty-fifth century.

Amanda had contributed a vibrating parapsychologist suit with a spiel about reincarnation and something called "morphic resonance," which, near as Jimmy could make out, had nothing to do with either special effects or the record industry.

Jimmy's memory of the ensuing dialog was mercifully vague, nor did he remember making much sense of it at the time, or there being much sense to make. His main attention had been on the audience.

Mr. Sci-Fi and the Resonating Morphodite were just the sort of kooky characters Ralf should've been able to work well off, but what few laughs there were seemed to be random accidents.

Mr. Sci-Fi went on about how his house full of moldy old books and magazines, tie-in merchandise, and bits and pieces of movie monsters made him an "archaeologist of the future." The Morphodite was into "the quantum transtemporality of spiritual transmigration." Ralf spent most of the show displaying his newfound ability to grin like an ape on Prozac, stare into space, and do voices.

Subject an ordinary audience to this tediously unfunny gibberish and if the bottles didn't start to fly or the hecklers didn't start to shout, then at least you'd hear the muttering and shuffling. But these zombies waited out the boredom in stony silence.

Weirder still, when two lines chanced to come together into something almost funny, they didn't pounce on it desperately with overeager laughter, they hardly laughed at all. Waiting for something to happen they were, but not for the jokes, folks.

What they were waiting for, Texas Jimmy couldn't figure until it happened.

Throughout all the voice changes, Ralf had maintained that not-silly-enough ghost of a grin, that empty bright-eyed look, no longer the wild-and-crazy-guy whose sanity had vacated the premises along with his comic instincts, leaving a psycho babbling random schtick.

". . . the resonance patterns are the essential structure of the universe, thoughts in the timeless mind of God, like foreshadows on the walls of Plato's famous cave—"

"*Plato's Cave?*" lisped Ralf. "The *leather bar*? Hey, sweetie, I didn't know you were into Greek culture!"

Blah, blah, blah . . .

"—have visions of things before they happen all the time, like the way Robert Heinlein predicted the water bed twenty years before there were any hippies, I've got the original edition in my—"

Yak, yak, yak . . .

And then—

"—your act is a kind of morphic resonance pattern itself, Ralf, a pure form predestined to incarnate itself in the present by the very future that will send you back here to do it later on."

"Close, but no cigar," said Ralf in a powerful voice that emerged from so deep inside of him that it seemed to be speaking *through* him.

Finally the audience had reacted, but it was more like what you'd get at a magician's signature capper or a trapeze artist's triple than what you'd expect at a comedy show; that gasp of breath that made the silence louder.

"Nothing is predestined. Nothing is written in the stars. Not even me."

Jimmy could detect no change in Ralf's expression. Nothing in the eyes. But somehow that voice changed everything. Somehow it rang with . . . *authenticity.*

"You don't get to blame it all on the Moving Finger of Mr. Pie in the Sky writing the script in stone. You can't even fob it off on some poor schmuck comedian. *You* dream me up, Starship Troupers. Or not, Monkey People."

Jimmy had the uncanny conviction that this was the Voice of the someone behind the mask to whom the Stare belonged. Someone who, while weird enough to have had him crossing himself if he were into such stuff, was *not* what you could call crazy.

"The dream you get is the dream you make. The Dreamer you get is the Dreamer you wake."

Like the reverse of the bit in *The Exorcist* where the demon starts babbling craziness through the sane girl he's possessed, the Voice had Texas Jimmy half-believing that a *sane* dybbuk was speaking through a lunatic.

"Think of all time as a week of Prime Time, Starship Troupers. No past, no present, no future. Just time slots to fill and an endless supply of formats forever competing for each of them. The names on the spaces in the producers' parking lot are written in whitewash. Think of evolution as the ratings in action."

Whoever or whatever had spoken through Ralf sat there making with the Stare for a long beat of silence.

Texas Jimmy wouldn't have been able to explain it to anyone, but he was somehow convinced that someone whose nature he could not comprehend had told him a truth that his nose now knew but that his brain couldn't quite understand. The stillness of the studio audience told Jimmy that this experience had been shared, or at least that the effect, whatever it was, had been worked on them too.

And then Mr. Sci-Fi piped up into the silence and totally fractured the elusively magical yet uncomfortable mood.

"That reminds me of a story by Jack Williamson that was published in *Astounding Science Fiction* way back in 1938—"

The groan was audible, a mixture of irritation and uneasy relief.

"Th-th-th-that's gall, folks!"

And Ralf had dropped right back into his voices routine via Porky Pig as if nothing had happened.

At which point, Jimmy could have almost convinced himself that it had just been an acting trick he didn't understand. The lines that had seemed so significant under the influence were gibberish when you tried to figure out what they really meant afterward.

Weren't they?

It was obvious that the audience didn't think so. You could just about hear them holding their breath waiting for it to happen again.

". . . so we can download our memories into computers and go to the stars as the brains of spaceships," Mr. Sci-Fi was saying. "As silicon instead of flesh, we'll be able to live forever."

"Somehow I don't think so," said Ralf, delivering the moldy oldie as Woody Allen, "but with no sex, no booze, no drugs, and not even a good delicatessen, it'll sure *seem* like it—"

"Seriously—"

"Eh, seriously, Doc?" said Ralf-as-Bugs-Bunny.

"Seriously, Mr. Man From the Future, a thousand years from now, *won't* we all live forever?"

"What do you mean *we*, White Man?" said Ralf.

But he hadn't delivered the pathetically decrepit punch line as Tonto addressing the Lone Ranger. Instead, that all-too-serious someone was there behind the comic mask again, turning it into something that made the audience gasp and gave Jimmy goose bumps by delivering it in that Voice resonating with utter conviction.

Ralf sat up straighter, lifted his chin, and opened his arms as if to present himself as Mr. Wonderful.

"Behold the man of the future," said the Voice.

And he did something with those eyes that went beyond the Stare. For a couple of beats, Jimmy felt that he was looking not *at* them but *through* them. . . .

"You and me and your caveman ancestor are the same animal. But between what's inside his head and what's inside yours is the difference between banging a couple of rocks together and Beethoven's Fifth Symphony, between Stonehenge and Disneyworld, between a chunk of raw mammoth and an Egg McMuffin. . . ."

. . . as if they were holes, or tunnels, or doorways, not into a man's head, but into someplace much larger whose nature Jimmy could not get a handle on.

"And between you and me and the lamppost . . ."

Texas Jimmy found that little shrug and pause somehow touching.

"How can I tell you all the things inside my head?" said the Voice.

And though Jimmy recognized it as a line from some old song, it carried sincerity. And though the Voice and the Stare and whatever was behind it seemed thoroughly Martian, he found himself feeling a kind of sympathy for whatever was trying to step through the doorway of those eyes.

For after all, he realized, if somehow there really *was* someone from the year 5000 in there, wouldn't it really be a ballbuster to explain himself to us? About as easy as me trying to explain the subsidiary rights clause in a film option contract to Jesus H. Christ!

"On the other hand," said Ralf, dropping suddenly down into W. C. Fields, "an entity that makes no sense to dogs and small children can't be all bad."

Jimmy blinked. The audience sighed. Ralf went back to being an ordinary gibbering loony.

Texas Jimmy still had no idea of what had really happened, but it was getting hard to convince himself that it was nothing but some previously unfamiliar acting trick. Because *that* time the Voice that had spoken through Ralf had made a kind of sense. Not that Jimmy really believed that some kind of spook from the future was trying to speak through him, hey come on, but whatever was happening, you had to admit that the ventriloquist sounded a whole lot smarter and a lot less crazy than the dummy.

It only happened twice during that show, but later on it would start to happen more often. A line from one of the guests, a beat of silence, who knew, and the Voice would emerge from Ralf's wall of noise, from the endless cutting from one imitation to another that his act had become.

Three, four, five, half a dozen times a show. And soon the studio audiences would seem to be calling for it, and not just with the T-shirts and banners and Captain suits, but in some elusive way Jimmy never could figure.

Lampkin swore that he wasn't writing the Voice, that he wasn't even *talking* to Ralf, which was not hard for Jimmy to believe, seeing as how there wasn't that much coherent Ralf left to talk to.

But he did admit that if he *were* writing the lines for someone from the far future trying to make sense of himself to the dimwits of the present, it couldn't be much different.

"A consciousness thousands of years of evolution more advanced than our own trying to explain itself to us would *have* to sound like you trying to give a chalk-talk on the audience demographics of *Dallas* reruns to a Doberman pincher. A science fiction writer *really* creating a character like that would be like Bonzo writing the lines for Ronald Reagan."

Jimmy had to admit that Lampkin's logic was convincing, except for the impossibility of a chimp coming up with lines like "If you've seen one tree, you've seen 'em all," and "If we're going to have a bloodbath, let's have one now."

Nor did the crap that started appearing in the sleazoid tabloids impress him as much beyond the literary powers of the inhabitants of the monkey house, running as it did to RALF POSSESSED BY COSMIC VOICES, and TV COMEDIAN CHANNELS FUTURE SCHLOCK.

In the absence of any reasonable expectation of consistent laughs, what seemed to be keeping the seats full were people waiting for the Voice From the Future to speak.

A lot of whom seemed to believe it was real.

Depending, of course, on your working definition of a lot of people.

Not enough to keep the ratings from sliding, but if only ten percent of the TV audience was taking Ralf seriously, that was still close to a million people. And while that wasn't jack shit by the standards of even a third-rate outfit like the Gold Network, it was the Major Leagues when it came to Nut Cult City.

Lampkin's tie-in book went into a third printing, the comic book rights went for a fancy price, the T-shirt and warm-up jacket and poster sales were holding up, and eight thousand Starship Captain suits had already been sold.

Three outfits who ran such operations for movie stars and ballplayers had approached Jimmy with deals to set up a dues-paying fan club. Twenty bucks a year, he was assured, was the bare minimum, which would get members a membership card, a discount on tie-in merchandise, and a newsletter. Meaning that even fifty thousand members would gross a cool million a year and the ad revenue and increased merchandising sales would more than cover the cost of the newsletter.

The numbers were to drool for. They kept bugging him to do it. Texas Jimmy Balaban had never imagined that he would ever hesitate to pluck such a plum from the money tree.

And yet . . .

And yet he kept procrastinating, he kept putting them off, and he couldn't say why. . . .

Maybe it had something to do with why he wouldn't let Ralf give interviews. He was certainly constantly being pestered by everyone from *People* to producers for major stops on the talk-show circuit to the big-city dailies.

If anyone had ever suggested that he would ever consider those who sought to shower such golden publicity on one of his clients pests, Texas Jimmy would've had them committed as obviously certifiable. If he had turned it all down, he would have had himself committed. Or so he previously would've thought.

But he had.

And he would.

Wasn't this only rational? The offstage Ralf was by now as crazy as what you saw on television. Interviews with him would be gibberish interspersed with the cryptic wisdom of the Voice. He had to protect his client, right?

Maybe.

Maybe not.

For Jimmy couldn't quite convince himself that the mystery of the plants had nothing to do with it. . . .

Jimmy's visits to Ralf's apartment had always been few and far between, and even more so since his star client had become so crazy that just being around him was enough to have Jimmy thinking maybe *he* was going nuts.

But an endorsement deal had required Ralf's signature on a release and Jimmy had been considering talking the fan club offers over with him anyway, so a couple weeks or so before the phone call from Archie Madden, Jimmy had found himself ringing the doorbell to Ralf's apartment.

The few times he *had* been inside the apartment had not been exactly pleasant experiences. Jimmy's own houseplants were limited to a rubber plant that seemed to be able to survive for weeks without water and a bunch of jade trees so tough you'd have to pound them with a hammer to kill them. But even Jimmy's mom, who refused to have plants in the house because she was convinced they made you sick by stealing your oxygen, would've been depressed by Ralf's botanical torture-chamber.

In some kind of attempt to convert the decor of the apartment from Deathship lifeboat to Starship greenhouse, he had crammed the place with plants. Cane trees and rubber trees and potted palms. Succulents and cacti. Spider plants and geraniums and ivy. Big ones and little ones. Hanging in pots from the ceiling. Occupying every inch of shelf space. If mom's theory had been right, you would've suffocated in five minutes.

But it had been like the *Night of the Living Vegetable Dead* in there. Yellowing leaves and browning palm-fronds. Vines hanging limp and nearly leafless in their pots. Even the jade trees were ready to expire, and as Jimmy knew from experience, killing those suckers was nearly impossible.

But this time . . .

When Ralf, wearing the Starship Captain's suit, opened the door, the fragrance that poured out into the hallway from the apartment blew him away.

It smelled like Laurel Canyon on a warm spring night right after the rain, like the shoreline of Biscayne Bay. Sweet with the scents of flowery perfumes, heavy with the sultry odor of abundant foliage, moist with the smell of undergrowth and loam. Jimmy had never been in a rain forest, but the complex of odors stirred up jungle visions in his brain.

Nor was he disappointed when Ralf led him through an entrance hall that had been turned into a tunnel of morning glory vines in full blue blossom and into the living room.

"Holy shit, Ralf, how did you do it?"

"A dying planet or a roomful of houseplants. A biosphere is a biosphere."

Jimmy was so entranced that he didn't even immediately notice that it was the Voice who had answered him.

Pots of flowering plants hung from the ceiling; vines, ivy, violets, geraniums, *orchids* fer chrissakes, dangling in such profusion, the foliage so green and luxuriant, that the effect was of a forest canopy. Big rubber trees, cane trees, palmettos, palms, in the peak of health, turned the room into a jungle clearing. Shelves and tables were crammed with exotics Jimmy couldn't identify, and—

Jesus Christ! Tiny brilliantly colored birds flying free like aerial tropical fish!

Jimmy never remembered how long he just stood there staring, but he knew he would never forget the moment he finally turned to look at Ralf.

There Ralf stood in his stupid green suit, smiling like the Happy Face having just eaten the hairy canary. Not looking back at him like your house-proud gardener, but making with the Stare, those eyes opening into . . . into . . .

Into someplace or something or somewhere that Jimmy simply couldn't understand.

"As the macrocosm, so in the microcosm," said the Voice.

Or believe in.

Or could he?

What was it Amanda Robin used to say? What is, is real?

You could hardly argue with that, now could you?

Time travelers from the future and flying saucers, Deathships and Starships and Elvis going bump-bump-a-doo-bump in the night, that was Lampkin's sci-fi fantasies.

Not real.

But this indoor jungle overgrown with healthy greenery, fragrant with floral perfumes and the loamy odors of growth and life, twittering with birdsong, *this* was real. If it wasn't, then neither was he, standing here with the previously black-thumbed guy who had created it.

"Who the fuck are you?" Jimmy demanded. "I mean, *really!*"

"I yam what I yam and that's all that I yam."

"Stop with the Popeye shit!" Jimmy shouted, and he could see something retreating behind the Stare, could sense the doorways of those eyes closing.

"Stick around for a minute, will you," Jimmy pleaded wheedlingly, doing a voice change of his own. "*Talk* to me."

"Here's lookin' at you, kid," Ralf Bogied, but now it was somehow the Voice doing the voices, and behind the Stare, Jimmy could sense someone at least *trying* to be human.

"But *who's* looking back at me, kiddo?" Jimmy said softly, afraid of fracturing an elusive and fragile something he could not quite name.

"That's the longest story ever told. It begins with a great Big Bang and if we grow up to be who I'm supposed to be, it never ends."

Jimmy stifled his exasperation with all this mumbo-jumbo by act of will. Lunatic, con artist, or Starship Captain, the nose didn't know, but all his instincts told him to humor him as you would humor even the most out-to-lunch producer when you had to.

"Come on, enough with the stories," he said carefully. "Can't we get to the bottom line?"

"The bottom line *is* the story," said the Voice. "I *am* the story. The one we keep trying to tell ourselves."

The smile didn't waver. The eyes remained locked on Jimmy's as Ralf opened his arms in a gesture to encompass the room, the magic mini indoor forest.

"I'm the version where we get it right. Believe in me, and Tinkerbell lives."

Jimmy might not understand what he was being told, but in that moment, just for a beat there, maybe, he believed it.

"On the other hand, if the show gets canceled," said the Voice, "then I was just a wild and crazy guy."

And something seemed to slip away down the zoom lenses of those eyes and it was gone.

Jimmy had forgotten all about talking over the fan club proposals with Ralf, had gotten the endorsement releases signed and gotten his ass out of there as soon as possible.

He couldn't figure out why that experience had not only confirmed his intention not to grant interviews with Ralf, which under the circumstances seemed only rational, but to resist the temptation to do a fan club deal, which did not.

And even less so now, as he trooped in to Archie Madden's office behind his all-too-wild-and-crazy guy. For if the show got canceled, he was going to wish he had made that one big last sweetheart of a tie-in deal while there was a show out there to be tied to.

The Boy Genius sat behind his desk looking somewhat less Boy and a little less Genius. A little older. A little harder. A little less sure of himself.

Maybe it was the ax whose fall he anticipated turning the desktop into one of those Aztec altars designed for the ripping out of hearts. Maybe it was Madden's carefully cultivated five-day beard and the dark blue serge suit and white shirt with narrow black tie. The effect was of a Hollywood version of a gangster masquerading as a Suit. Or vice versa.

"Give me a reason not to cancel the show, Balaban," Madden said by way of greeting.

"Huh?" said Jimmy plopping himself down in one of those weird chairs shaped like giant hands.

"Give me a reason not to cancel the show," Archie Madden repeated in a dead flat voice that gave away nothing.

"You're serious?" Jimmy said, studying his face for a clue and coming up empty.

Against all showbiz reason, was there really hope? Or was this just the son of a bitch's way of being cute about it?

"*The Word According to Ralf* has ceased to be a laughing matter, Balaban," said Madden. "The ratings are in the shitter and since the star has forgotten how to be funny, I see only worse in sight. I would sincerely like you to give me a reason not to pull the plug."

Why? Jimmy almost blurted. But he caught himself in time.

All at once Archie Madden had become much more ordinary, and the nose knew that the bloom was off his rose. The Biz was not an environment where very many Boy Geniuses became adults of the species when they grew up.

Madden was running a little scared. His job wasn't riding on *The Word Accord-*

ing to Ralf, but the previous glow of his rep was. To cancel a show that he himself had solicited in the middle of a season would be to admit that he had been wrong. Boy Geniuses were not supposed to be wrong. Much better to let the show play out the season, fade away over the summer, and simply never be renewed in the fall.

Jimmy began to have hope.

The bottom line interest of the Gold Network said cancel this bomb now, but it was in *Madden's* interest not to do it, to let it expire quietly offstage later. So he really *did* want Jimmy to give him an excuse to play it that way. An excuse that would stand up to scrutiny by the corporate powers that be that were paying his considerable salary.

But it wouldn't pay to confront the guy on this level of truth.

"Money," he said instead.

"Whose?" said Madden, carefully allowing a little sarcasm to slip into his voice. "Yours or ours?"

Bingo!

For while the Gold Network's ad revenue off the show itself was going south with the dwindling ratings, the sales of the tie-ins were booming. And while Madden could blame most of the network's failure to dip more than the first inch of their wick in that unexpectedly sweet honeypot of the contracts department, some of it would rub off on him. And would enhance the fading rep of his geniushood if he managed to work some of the old magic on the situation.

Jimmy didn't smile, but he did lean back a bit.

"What we are talking about here is a trade that will help both ballclubs," he said. Then he leaned forward a tad, looked Madden in the eye, and ventured a teeny smile, the moral equivalent of a wink. "Or at least both managers."

Madden did likewise back.

"If out of the goodness of my own heart I was to agree to renegotiate our deal to give the Gold Network ten percent of our net of all ancillary rights," Jimmy said, "would that be the sort of reason you're looking for not to cancel the show?"

He flashed Archie Madden his best friendly tiger-shark smile. "Seeing as how the deal would only remain in effect while the show stays on. After which, of course, it all reverts to us. What do you say to that . . . Archie?"

"I say twenty-five," said Archie Madden.

"I don't see your twenty-five, but I raise to fifteen."

"Twenty."

Jimmy shrugged. "Let's just split the difference, call it seventeen and a half, and not be pikers about it," he suggested magnanimously. "After all," he ventured in a some harder and more knowing tone, "there's a little more riding on this than a couple of lousy points in these numbers."

Madden didn't smile. He didn't even shrug to acknowledge the done deal. "But we've got to change the format," he said instead.

"Change the format?" said Jimmy.

"Change the format?" said Ralf. "This is the version where we get it right. Consider the terminal alternatives."

Ralf had done what he had been told, kept his mouth shut, to the point where Jimmy had almost been able to forget about him. Now, just as Jimmy was about to do what he came in here thinking was the impossible, he had spoken in the Voice, and turned the Stare on Archie Madden.

"But I *have*," said Madden, giving him a ghost of the Boy Genius version back.

"What's wrong with the format?" Jimmy said, too loudly and he knew it, but since he wasn't seated close enough to Ralf to fetch him a kick in the shins to shut him up, there didn't seem to be any other alternative.

At least he recaptured Archie Madden's attention.

"It isn't working anymore," Madden told him. "It isn't working because your boy has lost it," Madden said as if Ralf wasn't even there. "He's lost it because he's gone crazy. Perhaps you've noticed?"

Before Jimmy could get a word out, Madden was motor-mouthing like a used-car salesman and smiling at Ralf with his hand in the air.

"Now don't get me wrong, Ralf, you've got a constitutional right to be crazy, some really great talents have spent time in mental institutions, we're an equal opportunity employer here, I've got nothing at all against the sanity-disadvantaged as long as you can hold it together well enough to keep the ratings up."

"You think of the ratings as evolution in action," said Ralf.

"I'm glad to see you're taking it in such a professional manner," said Madden. "And I hope you'll accept my solution in the same spirit."

"I'm an equal opportunity spirit myself, Archie," said Ralf, mirroring Madden's smile, but turning those eyes and the Voice on him in a manner that at least for a moment had him blinking.

"Uh, you've got a *solution*, Archie?" Jimmy said loudly into the beat of uneasy silence.

It took Madden another beat to break eye contact with Ralf and get back to monkey business. "Tried and true," he finally told Jimmy. "Celebrities."

"*Celebrities?*"

Madden nodded. "When the act was at the top of its form," he said, speaking again as if Ralf were an item of furniture, "you could get away with all these space cadets and New Age used-karma salesmen. It worked because these kooks were the crazy characters and a comic could play off them. . . ."

He paused, turned to Ralf. "Nothing personal, Ralf—"

"Nothing at all," said the Voice, pinning him with that unwavering stare. "We're all transpersonal on this bus."

"Strictly a professional evaluation, you understand," Madden babbled nervously, "but like Wolfgang Puck said, you are what you eat—"

"Or what eats you."

Madden blinked rapidly several times. He didn't look away, but Jimmy had the feeling he wanted to. Every professional instinct said *break this up fast*, but some other instinct which Jimmy hadn't even known he had made him sit back and watch Ralf run with it.

"Or both," said Madden. "You started out eating your guests, but you ate too much of their craziness, and now they're eating you. You with me?"

"Most interesting, Doctor," said Ralf, doing a dead flat Mr. Spock without breaking eye contact or changing expression. "The Dreamer they wake is the Dreamer they make," said the Voice.

"Uh . . . I suppose you could put it that way," Madden muttered uneasily.

"They can summon spirits from the vasty deep, but who comes when they call . . . ?"

"Uh yeah, right," said Madden, sliding into a relentless little monologue like a guy trying to humor a possibly dangerous lunatic or bullshit his way out of a traffic ticket.

"Don't take this wrong, but you just don't have it together to work off these characters anymore. You can't carry the show by yourself with all these amateur weirdos. You need guests who know how to work off *you*. Who can help you carry the show. Who can carry *you* when they have to. *Professional celebrities!*"

He paused, as if waiting for a reaction line.

Ralf just sat there staring at him like Mona Sphinx.

"Well," Madden finally said lamely, "what do you think?"

Something here just wasn't adding up.

"At least I'd still be in show business," Ralf finally said.

The voice in which he said it and what seemed to be looking out of those eyes at Archie Madden gave the moldiest line in existence some strange kind of unfunny resonance.

Madden seemed under the spell of the Stare like a bird in front of a cobra or a birdbrained starlet looking into the eyes of a horny producer.

"And I'm the only story left in town," said the Voice.

"Hey wait a minute!" said Jimmy, suddenly realizing he must've been in some kind of trance himself to take this long to see the obvious. "You're telling me you're now willing to spring for the budget to get *stars*?"

Whatever spell the Boy Genius had been under, that brought him out of it like a slap in the face with a wet codfish, and he looked at Jimmy as if *he* had gone crazy.

"Hey, no way!" Jimmy cried. "I certainly can't afford to pay them out of *my* end on the budget!"

"Sure you can," said Archie Madden. "We pay them scale."

"Scale! We're not gonna get stars for *scale*!"

Madden gave Jimmy a fairly good imitation of the Stare himself, though his version of Ralf's little smile was more in the nature of a shit-eating grin.

"Stars?" he said. "I don't remember saying anything about stars. I said *celebrities*. *Professional* celebrities. I've been talking to a booking agent who assures me she can get us all of those we want for scale. You pay them out of your end, I pay her out of mine. Sara Gimble's the name. She says you know her."

"Oh shit," moaned Texas Jimmy Balaban as it all fell into place.

He knew Sara Gimble all right. From further back than he cared to remember. He had even screwed her a few times. Sara did a cut-rate volume business filling bottom-end showbizzy talk-show slots with bottom-end talk-show rats.

Permanently out-of-work onetime character actors. Retired strippers trading on their funny names. Singers whose last gigs had been Puerto Rican bar mitzvahs.

This of course was what the Boy Genius meant by the delicate term "professional celebrities." These showbiz hangers-on would indeed work for scale. Most of them would work for beer money if Equity would let you get away with it.

"Low," observed Jimmy, though he had to admire the structure.

For peanuts, Madden was buying the Gold Network seventeen and a half percent of the tie-in rights for the rest of the season and buying himself a soft death for the show over the summer which would keep all but a minimum amount of shit from clinging to his Gucci boot heels.

"By definition," said Archie Madden, "there is nothing lower than the bottom line." At least he had the grace to deliver it deadpan.

"So that makes this an offer I can't refuse?" Jimmy replied in kind.

Or can I?

Jimmy made his own bottom-line calculations. If he *turned down* this cynical deal, he'd lose his end of the TV money for what remained of the season, but he'd keep that seventeen and half percent of the ancillary rights for the period that would otherwise go to the Gold Network. The bottom line was that when you tried to put numbers to it there *was* no bottom line. It was kind of a toss-up.

Texas Jimmy Balaban found himself struggling with the concept that how he would now make the biggest business decision of his life could *not* be determined by the dollars and cents of the sacred bottom line.

Strangely enough, there was something liberating about it.

"Tell you what, Archie," he said, "for once in my life, I think I'll just let my client decide."

He turned to Ralf, met the Stare, and in that moment, he could almost believe that whoever or whatever was looking back at him from the other side of those bottomless eyes really *was* some kind of spook from the future.

"It's *your* Starship, Captain," he said, flipping him an ironic little salute.

Ralf's smile seemed to become a tad warmer as he did a twinkling Kirk. "Thank you, Mr. Spock. I guess there's still something human in even the best of us, now isn't there?"

And for the first time, Jimmy felt a connection, if not what you could call a friendship, with the whoever who had created that magic indoor garden, who had dribbled the Boy Genius like a basketball and somehow clarified Jimmy's perception of this moment in the process.

And though he was surrendering a major business decision to the whim of the client in a way that agent's pride and street smarts said he shouldn't, he found that it made him feel wiser, not stupid; bigger, not smaller.

Archie Madden, on the other hand, was not amused at all. "Hey, come on, Balaban, this guy isn't playing with a full deck, we both know that," he said, coming perilously close to a whine.

"Maybe not," Jimmy said blithely, "though sometimes it seems to me he's playing with a deck and a half. But I'm the manager, Archie, and I say this is his ball-game to win or lose."

Madden glared at him for a beat, letting his frustration show. Then, with a sigh and a little shrug, he pulled himself together and got professional, which, under the loony circumstances, made him grow up a notch in Jimmy's eyes.

"Well, that's showbiz," he said.

"No business like it," said Ralf, turning the Stare and the Voice on Madden.

Madden glanced theatrically at his watch. "Look, I've just been told the way it comes out is up to you," he said, "but I've got another meeting in six minutes, so what's the story, Ralf, I've got to end this one now."

"If it comes out right, the story never ends," said the Voice.

"Bullshit," said Archie Madden, who Jimmy found he could no longer think of as either a genius or a boy. "We're talking three more months here. We're not talking forever."

"Speak for yourself, Monkey Boy," said Ralf, the Voice doing an eerie ironic take on the original refugee from Deathship Earth.

"Speaking for *the Gold Network*, wise-guy," Madden shot back like a good old-fashioned Hollywood exec finally becoming openly pissed off, "*this meeting* now ends with a yes or no from you."

"What can I say when you put it that way except bring on the clowns?" said Ralf. "The show must go on. We know what happens if the Fat Lady sings."

Amanda's answering machine was full when she returned from her pilgrimage and about a dozen of the messages were from Texas Jimmy Balaban. Her machine didn't date messages and Jimmy hadn't done it either, but from the messages left by people who had and the changes he had gone through, it was touchingly easy to relate the time frame of his passage along the stations of the way to hers.

After the show when the satori she had so long sought had emerged from the Dreamtime, Amanda had considered her work with Ralf done and this phase of her life over.

But she discovered that such an Enlightenment was but another doorway, on the other side of which was the proverbial first day of the rest of her life, and the only way to discover what that would be was to walk through it.

But in the realm of Maya, she would have to drive. Walking the ridge road in all its incarnations all the way up the great cordillera from the Hollywood Hills to Alaska had been a fantasy, but Dexter had transformed it into a possibility in the real world. For not only was it really the only way possible, he had taught her that a car, like any other artifact crafted by humans, could be worthy of whatever love you were willing to grant.

And so, when destiny presented her with the possibility of acquiring a seven-year-old Land Rover at a price that *The Word According to Ralf* now allowed her to afford, she took it as a sign, or at least a good deal, bought it, lined up eight weeks' worth of guests for the show to cover her longest possible absence, and set forth.

After her endless series of clunkers, the Rover was a revelation; an appropriate vehicle to bear her on this rite de passage, the four-wheel drive would take her anywhere, it was solid as a rock, and it was the best car she had ever owned. If she didn't love it as Dexter loved his Porsche, she respected it in the morning when it started with no back talk and carried her reliably through the day. Behind the wheel of her Rover, the mystic seeker discovered an appreciation for the zen of nuts and bolts.

The pilgrimage began with a drive along the coast road to Big Sur and then a whole week spent in the environs, visiting friends and attending the usual seminars and consciousness-raising sessions which now seemed a pale shadow of that which she had already attained.

Perhaps because the central topic of interest around the Circuit had become Ralf. This might not have displeased her had it been a sincere attempt to encompass what his advent might mean to the future destiny of the species, but it seemed that even the wisest of her old compadres were still chasing the same old dualistic wills-o'-the-wisps. Genuine apparition from the future or inspired madman? Time traveler or avatar of the Godhead?

To all of which the only answer she could give was *Yes*.

And to all the pleas that she give a seminar on the meaning of Ralf, the only answer she could give was *No*.

What else could she do? True, she had experienced a mighty satori. The seamless unity of the spiritual and physical realms had been revealed. That matter and consciousness emerged from the same Dreamtime dance of virtual pattern in the Void was no longer an article of faith.

That out of Cameron Carswell's future mathematical parsing of what had previously been her faith would evolve a level of consciousness capable of opening the doorway to the Dreamtime by conscious act of will she did not doubt. But understanding how to do it herself, let alone how to teach the technique to others, was beyond her present level of evolution.

There had been no messages from Texas Jimmy Balaban while she tarried fecklessly in these old familiar stomping grounds, and he must've left the first one about the time she was deciding half-ruefully that she had become something of a stranger here and headed north.

"Listen, Amanda, this is Jimmy Balaban, and I don't want you to think I did this because I'm pissed off at you for what happened, well maybe I *am* kinda pissed off, but that's not why I did it, actually I let Ralf decide, you had to be there, shit, I guess this isn't making much sense. . . ."

The nervously guilty voice paused for a beat, then firmed up.

"Look, if you're picking up your messages with your remote, you don't have to hurry back, 'cause, well, your services are no longer required, because Madden was gonna cancel the show unless I let him turn over booking the guests to this bimbo talk-show-rat agent and, well, the bottom line is I did it, but hey, I'll lay a fair severance package on you, give me a call. . . ."

Listening to the message now, Amanda found herself smiling, and had she been checking her messages in real time, she probably would've called him, just to tell him *no blame*, Jimmy.

For just as putting the Circuit behind her and heading into terra incognita had come as a wistful emancipation, so would she have welcomed his news in the same vein as a liberation from a contractual obligation to the karma of the past.

But even though her answering machine had come with a remote, no pilgrim would drag such an anchor with her on a vision quest like this.

If vision quest it was.

Beyond the Golden Gate, she had opted for the coastal road, a winding two-laner between San Francisco and Mendocino, carved for the most part on a narrow shelf running along the shoulders of the mountains that tumbled straight to the sea, one of the most beautiful coastlines in the world, all sea-cliff and rock-beach, fir trees and mist, a mighty landscape hard to imagine as capable of being slain by even the most profligate hand of man.

It was also the scariest road that Amanda had ever driven; narrow, serpentine, perched precariously above sheer drops to the foaming rocks below without benefit of safety railing. Never had she had to concentrate so totally on her driving, and this too was a liberation, for the mandatory fusion of mind and body, consciousness and matter, hardwired the satoric lesson she had learned into her flesh and bones on a level of somatic wisdom that required no knowledge of calculus or quantum cosmology to attain.

No, this was not a vision quest, for the vision had already been attained. In some way she could not expect to fully comprehend until the journey was over, this was her attempt to digest that enlightenment, to walk the path of the Bodhisattva, to bring it all back home.

"Listen, Amanda, this is Jimmy Balaban, I don't know where you are or if you're picking up your messages, or if you're pissed off at me, but if you are and you're not, please give me a call, you can call collect, but make it station-to-station, not person-to-person, no sense in throwing money away. . . ."

That one must've been made sometime between the two days she spent in Mendocino and her sojourn in the sequoias.

Mendocino had been a whaling station, a hippie haven, a dope-growers' market town, and somehow the ghosts thereof remained, turning the town into a time-warped Brigadoon perched on the seacoast edge of the forest primeval. A spirit message of the ectoplasmic nature of the works of man in the time frame of the biosphere itself.

And in the nearby woods she had encountered the "dwarf forest," a patch of ground whose high alkalinity had reduced pines and even redwoods to natural bonsai; adult trees, some of which did not come up to her knees, as if to remind her that from the indifferent geologic time frame of the planet itself, even these great forests, even the biosphere itself, was a rime of lichen on a ball of rock whose existence, always precarious, would always remain very much in doubt.

Had she heard Jimmy's message about then, she probably would've called him, for listening to his voice now, she heard something plaintively precarious in it too, which would have called out to her then as she headed northeast into the sequoia groves.

"Amanda, this is Jimmy, and this is not about business, I just want to talk to someone who can maybe help me make sense of what's going on. . . ."

In an earlier incarnation, the immensity of the trees in space and time might have restored Amanda's faith in the eternal majesty of Mother Gaia, were it not for the tourists, the presence of which would've seemed a desecration. But now that ecopolitically correct cliché stood revealed as another dualistic illusion. What is, is real. A three-thousand-year-old sequoia. A six-year-old kid with chocolate ice cream smeared across his face. That boom box blasting out rap. This four-billion-year-old ball of rock and magma floating in a twenty-billion-year-old universe.

What is, is real, for better and for worse. Matter. Energy. Spirit. Good. Evil. Moral indifference. It all emerges from the same Dreamtime dance of virtual pattern in the Void.

"Jeez, Amanda, will you pick up your messages already, look I admit it, okay, maybe I didn't do the right thing, I mean . . . aw shit, give me a call for crying out loud!"

There were a couple more messages from Jimmy Balaban in that same vein which must've been recorded some time between the sequoias and the Oregon border.

"Amanda, this is Jimmy again, I know I'm beginning to sound like a broken record, and I know you're probably not listening to me now, but jeez, did you just see the show?"

This one she could date exactly, and she knew just where she had been when he made it, returning to her room in a roadside motel well north of Medford, Oregon. The room had come equipped with satellite TV, and she had taken a long walk to avoid the otherwise inevitable head-game of will I or won't I turn it on.

". . . if you did, you gotta understand, I mean assuming you give a shit anymore, that the deal I made with Madden makes the rest of the season a lock no matter what Ralf does, I mean, unless he decides to whip his cock out on the air or something, don't even think about it. . . ."

Amanda stopped the playback at that point, the wisdom of not bringing the remote along forcefully confirmed, for if she had heard *that* message in real time, she would've made *sure* she was around a TV set to catch the next week's show.

She had spent that hour of Prime Time in the contemplation of temporal relativity instead.

She had been in the Cascades, well in sight of Mount Saint Helens, the volcano which an augenblick of geologic time ago had reduced these environs to a lifeless lunar landscape of rock and pumice with a titanic explosion.

Yet there she was, camped out on the margin of a young virgin of a forest that had already grown up in a Gaian night and a day to demonstrate the inexorable resilience of the biosphere.

But there were lights moving in the pristine wilderness night sky; satellites, airplanes, the works of man, quite capable of terminally poisoning that billenial biosphere in less time than *it* would take to fully reclaim this land, quite capable too of unleashing a Faustian power that would make the Mount Saint Helens's eruption seem like a child's popgun and frying the planet to a cinder between one episode of *The Word According to Ralf* and the next.

From this perspective, the virtuality of time, and the possibility that some immaterial spirit—a story, an archetype, a dybbuk of the eternal Dreamtime— could turn its temporal vector at right angles to the linear illusion of causality to manifest itself in a transtemporal now made perfect Dreamtime sense.

Consciousness *could* impose pattern on matter. If an acting coach and a science fiction writer could impose an archetype upon the matter of a comedian, why could not they be the agents of that which they had summoned forth, why could not the Zeitgeist impose the pattern that would create its future destiny upon *them*?

Had not such archetypes, such stories, resonated back and forth in the collective unconscious, in the Dreamtime, without regard to causality, since before they themselves turned monkeys into men?

Amanda went to the fridge, took out a half-full bottle of Chardonnay, opened it, sniffed it to see if it was still drinkable, poured herself a glass, and took it out onto the porch.

Night had now fallen in Topanga too. A coyote howled at the starry sky that was a pale shadow of the one above the Cascades, a breeze off the cooling arroyos brought the sweet winy odor of chaparral to her backbrain, the perfume of the natural realm, of the eternal Now.

Except that now she understood that Coyote's howl was the laughter of the Joker and there *was* no Now now.

Now she was standing on her porch at the end of her long pilgrimage to this very moment. Now she had paused in her playback of Jimmy Balaban's skein of nows past.

Now she was contemplating the now in the shadow of the volcano when she had realized that you didn't need to be a quantum cosmologist to understand that there was no now except the transtemporal now of showtime in the Dreamtime of the Void.

Now she was thinking that while the linearity of time might in some absolute sense be an illusion, the sequence with which consciousness experienced these constellations of nows shaped destiny.

Had she brought her remote and retrieved her phone messages regularly, she would have experienced Texas Jimmy Balaban's nows in synch with the real time of her pilgrimage instead of retrospectively. And probably watched *The Word According to Ralf* in some motel and never experienced that wilderness night in the Cascades.

And had the trajectory of her consciousness altered thereby.

Instead, because she *hadn't* brought her remote, she *hadn't* seen the terminal stage of *The Word According to Ralf* until a week later, a week after the now in the Cascades through which she had passed had somehow prepared her for the experience.

In the intervening week, she had meandered north through the high Cascades, scribing a wide semicircle around the metropolitan area of Seattle, a wilderness route that didn't take her to what passed for urban civilization, until Boundary Bay, almost literally within spitting distance of the Canadian border.

It was a long, beautiful, leisurely drive, and she had plenty of time in which to think. Having reached what she imagined was a state of satisfied digestion of that which she had embarked upon this pilgrimage to digest, mostly what she contemplated was the pilgrimage itself.

Why was she *really* doing this? Why, if it had been to achieve the understanding she believed she had already been granted, did she continue? To find the path of the Bodhisattva?

Maybe.

Or just to find what to do next?

For the story of her life thus far had been the long vision quest that been successfully completed.

Yet here she was, in the material prime, with no mate, no children, and currently no calling to which she was passionately devoted. Was this what was meant by a midlife crisis?

It didn't feel like it. People who suffered same bemoaned the lack of the very completion she had attained or the loss of the hope that it would ever come, not what lay beyond it.

Perhaps she was now seeking a Sign.

Such had been her thoughts on the day of the next show as the sun went down and Prime Time approached and the road debouched toward the coast through empty country.

And lo, a Sign was granted.

ELLIOT'S MOTEL, it proclaimed on raw pine planking in red neon letters. VACANCY. EATS.

SATELLITE TV.

She took it as the Cosmic Inevitable. And so there she was, reclining on a bed in a motel room with a remote connection to the wide world in her hand. It had been a long time since she had seen *The Word According to Ralf* and it was quite a shock.

The guests were an aging actress barely stuffed into a slinky black vampire gown last seen a decade or so ago playing victims in horror films, the onetime owner of a used-car business who had had his fifteen minutes doing his own commercials with a succession of large animals a decade and more ago, and a porn-film star known for the size of his dong.

At the time, not having had the benefit of Jimmy's phone messages, Amanda couldn't imagine why the format had been changed, why the guest list was now scraping the dregs from the bottom of the showbiz barrel.

Nor, after about ten minutes of excruciation, as the guests gabbled self-promotion for their pathetic current fantasy projects while Ralf gibbered in comic tongues, could she imagine why anyone would still be watching the show, or why a pro like Jimmy Balaban had apparently agreed to this act of hara-kiri, since she could scarcely imagine how anything this awful could remain on even the Gold Network for another three weeks.

But then . . .

"—why *couldn't* I do musical comedy or even Shakespeare, didn't *Arnie* start out famous for nothing but the size of his—"

"—you ever hear of *another* hippopotamus act—"

"—it's an interesting script, for once *I* get to play the monster—"

"*Personally*, if you'll pardon the expression," said Ralf right in the middle of this deadly showbizzy blather, "I'd rather be a story that exits gracefully with a happy ending than stand around when it's over waiting for the hook."

Stunned silence.

It wasn't just the line that suddenly shut them up, though that would've been enough to do the trick. The voice in which Ralf had delivered it had become a powerful projective instrument of which the greatest of Shakespearean masters might be proud.

"All *good* stories have a beginning, a middle, and an end."

The voice. The eyes. The Buddha smile.

A Presence had manifested itself and was in command.

"And what's a career but a show business story?"

Nor was this mere acting technique.

Amanda had long since become convinced of that.

The Lightbringer speaking from the Dreamtime, the Eagle Spirit of the Virtual Future; perceive it through whatever image system you chose, there it was in phosphor dots right there on the screen.

"What's a *life* but a story? A man. A woman. A species. A biosphere."

This was hardly the first time Amanda had witnessed such an advent. Waiting for *The Word According To* had become the major draw for the dwindling audience for the show.

But this was a new level.

"Even *me*."

What was speaking now wasn't even trying to pretend it was playing the talk-show game. Wasn't even shielding the viewing audience from its ability to command the guests' silence for as long as it chose.

"Does my show go on forever or does it just seem that way?"

In one of his Don Juan books, Carlos Castaneda had his virtual brujo declare that the Perfect Warrior's power derived from envisioning his own death, and encompassing that vision, and being willing to use it.

Voila, the Perfect Warrior of Prime Time!

For only a being who didn't give a damn about the ratings or the pickup could say a thing like that on the air and not even try to blur it by reaching for a laugh.

"Depends on what you mean by forever, doesn't it?" he said, as the camera moved in for a tight close-up.

An illusion?

A chance conjunction with the conundrums of her own spirit?

Depends on what you mean by *chance*, Amanda thought.

She *knew* there was nothing behind those eyes but the vacuum of the picture tube, but she could not escape the conviction that they were looking right into hers, and through them into her soul.

And though she *knew* there was a multitude out there quite convinced of the same thing, she could not escape the conviction that he was speaking directly to *her*.

"Depends on what you mean by time," said Ralf. "Is my time your time? Is time *really* like a river flowing gently to the sea—"

"—an' life is but a dream, tra-la," sang out the horror movie bimboid, a snatch of song that died away in embarrassment, as if she realized she had committed an act of lèse-majesté, whether she understood the concept or not.

But the camera had held its close-up on Ralf and his smile became beatific.

"Out of the mouth of . . . *babes*," he said, and the face on the screen actually winked.

"What if *time* is just a dream, tra-la, Starship Troupers?" he said. "And the Dream is a wish our hearts make when we're fast asleep? We all know *that* one, don't we? The story we keep telling ourselves over and over and over. . . ."

Amanda envisioned millions of hands changing the channel, for surely this cryptic and unfunny transcendentalism could hardly be knocking them dead in Peoria. But she also envisioned some smaller number of viewers caught by those eyes, caught as she was by this chance confluence between the imagery of their own Dreamtimes and *The Word According To*.

"You know the one I mean, don't you, Starship Troupers? Where we put on our white hats and crowns of thorns and ride into Dodge City on Rocinante with our light-sabers held high to rescue ourselves from Darth Vader?"

If chance had anything to do with it.

For the eyes on the screen had become doorways into the Dreamtime that Amanda only in that moment realized had always been there beneath the phosphor-dot surface of Prime Time.

And she, though fully conscious, was now in it.

"But the show keeps getting canceled. The savior has to be nailed to a cross, King Arthur must die, JFK has to be blown away in Dallas."

No, she saw, neither chance nor causality was the operative principle here, where the individual merged with the Zeitgeist and premonitions of the future were written in memories of the past, where in the timeless Now of the Dream-time, in the collective and individual mythos of the species, in the story of ourselves, we all are that Hero.

"And do you know why, Starship Troupers?"

Was this what Saul had felt on the road to Tarsus? Was this what Timothy Leary felt taking his first hit of acid? This clear light? This blindingly simple? This retrospectively self-evident? This cosmically funny?

For of course, the joke *is* on us.

Always has been.

For sure, we are all the Hero of our Dreamtime.

But we are all also the Enemy.

Who else is there?

"Because once we dream it right, the Dreamer wakes up in the magic kingdom of Starship Camelot and *that* story is over."

The winking light and dragonfly drone of a light plane moving across the sky brought Amanda back from the memory of that eternal now into the now of standing here on her porch in Topanga remembering it, just as Ralf had dropped her out of that Dreamtime epiphany between one line and the next.

"It hasn't happened yet, or I wouldn't be here hoping *this* time is *my* time to get offstage before my plug gets pulled again," the almost plaintive voice of the Lightbringer had said within the Dreamtime.

And then Ralf had looked upward as if for a transporter beam that wouldn't come.

"Beam me up already, Scotty!" said the voice of Captain Kirk in the schlocktime. "Scotty . . . ? *Scotty . . . ?*"

Amanda didn't remember much about the rest of the show, partly because there had been nothing memorable, but mostly because she *did* remember that epiphany, she *had* for once been able to bring a vision entire back from the Dreamtime.

She had known right then and there in Elliot's Motel that she had gotten what she came for, that the apogee having been reached, her pilgrimage was over, and it was time to return to Los Angeles and all that it implied.

Amanda took another sip of wine and went back inside the house, ready now to face the playback of the rest of her phone messages.

There were two or three things that sounded like they might lead to serious offers of work, and listening to them, Amanda found that she was ready at last to finally take a career as an actress and an acting coach as seriously as the craft deserved.

Why not?

For the story of Amanda the Seeker was over.

Having learned, blessed by fortune.

The story of Amanda Robin might now truly begin.

To teach when called upon to teach.

Hollywood might not be Camelot, but in this age, Prime Time was the collective Dreamtime, so the path of wisdom might as well be the Walk of the Stars as anywhere else.

Nor had she bothered to watch the show again.

Why should she?

The Word for this age of evolutionary transformation or death had been spoken. By the Great Spirit of the World? The Zeitgeist of the Collective Dreamtime? An avatar of the Godhead? A time traveler from Starship Camelot? The Laughing Buddha in baggy pants?

Would it matter when the Dreamer awoke into a maturity no one could expect to comprehend now?

It's not the Singer, it's the Song.

In the beginning, was the Word.

And it had been spoken.

And *The Word According to Ralf* was a story that was over.

He who had spoken it had said so himself.

Only the exit scene remained.

Prometheus must be bound. Lucifer must be cast down into the pit. Jesus must be nailed up. Faust must be damned. The Lightbringer must die. That's what it said in the script. This story always had to end in tragedy.

How else to get the Lightbringer offstage?

Because if you didn't . . .

Then what?

Then the story's over and we awake in the magic kingdom of Starship Camelot.

And no one knows what that will be.

No one?

Speak for yourselves, Monkey Boys and Girls.

There was one more message from Texas Jimmy Balaban on Amanda Robin's answering machine. There was no way for her to tell when he had recorded it, but it must've been fairly recently because it ran the memory out.

"Listen, Amanda, I've been doing a lot of thinking, jeez, I've even been reading a bunch of weird stuff, which believe me ain't my thing, but what can I tell you, I don't know whether you've been watching the show, but it's not that Ralf's gone nuts, or the show's going down the tubes . . ."

There was a pause, a tinkle of ice against glass, a slurping sound.

"I mean, he's *always* been nuts, from the first minute I saw him at Kapplemeyer's, and I don't remember all the stuff I've said, but if I been blaming you for what's happened, forget it, that was bullshit talking, and hey, the show had reached the end of the line *before* Madden shoved a collection of brain-dead losers down my throat, I mean it's dead already and what you've been seeing now is a kind of afterlife running out the string. . . ."

Another pause. "Jeez, did I say that?" Texas Jimmy continued in a slower, softer voice. A tinkle, a swallow, a sigh. "Guess I did. I wouldn't say this to no one else, Amanda, but I've been having thoughts like that lately."

Another silent beat. "Shit!" The sound of liquid being poured into a glass. "I guess the only way to say it is to say it . . ." A long gulping sound.

"What if it's real? Him. It. The schtick. I mean, time travel, spirits, nuclear physics, dybbuks, sci-fi, what do I know from this shit? But I've been seeing things, and I've been thinking . . ."

Another pause, another drink.

"I mean, after all, we sure are in the process of really fucking the world up, ain't we, the ozone, and the greenhouse, and our general state of shitheadedness, and all. . . . So maybe someone or something from wherever really *did* or *will* or *has* sent us something or someone to give us a well-needed kick in the pants. . . ."

No drinking sounds now, just a long sigh.

"It's late, and I must be pretty drunk, no bad thing, but I just had to say this to someone before I went completely bugfuck myself. Hey, maybe I have already, how would I know, right? But I guess . . . I guess . . . I guess I'm drunk enough to say I think I believe that Ralf is for real. Or I want to. Whatever."

There was a long silence.

"I mean, better the Starship than the Deathship, right?" said Texas Jimmy Balaban. "So better to believe that we got a chance to make Tinkerbell live, like the man says, I mean considering the alternative, know what I mean?"

Another silent beat.

"So what I'm saying . . . I mean, I don't think I've gone through life being a prick and an asshole, I mean I got my honor, I try to be a mensch . . . but I mean, face it, I don't know about you or Dex, but I can't exactly say I've done anything much for the world, know what I mean . . . boy am I loaded. . . . What I'm trying to say, Amanda, and I'm not so fucked up I don't know that this is gonna sound nuts, but what we done, you and me and Lampkin, I mean even if we *did* drive some poor schizo schnook over the edge to do it and line our pockets in the process, I think we did a good thing, I mean something good maybe comes out of it. . . ."

A long, long guzzling sound, and then the sound of heavy glass being smacked down on wood.

"So, I mean, I guess I'm just trying to say, no blame, Amanda, know—"

The answering machine memory ran out.

"Yeah, Jimmy," said Amanda lifting her wineglass in a time-warped phantom toast to the Texas Jimmy Balaban of *that* now before picking up the phone to tell the current incarnation much the same thing. "No blame. I know *just* what you mean."

Dexter Lampkin knew that he should've been suspicious when Texas Jimmy Balaban invited him to lunch at La Californie.

Should've been suspicious? Hell, he *was* suspicious.

La Californie was trendy and monstrously expensive, the sort of restaurant producers took starlets to for the purpose of securing entry to their pants via their stomachs, but lunch there was strictly business, with the tab picked up by corporate entities rather than mortal wallets.

And Texas Jimmy Balaban had never exactly impressed Dexter as the last of the big spenders.

Then too, Dexter had had hardly any contact with Texas Jimmy since control of the guest list for *The Word According to Ralf* had passed into the hands Sara Gimble. Until now, he had considered his involvement with the show a closed chapter in his life story.

Well, sort of . . .

True, *The Word According to Ralf* was still his main cash cow. The tie-in book had gone into a fifth printing, the merchandise was selling better than ever, and Jimmy had made a deal to release the entire run on both disk and cassette as soon as the show was canceled.

True, Dexter's agent kept pressuring him to come up with a proposal for a series of Ralf novels, assuring him of a low-to-medium six figures a pop if he made a deal now before the show was canceled.

True too, it would be a long time if ever before he could go to a science fiction convention without being crawled all over by Ralfies, one experience in San Diego had been more than enough.

But he found he didn't miss his forced self-exile from the con scene, the house was paid for, he had the Porsche of his dreams, and unless he started doing stupid things, such as eating regularly in joints like La Californie on his own money or jamming vast quantities of coke up his nose, the various rights to *The Word According to Ralf* of which he had pieces made him financially independent.

He had the Power.

The power to tell his agent where to stick his sweet deal for high-paid galley slavery. Never again would he have to write anything that didn't come from the heart. He was free to become the best Dexter D. Lampkin possible. He had money enough and time.

From this vantage he found that it was even possible to be at peace with the inescapable truth that he was indeed middle-aged. Any woman under twenty-five whom he managed to bed would be attracted only by his modest fame.

Any older woman comely enough to attract *him* would therefore have to be interested in something more than a one-night stand, and among the other things that he had learned from his singular assignation with Amanda Robin was that he wasn't interested. That he had not even been tempted to pursue anything further with a woman as physically and intellectually attractive as Amanda had taught him that, face it, Lampkin, you're a committed husband and father.

No doubt this was one of the reasons he did not suffer greatly from his enforced absence from the convention scene. Oh, he missed the intellectual shoulder-rubbing, but as any male science fiction writer would admit when he was drunk or stoned enough, he mostly went to science fiction conventions because his fame therein made it easy to get laid. By who or by what and why you could avoid thinking about by the injudicious use of brain-barbling substances.

A mature middle-aged husband and father Dexter might now consider himself, but he kidded himself not that he would sagely resist easy temptation when it was placed before him.

But his "affair" with Amanda Robin had turned him off his previous sporadic and feckless pursuit of low-grade fannish pussy. Perhaps because it *had* been something more than a straightforward fuck.

There were fucks that passed in the night and there were fucks that contained the potential for emotional involvement, but the sexual transaction between himself and Amanda had been a Fuck of the Third Kind.

A strangely unemotional fuck; a *transpersonal* fuck. Which was why they hadn't slid into an affair afterward, why he hadn't even entertained such fantasies. It was hard for Dexter to convince himself that it hadn't been a ceremonial fuck, a fuck of conjuration.

A *magical* fuck.

Which was probably why the thought of cruising the con circuit for egoboo pussy now caused his mature middle-aged pecker to do nothing but wilt.

For deeper and darker truth be told, and by the very word the fans themselves had in their sardonic wisdom coined, beneath and beyond the male tropism toward the easy dipping of one's wick in worshipful flesh, boo for the aching ego was what so many science fiction writers rode the con circuit in search of, Dexter D. Lampkin of recent yore included, now that that incarnation had been transcended and he could forthrightly admit it to himself.

One could not as a callow youth set out to brave the daunting odds against succeeding at all as a writer, one could not presume to bring forth stories from nothing more than the inner depths of one's own being, without plenty of ego, let alone set out on the visionary path of the serious-minded and idealistic writer of science fiction, creator of worlds, universes, realities entire, encumbered by ungod-like modesty.

What a wounding of your pride when you begin to succeed, only to find your work packaged in a manner that makes you want to wrap it in plain brown paper when reading it on airplanes, and has you shuffling and muttering when those whom the world considers *real* writers ask you what you do!

What boo for that wounded ego when you discover that secret world whose denizens believe science fiction is the light of the world and you are indeed the visionary seer you have always known you are in your heart of hearts!

This was what Dexter believed he had transcended via that fuck of conjuration. Via the instrumentality of what it had brought into the world, his need for such egoboo had been slaked, his wounded ego had been healed, his youthful dream of visionary destiny had been fulfilled.

With *The Word According to Ralf* Dexter had achieved what he had failed to do with *The Transformation*.

He had thrown his pebble into the Dirac sea. Indeed he could congratulate himself on heaving a nice-sized stone.

In youth, unsuccessful personal tragedy; in middle age, mature triumph with farce.

His vision of the Transformation Crisis through which the species was passing and how it might be transcended had become a part of the Schlockgeist as surely as Star Trek itself. Manifested in T-shirts and warm-up jackets, comic books and Starship Captain suits, posters and Starship Crunchies and hordes of Ralfies.

That the Monkey People were faced with the choice between the future Deathship and the future Starship had been trivialized into a marketing cliché of popular culture.

Mission accomplished.

And a personal liberation from the egoistic messianic impulse of all too many science fiction writers' permanently extended adolescence. For he had succeeded in getting out the Message without nominating himself as the Messenger. He had contented himself with booze and grass and the occasional snort of other people's coke and had not allowed himself to get hooked on that hardest of stuff.

And that was what visionary writers had better to do if they knew what was good for them.

He had not only lucked out, he *deserved* his good karmic fortune.

He had done well by doing good.

Still, Dexter asked himself uneasily as he entered La Californie, what the hell am I doing here?

Had all those years of relative poverty simply conditioned him never to turn down a free lunch?

But hadn't another science fiction writer impressed upon the Zeitgeist the declaration that there ain't no such thing? And why was Jimmy Balaban springing for it in a place like this?

He was met in a lobby done up in pink marble and green travertine by a hunk in full tux with blond shoulder-length hair. This was the maître d'. He consulted a palmtop computer, and personally escorted Dexter to the table.

The ceiling of the dining room was a geodesic greenhouse dome whose panes were polarized to cut the cruel blue of the Los Angeles sky to a richer azure hue. The room was a lush tropical garden. The walls were Mediterranean blue overgrown with bougainvillea and honeysuckle vines whose fragrant blossoms filled the air with a sultry perfume. The waitpersons, male and female alike, wore powder blue tuxedos. Recorded surf sounds and discreet seabird cries completed the effect.

It seemed to Dexter like some French director's concept of an exotic Californian restaurant on Mars.

Texas Jimmy Balaban was dressed in a white ice cream suit that didn't seem out of place, but Jimmy himself seemed to be as much as Dexter was, and the look the waiter gave him when he ordered Wild Turkey on the rocks caused Dexter to perversely order the same.

"Some joint, huh, Dex?"

"Not what I would've called your style, Jimmy."

Texas Jimmy shrugged and gave him the ingenuous smile of the unselfconscious hustler. "I figured you might take some major buttering up," he said.

"Say what . . . ?"

Jimmy held up his hand. "Like the Jewish mama always says in the movies," he said, "first eat."

The drinks arrived with the menus. Jimmy manfully choked back a moan and washed it down with a mighty slug of bourbon when he read the bad news.

By the time the waiter arrived again to take the order, Jimmy had finished his drink. He ordered Kobe Beef Tartar on a Bed of Sauteed Shiitake Mushrooms and Rack of Lamb à la Tandoori with Sauce Bordelaise, about the cheapest dishes on the menu. Taking the cue, Dexter contented himself with similarly modest-priced fare by the local outrageous standards: Camphor and Tea Smoked Duck and Corn Salad with Sesame Oil dressing, and Tornedos of Wild Boar Simmered in Bordeaux with Sweet and Sour Red Cabbage and Pureed Chestnut.

Jimmy ordered a bottle of Pomerol, and then, as the waiter was about to depart, ordered another bourbon. "And another for my friend while we wait."

"One might think you were trying to get me drunk, Jimmy."

"One might just be right, Dex."

"You wouldn't mind telling me what this is all about?"

"Well, Dex, there's simple news, and there's complicated news, and if you don't mind, I think I'll save the complicated news till we've both had more to drink. . . ."

And over two bourbons apiece, Texas Jimmy laid out the bottom line. The show was finished at the end of the season. Given the belly-flop in the ratings and the mental state of the star, the chances of it getting picked up by anyone else were zero and zilch. Forget a syndicated package. Forget even a live tank-town tour. If Madden hadn't locked himself into the rest of the season, a guy as unfunnily crazy as Ralf would be off the air and in the bin already.

By this time, the appetizers had arrived and Dexter had managed to gulp down his second drink before the waiter poured the wine to go with them. His smoked duck and corn salad was fantastic, and he was feeling no pain.

"I don't get it, Jimmy," he said. "You had to take me to lunch in a joint like this and get me plastered just to tell me what I already know?"

"Uh . . . there's a little more to it than that, Dex," Jimmy told him with a somewhat furtive look about the eyes, committing the faux pas of refilling both of their glasses himself before the waiter could do it, an occurrence that the worthy did not allow to happen twice.

"I been thinking, Dex," Jimmy announced. "I been thinking of all that stuff you told me about Star Trek, you know, how the tie-ins never died . . ."

Somehow this had Dexter draining half his glass of Pomerol in a single unseemly gulp.

"I been thinking that's maybe what we've got here, I mean the show is tube city, but the merchandise and the book are still moving, and the video disks and cassettes don't even get launched until it dies. . . ."

"So?" said Dexter, munching on the last of his duck salad, in the unreasonable hope that more food might clear his head.

The waiter glided smoothly to the table, topped up their glasses, and departed almost beneath conscious attention.

"So I figure, hey, why not take a tip from Dexter's old buddy Roddenberry, and kind of help it along. . . ."

Dexter doubted that the sudden sinking sensation in his stomach had anything to do with the food.

At this point, the main courses arrived. After removing the silver covers with a Hollywood flourish and refilling their glasses, the waiter cast a dubious eye at the remains in the bottle. "Another, sir?" he suggested suavely.

"Yeah, sure," Jimmy said airily with a boozy wave of his hand.

"Help it along, you were saying?"

"Yeah, you know, stage an event."

"An event?"

"Yeah, you know, one of your sci-fi conventions, like the Star Trek conventions, we call it Ralfcon—"

"Is there a hole somewhere for me to get sick in?" Dexter moaned, in the absence of which he belted down another hasty slug of wine.

"Hey, come on, Dex, we do the first one ourselves, and if we launch it right, the Ralfies will take it from there, isn't that the way you said—"

"What do you mean *we*, White Man?"

"Hey, come on, Dex, what do I know from this sci-fi stuff? This is *your* planet, not mine, Monkey Boy."

Dexter put down his glass. Although the turn of the conversation had just thoroughly killed his appetite, he forced himself to take a mouthful of food and slowly chew it down before he spoke.

"*This* is why you bought me lunch in a place like this?"

Jimmy's false little smile was somehow engaging. "Well, uh, like I said, I *did* figure it might take some major buttering up, and I don't think my bank account would stand up to buttering up much more major than this. . . ."

"This is the complicated news?"

Texas Jimmy's eyes became positively furtive. "Naw, this is still the simple stuff, I'm not drunk enough for *that* yet. . . ."

His eyes brightened when the waiter arrived with the second bottle of Pomerol, did the ceremony, filled the glasses, and departed.

Dexter took only a pro forma sip, concentrating on getting more food down, while Jimmy took two long swallows.

Jimmy smiled, shrugged, sighed, frowned. "Well," he said tentatively, "maybe I'm ready to give it the old college try. . . ."

He put down his cutlery, and looked straight into Dexter's eyes in a forthright and intense manner that as Dexter remembered had never been his style before.

"I'm a showbiz guy, Dex, always have been," he said. "I ain't no schmuck, I mean I *do* have Hollywood street smarts or I wouldn't have survived in the business this long, but I'm not one of your Harvard intellectuals or rocket scientists."

He favored Dexter with a strange little smile. "I'm no science fiction writer either, let alone one of Amanda Robin's vibrating mystics, but . . ."

"But?"

A positively haunted look had stolen into Texas Jimmy Balaban's eyes. "But what is, is real, now ain't it?" he said. "A real-flesh-and-blood guy stumbles onstage with a schtick about being a comic from the future. And I groom him and make moves and there he is with a TV show. And through all the changes, the guy never wavers, he *insists* he's the real thing."

"What are you trying to tell me, Jimmy?" Dexter found himself saying quite gently.

Texas Jimmy shrugged, threw up his hands, took a drink, but all the while maintaining eye contact. "What am I trying to tell you, Dex? You're the science fiction writer, you tell me, shit, *you* created this Deathship Starship schtick."

The narrow-eyed look he gave Dexter had him going back to his wineglass himself despite all prior better judgment to the contrary.

"Or so you think," Jimmy said.

"Or so I think?" Dexter repeated slowly, his voice sounding as hollow to himself as the pit of his gut was beginning to feel.

"Look, Dex, I don't know from time travel or chaos mechanics or quantum cosmology, and about all I know about psychiatry is what I got from a movie about Freud starring Farley Granger, but I been thinking, and I been reading, and it seems to me one of two things *has* to be going on. . . ."

The boozyness went out of Texas Jimmy's voice, and though his eyes were now bloodshot, there was a depth to them that Dexter was sure he had never seen there before.

"Either you and me and Amanda took a nutcase who was at least still more or less functioning and drove him all the way round the bend for our own purposes," he said in a firm, hard voice. "Or . . ."

"Or?"

"Or we're living in one of your science fiction stories, Lampkin, and Ralf's more or less what he says he is, and *he's* been using us for *his.*"

Jimmy exhaled, took a mere sip of wine, seemed somehow relieved. "There, I've said it," he said. "Can you think of a third alternative, Dex?"

Dexter could and he couldn't.

He could just about grasp Cam Carswell's theory about the virtuality of time, in which both possibilities could be virtually true. But aside from his inability to explain the physics to himself, let alone to Texas Jimmy, he could hardly fit it into the moral framework that Jimmy had just laid out with brutal clarity.

Either a virtual entity from a virtual future had used him as a vector to manifest itself in the present in order to bootstrap that future into existence out of the quantum flux, or *he* had used a schizoid comic as the mouthpiece for *his* transformational purposes and driven the poor schmuck over the edge into full-blown psychosis while making beaucoup bucks in the process.

And Texas Jimmy Balaban, as deeply implicated as he was, who had never before impressed Dexter as a heavy duty moral philosopher, had summoned up the courage to voice that unpleasant truth. No wonder he had to get shit-faced to do it!

"What do *you* believe, Jimmy?" was all Dexter could manage to ask respectfully, saying with tone of voice what he could not quite bring himself to put into words.

Namely, that Texas Jimmy Balaban, in this moment, had proven himself a better man than he was.

"Believe me, Dex, I've been driving myself crazy trying to figure that one out, I mean, Ralf ain't hardly there no more, I been thinking maybe he needs to be put away right now for his own good, I could get him committed in five minutes, but you should see what . . . what . . . what whatever *is* there has been able to do with the plants in his apartment, I mean making the desert bloom like the Bible says, it don't get much realer than that, and seeing is believing, according to Ripley."

"You're starting to drift, Jimmy."

"*Starting* to drift!" Jimmy said. He issued a mirthless little laugh. "No, Dex, I just *stopped* drifting a few days ago when I finally figured it out."

"You've . . . figured it all out?" Dexter said, regarding Texas Jimmy with no little sense of wonder.

"Yeah," Jimmy told him, "I finally got it through my head that it doesn't matter."

"Doesn't matter?"

"Yeah, believe me, I went through being plenty pissed at you and Amanda till I figured *that* one out! You and Amanda fuck with a schizo's head for your own purposes, or Uk-Ruppa-Tooty from the thirty-fifth century uses the three of us for *his*, so what difference does it make one way or the other?"

"How do you figure that, Jimmy?" Dexter said.

"'Cause whosoever it is, the *purpose* is the same!" Texas Jimmy proclaimed. "Which is to get us to do what we got to do to get the Monkey People show picked up for another couple million years instead of continuing to lay the current series of bombs that's doing us in! So whether it's a sci-fi guy and a vibrating lady and an agent just out to make a buck creating the Starship Captain out of bullshit and bailing wire, or the Great Spirit from Beyond the Planet of the Apes using *us* to get it done, seems to me, Dex, either way or both, *nobody* done the wrong thing."

"Fuck a duck . . ." Dexter could only mutter. Was he just drunk as a skunk or had the booze or something else really summoned up such unexpected wisdom from the depths of this ordinary Hollywood hustler?

"What is, is real, right?" said Texas Jimmy. "And it seems to me that any schmuck who watches *The Word According To* and has it upstairs to read the papers and chew gum at the same time can figure out by now that while the Captain's Starship is presently one of your sci-fi pipe dreams, the Deathship's as real as the San Fernando Valley smog."

Dexter found himself feeling both vindicated and shamed.

Vindicated because whether as machiavellian creator or instrument of some more highly evolved consciousness inherently beyond his complete understanding or some virtual combination of both, what he had brought into the world with *The Word According to Ralf* had succeeded in doing what *The Transformation* could not.

No scientist, no heavy thinker, no science fiction reader, a perfect example of the sort of ordinary guy the science fiction fans scorned as a "mundane," Texas Jimmy had *gotten* it.

Shamed because he was now forced to realize that he too had sold the Texas Jimmy Balabans of the world short.

Jimmy met Dexter's eyes man-to-man. "Look Dex, I maybe fucked around too much on too many wives, but I don't think I've been a bad guy, I mean I never stole from clients, generally kept my word, never went around trying to do people in . . ."

He shrugged. "On the other hand, I can't honestly say I've ever really risked my own bottom line before just to try to make the world a better place, so what can I tell you . . ."

"More, just now, I think," said Dexter, "than I've ever been able to tell you."

"Then you're in it with me, Dex? The tab for this lunch isn't going to be just more money flushed down the tubes?"

"In *what*, Jimmy?"

"Ralfcon, what *else* you think this has all been about!"

"Oh fer—"

"Yeah, yeah, I know, you don't want any part of such a sleazy cynical operation just to sell T-shirts and DVDs, you'll puke if you have to be crawled all over by these disgusting fans, the whole nine yards!" Jimmy interrupted in a passionate burst before Dexter could finish opening his mouth.

"I know the whole story, but for the price of a fancy meal, maybe you owe it to me to shut up and listen before you tell me to get stuffed?"

There was no honestly denying that, so Dexter did.

"I made a deal with Madden," Jimmy told him. "For ten percent of our share of the cassette and video disk money for the first five years after cancellation, the Gold Network runs a two-hour live special on Ralfcon in Prime Time on the Fourth of July when they figure to get creamed by ballgames and stuff anyway."

"Why, Jimmy?" Dexter managed to say. "What's—"

"What's in it for us?"

"That's not what—"

"What's in it for us is a two-hour commercial to launch the disks and cassettes and whatever other tie-ins we can think of to push, tell me we don't come out ahead if the Ralfcon just breaks even on the admissions, and—"

"—but—"

"—and instead of slinking offstage to the bughouse at the end of this long series of bombs, Ralf gets to extro the scene with a flourish, with a little dignity, we leave 'em with a legend to remember instead of a sad story to forget!"

Dexter found himself taking yet another drink of wine, for, whatever gods there be help him or not, this was starting to make more kinds of sense than he really cared to think about.

"If we're dealing with a guy we've driven to the nuthatch, I'd say maybe we owe him that much, wouldn't you?" Jimmy told him. "And if not . . ."

"If not?"

Texas Jimmy Balaban actually pushed a half-full glass of wine away from him before he spoke.

"Look, whatever you and me are dealing with here, whoever's watching on television is seeing what they're seeing on television, period. Showbiz. TV. A story. And without the Ralfcon special, the story is the show goes off the air at the end of the season and it never comes back in the fall 'cause Ralf's had to be committed, and no matter how cool we try to play it, the tabloids'll find out, need I say more?"

Jimmy shrugged. A hard light of clarity seemed to come into his bloodshot eyes.

"Or we give 'em a real Hollywood ending and leave 'em with a legend that they'll remember long after the final curtain, we make out like bandits by doing good, hey, there's more Elvis merchandise moving now than there ever was while the King was alive, and last time I looked, Jesus Christ was still selling like a superstar after not even having made a single live appearance for two thousand years."

He laughed to take the edge off, but Dexter had never looked into a more serious pair of eyes. "You're the writer, Dex, if you're writing the end to the story, which way is it gonna to be?"

Dexter sighed, already feeling himself on the downhill slide to the inevitable. "Well, when you put it that way . . ."

"Then you're with me?"

Dexter hesitated; resigned, however, to the fact that that was all he was doing.

Jimmy's hands fidgeted nervously on the tablecloth. "I sure hope so, Dex," he said in his more familiar mode. "I mean, after all the money I'm blowing on this lunch . . ."

"Oh hell, Jimmy . . ." Dexter moaned.

"It'd be a ballbuster without you," Jimmy told him, "but if you turn me down I'm gonna have to try." He shrugged, threw up his hands. "Asshole that I am, I already booked a hotel in New York."

His endearing little smile was the clincher.

"Maybe the guys in the white coats should throw their net over me," he said, "'cause I fronted the guarantee with my own bread."

Dexter managed a woozy wan grin back. "I guess you should send them to my place instead," he said, "'cause not only am I with you, my good man, I'm gonna pick up the tab for this lunch!"

Texas Jimmy Balaban laughed. He clinked glasses with Dexter. "I'd drink to that, ol' buddy, if what you just said didn't already prove we were both so shit-faced drunk!"

He winked. He waved his hand to summon the waiter. He reached for his wallet.

"Tell you what, let's do the right thing, and be mensches about it, partner," he said. "Let's go Dutch."

No point in sendin' Rat Girl outa the rathole more'n you hadda these days, meanin' like when the fuckin' asshole onna desk banged onna door to remind her the Heroin Hilton ain't no city shelter and you ain't got the rent bein' paid by the Welfare either, y'stupid fuckin' junkie, so pay up or get out.

Think Rat, an' was there some fuckin' other way t'think, it was kinda hard t're-member, an' this was a pain in the ass, but whaddya gonna do, the monkey downstairs hadda baseball bat probably a fuckin' Uzi too anna cops was onna pad, would kite you maybe a day or two, but if y'didn't fork over by then, your rat's ass was out onna street.

Which wouldn'ta been no big fuckin' deal, save ya the trouble a scroungin' for money, 'cept then where the fuck do ya plug in your television?

Thinkin' Rat never seemed t'figure *that* one out, an' the monkey meat didn't know either, an' what they sent y'here inta this piecea meatware t'do was t'be then an' there at the nice sharp pivot point where y'could stick in that big steel tooth when an' where it was gonna do the most good, when you could just kinda flick th' Rat Girl's wrist an' twirl th' Monkey World off th' screen an' inta the Dumpster, hee, hee, hee, makin' the necessary room for a million years of a cool clean garbage can floatin' on a silver platter in space, scree, scree, scree, what the fuck *else* would a nice Rat Thing like you be doin' back here stuck like a rusty coat hanger inna disgustin' brain of a monkey girl like this!

But t'do that, y'hadda be there when th' time-line crossed th' slime-line, when it came down to a million years of meat or a million years of metal, y'hadda be there t'do the Dead World Destroyer before th' Enemy did *you*.

So you hadda watch TV.

'Cause that was where th' motherfucker hung out.

An' that was where it was gonna happen.

An' *that* was where you hadda figure out how t'be when it did.

On television.

That was where everything that was anything happened in the Monkey World.

Th' monkey meat had a lotta trouble gettin' it, Rat Things an' coat hangers was about what it could handle, there *ain't* no little people inside the fuckin' thing so we *can't* go there, ya stupid ratfuck bastid, it's pictures a full-sized humans they broadcast through the air with these gizmos, was about the size of its meatware data processing machinery.

No, monkey girl, not the place where they make the pictures onna glass.

On television.

Where waves in the invisible ocean of the air wait t'become pictures an' words. Where gonnabes in the invisible ocean of time fight it out to happen. To become real.

On television.

Like th' song onna TV says, Rat Girl, *you* are livin' in a material world, and *you* are a material girl, but there's others what ain't, floatin' around like stories tryin' t'get told, zillions and zillions of 'em, like there's thirty fuckin' channels a TV out there no one sees or hears till y'tune one in, but *they're still out there* waitin' t'happen when the channel gets changed hee, hee, hee!

An' that's what we're gonna do, monkey meat, we're gonna change th' channel, we're gonna tune out Captain Starship Planet of the Apes and tune in a *much* better program, y'd really love this one, Monkey Girl, was there any meatware creatures oozing around t'see it, hee, hee, hee, none a this awful pimply flesh stuff drippin' pus an' piss an' shit an' all don't it disgust you t'be it, scree, scree, scree, no things bitin' pieces outa other things inna biospheric daisy chain up its own asshole, nice clean chips an' metal an' machine oil instead, world runs like clockwork, hee, hee, hee, tick-tock, tick-tock, the Rat Things *are* the clock, scree, scree, scree, an' 'cause it ain't alive inna first place, the Dead World goes on forever, hee, hee, hee. . . .

An' if t'do that, y' gotta get out there witha monkeys every couple a three days so's y'can boost the money t'keep this rathole which gotta place t'plug in the television, well tough shit, besides which the fuckin' sparkly things was floatin' in fronta her face again like the static onna fuckin' crummy TV only had these goddamn rabbit ears an' that suckin' hole inna guts was reminding her again that the monkey meat couldn't keep goin' on cockroaches forever.

True, they was swarmin' all over the place, protein on six legs, but it took hours an' hours t'catch enough t'make a mouthful, a big fuckin' waste a time, an' you probably didn't even break even on th' energy, so you hadda skitter out onta the streets again t'score a couple three day's worth a food t'feed th' meatware an' money t'feed the juice t'the television. . . .

Things bein' what they was, wasn't much t'be had on Third Avenue, just her fuckin' luck they just picked up the garbage, all she was able t'find was a pigeon been run over by a garbage truck least it was fresh an' hadn't been pissed on but gettin' the feathers down wasn't so easy, an' t'fuck things up worse, some asshole inna delivery van had broadsided a bus, an' the street was swarmin' with cops, alla gypsies an' beggars had headed for elsewhere, anna Rat Girl figured likewise, skitterin' inna general direction of Madison Square Park, which figured t'be fulla nice OD'ed junkies an' dead t'the world crackheads an' winos as usual.

She was crossin' Madison when this whole fuckin' commotion in fronta the Grand Duke Plaza caught her attention.

The Grand Duke, better known as the Grand Puke an' not without reason, useta be a hooker hotel where y'could score this an' that too till it went downhill from there when they started stuffin' thirty spics inta each room t'cop th' steady an' bigger money from the Welfare.

Ordinarily, this was not a block y'figured t'score nothin' offa the animal life spilled out onta th' street, but somethin' was goin' on now an' y'never knew, now didya, Rat Girl. . . .

There was a couple big vans parked in fronta th' Grand Puke an' insteada roustin' 'em, the cops was holdin' a little crowd of rubberneckers behind sawhorses, looked like y'might be able t'slip y'fingers inside somethin' besides their stupid fuckin' ass-holes while none of 'em was lookin'.

And—

What the fuck?

Th' outside a th' Grand Puke useta be this faded brown paint-job all crackin' an' peelin', but now the walls been freshly painted Empire State Building gray with this tinfoil trim, not such a terrific job, y'can still sorta see the brown showin' through here an' there like the hotel shit inna pair a gray flannel pants, probably not that far from the fuckin' truth.

An' th' entrance marquees been given the same sleazy once-over, an' it don't say "Grand Duke" no more, sez "Hotel Metropolis."

An' on top a one a the vans is this big fuckin' satellite TV dish an' a buncha other crap looks like TV antennas and stuff and there's all this fuckin' cable shit coming outa the back end up the steps an' inta the lobby.

"What th' fuck's goin' on?" Rat Girl yelled at no one in particular, pushin' through the crowda assholes.

"Fuck you!"

"Jeez!"

A lotta gruntin' an' cursin' but none a these motherfuckers give her no straight answer, but at least none of 'em give her no shit neither when she squeezes by 'em, just sorta shrink back an' get outa her way like they can see she got the Big Ripper under her raincoat an' they know what's good for 'em.

She gets t'the sawhorses, still no one'll tell her what the fuck's happenin', just as these two guys wheel a big mother TV camera outa the other van.

There's a big black cop th' other side a the sawhorse.

"Hey, what's goin' on, man?"

Th' motherfucker gives her this look like she was a giant walkin' booger.

"It's *Ralfcon!*" sez this voice behind her sounds like Donald Duck.

Rat Girl turned, and there was this guy, maybe, kinda hard t'tell, 'cause he musta weighed three hundred fuckin' pounds, shaped like a fuckin' bowling pin, an ass y'wouldn't believe, a gut t'match, an' kinda *boobs* almost, stuffed inta this quadruple XXX-tra large T-shirt with th' Earth blastin' through space onna tail a fire like some fuckin' rocket ship.

"What the fuck's *Ralfcon?*"

"It's a *science fiction convention!*" the fat guy told her, grinning like he's real happy t'see her for some fuckin' reason. "Registration opens at five!" There's some-thing weird about his eyes, like they're kinda too close together. "It's going to be on television, and he's—"

Th' fat guy don't finish whatever the fuck he's sayin', 'cause there's this sound from th' rubberneckers kinda like squealin' an' kinda like barkin', an' he's makin' it too—

"Ralf! Ralf! Ralf!"

An' when Rat Girl turned t'look, she saw this cab had pulled up t'the curb, an' some guy in a tan suit had gotten out, followed by a man inna weird green suit looked like th' hotel doorman—

A man?

Think monkey meat, was a man maybe.

Think Rat, was th' Enemy, th' Dead World Destroyer.

The Starship Captain.

Right there in front of her like they was both *on television*.

Th' guy inna tan suit says somethin' that she don't hear an' a couple a cops come over t'guard him as th' Starship Captain walks past the sawhorses toward th' hotel entrance, an' then—

—and then th' motherfucker's walkin' right past her maybe three fuckin' feet away!

—she reaches inside th' raincoat, grabs th' handle a th' Big Ripper, starts t'whip it out as she shoves against the fuckin' sawhorse, an—

—the cop standin' there whacks her inna chest witha palm of his fuckin' ham of a hand, knockin' her staggerin' backwards inta the fat guy before she can get th' knife out, an—

And those eyes are lookin' *right at her* as he goes bye bye.

Like right *through* th' fuckin' raincoat can see Ol' Rip just waitin' t'say hello. Right through the monkey meat t'what's inside.

Grinnin' this stupid fuckin' grin says peek-a-boo Rat Girl I see you not a fuckin' thing you can do about at now can you, hee, hee, hee!

"We'll see about *that*, motherfucker!"

See about it where it counts.

"See ya on television, asshole!"

14

Texas Jimmy Balaban couldn't plead innocence of third-rate New York hotels, so except for the weirdness of the cut-rate decor, the Hotel Metropolis was more or less what he had expected. This neighborhood was not what people who knew New York only from movies pictured when they heard the words "Madison Avenue," but Jimmy wasn't one of them so he had known damn well the Metropolis was not going to be the Plaza or even the Sheraton as soon as the convention bureau put him onto it.

But the manager's spiel had won him over. The guy had forthrightly admitted that the Metropolis was a brand-new renovation of a truly disgusting dump called the Grand Duke and the only reason he was being offered such a sweetheart deal was because they sorely need some kind of event to start wiping clean the joint's well-deserved odious reputation.

Try finding a room rate and a deal like this on your function space in any other hotel in Manhattan with a restaurant, a coffee shop, a bar, room service, and no resident crack dealers, Mr. Balaban, and believe me, in six months, you won't find it at the Metropolis either. This had the ring of New York truth, and a day of calling around town had confirmed it, so here they were.

Namely in the top VIP suite on the tenth floor—a so-called parlor sandwiched in between two bedrooms—which had obviously been cobbled together out of three singles. The furnishings in the parlor looked like they had just been bought from some joint specializing in dentists' waiting rooms and the new cheapjack fixtures in the bathrooms were connected to ancient plumbing already starting to sweat through the cosmetic paint-job. Like the rest of the hotel, the suite was done up in pale gray, dim white, and matte black, with accents in silver, some sleazoid interior decorator's idea of Dreko Deco.

"Well, what do you think, Ralf?"

Ralf looked like he belonged in this set for a low-budget remake of *Flash Gordon* as he stood there in his Starship Captain's uniform with eyes from outer space and that semipermanent fixed smile.

"It's a hotel room on pre-Deathship Earth," Ralf said in the flat zombified tone that had become all too familiar.

"You're sure of that, huh?" Jimmy said sourly.

Ralf looked right at him, and something behind the eyes made contact, and the Presence that these days was doing all the significant talking let him know it was still in there with a one-word line delivered with a phantom wink.

"Virtually," said the Voice.

Gave you goose bumps.

And it made Jimmy glad for the layout of this crummy suite. Leaving Ralf alone in a self-contained single did not seem like a swift idea, but having this parlor in between their bedrooms did, and not because Jimmy entertained serious thoughts of chasing after pussy.

Flying out from the Coast with Ralf had been a little good news and a lot of bad. Jimmy had sprung for business class, hey why not, but when Ralf showed up in full costume, drawing the kind of attention one might expect, they had been hustled into the VIP lounge and bumped to First real quick. That had been the good news.

The bad news had been that Amanda Robin had refused to come along to try to help keep Ralf on the rails for the duration, even when he had offered her a business-class ticket and a room at the Plaza. Even when he upped it to all expenses plus two grand for three lousy days' work.

"As far as I'm concerned, *The Word According to Ralf* has been spoken, and the exit scene is not really something I want to be around for," she had told him.

Under the circumstances, it was kind of hard for Jimmy to argue with this, but of course he had tried anyway.

"That part of my life is over," she finally told him. "Anyway, I've signed to do a seven-day shoot in a feature that week, so I'm unavailable . . . but I promise I *will* watch it on television."

"Terrific, just terrific!"

So Jimmy had spent the whole flight watching a dumb movie and dumber videos, manfully refraining from lapping up too much of the unlimited free booze, and hoping that this Ralfcon thing wasn't going to turn out to be a terrible mistake.

For between the time he had written the deposit check to the Metropolis and the termination of the season, Ralf had given up entirely. No more voice imitations. No more jokes that mere Monkey People could understand, let alone laugh at. The final few shows consisted of long stretches of birdbrained celebrity babble punctuated by manifestations of the Voice preaching to the True Believers.

Okay, so the show was dead and there was nothing left to do but wait for the wake, but this untrouperlike behavior outraged Texas Jimmy's sense of show business honor.

Ernie Kovacs had once been given a deathslot opposite Berle when Uncle Miltie was Mr. Television. When the inevitable came, Kovacs, the master of live special comic effects, proclaimed: "If *we* can't have this studio, *nobody* can have it!" And spent the last half-hour of the very last show running a hilarious mock demolition of the premises.

That was class.

Throwing in the towel on the air was not.

If that was what it was.

Classless or not, Jimmy hoped so.

Because the alternative explanation was a lot worse.

Namely that Ralf had lost it completely.

There had been no point in reading Ralf the riot act about it either, because there was no getting through now. There didn't even exactly seem to be a Ralf to get through to of late.

Except when the Voice spoke through him, he walked, he ate, no doubt he used the john, he spoke a little when spoken to, but it was like there was nobody at home at all. Like he had been switched off for all but the most necessary functions.

The psych books Jimmy tried to plow through called it "intermittent catatonic fugue" and according to them it had a strong tendency to progress to a permanent condition, an act that did not exactly figure to go over too well on Sunday night's televised live performance. Ralf had passed so much of the flight in this state that he had Jimmy in a perpetual state of dread that it had happened already.

But occasionally, Ralf's expression would snap into focus, his eyes would come alive as if pinlights had been switched on inside his skull, and out would pour the kind of star presence that no one could fake and any performer would sell his soul for and gladly throw in his agent's in the bargain, and the Voice would deliver a line or so seemingly just to reassure him.

"Don't worry Jimmy, I *have* to get it right, 'cause if I bomb out *this* time, there's nothing left backstage to go on but a chimp act and a gypsy violinist."

None of the shrink books had any hundred-dollar-an-hour words to slap on that!

So Jimmy had nursed his drinks while praying to the gods of showbiz to keep Ralf at least *this* functional through Ralfcon. Come on, guys, just let me get him through a few appearances in crowd shots with no speaking lines to dress the taped footage during the next couple of days, an hour's live appearance on Sunday that's not a total disaster, and an autograph session on Monday, and it's off into the sunset, I promise.

Give us a break, will you, a *hit* I'm not even asking for!

Most science fiction conventions devoted to singular objects of worship like Star Trek, rather than being the creation of idealistic fannish enthusiasm, were moneymaking operations for the promoters, something which Dexter Lampkin had always found questionable, and not being even a minor deity in any such pocket universes made keeping his distance from such cons no sacrifice.

Which could be said in spades for even the thought of having anything to do with *running* a convention. Dexter, as a professional writer, had always considered such fannish activity several light-years beneath his dignity. Yet here he was in a crummy hotel in New York, up to his ass in just the sort of mercenary convention operation he had always so righteously scorned, and as the Secret Master of Ralfcon!

At first, all Jimmy Balaban had asked him to do was set up the program, something about which Jimmy knew jack shit, and which any science fiction writer who had been to enough of these things could do drunk and stoned in bed with a fan girl in his sleep.

Some phone calls and e-mail messages holding out a free trip to New York as the prize easily secured enough bodies to fill three days' worth of panels. And someone had to set the topics, didn't they?

And this was *Ralfcon,* wasn't it?

The theme of which was the successful negotiation of the Transformation Crisis as exemplified by the Starship Captain himself, so who was as qualified to lay out panel topics as the author of both *The Transformation* and *The Word According to Ralf*?

The Metropolis was otherwise the bare minimum for a convention hotel, two hundred and fifty-four rooms into which you could squeeze maybe eight hundred people if you got disgusting about it, which the fans surely would. Dexter had groaned when Jimmy had told him he hadn't made a deal with the hotel to comp him the function space in return for a guarantee to fill the rooms, and Jimmy had groaned even louder when Dexter explained this fact of convention life.

So Dexter had slid further down the slippery slope by telling Jimmy that with enough fans within easy commuting distance to draw minimum fifteen hundred people a day, he could recoup by offering day passes at say twenty bucks a pop.

It had seemed like a good idea at the time. But now, wandering around the main floor on Friday night, with the place only beginning to fill up with people checking in for the whole con, he was beginning to wonder.

The only real function space the Metropolis had was a ballroom into which you could maybe shoehorn a thousand people in a sardine can standing room situation. A hundred people would fill the bar, though probably not at the prices they were charging for watered booze. There were only half a dozen so-called suites, none of which were really adequate for a major party. If you stuffed fifteen hundred fans in here, every square inch of this joint was going to be jammed with flesh like the subway rush hour.

Ellie had turned down his offer to take her with him to Ralfcon, as Dexter had known she would, on wifely grounds that she had had enough of Ralf and *The Word According To* to last her several lifetimes and fannish grounds that no True Fan would be caught dead at such a cynical for-profit con. And Dexter had to admit that her fannish instincts seemed likely to be proven righter than even she had imagined when it came to Ralfcon.

Not my job, Monkey Boy, Dexter told himself, elbowing his way through the already crowded lobby toward the stairs to the basement.

But it was harder to convince himself that it wasn't his *doing*. Still harder to absolve himself of responsibility for what was surely going to be the usual sci-fi freak-show media coverage writ large.

For after he had presented Texas Jimmy with his panel program, Jimmy had pointed out that the main purpose of Ralfcon was to provide visuals for the two-hour TV show on Sunday and talking heads were not what the network programmer ordered.

Didn't you say something about these things having art shows and masquerades?

Oh shit.

Indeed Dexter had.

So in return for a promise that a minimum of twelve minutes of serious discussion of the future destiny of the species would be intercut into the broadcast in sixty-second sound bites, Dexter had let himself be conned into making the calls necessary to find some New York area fans to run the art show and the masquerade.

And while he was at it, why not the dealer's room too, after all, *his* books were going to be on sale there, now weren't they?

The only room the Metropolis had for both the art show and the huckster room was the basement storage area, which the management had insisted was adequate to the task.

When Dexter reached the bottom of the stairs he saw what they meant.

When the hotel was renovated, no one had apparently seen any point on wasting money redoing the basement. The naked gray concrete walls were tinted green here and there with fungus, and there was a background odor of rat poison and roach spray. It had been divided up into two by fiberboard partitions. The smaller of these held the art show; the usual amateur efforts, herein dominated by portraits of Ralf and renderings of future Earthscapes, which at least, Dexter was gratified to see, trended much more to the Starship than the Deathship.

In bottom-line terms, the huckster room should've delighted him, utterly dominated as it was by stands hawking every licensed Ralf tie-in extant, from the comics and posters and cheap T-shirts on up through the satin warm-up jackets and top-of-the-line Starship Captain suits, every sale of which was an incremental contribution to his bank account.

Instead it made him feel like just the sort of exploitative schlockmeister he had previously disdained. As one of those sarcastic Sixties slogans had it, he had turned into one of the people he had warned himself about.

When he checked out the book stands, of which there were only five in a sea of Ralf merchandising, he discovered to both his chagrin and sardonic amusement that poetic justice had not entirely vanished from the world.

The Transformation had been reissued in a modest printing. A thorough search of the bookstands revealed all of thirty-four copies in the entire room.

All the book stands, however, featured the twenty-four-pocket dump of *The Word According to Ralf*, with an abundance of copies in reserve behind the tables. And affixed to the fiberboard of each wall was an enormous blow-up of the cover, featuring Ralf in full cry, overprinted with an announcement of Monday's autograph session.

Which figured to move hundreds if not thousands of copies, each one of which would be money in Dexter's pocket.

For it wouldn't be the mere author of the book doing the signing.

It would be the Starship Captain.

———

Was enough t'make a Rat Girl puke. The lobby a th' Hotel Metropolis was wall-to-wall monkey meat, like it was rush hour inna subway, an' y'never saw so much fuckin' blubber in your life, they was all quackin' an' babblin' an' linin' up, well sorta, in fronta the check-in counter an' these desks they had set up with more weirdos behind 'em, so's y'almost had t'cut your way through it all with th' Big Ripper t'get to where this fat rentacop is standin' inna narrow hallway goes inside.

Even there, it's a mob a these weirdos with funny eyes an' asses like watermelons oozin' past him, but hey, this must be the place all right, 'cause a lotta them got on these T-shirts witha Starship Captain's face, somea them even stuffed into the fuckin' green uniform.

"Where do you think *you're* going?" said the rentacop when she finally managed t'shove her way through.

"Inside, whaddya think!"

The rentacop took a half-step sideways t'block her, put his hand on the handle of his billy like he was strokin' th' head of his dick.

"You don't get no further without a badge."

"What th' fuck y'mean I don't go no further! You're lettin' in all these disgustin' creeps, now ain'tcha!"

"You heard me," he said inna dead voice sounded like a dealer faced with the twenty-fifth junkie not makin' his day tryin' t'score on credit. "No one without a badge gets past the lobby."

"But I gotta real important message for th' Starship Captain," Rat Girl told him, reachin' inside her raincoat t'stroke th' handle a th' Big Ripper.

The rentacop kinda ran his eyes over th' fuckin' weirdos jammed inta th' lobby a th' Grand Puke.

"Yeah, right, you and the rest of these creeps," he said, wrinklin' up his nose like a buncha bad farts just been blown off, an' cometa think of it, it *did* stink in here.

"Well what th' fuck I gotta do t'get in there, suck your cock, hey, no problem, there's gotta be a toilet around somewheres. . . ."

The rentacop gave her this look like her mouth was drippin' with maggots an' AIDS pus or somethin', made ya wanna whip out ol' Rip an' let him suck on *that* for a while, somehow, though, she figured it might not be too terrific an idea in fronta all this monkey meat.

"So what I gotta do t'get onea these badge things?"

"You have to buy a convention membership," says this guy's voice behind her so bright an' friendly makes y' wanna sink ol' Rip inta his fuckin' cheerful guts.

When she turned an' looked, though, easier said than done, 'cause you coulda shoved a fuckin' samurai sword up t' the handle inta th' belly in question without hittin' bottom.

"This is your very first convention, I'll bet, now, isn't it?"

He's wearin' these Coke-bottle-bottom glasses make his eyes look like somethin' inna fish tank an' he's grinnin' from ear to ear.

"Yeah, I guess."

"Well, let *me* be the *very first* to welcome *you* to Fandom!" he sez, as he sorta takes her by the elbow an' leads her outa the crush a little. "You buy your membership over there at the registration desk," he tells her.

"Yeah? How much?"

"Fifty dollars."

"*Fifty fuckin' bucks!*"

"It sounds like a lot of money, but it gets you into *everything*—the panels, the art show, the masquerade, the big show on Sunday, and an all-night film program, the movies alone make it a bargain."

Fifty bucks! It'd take two or three fuckin' days t'snatch that much outa gypsies' hats an' blind beggars' paper cups!

She looked Mr. Friendly Fatso up an' down. Odds were real good that a guy like this got laid about as often as he took a fuckin' bath, which by the smell sure hadn't been lately. Well, it had been awhile, but what the fuck. . . .

"Hey, look, I really wanna go to my first convention an' all," she told him, "but I ain't got no money. So how about we go outside, an' find some alley, an' you give me five bucks, an' I suck your cock?"

His eyes bugged out even more, which was sayin' somethin', an' his face actually turned red, as soon as he noticed, he was probably gonna wipe the fuckin' *drool* offa his chin.

"You're . . . you're . . . serious?" he squeaked like he was about t'come already, would probably take about thirty seconds t'get him off once she found it under all that blubber.

"Tell y'what," she told him, "'cause you're sucha nice guy an' all, you find me ten a your friends, an' *you* I'll do for two-fifty."

Texas Jimmy Balaban had to have a serious talk with Dexter Lampkin about how to handle tomorrow's public appearances for the benefit of the cameras, but the last thing he wanted was Ralf walking in on the conversation. So after a room service dinner, he told Ralf to stay put, called Dexter's room, and told him to meet him in the bar.

Jimmy had given Dex's war stories about these sci-fi conventions a thirty-five percent discount for exaggeration, but even if he hadn't, it still wouldn't have prepared him for what was out there on the other side of the hotel room door.

The hall was full of people. Schlepping suitcases and boxes and cases of beer into rooms. Drinking and gabbling right there in the hallway. Sitting on the *floor*. Smoking *dope*. Wearing Starship Earth T-shirts, Starship Captain T-shirts, Starship Captain suits, homemade costumes of their own—Spocks, barbarians, space Nazis, grossly overweight little green men, jeez, a giant blue *rabbit*.

Jimmy had to step around and over them to get to the elevator, and when it arrived, the first thing that came sashaying out of it was about three hundred and fifty pounds of harem girl whose costume allowed the imagination absolutely no mercy.

As the elevator began its torturous floor-by-floor descent to the lobby, more and more of these sci-fi fans crammed themselves into it; in Ralf tie-in items, in chainmail jockstraps, with car antennas coming out of chartreuse hairdos, Viking broads from Venus.

And just as Lampkin had claimed, the proportion of the grossly overweight and weird around the eyeballs was amazingly large, to the point that Jimmy *hoped* he imagined the elevator cable groaning under the strain.

But Dex hadn't told him how unselfconscious these people were; flaunting all of what they had, which was plenty, as if a hairy belly bursting through a chainmail vest or an ass the size of the Ritz in skintight neon-pink Spandex were the most natural sights in the world.

In some crazy way, Jimmy found himself *admiring* them. Hey, if these bods and faces was what you got dealt, you could do a lot worse than summoning up the brass balls to play your crummy hand this way.

He might've almost found it charming, were it not for the overpowering smell of armpits and moldy sneakers underlaid by the musk of hopelessly frustrated locker room lust.

So Jimmy exhaled a sigh of more than relief at the fact that the elevator hadn't dropped like stone down the shaft when it finally reached the lobby and emptied out in a tide of sweaty flesh. But what greeted him there almost made him believe that one of Scotty's transporter beams had dropped him down elsewhere than Planet Earth.

The outer lobby between the street entrance and the registration desk was totally crammed with people checking in and registering, the contents of the elevator writ large. Pouring past each other up and down the steps to the basement, filling every square inch of standing room, posting messages on a wall of corkboards, taping up posters, babbling, yelling, playing handheld keyboards and kazoos, were people dressed as witches and wizards, space monsters and heavy metal disco queens, tinfoil robots, and even something that Jimmy would swear was supposed to be a giant walking *piece of shit*.

And Ralfs.

Dozens of them.

Male Ralfs. Female Ralfs. Ralfs of indeterminant sex. Normally shaped Ralfs. Fat Ralfs. Grossly fat Ralfs. Enormously fat Ralfs. Even the occasional skinny Ralfs. Ralfs in official Starship Captain uniforms. Ralfs in amateurish home-made rip-offs. Ralfs in full face makeup and fright wig.

Texas Jimmy Balaban fought his way to the bar through the Planet of the Ralfs with his mouth hanging open and every cell in his body screaming for booze.

For some merciful reason Jimmy found this refuge half-empty—a bunch of people in Starship T-shirts, a trio of airline stewardesses who looked like they had landed on Mars, only three Ralfs—and Lampkin was already there on a barstool.

"Double Wild Turkey on the rocks" were Jimmy's first words, as he sat down, to a bartender who was looking about as shell-shocked as he felt. "On second thought, maybe you got a big enough glass for a triple?"

"And what name do you want on your badge?" said the creature behind th' desk when the monkey meat finally got there an' plunked down ten five-dollar bills took less than an hour behinda Dumpster t'score off these creeps couple of 'em even came as they was unzipping their fuckin' flies back t'the enda the line buster y'wanna try again.

"Uh . . . Rat Girl . . ."

"Rat Girl?"

"Whatsa matter, you got a fuckin' problem with that?" the Rat Girl snarled, halfway t'flippin' open th' raincoat an' let the stupid cunt argue with ol' Rip.

Suckin' ten cocks inna row like that was easier work than rippin' off fifty beggars an' winos an' all, but what was onna other end of 'em didn't do much good for ya temper.

"Oh no," sez the monkey behinda desk in this fuckin' Have a Nice Day voice y'just wanna kill, "a lot of people put fan names on their badges."

And she looked the Rat Girl up an' down with a disgustin' Happy Face grin t'match.

"Nice hall costume," she said.

"I thought the masquerade was supposed to be *tomorrow* night," Texas Jimmy Balaban said after he had gulped down not quite enough bourbon to wipe the pole-axed and queasy disbelieving look of Mr. Mundane Jones's first encounter with Fandom off his face.

Dexter laughed. "You can't say I didn't warn you, Jimmy," he said.

"Very funny, Lampkin," Jimmy said sourly, "but I think maybe we got a problem."

"What do you mean *we,* Monkey Boy?"

"Can it, will you, Dex, you've had your fun, so let's get serious."

"So what's the problem, Jimmy?"

Texas Jimmy Balaban shrugged, sighed, took a calmer sip of bourbon before he spoke again. "Ralf, tomorrow, these people . . . Look, the way the show comes down on Sunday night, we open with a taped minidoc before we go to the live perfor-mance, twelve minutes of your precious talking heads just like I promised, but the *other* forty-eight . . ."

He paused, took another sip of whiskey, looked somewhat furtively around the bar.

"I suppose we can use five or ten minutes of this masquerade thing, a few more of, uh, local color, and you said there was some kind of art show, but we need a minimum of twenty, twenty-five minutes of Ralf on camera with these people, means we have to shoot an hour at least."

"So?" said Dexter.

"So," said Texas Jimmy Balaban, his face creased in a frown of concern, "I don't know if he can take it. I was out there for about ten minutes, Dex, and I don't know if *I* could take it. And it ain't a hundred and fifty-seven Texas Jimmy Balabans in all weird shapes and sizes out there. And *I'm* not on the edge of a complete catatonic breakdown."

Dexter eyed him narrowly. "*Catatonic breakdown . . . ?*" he said slowly. This did not seem like a natural part of Jimmy's vocabulary.

"I'm not a *complete* maroon, Dexter," Jimmy said testily. "I *can* plow my way through something a little heavier than the trades if I really have to."

He sighed, he shrugged, an uncharacteristic guilty look stole onto his face. "To tell you the truth, Dex, if it wasn't way too late, maybe I'd call the whole thing off," he said. "I mean, he's gotten a whole lot worse since I set this thing up, like a zombie most of the time, and when he isn't . . . when he isn't . . ."

Texas Jimmy Balaban took a long, slow sip at his bourbon.

"I may have phumphered around the bottom end of the biz most of my career, Dex," he said, "but you end up meeting a lot of big stars anyway over the years, maybe just for a minute at a party, but it's enough to know they got something you and me don't. Star quality, presence, something that makes 'em larger than life even when they don't have real talent, and believe me, a lot of 'em don't."

"What are you trying to tell me, Jimmy?" Dexter said softly, but he was beginning to think he knew.

"What I'm trying to tell you, Dex, is there's something like that sort of hiding inside Ralf these days, comes out to play when it wants to . . ."

"A split personality?" Dexter suggested unconvincingly.

"You know better than that, Lampkin," Texas Jimmy snapped harshly. "You've seen it happen on the air. You've heard the Voice."

"Yeah, well—"

"It's something like star quality, but it's . . . it's . . . it's bigger than that, stronger. . . ."

"As if it really *is* a more highly evolved consciousness from the future, Jimmy?" Dexter said only half-teasingly.

There was an intellectual courage in Jimmy Balaban's little laugh and shrug that Dexter could not but admire. "After what I've just seen between my room and this saloon, I mean when a goddamn giant *turd* goes walking by you . . ."

"But what's the point of all this, Jimmy?"

"The point is we got a guy who's walking around in a catatonic fugue except when whatever it is takes him over to do its Starship Captain act. And before we shove him out live onstage on a wing and a prayer, we need to shoot an hour of him in the middle of what I just seen out there. I mean six-hundred-pound bimbos and giant blue rabbits ain't enough, there's got to be a few dozen versions of *him* fer chrissakes!"

Jimmy drained the last of his huge glass of bourbon.

"The point is we have to walk Ralf through a scene that's crazier than *he* is to get that footage, and it would be kind of nice if you would help me scout out a few locations where we can at least *minimize* the chances of driving him *completely* bugfuck bananas before the live performance."

He laughed. "Or at least maybe you can keep *me* from flipping out when I leave the relative sanity of this bar."

A heavily watered triple bourbon couldn't truly prepare Texas Jimmy Balaban for it, but at least the glow cushioned the shock a little as Dexter led him back into the Planet of the Sci-Fi Fans, running interference for him like a lineman leading the ball-carrier through the mob scene.

Around a half a dozen or so Ralfs of various degrees of obesity they snake-danced, past a three-hundred-pound weakling in a leopard-skin bathing suit masquerading as Charles Atlas, they shoved between the guy in the tinfoil robot suit and a girl in long brown flasher raincoat that looked like it had served as a Kleenex for a herd of elephants with eyes looked like she bit the heads off live kittens, and down the stairs to the basement.

It was crowded down here too, and the stink was even riper, but at least the "art show" gave Jimmy some hope.

What wasn't amateur night renditions of Ralf—riding a rocket like a broom-stick, standing atop the world with his hands on his hips like that old logo of Superman—was World's Fair City of the Future or Deathship Diorama.

"Not bad."

"Just pose him in front of this stuff and dress the set with a few fans," Dexter suggested. "No sound, voice-over narration added later. . . ."

"Yeah, maybe we could come away with five usable minutes. . . ."

The "dealers' room" was even better, mostly devoted as it was to the sale of Ralf tie-in items. Ralf could pose with the stacks of books, the posters, try on a T-shirt, maybe hold up a Starship Captain suit and grab a customer like a haberdashery puller, might be a gag in that, and you could come away with another usable three to five minutes that would actually be a commercial for the stuff.

"Okay, pretty good, Dex, that gives us nearly half of what we need without getting him really *involved* with these loonies," Jimmy told him. "What else we got to use for visuals?"

Lampkin's blank look was less than reassuring.

"Well, uh, the panels—"

"Your talking heads don't count."

"The scenes in the halls and lobby . . ."

Jimmy sighed. "Yeah, I guess we're gonna have to risk some walk throughs . . ."

"Leaving—"

"An appearance at the masquerade as the capper, of course, what else!" Jimmy realized. It was obvious, wasn't it? He wondered why Lampkin hadn't thought of it right up front.

He wondered why Dex was groaning now.

Float and fade, Rat Girl, 'cause here we are, scree, scree, scree, fade and float, 'cause this is *just* where we wanna be, th' *other* side a the screen, th' place what ain't exactly a *place*, y'unnerstan, right inna middle of a thousand channels of television, hee, hee, hee, where all these maybes are waitin' t'be tuned in an' become real. . . .

Whatever th' fuck *that* means unner the circumstances!

Yeah, was like a zillion channels a television all tuned in at th' same time, what with Star Trek anna Star Wars, Count Drac, an' Tarzan th' fuckin' ape, robots an' witches, monsters an' lizards an' astronuts, Dr. Who an' Prof. What The Fuck Is That, but it was also like the fuckin' subway inna middle a th' rush hour, 'cause it was *monkey meat* crammed in here, y'could sorta tell by the *smell* enough t'blow you away was there a fuckin' incha clear space t'blow you *into* . . .

A thousand channels of maybe waitin' t'be tuned in and become real? Hey, why not, *anythin'* could be hidin' here inside all this monkey meat television, an' it probably was—aliens from the flyin' saucers, dead fuckin' Elvis zombies, gorillas in human suits, Bat Girls with hollow teeth fulla AIDS faggot cum, Cat Girls with rusty razor-blade claws, hey, why not, even *Rat Girls* with great big beautiful fuckin' knives unner their raincoats, hee, hee, surprise, surprise, motherfucker!

Everything that was maybe *anything* was hiding in here right inna middle of a thousand channels a Monkey Meat TV!

Including th' Dead World Destroyer.

But th' fuckin' Starship Captain was bein' cute about it.

Real cute.

Like hidin' in plain sight.

'Cause while y'didn't even hafta think Rat t'smell he was here, stupid fuckin' monkey meat could figure *that* much out, *findin'* the motherfucker was somethin' else again, 'cause there was *hunnerds* of him walkin' around!

All wearin' that fuckin' stupid green uniform—fat ones, fatter ones, skinny ones with weird eyeballs, in all kindsa disgustin' shapes an' sizes, like th' *real* Starship Captain, the Enemy, hired himself a buncha fuckin' wind-up winos, stuffed 'em in all those cheap costumes a himself, an' turned 'em all loose t'hide behind, peek-a-boo, I see you, the fuck you do—

"Hi, Rat Girl, *I'm* Captain Ralf of Starship Earth!"

Rat Girl finds herself squashed up against one a these Starship Captain things starin' with a big stupid grin at the badge pinned t'her raincoat, squealin' an quackin', and the monkey meat starts t'whip out ol Rip an' sink it as far as it'll go inta all that blubber, seems like a good idea t'slice open this big fuckin' belly t'see what's *really* inside, hey, y'never know, y'can't be too fuckin' careful. . . .

"If you say so, asshole!"

But somethin' feels like a steel ice cube in her brain where they stuck in th' coat hanger sends this cold electric shock down her skull inta her bones, feels like she's some kinda stone statue got bonged onna head with a fuckin' hammer sent these cracks all through her like fuckin' spiderwebs an' all these crystal metal spiders come crawlin' down 'em takin' over an' inta her arm her knife-hand freezes it right there on the handle a th' Big Ripper an' not a fuckin' thing she can do about it. . . .

Not that there's exactly a Rat Girl there to think about it, you unnerstand, 'cause . . .

It's time t'*be* Rat, monkey meat, time t'change the channel an' let the Dead World show take over, you'd love this one was you gonna be around to see it, Loxy Foxy, time t'stop thinking meat, Foxy Loxy, time t'stop *being* meat, Rat Girl, don't worry, you don't have to think about it, it's a perfect circuit, a reflex arc, stimulus and response like they used to say in the disgusting protoplasmic biosphere, you'll know the Enemy when you see the empty black holes of his eyes like windows into nowhere, he can hide, but he can't run, not from your only friend and ours, the Big steel Ripper.

"Were you at Balticon?" sez the fat guy inna green uniform who ain't the Starship Captain.

Just turn the monkey meat's eyes on him to let him see what's behind them.

He freezes, he blinks four or five times. He don't even wipe the dumb smile off his face.

"Uh . . . well, have a nice con," he says.

"Who knows," Texas Jimmy Balaban said when Dexter finished showing him the ballroom setup, "maybe we get away with it."

A runway had been added to the stage for the masquerade, and since it would be kept in place for Sunday's live performance, Dexter was stuck with its useless presence for the panels too.

There wasn't enough room backstage to line up the costumers, they'd have to traipse up the aisles right past the audience, but there *was* enough room to keep

Ralf behind the curtain and get him on and off without running him through the fannish gauntlet.

"Back to the bar?" Dexter suggested. "Unless you want to try out some of the room parties . . ."

"Pass and double pass," Jimmy groaned.

Dexter couldn't help laughing inside as he escorted Jimmy through the hordes to the elevators still glassy-eyed from his first Close Encounter of the Fannish Kind.

Poor Jimmy!

Poor Jimmy?

Poor me, Dexter thought as the elevator door slid closed behind Jimmy, leaving him all alone.

With about a thousand fans, that is.

Wizards and barbarians, Spocks and heavy-metal cyborgs, the Rabbit Lady and the Toad Man, and someone done up in a filthy raincoat with eyes from the dark side of the Moon and a badge with the fan name of Rat Girl.

Dexter tried to imagine this scene through Jimmy's eyes, but his extrapolative talent failed him. Many were the tales told around convention bars of writers' first encounters with this alternate reality. Certain of them had supposedly stayed blind drunk for a week. Others had blocked for a year. Still others had purportedly given up on science fiction entirely in favor of a career selling aluminum siding.

And these were *science fiction* writers.

There was also an abundance of fannish folklore about the pole-axed reaction of the science fictionally innocent transported by humorous chance into the same hotel as a science fiction convention.

But Jimmy Balaban wasn't quite either.

Jimmy might not have known what a science fiction convention was really like except the unbelievable stories Dexter himself had told him, but *he* had brought Ralfcon into being.

Forgive yourself whatever happens, Jimmy, Dexter thought, for boy oh boy, you knew not what you do!

And what about *you*, Dexter D. Lampkin?

Forgiving himself seemed more difficult as Dexter wandered through the fannish masses in their hall costumes—the strange shapes, the Rabbit Ladies, Chicken Men, and Rat Girls, Starship Cyborgs—for now he realized exactly what he had done.

He had collaborated in turning media coverage of a science fiction convention into a freak show.

On the other hand . . .

Dexter had once seen an interview of Norman Mailer by William F. Buckley in which Mailer had woundedly complained that an article in Buckley's magazine had called him a freak.

And Buckley had slouched there giving Mailer his best reptilian smirk as he slyly but truthfully pinned him.

"But Norman," he said in the voice of sweet reason, "you *are* a freak."

And so were they.

And yet, just as Mailer's very freakiness was what upon occasion allowed him to speak truly for the Zeitgeist, so too was there an upside flipside to the fannish freak show.

It might be going too far to claim a line of direct linear causality from 1930s fandom in propeller beanies to Neal Armstrong's footstep on the Moon, but without that goofy fannish pebble tossed in the virtual sea of the quantum flux it might never have happened.

And here, among the rest of the weirdly costumed fannish pretenders, were the Ralfs, transmuting the Starship Captain into an archetype that would incarnate itself in hall costumes and T-shirts as long as there were fans who shared the collective vision it embodied.

Dexter's vision.

And while this might not be enough to transmute the current planetary Deathship into the Starship Earth, it didn't take much faith in the slannishness of Fandom to believe that the chances of it happening had looked worse without it.

But if so, it was both cosmic and fannish justice that the joke was on him.

That he had to walk among them as the Secret Master of Ralfcon to do it.

Texas Jimmy Balaban had no belief in the power of prayer and plenty in the stupidity of booze before the sun was past the yardarm, but right now he would've gladly swapped the one for the other.

The Gold Network had given him a three-camera setup to cover Sunday night's live performance: two floor cameras, and a handheld job with Steadicam mount. This would be enough to cover Ralf's live hour and tonight's masquerade, but it made getting this afternoon's taped footage a nightmare.

The price of Lampkin's cooperation had been the installation of one of the floor cameras in the ballroom to cover his precious panels. Meaning that the other floor camera and its lighting would have to be moved from the first setup in the art show to the second one in the huckster room. Meaning everything else would have to be done with the Steadicam.

Also meaning that with the director in the van and the lighting guy and sound man occupied, Jimmy had a crew of one to get the Steadicam footage, and had to give *himself* a battlefield commission as second-unit director.

"Ready to face your fans, kiddo?" he asked Ralf.

Yeah, sure.

It was hard to imagine anyone being ready for what was out there beyond the suite. And this was, after all, *Ralf* he was talking to. Well, at least his Starship Captain uniform was freshly pressed and the fly wasn't open.

"Ready when you are, C.B.," Ralf said.

Hey, wasn't that actually an attempt at *humor*?

Hadn't that maybe been the Voice speaking?

Relax, will you, break a leg and all that good stuff, Jimmy told himself. Piece of cake. We won't even be shooting sound. What can go wrong?

Don't ask, he thought, knocking on the plywood lamp table, the closest piece of wood to hand.

"Okay, lights, camera," Texas Jimmy Balaban said, "let's get out there, and get it over with!"

And opened the door into Ralfcon.

"Action!" said Texas Jimmy.

Action all right!

The scene in the hallway was like a Roger Corman remake of the famous Star Wars bar scene. Sci-fi fans in their costumes and T-shirts paraded up and down, more or less managing not to trip over the ones sitting in the middle of the floor. Wookies and wonkies and things that go burp in the night. And of course, an assortment of Starship Captains.

Ralf stepped through the doorway in a blaze of kleig light and a bedlam like the barking of a pack of junkyard dogs.

"RALF! RALF! RALF! RALF!"

Ralf stood there as wooden and blank-eyed as a cigar store Indian for a long beat, as Jimmy's stomach sank.

"RALF! RALF! RALF! RALF!"

But then—

Ralf seemed to unfold like a flower within the spotlight. Become larger. Shine with its reflected limelight glow.

This was a piece of business with which Jimmy was quite familiar. He couldn't do it himself, but if you were an actor or a comic, you had *better* know how to pull it off.

But the way Ralf managed to command a beat of silence with nothing more than a teeny tilt of the head to use the lighting to paint highlights on his eyeballs and two slow steps forward was something else again.

"I'm *here*," said the Voice.

No shit.

Jimmy had heard it said of Richard Burton that he could hold an audience reading the phone book, and he had witnessed Professor Irwin Corey getting laughs with double-talk that meant nothing at all.

Something like that was happening now.

"The Dreamer awakes."

Slowly, deliberately, apparently conscious of the camera, and moving no faster than a man backing before him could handle, Ralf walked forward into the hallway.

"And so do you, Starship Troupers."

Haloed in the glory of the shooting light, spouting this stuff in a mighty voice like the Big Enchilada preaching to the multitude of costumed extras in one of those Biblical epics but wearing a silly green suit instead of a long flowing white robe, he walked among them.

"You have summoned your own spirit from the vasty quantum deeps and behold you come when I call!"

And fer chrissakes, they *did*!

A half dozen or so of the sci-fi fans in Starship Captain suits sort of slid into the spotlight circle and entered the shot. And stood there flanking Ralf, blinking and fidgeting nervously like an assortment of department store Santa Clauses in cheap costumes summoned to the North Pole for a photo op with the real thing.

"Get this! Get this!" Jimmy shouted superfluously into the cameraman's ear. "Keep shooting!"

It was as if the King himself had showed up to make an appearance at one of those amateur nights for Elvis impersonators.

Jimmy pulled the cameraman backward with one hand and gave frantic bringalong signals to Ralf with the other.

Ralf gave him no sign back, but he started walking forward again, the Starship Captain impersonators forming up into a guard of honor in a semicircle behind him just within the moving spotlight, their assorted weird-looking eyes glowing at the camera as if they were worshipful groupies wetting their panties.

The shot was so perfect that Texas Jimmy supposed that some wise-guy French film critic out there was probably going to call him a directing genius.

So much for *that* theory!

For Jimmy was under no illusion as to who the auteur was here.

And here comes somethin' *real* kinda of pushin' its way through th' thousand channels of wannabe monkey meat TV, realer than the Spocks an' Razor Lizards from th' Green Latrine an' three-hunnerd-pound chickens from th' flyin' saucers crammed like fuckin' sardines inta th' lobby. . . .

Here it comes, monkey meat, you can feel it, you can kinda see it comin' right atcha without knowin' what it's gonna be, guess who, scree, scree, scree, movin' th' fuckin' monkeys outa its way like a maniac's wavin' a great big bloody butcher knife back there inna crowd, like someone dropped a shark in th' other end of the tropical fish tank, hee, hee, hee. . . .

An' then—

An' then a bright bubble of light explodes out of the mob scene maybe five feet away, like a train comin' round a bend an' up the subway tunnel an' right inta your face!

A circle of light like what follows the singer onna MTV, an' all these fuckin' weirdos in their stupid Starship Captain suits is dancing around what's in the middle of it—

The Starship Captain.

The Real Thing.

Lookin' out from the light at what's lookin' back from the dark.

All th' other channels a monkey meat TV kinda fade. Floatin' in a nowhere space where things go that ain't gonna get t'happen.

'Cause there's only two channels of TV left now, meatware motherfuckers, and they're lookin' right at each other at either end of a million-year-long rathole, waitin' t'happen.

Waitin' t'happen.

Peek-a-boo, I see you.

An' you're another.

And so's your mother.

Only one of 'em gonna.

Only one of 'em can.

What's givin' that shit-eating grin outa the light at the Starship end of th' rathole.

Or what's lookin' back from th' cool clean dark at *this* end of th' rathole with a big steel tooth t'wipe it off his fuckin' face!

Guess which, motherfucker!

An' out comes the Big Ripper—

—and a big ham of a hand grabs her wrist.

A hand she pushes against with all her weight, but *still* can't stop from pullin' the Big Ripper down outa the air, while th' Starship Captain flies away grinnin' outa sight in his bubble a' light doin' everything but givin' her the finger!

Leavin' Rat Girl standin' there t'deal with what's on th' other end of the hand tryin' t'grab away her knife!

Which is this enormous fuckin' guy in some kinda chain shirt, helmet with fuckin' horns stickin' out, leather jockstrap, anna sword strapped in a plastic belt around his big hairy belly makes ol' Rip look like a toothpick.

"A thousand pardons, My Lady," he sez in this high squeaky voice, "but the weapons policy at Ralfcon permits not the brandishing of edged weapons save at the masquerade or private parties."

An' he puts his other hand on the handle of his huge fuckin' sword would take a gorilla t'swing it.

Oh shit.

But he don't whip it out.

Instead, he squints at her badge like maybe he don't see too good, an' flashes her this friendly asshole smile fulla rotten teeth.

"'Tis not Melmar's edict, Rat Girl, me thinks it's a stupid rule too, yea, my own Doom Sword longs to leap free from the prison of its scabbard!"

He shrugs. He lets go of her hand. He gives her this look like of course she knows what the fuck he's talkin' about.

"But what can you do, if we don't save it for the masquerade," he sez, "there are dweebs on *every* con committee just looking for *any* excuse to ban weapons entirely!"

"Here he is, folks," Dexter Lampkin shouted, "let him through, will you!"

A superfluous request as it turned out.

For, bathed in glory by the shooting light of the shoulder-mounted camera, Ralf parted the fannish masses before him as he strode into the art show room all-too-literally like Jesus through Jerusalem.

Surrounded not by mere apostles but tackily cloned avatars of his very own self.

The whole room oohed and aahed like a science fictional hive mind experiencing a collective orgasm.

Dexter gave ten points to the guy on the floor camera for the presence of mind to turn it around to catch about thirty seconds of this grand entrance of the Starship Captain before the shoulder-mounted camera's shooting light was turned off.

The blocking called for Ralf to make a slow tour around the art show tracked by the floor camera, pausing for a beat or two beside each painting for a reaction shot.

This he did, accreting more and more fans costumed in his own image at each station of the way, so that by the time he reached the one that Jimmy had saved for last—a huge and amateurish painting of the Starship Earth logo—the shot was entirely filled with Starship Captains.

Dexter didn't know whether to laugh or shiver.

There they stood in their official items and homemade rip-offs, the long and the short and the tall, the thin and the fat and the victims of advanced globulosis.

Behind them was the backdrop for living movie poster, the Big Blue Marble rocketing in triumph through a cosmos impossibly crammed with badly rendered ringed planets, moons, and spiral nebulae.

And overarching the shot in flowing letters of flame the title: STARSHIP EARTH.

And framed dead-center was Mr. Great Spirit of This World himself, slowly scanning the room with eyes like planetary probe cameras.

The Ralfies. The fans. The faithful.

Eyes that finally locked on Dexter's as if the two of them were attractors upon which the chaotic wave function of probability had been fated in this moment to collapse.

They weren't shooting sound and no lines had been scripted, but Ralf spoke anyway, in a voice which to Dexter carried total conviction, even though it was virtually the voice of a character he himself had created. Even though the eyes behind the mask of that character were windows into nothing but the virtual void of the quantum flux.

"Thank you for bringing me here. And you *do* know that you *have*, now don't you, Starship Troupers? Where is *here*, but your convention of a Starship future? And who am *I*, but a story you're telling to call that future into being? So who can *you* be, but the Starship Dreamers?"

Dexter couldn't quite say what, but it *did* seem to say everything.

For while whatever had spoken from this virtual future struggling to be born might in a linear literary sense be *his* creation, should that future thereby be called into being, he too would have been but an instrument of a transtemporal collectivity, call it what you will, the Collective Unconscious, the Zeitgeist, the Great Spirit of the World itself.

Dexter looked around at the pathetic fannish flesh crammed into the art show of a cynically crafted-for-profit science fiction convention in the moldy-smelling basement of the usual crummy con hotel.

Could *this* be the instrumentality by means of which the transtemporal consciousness of the Transformational future reached back to bootstrap itself into existence?

Could *these* be the Starship Dreamers?

"Who else is there?" said Ralf.

In that moment, God help him, Dexter Lampkin knew that he was one of them too.

"After all," said Ralf, "we all *know* that time travel is *absolutely* impossible."

"Except of course in the wonderful world of *Ralfcon*, where virtually anything is *virtually* possible," he said with a wink, a bow, a flourish. "Even me!"

And quite unexpectedly, he exited stage left.

Exited the shot, the art show, the best-laid plans of monkeys and men, up toward the quantum chaos of the lobby, surrounded by his satellite system of Starship Dreamers, trailed by the mobile cameraman and an outraged and shouting Texas Jimmy Balaban, all but tearing the hair out of his head.

The chief lunatic had taken over the asylum, there were no boys in white coats around to throw a net over him, and the way things were going, Texas Jimmy Balaban suspected it would've started a riot if they tried. So like they say, if you get lemons thrown your way, make lemonade, if it's rotten eggs, make a rotten omelet, if it's a disaster, shoot disaster movie footage.

The shoot in the huckster room having been flushed down the toilet by Ralf, Jimmy found himself chasing him around the convention with the mobile cameraman instead, nor could he be said to be calling the shots.

Call the shots?

With a dozen or more overweight bozos in Starship Captain suits surrounding Ralf like an army of Sinatra bodyguards in Vegas as he made the grand tour of the Planet of the Sci-fi Fans pressing the flesh and dispensing the wonderfulness of his presence like Danny DeVito playing the pope?

Through the lobby, into an elevator to the top floor, and then down successive stairwells to lower and lower floors, touring every goddamn foot of every jam-packed hallway, like a Chicago ward-heeler cruising for votes.

Jimmy couldn't even get near enough to Ralf to beg him to cut this shit out before things got out of hand to the point where they started getting dangerous.

After all, this was a *convention*, wasn't it? In Jimmy's previous experience with hotels full of conventioneers, that meant a minimum of a hundred or so belligerent drunks. Worse still, the Metropolis was stuffed to the gills with sci-fi fans, and it did not seem unreasonable to assume that the proportion of unstable weirdos was somewhat high, given that close to a quarter of them were dressed for Mardi Gras on Mars.

Nor did Jimmy find it reassuring that quite a few of them were armed. Okay, the rayguns and neon-tube light-sabers were for sure harmless, but some of that space-mercenary equipment looked suspiciously realistic and some of those swords and battle-axes were *definitely* real.

But though the star attraction moved through Ralfcon in the eye of his own self-created storm of flesh and noise and pandemonium, considering that this was a hotel full of armed and costumed loonies under the influence of much booze and maybe stronger stuff, it was a remarkably good-natured mob scene, and the fisticuffs or worse that Jimmy had expected never broke out.

Ralf managed to make it back to the lobby without encountering Charlie Manson in Star Trek drag or a beered-out barbarian with a broadsword and a bad attitude.

But Jimmy didn't believe in pressing their luck.

For the moment, Ralf was pinned up against the elevator bank by wall-to-wall Starship Captains, the first chance Jimmy had had to get to him with the hook.

"Turn on the shooting light," he told the cameraman.

"I ran out of tape twenty minutes ago."

"Yeah, yeah, I know, but we gotta get outa here in one piece," Jimmy told him, snatching the camera's detachable hand-mike out of its cradle. "Just pretend you're shooting this."

Jimmy advanced into the spotlight circle thrusting the mike into phony Starship Captains' faces, cuing their sound bites, whipping it away, using the equally phony man-in-the-street schtick to make his way to Ralf.

"What do you think of this terrific convention, Captain?"

"Well, actually at Boscon—"

"That thing official, looks like you made it yourself?"

"Duh—"

"And you, you believe in flying saucers? Little green men from Mars?"

It worked like a show business charm.

How could it not?

Who would not make way for *television coverage*? Who could resist the chance of being on the tube for ten seconds themselves?

Jimmy had seen footage of guys being carried out of battle zones half dead on stretchers rise and shine and make like wannabe professionals when a TV camera was turned on them and a microphone shoved in their face.

"And tell me, Captain Ralf," he went on in similar vein, thrusting the mike in the smiling puss of the real thing, "what do you think of all your fantastic fans here who want to be you?"

Ralf played it to the crowd pressed up against the magic spotlight circle like heavyweight fressers with their noses up against the bake shop window.

"Evolution is the sincerest form of flattery," he said.

"And what do you think of all these Starship Captains here?" Jimmy yammered as the elevator finally arrived.

"Flattery is the sincerest form of evolution," said Ralf.

The elevator doors slid open and an impossible number of weirdly dressed sci-fi fans tumbled out blinking into the spotlight like one of those old circus numbers where a zillion clowns poured out of a Volkswagen Beetle.

Jimmy grabbed the cameraman by the belt, pulled him forward, used his mike hand to shove Ralf backwards through the open elevator door, yanking the cameraman in behind him to block further entry long enough to hit the door close button and make their escape.

"This is *crazy*, Ralf," Jimmy said as the elevator moved upward. "A major star can't just run around a hotel full of weirdos like a chicken with his head cut off."

"I am the Lizard King. I can do anything."

"It could get *dangerous*!"

"To take a walkabout through the Dreamtime in real time?" said the Voice. "I've just done it, and as you can't help but notice, *here I am*."

"Yeah, okay, whatever you say, but *I'm* your agent, and I say you don't pull a number like that again!"

"Whatever you say, C.B.," Ralf said with a Trust Me grin that somehow inspired anything but confidence.

So, after getting Ralf up ten floors and into the suite by using the cameraman as a blocking back, Jimmy phoned for a rentacop, and told him nobody got in or out while he was gone before going to the van to view the rushes.

Which sucked.

The exit from the suite and the stuff in the art show were golden. They were also about six minutes' worth of usable running time, and stretching it at that when Jimmy clocked it.

The rest of the footage was shit.

The key shoot in the huckster room to promo the merchandise hadn't happened.

At least half the footage they had shot chasing Ralf around the hotel was technically crap except for five- or ten-second cuts here and there—out of focus, badly lit, impossibly framed, or all three at once. And most of what *was* at least marginally air-quality was Ralf moving through mob-scene shots of sci-fi fans in their homemade costumes half-hidden by his surrounding Starship Captain impersonators.

Trying to reshoot tomorrow and get it cut before airtime was out of the question. There wouldn't be time enough, and anyway, given Ralf's mental condition, they'd be lucky to get him through tonight's masquerade shoot.

They?

Lampkin sure wasn't being much help.

He was supposed to be the expert on this scene, wasn't he?

But all he wanted to do was sit here and edit his goddamn talking-head footage, he acted like it was some a gross imposition whenever Jimmy asked him for a simple piece of advice.

Not that Jimmy didn't know what he was thinking when he curled his lip and scrunched up his nose at the action footage. At least, to give Dex credit, he was enough of a mensch not to say it.

Why don't you just shitcan this crap, Jimmy and give my stuff more than a lousy twelve minutes of running time instead?

If he had, things being what they were, Jimmy probably would've popped him in the mouth.

Texas Jimmy Balaban had been constantly interrupting the engineer who had to do Dexter's actual editing to key up more of his own convention footage. And Dexter had to endure not only Jimmy's pissing and moaning but his repeated insistence that he interrupt his own work to view some choice footage of costumed fans make embarrassing fools of themselves while Ralf played King of the Pig People.

Nor was his mood improved by the perversely self-defeating task of boiling down four hours of a symposium on the nature of a Transformational space-going civilization capable of surviving a million years of its own history into twelve lousy one-minute commercials that would make it all comprehensible on a dog food and deodorant level in Peoria.

Nevertheless he *had* done it.

Well, sort of.

Unlimited electric power from fusion technology fueled only by water. From the sun itself via solar power satellites. Throw your garbage into a fusion torch, folks, and out the other end comes free clean raw materials. Unlimited power means unlimited Animal and People Chow from artificial photosynthesis. No more need to plant vast monocultures of grain means planting more trees and cleaning up the atmosphere. Moving heavy industry into space finishes the job. Mining the moons and asteroids means unlimited raw materials and unlimited power means the ability to turn anything into anything. Which means the ability to build whole new worlds in space or terraform planets. Which means the ability to do likewise with the mess we've made of *this* one. No more hunger or poverty or overpopulation means no more reasons for war.

Voila, Starship Earth, able and worthy to take its place among those advanced galactic civilizations who have transcended their Transformation Crises.

Twelve one-minute commercials on national Prime Time television for the survival of human civilization.

With no production values. With zero visuals.

Twelve minutes of mostly untelegenic talking heads.

Surrounded by forty-eight excruciating minutes of convention freak-show footage.

Pathetic, Lampkin, considering the bargain you had to make to get them. All you had to do was collaborate in turning this convention into a set for the longest continuous piece of national television time ever devoted to science fiction.

And what is that national audience going to see?

What else but the usual sixty-second photo op coverage writ enormous?

Weirdos and globuloids. Merchandising tie-in items and tacky hall costumes. Ralf culties and the Starship Captain himself gone over the top and of course the goddamn masquerade.

What else but a king-sized dose of the usual sniggering visual shit smeared all over the visionary literature so dear to your heart, what else but yet more "sci-fi" heaped on the already putrid public image of science fiction.

How's *that* for your Deal-with-the-Devil story, Lampkin?

So this was the fuckin' *masquerade*!

Hard t'tell the scene down here in th' audience from rush-hour onna D-train, crammed tits t'back an' ass t'cock so fuckin' tight an' stinkin' you could just about lift your feet off the floor an' hang there inna monkey meat sandwich, disgustin' job, so let the Rat Girl do th' walkin', scree, scree, scree.

Could just about see th' stage up there in front, a kinda strip-joint runway thing runnin' out inta the audience, an'—an' up there onna stage is this fuckin' green octopus thing with a buncha stupid plastic swords hangin' like limp dicks from these phony tentacles fightin' a guy inna jockstrap an' a cloak with a fuckin' *fishbowl* on his head—

—an' there's a lotta noise, an' th' action moves out onta th' runway, an' th' Rat Girl can sorta see what's standin' back there onna stage outa the spotlight watchin' it. Can just make out the green suit—

An' then just get a flash a those eyes whena spotlight moves across his face tryin' t'follow th' octopus bein' dragged off stage by th' asshole wearin' th' fishbowl.

Nothin' else got eyes like that see you there at the other enda th' rathole even through all this monkey meat, knows you're there an' likewise, motherfucker!

It's him.

The Enemy.

The Starship Captain.

Somethin' moves th' Rat Girl's hand inside her raincoat t'grab th' handle a the Big Ripper, same somethin' that's movin' th' legs, churnin' th' feet forward in place like onea those windup toys stuck up against a wall an' goin' nowhere.

Cool it, ya dumb Ratfuck, willya!

Th' Rat Girl's way inna back, she'd have t'hack her way through th' wall-to-wall monkey meat with th' Big Ripper like th' White Hunter witha machete in onea those jungle movies take all fuckin' night t'do it, an' what witha screams an' all would be kinda hard t'sneak up on the fucker. . . .

Disgust ya t'do it, but let th' Rat Girl think *human* fer a minute!

'Cause lined up against th' wall from way back here alla way to th' stairs climbin' to the stage was somethin' a little like a fuckin' circus parade inna garbage dump an' a lot like the stuff winos must be seein' climbin' th' back alley walls.

Knights in fuckin' tinfoil armor, slime monsters from outer space, robots an' bird-things, lizards in black leather, three-hunnerd-pound ladies with Ping-Pong balls on coat hangers stickin' outa their heads, plastic garbage bags an' feathers, pieces a metal crap outa junkyards, was like a fuckin' explosion inna bargain basement Disneyland shit factory, like a thousand channels a late-night monster movie TV shoved through a meat grinder. . . .

Gibberin' an' jabberin', an' waddlin' a step at a time as fuckin' ugly as you please as they wait their turn t'slither up onta th' stage like it was some kinda supermarket checkout line in Bugfuck City.

"Fer chrissakes, Dex, what's eating you?" Texas Jimmy Balaban said as they stood there backstage in what passed for the wings in this dump of a setup.

Lampkin gave him another of those looks that would melt glass.

"If I have to explain it to you, Jimmy, you'll never get it," he groused.

Onstage, a not-too-bad-looking and only slightly overweight babe in skintight silver leotards was doing a soft-core obscene snake-charming act with a green puppet that looked vaguely like Mr. Spock's schlong with purple liver-lips and Donald Duck's eyeballs.

"Come on, Dex, cheer up, this is great footage!" He shrugged. "Well anyway," he admitted, "considering the rest of the crap we got in the can . . ."

Jimmy just didn't get it. What was Lampkin's problem?

After this afternoon's disaster, this masquerade thing was a godsend. All three cameras in the same place at the same time. Ralf standing there at the back of the stage with the judges where they could get him into long shots and shoot cutaway reaction shots. Finally, nice safe controlled conditions with knockout visuals!

The Schlong-Taming act finished her parade down and up the runway, and on came three guys done up as punk dinosaurs, complete with neon-pink headcrests, rings in their noses, and futuristic sci-fi guitars.

For amateur night, these sci-fi convention costumes weren't all that bad, Jimmy had seen worse in what passed for professional shows in the crummier joints in Atlantic City and Vegas. These sci-fi fans might not be working with Circus-Circus-class budgets, the girls would have a hard time breaking into the chorus line in a beer-bar in Pismo Beach, but you had to give 'em points for outrageous imagination.

A giant walking turd made out of peanut butter and candy corn smeared on a tarp. A bird-girl costume with wings of tie-dyed chicken feathers almost looked real. A pantomime-horse of a dragon with dry ice smoke and lighter-fluid flames coming out of its mouth. A couple stuffed into the same costume doing a pretty good two-headed mutant arguing with itself.

And—what's this?

Up on the stage came a guy with a huge belly in a white karate suit with a sword strapped to his waist looking like John Belushi doing a three-hundred-pound samurai. He waddled to the center of the stage. He bowed to the audience. He spread a big white beach towel down on the stage. He kneeled on it. He bowed again. He drew the sword. He held it out before him, pointed squarely at his enormous gut—

Oh no!

Oh yes!

"AAAAYAAH!" he screamed—

—and plunged the samurai sword into his stomach!

And swirled it around inside what must've been a plastic garbage bag, twitching, jerking, rolling his eyes, and gurgling, as out of it slopped and slithered about fifty pounds of cherry and lime Jell-O larded with butchershop scraps, raw sausages, squid bodies, and better you don't ask, while the audience roared, and Texas Jimmy nearly split a gut laughing.

As Mr. Hara-Kiri folded the mess into the towel to make way for the next act, however, Dexter gave Jimmy a look like he wished *he* would do the real thing and was more than ready to help him.

"Hey, come on, Dex, lighten up, where's your sense of humor?"

Dexter just glowered at him as the next act came up onstage, whatever *this* was supposed to be.

A girl in a filthy raincoat so smeared with grunge and dirt and mung Jimmy couldn't even tell what color the cloth had once been. Hair matted and knotted and grayed and greased till it looked like an old mop-head used to clean cesspools. Eyes like green marbles that had been cracked with a hammer. A set of false teeth that looked like they belonged in a dead rat. Her face done up with scabs and scratches as if she had spent the last few years with her head in a garbage can fighting alley cats for fish heads.

"Will you look at that, Dex!" Jimmy said in no little admiration. "Now *that's* what I call a professional job of makeup!"

Th' Rat Girl stepped onta th' stage, an'—

—inta a fuckin' white light fried her eyeballs!

Like a cockroach inna kitchen at night when a light gets flipped on, only there's no scummy sink fulla dirty dishes t'hide under.

"Turn it *off*, you stupid motherfucker, or I'll slice your dick off!" she screamed, flipping open th' raincoat an' whipping out the Big Ripper.

There's this huge oohing sound sorta like a thousand johns coming behinda Dumpster—

—an' it's like she's a fuckin' mugger inna dark alley's got his hands around sweet granny's throat suddenly pinned inna cop car's headlights, well ya see, officer, it's like this, duh. . . .

This ain't exactly goin' accordin' t'plan, now is it, Rat Girl?

Think *Rat*! Turn away from the light an' toward the dark a th' nearest available hole, right, doin' what comes natural, but—

There's a zillion eyes starin' up outa the darkness.

Eyes glistening with slimy wetness. Live eyeballs fulla snotty goo. Oozin' outa holes in bony skulls fulla rotten gray brains. On top of sweatin' bags of meat made a pulsin' tubes thick with blood an' pus an' putrid green guts.

Disgust a Dead World Rat Thing t'see it.

An' the meat can *smell* it, smell the shit in the guts, th' farts leakin' outa all those rancid assholes, wino breath steamin' stinkin' outa the wet holes inna faces, smell a tide pool muck spent a billion years a rottin' inna sun, bitin', an' clawin', eatin' and pissin' an' shittin', fuckin' an' squeezin' more of itself outa cunts just t'turn itself inta *this*.

Protoplasm crawlin' up outa the cesspool a th' ocean t'walk around like monkeys.

Jibberin' and jabberin' like *they* was the ones seen th' fuckin' monster!

"Whaddya think *you're* starin' at, monkey meat?"

Gabblin' and screechin' an' laughin' out there in th' darkness belongs to *us*, monkey things, you can just about see 'em jumpin' up an' down on their tree limbs an' scratchin' their hairy armpits.

"You want me t'tell ya?"

"Gabble, gobble, blabble, ook, ook, ook . . ."

"You *really* wanna know, do ya?"

And something made a machine-oiled metal an' silicon glass slid down the coat hanger jammed inta the monkey girl's brain, hee, hee, hee, slid down through the Rat Girl, scree, scree, scree, down through the Rat Thing program, down through the timelines from a pure world of airless void and electronic perfection hadn't been slimed by blood or shit or snot for a million years, burning its way through the meat and pus and corruption with a cold blue fire as clear and sharp and clean as the great big sharp blade of steel, its only friend under the circumstances, the Big Ripper.

"I ain't no monkey meat, I ain't no Rat Girl, and I ain't no Rat Thing neither, I ain't nothing *ever* made outa meat an' guts an' pus, Meatship Motherfuckers, nothin' lefta that but piecesa rats an' cockroaches sewn inta the machinery a million years from now when it's all rock an' steel and aluminum floating and fading and following the little blue lights down into the lovely cold hard darkness too bad you ain't gonna be around to enjoy it—"

A loud booing like the hooting of bass baboons.

"Next! Next!"

"The hook! The hook!"

The heavy stomping of hundreds of feet.

And then—

"Give the lady a break, Starship Troupers," says a voice behind her. "It's a perfect costume. It's the truest one here."

The stomping and the shouting stops. Dead silence. No need to turn to know what's talking. But do it anyway, monkey meat.

The Starship Captain walks up out of the shadows toward her. The light from the other end of time's rathole follows him like he owns it. Or vice versa.

"We know where you're coming from. We know who you really are," says the Enemy.

Eyes like doorways.

"You're coming from what's waiting out there in the darkness. You're what's left when all our hopes are gone."

The smile of a wise old cannibal cat.

"You're Deathship Earth in a flasher's raincoat, isn't that right, Rat Girl?"

Feel the thick hard handle of the cold steel knife!

"An' *you're* dead meat, Starship Boy!"

Amanda had to admit that this was a convincing costume. Maybe *too* convincing, she thought, hunching closer to her TV set to watch the Deathship Streetgirl dance a step forward, waving her prop knife like something out of *West Side Story*.

Prop knife?

On the screen, anyway, that knife looked a little *too* real.

But Ralf didn't seem afraid.

He spread his arms out wide, hung his head to one side, looked heavenward in comic supplication, thrust his chest forward—a pantomime Jesus offering himself up to an Aztec sacrificial knife.

The audience gasped and muttered.

The Deathship Streetgirl raised the knife higher, oh my God, is that a glint of real steel—

And three fat men in silver suits wearing green lizard masks and carrying hockey sticks with giant cardboard chain-saw teeth taped to the blades surged up onto the stage between her and Ralf.

"Cut!" shouted Ralf, dropping down out of the Jesus pose and becoming an irate director rounding on his crew.

"She forgot the hammer *and* the nails! Come on, people, aren't you *ever* gonna get this shot right?"

Cut to another of Dexter Lampkin's talking heads.

"Stewardship of the Earth and a visionary space program are the meat and po-tatoes of an enlightened and mature civilization. The technology we need to bring a dead planet like Mars to life is exactly what we need to clean up the mess we've made on this one."

Cut to a shaky and badly lit shot of a corridor jammed with peculiar-looking people, many of them in amateurish costumes. Who break into cheers as Ralf, barely visible inside a bodyguard circle of Starship Captain clones, moves past the camera, pantomiming a papal blessing. For a beat, the camera manages to catch his face, Buddha-smile fixed on his lips, eyes humorlessly unamused.

"Stay tuned, Starship Troupers," says an announcer's fruity voice-over, "we'll be right back with Ralf, with the Starship Captain himself, coming to you live as he'll ever be, direct from Ralfcon!"

On came a commercial for Starship Captain suits.

Amanda aimed her remote and muted it.

She shook her head. She took a sip of wine.

Oh yes, she had done the right thing turning down Texas Jimmy Balaban's two thousand dollars to help him nursemaid Ralf through this swan-song appearance. If she hadn't, she would have missed the *true* experience, for *this* was how it would pass into the collective memory of the Zeitgeist.

On television.

What was being experienced by the millions in the Dreamtime of Prime Time.

No one in the Hotel Metropolis could have experienced this first hour as she had. Yet millions of people outside of the Ralfcon hotel had shared the collective reality thereof with her. And *that* would be the one which resonated down the timelines.

They might nod out during Dexter's attempts to convey the complexity of his transformational visions in tendentious one-minute sound bites, but they would have *experienced* them anyway.

All of it.

The sci-fi fans in their strange costumes. The heads spieling sixty-second sound bites of a visionary future their familiarity with Ralf's Starship could just about let most of them comprehend. The pitches for the merchandising items. The crazy masquerade. Ralf launching himself fearlessly into the sea of his fans like a rock star crowd-diving off the stage.

What is, is real.

Of course it is.

Aren't we seeing it on television?

———

"Break a leg, kiddo," said Texas Jimmy Balaban, shoving Ralf gently onstage with a palm to the small of his back, a wing and a prayer, and one of the long shotgun mikes that had been his signature way back when.

Call it inspiration, call it nostalgia, it seemed the *only* thing to do.

Back when Ralf was a just wild-and-crazy guy from the future starting a show on a zilcho budget, working an audience of weirdos with a shotgun mike had been a comic virtue born of budgetary necessity. Now that the final curtain was coming down on whatever he had become, ad-libbing off *this* audience of weirdos which he had somehow created seemed the only format he had even a hope of handling.

The standing-room-only crowd shoehorned into the ballroom roared as the Starship Captain emerged into the spotlight. As the lions might have done upon the entrance of the next Christian onto the floor of the Roman Coliseum.

Was that part of the act, Amanda wondered, or had someone *really* shoved Ralf onto the stage?

It was hard to tell, because instead of doing a comic stumble, he recovered without even mugging at the camera, and stood there, silent and immobile in the spotlight, taking the cheers and applause for what seemed a small eternity.

The director cut away to a sweeping panorama around the audience, on its collective feet, cheering and boogeying after its overweight nerdish fashion, a shot eerily reminiscent of crowd shots in the *Woodstock* movie, but here dominated by Starship Earth T-shirts, not tie-dyes; Starship Captain suits, not blue denim; images of Ralf, not mandalas or peace signs.

And when the shot returned to the stage, Ralf's carriage was bantam cock upright, the bright green and gold uniform glistened in the spotlight, his smile was radiant, and he held his shotgun mike like a scepter, a science fictional version of rock star glamour, of Jimi Hendrix and his magic electric guitar.

"I'm here, Starship Troupers!" he proclaimed in that resonant lordly voice. "Yes, I'm really here, in this flesh, the hero of the lastest version of the tale you've been telling yourselves since you stumbled out of the trees, the Captain of your future Starship, and you've bent the laws of prime time and space to bring me here tonight, so let's have a big Ralfcon welcome for . . . the Giant Turnip God himself!"

It should've come off as self-parody. But it didn't. There should've been laughter. But there wasn't.

Instead, the cheering and applause peaked again and then died away into the silence of a congregation in the Presence. Of who or of what depended on your own symbol system.

But whatever archetypes arose in each individual internal dreamscape, the Presence in the spotlight encompassed them all in the *collective* Dreamtime. For there it was on millions of screens.

A Presence that Amanda could only call numinous.

You didn't have to be there in the flesh to believe it.

It was quite capable of manifesting itself on television.

Ralf walked out onto the runway.

"Who am I?" he said, those eyes doorways. "The star of the show? Just another one of *you* in a fancy Starship Captain uniform?"

He walked farther out onto the runway, the spotlight circle following him, deeper and deeper out into the audience.

"Would you believe those questions make no sense when I come from? Would you believe that there can be a time when each of us knows we are all waves on a sea of dreams? That the same story tells itself through all of us? That we are all the instrumentality by which the Great Spirit of the World reaches out through time to be born? That each of us contains the whole? That *I* am the Dream and *we* are the Dreamer?"

He stopped near the end of the runway, glowing in green and gold above a sea of faces, of bodies swaying and surging below him in the depths of the communal darkness.

Ralf looked around slowly, silently, doing a full three-hundred-and-sixty-degree pirouette, gazing out into the audience with that little smile, those eyes deeper doorways into the ocean of elsewhere than ever, but though the voice was that of some unknowable multitude therefrom, when he spoke again, it was with a human warmth.

"*Sure* you would, Starship Troupers. Sure *you* do. Look at you! Space men! Witchy women! *Starship Captains!* You have to, don't you? Because here we are, the virtual heroes of the story we all tell ourselves! Or else just a bunch of nuts in silly costumes making fools of ourselves on TV!"

He laughed, a more human sound of merriment than Amanda remembered ever having come from the mask of Ralf.

"Tell you what, Starship Troupers," he said, "let's play *Let's Make a Deal*. If you believe that Tinkerbell lives, then Tinkerbell will believe in *you*. After all, *we're* the captain and the crew of the Starship, who else is there, so let's take it past the Deathship on the right, and straight on into Tomorrowland's morning!"

A camera panned slowly across the upturned faces, the costumed bodies, the T-shirts, the Starship Captains in every shape and form.

It was a moment of television unlike anything Amanda had ever experienced before. A moment in which it didn't seem to take such a great leap into the Dreamtime to imagine this hotel ballroom full of science fiction fans as the now and future crew of Starship Earth.

There must be something wrong with the air-conditioning, Dexter Lampkin told himself. For surely his eyes couldn't be smarting just from this fannish schmaltz, you *hate* it when one of your colleagues stands up there at a con and panders to them like this, you'd *never* do it yourself.

"So here we are on Starship Earth," said Ralf, taking several long paces back toward the stage, then to turning again, and walking back deeper into the audience.

"The Tomorrowland we dreamed up together when men were still monkeys standing up to their shinbones in their own crap on a dying planet and looking up at the stars. Dreaming that some day somehow we'd get there, that if we got one last chance to get it right, we'd make it, we'd reach the Starship Dreamtime where we are right . . . *now!*"

Deeper and deeper into the pocket universe of Fandom.

Of, face it, Lampkin, science fiction itself, where the multiplexity of the future was a self-fulfilling prophecy, where the virtuality of reality was the only article of faith.

The Starship Captain stood in the spotlight at the end of the runway turning round, round, round, looking out over the Ralfies and the globuloids, the computer nerds and the costumers, the brilliant intellectual misfits and the teenage malcontents, the fans who would be slans.

And, like some kid playing spin the bottle, when he stopped, the shotgun mike was pointed squarely at a fat fan with thick spectacles and a cheap homemade Ralf wig stuffed into an off-the-rack Starship Captain suit a size or two too small for his belly.

"Sensor readings indicate we have reached Starship Earth, Captain," Ralf said, doing Spock. "Beamin' ya aboard," said Scotty. "Report please, Captain," said Spock again. "We're getting abundant indications of highly evolved life-forms. What's it like out there?"

Caught like a bug in the spotlight, the poor nerd squirmed with embarrassment.

Ralf leaned out over a frowzy woman in a Starship Earth T-Shirt, to mike him more intimately, to meet his eyes and flash him a tender smile never seen on mortal Vulcan face.

"Come on, *you're* the Captain in this story, the Great Spirit of the World is telling you so, so it *must* be at least virtually true," Ralf told him gently. "What's it like in *your* Tomorrowland?"

The fan in the Starship Captain suit blinked his way out of it, plastered a silly grin across his face, and while it was truly an embarrassingly amateurish attempt, he drew applause anyway after the laughter when he did Dr. McCoy.

"Well . . . it's *not* dead, Jim," he said.

The ridiculously dressed fat fan boy blossomed visibly with this ovation and began to gabble in a high squeaky voice.

"It's *alive*, Captain, forests full of animals, oceans full of whales and dolphins and fish, the planet's more alive than it's ever been, the biomass is bigger than it ever was before we terraformed the Earth, because the factories are all in orbit, so the air is sweet and clean and there's mirrors in orbit too turning the whole world into springtime in *Southern California*, so you have to go to *Mars* for a white Christmas. . . ."

The Starship Captain turned, twirled the shotgun mike around again, and thrust into the spotlight circle a green-faced woman with Ping-Pong balls painted as eyes boinging out of her frizzy purple hairdo on miniature slinkies.

This one needed no cue.

"Out there in the Asteroid Belt, where they've got a big antenna downloading television broadcasts from the stars, they're building generation starships to take us there," she gushed in a husky voice that might have been sexy if she blew off about fifty pounds.

"It'll take hundreds of years to get there, but that's no problem, because the nanotechnology in our bodies keeps us young and healthy and beautiful for thousands of years . . ."

Dexter Lampkin imagined these sights through the camera's eye as they were now appearing on those millions of television sets out there in the mundane world and his gorge rose with the shame of it.

". . . tiny computer terminals implanted in our brains giving us full access to all human knowledge in three dimensions and quadraphonic sound anywhere we go, and full-sensory *movies*, too . . ."

But God help him, there was also a horrendous pride in Dexter's heart as he accepted the full, glorious, and nauseating truth.

"... drugs designed for specific receptors, and nanotechnology lets us *choose* the style of our consciousness, sometimes we even make ourselves feel *bored*, so we can remember what it was like for our ancestors. ..."

Most of this spontaneously recited fannish folklore came straight from *The Transformation*, or from his best-selling tie-in item, *The Word According to Ralf*.

And these publicly embarrassing poor pathetic jerks who dared to believe themselves the mutated cutting edge of evolution and the secret hope of the species' survival had one thing in common with the author thereof and with unknown millions who would be mortified to be caught dead at a science fiction convention.

They read science fiction.

They could therefore believe that all this was possible.

And Dexter D. Lampkin found that in the end he could not escape the science fiction writer's bittersweet destiny.

He wrote science fiction.

And therefore was one of them.

For he believed it too.

"... upload our software into computers, store ourselves on silicon, and then download it later when our bodies die into new cloned *designer* bodies ..."

What with the monkeys all starin' up outa the dark at what was goin' on inna bright light, movin' the meatware through the subway rush hour was easy now, easy as a razor-sharp blade slippin' and slidin' inta a fuckin' pimp's belly wouldn't even know it was happenin' till you was gone back up the alley behind the Dumpster anna guts spilled out.

"... dinosaurs and dodos sure, but if you can do that, you can make species that never were, unicorns, and dragons, elves and leprechauns, why not. ..."

Closer t'the stage, Rat Girl, that's the way, closer t'the yellow light up there at the other end of the subway tunnel, fade and float, float and fade, follow the little blue lights, what fuck was that, who wantsa know asshole or I'll slice your fuckin' dick off, hee, hee, hee, you can say it with your eyes when you're the White Tornado from a million years of perfect razor-blade steel and cold oiled rock-hard darkness. ...

"... in contact with advanced galactic civilizations that had transcended this crisis while we were still trying to figure out how to light our little fires to keep back those hungry eyes looking back at us out of the dark. ..."

———

"This," Texas Jimmy Balaban told Lampkin as they stood backstage watching the proceedings, "is *not* funny." The lack of laughter made it a statement of the obvious, but he felt compelled to say it anyway.

"But they're not throwing rotten eggs either, are they?" Dex said, and Jimmy had to admit he had a point.

Ralf's current act was not funny.

But it was holding the live audience anyway.

How much of the television audience it was holding, he couldn't even imagine. In all his years in the biz, Jimmy had never seen anything like it.

Okay, working a studio audience with a shotgun mike for other than laughter was the stock-in-trade of talk-show hosts, and playing the Great I Am to the rubes was as old as the first tent-show preacher act, and using a runway to get right in there among 'em was a burlesque staple.

But Ralf was a comedian, not the second coming of Donahue, and the *strippers* were supposed to work the runway, not the comedian, and Jimmy had never seen an act like this where the *televangelist* let the *congregation* do the preaching.

Of course there had never been a tent-show congregation like this on the tube before either.

When he had shoved Ralf out there he had expected, or at least hoped for, a live version of the freak-show footage they had shot in the corridors and the lobby and the masquerade. The sort of stuff that would have them laughing out there in Nielsenland at these sci-fi fans' expense.

Instead he had gotten a lot less than he had bargained for.

But just maybe something more.

For over half an hour now, Ralf had been working the weirdos in the audience, *interviewing* them, as if he were doing man-in-the-street footage for the six o'clock news.

Making *them* do the work for him. Coaxing them into ad-libbing their own sci-fi story, making up their own Ralfcon version of Starship Earth.

Until this weekend, Jimmy had found Dexter's endless pissing and moaning about these sci-fi fans sort of unprofessional. Contempt for your audience was a real bad attitude in his book.

His all-too-close encounter with sci-fi fandom on his very first trip from the suite to the bar, however, had been enough to give it to *him*.

But now Jimmy found his attitude changing again.

Turning the whole world into a botanical garden with a climate ordered up from special weather effects. Bringing back the dinosaurs and the whales and the dodos. Full-sensory movies. New bodies custom tailored to your specs on Saville

Row whenever you wanted. Feeding the famous starving children in Africa your mother always hocked you about when you wouldn't finish your spinach. No more war. Living forever. Meeting strange new worlds out there in the stars, a future that went on, and on forever, boldly going where it had never gone before. . . .

What's not to like?

Yeah, these people wore tacky costumes, a lot of them did look not right around the eyeballs, and Jimmy had never seen so many grossly overweight people in one place in his life. Nor would he have believed that he could find himself in a hotel with several hundred women and a dick that shriveled at the thought of fucking any of them.

And yet . . .

And yet, while these sci-fi fans lacked most of everything that Texas Jimmy would have called class, they had something that they had taught him tonight to feel the lack of in himself.

Lacking it, it was hard for Jimmy to figure out exactly what it was.

Some kind of goofy innocence he must've lost when he was about fourteen?

Something, like virginity, perhaps best admired from afar?

Not my planet, Monkey Boy!

These strange folks seemed to feel otherwise.

Whose else was it?

Oddly enough, it felt good to know they were there.

Ralf finally let his shotgun mike hang detumescent as he slowly strode to the very end of the runway. Out into the midst of the corporeal incarnation of the science fictional Dreamtime which had opened a doorway to Starship Earth for Amanda and several million other Monkey People huddled around the collective electronic campfire of their TV sets in the dark.

"*We* are the Dream," he said. "*We* are the Dreamers."

The camera moved in for a close-up on the mask of his face, transformed into the warmly enlightened visage of the Buddha-Who-Laughs.

If one picture was worth a thousand words then surely the footage of sci-fans cavorting around a hotel in silly costumes that had dominated the first hour had made a millionfold greater impression on most viewers than Dexter's earnest intellectual talking heads.

But what had the *second* hour done?

How many *pictures* was a live broadcast of . . . an Advent worth?

And Amanda knew that that was what this was.

For together the Starship Captain and his Ralfies had opened the doorways of all those television screens out there. And through it had emerged from the collective Dreamtime a sci-fi Schlocktime avatar of Dexter's vision simple and silly enough for the demographic mean to share.

Which in this electronically enlightened age was precisely how new archetype was graven into the collective unconscious of the Zeitgeist.

In full sight on television. While millions watched it happen.

"Dreaming up the story we've been trying to tell ourselves since we woke out of the dreamless sleep of the trees. The one that takes a tribe of dreaming monkeys from there to the stars."

"Oh yes!" Amanda exclaimed aloud in the solitude of her own living room.

For in the beginning, was the Word.

And through the Word was the World and the dance of matter and energy within it made manifest.

And while the pictures might hold the attention and the ratings, it was the Word, *The Word According To*, that was the doorway through which this new archetype from a Dreamtime future made itself manifest in the Maya of the now.

It was happening.

It was real.

Millions of spiritually naive people were experiencing it and so in some small way at least would never be the same.

"Ever notice, Starship Troupers," said Ralf, "how what goes around comes around? Who am I, star of the show or just another one of you in a fancier Starship Captain suit?"

He put his hands on his hips. He shook his head. But the warmth of that smile never wavered. "You want to know what the future is *really* like?" he said.

Scattered imploring sounds from the audience.

"The masters of time and space bit is the just the opening act," said Ralf. "The star turn comes when we become masters of *ourselves*. When we awake within the World beholding the crown of creation. When we awake within the Dream and behold the Dreamer. And who is that, Starship Troupers? Say the magic word, and Captain Tinkerbell lives!"

"*US!*" shouted the voice of the multitude.

Ralf laughed a quite human laugh. He raised his right foot, brought it down with exaggerated slowness, as if moving through molasses.

"That's one small step for the Great I Am," he said, doing a magically perfect Neil Armstrong. "One giant leap for the Great You're Gonna Be."

"Gonna be nothin' but the cold blue steel at the end of the subway tunnel, motherfucker!"

Shouts, screams, confused swipes of more than one camera, jagged jump-cuts, then—

A full-shot on a shadowy shambling figure standing in the darkness on the runway between Ralf and the stage. Then a spotlight was thrown on it to reveal:

An ancient girl.

The Deathship Streetgirl from the masquerade.

A filthy flasher's raincoat hanging open to reveal a skeletal body clad in shreddy gray rags like something you might see in a state between sleep and death in a Calcutta gutter.

This was no costume.

She couldn't have been twenty-five, but by the muck-grayed witch's hair, the scratches and scabs scarring her pasty face, and most of all by what glared out from those blackly hollowed eyes, she was the eternal evil crone.

And that face was no mask.

And the big sharp knife she brandished was all too real.

"Peek-a-boo, guess who sees you," she gabbled in a scratchy metallic howl. "Here's the Dead World's only friend the Big Ripper comin' right atcha, hee, hee, hee, down through the centuries of a garbage can of a planet floating onna silver platter in the void, following the little blue lights down through the subway rathole inta the coat hanger in th' disgustin' meatware brain a this Rat Girl t'slice out the shit an' pus and putrid fuckin' green fish guts . . ."

A cut to a shot on Ralf in his own spotlight circle.

"I thought you'd never get here," he said.

Weirdly enough under the circumstances, that smile never wavered, fear never chilled the humanity of its warmth, and his eyes addressed only the camera.

"Well not really. Hammers and nails, chains or butcher knives, Mannlicher-Carcanos or Saturday-night Specials, you always show up with the hook in the nick of time."

And Amanda understood that Buddha smile of acceptance, that visage of serenity.

Nemesis must always arrive with the blade of destiny.

This is the way the story always ends.

The way it *must*.

Arthur *must* die at the hand of Mordred.

Prometheus *must* be bound to the rock of eternal torment.

Christ *must* be crucified.

The Sun King of the Second Lost Camelot *must* be shot down.

Lucifer *must* be cast into the pit.

The Lightbringer *must* die.

How else to end the story?

How else to leave the stage and pass into the crystal mists of legend?

Rat Girl stood there at th' end of th' long long tunnel where th' little blue lights had led her, th' dark end a th' million-year-old rathole unner the Pig a' th' Apple, subway tunnel unner th' meat a th' world, float and fade, fade an' float, monkey meat . . .

An' up there at th' other end, up there inna subway station inna yellow light was a cop witha great big fuckin' billie club, th' Enemy right, fuckin' mother of all pimps witha razor, wouldn't letya suck an honest cock . . .

Follow the blue lights, Rat Girl, float an' fade . . .

"Who do you think you're supposed to be?" said the Dead World Destroyer.

Bright green suit shining in the light like Central Park in springtime.

"*We* know, don't we, Starship Troupers? We've all seen this masquerade costume before."

That fuckin' smile like Mr. Sunshine Happy Face should make a Rat Girl wanna puke.

But—

"You're the dark at the end of the tunnel. You're what we made. You're what something thinks we deserve. You're what's left when all hope dies. Deathship Earth in a flasher's raincoat."

Move forward, monkey meat, lift the knife higher, Rat Girl, one foot after the other, just follow the little blue lights, see, it's not so hard to do when you've got a coat hanger in your brain . . .

But—

"That's who you think you're supposed to be . . ."

Those eyes, wide open an' comin' right atcha, eyes like doorways inta someplace didn't seem so fuckin' bad unner the circumstances, eyes like mirrors, y'could sorta see this little girl someone once been a long long time ago . . .

"But I know who you are."

"I am the ratbrain cockroach hardware with a butcherknife!" she found herself screaming.

Hey, wait a minute—

"I'm Freddy fuckin' Krueger with a dirty steel hard-on for your fuckin' ass! I am the Dead World program for a million years of a cold garbage can floating on a silver platter comin' t'take you away!"

Hey come on, Rat Thing, this don't—

"And I am the Great Tinkerbell Spirit of the World," said the Starship Captain, still smiling. "And seeing as how that *is* a knife you're holding, I don't suppose you're glad to see me."

Those eyes like little blue lights leading up out of the darkness . . .

"But strange as it seems if you don't know the way the story ends," he said, "*I'm* here for *you*."

And he opened his arms wide like Jesus onna cross, like the wings a some fuckin' eagle, like he was darin' her to do it, like he was trustin' her not to, like he was offerin' himself to the knife.

Anna Rat Girl's eyes was gettin' blurry, what did they call this onna Planet a th' Monkeys, tears, what happened t'your eyes when ya stumbled outa th' dark inta the light, hey ratfuck, maybe—

But somethin' jams a fuckin' ice pick inta the meat a her brain fuckin' biggest spike fulla crack a crummy shooting gallery inna cellar unner the wormy Apple's ever seen, hey never *mainlined* this shit before, an' roarin' up the fuckin' tunnel like the D Train of Death on th' express track, do it, Rat Girl, believe it, motherfucker, comes the White Tornado, whoo-ee, scree, scree, scree!

In real time, seconds, but in Amanda's television Dreamtime, in the amazing grace of slomo legend.

Nemesis, the Angel of Death, avatar of the Darkness howling up the runway with the Sword of Doom.

The Bringer of the Light, the Sun King Who Must Die, the Great Eagle spreading his wings to accept the fated thanatotic lover, offering up the blood sacrifice of the flesh once more that the Spirit might pass into legend.

The shouts of the multitude as the knife plunges toward his breast through the golden spotlight circle—

The crack of metal against metal as he swings the shotgun mike two-handed like a baseball bat and knocks it flying.

"On second thought," said Ralf, in a W. C. Fields voice and mugging a cynical sneer to match, "I'd rather be in Philadelphia."

———

What th' fuck?

Rat Girl found herself suddenly blinkin' in th' bright light, alla people jibberin' an jabberin', up outa the dark a the subway station empty-handed . . .

Empty-handed?

What th' fuck's goin' on, Rat Thing, didn't ya snatch it for me, ain't I supposed t'have a pretzel?

A long shot on Ralf and the street girl standing there dazed and squinting in the circle of light at the end of the runway.

In the shadows of the stage, movement that Amanda could not quite make out.

And then out onto the runway, grunting and puffing, came two out-of-shape-middle-aged rentacops in baggy gray uniforms.

Ralf shot them a quick look over his shoulder, mugged at the camera.

"Terrific," he rasped, "the Keystone Kops arrive right behind the tick of time as usual."

"What now, ya stupid ratfuck?" the street girl screamed into Ralf's open shotgun mike as they hesitantly drew their pistols.

The rentacops took a few uncertain steps forward.

"Rat Thing! Rip! Where th' fuck are you? Where's my only friend?"

"Hey, come on, give the kid a break," Ralf said, raising his free hand to stay them. "Don't you think *that's* an act worth its famous fifteen minutes?"

The rentacops looked all too relieved to give him any argument.

Jesus fuckin' Christ, the cops was chasin' her again, wouldya believe it, least there was only two of 'em this time, but seems like I been goin' through this shit for a million years, like some kinda bad fuckin' dream, ain't it, hee, hee, hee, disgust ya t'be it . . .

Amanda would not have called the smile Ralf turned on his would-be slayer solemn enough to convince as Christ-like forgiveness. In fact it was the smirk of the Borscht Belt wise-guy. Thus might Mel Brooks have played the Laughing Buddha in this moment. Thus might Steve Martin playing Jesus have regarded Pilate from the bridge of the Enterprise had Scotty beamed him up from his Calvary on comic cue right before the fade out.

"Well, ex-*cuse* me for living the last time around," he said. "But what can I tell you, don't you think the martyr act was getting awful old?"

"Rat Thing? Rat Thing?"

Nobody home, Foxy Loxy, nothin' in her head but a fuckin' headache felt like someone jammed a coat hanger inta her brain, an' up there inna light behind the Dumpster in the alley wasa john shovin' th' biggest weirdest dick she had ever seen in her face, all gray an' rubbery, musta been two fuckin' feet long!

"Hey, I ain't gonna suck *that* for ten bucks, no way, run ya twenny-five, whaddya think I am, Mother Teresa!"

Amanda watched in fascination as, with a little shrug and mug of reaction, Ralf actually cued a spattering of *laughter* at this line.

He mimed the perusal of a phantom sheaf of paper.

"Well, according to the script, you're the Bad Little Match Girl with the Hook to yank me off the stage," he said.

He shrugged.

"But we've *already* canned that moldy oldie, now ain't we, Starship Troupers?" he said, shooting a confidential glance at the camera, a ghost of a wink.

He mimed tearing up the script and throwing it away.

"And I see by the old handwriting on the wall that the masquerade is finally over."

He took the street girl by the hand. He raised her arm high in the manner of a victorious prizefighter.

"The winner and Ralfcon champion!" he proclaimed in the quavery grandeur of a boxing referee. "The Deathworld Streetgirl! So let's have a big hand for the little lady!"

Like wakin' up th' mornin' after a night a smokin' a rock in Tompkins Square Park, suckin' thirty or forty rat dicks inna subway tunnel, Rats Things an' coat hangers an' butcher knives an' some kinda place made a cold black and metal where she was dead an' eatin' garbage outa Dumpsters for a million years a razor blades . . .

Jeez!

The Starship Captain was holdin' Foxy Loxy's hand, that's who she was, wasn't she, and then he was raisin' it way up in the air.

Felt like she was gonna puke, like she'd been eatin' fish heads an' dog turds for th' last ten years, an' this awful sound sent a toothache pain through her like someone was pullin' a fuckin' rusty coat hanger outa her brain . . .

Whatta fuckin' awful dream t'wake up outa!

Wake up outa?

Inta this?

This hadda be the dream, didn't it?

"The winner and Ralfcon champion! The Deathworld Streetgirl! So let's have a big hand for the little lady!"

'Cause there she was, standin' in this bright fuckin' light like a rock star onna MTV. Onna fuckin' stage. Inna middle of a crowd a people.

And they were clappin' an' cheerin'.

"Baby, you were great, hey, that was an Oscar-class performance!" said the Starship Captain.

The cheerin' and clappin' sorta stopped or anyway almost.

"We all know the act couldn't have worked without you, don't we Starship Troupers?"

An' he fuckin' kissy-kissed her on both cheeks like they did inna Hollywood talk shows.

An' the cheerin' and the clappin' started again.

An' Foxy Loxy stood up there inna bright white light where not alla crack inna world ever let her dream she would ever be. Up there onna stage witha camera lookin' at her, in fronta thousands a fuckin' people like she was some kinda TV star or somethin'.

An' it was *her* they was cheerin'.

An' it was *her* who was cryin' an' fuck you who cares if the whole world sees it.

'Cause nobody had ever cheered for Foxy Loxy before.

Odds were nobody ever would again.

But hey, she was ahead a the game already.

She was one in a million.

There they were cheerin'.

Here she was on stage.

An' there was a microphone stuck in her face.

T'die for, now wasn't it?

Betcha a lotta people had.

"What the fuck am I supposedta say?" she said. "Hey, what would you say if you was me? Who the fuck ever thought I'd make it t'here? Who the fuck ever thought I'd be *on television*?"

———

Ralf walked the street girl down the runway past the rentacops and into the wings. After which there was a long deadly silence as he stood there alone in the spotlight on the empty stage.

There was also about ten minutes of airtime left.

Amanda could not possibly imagine what Ralf could fill it with after a capper like *that*.

He stood there for a few long beats as if wondering the same thing himself.

Then—

"Brrring!"

Ralf did a vocal version of a telephone ring.

And a take.

He turned, letting the shotgun mike hang, picked up a phantom phone receiver.

"Yeah, hello, what do you want . . . ?"

Another take.

Ralf looked up, tucked the shotgun mike into his armpit, covered the speaking end of the pantomime phone, mugged confidentiality at the audience.

"It's my agent," he said. "The one that won't be born for another hundred years." He shrugged. "What *other* kind is there?"

What's going on? Amanda wondered. He had never done a piece of business like this.

"Listen, kiddo, I got great news for you," Ralf said through the semi-immobile lips of the unprofessional ventriloquist. "I got you a sweetheart of a gig at the Starship Hilton, so you can forget the tank town tour of the Planet of the Monkey People and boogie on back to the Big Time!"

Amanda laughed, far harder than just about anyone else would.

It was pretty much an inside joke.

There couldn't be *that* many people who could have appreciated his perfect Texas Jimmy Balaban.

"The Starship Hilton? I *can*? What happened?"

"*You* happened, what do you think, kiddo, you're a big star here now!"

"I *am*?" said Ralf doing the perfectly befuddled innocent. "But when you talked me into *this* gig, you told me if I whipped it out in public I'd *still* have a hard time getting arrested."

"That was before you did your Elvis, Ralf! When you take your powder, they pick up the old shows for a syndicate package. You can *still* catch the reruns if you stay up late enough. The DVDs and the CDs are still moving, though what can I say, the movie they made of your life story was a stinker, I don't even want to *tell* you who played the part, I tried, but there was *no way* I could get Robin Williams."

Ralf mugged a look of perfect stupefaction.

"You *did it*, kiddo!" he mouthed in the voice of Texas Jimmy. "You turned the Deathship into the Starship! You changed history, Ralf! You're a hero! You're a legend! Imagine what Elvis could command in Vegas if he *really* came back in a pink and chrome flying saucer! Some people think you really *are* the Giant Turnip God!"

"They do?"

"Better than that!"

"*Better than that?*"

"For the first time in your crappy career, you're finally *bankable!*"

Ralf did another take. He hung up the phantom phone.

He shrugged.

He looked up into the camera.

The eyes were as empty as the Void at the Center of the Great Wheel. But the smile was the perfect comic opera Buddha.

He saluted. He waved. He blew a farewell kiss.

Then the camera pulled back into a long shot.

A spotlight tracking a jaunty vaudevillian as he slowly cakewalked toward the wings twirling the shotgun mike like a cane.

Amanda could not have dreamed of an exit more perfect.

Once, twice, thrice, he paused, turned, tipped a phantom hat, before the spotlight irised down to the final blackout.

Texas Jimmy Balaban would remember the last time he saw his comedian from the future for the rest of his life. How could he forget it? How could he not believe that Ralf's extro was a tip of the hat just for him?

How many *other* people watching would know that it couldn't have been more perfect if Jimmy Durante himself had done that tip of the hat?

How many *other* people out there would've gotten teary-eyed to hear him do that gravelly voice leaving the stage with a "Goodnight, Mrs. Calabash, wherever you are?"

It took a long beat for Jimmy to remember that there were still five minutes of airtime left.

Long enough for Ralf to toss the shotgun mike to him and make for the backstage toilet.

"Hey what the fuck are you doing?" Jimmy managed to shout at him. "The show ain't *over* yet!"

"Speak for yourself, Monkey Boy, when you gotta go, you gotta go," said Ralf. "Or ain't you just noticed the Fat Lady sing?"

And disappeared inside.

It took Jimmy another beat to chase after him, not that he really thought it was going to matter.

The nose knew.

Jimmy had had several occasions to piss in that toilet.

It had the one door and a small window looking out on an airshaft.

And sure enough, when he checked it out, the window was open, and there was no one inside.